THE MIDNIGHT RAYMOND CHANDLER

with an Introduction by
JOAN KAHN

HOUGHTON MIFFLIN COMPANY BOSTON
1971

CON

78
84
90
95

THE
MIDNIGHT
RAYMOND
CHANDLER

with an Introduction by

JOAN KAHN

HOUGHTON MIFFLIN COMPANY BOSTON
1971

ISBN: 0-395-12712-2
Library of Congress Catalog Card Number:
74-162005

Printed in the United States of America

INTRODUCTION
by Joan Kahn

IN 1929 IT WAS POSSIBLE for Father Ronald Knox, a classical scholar, a theologian, a professor and a detective story writer, to introduce a collection of short stories which included Agatha Christie, E. Phillips Oppenheim and Marie Belloc Lowndes with, "The detective story differs essentially from every other type of fiction . . . Ordinary fiction appeals to the synthetic in our natures, detective fiction to the analytic." Then Father Knox gave his rules for the detective field, among them:

> The criminal must be someone mentioned in the early part of the story, but must not be anyone whose thoughts the reader has been allowed to follow.
>
> No more than one secret room or passage is allowable.
>
> No Chinaman must figure in the story.
>
> No accident must ever help the detective, nor must he ever have an unaccountable intuition which proves to be right.
>
> The detective must not himself commit the crime.

"Rules so numerous and so stringent," Knox admits, "cannot fail to cramp the style of the author and make the practice of the art not difficult only, but progressively more difficult . . . Nobody can have failed to notice that while the public demand for mystery stories remains unshaken, the faculty for writing one with any symptom of originality about it becomes rarer with each succeeding year. The game is getting played out; before long, it is to be feared, all the possible combinations will have been used up."

Father Knox had not, perhaps, noted that the same year a writer named Dashiell Hammett had published two books, *The*

Dain Curse and *Red Harvest.* That man, and a number of writers who followed him, helped make sure that the field of the mystery was going to continue to flourish, was going to permit a man named Raymond Chandler to write his own set of rules twenty years later. So in 1950 Chandler could say, "The mystery story is a kind of writing that needs not dwell in the shadow of the past and owes little if any allegiance to the cult of the classic . . . There are no 'classics' of crime and detection. Not one. Within its frame of reference, which is the only way it should be judged, a classic is a piece of writing which exhausts the possibilities of its form and can hardly be surpassed. No story or novel of mystery has done that yet. Few have come close. Which is why otherwise reasonable people continue to assault the citadel."

Raymond Chandler didn't begin to write in the mystery field until he was in his mid-forties. Born in America in 1888, in Chicago, he was taken to London by his Irish-born mother when he was seven, after his Quaker parents were divorced. (He never saw his father again.)

As a young man he worked as a journalist. He served with the Canadian Army and the R.A.F. in World War I. After the Armistice he and his mother returned to the United States and lived in California. When his mother died Chandler, then thirty-six, married twice-divorced Pearl Cecily Bowen, who was beautiful and fifty-three years old. She died while he was writing *The Long Goodbye.* He was heartbroken after her death, and even attempted suicide. He wrote of her: "For thirty years, ten months and four days, she was the light of my life, my whole ambition."

Chandler had arrived in California with, he wrote, "an English public school accent and a beautiful wardrobe." To support himself initially he picked apricots, sold sporting goods and took a book-keeping course. It was a three-year course and he did it in six weeks. Eventually he became a director of a number of independent oil companies. "They were small companies but very rich," he said. When the depression came the companies faltered and Chandler again had to find a means of supporting himself. He had read a number of pulp magazines, and one of them, *Black Mask* impressed him, quite rightly. He tried a story for it — or rather a novelette of

18,000 words. *Black Mask* bought the story for $180. After that, Chandler said, he never looked back. (The story, "Blackmailers Don't Shoot," is included in this collection, marking its first appearance in book form in this country.)

He sold his first novel *The Big Sleep* to Alfred Knopf in the United States and Hamish Hamilton in England. It was published in 1939. He was fifty-one years old.

Of the business world, now safely behind him, Chandler had observed, "Business is very tough and I hate it. But whatever you set out to do, you have to do it as well as you know how."

He approached his new career as an author in the same manner. At first his reception in England was greater than his reception in the United States. He wrote from London: "A thriller writer in England, if he is good enough, is just as good as anyone else."

Chandler intended to be at least as good as anyone else. He had, as every writer does, times of struggle with his work. He hated, as almost all writers do (probably *all* writers), rewriting. He felt he was a poor plotter and bad at construction. But he said, "Do I read my stuff when published? Yes, and at very great risk of being called an egotistical twerp, I find it damn hard to put down. Even me, that knows all about it. There must be some magic in the writing after all, but I take no credit for it. It just happens, like red hair."

Chandler and his novels (there were only seven of them published), his numerous short stories, and his detective Philip Marlowe helped advance the detective story field enormously. He could, and did, set a scene quickly and simply, and with authority. Rich, varied scenes such as: "I pushed the bell to number fourteen, went on through the patio where scarlet Chinese honeysuckle was lit by a peanut spotlight. Another light glowed down on the big ornamented pool full of fat goldfish and silent lily pads, the lilies folded for the night. There were a couple of stone seats and a lawn swing. The place didn't look very expensive except that every place was expensive that year."

Or, he could write: "He looked at some dusty antlers, a big rough table spattered with magazines, an old-fashioned battery-type radio, a box-shaped phonograph with a disheveled pile of records beside it. There were tall glasses that hadn't been washed and a half-bottle of Scotch beside them, on a table near the big stone fireplace. A car went along the road above and stopped not far off."

There is loneliness, and a sense of something imminent in both these scenes. And when Chandler took you into a scene with him you were there. When Chandler introduced you to someone alive you knew her: "A very pretty black-haired, gray-eyed girl stepped out of the clothes closet and poked a .32 at me. She wore a blue suit cut with a lot of snap. An inverted saucer of a hat came down across her forehead. Shiny black hair showed at the sides. Her eyes were slate-gray, cold and yet light-hearted. Her face was young and delicate, and as hard as a chisel." Or if he showed you someone dying you remembered him: "He was braced to the doorframe by four hooked fingers made of white wax. He had eyes an eighth of an inch deep, pale gray-blue, wide open. They looked at me but they didn't see me. Our faces were inches apart. Our breathing met in midair. Mine was quick and harsh, his was the far-off whisper which had not yet begun to rattle. Blood bubbled from his mouth and ran down his chin."

Chandler admits that his detective Marlowe is a romantic whose toughness has always been more or less of a surface bluff. And though no one has the right to assign to an author his creation's characteristics, it's very probable that in these respects the author and his creation overlapped.

In their tough romantic, observant way Chandler and his detective Marlowe are going to move together through the years, holding their own as the field Chandler admired so much, and did so much for, moves on, keeps advancing, as it has since his time and will continue to do.

Twenty years after Father Knox set down his rules Chandler made up some of his own, which were very different. In 1949 Chandler wrote:

> The mystery novel must be credibly motivated both as to the original situation and the denouement.
> The mystery novel must be technically sound about the methods of murder and detection.
> The mystery novel must be realistic as to character, setting and atmosphere.

The mystery novel must have a sound story value apart from the mystery element.

The mystery novel must not try to do everything at once.

The mystery novel must punish the criminal in one way or another, not necessarily by operation of the law courts.

Raymond Chandler wrote by his rules — and, in a field that will often, as it stretches and experiments and grows, need no set of rules, and perhaps even feature an occasional Chinaman, his rules are still sound and sensible.

If this is your first Chandler reading remember that Chandler says his writing is damn hard to put down. And I can assure you it is. If you are an old Chandler fan, you probably haven't been able to read most of what's in this book for far too many years. So sample the magic again — and have a fine time.

THE MIDNIGHT
RAYMOND CHANDLER

RAYMOND CHANDLER
INTRODUCES
The Simple Art of Murder

SOME LITERARY ANTIQUARIAN of a rather special type may one day think it worth while to run through the files of the pulp detective magazines which flourished during the late twenties and early thirties, and determine just how and when and by what steps the popular mystery story shed its refined good manners and went native. He will need sharp eyes and an open mind. Pulp paper never dreamed of posterity and most of it must be a dirty brown color by now. And it takes a very open mind indeed to look beyond the unnecessarily gaudy covers, trashy titles and barely acceptable advertisements and recognize the authentic power of a kind of writing that, even at its most mannered and artificial, made most of the fiction of the time taste like a cup of luke-warm consommé at a spinsterish tearoom.

I don't think this power was entirely a matter of violence, although far too many people got killed in these stories and their passing was celebrated with a rather too loving attention to detail. It certainly was not a matter of fine writing, since any attempt at that would have been ruthlessly blue-penciled by the editorial staff. Nor was it because of any great originality of plot or character. Most of the plots were rather ordinary and most of the characters rather primitive types of people. Possibly it was the smell of fear which these stories managed to generate. Their characters lived in a world gone wrong, a world in which, long before the atom bomb, civilization had created the machinery for its own destruction, and was learning to use it with all the moronic delight of a gangster trying out his first machine gun. The law was something to be manipulated for profit and power. The streets were dark with something more than night. The mystery story grew hard and cynical about motive and character, but it was not cynical about the effects it tried to produce nor about its technique of producing them. A few unusual critics recognized this at the time, which was all one had any right to expect. The average critic never recognizes an achievement when it happens. He explains it after it has become respectable.

The emotional basis of the standard detective story was and had always been that murder will out and justice will be done. Its technical basis was the relative insignificance of everything except the final denouement. What led up to that was more or less passage-work. The denouement would justify everything. The technical basis of the *Black Mask* type of story on the other hand was that the scene outranked the plot, in the sense that a good plot was one which made good scenes. The ideal mystery was one you would read if the end was missing. We who tried to write it had the same point of view as the film makers. When I first went to work in Hollywood a very intelligent producer told me that you couldn't make a successful motion picture from a mystery story, because the whole point was a disclosure that took a few seconds of screen time while the audience was reaching for its hat. He was wrong, but only because he was thinking of the wrong kind of mystery.

As to the emotional basis of the hard-boiled story, obviously it does not believe that murder will out and justice will be done — unless some very determined individual makes it his business to see that justice is done. The stories were about the men who made that happen. They were apt to be hard men, and what they did, whether they were called police officers, private detectives or newspaper men, was hard, dangerous work. It was work they could always get. There was plenty of it lying around. There still is. Undoubtedly the stories about them had a fantastic element. Such things happened, but not so rapidly, nor to so close-knit a group of people, nor within so narrow a frame of logic. This was inevitable because the demand was for constant action; if you stopped to think you were lost. When in doubt have a man come through a door with a gun in his hand. This could get to be pretty silly, but somehow it didn't seem to matter. A writer who is afraid to overreach himself is as useless as a general who is afraid to be wrong.

As I look back on my own stories it would be absurd if I did not wish they had been better. But if they had been much better they would not have been published. If the formula had been a little less rigid, more of the writing of that time might have survived. Some of us tried pretty hard to break out of the formula, but we usually got caught and sent back. To exceed the limits of a formula without destroying it is the dream of every magazine writer who is not a hopeless hack. There are things in my stories which I might like to change or leave out altogether. To do this may look simple, but if you try, you find you cannot do it at all. You will only destroy what is good without having any noticeable effect on what is bad. You cannot recapture the mood, the state of innocence, much less the animal gusto you had when you had very little else. Everything a writer learns about the art or craft of fiction takes just a little away from his need or desire to write at all. In the end he knows all the tricks and has nothing to say.

As for the literary quality of these exhibits, I am entitled to assume from the imprint of a distinguished publisher that I need not be sickeningly humble. As a writer I have never been able to take myself with that enormous earnestness which is one of the trying characteristics of the craft. And I have been fortunate to escape what has been called "that form of snobbery which can accept the Literature of Entertainment in the Past, but only the Literature of Enlightenment in the Present." Between the one-syllable humors of the comic strip and the anemic subtleties of the litterateurs there is a wide stretch of country, in which the mystery story may or may not be an important landmark. There are those who hate it in all its forms. There are those who like it when it is about nice people ("that charming Mrs. Jones, whoever would have thought she would cut off her husband's head with a meat saw? Such a handsome man, too!"). There are those who think violence and sadism interchangeable terms, and those who regard detective fiction as sub-literary on no better grounds than that it does not habitually get itself jammed up with subordinate clauses, tricky punctuation and hypothetical subjunctives. There are those who read it only when they are tired or sick, and, from the number of mystery novels they consume, they must be tired and sick most of the time. There are the aficionados of deduction (with whom I have had words elsewhere) and the aficionados of sex who can't get it into their hot little heads that the fictional detective is a catalyst, not a Casanova. The former demand a ground plan of Greythorpe Manor, showing the study, the gun room, the main hall and staircase and the passage to that grim little room where the butler polishes the Georgian silver, thin-lipped and silent, hearing the murmur of doom. The latter think the shortest distance between two points is from a blonde to a bed.

No writer can please them all, no writer should try. The stories in this book certainly had no thought of being able to please anyone ten or fifteen years after they were written. The mystery story is a kind of writing that need not dwell in the shadow of the past and owes little if any allegiance to the cult of the classics. It is a good deal more than unlikely that any writer now living will produce a better historical novel than *Henry Esmond,* a better tale of children than *The Golden Age,* a sharper social vignette than *Madame Bovary,* a more graceful and elegant evocation than *The Spoils of Poynton,* a wider and richer canvas than *War and Peace* or *The Brothers Karamazov.* But to devise a more plausible mystery than *The Hound of the Baskervilles* or *The Purloined Letter* should not be too difficult. Nowadays it would be rather more difficult not to. There are no "classics" of crime and detection. Not one. Within its frame of reference, which is the only way it should be judged, a classic is a piece of writing which exhausts the possibilities of its form and can hardly be surpassed. No story or novel of mystery has done that yet. Few have come close. Which is one of the principal reasons why otherwise reasonable people continue to assault the citadel.

RED WIND

1

THERE WAS A DESERT WIND blowing that night. It was one of those hot dry Santa Anas that come down through the mountain passes and curl your hair and make your nerves jump and your skin itch. On nights like that every booze party ends in a fight. Meek little wives feel the edge of the carving knife and study their husbands' necks. Anything can happen. You can even get a full glass of beer at a cocktail lounge.

I was getting one in a flossy new place across the street from the apartment house where I lived. It had been open about a week and it wasn't doing any business. The kid behind the bar was in his early twenties and looked as if he had never had a drink in his life.

There was only one other customer, a souse on a bar stool with his back to the door. He had a pile of dimes stacked neatly in front of him, about two dollars' worth. He was drinking straight rye in small glasses and he was all by himself in a world of his own.

I sat farther along the bar and got my glass of beer and said: "You sure cut the clouds off them, buddy. I will say that for you."

"We just opened up," the kid said. "We got to build up trade. Been in before, haven't you, mister?"

"Uh-huh."

"Live around here?"

"In the Berglund Apartments across the street," I said. "And the name is Philip Marlowe."

"Thanks, mister. Mine's Lew Petrolle." He leaned close to me across the polished dark bar. "Know that guy?"

"No."

"He ought to go home, kind of. I ought to call a taxi and send him home. He's doing his next week's drinking too soon."

"A night like this," I said. "Let him alone."

"It's not good for him," the kid said, scowling at me.

"Rye!" the drunk croaked, without looking up. He snapped his fingers so as not to disturb his piles of dimes by banging on the bar.

The kid looked at me and shrugged. "Should I?"

"Whose stomach is it? Not mine."

The kid poured him another straight rye and I think he doctored it with water down behind the bar because when he came up with it he looked as guilty as if he'd kicked his grandmother. The drunk paid no attention. He lifted coins off his pile with the exact care of a crack surgeon operating on a brain tumor.

The kid came back and put more beer in my glass. Outside the wind howled. Every once in a while it blew the stained-glass door open a few inches. It was a heavy door.

The kid said: "I don't like drunks in the first place and in the second place I don't like them getting drunk in here, and in the third place I don't like them in the first place."

"Warner Brothers could use that," I said.

"They did."

Just then we had another customer. A car squeaked to a stop outside and the swinging door came open. A fellow came in who looked a little in a hurry. He held the door and ranged the place quickly with flat, shiny, dark eyes. He was well set up, dark, good-looking in a narrow-faced, tight-lipped way. His clothes were dark and a white handkerchief peeped coyly from his pocket and he looked cool as well as under a tension of some sort. I guessed it was the hot wind. I felt a bit the same myself only not cool.

He looked at the drunk's back. The drunk was playing checkers with his empty glasses. The new customer looked at me, then he looked along the line of half-booths at the other side of the place. They were all empty. He came on in — down past where the drunk sat swaying and muttering to himself — and spoke to the bar kid.

"Seen a lady in here, buddy? Tall, pretty, brown hair, in a print bolero jacket over a blue crêpe silk dress. Wearing a wide-brimmed straw hat with a velvet band." He had a tight voice I didn't like.

"No, sir. Nobody like that's been in," the bar kid said.

"Thanks. Straight Scotch. Make it fast, will you?"

The kid gave it to him and the fellow paid and put the drink down in a gulp and started to go out. He took three or four steps and stopped, facing the drunk. The drunk was grinning. He swept a gun from somewhere so fast that it was just a blur coming out. He held it steady and he didn't look any drunker than I was. The tall dark guy stood quite still and then his head jerked back a little and then he was still again.

A car tore by outside. The drunk's gun was a .22 target automatic, with a large front sight. It made a couple of hard snaps and a little smoke curled — very little.

"So long, Waldo," the drunk said.

Then he put the gun on the barman and me.

The dark guy took a week to fall down. He stumbled, caught himself, waved one arm, stumbled again. His hat fell off, and then he hit the floor with his face. After he hit it he might have been poured concrete for all the fuss he made.

The drunk slid down off the stool and scooped his dimes into a pocket and slid towards the door. He turned sideways, holding the gun across his body. I didn't have a gun. I hadn't thought I needed one to buy a glass of beer. The kid behind the bar didn't move or make the slightest sound.

The drunk felt the door lightly with his shoulder, keeping his eyes on us, then pushed through it backwards. When it was wide a hard gust of air slammed in and lifted the hair of the man on the floor. The drunk said: "Poor Waldo. I bet I made his nose bleed."

The door swung shut. I started to rush it — from long practice in doing the wrong thing. In this case it didn't matter. The car outside let out a roar and when I got onto the sidewalk it was flicking a red smear of taillight around the nearby corner. I got its license number the way I got my first million.

There were people and cars up and down the block as usual. Nobody acted as if a gun had gone off. The wind was making enough noise to make the hard quick rap of .22 ammunition sound like a slammed door, even if anyone heard it. I went back into the cocktail bar.

The kid hadn't moved, even yet. He just stood with his hands flat on the bar, leaning over a little and looking down at the dark guy's back. The dark guy hadn't moved either. I bent down and felt his neck artery. He wouldn't move — ever.

The kid's face had as much expression as a cut of round steak and was about the same color. His eyes were more angry than shocked.

I lit a cigarette and blew smoke at the ceiling and said shortly: "Get on the phone."

"Maybe he's not dead," the kid said.

"When they use a twenty-two that means they don't make mistakes. Where's the phone?"

"I don't have one. I got enough expenses without that. Boy, can I kick eight hundred bucks in the face!"

"You own this place?"

"I did till this happened."

He pulled his white coat off and his apron and came around the inner end of the bar. "I'm locking this door," he said, taking keys out.

He went out, swung the door to and juggled the lock from the outside until the bolt clicked into place. I bent down and rolled Waldo over. At first I couldn't even see where the shots went in. Then I could. A couple of tiny holes in his coat, over his heart. There was a little blood on his shirt.

The drunk was everything you could ask — as a killer.

The prowl-car boys came in about eight minutes. The kid, Lew Petrolle, was back behind the bar by then. He had his white coat on again and he was counting his money in the register and putting it in his pocket and making notes in a little book.

I sat at the edge of one of the half-booths and smoked cigarettes and watched Waldo's face get deader and deader. I wondered who the girl in the print coat was, why Waldo had left the engine of his car running outside, why he was in a hurry, whether the drunk had been waiting for him or just happened to be there.

The prowl-car boys came in perspiring. They were the usual large size and one of them had a flower stuck under his cap and his cap on a bit crooked. When he saw the dead man he got rid of the flower and leaned down to feel Waldo's pulse.

"Seems to be dead," he said, and rolled him around a little more. Oh yeah, I see where they went in. Nice clean work. You two see im get it?"

I said yes. The kid behind the bar said nothing. I told nem about it, that the killer seemed to have left in Waldo's car.

The cop yanked Waldo's wallet out, went through it rapidly and rhistled. "Plenty of jack and no driver's license." He put the wal-et away. "Okay, we didn't touch him, see? Just a chance we could nd did he have a car and put it on the air."

"The hell you didn't touch him," Lew Petrolle said.

The cop gave him one of those looks. "Okay, pal," he said softly. We touched him."

The kid picked up a clean highball glass and began to polish it. Ie polished it all the rest of the time we were there.

In another minute a homicide fast-wagon sirened up and creeched to a stop outside the door and four men came in, two dicks, a photographer and a laboratory man. I didn't know either of he dicks. You can be in the detecting business a long time and not now all the men on a big city force.

One of them was a short, smooth, dark, quiet, smiling man, with urly black hair and soft intelligent eyes. The other was big, raw-boned, long-jawed, with a veined nose and glassy eyes. He looked ike a heavy drinker. He looked tough, but he looked as if he hought he was a little tougher than he was. He shooed me into he last booth against the wall and his partner got the kid up front nd the bluecoats went out. The fingerprint man and photog-apher set about their work.

A medical examiner came, stayed just long enough to get sore because there was no phone for him to call the morgue wagon.

The short dick emptied Waldo's pockets and then emptied his wallet and dumped everything into a large handkerchief on a booth table. I saw a lot of currency, keys, cigarettes, another handkerchief, very little else.

The big dick pushed me back into the end of the half-booth. "Give," he said. "I'm Copernik, Detective Lieutenant."

I put my wallet in front of him. He looked at it, went through it, tossed it back, made a note in a book.

"Philip Marlowe, huh? A shamus. You here on business?"

"Drinking business," I said. "I live just across the street in th
Berglund."

"Know this kid up front?"

"I've been in here once since he opened up."

"See anything funny about him now?"

"No."

"Takes it too light for a young fellow, don't he? Never min
answering. Just tell the story."

I told it — three times. Once for him to get the outline, onc
for him to get the details and once for him to see if I had it too pa
At the end he said: "This dame interests me. And the killer calle
the guy Waldo, yet didn't seem to be anyways sure he would be in.
mean, if Waldo wasn't sure the dame would be here, nobody coul
be sure Waldo would be here."

"That's pretty deep," I said.

He studied me. I wasn't smiling. "Sounds like a grudge job
don't it? Don't sound planned. No getaway except by accident. A
guy don't leave his car unlocked much in this town. And the kille
works in front of two good witnesses. I don't like that."

"I don't like being a witness," I said. "The pay's too low."

He grinned. His teeth had a freckled look. "Was the kille
drunk really?"

"With that shooting? No."

"Me too. Well, it's a simple job. The guy will have a record and
he's left plenty prints. Even if we don't have his mug here we'll
make him in hours. He had something on Waldo, but he wasn't
meeting Waldo tonight. Waldo just dropped in to ask about a dame
he had a date with and had missed connections on. It's a hot night
and this wind would kill a girl's face. She'd be apt to drop in somewhere to wait. So the killer feeds Waldo two in the right place and
scrams and don't worry about you boys at all. It's that simple."

"Yeah," I said.

"It's so simple it stinks," Copernik said.

He took his felt hat off and tousled up his ratty blond hair and
leaned his head on his hands. He had a long mean horse face. He
got a handkerchief out and mopped it, and the back of his neck and
the back of his hands. He got a comb out and combed his hair —
he looked worse with it combed — and put his hat back on.

"I was just thinking," I said.

"Yeah? What?"

"This Waldo knew just how the girl was dressed. So he must already have been with her tonight."

"So, what? Maybe he had to go to the can. And when he came back she's gone. Maybe she changed her mind about him."

"That's right," I said.

But that wasn't what I was thinking at all. I was thinking that Waldo had described the girl's clothes in a way the ordinary man wouldn't know how to describe them. Printed bolero jacket over blue crêpe silk dress. I didn't even know what a bolero jacket was. And I might have said blue dress or even blue silk dress, but never blue crêpe silk dress.

After a while two men came with a basket. Lew Petrolle was still polishing his glass and talking to the short dark dick.

We all went down to headquarters.

Lew Petrolle was all right when they checked on him. His father had a grape ranch near Antioch in Contra Costa County. He had given Lew a thousand dollars to go into business and Lew had opened the cocktail bar, neon sign and all, on eight hundred flat.

They let him go and told him to keep the bar closed until they were sure they didn't want to do any more printing. He shook hands all around and grinned and said he guessed the killing would be good for business after all, because nobody believed a newspaper account of anything and people would come to him for the story and buy drinks while he was telling it.

"There's a guy won't ever do any worrying," Copernik said, when he was gone. "Over anybody else."

"Poor Waldo," I said. "The prints any good?"

"Kind of smudged," Copernik said sourly. "But we'll get a classification and teletype it to Washington some time tonight. If it don't click, you'll be in for a day on the steel picture racks downstairs."

I shook hands with him and his partner, whose name was Ybarra, and left. They didn't know who Waldo was yet either. Nothing in his pockets told.

2

I GOT BACK TO MY STREET about 9 P.M. I looked up and down the block before I went into the Berglund. The cocktail bar was farther down on the other side, dark, with a nose or two against the glass but no real crowd. People had seen the law and the morgue wagon but they didn't know what had happened. Except the boys playing pinball games in the drugstore on the corner. They know everything, except how to hold a job.

The wind was still blowing, oven-hot, swirling dust and torn paper up against the walls.

I went into the lobby of the apartment house and rode the automatic elevator up to the fourth floor. I unwound the door and stepped out and there was a tall girl standing there waiting for the car.

She had brown wavy hair under a wide-brimmed straw hat with a velvet band and loose bow. She had wide blue eyes and eyelashes that didn't quite reach her chin. She wore a blue dress that might have been crêpe silk, simple in lines but not missing any curves. Over it she wore what might have been a print bolero jacket.

I said: "Is that a bolero jacket?"

She gave me a distant glance and made a motion as if to brush a cobweb out of the way.

"Yes. Would you mind — I'm rather in a hurry. I'd like —"

I didn't move. I blocked her off from the elevator. We stared at each other and she flushed very slowly.

"Better not go out on the street in those clothes," I said.

"Why, how dare you —"

The elevator clanked and started down again. I didn't know what she was going to say. Her voice lacked the edgy twang of a beer parlor frill. It had a soft light sound, like spring rain.

"It's not a make," I said. "You're in trouble. If they come to this floor in the elevator, you have just that much time to get off the hall. First take off the hat and jacket — and snap it up!"

She didn't move. Her face seemed to whiten a little behind the not-too-heavy make-up.

"Cops," I said, "are looking for you. In those clothes. Give me the chance and I'll tell you why."

She turned her head swiftly and looked back along the corridor. With her looks I didn't blame her for trying one more bluff.

"You're impertinent, whoever you are. I'm Mrs. Leroy in apartment thirty-one. I can assure —"

"That you're on the wrong floor," I said. "This is the fourth." The elevator had stopped down below. The sound of doors being wrenched open came up the shaft.

"Off!" I rapped. "Now!"

She switched her hat off and slipped out of the bolero jacket, fast. I grabbed them and wadded them into a mess under my arm. I took her elbow and turned her and we were going down the hall.

"I live in forty-two. The front one across from yours, just a floor up. Take your choice. Once again — I'm not on the make."

She smoothed her hair with that quick gesture, like a bird preening itself. Ten thousand years of practice behind it.

"Mine," she said, and tucked her bag under her arm and strode down the hall fast. The elevator stopped at the floor below. She stopped when it stopped. She turned and faced me.

"The stairs are back by the elevator shaft," I said gently.

"I don't have an apartment," she said.

"I didn't think you had."

"Are they searching for me?"

"Yes, but they won't start gouging the block stone by stone before tomorrow. And then only if they don't make Waldo."

She stared at me. "Waldo?"

"Oh, you don't know Waldo," I said.

She shook her head slowly. The elevator started down in the shaft again. Panic flicked in her blue eyes like a ripple on water.

"No," she said breathlessly, "but take me out of this hall."

We were almost at my door. I jammed the key in and shook the lock around and heaved the door inward. I reached in far enough to switch lights on. She went in past me like a wave. Sandalwood floated on the air, very faint.

I shut the door, threw my hat into a chair and watched her stroll over to a card table on which I had a chess problem set out that I couldn't solve. Once inside, with the door locked, her panic had left her.

"So you're a chess player," she said, in that guarded tone, as if she had come to look at my etchings. I wished she had.

We both stood still then and listened to the distant clang of elevator doors and then steps — going the other way.

I grinned, but with strain, not pleasure, went out into the kitchenette and started to fumble with a couple of glasses and then realized I still had her hat and bolero jacket under my arm. I went into the dressing room behind the wall bed and stuffed them into a drawer, went back out to the kitchenette, dug out some extra-fine Scotch and made a couple of highballs.

When I went in with the drinks she had a gun in her hand. It was a small automatic with a pearl grip. It jumped up at me and her eyes were full of horror.

I stopped, with a glass in each hand, and said: "Maybe this hot wind has got you crazy too. I'm a private detective. I'll prove it if you let me."

She nodded slightly and her face was white. I went over slowly and put a glass down beside her, and went back and set mine down and got a card out that had no bent corners. She was sitting down, smoothing one blue knee with her left hand, and holding the gun on the other. I put the card down beside her drink and sat with mine.

"Never let a guy get that close to you," I said. "Not if you mean business. And your safety catch is on."

She flashed her eyes down, shivered, and put the gun back in her bag. She drank half the drink without stopping, put the glass down hard and picked the card up.

"I don't give many people that liquor," I said. "I can't afford to."

Her lips curled. "I supposed you would want money."

"Huh?"

She didn't say anything. Her hand was close to her bag again.

"Don't forget the safety catch," I said. Her hand stopped. I went on: "This fellow I called Waldo is quite tall, say five-eleven, slim, dark, brown eyes with a lot of glitter. Nose and mouth too thin.

Dark suit, white handkerchief showing, and in a hurry to find you. Am I getting anywhere?"

She took her glass again. "So that's Waldo," she said. "Well, what about him?" Her voice seemed to have a slight liquor edge now.

"Well, a funny thing. There's a cocktail bar across the street . . . Say, where have you been all evening?"

"Sitting in my car," she said coldly, "most of the time."

"Didn't you see a fuss across the street up the block?"

Her eyes tried to say no and missed. Her lips said: "I knew there was some kind of disturbance. I saw policemen and red searchlights. I supposed someone had been hurt."

"Someone was. And this Waldo was looking for you before that. In the cocktail bar. He described you and your clothes."

Her eyes were set like rivets now and had the same amount of expression. Her mouth began to tremble and kept on trembling.

"I was in there," I said, "talking to the kid that runs it. There was nobody in there but a drunk on a stool and the kid and myself. The drunk wasn't paying any attention to anything. Then Waldo came in and asked about you and we said no, we hadn't seen you and he started to leave."

I sipped my drink. I like an effect as well as the next fellow. Her eyes ate me.

"Just started to leave. Then this drunk that wasn't paying any attention to anyone called him Waldo and took a gun out. He shot him twice" — I snapped my fingers twice — "like that. Dead."

She fooled me. She laughed in my face. "So my husband hired you to spy on me," she said. "I might have known the whole thing was an act. You and your Waldo."

I gawked at her.

"I never thought of him as jealous," she snapped. "Not of a man who had been our chauffeur anyhow. A little about Stan, of course — that's natural. But Joseph Coates —"

I made motions in the air. "Lady, one of us has this book open at the wrong page," I grunted. "I don't know anybody named Stan or Joseph Coates. So help me, I didn't even know you had a chauffeur. People around here don't run to them. As for husbands — yeah, we do have a husband once in a while. Not often enough."

She shook her head slowly and her hand stayed near her bag and her blue eyes had glitters in them.

"Not good enough, Mr. Marlowe. No, not nearly good enough. I know you private detectives. You're all rotten. You tricked me into your apartment, if it is your apartment. More likely it's the apartment of some horrible man who will swear anything for a few dollars. Now you're trying to scare me. So you can blackmail me — as well as get money from my husband. All right," she said breathlessly, "how much do I have to pay?"

I put my empty glass aside and leaned back. "Pardon me if I light a cigarette," I said. "My nerves are frayed."

I lit it while she watched me without enough fear for any real guilt to be under it. "So Joseph Coates is his name," I said. "The guy that killed him in the cocktail bar called him Waldo."

She smiled a bit disgustedly, but almost tolerantly. "Don't stall. How much?"

"Why were you trying to meet this Joseph Coates?"

"I was going to buy something he stole from me, of course. Something that's valuable in the ordinary way too. Almost fifteen thousand dollars. The man I loved gave it to me. He's dead. There! He's dead! He died in a burning plane. Now, go back and tell my husband that, you slimy little rat!"

"I'm not little and I'm not a rat," I said.

"You're still slimy. And don't bother about telling my husband. I'll tell him myself. He probably knows anyway."

I grinned. "That's smart. Just what was I supposed to find out?"

She grabbed her glass and finished what was left of her drink. "So he thinks I'm meeting Joseph. Well, perhaps I was. But not to make love. Not with a chauffeur. Not with a bum I picked off the front step and gave a job to. I don't have to dig down that far, if I want to play around."

"Lady," I said, "you don't indeed."

"Now I'm going," she said. "You just try and stop me." She snatched the pearl-handled gun out of her bag. I didn't move.

"Why, you nasty little string of nothing," she stormed. "How do I know you're a private detective at all? You might be a crook. This card you gave me doesn't mean anything. Anybody can have cards printed."

"Sure," I said. "And I suppose I'm smart enough to live here two years because you were going to move in today so I could blackmail you for not meeting a man named Joseph Coates who was bumped off across the street under the name of Waldo. Have you got the money to buy this something that cost fifteen grand?"

"Oh! You think you'll hold me up, I suppose!"

"Oh!" I mimicked her. "I'm a stick-up artist now, am I? Lady, will you please either put that gun away or take the safety catch off? It hurts my professional feelings to see a nice gun made a monkey of that way."

"You're a full portion of what I don't like," she said. "Get out of my way."

I didn't move. She didn't move. We were both sitting down — and not even close to each other.

"Let me in on one secret before you go," I pleaded. "What in hell did you take the apartment down on the floor below for? Just to meet a guy down on the street?"

"Stop being silly," she snapped. "I didn't. I lied. It's his apartment."

"Joseph Coates'?"

She nodded sharply.

"Does my description of Waldo sound like Joseph Coates?"

She nodded sharply again.

"All right. That's one fact learned at last. Don't you realize Waldo described your clothes before he was shot — when he was looking for you — that the description was passed on to the police — that the police don't know who Waldo is — and are looking for somebody in those clothes to help tell them? Don't you get that much?"

The gun suddenly started to shake in her hand. She looked down at it, sort of vacantly, slowly put it back in her bag.

"I'm a fool," she whispered, "to be even talking to you." She stared at me for a long time, then pulled in a deep breath. "He told me where he was staying. He didn't seem afraid. I guess blackmailers are like that. He was to meet me on the street, but I was late. It was full of police when I got here. So I went back and sat in my car for a while. Then I came up to Joseph's apartment and knocked. Then I went back to my car and waited again. I came up here three times in all. The last time I walked up a flight to take the elevator. I had already been seen twice on the third floor. I met you. That's all."

"You said something about a husband," I grunted. "Where is he?"

"He's at a meeting."

"Oh, a meeting," I said nastily.

"My husband's a very important man. He has lots of meetings. He's a hydroelectric engineer. He's been all over the world. I'd have you know —"

"Skip it," I said. "I'll take him to lunch some day and have him tell me himself. Whatever Joseph had on you is dead stock now. Like Joseph."

"He's really dead?" she whispered. "Really?"

"He's dead," I said. "Dead, dead, dead. Lady, he's dead."

She believed it at last. I hadn't thought she ever would somehow. In the silence, the elevator stopped at my floor.

I heard steps coming down the hall. We all have hunches. I put my finger to my lips. She didn't move now. Her face had a frozen look. Her big blue eyes were as black as the shadows below them. The hot wind boomed against the shut windows. Windows have to be shut when a Santa Ana blows, heat or no heat.

The steps that came down the hall were the casual ordinary steps of one man. But they stopped outside my door, and somebody knocked.

I pointed to the dressing room behind the wall bed. She stood up without a sound, her bag clenched against her side. I pointed again, to her glass. She lifted it swiftly, slid across the carpet, through the door, drew the door quietly shut after her.

I didn't know just what I was going to all this trouble for.

The knocking sounded again. The backs of my hands were wet. I creaked my chair and stood up and made a loud yawning sound. Then I went over and opened the door — without a gun. That was a mistake.

3

I DIDN'T KNOW HIM AT FIRST. Perhaps for the opposite reason Waldo hadn't seemed to know him. He'd had a hat on all the time over at the cocktail bar and he didn't have one on now. His hair ended completely and exactly where his hat would start. Above that line was hard white sweatless skin almost as glaring as scar tissue. He wasn't just twenty years older. He was a different man.

But I knew the gun he was holding, the .22 target automatic with the big front sight. And I knew his eyes. Bright, brittle, shallow eyes like the eyes of a lizard.

He was alone. He put the gun against my face very lightly and said between his teeth: "Yeah, me. Let's go on in."

I backed in just far enough and stopped. Just the way he would want me to, so he could shut the door without moving much. I knew from his eyes that he would want me to do just that.

I wasn't scared. I was paralyzed.

When he had the door shut he backed me some more, slowly, until there was something against the back of my legs. His eyes looked into mine.

"That's a card table," he said. "Some goon here plays chess. You?"

I swallowed. "I don't exactly play it. I just fool around."

"That means two," he said with a kind of hoarse softness, as if some cop had hit him across the windpipe with a blackjack once, in a third-degree session.

"It's a problem," I said. "Not a game. Look at the pieces."

"I wouldn't know."

"Well, I'm alone," I said, and my voice shook just enough.

"It don't make any difference," he said. "I'm washed up anyway. Some nose puts the bulls on me tomorrow, next week, what the hell? I just didn't like your map, pal. And that smug-faced pansy in the bar coat that played left tackle for Fordham or something. To hell with guys like you guys."

I didn't speak or move. The big front sight raked my cheek lightly, almost caressingly. The man smiled.

"It's kind of good business too," he said. "Just in case. An old con like me don't make good prints, all I got against me is two witnesses. The hell with it."

"What did Waldo do to you?" I tried to make it sound as if I wanted to know, instead of just not wanting to shake too hard.

"Stooled on a bank job in Michigan and got me four years. Got himself a nolle prosse. Four years in Michigan ain't no summer cruise. They make you be good in them lifer states."

"How'd you know he'd come in there?" I croaked.

"I didn't. Oh yeah, I was lookin' for him. I was wanting to see him all right. I got a flash of him on the street night before last but I lost him. Up to then I wasn't lookin' for him. Then I was. A cute guy, Waldo. How is he?"

"Dead," I said.

"I'm still good," he chuckled. "Drunk or sober. Well, that don't make no doughnuts for me now. They make me downtown yet?"

I didn't answer him quick enough. He jabbed the gun into my throat and I choked and almost grabbed for it by instinct.

"Naw," he cautioned me softly. "Naw. You ain't that dumb."

I put my hands back, down at my sides, open, the palms towards him. He would want them that way. He hadn't touched me, except with the gun. He didn't seem to care whether I might have one too. He wouldn't — if he just meant the one thing.

He didn't seem to care very much about anything, coming back on that block. Perhaps the hot wind did something to him. It was booming against my shut windows like the surf under a pier.

"They got prints," I said. "I don't know how good."

"They'll be good enough — but not for teletype work. Take 'em airmail time to Washington and back to check 'em right. Tell me why I came here, pal."

"You heard the kid and me talking in the bar. I told him my name, where I lived."

"That's how, pal. I said why." He smiled at me. It was a lousy smile to be the last one you might see.

"Skip it," I said. "The hangman won't ask you to guess why he's there."

"Say, you're tough at that. After you, I visit that kid. I tailed him home from headquarters, but I figure you're the guy to put the bee on first. I tail him home from the city hall, in the rent car Waldo had. From headquarters, pal. Them funny dicks. You can sit in their laps and they don't know you. Start runnin' for a streetcar and they open up with machine guns and bump two pedestrians, a hacker asleep in his cab, and an old scrubwoman on the second floor workin' a mop. And they miss the guy they're after. Them funny lousy dicks."

He twisted the gun muzzle in my neck. His eyes looked madder than before.

"I got time," he said. "Waldo's rent car don't get a report right away. And they don't make Waldo very soon. I know Waldo. Smart he was. A smooth boy, Waldo."

"I'm going to vomit," I said, "if you don't take that gun out of my throat."

He smiled and moved the gun down to my heart. "This about right? Say when."

I must have spoken louder than I meant to. The door of the dressing room by the wall bed showed a crack of darkness. Then an inch. Then four inches. I saw eyes, but didn't look at them. I stared hard into the bald-headed man's eyes. Very hard. I didn't want him to take his eyes off mine.

"Scared?" he asked softly.

I leaned against his gun and began to shake. I thought he would enjoy seeing me shake. The girl came out through the door. She had her gun in her hand again. I was sorry as hell for her. She'd try to make the door — or scream. Either way it would be curtains — for both of us.

"Well, don't take all night about it," I bleated. My voice sounded far away, like a voice on a radio on the other side of a street.

"I like this, pal," he smiled. "I'm like that."

The girl floated in the air, somewhere behind him. Nothing was ever more soundless than the way she moved. It wouldn't do any good though. He wouldn't fool around with her at all. I had known him all my life but I had been looking into his eyes for only five minutes.

"Suppose I yell," I said.

"Yeah, suppose you yell. Go ahead and yell," he said with his killer's smile.

She didn't go near the door. She was right behind him.

"Well — here's where I yell," I said.

As if that was the cue, she jabbed the little gun hard into his short ribs, without a single sound.

He had to react. It was like a knee reflex. His mouth snapped open and both his arms jumped out from his sides and he arched his back just a little. The gun was pointing at my right eye.

I sank and kneed him with all my strength, in the groin.

His chin came down and I hit it. I hit it as if I was driving the last spike on the first transcontinental railroad. I can still feel it when I flex my knuckles.

His gun raked the side of my face but it didn't go off. He was already limp. He writhed down gasping, his left side against the floor. I kicked his right shoulder — hard. The gun jumped away from him, skidded on the carpet, under a chair. I heard the chessmen tinkling on the floor behind me somewhere.

The girl stood over him, looking down. Then her wide dark horrified eyes came up and fastened on mine.

"That buys me," I said. "Anything I have is yours — now and forever."

She didn't hear me. Her eyes were strained open so hard that the whites showed under the vivid blue iris. She backed quickly to the door with her little gun up, felt behind her for the knob and twisted it. She pulled the door open and slipped out.

The door shut.

She was bareheaded and without her bolero jacket.

She had only the gun, and the safety catch on that was still set so that she couldn't fire it.

It was silent in the room then, in spite of the wind. Then I heard him gasping on the floor. His face had a greenish pallor. I moved behind him and pawed him for more guns, and didn't find any. I got a pair of store cuffs out of my desk and pulled his arms in front of him and snapped them on his wrists. They would hold if he didn't shake them too hard.

His eyes measured me for a coffin, in spite of their suffering. He lay in the middle of the floor, still on his left side, a twisted, wizened, bald-headed little guy with drawn-back lips and teeth spotted with cheap silver fillings. His mouth looked like a black pit and his breath came in little waves, choked, stopped, came on again, limping.

I went into the dressing room and opened the drawer of the chest. Her hat and jacket lay there on my shirts. I put them underneath, at the back, and smoothed the shirts over them. Then I went out to the kitchenette and poured a stiff jolt of whiskey and put it down and stood a moment listening to the hot wind howl against the window glass. A garage door banged, and a power-line wire with too much play between the insulators thumped the side of the building with a sound like somebody beating a carpet.

The drink worked on me. I went back into the living room and opened a window. The guy on the floor hadn't smelled her sandalwood, but somebody else might.

I shut the window again, wiped the palms of my hands and used the phone to dial headquarters.

Copernik was still there. His smart-aleck voice said: "Yeah? Marlowe? Don't tell me. I bet you got an idea."

"Make that killer yet?"

"We're not saying, Marlowe. Sorry as all hell and so on. You know how it is."

"Okay. I don't care who he is. Just come and get him off the floor of my apartment."

"Holy Christ!" Then his voice hushed and went down low. "Wait a minute, now. Wait a minute." A long way off I seemed to hear a door shut. Then his voice again. "Shoot," he said softly.

"Handcuffed," I said. "All yours. I had to knee him, but he'll be all right. He came here to eliminate a witness."

Another pause. The voice was full of honey. "Now listen, boy, who else is in this with you?"

"Who else? Nobody. Just me."

"Keep it that way, boy. All quiet. Okay?"

"Think I want all the bums in the neighborhood in here sightseeing?"

"Take it easy, boy. Easy. Just sit tight and sit still. I'm practically there. No touch nothing. Get me?"

"Yeah." I gave him the address and apartment number again to save him time.

I could see his big bony face glisten. I got the .22 target gun from under the chair and sat holding it until feet hit the hallway outside my door and knuckles did a quiet tattoo on the door panel.

Copernik was alone. He filled the doorway quickly, pushed me back into the room with a tight grin and shut the door. He stood with his back to it, his hand under the left side of his coat. A big hard bony man with flat cruel eyes.

He lowered them slowly and looked at the man on the floor. The man's neck was twitching a little. His eyes moved in short stabs — sick eyes.

"Sure it's the guy?" Copernik's voice was hoarse.

"Positive. Where's Ybarra?"

"Oh, he was busy." He didn't look at me when he said that. "Those your cuffs?"

"Yeah."

"Key."

I tossed it to him. He went down swiftly on one knee beside the killer and took my cuffs off his wrists, tossed them to one side. He got his own off his hip, twisted the bald man's hands behind him and snapped the cuffs on.

"All right, you bastard," the killer said tonelessly.

Copernik grinned and balled his fist and hit the handcuffed man in the mouth a terrific blow. His head snapped back almost enough to break his neck. Blood dribbled from the lower corner of his mouth.

"Get a towel," Copernik ordered.

I got a hand towel and gave it to him. He stuffed it between the handcuffed man's teeth, viciously, stood up and rubbed his bony fingers through his ratty blond hair.

"All right. Tell it."

I told it — leaving the girl out completely. It sounded a little funny. Copernik watched me, said nothing. He rubbed the side of his veined nose. Then he got his comb out and worked on his hair just as he had done earlier in the evening, in the cocktail bar.

I went over and gave him the gun. He looked at it casually,

dropped it into his side pocket. His eyes had something in them and his face moved in a hard bright grin.

I bent down and began picking up my chessmen and dropping them into the box. I put the box on the mantel, straightened out a leg of the card table, played around for a while. All the time Copernik watched me. I wanted him to think something out.

At last he came out with it. "This guy uses a twenty-two," he said. "He uses it because he's good enough to get by with that much gun. That means he's good. He knocks at your door, pokes that gat in your belly, walks you back into the room, says he's here to close your mouth for keeps — and yet you take him. You not having any gun. You take him alone. You're kind of good yourself, pal."

"Listen," I said, and looked at the floor. I picked up another chessman and twisted it between my fingers. "I was doing a chess problem," I said. "Trying to forget things."

"You got something on your mind, pal," Copernik said softly. "You wouldn't try to fool an old copper, would you, boy?"

"It's a swell pinch and I'm giving it to you," I said. "What the hell more do you want?"

The man on the floor made a vague sound behind the towel. His bald head glistened with sweat.

"What's the matter, pal? You been up to something?" Copernik almost whispered.

I looked at him quickly, looked away again. "All right," I said. "You know damn well I couldn't take him alone. He had the gun on me and he shoots where he looks."

Copernik closed one eye and squinted at me amiably with the other. "Go on, pal. I kind of thought of that too."

I shuffled around a little more, to make it look good. I said, slowly: "There was a kid here who pulled a job over in Boyle Heights, a heist job. It didn't take. A two-bit service station stick-up. I know his family. He's not really bad. He was here trying to beg train money off me. When the knock came he sneaked in — there."

I pointed at the wall bed and the door beside. Copernik's head swiveled slowly, swiveled back. His eyes winked again. "And this kid had a gun," he said.

I nodded. "And he got behind him. That takes guts, Copernik. You've got to give the kid a break. You've got to let him stay out of it."

"Tag out for this kid?" Copernik asked softly.

"Not yet, he says. He's scared there will be."

Copernik smiled. "I'm a homicide man," he said. "I wouldn't know — or care."

I pointed down at the gagged and handcuffed man on the floor. "You took him, didn't you?" I said gently.

Copernik kept on smiling. A big whitish tongue came out and massaged his thick lower lip. "How'd I do it?" he whispered.

"Get the slugs out of Waldo?"

"Sure. Long twenty-two's. One smashed a rib, one good."

"You're a careful guy. You don't miss any angles. You know anything about me? You dropped in on me to see what guns I had."

Copernik got up and went down on one knee again beside the killer. "Can you hear me, guy?" he asked with his face close to the face of the man on the floor.

The man made some vague sound. Copernik stood up and yawned. "Who the hell cares what he says? Go on, pal."

"You wouldn't expect to find I had anything, but you wanted to look around my place. And while you were mousing around in there" — I pointed to the dressing room — "and me not saying anything, being a little sore, maybe, a knock came on the door. So he came in. So after a while you sneaked out and took him."

"Ah." Copernik grinned widely, with as many teeth as a horse. "You're on, pal. I socked him and I kneed him and I took him. You didn't have no gun and the guy swiveled on me pretty sharp and I left-hooked him down the backstairs. Okay?"

"Okay," I said.

"You'll tell it like that downtown?"

"Yeah," I said.

"I'll protect you, pal. Treat me right and I'll always play ball. Forget about that kid. Let me know if he needs a break."

He came over and held out his hand. I shook it. It was as clammy as a dead fish. Clammy hands and the people who own them make me sick.

"There's just one thing," I said. "This partner of yours —

Ybarra. Won't he be a bit sore you didn't bring him along on this?"

Copernik tousled his hair and wiped his hatband with a large yellowish silk handkerchief.

"That guinea?" he sneered. "To hell with him!" He came close to me and breathed in my face. "No mistakes, pal — about that story of ours."

His breath was bad. It would be.

4

THERE WERE JUST FIVE OF US in the chief of detectives' office when Copernik laid it before them. A stenographer, the chief, Copernik, myself, Ybarra. Ybarra sat on a chair tilted against the side wall. His hat was down over his eyes but their softness loomed underneath, and the small still smile hung at the corners of the clean-cut Latin lips. He didn't look directly at Copernik. Copernik didn't look at him at all.

Outside in the corridor there had been photos of Copernik shaking hands with me, Copernik with his hat on straight and his gun in his hand and a stern, purposeful look on his face.

They said they knew who Waldo was, but they wouldn't tell me. I didn't believe they knew, because the chief of detectives had a morgue photo of Waldo on his desk. A beautiful job, his hair combed, his tie straight, the light hitting his eyes just right to make them glisten. Nobody would have known it was a photo of a dead man with two bullet holes in his heart. He looked like a dance-hall sheik making up his mind whether to take the blonde or the red-head.

It was about midnight when I got home. The apartment door was locked and while I was fumbling for my keys a low voice spoke to me out of the darkness.

All it said was "Please!" but I knew it. I turned and looked at a dark Cadillac coupe parked just off the loading zone. It had no lights. Light from the street touched the brightness of a woman's eyes.

I went over there. "You're a darn fool," I said.

She said: "Get in."

I climbed in and started the car and drove it a block and a half along Franklin and turned down Kingsley Drive. The hot wind still burned and blustered. A radio lilted from an open, sheltered side window of an apartment house. There were a lot of parked cars but she found a vacant space behind a small brand-new Packard cabriolet that had the dealer's sticker on the windshield glass. After she'd jockeyed us up to the curb she leaned back in the corner with her gloved hands on the wheel.

She was all in black now, or dark brown, with a small foolish hat. I smelled the sandalwood in her perfume.

"I wasn't very nice to you, was I?" she said.

"All you did was save my life."

"What happened?"

"I called the law and fed a few lies to a cop I don't like and gave him all the credit for the pinch and that was that. That guy you took away from me was the man who killed Waldo."

"You mean — you didn't tell them about me?"

"Lady," I said again, "all you did was save my life. What else do you want done? I'm ready, willing, and I'll try to be able."

She didn't say anything, or move.

"Nobody learned who you are from me," I said. "Incidentally, I don't know myself."

"I'm Mrs. Frank C. Barsaly, two-twelve Fremont Place, Olympia two-four-five-nine-six. Is that what you wanted?"

"Thanks," I mumbled, and rolled a dry unlit cigarette around in my fingers. "Why did you come back?" Then I snapped the fingers of my left hand. "The hat and jacket," I said. "I'll go up and get them."

"It's more than that," she said. "I want my pearls." I might have jumped a little. It seemed as if there had been enough without pearls.

A car tore by down the street going twice as fast as it should. A thin bitter cloud of dust lifted in the streetlights and whirled and vanished. The girl ran the window up quickly against it.

"All right," I said. "Tell me about the pearls. We have had a murder and a mystery woman and a mad killer and a heroic rescue and a police detective framed into making a false report. Now we will have pearls. All right — feed it to me."

"I was to buy them for five thousand dollars. From the man you call Waldo and I call Joseph Coates. He should have had them."

"No pearls," I said. "I saw what came out of his pockets. A lot of money, but no pearls."

"Could they be hidden in his apartment?"

"Yes," I said. "So far as I know he could have had them hidden anywhere in California except in his pockets. How's Mr. Barsaly this hot night?"

"He's still downtown at his meeting. Otherwise I couldn't have come."

"Well, you could have brought him," I said. "He could have sat in the rumble seat."

"Oh, I don't know," she said. "Frank weighs two hundred pounds and he's pretty solid. I don't think he would like to sit in the rumble seat, Mr. Marlowe."

"What the hell are we talking about anyway?"

She didn't answer. Her gloved hands tapped lightly, provokingly on the rim of the slender wheel. I threw the unlit cigarette out the window, turned a little and took hold of her.

When I let go of her, she pulled as far away from me as she could against the side of the car and rubbed the back of her glove against her mouth. I sat quite still.

We didn't speak for some time. Then she said very slowly: "I meant you to do that. But I wasn't always that way. It's only been since Stan Phillips was killed in his plane. If it hadn't been for that, I'd be Mrs. Phillips now. Stan gave me the pearls. They cost fifteen thousand dollars, he said once. White pearls, forty-one of them, the largest about a third of an inch across. I don't know how many grains. I never had them appraised or showed them to a jeweler, so I don't know those things. But I loved them on Stan's account. I loved Stan. The way you do just the one time. Can you understand?"

"What's your first name?" I asked.

"Lola."

"Go on talking, Lola." I got another dry cigarette out of my pocket and fumbled it between my fingers just to give them something to do.

"They had a simple silver clasp in the shape of a two-bladed propeller. There was one small diamond where the boss would be. I told Frank they were store pearls I had bought myself. He didn't know the difference. It's not so easy to tell, I dare say. You see — Frank is pretty jealous."

In the darkness she came closer to me and her side touched my side. But I didn't move this time. The wind howled and the trees shook. I kept on rolling the cigarette around in my fingers.

"I suppose you've read that story," she said. "About the wife and the real pearls and her telling her husband they were false?"

"I've read it," I said, "Maugham."

"I hired Joseph. My husband was in Argentina at the time. I was pretty lonely."

"*You* should be lonely," I said.

"Joseph and I went driving a good deal. Sometimes we had a drink or two together. But that's all. I don't go around —"

"You told him about the pearls," I said. "And when your two hundred pounds of beef came back from Argentina and kicked him out — he took the pearls, because he knew they were real. And then offered them back to you for five grand."

"Yes," she said simply. "Of course I didn't want to go to the police. And of course in the circumstance Joseph wasn't afraid of my knowing where he lived."

"Poor Waldo," I said. "I feel kind of sorry for him. It was a hell of a time to run into an old friend that had a down on you."

I struck a match on my shoe sole and lit the cigarette. The tobacco was so dry from the hot wind that it burned like grass. The girl sat quietly beside me, her hands on the wheel again.

"Hell with women — these fliers," I said. "And you're still in love with him, or think you are. Where did you keep the pearls?"

"In a Russian malachite jewelry box on my dressing table. With some other costume jewelry. I had to, if I ever wanted to wear them."

"And they were worth fifteen grand. And you think Joseph might have hidden them in his apartment. Thirty-one, wasn't it?"

"Yes," she said. "I guess it's a lot to ask."

I opened the door and got out of the car. "I've been paid," I said. "I'll go look. The doors in my apartment are not very obstinate. The cops will find out where Waldo lived when they publish his photo, but not tonight, I guess."

"It's awfully sweet of you," she said. "Shall I wait here?"

I stood with a foot on the running board, leaning in, looking at her. I didn't answer her question. I just stood there looking in at the shine of her eyes. Then I shut the car door and walked up the street towards Franklin.

Even with the wind shriveling my face I could still smell the sandalwood in her hair. And feel her lips.

I unlocked the Berglund door, walked through the silent lobby to the elevator, and rode up to 3. Then I soft-footed along the silent corridor and peered down at the sill of apartment 31. No light. I rapped — the old light, confidential tattoo of the bootlegger with the big smile and the extra-deep hip pockets. No answer. I took the piece of thick hard celluloid that pretended to be a window over the driver's license in my wallet, and eased it between the lock and the jamb, leaning hard on the knob, pushing it towards the hinges. The edge of the celluloid caught the slope of the spring lock and snapped it back with a small brittle sound, like an icicle breaking. The door yielded and I went into near darkness. Street light filtered in and touched a high spot here and there.

I shut the door and snapped the light on and just stood. There was a queer smell in the air. I made it in a moment — the smell of dark-cured tobacco. I prowled over to a smoking stand by the window and looked down at four brown butts — Mexican or South American cigarettes.

Upstairs, on my floor, feet hit the carpet and somebody went into a bathroom. I heard the toilet flush. I went into the bathroom of apartment 31. A little rubbish, nothing, no place to hide anything. The kitchenette was a longer job, but I only half searched. I knew there were no pearls in that apartment. I knew Waldo had been on his way out and that he was in a hurry and that something was riding him when he turned and took two bullets from an old friend.

I went back to the living room and swung the wall bed and looked past its mirror side into the dressing room for signs of still current occupancy. Swinging the bed farther I was no longer looking for pearls. I was looking at a man.

He was small, middle-aged, iron-gray at the temples, with a very dark skin, dressed in a fawn-colored suit with a wine-colored tie. His neat little brown hands hung limply by his sides. His small feet, in pointed polished shoes, pointed almost at the floor.

He was hanging by a belt around his neck from the metal top of the bed. His tongue stuck out farther than I thought it possible for a tongue to stick out.

He swung a little and I didn't like that, so I pulled the bed shut and he nestled quietly between the two clamped pillows. I didn't touch him yet. I didn't have to touch him to know that he would be cold as ice.

I went around him into the dressing room and used my handkerchief on drawer knobs. The place was stripped clean except for the light litter of a man living alone.

I came out of there and began on the man. No wallet. Waldo would have taken that and ditched it. A flat box of cigarettes, half full, stamped in gold:

LOUIS TAPIA Y CIA
CALLE DE PAYSANDÚ, 19
MONTEVIDEO

Matches from the Spezzia Club. An underarm holster of dark-grained leather and in it a 9-millimeter Mauser.

The Mauser made him a professional, so I didn't feel so badly. But not a very good professional, or bare hands would not have finished him, with the Mauser — a gun you can blast through a wall with — undrawn in his shoulder holster.

I made a little sense of it, not much. Four of the brown cigarettes had been smoked, so there had been either waiting or discussion. Somewhere along the line Waldo had got the little man by the throat and held him in just the right way to make him pass out in a matter of seconds. The Mauser had been less useful to him than a toothpick. Then Waldo had hung him up by the strap, probably dead already. That would account for haste, cleaning out the apartment, for Waldo's anxiety about the girl. It would account for the car left unlocked outside the cocktail bar.

That is, it would account for these things if Waldo had killed him, if this was really Waldo's apartment — if I wasn't just being kidded.

I examined some more pockets. In the left trouser one I found a gold penknife, some silver. In the left hip pocket a handkerchief, folded, scented. On the right hip another, unfolded but clean. In the right leg pocket four or five tissue handkerchiefs. A clean little guy. He didn't like to blow his nose on his handkerchief. Under these there was a small new keytainer holding four new keys — car keys. Stamped in gold on the keytainer was:

COMPLIMENTS OF R. K. VOGELSANG, INC.
"THE PACKARD HOUSE."

I put everything as I had found it, swung the bed back, used my handkerchief on knobs and other projections, and flat surfaces, killed the light and poked my nose out the door. The hall was empty. I went down to the street and around the corner to Kingsley Drive. The Cadillac hadn't moved.

I opened the car door and leaned on it. She didn't seem to have moved, either. It was hard to see any expression on her face. Hard to see anything but her eyes and chin, but not hard to smell the sandalwood.

"That perfume," I said, "would drive a deacon nuts . . . no pearls."

"Well, thanks for trying," she said in a low, soft vibrant voice. "I guess I can stand it. Shall I . . . Do we . . . Or . . .?"

"You go on home now," I said. "And whatever happens you never saw me before. Whatever happens. Just as you may never see me again."

"I'd hate that."

"Good luck, Lola." I shut the car door and stepped back.

The lights blazed on, the motor turned over. Against the wind at the corner the big coupe made a slow contemptuous turn and was gone. I stood there by the vacant space at the curb where it had been.

It was quite dark there now. Windows had become blanks in the apartment where the radio sounded. I stood looking at the back of a Packard cabriolet which seemed to be brand-new. I had seen it before — before I went upstairs, in the same place, in front of

Lola's car. Parked, dark, silent, with a blue sticker pasted to the right-hand corner of the shiny windshield.

And in my mind I was looking at something else, a set of brand-new car keys in a keytainer stamped "THE PACKARD HOUSE," upstairs, in a dead man's pocket.

I went up to the front of the cabriolet and put a small pocket flash on the blue slip. It was the same dealer all right. Written in ink below his name and slogan was a name and address — Eugénie Kolchenko, 5315 Arvieda Street, West Los Angeles.

It was crazy. I went back up to apartment 31, jimmied the door as I had done before, stepped in behind the wall bed and took the keytainer from the trousers pocket of the neat brown dangling corpse. I was back down on the street beside the cabriolet in five minutes. The keys fitted.

5

IT WAS A SMALL HOUSE, near a canyon rim out beyond Sawtelle, with a circle of writhing eucalyptus trees in front of it. Beyond that, on the other side of the street, one of those parties was going on where they come out and smash bottles on the sidewalk with a whoop like Yale making a touchdown against Princeton.

There was a wire fence at my number and some rose trees, and a flagged walk and a garage that was wide open and had no car in it. There was no car in front of the house either. I rang the bell. There was a long wait, then the door opened rather suddenly.

I wasn't the man she had been expecting. I could see it in her glittering kohl-rimmed eyes. Then I couldn't see anything in them. She just stood and looked at me, a long, lean, hungry brunette, with rouged cheekbones, thick black hair parted in the middle, a mouth made for three-decker sandwiches, coral-and-gold pajamas, sandals —

and gilded toenails. Under her ear lobes a couple of miniature temple bells gonged lightly in the breeze. She made a slow disdainful motion with a cigarette in a holder as long as a baseball bat.

"We-el, what ees it, little man? You want sometheeng? You are lost from the bee-ootiful party across the street, hein?"

"Ha-ha," I said. "Quite a party, isn't it? No, I just brought your car home. Lost it, didn't you?"

Across the street somebody had delirium tremens in the front yard and a mixed quartet tore what was left of the night into small strips and did what they could to make the strips miserable. While this was going on the exotic brunette didn't move more than one eyelash.

She wasn't beautiful, she wasn't even pretty, but she looked as if things would happen where she was.

"You have said what?" she got out, at last, in a voice as silky as a burnt crust of toast.

"Your car." I pointed over my shoulder and kept my eyes on her. She was the type that uses a knife.

The long cigarette holder dropped very slowly to her side and the cigarette fell out of it. I stamped it out, and that put me in the hall. She backed away from me and I shut the door.

The hall was like the long hall of a railroad flat. Lamps glowed pinkly in iron brackets. There was a bead curtain at the end, a tiger skin on the floor. The place went with her.

"You're Miss Kolchenko?" I asked, not getting any more action.

"Ye-es. I am Mees Kolchenko. What the 'ell you want?"

She was looking at me now as if I had come to wash the windows, but at an inconvenient time.

I got a card out with my left hand, held it out to her. She read it in my hand, moving her head just enough. "A detective?" she breathed.

"Yeah."

She said something in a spitting language. Then in English: "Come in! Theese damn wind dry up my skeen like so much teesue paper."

"We're in," I said. "I just shut the door. Snap out of it, Nazimova. Who was he? The little guy?"

Beyond the bead curtain a man coughed. She jumped as if she had been stuck with an oyster fork. Then she tried to smile. It wasn't very successful.

"A reward," she said softly. "You weel wait 'ere? Ten dollars it is fair to pay, no?"

"No," I said.

I reached a finger towards her slowly and added: "He's dead."

She jumped about three feet and let out a yell.

A chair creaked harshly. Feet pounded beyond the bead curtain, a large hand plunged into view and snatched it aside, and a big hard-looking blond man was with us. He had a purple robe over his pajamas, his right hand held something in his robe pocket. He stood quite still as soon as he was through the curtain, his feet planted solidly, his jaw out, his colorless eyes like gray ice. He looked like a man who would be hard to take out on an off-tackle play.

"What's the matter, honey?" He had a solid, burring voice, with just the right sappy tone to belong to a guy who would go for a woman with gilded toenails.

"I came about Miss Kolchenko's car," I said.

"Well, you could take your hat off," he said. "Just for a light work-out."

I took it off and apologized.

"Okay," he said, and kept his right hand shoved down hard in the purple pocket. "So you came about Miss Kolchenko's car. Take it from there."

I pushed past the woman and went closer to him. She shrank back against the wall and flattened her palms against it. Camille in a high-school play. The long holder lay empty at her toes.

When I was six feet from the big man he said easily: "I can hear you from there. Just take it easy. I've got a gun in this pocket and I've had to learn to use one. Now about the car?"

"The man who borrowed it couldn't bring it," I said, and pushed the card I was still holding towards his face. He barely glanced at it. He looked back at me.

"So what?" he said.

"Are you always this tough?" I asked. "Or only when you have your pajamas on?"

"So why couldn't he bring it himself?" he asked. "And skip the mushy talk."

The dark woman made a stuffed sound at my elbow.

"It's all right, honeybunch," the man said. "I'll handle this. Go on."

She slid past both of us and flicked through the bead curtain. I waited a little while. The big man didn't move a muscle. He didn't look any more bothered than a toad in the sun.

"He couldn't bring it because somebody bumped him off," I said. "Let's see you handle that."

"Yeah?" he said. "Did you bring him with you to prove it?"

"No," I said. "But if you put your tie and crush hat on, I'll take you down and show you."

"Who the hell did you say you were, now?"

"I didn't say. I thought maybe you could read." I held the card at him some more.

"Oh, that's right," he said. "Philip Marlowe, private investigator. Well, well. So I should go with you to look at who, why?"

"Maybe he stole the car," I said.

The big man nodded. "That's a thought. Maybe he did. Who?"

"The little brown guy who had the keys to it in his pocket, and had it parked around the corner from the Berglund Apartments."

He thought that over, without any apparent embarrassment. "You've got something there," he said. "Not much. But a little. I guess this must be the night of the Police Smoker. So you're doing all their work for them."

"Huh?"

"The card says private detective to me," he said. "Have you got some cops outside that were too shy to come in?"

"No, I'm alone."

He grinned. The grin showed white ridges in his tanned skin. "So you find somebody dead and take some keys and find a car and come riding out here — all alone. No cops. Am I right?"

"Correct."

He sighed. "Let's go inside," he said. He yanked the bead curtain aside and made an opening for me to go through. "It might be you have an idea I ought to hear."

I went past him and he turned, keeping his heavy pocket towards me. I hadn't noticed until I got quite close that there were beads of sweat on his face. It might have been the hot wind but I didn't think so.

We were in the living room of the house.

We sat down and looked at each other across a dark floor, on which a few Navajo rugs and a few dark Turkish rugs made a decorating combination with some well-used overstuffed furniture. There was a fireplace, a small baby grand, a Chinese screen, a tall Chinese lantern on a teakwood pedestal, and gold net curtains against lattice windows. The windows to the south were open. A fruit tree with a whitewashed trunk whipped about outside the screen, adding its bit to the noise from across the street.

The big man eased back into a brocaded chair and put his slippered feet on a footstool. He kept his right hand where it had been since I met him — on his gun.

The brunette hung around in the shadows and a bottle gurgled and her temple bells gonged in her ears.

"It's all right, honeybunch," the man said. "It's all under control. Somebody bumped somebody off and this lad thinks we're interested. Just sit down and relax."

The girl tilted her head and poured half a tumbler of whiskey down her throat. She sighed, said, "Goddam," in a casual voice, and curled up on a davenport. It took all of the davenport. She had plenty of legs. Her gilded toenails winked at me from the shadowy corner where she kept herself quiet from then on.

I got a cigarette out without being shot at, lit it and went into my story. It wasn't all true, but some of it was. I told them about the Berglund Apartments and that I had lived there and that Waldo was living there in apartment 31 on the floor below mine and that I had been keeping an eye on him for business reasons.

"Waldo what?" the blond man put in. "And what business reasons?"

"Mister," I said, "have you no secrets?" He reddened slightly.

I told him about the cocktail lounge across the street from the Berglund and what had happened there. I didn't tell him about the printed bolero jacket or the girl who had worn it. I left her out of the story altogether.

"It was an undercover job — from my angle," I said. "If you

know what I mean." He reddened again, bit his teeth. I went on: "I got back from the City Hall without telling anybody I knew Waldo. In due time, when I decided they couldn't find out where he lived that night, I took the liberty of examining his apartment."

"Looking for what?" the big man said thickly.

"For some letters. I might mention in passing there was nothing there at all — except a dead man. Strangled and hanging by a belt to the top of the wall bed — well out of sight. A small man, about forty-five, Mexican or South American, well-dressed in a fawn-colored —"

"That's enough," the big man said. "I'll bite, Marlowe. Was it a blackmail job you were on?"

"Yeah. The funny part was this little brown man had plenty of gun under his arm."

"He wouldn't have five hundred bucks in twenties in his pocket, of course? Or are you saying?"

"He wouldn't. But Waldo had over seven hundred in currency when he was killed in the cocktail bar."

"Looks like I underrated this Waldo," the big man said calmly. "He took my guy and his pay-off money, gun and all. Waldo have a gun?"

"Not on him."

"Get us a drink, honeybunch," the big man said. "Yes, I certainly did sell this Waldo person shorter than a bargain-counter shirt."

The brunette unwound her legs and made two drinks with soda and ice. She took herself another gill without trimmings, wound herself back on the davenport. Her big glittering black eyes watched me solemnly.

"Well, here's how," the big man said, lifting his glass in salute. "I haven't murdered anybody, but I've got a divorce suit on my hands from now on. You haven't murdered anybody, the way you tell it, but you laid an egg down at police headquarters. What the hell! Life's a lot of trouble, anyway you look at it. I've still got honeybunch here. She's a white Russian I met in Shanghai. She's safe as a vault and she looks as if she could cut your throat for a nickel. That's what I like about her. You get the glamour without the risk."

"You talk damn foolish," the girl spat him.

"You look okay to me." The big man went on ignoring her. "That is, for a keyhole peeper. Is there an out?"

"Yeah. But it will cost a little money."

"I expected that. How much?"

"Say another five hundred."

"Goddam, thees hot wind make me dry like the ashes of love," the Russian girl said bitterly.

"Five hundred might do," the blond man said. "What do I get for it?"

"If I swing it — you get left out of the story. If I don't — you don't pay."

He thought it over. His face looked lined and tired now. The small beads of sweat twinkled in his short blond hair.

"This murder will make you talk," he grumbled. "The second one, I mean. And I don't have what I was going to buy. And if it's a hush, I'd rather buy it direct."

"Who was the little brown man?" I asked.

"Name's Leon Valesanos, a Uruguayan. Another of my importations. I'm in a business that takes me a lot of places. He was working in the Spezzia Club in Chiseltown — you know, the strip of Sunset next to Beverly Hills. Working on roulette, I think. I gave him the five hundred to go down to this — this Waldo — and buy back some bills for stuff Miss Kolchenko had charged to my account and delivered here. That wasn't bright, was it? I had them in my briefcase and this Waldo got a chance to steal them. What's your hunch about what happened?"

I sipped my drink and looked at him down my nose. "Your Uruguayan pal probably talked cut and Waldo didn't listen good. Then the little guy thought maybe that Mauser might help his argument — and Waldo was too quick for him. I wouldn't say Waldo was a killer — not by intention. A blackmailer seldom is. Maybe he lost his temper and maybe he just held on to the little guy's neck too long. Then he had to take it on the lam. But he had another date, with more money coming up. And he worked the neighborhood looking for the party. And accidentally he ran into a pal who was hostile enough and drunk enough to blow him down."

"There's a hell of a lot of coincidence in all this business," the big man said.

"It's the hot wind." I grinned. "Everybody's screwy tonight."

"For the five hundred you guarantee nothing? If I don't get my cover-up, you don't get your dough. Is that it?"

"That's it," I said, smiling at him.

"Screwy is right," he said, and drained his highball. "I'm taking you up on it."

"There are just two things," I said softly, leaning forward in my chair. "Waldo had a getaway car parked outside the cocktail bar where he was killed, unlocked with the motor running. The killer took it. There's always the chance of a kickback from that direction. You see, all Waldo's stuff must have been in that car."

"Including my bills, and your letters."

"Yeah. But the police are reasonable about things like that — unless you're good for a lot of publicity. If you're not, I think I can eat some stale dog downtown and get by. If you are — that's the second thing. What did you say your name was?"

The answer was a long time coming. When it came I didn't get as much kick out of it as I thought I would. All at once it was too logical.

"Frank C. Barsaly," he said.

After a while the Russian girl called me a taxi. When I left, the party across the street was doing all that a party could do. I noticed the walls of the house were still standing. That seemed a pity.

6

WHEN I UNLOCKED THE GLASS ENTRANCE DOOR of the Berglund I smelled policeman. I looked at my wrist watch. It was nearly 3 A.M. In the dark corner of the lobby a man dozed in a chair with a newspaper over his face. Large feet stretched out before him. A corner of the paper lifted an inch, dropped again. The man made no other movement.

I went on along the hall to the elevator and rode up to my floor. I soft-footed along the hallway, unlocked my door, pushed it wide and reached in for the light switch.

A chain switch tinkled and light glared from a standing lamp by the easy chair, beyond the card table on which my chessmen were still scattered.

Copernik sat there with a stiff unpleasant grin on his face. The short dark man, Ybarra, sat across the room from him, on my left, silent, half smiling as usual.

Copernik showed more of his big yellow horse teeth and said: "Hi. Long time no see. Been out with the girls?"

I shut the door and took my hat off and wiped the back of my neck slowly, over and over again. Copernik went on grinning. Ybarra looked at nothing with his soft dark eyes.

"Take a seat, pal," Copernik drawled. "Make yourself to home. We got pow-wow to make. Boy, do I hate this night sleuthing. Did you know you were low on hooch?"

"I could have guessed it," I said. I leaned against the wall.

Copernik kept on grinning. "I always did hate private dicks," he said, "but I never had a chance to twist one like I got tonight."

He reached down lazily beside his chair and picked up a printed bolero jacket, tossed it on the card table. He reached down again and put a wide-brimmed hat beside it.

"I bet you look cuter than all hell with these on," he said.

I took hold of a straight chair, twisted it around and straddled it, leaned my folded arms on the chair and looked at Copernik.

He got up very slowly — with an elaborate slowness, walked across the room and stood in front of me smoothing his coat down. Then he lifted his open right hand and hit me across the face with it — hard. It stung but I didn't move.

Ybarra looked at the wall, looked at the floor, looked at nothing.

"Shame on you, pal," Copernik said lazily. "The way you was taking care of this nice exclusive merchandise. Wadded down behind your old shirts. You punk peepers always did make me sick."

He stood there over me for a moment. I didn't move or speak. I looked into his glazed drinker's eyes. He doubled a fist at his side, then shrugged and turned and went back to the chair.

"Okay," he said. "The rest will keep. Where did you get these things?"

"They belong to a lady."

"Do tell. They belong to a lady. Ain't you the lighthearted bastard! I'll tell you what lady they belong to. They belong to the lady a guy named Waldo asked about in a bar across the street — about two minutes before he got shot kind of dead. Or would that have slipped your mind?"

I didn't say anything.

"You was curious about her yourself," Copernik sneered on. "But you were smart, pal. You fooled me."

"That wouldn't make me smart," I said.

His face twisted suddenly and he started to get up. Ybarra laughed, suddenly and softly, almost under his breath. Copernik's eyes swung on him, hung there. Then he faced me again, bland-eyed.

"The guinea likes you," he said. "He thinks you're good."

The smile left Ybarra's face, but no expression took its place. No expression at all.

Copernik said: "You knew who the dame was all the time. You knew who Waldo was and where he lived. Right across the hall a floor below you. You knew this Waldo person had bumped a guy off and started to lam, only this broad came into his plans somewhere and he was anxious to meet up with her before he went away. Only he never got the chance. A heist guy from back east named Al Tessilore took care of that by taking care of Waldo. So you met the gal and hid her clothes and sent her on her way and kept your trap glued. That's the way guys like you make your beans. Am I right?"

"Yeah," I said. "Except that I only knew these things very recently. Who was Waldo?"

Copernik bared his teeth at me. Red spots burned high on his sallow cheeks. Ybarra, looking down at the floor, said very softly: "Waldo Ratigan. We got him from Washington by teletype. He was a two-bit porch climber with a few small terms on him. He drove a car in a bank stick-up job in Detroit. He turned the gang in later and got a nolle prosse. One of the gang was this Al Tessilore.

He hasn't talked a word, but we think the meeting across the street was purely accidental."

Ybarra spoke in the soft quiet modulated voice of a man for whom sounds have a meaning. I said: "Thanks, Ybarra. Can I smoke — or would Copernik kick it out of my mouth?"

Ybarra smiled suddenly. "You may smoke, sure," he said.

"The guinea likes you all right," Copernik jeered. "You never know what a guinea will like, do you?"

I lit a cigarette. Ybarra looked at Copernik and said very softly: "The word guinea — you overwork it. I don't like it so well applied to me."

"The hell with what you like, guinea."

Ybarra smiled a little more. "You are making a mistake," he said. He took a pocket nail file out and began to use it, looking down.

Copernik blared: "I smelled something rotten on you from the start, Marlowe. So when we make these two mugs, Ybarra and me think we'll drift over and dabble a few more words with you. I bring one of Waldo's morgue photos — nice work, the light just right in his eyes, his tie all straight and a white handkerchief showing just right in his pocket. Nice work. So on the way up, just as a matter of routine, we rout out the manager here and let him lamp it. And he knows the guy. He's here as A. B. Hummel, apartment thirty-one. So we go in there and find a stiff. Then we go round and round with that. Nobody knows him yet, but he's got some swell finger bruises under that strap and I hear they fit Waldo's fingers very nicely."

"That's something," I said. "I thought maybe I murdered him."

Copernik stared at me a long time. His face had stopped grinning and was just a hard brutal face now. "Yeah. We got something else even," he said. "We got Waldo's getaway car — and what Waldo had in it to take with him."

I blew cigarette smoke jerkily. The wind pounded the shut windows. The air in the room was foul.

"Oh, we're bright boys," Copernik sneered. "We never figured you with that much guts. Take a look at this."

He plunged his bony hand into his coat pocket and drew something up slowly over the edge of the card table, drew it along the green top and left it there stretched out, gleaming. A string of white pearls with a clasp like a two-bladed propeller. They shimmered softly in the thick smoky air.

Lola Barsaly's pearls. The pearls the flier had given her. The guy who was dead, the guy she still loved.

I stared at them, but I didn't move. After a long moment Copernik said almost gravely: "Nice, ain't they? Would you feel like telling us a story about now, Mis-ter Marlowe?"

I stood up and pushed the chair from under me, walked slowly across the room and stood looking down at the pearls. The largest was perhaps a third of an inch across. They were pure white, iridescent, with a mellow softness. I lifted them slowly off the card table from beside her clothes. They felt heavy, smooth, fine.

"Nice," I said. "A lot of the trouble was about these. Yeah, I'll talk now. They must be worth a lot of money."

Ybarra laughed behind me. It was a very gentle laugh. "About a hundred dollars," he said. "They're good phonies — but they're phony."

I lifted the pearls again. Copernik's glassy eyes gloated at me. "How do you tell?" I asked.

"I know pearls," Ybarra said. "These are good stuff, the kind women very often have made on purpose, as a kind of insurance. But they are slick like glass. Real pearls are gritty between the edges of the teeth. Try."

I put two or three of them between my teeth and moved my teeth back and forth, then sideways. Not quite biting them. The beads were hard and slick.

"Yes. They are very good," Ybarra said. "Several even have little waves and flat spots, as real pearls might have."

"Would they cost fifteen grand — if they were real?" I asked.

"Sí. Probably. That's hard to say. It depends on a lot of things."

"This Waldo wasn't so bad," I said.

Copernik stood up quickly, but I didn't see him swing. I was still looking down at the pearls. His fist caught me on the side of the face, against the molars. I tasted blood at once. I staggered back and made it look like a worse blow than it was.

"Sit down and talk, you bastard!" Copernik almost whispered.

I sat down and used a handkerchief to pat my cheek. I licked at the cut inside my mouth. Then I got up again and went over and picked up the cigarette he had knocked out of my mouth. I crushed it out in a tray and sat down again.

Ybarra filed at his nails and held one up against the lamp. There were beads of sweat on Copernik's eyebrows, at the inner ends.

"You found the beads in Waldo's car," I said, looking at Ybarra. "Find any papers?"

He shook his head without looking up.

"I'd believe you," I said. "Here it is. I never saw Waldo until he stepped into the cocktail bar tonight and asked about the girl. I knew nothing I didn't tell. When I got home and stepped out of the elevator this girl, in the printed bolero jacket and the wide hat and the blue silk crêpe dress — all as he had described them — was waiting for the elevator, here on my floor. And she looked like a nice girl."

Copernik laughed jeeringly. It didn't make any difference to me. I had him cold. All he had to do was know that. He was going to know it now, very soon.

"I knew what she was up against as a police witness," I said. "And I suspected there was something else to it. But I didn't suspect for a minute that there was anything wrong with her. She was just a nice girl in a jam — and she didn't even know she was in a jam. I got her in here. She pulled a gun on me. But she didn't mean to use it."

Copernik sat up very suddenly and he began to lick his lips. His face had a stony look now. A look like wet gray stone. He didn't make a sound.

"Waldo had been her chauffeur," I went on. "His name was then Joseph Coates. Her name is Mrs. Frank C. Barsaly. Her husband is a big hydroelectric engineer. Some guy gave her the pearls once and she told her husband they were just store pearls. Waldo got wise somehow there was a romance behind them and when Barsaly came home from South America and fired him, because he was too good-looking, he lifted the pearls."

Ybarra lifted his head suddenly and his teeth flashed. "You mean he didn't know they were phony?"

"I thought he fenced the real ones and had imitations fixed up," I said.

Ybarra nodded. "It's possible."

"He lifted something else," I said. "Some stuff from Barsaly's brief-case that showed he was keeping a woman — out in Brentwood. He was blackmailing wife and husband both, without either know-ing about the other. Get it so far?"

"I get it," Copernik said harshly, between his tight lips. His face was still wet gray stone. "Get the hell on with it."

"Waldo wasn't afraid of them," I said. "He didn't conceal where he lived. That was foolish, but it saved a lot of finagling, if he was willing to risk it. The girl came down here tonight with five grand to buy back her pearls. She didn't find Waldo. She came here to look for him and walked up a floor before she went back down. A wom-an's idea of being cagey. So I met her. So I brought here in here. So she was in that dressing room when Al Tessilore visited me to rub out a witness." I pointed to the dressing-room door. "So she came out with her little gun and stuck it in his back and saved my life," I said.

Copernik didn't move. There was something horrible in his face now. Ybarra slipped his nail file into a small leather case and slowly tucked it into his pocket.

"Is that all?" he said gently.

I nodded. "Except that she told me where Waldo's apartment was and I went in there and looked for the pearls. I found the dead man. In his pocket I found new car keys in a case from a Pack-ard agency. And down on the street I found the Packard and took it to where it came from. Barsaly's kept woman. Barsaly had sent a friend from the Spezzia Club down to buy something and he had tried to buy it with his gun instead of the money Barsaly gave him. And Waldo beat him to the punch."

"Is that all?" Ybarra said softly.

"That's all," I said, licking the torn place on the inside of my cheek.

Ybarra said slowly: "What do you want?"

Copernik's face convulsed and he slapped his long hard thigh. "This guy's good," he jeered. "He falls for a stray broad and breaks every law in the book and you ask him what does he want? I'll give him what he wants, guinea!"

Ybarra turned his head slowly and looked at him. "I don't think you will," he said. "I think you'll give him a clean bill of health and anything else he wants. He's giving you a lesson in police work."

Copernik didn't move or make a sound for a long minute. None of us moved. Then Copernik leaned forward and his coat fell open. The butt of his service gun looked out of his underarm holster.

"So what do you want?" he asked me.

"What's on the card table there. The jacket and hat and the phony pearls. And some names kept away from the papers. Is that too much?"

"Yeah — it's too much," Copernik said almost gently. He swayed sideways and his gun jumped neatly into his hand. He rested his forearm on his thigh and pointed the gun at my stomach.

"I like better that you get a slug in the guts resisting arrest," he said. "I like that better, because of a report I made out on Al Tessilore's arrest and how I made the pinch. Because of some photos of me that are in the morning sheets going out about now. I like it better that you don't live long enough to laugh about that baby."

My mouth felt suddenly hot and dry. Far off I heard the wind booming. It seemed like the sound of guns.

Ybarra moved his feet on the floor and said coldly: "You've got a couple of cases all solved, policeman. All you do for it is leave some junk here and keep some names from the papers. Which means from the D.A. If he gets them anyway, too bad for you."

Copernik said: "I like the other way." The blue gun in his hand was like a rock. "And God help you, if you don't back me up on it."

Ybarra said: "If the woman is brought out into the open, you'll be a liar on a police report and a chiseler on your own partner. In a week they won't even speak your name at Headquarters. The taste of it would make them sick."

The hammer clicked back on Copernik's gun and I watched his big finger slide in farther around the trigger.

Ybarra stood up. The gun jumped at him. He said: "We'll see how yellow a guinea is. I'm telling you to put that gun up, Sam."

He started to move. He moved four even steps. Copernik was a man without a breath of movement, a stone man.

Ybarra took one more step and quite suddenly the gun began to shake.

Ybarra spoke evenly: "Put it up, Sam. If you keep your head everything lies the way it is. If you don't — you're gone."

He took one more step. Copernik's mouth opened wide and made a gasping sound and then he sagged in the chair as if he had been hit on the head. His eyelids dropped.

Ybarra jerked the gun out of his hand with a movement so quick it was no movement at all. He stepped back quickly, held the gun low at his side.

"It's the hot wind, Sam. Let's forget it," he said in the same even, almost dainty voice.

Copernik's shoulders sagged lower and he put his face in his hands. "Okay," he said between his fingers.

Ybarra went softly across the room and opened the door. He looked at me with lazy, half-closed eyes. "I'd do a lot for a woman who saved my life, too," he said. "I'm eating this dish, but as a cop you can't expect me to like it."

I said: "The little man in the bed is called Leon Valesanos. He was a croupier at the Spezzia Club."

"Thanks," Ybarra said. "Let's go, Sam."

Copernik got up heavily and walked across the room and out of the open door and out of my sight. Ybarra stepped through the door after him and started to close it.

I said: "Wait a minute."

He turned his head slowly, his left hand on the door, the blue gun hanging down close to his right side.

"I'm not in this for money," I said. "The Barsalys live at two-twelve Fremont Place. You can take the pearls to her. If Barsaly's name stays out of the paper, I get five C's. It goes to the Police Fund. I'm not so damn smart as you think. It just happened that way — and you had a heel for a partner."

Ybarra looked across the room at the pearls on the card table. His eyes glistened. "You take them," he said. "The five hundred's okay. I think the fund has it coming."

He shut the door quietly and in a moment I heard the elevator doors clang.

7

I OPENED A WINDOW and stuck my head out into the wind and watched the squad car tool off down the block. The wind blew in hard and I let it blow. A picture fell off the wall and two chessmen rolled off the card table. The material of Lola Barsaly's bolero jacket lifted and shook.

I went out to the kitchenette and drank some Scotch and went back into the living room and called her — late as it was.

She answered the phone herself, very quickly, with no sleep in her voice.

"Marlowe," I said. "Okay your end?"

"Yes . . . yes," she said. "I'm alone."

"I found something," I said. "Or rather the police did. But your dark boy gypped you. I have a string of pearls. They're not real. He sold the real ones, I guess, and made you up a string of ringers, with your clasp."

She was silent for a long time. Then, a little faintly: "The police found them?"

"In Waldo's car. But they're not telling. We have a deal. Look at the papers in the morning and you'll be able to figure out why."

"There doesn't seem to be anything more to say," she said. "Can I have the clasp?"

"Yes. Can you meet me tomorrow at four in the Club Esquire bar?"

"You're really rather sweet," she said in a dragged-out voice. "I can. Frank is still at his meeting."

"Those meetings — they take it out of a guy," I said. We said goodbye.

I called a West Los Angeles number. He was still there, with the Russian girl.

"You can send me a check for five hundred in the morning," I told him. "Made out to the Police Relief Fund, if you want to. Because that's where it's going."

Copernik made the third page of the morning papers with two photos and a nice half-column. The little brown man in apartment 31 didn't make the paper at all. The Apartment House Association has a good lobby too.

I went out after breakfast and the wind was all gone. It was soft, cool, a little foggy. The sky was close and comfortable and gray. I rode down to the boulevard and picked out the best jewelry store on it and laid a string of pearls on a black velvet mat under a daylight-blue lamp. A man in a wing collar and striped trousers looked down at them languidly.

"How good?" I asked.

"I'm sorry, sir. We don't make appraisals. I can give you the name of an appraiser."

"Don't kid me," I said. "They're Dutch."

He focused the light a little and leaned down and toyed with a few inches of the string.

"I want a string just like them, fitted to that clasp, and in a hurry," I added.

"How, like them?" He didn't look up. "And they're not Dutch. They're Bohemian."

"Okay, can you duplicate them?"

He shook his head and pushed the velvet pad away as if it soiled him. "In three months, perhaps. We don't blow glass like that in this country. If you wanted them matched — three months at least. And this house would not do that sort of thing at all."

"It must be swell to be that snooty," I said. I put a card under his black sleeve. "Give me a name that will — and not in three months — and maybe not exactly like them."

He shrugged, went away with the card, came back in five minutes and handed it back to me. There was something written on the back.

The old Levantine had a shop on Melrose, a junk shop with everything in the window from a folding baby carriage to a French horn, from a mother-of-pearl lorgnette in a faded plush case to one of those .44 Special Single Action six-shooters they still make for Western peace officers whose grandfathers were tough.

The old Levantine wore a skull cap and two pairs of glasses and a full beard. He studied my pearls, shook his head sadly, and said: "For twenty dollars, almost so good. Not so good, you understand. Not so good glass."

"How like will they look?"

He spread his firm strong hands. "I am telling you the truth," he said. "They would not fool a baby."

"Make them up," I said. "With this clasp. And I want the others back, too, of course."

"Yah. Two o'clock," he said.

Leon Valesanos, the little brown man from Uruguay, made the afternoon papers. He had been found hanging in an unnamed apartment. The police were investigating.

At four o'clock I walked into the long cool bar of the Club Esquire and prowled along the row of booths until I found one where a woman sat alone. She wore a hat like a shallow soup plate with a very wide edge, a brown tailor-made suit with a severe mannish shirt and tie.

I sat down beside her and slipped a parcel along the seat. "You don't open that," I said. "In fact you can slip it into the incinerator as is, if you want to."

She looked at me with dark tired eyes. Her fingers twisted a thin glass that smelled of peppermint. "Thanks." Her face was very pale.

I ordered a highball and the waiter went away. "Read the papers?"

"Yes."

"You understand now about this fellow Copernik who stole your act? That's why they won't change the story or bring you into it."

"It doesn't matter now," she said. "Thank you, all the same. Please — please show them to me."

I pulled the string of pearls out of the loosely wrapped tissue paper in my pocket and slid them across to her. The silver propeller clasp winked in the light of the wall bracket. The little diamond winked. The pearls were as dull as white soap. They didn't even match in size.

"You were right," she said tonelessly. "They are not my pearls."

The waiter came with my drink and she put her bag on them

deftly. When he was gone she fingered them slowly once more, dropped them into the bag and gave me a dry mirthless smile.

"As you said — I'll keep the clasp."

I said slowly: "You don't know anything about me. You saved my life last night and we had a moment, but it was just a moment. You still don't know anything about me. There's a detective downtown named Ybarra, a Mexican of the nice sort, who was on the job when the pearls were found in Waldo's suitcase. That is in case you would like to make sure — "

She said: "Don't be silly. It's all finished. It was a memory. I'm too young to nurse memories. It may be for the best. I loved Stan Phillips — but he's gone — long gone."

I stared at her, didn't say anything.

She added quietly: "This morning my husband told me something I hadn't known. We are to separate. So I have very little to laugh about today."

"I'm sorry," I said lamely. "There's nothing to say. I may see you sometime. Maybe not. I don't move much in your circle. Good luck."

I stood up. We looked at each other for a moment. "You haven't touched your drink," she said.

"You drink it. That peppermint stuff will just make you sick."

I stood there a moment with a hand hard on the table.

"If anybody ever bothers you," I said, "let me know."

I went out of the bar without looking back at her, got into my car and drove west on Sunset and down all the way to the Coast Highway. Everywhere along the way gardens were full of withered and blackened leaves and flowers which the hot wind had burned.

But the ocean looked cool and languid and just the same as ever. I drove on almost to Malibu and then parked and went and sat on a big rock that was inside somebody's wire fence. It was about half-tide and coming in. The air smelled of kelp. I watched the water for a while and then I pulled a string of Bohemian glass imitation pearls out of my pocket and cut the knot at one end and slipped the pearls off one by one.

When I had them all loose in my left hand I held them like that for a while and thought. There wasn't really anything to think about. I was sure.

"To the memory of Mr. Stan Phillips," I said aloud. "Just another four-flusher."

I flipped her pearls out into the water one by one at the floating seagulls.

They made little splashes and the seagulls rose off the water and swooped at the splashes.

TROUBLE IS
MY BUSINESS

1

ANNA HALSEY WAS about two hundred and forty pounds of middle-aged putty-faced woman in a black tailor-made suit. Her eyes were shiny black shoe buttons, her cheeks were as soft as suet and about the same color. She was sitting behind a black glass desk that looked like Napoleon's tomb and she was smoking a cigarette in a black holder that was not quite as long as a rolled umbrella. She said: "I need a man."

I watched her shake ash from the cigarette to the shiny top of the desk where flakes of it curled and crawled in the draft from an open window.

"I need a man good-looking enough to pick up a dame who has a sense of class, but he's got to be tough enough to swap punches with a power shovel. I need a guy who can act like a bar lizard and backchat like Fred Allen, only better, and get hit on the head with a beer truck and think some cutie in the leg-line topped him with a breadstick."

"It's a cinch," I said. "You need the New York Yankees, Robert Donat, and the Yacht Club Boys."

"You might do," Anna said, "cleaned up a little. Twenty bucks a day and ex's. I haven't brokered a job in years, but this one is out of my line. I'm in the smooth angles of the detecting business and I make money without getting my can knocked off. Let's see how Gladys likes you."

She reversed the cigarette holder and tipped a key on a large black-and-chromium annunciator box. "Come in and empty Anna's ash tray, honey."

We waited.

The door opened and a tall blonde dressed better than the Duchess of Windsor strolled in.

She swayed elegantly across the room, emptied Anna's ash tray, patted her fat cheek, gave me a smooth rippling glance and went out again.

"I think she blushed," Anna said when the door closed. "I guess you still have It."

"She blushed — and I have a dinner date with Darryl Zanuck," I said. "Quit horsing around. What's the story?"

"It's to smear a girl. A red-headed number with bedroom eyes. She's shill for a gambler and she's got her hooks into a rich man's pup."

"What do I do to her?"

Anna sighed. "It's kind of a mean job, Philip, I guess. If she's got a record of any sort, you dig it up and toss it in her face. If she hasn't, which is more likely as she comes from good people, it's kind of up to you. You get an idea once in a while, don't you?"

"I can't remember the last one I had. What gambler and what rich man?"

"Marty Estel."

I started to get up from my chair, then remembered that business had been bad for a month and that I needed the money.

I sat down again.

"You might get into trouble, of course," Anna said. "I never heard of Marty bumping anybody off in the public square at high noon, but he don't play with cigar coupons."

"Trouble is my business," I said. "Twenty-five a day and a guarantee of two-fifty, if I pull the job."

"I gotta make a little something for myself," Anna whined.

"Okay. There's plenty of coolie labor around town. Nice to have seen you looking so well. So long, Anna."

I stood up this time. My life wasn't worth much, but it was worth that much. Marty Estel was supposed to be pretty tough people, with the right helpers and the right protection behind him. His place was out in West Hollywood, on the Strip. He wouldn't pull anything crude, but if he pulled at all, something would pop.

"Sit down, it's a deal," Anna sneered. "I'm a poor old broken-down woman trying to run a high-class detective agency on nothing but fat and bad health, so take my last nickel and laugh at me."

"Who's the girl?" I had sat down again.

"Her name is Harriet Huntress — a swell name for the part too. She lives in the El Milano, nineteen-hundred block on North Sycamore, very high-class. Father went broke back in thirty-one and jumped out of his office window. Mother dead. Kid sister in boarding school back in Connecticut. That might make an angle."

"Who dug up all this?"

"The client got a bunch of photostats of notes the pup had given to Marty. Fifty grand worth. The pup — he's an adopted son to the old man — denied the notes, as kids will. So the client had the photostats experted by a guy named Arbogast, who pretends to be good at that sort of thing. He said okay and dug around a bit, but he's too fat to do legwork, like me, and he's off the case now."

"But I could talk to him?"

"I don't know why not." Anna nodded several of her chins.

"This client — does he have a name?"

"Son, you have a treat coming. You can meet him in person — right now."

She tipped the key of her call box again. "Have Mr. Jeeter come in, honey."

"That Gladys," I said, "does she have a steady?"

"You lay off Gladys!" Anna almost screamed at me. "She's worth eighteen grand a year in divorce business to me. Any guy that lays a finger on her, Philip Marlowe, is practically cremated."

"She's got to fall some day," I said. "Why couldn't I catch her?" The opening door stopped that.

I hadn't seen him in the paneled reception room, so he must have been waiting in a private office. He hadn't enjoyed it. He came in quickly, shut the door quickly, and yanked a thin octagonal platinum watch from his vest and glared at it. He was a tall white-blond type in pin-striped flannel of youthful cut. There was a small pink rosebud in his lapel. He had a keen frozen face, a little pouchy under the eyes, a little thick in the lips. He carried an ebony cane with a silver knob, wore spats and looked a smart sixty, but I gave him close to ten years more. I didn't like him.

"Twenty-six minutes, Miss Halsey," he said icily. "My time happens to be valuable. By regarding it as valuable I have managed to make a great deal of money."

"Well, we're trying to save you some of the money," Anna drawled. She didn't like him either. "Sorry to keep you waiting, Mr. Jeeter, but you wanted to see the operative I selected and I had to send for him."

"He doesn't look the type to me," Mr. Jeeter said, giving me a nasty glance. "I think more of a gentleman —"

"You're not the Jeeter of *Tobacco Road*, are you?" I asked him. He came slowly towards me and half lifted the stick. His icy eyes tore at me like claws. "So you insult me," he said. "Me — a man in my position."

"Now wait a minute," Anna began.

"Wait a minute nothing," I said. "This party said I was not a gentleman. Maybe that's okay for a man in his position, whatever it is — but a man in my position doesn't take a dirty crack from anybody. He can't afford to. Unless, of course, it wasn't intended."

Mr. Jeeter stiffened and glared at me. He took his watch out again and looked at it. "Twenty-eight minutes," he said. "I apologize, young man. I had no desire to be rude."

"That's swell," I said. "I knew you weren't the Jeeter in *Tobacco Road* all along."

That almost started him again, but he let it go. He wasn't sure how I meant it.

"A question or two while we are together," I said. "Are you willing to give this Huntress girl a little money — for expenses?"

"Not one cent," he barked. "Why should I?"

"It's got to be a sort of custom. Suppose she married him. What would he have?"

"At the moment a thousand dollars a month from a trust fund established by his mother, my late wife." He dipped his head. "When he is twenty-eight years old, far too much money."

"You can't blame the girl for trying," I said. "Not these days. How about Marty Estel? Any settlement there?"

He crumpled his gray gloves with a purple-veined hand. "The debt is uncollectible. It is a gambling debt."

Anna sighed wearily and flicked ash around on her desk.

"Sure," I said. "But gamblers can't afford to let people welsh on them. After all, if your son had won, Marty would have paid *him*."

"I'm not interested in that," the tall thin man said coldly.

"Yeah, but think of Marty sitting there with fifty grand in notes. Not worth a nickel. How will he sleep nights?"

Mr. Jeeter looked thoughtful. "You mean there is danger of violence?" he suggested, almost suavely.

"That's hard to say. He runs an exclusive place, gets a good movie crowd. He has his own reputation to think of. But he's in a racket and he knows people. Things can happen — a long way off from where Marty is. And Marty is no bathmat. He gets up and walks."

Mr. Jeeter looked at his watch again and it annoyed him. He slammed it back into his vest. "All that is your affair," he snapped. "The district attorney is a personal friend of mine. If this matter seems to be beyond your powers —"

"Yeah," I told him. "But you came slumming down our street just the same. Even if the D.A. is in your vest pocket — along with that watch."

He put his hat on, drew on one glove, tapped the edge of his shoe with his stick, walked to the door and opened it.

"I ask results and I pay for them," he said coldly. "I pay promptly. I even pay generously sometimes, although I am not considered a generous man. I think we all understand one another."

He almost winked then and went on out. The door closed softly against the cushion of air in the door-closer. I looked at Anna and grinned.

"Sweet, isn't he?" she said. "I'd like eight of him for my cocktail set."

I gouged twenty dollars out of her — for expenses.

2

THE ARBOGAST I WANTED was John D. Arbogast and he had an office on Sunset near Ivar. I called him up from a phone booth. The voice that answered was fat. I wheezed softly, like the voice of a man who had just won a pie-eating contest.

"Mr. John D. Arbogast?"

"Yeah."

"This is Philip Marlowe, a private detective working on a case you did some experting on. Party named Jeeter."

"Yeah?"

"Can I come up and talk to you about it — after I eat lunch?"

"Yeah." He hung up. I decided he was not a talkative man.

I had lunch and drove out there. It was east of Ivar, an old two-story building faced with brick which had been painted recently. The street floor was stores and a restaurant. The building entrance was the foot of a wide straight stairway to the second floor. On the directory at the bottom I read: John D. Arbogast, Suite 212. I went up the stairs and found myself in a wide straight hall that ran parallel with the street. A man in a smock was standing in an open doorway down to my right. He wore a round mirror strapped to his forehead and pushed back, and his face had a puzzled expression. He went back to his office and shut the door.

I went the other way, about half the distance along the hall. A door on the side away from Sunset was lettered:

JOHN D. ARBOGAST,

EXAMINER OF QUESTIONED DOCUMENTS

PRIVATE INVESTIGATOR

ENTER

The door opened without resistance onto a small windowless anteroom with a couple of easy chairs, some magazines, two chromium smoking stands. There were two floor lamps and a ceiling fixture, all lighted. A door on the other side of the cheap but thick and new rug was lettered:

JOHN D. ARBOGAST,
EXAMINER OF QUESTIONED DOCUMENTS
PRIVATE

A buzzer had rung when I opened the outer door and gone on ringing until it closed. Nothing happened. Nobody was in the waiting room. The inner door didn't open. I went over and listened at the panel — no sound of conversation inside. I knocked. That didn't buy me anything either. I tried the knob. It turned, so I opened the door and went in.

This room had two north windows, both curtained at the sides and both shut tight. There was dust on the sills. There was a desk, two filing cases, a carpet which was just a carpet, and walls which were just walls. To the left another door with a glass panel was lettered:

JOHN D. ARBOGAST
LABORATORY
PRIVATE

I had an idea I might be able to remember the name.

The room in which I stood was small. It seemed almost too small even for the pudgy hand that rested on the edge of the desk, motionless, holding a fat pencil like a carpenter's pencil. The hand had a wrist, hairless as a plate. A buttoned shirt cuff, not too clean, came down out of a coat sleeve. The rest of the sleeve dropped over the far edge of the desk out of sight. The desk was less than six feet long, so he couldn't have been a very tall man. The hand and the ends of the sleeves were all I saw of him from where I stood. I went quietly back through the anteroom and fixed its door so that it couldn't be opened from the outside and put out the three lights and went back to the private office. I went around an end of the desk.

He was fat all right, enormously fat, fatter by far than Anna Halsey. His face, what I could see of it, looked about the size of a basketball. It had a pleasant pinkness, even now. He was kneeling on the floor. He had his large head against the sharp inner corner of the kneehole of the desk, and his left hand was flat on the floor with a piece of yellow paper under it. The fingers were outspread as much as such fat fingers could be, and the yellow paper showed between. He looked as if he were pushing hard on the floor, but he wasn't really. What was holding him up was his own fat. His body was folded down against his enormous thighs, and the thickness and fatness of them held him that way, kneeling, poised solid. It would have taken a couple of good blocking backs to knock him over. That wasn't a very nice idea at the moment, but I had it just the same. I took time out and wiped the back of my neck, although it was not a warm day.

His hair was gray and clipped short and his neck had as many folds as a concertina. His feet were small, as the feet of fat men often are, and they were in black shiny shoes which were sideways on the carpet and close together and neat and nasty. He wore a dark suit that needed cleaning. I leaned down and buried my fingers in the bottomless fat of his neck. He had an artery in there somewhere, probably, but I couldn't find it and he didn't need it any more anyway. Between his bloated knees on the carpet a dark stain had spread and spread —

I knelt in another place and lifted the pudgy fingers that were holding down the piece of yellow paper. They were cool, but not cold, and soft and a little sticky. The paper was from a scratch pad. It would have been very nice if it had had a message on it, but it hadn't. There were vague meaningless marks, not words, not even letters. He had tried to write something after he was shot — perhaps even thought he *was* writing something — but all he managed was some hen scratches.

He had slumped down then, still holding the paper, pinned it to the floor with his fat hand, held on to the fat pencil with his other hand, wedged his torso against his huge thighs, and so died. John D. Arbogast, Examiner of Questioned Documents. Private. Very damned private. He had said "yeah" to me three times over the phone.

And here he was.

I wiped doorknobs with my handkerchief, put off the lights in the anteroom, left the outer door so that it was locked from the outside, left the hallway, left the building and left the neighborhood. So far as I could tell nobody saw me go. So far as I could tell.

3

THE EL MILANO WAS, as Anna had told me, in the 1900 block on North Sycamore. It was most of the block. I parked fairly near the ornamental forecourt and went along to the pale blue neon sign over the entrance to the basement garage. I walked down a railed ramp into a bright space of glistening cars and cold air. A trim light-colored Negro in a spotless coverall suit with blue cuffs came out of a glass office. His black hair was as smooth as a bandleader's.

"Busy?" I asked him.

"Yes and no, sir."

"I've got a car outside that needs a dusting. About five bucks worth of dusting."

It didn't work. He wasn't the type. His chestnut eyes became thoughtful and remote. "That is a good deal of dusting, sir. May I ask if anything else would be included?"

"A little. Is Miss Harriet Huntress' car in?"

He looked. I saw him look along the glistening row at a canary-yellow convertible which was about as inconspicuous as a privy on the front lawn.

"Yes, sir. It is in."

"I'd like her apartment number and a way to get up there without going through the lobby. I'm a private detective." I showed him a buzzer. He looked at the buzzer. It failed to amuse him.

He smiled the faintest smile I ever saw. "Five dollars is nice money, sir, to a working man. It falls a little short of being nice enough to make me risk my position. About from here to Chicago short, sir. I suggest that you save your five dollars, sir, and try the customary mode of entry."

"You're quite a guy," I said. "What are you going to be when you grow up — a five-foot shelf?"

"I am already grown up, sir. I am thirty-four years old, married happily, and have two children. Good afternoon, sir."

He turned on his heel. "Well, goodbye," I said. "And pardon my whiskey breath. I just got in from Butte."

I went back up along the ramp and wandered along the street to where I should have gone in the first place. I might have known that five bucks and a buzzer wouldn't buy me anything in a place like the El Milano.

The Negro was probably telephoning the office right now.

The building was a huge white stucco affair, Moorish in style, with great fretted lanterns in the forecourt and huge date palms. The entrance was at the inside corner of an L, up marble steps, through an arch framed in California or dishpan mosaic.

A doorman opened the door for me and I went in. The lobby was not quite as big as the Yankee Stadium. It was floored with a pale blue carpet with sponge rubber underneath. It was so soft it made me want to lie down and roll. I waded over to the desk and put an elbow on it and was stared at by a pale thin clerk with one of those mustaches that get stuck under your fingernail. He toyed with it and looked past my shoulder at an Ali Baba oil jar big enough to keep a tiger in.

"Miss Huntress in?"

"Who shall I announce?"

"Mr. Marty Estel."

That didn't take any better than my play in the garage. He leaned on something with his left foot. A blue-and-gilt door opened at the end of the desk and a large sandy-haired man with cigar ash on his vest came out and leaned absently on the end of the desk and stared at the Ali Baba oil jar, as if trying to make up his mind whether it was a spittoon.

The clerk raised his voice. "You are Mr. Marty Estel?"

"From him."

"Isn't that a little different? And what is your name, sir, if one may ask?"

"One may ask," I said. "One may not be told. Such are my orders. Sorry to be stubborn and all that rot."

He didn't like my manner. He didn't like anything about me. "I'm afraid I can't announce you," he said coldly. "Mr. Hawkins, might I have your advice on a matter?"

The sandy-haired man took his eyes off the oil jar and slid along the desk until he was within blackjack range of me.

"Yes, Mr. Gregory?" He yawned.

"Nuts to both of you," I said. "And that includes your lady friends."

Hawkins grinned. "Come into my office, bo. We'll kind of see if we can get you straightened out."

I followed him into the doghole he had come out of. It was large enough for a pint-sized desk, two chairs, a knee-high cuspidor, and an open box of cigars. He placed his rear end against the desk and grinned at me sociably.

"Didn't play it very smooth, did you, bo? I'm the house man here. Spill it."

"Some days I feel like playing smooth," I said, "and some days I feel like playing it like a waffle iron." I got my wallet out and showed him the buzzer and the small photostat of my license behind a celluloid window.

"One of the boys, huh?" He nodded. "You ought to of asked for me in the first place."

"Sure. Only I never heard of you. I want to see this Huntress frail. She doesn't know me, but I have business with her, and it's not noisy business."

He made a yard and a half sideways and cocked his cigar in the other corner of his mouth. He looked at my right eyebrow. "What's the gag? Why try to apple polish the dinghe downstairs? You gettin' any expense money?"

"Could be."

"I'm nice people," he said. "But I gotta protect the guests."

"You're almost out of cigars," I said, looking at the ninety or so in the box. I lifted a couple, smelled them, tucked a folded ten-dollar bill below them and put them back.

"That's cute," he said. "You and me could get along. What you want done?"

"Tell her I'm from Marty Estel. She'll see me."

"It's the job if I get a kickback."

"You won't. I've got important people behind me."

I started to reach for my ten, but he pushed my hand away. "I'll take a chance," he said. He reached for his phone and asked for suite 814 and began to hum. His humming sounded like a cow being sick. He leaned forward suddenly and his face became a honeyed smile. His voice dripped.

"Miss Huntress? This is Hawkins, the house man. Hawkins. Yeah . . . Hawkins. Sure, you meet a lot of people, Miss Huntress. Say, there's a gentleman in my office wanting to see you with a message from Mr. Estel. We can't let him up without your say so, because he don't want to give us no name . . . Yeah, Hawkins, the house detective, Miss Huntress. Yeah, he says you don't know him personal, but he looks okay to me . . . Okay. Thanks a lot, Miss Huntress. Serve him right up."

He put the phone down and patted it gently.

"All you needed was some background music," I said.

"You can ride up," he said dreamily. He reached absently into his cigar box and removed the folded bill. "A darb," he said softly. "Every time I think of that dame I have to go out and walk around the block. Let's go."

We went out to the lobby again and Hawkins took me to the elevator and highsigned me in.

As the elevator doors closed I saw him on his way to the entrance, probably for his walk around the block.

The elevator had a carpeted floor and mirrors and indirect lighting. It rose as softly as the mercury in a thermometer. The doors whispered open, I wandered over the moss they used for a hall carpet and came to a door marked 814. I pushed a little button beside it, chimes rang inside and the door opened.

She wore a street dress of pale green wool and a small cockeyed hat that hung on her ear like a butterfly. Her eyes were wide-set and there was thinking room between them. Their color was lapis-lazuli blue and the color of her hair was dusky red, like a fire under control but still dangerous. She was too tall to be cute. She wore plenty of make-up in the right places and the cigarette she was poking at me had a built-on mouthpiece about three inches long. She didn't look hard, but she looked as if she had heard all the answers and remembered the ones she thought she might be able to use sometime.

She looked me over coolly. "Well what's the message, brown eyes?"

"I'd have to come in," I said. "I never could talk on my feet."

She laughed disinterestedly and I slid past the end of her cigarette into a long rather narrow room with plenty of nice furniture, plenty of windows, plenty of drapes, plenty of everything. A fire blazed behind a screen, a big log on top of a gas teaser. There was a silk Oriental rug in front of a nice rose davenport in front of the nice fire, and beside that there was Scotch and swish on a tabouret, ice in a bucket, everything to make a man feel at home.

"You'd better have a drink," she said. "You probably can't talk without a glass in your hand."

I sat down and reached for the Scotch. The girl sat in a deep chair and crossed her knees. I thought of Hawkins walking around the block. I could see a little something in his point of view.

"So you're from Marty Estel," she said, refusing a drink.

"Never met him."

"I had an idea to that effect. What's the racket, bum? Marty will love to hear how you used his name."

"I'm shaking in my shoes. What made you let me up?"

"Curiosity. I've been expecting lads like you any day. I never dodge trouble. Some kind of a dick, aren't you?"

I lit a cigarette and nodded. "Private. I have a little deal to propose."

"Propose it." She yawned.

"How much will you take to lay off young Jeeter?"

She yawned again. "You interest me — so little I could hardly tell you."

"Don't scare me to death. Honest, how much are you asking? Or is that an insult?"

She smiled. She had a nice smile. She had lovely teeth. "I'm a bad girl now," she said. "I don't have to ask. They bring it to me, tied up with ribbon."

"The old man's a little tough. They say he draws a lot of water."

"Water doesn't cost much."

I nodded and drank some more of my drink. It was good Scotch. In fact it was perfect. "His idea is you get nothing. You get smeared. You get put in the middle. I can't see it that way."

"But you're working for him."

"Sounds funny, doesn't it? There's probably a smart way to play this, but I just can't think of it at the moment. How much would you take — or would you?"

"How about fifty grand?"

"Fifty grand for you and another fifty for Marty?"

She laughed. "Now, you ought to know Marty wouldn't like me to mix in his business. I was just thinking of my end."

She crossed her legs the other way. I put another lump of ice in my drink.

"I was thinking of five hundred," I said.

"Five hundred what?" She looked puzzled.

"Dollars — not Rolls-Royces."

She laughed heartily. "You amuse me. I ought to tell you to go to hell, but I like brown eyes. Warm brown eyes with flecks of gold in them."

"You're throwing it away. I don't have a nickel."

She smiled and fitted a fresh cigarette between her lips. I went over to light it for her. Her eyes came up and looked into mine. Hers had sparks in them.

"Maybe I have a nickel already," she said softly.

"Maybe that's why he hired the fat boy — so you couldn't make him dance." I sat down again.

"Who hired what fat boy?"

"Old Jeeter hired a fat boy named Arbogast. He was on the case before me. Didn't you know? He got bumped off this afternoon."

I said it quite casually for the shock effect, but she didn't move. The provocative smile didn't leave the corners of her lips. Her eyes didn't change. She made a dim sound with her breath.

"Does it have to have something to do with me?" she asked quietly.

"I don't know. I don't know who murdered him. It was done in his office, around noon or a little later. It may not have anything to do with the Jeeter case. But it happened pretty pat — just after I had been put on the job and before I got a chance to talk to him."

She nodded. "I see. And you think Marty does things like that. And of course you told the police?"

"Of course I did not."

"You're giving away a little weight there, brother."

"Yeah. But let's get together on a price and it had better be low. Because whatever the cops do to me they'll do plenty to Marty Estel and you when they get the story — if they get it."

"A little spot of blackmail," the girl said coolly. "I think I might call it that. Don't go too far with me, brown eyes. By the way, do I know your name?"

"Philip Marlowe."

"Then listen, Philip. I was in the Social Register once. My family were nice people. Old Man Jeeter ruined my father — all proper and legitimate, the way that kind of heel ruins people — but he ruined him, and my father committed suicide, and my mother died and I've got a kid sister back east in school and perhaps I'm not too damn particular how I get the money to take care of her. And maybe I'm going to take care of old Jeeter one of these days, too — even if I have to marry his son to do it."

"Stepson, adopted son," I said. "No relation at all."

"It'll hurt him just as hard, brother. And the boy will have plenty of the long green in a couple of years. I could do worse — even if he does drink too much."

"You wouldn't say that in front of him, lady."

"No? Take a look behind you, gumshoes. You ought to have the wax taken out of your ears."

I stood up and turned fast. He stood about four feet from me. He had come out of some door and sneaked across the carpet and I had been too busy being clever with nothing on the ball to hear him. He was big, blond, dressed in a rough sporty suit, with a scarf and open-neck shirt. He was red-faced and his eyes glittered and they were not focusing any too well. He was a bit drunk for that early in the day.

"Beat it while you can still walk," he sneered at me. "I heard it. Harry can say anything she likes about me. I like it. Dangle, before I knock your teeth down your throat!"

The girl laughed behind me. I didn't like that. I took a step towards the big blond boy. His eyes blinked. Big as he was, he was a pushover.

"Ruin him, baby," the girl said coldly behind my back. "I love to see these hard numbers bend at the knees."

I looked back at her with a leer. That was a mistake. He was wild, probably, but he could still hit a wall that didn't jump. He hit me while I was looking back over my shoulder. It hurts to be hit that way. He hit me plenty hard, on the back end of the jawbone.

I went over sideways, tried to spread my legs, and slid on the silk rug. I did a nose dive somewhere or other and my head was not as hard as the piece of furniture it smashed into.

For a brief blurred moment I saw his red face sneering down at me in triumph. I think I was a little sorry for him — even then. Darkness folded down and I went out.

4

WHEN I CAME TO, the light from the windows across the room was hitting me square in the eyes. The back of my head ached. I felt it and it was sticky. I moved around slowly, like a cat in a strange house, got up on my knees and reached for the bottle of Scotch on the tabouret at the end of the davenport. By some miracle I hadn't knocked it over. Falling I had hit my head on the clawlike leg of a chair. That had hurt me a lot more than young Jeeter's haymaker. I could feel the sore place on my jaw all right, but it wasn't important enough to write in my diary.

I got up on my feet, took a swig of the Scotch and looked around. There wasn't anything to see. The room was empty. It was full of silence and the memory of a nice perfume. One of those perfumes you don't notice until they are almost gone, like the last leaf on a tree. I felt my head again, touched the sticky place with my handkerchief, decided it wasn't worth yelling about, and took another drink.

I sat down with the bottle on my knees, listening to traffic noise somewhere, far off. It was a nice room. Miss Harriet Huntress was a nice girl. She knew a few wrong numbers, but who didn't? I should criticize a little thing like that. I took another drink. The level in the bottle was a lot lower now. It was smooth and you hardly noticed it going down. It didn't take half your tonsils with it, like some of the stuff I had to drink. I took some more. My head felt all right now. I felt fine. I felt like singing the Prologue to *Pagliacci*. Yes, she was a nice girl. If she was paying her own rent, she was doing right well. I was for her. She was swell. I used some more of her Scotch.

The bottle was still half full. I shook it gently, stuffed it in my overcoat pocket, put my hat somewhere on my head and left. I made the elevator without hitting the walls on either side of the corridor, floated downstairs, strolled out into the lobby.

Hawkins, the house dick, was leaning on the end of the desk again, staring at the Ali Baba oil jar. The same clerk was nuzzling at the same itsy-bitsy mustache. I smiled at him. He smiled back. Hawkins smiled at me. I smiled back. Everybody was swell.

I made the front door the first time and gave the doorman two bits and floated down the steps and along the walk to the street and my car. The swift California twilight was falling. It was a lovely night. Venus in the west was as bright as a streetlamp, as bright as life, as bright as Miss Huntress' eyes, as bright as a bottle of Scotch. That reminded me. I got the square bottle out and tapped it with discretion, corked it, and tucked it away again. There was still enough to get home on.

I crashed five red lights on the way back but my luck was in and nobody pinched me. I parked more or less in front of my apartment house and more or less near the curb. I rode to my floor in the elevator, had a little trouble opening the doors and helped myself out with my bottle. I got the key into my door and unlocked it and stepped inside and found the light switch. I took a little more of my medicine before exhausting myself any further. Then I started for the kitchen to get some ice and ginger ale for a real drink.

I thought there was a funny smell in the apartment — nothing I could put a name to offhand — a sort of medicinal smell. I hadn't put it there and it hadn't been there when I went out. But I felt too well to argue about it. I started for the kitchen, got about halfway there.

They came out at me, almost side by side, from the dressing room beside the wall bed — two of them — with guns. The tall one was grinning. He had his hat low on his forehead and he had a wedge-shaped face that ended in a point, like the bottom half of the ace of diamonds. He had dark moist eyes and a nose so bloodless that it might have been made of white wax. His gun was a Colt Woodsman with a long barrel and the front sight filed off. That meant he thought he was good.

The other was a little terrierlike punk with bristly reddish hair and no hat and watery blank eyes and bat ears and small feet in dirty white sneakers. He had an automatic that looked too heavy for him to hold up, but he seemed to like holding it. He breathed open-mouthed and noisily and the smell I had noticed came from him in waves — menthol.

"Reach, you bastard," he said.

I put my hands up. There was nothing else to do.

The little one circled around to the side and came at me from the side. "Tell us we can't get away with it," he sneered.

"You can't get away with it," I said.

The tall one kept on grinning loosely and his nose kept on looking as if it was made of white wax. The little one spat on my carpet. "Yah!" He came close to me, leering, and made a pass at my chin with the big gun.

I dodged. Ordinarily that would have been just something which, in the circumstances, I had to take and like. But I was feeling better than ordinary. I was a world-beater. I took them in sets, guns and all. I took the little man around the throat and jerked him hard against my stomach, put a hand over his little gun hand and knocked the gun to the floor. It was easy. Nothing was bad about it but his breath. Blobs of saliva came out on his lips. He spit curses.

The tall man stood and leered and didn't shoot. He didn't move. His eyes looked a little anxious, I thought, but I was too busy to make sure. I went down behind the little punk, still holding him, and got hold of his gun. That was wrong. I ought to have pulled my own.

I threw him away from me and he reeled against a chair and fell down and began to kick the chair savagely. The tall man laughed.

"It ain't got any firing pin in it," he said.

"Listen," I told him earnestly, "I'm half full of good Scotch and ready to go places and get things done. Don't waste much of my time. What do you boys want?"

"It still ain't got any firing pin in it," Waxnose said. "Try and

see. I don't never let Frisky carry a loaded rod. He's too impulsive.
You got a nice arm action there, pal. I will say that for you."

Frisky sat up on the floor and spat on the carpet again and
laughed. I pointed the muzzle of the big automatic at the floor and
squeezed the trigger. It clicked dryly, but from the balance it felt
as if it had cartridges in it.

"We don't mean no harm," Waxnose said. "Not this trip. Maybe
next trip? Who knows? Maybe you're a guy that will take a hint.
Lay off the Jeeter kid is the word. See?"

"No."

"You won't do it?"

"No, I don't see. Who's the Jeeter kid?"

Waxnose was not amused. He waved his long .22 gently. "You
oughta get your memory fixed, pal, about the same time you get
your door fixed. A pushover that was. Frisky just blew it in with
his breath."

"I can understand that," I said.

"Gimme my gat," Frisky yelped. He was up off the floor again,
but this time he rushed his partner instead of me.

"Lay off, dummy," the tall one said. "We just got a message for
a guy. We don't blast him. Not today."

"Says you!" Frisky snarled and tried to grab the .22 out of Waxnose's hand. Waxnose threw him to one side without trouble but
the interlude allowed me to switch the big automatic to my left
hand and jerk out my Luger. I showed it to Waxnose. He nodded,
but did not seem impressed.

"He ain't got no parents," he said sadly. "I just let him run
around with me. Don't pay him no attention unless he bites you.
We'll be on our way now. You get the idea. Lay off the Jeeter kid."

"You're looking at a Luger," I said. "Who is the Jeeter kid? And
maybe we'll have some cops before you leave."

He smiled wearily. "Mister, I pack this small-bore because I can
shoot. If you think you can take me, go to it."

"Okay," I said. "Do you know anybody named Arbogast?"

"I meet such a lot of people," he said, with another weary smile.
"Maybe yes, maybe no. So long, pal. Be pure."

He strolled over to the door, moving a little sideways, so that he
had me covered all the time, and I had him covered, and it was just

a case of who shot first and straightest, or whether it was worthwhile to shoot at all, or whether I could hit anything with so much nice warm Scotch in me. I let him go. He didn't look like a killer to me, but I could have been wrong.

The little man rushed me again while I wasn't thinking about him. He clawed his big automatic out of my left hand, skipped over to the door, spat on the carpet again, and slipped out. Waxnose backed after him — long sharp face, white nose, pointed chin, weary expression. I wouldn't forget him.

He closed the door softly and I stood there, foolish, holding my gun. I heard the elevator come up and go down again and stop. I still stood there. Marty Estel wouldn't be very likely to hire a couple of comics like that to throw a scare into anybody. I thought about that, but thinking got me nowhere. I remembered the half-bottle of Scotch I had left and went into executive session with it.

An hour and a half later I felt fine, but I still didn't have any ideas. I just felt sleepy.

The jarring of the telephone bell woke me. I had dozed off in the chair, which was a bad mistake, because I woke up with two flannel blankets in my mouth, a splitting headache, a bruise on the back of my head and another on my jaw, neither of them larger than a Yakima apple, but sore for all that. I felt terrible. I felt like an amputated leg.

I crawled over to the telephone and humped myself in a chair beside it and answered it. The voice dripped icicles.

"Mr. Marlowe? This is Mr. Jeeter. I believe we met this morning. I'm afraid I was a little stiff with you."

"I'm a little stiff myself. Your son poked me in the jaw. I mean your stepson, or your adopted son — or whatever he is."

"He is both my stepson and my adopted son. Indeed?" He sounded interested. "And where did you meet him?"

"In Miss Huntress' apartment."

"Oh I see." There had been a sudden thaw. The icicles had melted. "Very interesting. What did Miss Huntress have to say?"

"She liked it. She liked him poking me in the jaw."

"I see. And why did he do that?"

"She had him hid out. He overheard some of our talk. He didn't like it."

"I see. I have been thinking that perhaps some consideration —
not large, of course — should be granted to her for her co-operation.
That is, if we can secure it."

"Fifty grand is the price."

"I'm afraid I don't —"

"Don't kid me," I snarled. "Fifty thousand dollars. Fifty grand.
I offered her five hundred — just for a gag."

"You seem to treat this whole business in a spirit of considerable levity," he snarled back. "I am not accustomed to that sort of
thing and I don't like it."

I yawned. I didn't give a damn if school kept in or not.
"Listen, Mr. Jeeter, I'm a great guy to horse around, but I have
my mind on the job just the same. And there are some very unusual angles to this case. For instance a couple of gunmen just
stuck me up in my apartment here and told me to lay off the Jeeter
case. I don't see why it should get so tough."

"Good heavens!" He sounded shocked. "I think you had better
come to my house at once and we will discuss matters. I'll send my
car for you. Can you come right away?"

"Yeah. But I can drive myself. I —"

"No. I'm sending my car and chauffeur. His name is George;
you may rely upon him absolutely. He should be there in about
twenty minutes."

"Okay," I said. "That just gives me time to drink my dinner.
Have him park around the corner of Kenmore, facing towards
Franklin." I hung up.

When I'd had a hot-and-cold shower and put on some clean
clothes I felt more respectable. I had a couple of drinks, small ones
for a change, and put a light overcoat on and went down to the
street.

The car was there already. I could see it half a block down the
side street. It looked like a new market opening. It had a couple
of head lamps like the one on the front end of a streamliner, two
amber foglights hooked to the front fender, and a couple of sidelights as big as ordinary headlights. I came up beside it and stopped
and a man stepped out of the shadows, tossing a cigarette over his
shoulder with a neat flip of the wrist. He was tall, broad, dark,
wore a peaked cap, a Russian tunic with a Sam Browne belt, shiny

leggings and breeches that flared like an English staff major's whipcords.

"Mr. Marlowe?" He touched the peak of his cap with a gloved forefinger.

"Yeah," I said. "At ease. Don't tell me that's Old Man Jeeter's car."

"One of them." It was a cool voice that could get fresh.

He opened the rear door and I got in and sank down into the cushions and George slid under the wheel and started the big car. It moved away from the curb and around the corner with as much noise as a bill makes in a wallet. We went west. We seemed to be drifting with the current, but we passed everything. We slid through the heart of Hollywood, the west end of it, down to the Strip and along the glitter of that to the cool quiet of Beverly Hills where the bridle path divides the boulevard.

We gave Beverly Hills the swift and climbed along the foothills, saw the distant lights of the university buildings and swung north into Bel-Air. We began to slide up long narrow streets with high walls and no sidewalks and big gates. Lights on mansions glowed politely through the early night. Nothing stirred. There was no sound but the soft purr of the tires on concrete. We swung left again and I caught a sign which read Calvello Drive. Halfway up this George started to swing the car wide to make a left turn in at a pair of twelve-foot wrought-iron gates. Then something happened.

A pair of lights flared suddenly just beyond the gates and a horn screeched and a motor raced. A car charged at us fast. George straightened out with a flick of the wrist, braked the car and slipped off his right glove, all in one motion.

The car came on, the lights swaying. "Damn drunk," George swore over his shoulder.

It could be. Drunks in cars go all kinds of places to drink. It could be. I slid down onto the floor of the car and yanked the Luger from under my arm and reached up to open the catch. I opened the door a little and held it that way, looking over the sill. The headlights hit me in the face and I ducked, then came up again as the beam passed.

The other car jammed to a stop. Its door slammed open and a figure jumped out of it, waving a gun and shouting. I heard the voice and knew.

"Reach, you bastards!" Frisky screamed at us.

George put his left hand on the wheel and I opened my door a little more. The little man in the street was bouncing up and down and yelling. Out of the small dark car from which he had jumped came no sound except the noise of its motor.

"This is a heist!" Frisky yelled. "Out of there and line up, you sons of bitches!"

I kicked my door open and started to get out, the Luger down at my side.

"You asked for it!" the little man yelled.

I dropped — fast. The gun in his hand belched flame. Somebody must have put a firing pin in it. Glass smashed behind my head. Out of the corner of my eye, which oughtn't to have had any corners at that particular moment, I saw George make a movement as smooth as a ripple of water. I brought the Luger up and started to squeeze the trigger, but a shot crashed beside me — George.

I held my fire. It wasn't needed now.

The dark car lurched forward and started down the hill furiously. It roared into the distance while the little man out in the middle of the pavement was still reeling grotesquely in the light reflected from the walls.

There was something dark on his face that spread. His gun bounded along the concrete. His little legs buckled and he plunged sideways and rolled and then, very suddenly, became still.

George said, "Yah!" and sniffed at the muzzle of his revolver.

"Nice shooting." I got out of the car, stood there looking at the little man — a crumpled nothing. The dirty white of his sneakers gleamed a little in the side glare of the car's lights.

George got out beside me. "Why me, brother?"

"I didn't fire. I was watching that pretty hip draw of yours. It was sweeter than honey."

"Thanks, pal. They were after Mister Gerald, of course. I usually ferry him home from the club about this time, full of liquor and bridge losses."

We went over to the little man and looked down at him. He wasn't anything to see. He was just a little man who was dead, with a big slug in his face and blood on him.

"Turn some of those damn lights off," I growled. "And let's get away from here fast."

"The house is just across the street." George sounded as casual as if he had just shot a nickel in a slot machine instead of a man.

"The Jeeters are out of this, if you like your job. You ought to know that. We'll go back to my place and start all over."

"I get it," he snapped, and jumped back into the big car. He cut the foglights and the sidelights and I got in beside him in the front seat.

We straightened out and started up the hill, over the brow. I looked back at the broken window. It was the small one at the extreme back of the car and it wasn't shatterproof. A large piece was gone from it. They could fit that, if they got around to it, and make some evidence. I didn't think it would matter, but it might.

At the crest of the hill a large limousine passed us going down. It's dome light was on and in the interior, as in a lighted showcase, an elderly couple sat stiffly, taking the royal salute. The man was in evening clothes, with a white scarf and a crush hat. The woman was in furs and diamonds.

George passed them casually, gunned the car and we made a fast right turn into a dark street. "There's a couple of good dinners all shot to hell," he drawled. "And I bet they don't even report it."

"Yeah. Let's get back home and have a drink," I said. "I never really got to like killing people."

5

WE SAT WITH SOME of Miss Harriet Huntress' Scotch in our glasses and looked at each other across the rims. George looked nice with his cap off. His head was clustered over with wavy dark-brown hair and his teeth were very white and clean. He sipped his drink and nibbled a cigarette at the same time. His snappy black eyes had a cool glitter in them.

"Yale?" I asked.

"Dartmouth, if it's any of your business."

"Everything's my business. What's a college education worth these days?"

"Three squares and a uniform," he drawled.

"What kind of guy is young Jeeter?"

"Big blond bruiser, plays a fair game of golf, thinks he's hell with the women, drinks heavy but hasn't sicked up on the rugs so far."

"What kind of guy is old Jeeter?"

"He'd probably give you a dime — if he didn't have a nickel with him."

"Tsk, tsk, you're talking about your boss."

George grinned. "He's so tight his head squeaks when he takes his hat off. I always took chances. Maybe that's why I'm just somebody's driver. This is good Scotch."

I made another drink, which finished the bottle. I sat down again.

"You think those two gunnies were stashed out for Mister Gerald?"

"Why not? I usually drive him home about that time. Didn't today. He had a bad hangover and didn't go out until late. You're a dick, you know what it's all about, don't you?"

"Who told you I was a dick?"

"Nobody but a dick ever asked so goddam many questions."

I shook my head. "Uh-uh. I've asked you just six questions. Your boss has a lot of confidence in you. He must have told you."

The dark man nodded, grinned faintly and sipped. "The whole set-up is pretty obvious," he said. "When the car started to swing for the turn into the driveway these boys went to work. I don't figure they meant to kill anybody, somehow. It was just a scare. Only that little guy was nuts."

I looked at George's eyebrows. They were nice black eyebrows, with a gloss on them like horsehair.

"It doesn't sound like Marty Estel to pick that sort of helpers."

"Sure. Maybe that's why he picked that sort of helpers."

"You're smart. You and I can get along. But shooting that little punk makes it tougher. What will you do about that?"

"Nothing."

"Okay. If they get to you and tie it to your gun, if you still have the gun, which you probably won't, I suppose it will be passed off as an attempted stick-up. There's just one thing."

"What?" George finished his second drink, laid the glass aside, lit a fresh cigarette and smiled.

"It's pretty hard to tell a car from in front — at night. Even with all those lights. It might have been a visitor."

He shrugged and nodded. "But if it's a scare, that would do just as well. Because the family would hear about it and the old man would guess whose boys they were — and why."

"Hell, you really are smart," I said admiringly, and the phone rang.

It was an English-butler voice, very clipped and precise, and it said that if I was Mr. Philip Marlowe, Mr. Jeeter would like to speak to me. He came on at once, with plenty of frost.

"I must say that you take your time about obeying orders," he barked. "Or hasn't that chauffeur of mine —"

"Yeah, he got here, Mr. Jeeter," I said. "But we ran into a little trouble. George will tell you."

"Young man, when I want something done —"

"Listen, Mr. Jeeter, I've had a hard day. Your son punched me on the jaw and I fell and cut my head open. When I staggered back to my apartment, more dead than alive, I was stuck up by a couple of hard guys with guns who told me to lay off the Jeeter case. I'm doing my best but I'm feeling a little frail, so don't scare me."

"Young man —"

"Listen," I told him earnestly, "if you want to call all the plays in this game, you can carry the ball yourself. Or you can save your-self a lot of money and hire an order taker. I have to do things my way. Any cops visit you tonight?"

"Cops?" he echoed in a sour voice. "You mean policemen?"

"By all means — I mean policemen."

"And why should I see any policemen?" he almost snarled.

"There was a stiff in front of your gates half an hour ago. Stiff meaning dead man. He's quite small. You could sweep him up in a dustpan, if he bothers you."

"My God! Are you serious?"

"Yes. What's more he took a shot at George and me. He recognized the car. He must have been all set for your son, Mr. Jeeter."

A silence with barbs on it. "I thought you said a dead man," Mr. Jeeter's voice said very coldly. "Now you say he shot at you."

"That was while he wasn't dead," I said. "George will tell you. George —"

"You come out here at once!" he yelled at me over the phone. "At once, do you hear? At once!"

"George will tell you," I said softly and hung up.

George looked at me coldly. He stood up and put his cap on. "Okay, pal," he said. "Maybe some day I can put you on to a soft thing." He started for the door.

"It had to be that way. It's up to him. He'll have to decide."

"Nuts," George said, looking back over his shoulder. "Save your breath, shamus. Anything you say to me is just so much noise in the wrong place."

He opened the door, went out, shut it, and I sat there still holding the telephone, with my mouth open and nothing in it but my tongue and a bad taste on that.

I went out to the kitchen and shook the Scotch bottle, but it was still empty. I opened some rye and swallowed a drink and it tasted sour. Something was bothering me. I had a feeling it was going to bother me a lot more before I was through.

They must have missed George by a whisker. I heard the elevator come up again almost as soon as it had stopped going down. Solid steps grew louder along the hallway. A fist hit the door. I went over and opened it.

One was in brown, one in blue, both large, hefty and bored.

The one in brown pushed his hat back on his head with a freckled hand and said: "You Philip Marlowe?"

"Me," I said.

They rode me back into the room without seeming to. The one in blue shut the door. The one in brown palmed a shield and let me catch a glint of the gold and enamel.

"Finlayson, Detective Lieutenant working out of Central Homicide," he said. "This is Sebold, my partner. We're a couple of swell guys not to get funny with. We hear you're kind of sharp with a gun."

Sebold took his hat off and dusted his salt-and-pepper hair back with the flat of his hand. He drifted noiselessly out to the kitchen.

Finlayson sat down on the edge of a chair and flicked his chin with a thumbnail as square as an ice cube and yellow as a mustard plaster. He was older than Sebold, but not so good-looking. He had the frowsy expression of a veteran cop who hadn't got very far.

I sat down. I said: "How do you mean, sharp with a gun?"

"Shooting people is how I mean."

I lit a cigarette. Sebold came out of the kitchen and went into the dressing room behind the wall bed.

"We understand you're a private-license guy," Finlayson said heavily.

"That's right."

"Give." He held his hand out. I gave him my wallet. He chewed it over and handed it back. "Carry a gun?"

I nodded. He held out his hand for it. Sebold came out of the dressing room. Finlayson sniffed at the Luger, snapped the magazine out, cleared the breech and held the gun so that a little light shone up through the magazine opening into the breech end of the barrel. He looked down the muzzle, squinting. He handed the gun to Sebold. Sebold did the same thing.

"Don't think so," Sebold said. "Clean, but not that clean. Couldn't have been cleaned within the hour. A little dust."

"Right."

Finlayson picked the ejected shell off the carpet, pressed it into the magazine and snapped the magazine back in place. He handed me the gun. I put it back under my arm.

"Been out anywhere tonight?" he asked tersely.

"Don't tell me the plot," I said. "I'm just a bit-player."

"Smart guy," Sebold said dispassionately. He dusted his hair again and opened a desk drawer. "Funny stuff. Good for a column. I like 'em that way — with my blackjack."

Finlayson sighed. "Been out tonight, shamus?"

"Sure. In and out all the time. Why?"

He ignored the question. "Where you been?"

"Out to dinner. Business call or two."

"Where at?"

"I'm sorry, boys. Every business has its private files."

"Had company, too," Sebold said, picking up George's glass and niffing it. "Recent — within the hour."

"You're not that good," I told him sourly.

"Had a ride in a big Caddy?" Finlayson bored on, taking a deep breath. "Over West L.A. direction?"

"Had a ride in a Chrysler — over Vine Street direction."

"Maybe we better just take him down," Sebold said, looking at his fingernails.

"Maybe you better skip the gang-buster stuff and tell me what's stuck in your nose. I get along with cops — except when they act as if the law is only for citizens."

Finlayson studied me. Nothing I had said made an impression on him. Nothing Sebold said made any impression on him. He had an idea and he was holding it like a sick baby.

"You know a little rat named Frisky Lavon?" he sighed. "Used to be a dummy-chucker, then found out he could bug his way outa raps. Been doing that for say twelve years. Totes a gun and acts simple. But he quit acting tonight at seven-thirty about. Quit cold — with a slug in his head."

"Never heard of him," I said.

"You bumped anybody off tonight?"

"I'd have to look at my notebook."

Sebold leaned forward politely. "Would you care for a smack in the kisser?" he inquired.

Finlayson held his hand out sharply. "Cut it, Ben. Cut it. Listen, Marlowe. Maybe we're going at this wrong. We're not talking about murder. Could have been legitimate. This Frisky Lavon got froze off tonight on Calvello Drive in Bel-Air. Out in the middle of the street. Nobody seen or heard anything. So we kind of want to know."

"All right," I growled. "What makes it my business? And keep that piano tuner out of my hair. He has a nice suit and his nails are clean, but he bears down on his shield too hard."

"Nuts to you," Sebold said.

"We got a funny phone call," Finlayson said. "Which is where you come in. We ain't just throwing our weight around. And we want a forty-five. They ain't sure what kind yet."

"He's smart. He threw it under the bar at Levy's," Sebold sneered.

"I never had a forty-five," I said. "A guy who needs that much gun ought to use a pick."

Finlayson scowled at me and counted his thumbs. Then he took a deep breath and suddenly went human on me. "Sure, I'm just a dumb flatheel," he said. "Anybody could pull my ears off and I wouldn't even notice it. Let's all quit horsing around and talk sense.

"This Frisky was found dead after a no-name phone call to West L.A. police. Found dead outside a big house belonging to a man named Jeeter who owns a string of investment companies. He wouldn't use a guy like Frisky for a penwiper, so there's nothing in that. The servants didn't hear nothing, nor the servants at any of the four houses on the block. Frisky is lying in the street and somebody run over his foot, but what killed him was a forty-five slug smack in his face. West L.A. ain't hardly started the routine when some guy calls up Central and says to tell Homicide if they want to know who got Frisky Lavon, ask a private eye named Philip Marlowe, complete with address and everything, then a quick hang-up.

"Okay. The guy on the board gives me the dope and I don't know Frisky from a hole in my sock, but I ask Identification and sure enough they have him and just about the time I'm looking it over the flash comes from West L.A. and the description seems to check pretty close. So we get together and it's the same guy all right and the chief of detectives has us drop around here. So we drop around."

"So here you are," I said. "Will you have a drink?"

"Can we search the joint, if we do?"

"Sure. It's a good lead — that phone call, I mean — if you put in about six months on it."

"We already got that idea," Finlayson growled. "A hundred guys could have chilled this little wart, and two-three of them maybe could have thought it was a smart rib to pin it on you. Them two-three is what interests us."

I shook my head.

"No ideas at all, huh?"

"Just for wisecracks," Sebold said.

Finlayson lumbered to his feet. "Well, we gotta look around."

"Maybe we had ought to have brought a search warrant," Sebold said, tickling his upper lip with the end of his tongue.

"I don't *have* to fight this guy, do I?" I asked Finlayson. "I mean, is it all right if I leave him his gag lines and just keep my temper?"

Finlayson looked at the ceiling and said dryly: "His wife left him day before yesterday. He's just trying to compensate, as the fellow says."

Sebold turned white and twisted his knuckles savagely. Then he laughed shortly and got to his feet.

They went at it. Ten minutes of opening and shutting drawers and looking at the backs of shelves and under seat cushions and letting the bed down and peering into the electric refrigerator and the garbage pail fed them up.

They came back and sat down again. "Just a nut," Finlayson said wearily. "Some guy that picked your name outa the directory maybe. Could be anything."

"Now I'll get that drink."

"I don't drink," Sebold snarled.

Finlayson crossed his hands on his stomach. "That don't mean any liquor gets poured in the flowerpot, son."

I got three drinks and put two of them beside Finlayson. He drank half of one of them and looked at the ceiling. "I got another killing, too," he said thoughtfully. "A guy in your racket, Marlowe. A fat guy on Sunset. Name of Arbogast. Ever hear of him?"

"I thought he was a handwriting expert," I said.

"You're talking about police business," Sebold told his partner coldly.

"Sure. Police business that's already in the morning paper. This Arbogast was shot three times with a twenty-two. Target gun. You know any crooks that pack that kind of heat?"

I held my glass tightly and took a long slow swallow. I hadn't thought Waxnose looked dangerous enough, but you never knew.

"I did," I said slowly. "A killer named Al Tessilore. But he's in Folsom. He used a Colt Woodsman."

Finlayson finished the first drink, used the second in about the same time, and stood up. Sebold stood up, still mad.

Finlayson opened the door. "Come on, Ben." They went out.

I heard their steps along the hall, the clang of the elevator once more. A car started just below in the street and growled off into the night.

"Clowns like that don't kill," I said out loud. But it looked as if they did.

I waited fifteen minutes before I went out again. The phone rang while I was waiting, but I didn't answer it.

I drove towards the El Milano and circled around enough to make sure I wasn't followed.

6

THE LOBBY HADN'T CHANGED ANY. The blue carpet still tickled my ankles while I ambled over to the desk, the same pale clerk was handing a key to a couple of horse-faced females in tweeds, and when he saw me he put his weight on his left foot again and the door at the end of the desk popped open and out popped the fat and erotic Hawkins, with what looked like the same cigar stub in his face.

He hustled over and gave me a big warm smile this time, took hold of my arm. "Just the guy I was hoping to see," he chuckled. "Let's us go upstairs a minute."

"What's the matter?"

"Matter?" His smile became broad as the door to a two-car garage. "Nothing ain't the matter. This way."

He pushed me into the elevator and said, "Eight" in a fat cheerful voice and up we sailed and out we got and slid along the corridor. Hawkins had a hard hand and knew where to hold an arm. I was interested enough to let him get away with it. He pushed the buzzer beside Miss Huntress' door and Big Ben chimed inside and the door opened and I was looking at a deadpan in a derby hat and a dinner coat. He had his right hand in the side pocket of the coat, and under the derby a pair of scarred eyebrows and under the eyebrows a pair of eyes that had as much expression as the cap on a gas tank.

The mouth moved enough to say: "Yeah?"

"Company for the boss," Hawkins said expansively.

"What company?"

"Let me play too," I said. "Limited Liability Company. Gimme the apple."

"Huh?" The eyebrows went this way and that and the jaw came out. "Nobody ain't kiddin' nobody, I hope."

"Now, now, gents — " Hawkins began.

A voice behind the derby-hatted man interrupted him. "What's the matter, Beef?"

"He's in a stew," I said.

"Listen, mugg — "

"Now, now, gents — " as before.

"Ain't nothing the matter," Beef said, throwing his voice over his shoulder as it were a coil of rope. "The hotel dick got a guy up here and he says he's company."

"Show the company in, Beef." I liked this voice. It was smooth quiet, and you could have cut your name in it with a thirty-pound sledge and a cold chisel.

"Lift the dogs," Beef said, and stood to one side.

We went in. I went first, then Hawkins, then Beef wheeled neatly behind us like a door. We went in so close together that we must have looked like a three-decker sandwich.

Miss Huntress was not in the room. The log in the fireplace had almost stopped smoldering. There was still that smell of sandalwood on the air. With it cigarette smoke blended.

A man stood at the end of the davenport, both hands in the pockets of a blue camel's-hair coat with the collar high to a black snap-brim hat. A loose scarf hung outside his coat. He stood motionless, the cigarette in his mouth lisping smoke. He was tall, black-haired, suave, dangerous. He said nothing.

Hawkins ambled over to him. "This is the guy I was telling you about, Mr. Estel," the fat man burbled. "Come in earlier today and said he was from you. Kinda fooled me."

"Give him a ten, Beef."

The derby hat took its left hand from somewhere and there was a bill in it. It pushed the bill at Hawkins. Hawkins took the bill, blushing.

"This ain't necessary, Mr. Estel. Thanks a lot just the same."

"Scram."

"Huh?" Hawkins looked shocked.

"You heard him," Beef said truculently. "Want your fanny out the door first, huh?"

Hawkins drew himself up. "I gotta protect the tenants. You gentlemen know how it is. A man in a job like this."

"Yeah. Scram," Estel said without moving his lips.

Hawkins turned and went out quickly, softly. The door clicked gently shut behind him. Beef looked back at it, then moved behind me.

"See if he's rodded, Beef."

The derby hat saw if I was rodded. He took the Luger and went away from me. Estel looked casually at the Luger, back at me. His eyes held an expression of indifferent dislike.

"Name's Philip Marlowe, eh? A private dick."

"So what?" I said.

"Somebody's goin' to get somebody's face pushed into somebody's floor," Beef said coldly.

"Aw, keep that crap for the boiler room," I told him. "I'm sick of hard guys for this evening. I said 'so what,' and 'so what' is what I said."

Marty Estel looked mildly amused. "Hell, keep your shirt in. I've got to look after my friends, don't I? You know who I am. Okay, I know what you talked to Miss Huntress about. And I know something about you that you don't know I know."

"All right," I said. "This fat slob Hawkins collected ten from me for letting me up here this afternoon — knowing perfectly well who I was — and he has just collected ten from your iron man for slipping me the nasty. Give me back my gun and tell me what makes my business your business."

"Plenty. First off, Harriet's not home. We're waiting for her on account of a thing that happened. I can't wait any longer. Got to go to work at the club. So what did you come after this time?"

"Looking for the Jeeter boy. Somebody shot at his car tonight. From now on he needs somebody to walk behind him."

"You think I play games like that?" Estel asked me coldly.

I walked over to a cabinet and opened it and found a bottle of

Scotch. I twisted the cap off, lifted a glass from the tabouret and poured some out. I tasted it. It tasted all right.

I looked around for ice, but there wasn't any. It had all melted long since in the bucket.

"I asked you a question," Estel said gravely.

"I heard it. I'm making my mind up. The answer is, I wouldn't have thought it — no. But it happened. I was there. I was in the car — instead of young Jeeter. His father had sent for me to come to the house to talk things over."

"What things?"

I didn't bother to look surprised. "You hold fifty grand of the boy's paper. That looks bad for you, if anything happens to him."

"I don't figure it that way. Because that way I would lose my dough. The old man won't pay — granted. But I wait a couple of years and I collect from the kid. He gets his estate out of trust when he's twenty-eight. Right now he gets a grand a month and he can't even will anything, because it's still in trust. Savvy?"

"So you wouldn't knock him off," I said, using my Scotch. "But you might throw a scare into him."

Estel frowned. He discarded his cigarette into a tray and watched it smoke a moment before he picked it up again and snubbed it out. He shook his head.

"If you're going to bodyguard him, it would almost pay me to stand part of your salary, wouldn't it? Almost. A man in my racket can't take care of everything. He's of age and it's his business who he runs around with. For instance, women. Any reason why a nice girl shouldn't cut herself a piece of five million bucks?"

I said: "I think it's a swell idea. What was it you knew about me that I didn't know you knew?"

He smiled, faintly. "What was it you were waiting to tell Miss Huntress — the thing that happened?"

He smiled faintly again.

"Listen, Marlowe, there are lots of ways to play any game. I play mine on the house percentage, because that's all I need to win. What makes me get tough?"

I rolled a fresh cigarette around in my fingers and tried to roll it around my glass with two fingers. "Who said you were tough? I always heard the nicest things about you."

Marty Estel nodded and looked faintly amused. "I have sources of information," he said quietly. "When I have fifty grand invested in a guy, I'm apt to find out a little about him. Jeeter hired a man named Arbogast to do a little work. Arbogast was killed in his office today — with a twenty-two. That could have nothing to do with Jeeter's business. But there was a tail on you when you went there and you didn't give it to the law. Does that make you and me friends?"

I licked the edge of my glass, nodded. "It seems it does."

"From now on just forget about bothering Harriet, see?"

"Okay."

"So we understand each other real good, now."

"Yeah."

"Well, I'll be going. Give the guy back his Luger, Beef."

The derby hat came over and smacked my gun into my hand hard enough to break a bone.

"Staying?" Estel asked, moving towards the door.

"I guess I'll wait a little while. Until Hawkins comes up to touch me for another ten."

Estel grinned. Beef walked in front of him wooden-faced to the door and opened it. Estel went out. The door closed. The room was silent. I sniffed at the dying perfume of sandalwood and stood motionless, looking around.

Somebody was nuts. I was nuts. Everybody was nuts. None of it fitted together worth a nickel. Marty Estel, as he said, had no good motive for murdering anybody, because that would be the surest way to kill his chances to collect his money. Even if he had a motive for murdering anybody, Waxnose and Frisky didn't seem like the team he would select for the job. I was in bad with the police, I had spent ten dollars of my twenty expense money, and I didn't have enough leverage anywhere to lift a dime off a cigar counter.

I finished my drink, put the glass down, walked up and down the room, smoked a third cigarette, looked at my watch, shrugged and felt disgusted. The inner doors of the suite were closed. I went across to the one out of which young Jeeter must have sneaked that afternoon. Opening it I looked into a bedroom done in ivory and ashes of roses. There was a big double bed with no footboard, covered with figured brocade. Toilet articles glistened on a built-in dressing table with a panel light. The light was lit. A small lamp on a table beside the door was lit also. A door near the dressing table showed the cool green of bathroom tiles.

I went over and looked in there. Chromium, a glass stall shower, monogrammed towels on a rack, a glass shelf for perfume and bath salts at the foot of the tub, everything nice and refined. Miss Huntress did herself well. I hoped she was paying her own rent. It didn't make any difference to me — I just liked it that way.

I went back towards the living room, stopped in the doorway to take another pleasant look around, and noticed something I ought to have noticed the instant I stepped into the room. I noticed the sharp tang of cordite on the air, almost, but not quite gone. And then I noticed something else.

The bed had been moved over until its head overlapped the edge of a closet door which was not quite closed. The weight of the bed was holding it from opening. I went over there to find out why it wanted to open. I went slowly and about halfway there I noticed that I was holding a gun in my hand.

I leaned against the closet door. It didn't move. I threw more weight against it. It still didn't move. Braced against it I pushed the bed away with my foot, gave ground slowly.

A weight pushed against me hard. I had gone back a foot or so before anything else happened. Then it happened suddenly. He came out — sideways, in a sort of roll. I put some more weight back on the door and held him like that a moment, looking at him.

He was still big, still blond, still dressed in rough sporty material, with scarf and open-necked shirt. But his face wasn't red any more.

I gave ground again and he rolled down the back of the door, turning a little like a swimmer in the surf, thumped the floor and lay there, almost on his back, still looking at me. Light from the bedside lamp glittered on his head. There was a scorched and soggy stain on the rough coat — about where his heart would be. So he wouldn't get that five million after all. And nobody would get anything and Marty Estel wouldn't get his fifty grand. Because young Mister Gerald was dead.

I looked back into the closet where he had been. Its door hung wide open now. There were clothes on racks, feminine clothes, nice clothes. He had been backed in among them, probably with his hands in the air and a gun against his chest. And then he had been shot dead, and whoever did it hadn't been quite quick enough or quite strong enough to get the door shut. Or had been scared and had just yanked the bed over against the door and left it that way.

Something glittered down on the floor. I picked it up. A small automatic, .25 caliber, a woman's purse gun with a beautifully engraved butt inlaid with silver and ivory. I put the gun in my pocket. That seemed a funny thing to do, too.

I didn't touch him. He was as dead as John D. Arbogast and looked a whole lot deader. I left the door open and listened, walked quickly back across the room and into the living room and shut the bedroom door, smearing the knob as I did it.

A lock was being tinkled at with a key. Hawkins was back again, to see what delayed me. He was letting himself in with his passkey.

I was pouring a drink when he came in.

He came well into the room, stopped with his feet planted and surveyed me coldly.

"I seen Estel and his boy leave," he said. "I didn't see you leave. So I come up. I gotta—"

"You gotta protect the guests," I said.

"Yeah. I gotta protect the guests. You can't stay up here, pal. Not without the lady of the house is home."

"But Marty Estel and his hard boy can."

He came a little closer to me. He had a mean look in his eye. He had always had it, probably, but I noticed it more now.

"You don't want to make nothing of that, do you?" he asked me.

"No. Every man to his own chisel. Have a drink."

"That ain't your liquor."

"Miss Huntress gave me a bottle. We're pals. Marty Estel and I are pals. Everybody is pals. Don't you want to be pals?"

"You ain't trying to kid me, are you?"

"Have a drink and forget it."

I found a glass and poured him one. He took it.

"It's the job if anybody smells it on me," he said.

"Uh-huh."

He drank slowly, rolling it around on his tongue. "Good Scotch."

"Won't be the first time you tasted it, will it?"

He started to get hard again, then relaxed. "Hell, I guess you're just a kidder." He finished the drink, put the glass down, patted his lips with a large and very crumpled handkerchief and sighed.

"Okay," he said. "But we'll have to leave now."

"All set. I guess she won't be home for a while. You see them go out?"

"Her and the boy friend. Yeah, long time ago."

I nodded. We went towards the door and Hawkins saw me out. He saw me downstairs and off the premises. But he didn't see what was in Miss Huntress' bedroom. I wondered if he would go back up. If he did, the Scotch bottle would probably stop him.

I got into my car and drove off home — to talk to Anna Halsey on the phone. There wasn't any case any more — for us. I parked close to the curb this time. I wasn't feeling gay any more. I rode up in the elevator and unlocked the door and clicked the light on.

Waxnose sat in my best chair, an unlit hand-rolled brown cigarette between his fingers, his bony knees crossed, and his long Woodsman resting solidly on his leg. He was smiling. It wasn't the nicest smile I ever saw.

"Hi, pal," he drawled. "You still ain't had that door fixed. Kind of shut it, huh?" His voice, for all the drawl, was deadly.

I shut the door, stood looking across the room at him.

"So you killed my pal," he said.

He stood up slowly, came across the room slowly and leaned the .22 against my throat. His smiling thin-lipped mouth seemed as expressionless, for all its smile, as his wax-white nose. He reached quietly under my coat and took the Luger. I might as well leave it home from now on. Everybody in town seemed to be able to take it away from me.

He stepped back across the room and sat down again in the chair.

"Steady does it," he said almost gently. "Park the body, friend. No false moves. No moves at all. You and me are at the jumping-off place. The clock's tickin' and we're waiting to go."

I sat down and stared at him. A curious bird. I moistened my dry lips. "You told me his gun had no firing pin," I said.

"Yeah. He fooled me on that, the little so-and-so. And I told you to lay off the Jeeter kid. That's cold now. It's Frisky I'm thinking about. Crazy, ain't it? Me bothering about a dimwit like that, packin' him around with me, and letting him get hisself bumped off." He sighed and added simply, "He was my kid brother."

"I didn't kill him," I said.

He smiled a little more. He had never stopped smiling. The corners of his mouth just tucked in a little deeper.

"Yeah?"

He slid the safety catch off the Luger, laid it carefully on the arm of the chair at his right, and reached into his pocket. What he brought out made me as cold as an ice bucket.

It was a metal tube, dark and rough-looking, about four inches long and drilled with a lot of small holes. He held his Woodsman in his left hand and began to screw the tube casually on the end of it.

"Silencer," he said. "They're the bunk, I guess you smart guys think. This one ain't the bunk — not for three shots. I oughta know. I made it myself."

I moistened my lips again. "It'll work for one shot," I said. "Then it jams your action. That one looks like cast-iron. It will probably blow your hand off."

He smiled his waxy smile, screwed it on, slowly, lovingly, gave it a last hard turn and sat back relaxed. "Not this baby. She's packed with steel wool and that's good for three shots, like I said. Then you got to repack it. And there ain't enough back pressure to jam the action of this gun. You feel good? I'd like you to feel good."

"I feel swell, you sadistic son of a bitch," I said.

"I'm having you lie down on the bed after a while. You won't feel nothing. I'm kind of fussy about my killings. Frisky didn't feel nothing, I guess. You got him neat."

"You don't see good," I sneered. "The chauffeur got him with a Smith and Wesson forty-four. I didn't even fire."

"Uh-huh."

"Okay, you don't believe me," I said. "What did you kill Arbogast for? There was nothing fussy about that killing. He was just shot at his desk, three times with a twenty-two and he fell down on the floor. What did he ever do to your filthy little brother?"

He jerked the gun up, but his smile held. "You got guts," he said. "Who is this here Arbogast?"

I told him. I told him slowly and carefully, in detail. I told him a lot of things. And he began in some vague way to look worried. His eyes flickered at me, away, back again, restlessly, like a hummingbird.

"I don't know any party named Arbogast, pal," he said slowly. "Never heard of him. And I ain't shot any fat guys today."

"You killed him," I said. "And you killed young Jeeter — in the girl's apartment at the El Milano. He's lying there dead right now. You're working for Marty Estel. He's going to be awfully damn sorry about that kill. Go ahead and make it three in a row."

His face froze. The smile went away at last. His whole face looked waxy now. He opened his mouth and breathed through it, and his breath made a restless worrying sound. I could see the faint glitter of sweat on his forehead, and I could feel the cold from the evaporation of sweat on mine.

Waxnose said very gently: "I ain't killed anybody at all, friend. Not anybody. I wasn't hired to kill people. Until Frisky stopped that slug I didn't have no such ideas. That's straight."

I tried not to stare at the metal tube on the end of the Woodsman.

A flame flickered at the back of his eyes, a small, weak, smoky flame. It seemed to grow larger and clearer. He looked down at the floor between his feet. I looked around at the light switch, but it was too far away. He looked up again. Very slowly he began to unscrew the silencer. He had it loose in his hand. He dropped it back into his pocket, stood up, holding the two guns, one in each hand. Then he had another idea. He sat down again, took all the shells out of the Luger quickly and threw it on the floor after them.

He came towards me softly across the room. "I guess this is your lucky day," he said. "I got to go a place and see a guy."

"I knew all along it was my lucky day. I've been feeling so good."

He moved delicately around me to the door and opened it a foot and started through the narrow opening, smiling again.

"I gotta see a guy," he said very gently, and his tongue moved along his lips.

"Not yet," I said, and jumped.

His gun hand was at the edge of the door, almost beyond the

edge. I hit the door hard and he couldn't bring it in quickly enough. He couldn't get out of the way. I pinned him in the doorway and used all the strength I had. It was a crazy thing. He had given me a break and all I had to do was to stand still and let him go. But I had a guy to see too — and I wanted to see him first.

Waxnose leered at me. He grunted. He fought with his hand beyond the door edge. I shifted and hit his jaw with all I had. It was enough. He went limp. I hit him again. His head bounced against the wood. I heard a light thud beyond the door edge. I hit him a third time. I never hit anything any harder.

I took my weight back from the door then and he slid towards me, blank-eyed, rubber-kneed, and I caught him and twisted his empty hands behind him and let him fall. I stood over him panting. I went to the door. His Woodsman lay almost on the sill. I picked it up, dropped it into my pocket — not the pocket that held Miss Huntress' gun. He hadn't even found that.

There he lay on the floor. He was thin, he had no weight, but I panted just the same. In a little while his eyes flickered open and looked up at me.

"Greedy guy," he whispered wearily. "Why did I ever leave Saint Looey?"

I snapped handcuffs on his wrists and pulled him by the shoulders into the dressing room and tied his ankles with a piece of rope. I left him lying on his back, a little sideways, his nose as white as ever, his eyes empty now, his lips moving a little as if he were talking to himself. A funny lad, not all bad, but not so pure I had to weep over him either.

I put my Luger together and left with my three guns. There was nobody outside the apartment house.

7

THE JEETER MANSION WAS on a nine- or ten-acre knoll, a big colonial pile with fat white columns and dormer windows and magnolias and a four-car garage. There was a circular parking space at the top of the driveway with two cars parked in it — one was the big dreadnought in which I'd ridden and the other a canary-yellow sports convertible I had seen before.

I rang a bell the size of a silver dollar. The door opened and a tall narrow cold-eyed bird in dark clothes looked out at me.

"Mr. Jeeter home? Mr. Jeeter, senior?"

"May I arsk who is calling?" The accent was a little too thick, like cut Scotch.

"Philip Marlowe. I'm working for him. Maybe I had ought to of gone to the servant's entrance."

He hitched a finger at a wing collar and looked at me without pleasure. "Aw, possibly. You may step in. I shall inform Mr. Jeeter. I believe he is engaged at the moment. Kindly wait 'ere in the 'all."

"The act stinks," I said. "English butlers aren't dropping their h's this year."

"Smart guy, huh?" he snarled, in a voice from not any farther across the Atlantic than Hoboken. "Wait here." He slid away.

I sat down in a carved chair and felt thirsty. After a while the butler came cat-footing back along the hall and jerked his chin at me unpleasantly.

We went along a mile of hallway. At the end it broadened without any doors into a huge sunroom. On the far side of the sunroom the butler opened a wide door and I stepped past him into an oval room with a black-and-silver oval rug, a black marble table in the middle of the rug, stiff high-backed carved chairs against the walls, a huge oval mirror with a rounded surface that made me look like a pygmy with water on the brain, and in the room three people.

By the door opposite where I came in, George the chauffeur stood stiffly in his neat dark uniform, with his peaked cap in his hand. In the least uncomfortable of the chairs sat Miss Harriet Huntress holding a glass in which there was half a drink. And around the silver margin of the oval rug, Mr. Jeeter, senior, was trying his legs out in a brisk canter, still under wraps, but mad inside. His face was red and the veins on his nose were distended. His hands were in the pockets of a velvet smoking jacket. He wore a pleated shirt with a black pearl in the bosom, a batwing black tie and one of his patent-leather oxfords was unlaced.

He whirled and yelled at the butler behind me: "Get out and keep those doors shut! And I'm not at home to anybody, understand? Nobody!"

The butler closed the doors. Presumably, he went away. I didn't hear him go.

George gave me a cool one-sided smile and Miss Huntress gave me a bland stare over her glass. "You made a nice comeback," she said demurely.

"You took a chance leaving me alone in your apartment," I told her. "I might have sneaked some of your perfume."

"Well, what do you want?" Jeeter yelled at me. "A nice sort of detective you turned out to be. I put you on a confidential job and you walk right in on Miss Huntress and explain the whole thing to her."

"It worked, didn't it?"

He stared. They all stared. "How do you know that?" he barked.

"I know a nice girl when I see one. She's here telling you she had an idea she got not to like, and for you to quit worrying about it. Where's Mister Gerald?"

Old Man Jeeter stopped and gave me a hard level stare. "I still regard you as incompetent," he said. "My son is missing."

"I'm not working for you. I'm working for Anna Halsey. Any complaints you have to make should be addressed to her. Do I pour my own drink or do you have a flunky in a purple suit to do it? And what do you mean, your son is missing?"

"Should I give him the heave, sir?" George asked quietly.

Jeeter waved his hand at a decanter and siphon and glasses on the black marble table and started around the rug again. "Don't be silly," he snapped at George.

George flushed a little, high on his cheekbones. His mouth looked tough.

I mixed myself a drink and sat down with it and tasted it and asked again: "What do you mean your son is missing, Mr. Jeeter?"

"I'm paying you good money," he started to yell at me, still mad.

"When?"

He stopped dead in his canter and looked at me again. Miss Huntress laughed lightly. George scowled.

"What do you suppose I mean — my son is missing?" he snapped. "I should have thought that would be clear enough even to you. Nobody knows where he is. Miss Huntress doesn't know. I don't know. No one at any of the places where he might be known."

"But I'm smarter than they are," I said. "*I* know."

Nobody moved for a long minute. Jeeter stared at me fish-eyed. George stared at me. The girl stared at me. She looked puzzled. The other two just stared.

I looked at her. "Where did you go when you went out, if you're telling?"

Her dark blue eyes were water-clear. "There's no secret about it. We went out together — in a taxi. Gerald had had his driving license suspended for a month. Too many tickets. We went down towards the beach and I had a change of heart, as you guessed. I decided I was just being a chiseler after all. I didn't want Gerald's money really. What I wanted was revenge. On Mr. Jeeter here for ruining my father. Done all legally of course, but done just the same. But I got myself in a spot where I couldn't have my revenge and not look like a cheap chiseler. So I told George to find some other girl to play with. He was sore and we quarreled. I stopped the taxi and got out in Beverly Hills. He went on. I don't know where. Later I went back to the El Milano and got my car out of the garage and came here. To tell Mr. Jeeter to forget the whole thing and not bother to sic sleuths on to me."

"You say you went with him in a taxi," I said. "Why wasn't George driving him, if he couldn't drive himself?"

I stared at her, but I wasn't talking to her. Jeeter answered me, frostily. "George drove me home from the office, of course. At that time Gerald had already gone out. Is there anything important about that?"

I turned to him. "Yeah. There's going to be. Mister Gerald is at the El Milano. Hawkins the house dick told me. He went back there to wait for Miss Huntress and Hawkins let him into her apartment. Hawkins will do you those little favors — for ten bucks. He may be there still and he may not."

I kept on watching them. It was hard to watch all three of them. But they didn't move. They just looked at me.

"Well — I'm glad to hear it," Old Man Jeeter said. "I was afraid he was off somewhere getting drunk."

"No. He's not off anywhere getting drunk," I said. "By the way, among these places you called to see if he was there, you didn't call the El Milano?"

George nodded. "Yes, I did. They said he wasn't there. Looks like the house peeper tipped the phone girl off not to say anything."

"He wouldn't have to do that. She'd just ring the apartment and he wouldn't answer — naturally." I watched Old Man Jeeter hard then, with a lot of interest. It was going to be hard for him to take that up, but he was going to have to do it.

He did. He licked his lips first. "Why — naturally, if I may ask?" he said coldly.

I put my glass down on the marble table and stood against the wall, with my hands hanging free. I still tried to watch them — all three of them.

"Let's go back over this thing a little," I said. "We're all wise to the situation. I know George is, although he shouldn't be, being just a servant. I know Miss Huntress is. And of course *you* are, Mr. Jeeter. So let's see what we have got. We have a lot of things that don't add up, but I'm smart. I'm going to add them up anyhow. First-off a handful of photostats of notes from Marty Estel. Gerald denies having given these and Mr. Jeeter won't pay them, but he has a handwriting man named Arbogast check the signatures, to see if they look genuine. They do. They are. This Arbogast may have done other things. I don't know. I couldn't ask him. When I went to see him, he was dead — shot three times — as I've since heard — with a twenty-two. No, I didn't tell the police, Mr. Jeeter."

The tall silver-haired man looked horribly shocked. His lean body shook like a bulrush. "Dead?" he whispered. "Murdered?"

I looked at George. George didn't move a muscle. I looked at the girl. She sat quietly, waiting, tight-lipped.

I said: "There's only one reason to suppose his killing had anything to do with Mr. Jeeter's affairs. He was shot with a twenty-two — and there is a man in this case who wears a twenty-two."

I still had their attention. And their silence.

"Why he was shot I haven't the faintest idea. He was not a dangerous man to Miss Huntress or Marty Estel. He was too fat to get around much. My guess is he was a little too smart. He got a simple case of signature identification and he went on from there to find out more than he should. And after he had found out more than he should — he guessed more than he ought — and maybe he even tried a little blackmail. And somebody rubbed him out this afternoon with a twenty-two. Okay, I can stand it. I never knew him.

"So I went over to see Miss Huntress and after a lot of finagling around with this itchy-handed house dick I got to see her and we had a chat, and then Mister Gerald stepped neatly out of hiding and bopped me a nice one on the chin and over I went and hit my head on a chair leg. And when I came out of that the joint was empty. So I went on home.

"And home I found the man with the twenty-two and with him a dimwit called Frisky Lavon, with a bad breath and a very large gun, neither of which matters now as he was shot dead in front of your house tonight, Mr. Jeeter — shot trying to stick up your car. The cops know about that one — they came to see me about it — because the other guy, the one that packs the twenty-two, is the little dimwit's brother and he thought I shot Dimwit and tried to put the bee on me. But it didn't work. That's two killings.

"We now come to the third and most important. I went back to the El Milano because it no longer seemed a good idea for Mister Gerald to be running around casually. He seemed to have a few enemies. It even seemed that he was supposed to be in the car this evening when Frisky Lavon shot at it — but of course that was just a plant."

Old Jeeter drew his white eyebrows together in an expression of puzzlement. George didn't look puzzled. He didn't look anything. He was as wooden-faced as a cigar-store Indian. The girl looked a little white now, a little tense. I plowed on.

"Back at the El Milano I found that Hawkins had let Marty Estel and his bodyguard into Miss Huntress' apartment to wait for her. Marty had something to tell her — that Arbogast had been killed.

That made it a good idea for her to lay off young Jeeter for a while — until the cops quieted down anyhow. A thoughtful guy, Marty. A much more thoughtful guy than you would suppose. For instance, he knew about Arbogast and he knew Mr. Jeeter went to Anna Halsey's office this morning and he knew somehow — Anna might have told him herself, I wouldn't put it past her — that I was working on the case now. So he had me tailed to Arbogast's place and away, and he found out later from his cop friends that Arbogast had been murdered, and he knew I hadn't given it out. So he had me there and that made us pals. He went away after telling me this and once more I was left alone in Miss Huntress' apartment. But this time for no reason at all I poked around. And I found young Mister Gerald, in the bedroom, in a closet."

I stepped quickly over to the girl and reached into my pocket and took out the small fancy .25 automatic and laid it down on her knee. "Ever see this before?"

Her voice had a curious tight sound, but her dark blue eyes looked at me levelly.

"Yes. It's mine."

"You kept it where?"

"In the drawer of a small table beside the bed."

"Sure about that?"

She thought. Neither of the two men stirred.

George began to twitch the corner of his mouth. She shook her head suddenly, sideways.

"No. I have an idea now I took it out to show somebody — because I don't know much about guns — and left it lying on the mantel in the living room. In fact, I'm almost sure I did. It was Gerald I showed it to."

"So he might have reached for it there, if anybody tried to make a wrong play at him?"

She nodded, troubled. "What do you mean — he's in the closet?" she asked in a small quick voice.

"You know. Everybody in this room knows what I mean. They know that I showed you that gun for a purpose." I stepped away from her and faced George and his boss. "He's dead, of course. Shot through the heart — probably with this gun. It was left there with him. That's why it would be left."

The old man took a step and stopped and braced himself against the table. I wasn't sure whether he had turned white or whether he had been white already. He stared stonily at the girl. He said very slowly, between his teeth: "You damned murderess!"

"Couldn't it have been suicide?" I sneered.

He turned his head enough to look at me. I could see that the idea interested him. He half nodded.

"No," I said. "It couldn't have been suicide."

He didn't like that so well. His face congested with blood and the veins on his nose thickened. The girl touched the gun lying on her knee, then put her hand loosely around the butt. I saw her thumb slide very gently towards the safety catch. She didn't know much about guns, but she knew that much.

"It couldn't be suicide." I said again, very slowly. "As an isolated event — maybe. But not with all the other stuff that's been happening. Arbogast, the stick-up down on Calvello Drive outside this house, the thugs planted in my apartment, the job with the twenty-two."

I reached into my pocket again and pulled out Waxnose's Woodsman. I held it carelessly on the flat of my left hand. "And curiously enough, I don't think it was *this* twenty-two — although this happens to be the gunman's twenty-two. Yeah, I have the gunman, too. He's tied up in my apartment. He came back to knock me off, but I talked him out of it. I'm a swell talker."

"Except that you overdo it," the girl said coolly, and lifted the gun a little.

"It's obvious who killed him, Miss Huntress," I said. "It's simply a matter of motive and opportunity. Marty Estel didn't, and didn't have it done. That would spoil his chances to get his fifty grand. Frisky Lavon's pal didn't, regardless of who he was working for, and I don't think he was working for Marty Estel. He couldn't have got into the El Milano to do the job, and certainly not into Miss Huntress' apartment. Whoever did it had something to gain by it and an opportunity to get to the place where it was done. Well, who had something to gain? Gerald had five million coming to him in two years out of a trust fund. He couldn't will it until he got it. So if he died, his natural heir got it. Who's his natural heir? You'd be surprised. Did you know that in the state of California and some others, but not in all, a man can by his own act become a natural heir? Just by adopting somebody who has money and no heirs!"

George moved then. His movement was once more as smooth as a ripple of water. The Smith & Wesson gleamed dully in his hand, but he didn't fire it. The small automatic in the girl's hand cracked. Blood spurted from George's brown hard hand. The Smith & Wesson dropped to the floor. He cursed. She didn't know much about guns — not very much.

"Of course!" she said grimly. "George could get into the apartment without any trouble, if Gerald was there. He would go in through the garage, a chauffeur in uniform, ride up in the elevator and knock at the door. And when Gerald opened it, George would back him in with that Smith and Wesson. But how did he know Gerald was there?"

I said: "He must have followed your taxi. We don't know where he has been all evening since he left me. He had a car with him. The cops will find out. How much was in it for you, George?"

George held his right wrist with his left hand, held it tightly, and his face was twisted, savage. He said nothing.

"George would back him in with the Smith and Wesson," the girl said wearily. "Then he would see my gun on the mantelpiece. That would be better. He would use that. He would back Gerald into the bedroom, away from the corridor, into the closet, and there, quietly, calmly, he would kill him and drop the gun on the floor."

"George killed Arbogast, too. He killed him with a twenty-two because he knew that Frisky Lavon's brother had a twenty-two, and he knew that because he had hired Frisky and his brother to put over a big scare on Gerald — so that when he was murdered it would look as if Marty Estel had had it done. That was why I was brought out here tonight in the Jeeter car — so that the two thugs who had been warned and planted could pull their act and maybe knock me off, if I got too tough. Only George likes to kill people. He made a neat shot at Frisky. He hit him in the face. It was so good a shot I think he meant it to be a miss. How about it, George?"

Silence.

I looked at old Jeeter at last. I had been expecting him to pull a gun himself, but he hadn't. He just stood there, open-mouthed, appalled, leaning against the black marble table, shaking.

"My God!" he whispered. "My God!"

"You don't have one — except money."

A door squeaked behind me. I whirled, but I needn't have bothered. A hard voice, about as English as Amos and Andy, said: "Put 'em up, bud."

The butler, the very English butler, stood there in the doorway, a gun in his hand, tight-lipped. The girl turned her wrist and shot him just kind of casually, in the shoulder or something. He squealed like a stuck pig.

"Go away, you're intruding," she said coldly.

He ran. We heard his steps running.

"He's going to fall," she said.

I was wearing my Luger in my right hand now, a little late in the season, as usual. I came around with it. Old Man Jeeter was holding on to the table, his face gray as a paving block. His knees were giving. George stood cynically, holding a handkerchief around his bleeding wrist, watching him.

"Let him fall," I said. "Down is where he belongs."

He fell. His head twisted. His mouth went slack. He hit the carpet on his side and rolled a little and his knees came up. His mouth drooled a little. His skin turned violet.

"Go call the law, angel," I said. "I'll watch them now."

"All right," she said standing up. "But you certainly need a lot of help in your private-detecting business, Mr. Marlowe."

8

I HAD BEEN IN THERE for a solid hour, alone. There was the scarred desk in the middle, another against the wall, a brass spittoon on a mat, a police loudspeaker box on the wall, three squashed flies, a smell of cold cigars and old clothes. There were two hard arm-chairs with felt pads and two hard straight chairs without pads. The electric-light fixture had been dusted about Coolidge's first term.

The door opened with a jerk and Finlayson and Sebold came in. Sebold looked as spruce and nasty as ever, but Finlayson looked older, more worn, mousier. He held a sheaf of papers in his hand. He sat down across the desk from me and gave me a hard bleak stare.

"Guys like you get in a lot of trouble," Finlayson said sourly. Sebold sat down against the wall and tilted his hat over his eyes and yawned and looked at his new stainless-steel wrist watch.

"Trouble is my business," I said. "How else would I make a nickel?"

"We oughta throw you in the can for all this cover-up stuff. How much you making on this one?"

"I was working for Anna Halsey who was working for Old Man Jeeter. I guess I made a bad debt."

Sebold smiled his blackjack smile at me. Finlayson lit a cigar and licked at a tear on the side of it and pasted it down, but it leaked smoke just the same when he drew on it. He pushed papers across the desk at me.

"Sign three copies."

I signed three copies.

He took them back, yawned and rumpled his old gray head. "The old man's had a stroke," he said. "No dice there. Probably won't know what time it is when he comes out. This George Haster-man, this chauffeur guy, he just laughs at us. Too bad he got pinked. I'd like to wrastle him a bit."

"He's tough," I said.

"Yeah. Okay, you can beat it for now."

I got up and nodded to them and went to the door. "Well, good-night, boys."

Neither of them spoke to me.

I went out, along the corridor and down in the night elevator to the City Hall lobby. I went out the Spring Street side and down the long flight of empty steps and the wind blew cold. I lit a ciga-rette at the bottom. My car was still out at the Jeeter place. I lifted a foot to start walking to a taxi half a block down across the street. A voice spoke sharply from a parked car.

"Come here a minute."

It was a man's voice, tight, hard. It was Marty Estel's voice. It came from a big sedan with two men in the front seat. I went over there. The rear window was down and Marty Estel leaned a gloved hand on it.

"Get in." He pushed the door open. I got in. I was too tired to argue. "Take it away, Skin."

The car drove west through dark, almost quiet streets, almost clean streets. The night air was not pure but it was cool. We went up over a hill and began to pick up speed.

"What they get?" Estel asked coolly.

"They didn't tell me. They didn't break the chauffeur yet."

"You can't convict a couple million bucks of murder in this man's town." The driver called Skin laughed without turning his head. "Maybe I don't even touch my fifty grand now . . . she likes you."

"Uh-huh. So what?"

"Lay off her."

"What will it get me?"

"It's what it'll get you if you don't."

"Yeah, sure," I said. "Go to hell, will you please. I'm tired." I shut my eyes and leaned in the corner of the car and just like that went to sleep. I can do that sometimes, after a strain.

A hand shaking my shoulder woke me. The car had stopped. I looked out at the front of my apartment house.

"Home," Marty Estel said. "And remember. Lay off her."

"Why the ride home? Just to tell me that?"

"She asked me to look out for you. That's why you're loose. She likes you. I like her. See? You don't want any more trouble."

"Trouble — " I started to say, and stopped. I was tired of that gag for that night. "Thanks for the ride, and apart from that, nuts to you." I turned away and went into the apartment house and up.

The door lock was still loose but nobody waited for me this time. They had taken Waxnose away long since. I left the door open and threw the windows up and I was still sniffing at policemen's cigar butts when the phone rang. It was her voice, cool, a little hard, not touched by anything, almost amused. Well, she'd been through enough to make her that way, probably.

"Hello, brown eyes. Make it home all right?"

"Your pal Marty brought me home. He told me to lay off you. Thanks with all my heart, if I have any, but don't call me up any more."

"A little scared, Mr. Marlowe?"

"No. Wait for me to call you," I said. "Goodnight, angel."

"Goodnight, brown eyes."

The phone clicked. I put it away and shut the door and pulled the bed down. I undressed and lay on it for a while in the cold air.

Then I got up and had a drink and a shower and went to sleep.

They broke George at last, but not enough. He said there had been a fight over the girl and young Jeeter had grabbed the gun off the mantel and George had fought with him and it had gone off. All of which, of course, looked possible — in the papers. They never pinned the Arbogast killing on him or on anybody. They never found the gun that did it, but it was not Waxnose's gun. Waxnose disappeared — I never heard where. They didn't touch Old Man Jeeter, because he never came out of his stroke, except to lie on his back and have nurses and tell people how he hadn't lost a nickel in the depression.

Marty Estel called me up four times to tell me to lay off Harriet Huntress. I felt kind of sorry for the poor guy. He had it bad. I went out with her twice and sat with her twice more at home, drinking her Scotch. It was nice, but I didn't have the money, the clothes, the time or the manners. Then she stopped being at the El Milano and I heard she had gone to New York.

I was glad when she left — even though she didn't bother to tell me goodbye.

BLACKMAILERS DON'T SHOOT

BLACKMAILERS
DON'T SHOOT

Publisher's Note:

"Blackmailers Don't Shoot" was Raymond Chandler's first published story and has never before appeared in book form in the United States. It was originally published in the magazine *Black Mask* in December 1933.

1

THE MAN IN THE POWDER-BLUE SUIT — which wasn't powder-blue under the lights of the Club Bolivar — was tall, with wide-set gray eyes, a thin nose, a jaw of stone. He had a rather sensitive mouth. His hair was crisp and black, ever so faintly touched with gray, as by an almost diffident hand. His clothes fitted him as though they had a soul of their own, not just a doubtful past. His name happened to be Mallory.

He held a cigarette between the strong, precise fingers of one hand. He put the other hand flat on the white tablecloth, and said:

"The letters will cost you ten grand, Miss Farr. That's not too much."

He looked at the girl opposite him very briefly; then he looked across empty tables towards the heart-shaped space of floor where the dancers prowled under shifting colored lights.

They crowded the customers around the dance floor so closely that the perspiring waiters had to balance themselves like tightrope walkers to get between the tables. But near where Mallory sat were only four people.

A slim, dark woman was drinking a highball across the table from a man whose fat red neck glistened with damp bristles. The woman stared into her glass morosely, and fiddled with a big silver flask in her lap. Farther along two bored, frowning men smoked long thin cigars, without speaking to each other.

Mallory said thoughtfully: "Ten grand does it nicely, Miss Farr."

Rhonda Farr was very beautiful. She was wearing, for this occasion, all black, except a collar of white fur, light as thistledown, on her evening wrap. Except also a white wig which, meant to disguise her, made her look very girlish. Her eyes were cornflower blue, and she had the sort of skin an old rake dreams of.

She said nastily, without raising her head: "That's ridiculous."

"Why is it ridiculous?" Mallory asked, looking mildly surprised and rather annoyed.

Rhonda Farr lifted her face and gave him a look as hard as marble. Then she picked a cigarette out of a silver case that lay open on the table, and fitted it into a long slim holder, also black. She went on:

"The love letters of a screen star? Not so much any more. The public has stopped being a sweet old lady in long lace panties."

A light danced contemptuously in her purplish blue eyes. Mallory gave her a hard look.

"But you came here to talk about them quick enough," he said, "with a man you never heard of."

She waved the cigarette holder, and said: "I must have been nuts."

Mallory smiled with his eyes, without moving his lips. "No, Miss Farr. You had a damn good reason. Want me to tell you what it is?"

Rhonda Farr looked at him angrily. Then she looked away, almost appeared to forget him. She held up her hand, the one with the cigarette holder, looked at it, posing. It was a beautiful hand, without a ring. Beautiful hands are as rare as jacaranda trees in bloom, in a city where pretty faces are as common as runs in dollar stockings.

She turned her head and glanced at the stiff-eyed woman, beyond her towards the mob around the dance floor. The orchestra went on being saccharine and monotonous.

"I loathe these dives," she said thinly. "They look as if they only existed after dark, like ghouls. The people are dissipated without grace, sinful without irony." She lowered her hand to the white cloth. "Oh yes, the letters, what makes them so dangerous, blackmailer?"

Mallory laughed. He had a ringing laugh with a hard quality in it, a grating sound. "You're good," he said. "The letters are not so much perhaps. Just sexy tripe. The memoirs of a schoolgirl who's been seduced and can't stop talking about it."

"That's lousy," Rhonda Farr said in a voice like iced velvet.

"It's the man they're written to that makes them important," Mallory said coldly. "A racketeer, a gambler, a fast-money boy. And all that goes with it. A guy you couldn't be seen talking to — and stay in the cream."

"I don't talk to him, blackmailer. I haven't talked to him in years. Landrey was a pretty nice boy when I knew him. Most of us have something behind us we'd rather not go into. In my case it *is* behind."

"Oh, yes? Make mine strawberry," Mallory said with a sudden sneer. "You just got through asking him to help you get your letters back."

Her head jerked. Her face seemed to come apart, to become merely a set of features without control. Her eyes looked like the prelude to a scream — but only for a second.

Almost instantly she got her self-control back. Her eyes were drained of color, almost as gray as his own. She put the black cigarette holder down with exaggerated care, laced her fingers together. The knuckles looked white.

"You know Landrey that well?" she said bitterly.

"Maybe I just get around, find things out . . . Do we deal, or do we just go on snarling at each other?"

"Where did you get the letters?" Her voice was still rough and bitter.

Mallory shrugged. "We don't tell things like that in our business."

"I had a reason for asking. Some other people have been trying to sell me these same damned letters. That's why I'm here. It made me curious. But I guess you're just one of them trying to scare me into action by stepping the price."

Mallory said: "No. I'm on my own."

She nodded. Her voice was scarcely more than a whisper. "That makes it nice. Perhaps some bright mind thought of having a private edition of my letters made. Photostats . . . Well, I'm not paying. It wouldn't get me anywhere. I don't deal, blackmailer. So far as I'm concerned you can go out some dark night and jump off the dock with your lousy letters!"

Mallory wrinkled his nose, squinted down it with an air of deep concentration. "Nicely put, Miss Farr. But it doesn't get us anywhere."

She said deliberately: "It wasn't meant to. I could put it better. And if I'd thought to bring my little pearl-handled gun I could say it with slugs and get away with it! But I'm not looking for that kind of publicity."

Mallory held up two lean fingers and examined them critically. He looked amused, almost pleased. Rhonda Farr put her slim hand up to her white wig, held it there a moment, and dropped it.

A man sitting at a table some way off got up at once and came towards them.

He came quickly, walking with a light, lithe step and swinging a soft black hat against his thigh. He was sleek in dinner clothes.

While he was coming Rhonda Farr said: "You didn't expect me to walk in here alone, did you? Me, I don't go to nightclubs alone."

Mallory grinned. "You shouldn't ought to have to, baby," he said dryly.

The man came up to the table. He was small, neatly put together, dark. He had a little black mustache, shiny like satin, and the clear pallor that Latins prize above rubies.

With a smooth gesture, a hint of drama, he leaned across the table and took one of Mallory's cigarettes out of the silver case. He lit it with a flourish.

Rhonda Farr put her hand to her lips and yawned. She said, "This is Erno, my bodyguard. He takes care of me. Nice, isn't it?"

She stood up slowly. Erno helped her with her wrap. Then he spread his lips in a mirthless smile, looked at Mallory, said:

"Hello, baby."

He had dark, almost opaque eyes with hot lights in them.

Rhonda Farr gathered her wrap about her, nodded slightly, sketched a brief sarcastic smile with her delicate lips, and turned off along the aisle between the tables. She went with her head up and proud, her face a little tense and wary, like a queen in jeopardy. Not fearless, but disdaining to show fear. It was nicely done.

The two bored men gave her an interested eye. The dark woman brooded glumly over the task of mixing herself a highball that would have floored a horse. The man with the fat sweaty neck seemed to have gone to sleep.

Rhonda Farr went up the five crimson-carpeted steps to the lobby, past a bowing headwaiter. She went through looped-back gold curtains, and disappeared.

Mallory watched her out of sight, then he looked at Erno. He said: "Well, punk, what's on your mind?"

He said it insultingly, with a cold smile. Erno stiffened. His gloved left hand jerked the cigarette that was in it so that some ash fell off.

"Kiddin' yourself, baby?" he inquired swiftly.

"About what, punk?"

Red spots came into Erno's pale cheeks. His eyes narrowed to black slits. He moved his ungloved right hand a little, curled the fingers so that the small pink nails glittered. He said thinly:

"About some letters, baby. Forget it! It's out, baby, out!"

Mallory looked at him with elaborate, cynical interest, ran his fingers through his crisp black hair. He said slowly:

"Perhaps I don't know what you mean, little one."

Erno laughed. A metallic sound, a strained deadly sound. Mallory knew that kind of laugh: the prelude to gun music in some places. He watched Erno's quick little right hand. He spoke raspingly.

"On your way, red hot. I might take a notion to slap that fuzz off your lip."

Erno's face twisted. The red patches showed startlingly in his cheeks. He lifted the hand that held his cigarette, lifted it slowly, and snapped the burning cigarette straight at Mallory's face. Mallory moved his head a little, and the white tube arched over his shoulder.

There was no expression on his lean, cold face. Distantly, dimly, as though another voice spoke, he said:

"Careful, punk. People get hurt for things like that."

Erno laughed the same metallic, strained laugh. "Blackmailers don't shoot, baby," he snarled. "Do they?"

"Beat it, you dirty little wop!"

The words, the cold sneering tone, stung Erno to fury. His right hand shot up like a striking snake. A gun whisked into it from a shoulder holster. Then he stood motionless, glaring. Mallory bent forward a little, his hands on the edge of the table, his fingers curled below the edge. The corners of his mouth sketched a dim smile.

There was a dull screech, not loud, from the dark woman. The color drained from Erno's cheeks, leaving them pallid, sunk in. In a voice that whistled with fury he said:

"Okay, baby. We'll go outside. March, you ———— !"

One of the bored men three tables away made a sudden movement of no significance. Slight as it was it caught Erno's eye. His glance flickered. Then the table rose into his stomach, knocked him sprawling.

It was a light table, and Mallory was not a lightweight. There was a complicated thudding sound. A few dishes clattered, some silver. Erno was spread on the floor with the table across his thighs. His gun settled a foot from his clawing hand. His face was convulsed.

For a poised instant of time it was as though the scene were imprisoned in glass, and would never change. Then the dark woman screeched again, louder. Everything became a swirl of movement. People on all sides came to their feet. Two waiters put their arms straight up in the air and began to spout violent Neapolitan. A moist, overdriven busboy charged up, more afraid of the headwaiter than of sudden death. A plump, reddish man with corn-colored hair hurried down steps, waving a bunch of menus.

Erno jerked his legs clear, weaved to his knees, snatched up his gun. He swiveled, spitting curses. Mallory, alone, indifferent in the center of the babel, leaned down and cracked a hard fist against Erno's flimsy jaw.

Consciousness evaporated from Erno's eyes. He collapsed like a half-filled sack of sand.

Mallory observed him carefully for a couple of seconds. Then he picked his cigarette case up off the floor. There were still two cigarettes in it. He put one of them between his lips, put the case away. He took some bills out of his trouser pocket, folded one lengthwise and poked it at a waiter.

He walked away without haste, towards the five crimson-carpeted steps and the entrance.

The man with a fat neck opened a cautious and fishy eye. The drunken woman staggered to her feet with a cackle of inspiration, picked up a bowl of ice cubes in her thin jeweled hands, and dumped it on Erno's stomach, with fair accuracy.

2

MALLORY CAME OUT from under the canopy with his soft hat under his arm. The doorman looked at him inquiringly. He shook his head and walked a little way down the curving sidewalk that bordered the semicircular private driveway. He stood at the edge of the curbing, in the darkness, thinking hard. After a little while an Osotta-Fraschini went by him slowly.

It was an open phaeton, huge even for the calculated swank of Hollywood. It glittered like a Ziegfeld chorus as it passed the entrance lights, then it was dull gray and silver. A liveried chauffeur sat behind the wheel as stiff as a poker, with a peaked cap cocked rakishly over one eye. Rhonda Farr sat in the back seat, under the half-deck, with the rigid stillness of a wax figure.

The car slid soundlessly down the driveway, passed between a couple of squat stone pillars and was lost among the lights of the boulevard. Mallory put on his hat absently.

Something stirred in the darkness behind him, between tall Italian cypresses. He swung around, looked at faint light on a gun barrel.

The man who held the gun was very big and broad. He had a shapeless felt hat on the back of his head, and an indistinct overcoat hung away from his stomach. Dim light from a high-up, narrow window outlined bushy eyebrows, a hooked nose. There was another man behind him.

He said: "This is a gun, buddy. It goes boom-boom, and guys fall down. Want to try it?"

Mallory looked at him emptily, and said: "Grow up, flattie! What's the act?"

The big man laughed. His laughter had a dull sound, like the sea breaking on rocks in a fog. He said with heavy sarcasm:

"Bright boy has us spotted, Jim. One of us must look like a cop." He eyed Mallory, and added: "Saw you pull a rod on a little guy inside. Was that nice?"

Mallory tossed his cigarette away, watched it arc through the darkness. He said carefully:

"Would twenty bucks make you see it some other way?"

"Not tonight, mister. Most any other night, but not tonight."

"A C note?"

"Not even that, mister."

"That," Mallory said gravely, "must be damn tough."

The big man laughed again, came a little closer. The man behind him lurched out of the shadows and planted a soft fattish hand on Mallory's shoulder. Mallory slid sideways without moving his feet. The hand fell off. He said:

"Keep your paws off me, gumshoe!"

The other man made a snarling sound. Something swished through the air. Something hit Mallory very hard behind his left ear. He went to his knees. He kneeled swaying for a moment, shaking his head violently. His eyes cleared. He could see the lozenge design in the sidewalk. He got to his feet again rather slowly.

He looked at the man who had blackjacked him and cursed him in a thick, dull voice, with a concentration of ferocity that set the man back on his heels with his slack mouth working like melting rubber.

The big man said: "Damn your soul, Jim! What in hell'd you do that for?"

The man called Jim put his soft fat hand to his mouth and gnawed at it. He shuffled the blackjack into the side pocket of his coat.

"Forget it!" he said. "Let's take the —————— and get on with it. I need a drink."

He plunged down the walk. Mallory turned slowly, followed him with his eyes, rubbing the side of his head. The big man moved his gun in a businesslike way and said:

"Walk, buddy. We're takin' a little ride in the moonlight."

Mallory walked. The big man fell in beside him. The man called Jim fell in on the other side. He hit himself hard in the pit of the stomach, said:

"I need a drink, Mac. I've got the jumps."

The big man said peacefully: "Who don't, you poor egg?"

They came to a touring car that was double-parked near the squat pillars at the edge of the boulevard. The man who had hit Mallory got in behind the wheel. The big man prodded Mallory into the back seat and got in beside him. He held his gun across his big thigh, tilted his hat a little further back, and got out a crumpled pack of cigarettes. He lit one carefully, with his left hand.

The car went out into the sea of lights, rolled east a short way, then turned south down the long slope. The lights of the city were an endless glittering sheet. Neon signs glowed and flashed. The languid ray of a searchlight prodded about among high faint clouds.

"It's like this," the big man said, blowing smoke from his wide nostrils. "We got you spotted. You were tryin' to peddle some phony letters to this Farr twist."

Mallory laughed shortly, mirthlessly. He said: "You flatties give me an ache."

The big man appeared to think it over, staring in front of him. Passing streetlights threw quick waves of light across his broad face. After a while he said:

"You're the guy all right. We got to know these things in our business."

Mallory's eyes narrowed in the darkness. His lips smiled. He said: "What business, copper?"

The big man opened his mouth wide, shut it with a click. He said:

"Maybe you better talk, bright boy. Now would be a hell of a good time. Jim and me ain't tough to get on with, but we got friends who ain't so dainty."

Mallory said: "What would I talk about, Lieutenant?"

The big man shook with silent laughter, made no answer. The car went past the oil well that stands in the middle of La Cienega Boulevard, then turned off onto a quiet street fringed with palm trees. It stopped halfway down the block, in front of an empty lot.

Jim cut the motor and the lights. Then he got a flat bottle out of the door pocket and held it to his mouth, sighed deeply, passed the bottle over his shoulder.

The big man took a drink, waved the bottle, said:

"We got to wait here for a friend. Let's talk. My name's Macdonald — detective bureau. You was tryin' to shake the Farr girl down. Then her protection stepped in front of her. You bopped him. That was nice routine and we liked it. But we didn't like the other part."

Jim reached back for the whiskey bottle, took another drink, sniffed at the neck, said: "We was stashed out for you. But we don't figure your play out in the open like that. It don't listen."

Mallory leaned an arm on the side of the car, and looked out and up at the calm, blue, star-spattered sky. He said:

"You know too much, copper. And you didn't get your dope from Miss Farr. No screen star would go to the police on a matter of blackmail."

Macdonald jerked his big head around. His eyes gleamed faintly in the dark interior of the car.

"We didn't say how we got our dope, bright boy. So you *was* tryin' to shake her down, huh?"

Mallory said gravely: "Miss Farr is an old friend of mine. Somebody is trying to blackmail her, but not me. I just have a hunch."

Macdonald said swiftly: "What the wop pull a gun on you for?"

"He didn't like me," Mallory said in a bored voice. "I was mean to him."

Macdonald said: "Horse-feathers!" He rumbled angrily. The man in the front seat said: "Smack him in the kisser, Mac. Make the ——— like it!"

Mallory stretched his arms downward, twisting his shoulders like a man cramped from sitting. He felt the bulge of his Luger under his left arm. He said slowly:

"You said I was trying to peddle some phony letters. What makes you think the letters would be phony?"

Macdonald said softly: "Maybe we know where the right ones are."

Mallory drawled: "That's what I thought, copper," and laughed.

Macdonald moved suddenly, jerked his balled fist up, hit him in the face, but not very hard. Mallory laughed again, then he touched the bruised place behind his ear with careful fingers.

"That went home, didn't it?" he said.

Macdonald swore dully. "Maybe you're just a bit too damn smart, bright boy. I guess we'll find out after a while."

He fell silent. The man in the front seat took off his hat and scratched at a mat of gray hair. Staccato horn blasts came from the boulevard a half block away. Headlights streamed past the end of the street. After a time a pair of them swung around in a wide curve, speared white beams along below the palm trees. A dark bulk drifted down the half block, slid to the curb in front of the touring car. The lights went off.

A man got out and walked back. Macdonald said: "Hi, Slippy. How'd it go?"

The man was a tall thin figure with a shadowy face under a pulled-down cap. He lisped a little when he spoke. He said: "Nothin' to it. Nobody got mad."

"Okay," Macdonald grunted. "Ditch the hot one and drive this heap."

Jim got into the back of the touring car and sat on Mallory's left, digging a hard elbow into him. The lanky man slid under the wheel, started the motor, and drove back to La Cienega, then south to Wilshire, then west again. He drove fast and roughly.

They went casually through a red light, passed a big movie palace with most of its lights out and its glass cashier's cage empty; then through Beverly Hills, over interurban tracks. The exhaust got louder on a hill with high banks paralleling the road. Macdonald spoke suddenly:

"Hell, Jim, I forgot to frisk this baby. Hold the gun a minute."

He leaned in front of Mallory, close to him, blowing whiskey breath in his face. A big hand went over his pockets, down inside his coat around the hips, up under his left arm. It stopped there a moment, against the Luger in the shoulder holster. It went on to the other side, went away altogether.

"Okay, Jim. No gun on bright boy."

A sharp light of wonder winked into being deep in Mallory's brain. His eyebrows drew together. His mouth felt dry.

"Mind if I light up a cigarette?" he asked, after a pause.

Macdonald said with mock politeness: "Now why would we mind a little thing like that, sweetheart?"

3

THE APARTMENT HOUSE STOOD on a hill above Westward Village, and was new and rather cheap-looking. Macdonald and Mallory and Jim got out in front of it, and the touring car went on around the corner, disappeared.

The three men went through a quiet lobby past a switchboard where no one sat at the moment, up to the seventh floor in the automatic elevator. They went along a corridor, stopped before a door. Macdonald took a loose key out of his pocket, unlocked the door. They went in.

It was a very new room, very bright, very foul with cigarette smoke. The furniture was upholstered in loud colors, the carpet was a mess of fat green and yellow lozenges. There was a mantel with bottles on it.

Two men sat at an octagonal table with tall glasses at their elbows. One had red hair, very dark eyebrows, and a dead white face with deep-set dark eyes. The other one had a ludicrous big bulbous nose, no eyebrows at all, hair the color of the inside of a sardine can. This one put some cards down slowly and came across the room with a wide smile. He had a loose, good-natured mouth, an amiable expression.

"Have any trouble, Mac?" he said.

Macdonald rubbed his chin, shook his head sourly. He looked at the man with the nose as if he hated him. The man with the nose went on smiling. He said:

"Frisk him?"

Macdonald twisted his mouth to a thick sneer and stalked across the room to the mantel and the bottles. He said in a nasty tone:

"Bright boy don't pack a gun. He works with his head. He's smart."

He re-crossed the room suddenly and smacked the back of his rough hand across Mallory's mouth. Mallory smiled thinly, did not stir. He stood in front of a big bile-colored davenport spotted with angry-looking red squares. His hands hung down at his sides, and cigarette smoke drifted up from between his fingers to join the haze that already blanketed the rough, arched ceiling.

"Keep your pants on, Mac," the man with the nose said. "You've done your act. You and Jim check out now. Oil the wheels and check out."

Macdonald snarled: "Who you givin' orders to, big shot? I'm stickin' around till this chiseler gets what's coming to him, Costello."

The man called Costello shrugged his shoulders briefly. The red-haired man at the table turned a little in his chair and looked at Mallory with the impersonal air of a collector studying an impaled beetle. Then he took a cigarette out of a neat black case and lit it carefully with a gold lighter.

Macdonald went back to the mantel, poured some whiskey out of a square bottle into a glass, and drank it raw. He leaned, scowling, with his back to the mantel.

Costello stood in front of Mallory, cracking the joints of long, bony fingers.

He said: "Where do you come from?"

Mallory looked at him dreamily and put his cigarette in his mouth. "McNeil's Island," he said with vague amusement.

"How long since?"

"Ten days."

"What were you in for?"

"Forgery." Mallory gave the information in a soft, pleased voice.

"Been here before?"

Mallory said: "I was born here. Didn't you know?"

Costello's voice was gentle, almost soothing. "No-o, I didn't know that," he said. "What did you come for — ten days ago?"

Macdonald heaved across the room again, swinging his thick

arms. He slapped Mallory across the mouth a second time, leaning past Costello's shoulder to do it. A red mark showed on Mallory's face. He shook his head back and forth. Dull fire was in his eyes.

"Jeeze, Costello, this crumb ain't from McNeil. He's ribbin' you." His voice blared. "Bright boy's just a cheap chiseler from Brooklyn or K.C. — one of those hot towns where the cops are all cripples."

Costello put a hand up and pushed gently at Macdonald's shoulder. He said: "You're not needed in this, Mac," in a flat, toneless voice.

Macdonald balled his fist angrily. Then he laughed, lunged forward and ground his heel on Mallory's foot. Mallory said: "—— damn!" and sat down hard on the davenport.

The air in the room was drained of oxygen. Windows were in one wall only, and heavy net curtains hung straight and still across them. Mallory got out a handkerchief and wiped his forehead, patted his lips.

Costello said: "You and Jim check out, Mac," in the same flat voice.

Macdonald lowered his head, stared at him steadily through a fringe of eyebrow. His face was shiny with sweat. He had not taken his shabby, crumpled overcoat off. Costello didn't even turn his head. After a moment Macdonald barged back to the mantel, elbowed the gray-haired cop out of the way and grabbed at the square bottle of Scotch.

"Call the boss, Costello," he blared over his shoulder. "You ain't got the brains for this deal. For —— sake do something besides talk!" He turned a little towards Jim, thumped him on the back, said sneeringly: "Did you want just one more drink, copper?"

"What did you come here for?" Costello asked Mallory again.

"Looking for a connection." Mallory stared up at him lazily. The fire had died out of his eyes.

"Funny way you went about it, boy."

Mallory shrugged. "I thought if I made a play I might get in touch with the right people."

"Maybe you made the wrong kind of play," Costello said quietly. He closed his eyes and rubbed his nose with a thumbnail. "These things are hard to figure sometimes."

Macdonald's harsh voice boomed across the close room. "Bright boy don't make mistakes, mister. Not with his brains."

Costello opened his eyes and glanced back over his shoulder at the red-haired man. The red-haired man swiveled loosely in his chair. His right hand lay along his leg, slack, half-closed. Costello turned the other way, looked straight at Macdonald.

"Move out!" he snapped coldly. "Move out now. You're drunk, and I'm not arguing with you."

Macdonald ground his shoulders against the mantel and put his hands in the side pockets of his suit coat. His hat hung formless and crumpled on the back of his big, square head. Jim, the gray-haired cop, moved a little away from him, stared at him strainedly, his mouth working.

"Call the boss, Costello!" Macdonald shouted. "You ain't givin' me orders. I don't like you well enough to take 'em."

Costello hesitated, then moved across to the telephone. His eyes stared at a spot high up on the wall. He lifted the instrument off the prongs and dialed with his back to Macdonald. Then he leaned against the wall, smiling thinly at Mallory over the cup. Waiting.

"Hello . . . yes . . . Costello. Everything's oke except Mac's loaded. He's pretty hostile . . . won't move out. Don't know yet . . . some out-of-town boy. Okay."

Macdonald made a motion, said: "Hold it . . ."

Costello smiled and put the phone aside without haste. Macdonald's eyes gleamed at him with a greenish fire. He spit on the carpet, in the corner between a chair and the wall. He said:

"That's lousy. Lousy. You can't dial Montrose from here." Costello moved his hands vaguely. The red-haired man got to his feet. He moved away from the table and stood laxly, tilting his head back so that the smoke from his cigarette rose clear of his eyes.

Macdonald rocked angrily on his heels. His jawbone was a hard white line against his flushed face. His eyes had a deep, hard glitter.

"I guess we'll play it this way," he stated. He took his hands out of his pockets in a casual manner, and his blued service revolver moved in a tight, businesslike arc.

Costello looked at the red-haired man and said: "Take him, Andy."

The red-haired man stiffened, spat his cigarette straight out from between his pale lips, flashed a hand up like lightning.

Mallory said: "Not fast enough. Look at this one."

He had moved so quickly and so little that he had not seemed to move at all. He leaned forward a little on the davenport. The long black Luger lined itself evenly on the red-haired man's belly.

The red-haired man's hand came down slowly from his lapel, empty. The room was very quiet. Costello looked once at Macdonald with infinite disgust, then he put his hands out in front of him, palms up, and looked down at them with a blank smile.

Macdonald spoke slowly, bitterly. "The kidnaping is one too many for me, Costello. I don't want any part of it. I'm takin' a powder from this toy mob. I took a chance that bright boy might side me."

Mallory stood up and moved sideways towards the red-haired man. When he had gone about half the distance the gray-haired cop, Jim, let out a strangled sort of yell and jumped for Macdonald, clawing at his pocket. Macdonald looked at him with quick surprise. He put his big left hand out and grabbed both lapels of Jim's overcoat tight together, high up. Jim flailed at him with both fists, hit him in the face twice. Macdonald drew his lips back over his teeth. Calling to Mallory, "Watch those birds," he very calmly laid his gun down on the mantel, reached down into the pocket of Jim's coat and took out the woven leather blackjack. He said:

"You're a louse, Jim. You always were a louse."

He said it rather thoughtfully, without rancor. Then he swung the blackjack and hit the gray-haired man on the side of the head. The gray-haired man sagged slowly to his knees. He clawed freely at the skirts of Macdonald's coat. Macdonald stooped over and hit him again with the blackjack, in the same place, very hard.

Jim crumpled down sideways and lay on the floor with his hat off and his mouth open. Macdonald swung the blackjack slowly from side to side. A drop of sweat ran down the side of his nose.

Costello said: "Rough boy, ain't you, Mac?" He said it dully, absently, as though he had very little interest in what went on.

Mallory went on towards the red-haired man. When he was behind him he said:

"Put the hands way up, wiper."

When the red-haired man had done this, Mallory put his free hand over his shoulder, down inside his coat. He jerked a gun loose from a shoulder holster and dropped it on the floor behind him. He felt the other side, patted pockets. He stepped back and circled to Costello. Costello had no gun.

Mallory went to the other side of Macdonald, stood where everyone in the room was in front of him. He said:

"Who's kidnaped?"

Macdonald picked up his gun and glass of whiskey. "The Farr girl," he said. "They got her on her way home, I guess. It was planned when they knew from the wop bodyguard about the date at the Bolivar. I don't know where they took her."

Mallory planted his feet wide apart and wrinkled his nose. He held his Luger easily, with a slack wrist. He said:

"What does your little act mean?"

Macdonald said grimly: "Tell me about yours. I gave you a break."

Mallory nodded, said: "Sure — for your own reasons. I was hired to look for some letters that belong to Rhonda Farr." He looked at Costello. Costello showed no emotion.

Macdonald said: "Okay by me. I thought it was some kind of a plant. That's why I took the chance. Me, I want an out from this connection, that's all." He waved his hand around to take in the room and everything in it.

Mallory picked up a glass, looked into it to see if it was clean, then poured a little Scotch into it and drank it in sips, rolling his tongue around in his mouth.

"Let's talk about kidnaping," he said. "Who was Costello phoning to?"

"Atkinson. Big Hollywood lawyer. Front for the boys. He's the Farr girl's lawyer, too. Nice guy, Atkinson. A louse."

"He in on the kidnaping?"

Macdonald laughed and said: "Sure."

Mallory shrugged, said: "It seems like a dumb trick — for him."

He went past Macdonald, along the wall to where Costello stood. He stuck the muzzle of the Luger against Costello's chin, pushed his head back against the rough plaster.

"Costello's a nice old boy," he said thoughtfully. "He wouldn't kidnap a girl. Would you, Costello? A little quiet extortion maybe, but nothing rough. That right, Costello?"

Costello's eyes went blank. He swallowed. He said between his teeth: "Can it. You're not funny."

Mallory said: "It gets funnier as it goes on. But perhaps you don't know it all."

He lifted the Luger and drew the muzzle down the side of Costello's big nose, hard. It left a white mark that turned to a red weal. Costello looked a little worried.

Macdonald finished pushing a nearly full bottle of Scotch into his overcoat pocket, and said:

"Let me work on the ——— !"

Mallory shook his head gravely from side to side, looking at Costello.

"Too noisy. You know how these places are built. Atkinson is the boy to see. Always see the head man — if you can get to him."

Jim opened his eyes, flapped his hands on the floor, tried to get up. Macdonald lifted a large foot and planted it carelessly in the gray-haired man's face. Jim lay down again. His face was a muddy gray color.

Mallory glanced at the red-haired man and went over to the telephone stand. He lifted the instrument down and dialed a number awkwardly, with his left hand.

He said: "I'm calling the man who hired me . . . He has a big fast car . . . We'll put these boys in soak for a while."

4

LANDREY'S BIG BLACK CADILLAC rolled soundlessly up the long grade to Montrose. Lights shone low on the left, in the lap of the valley. The air was cool and clear, and the stars were very bright. Landrey looked back from the front seat, draped an arm over the back of the seat, a long black arm that ended in a white glove.

He said, for the third or fourth time: "So it's her own mouth-piece shaking her down. Well, well, well."

He smiled smoothly, deliberately. All his movements were smooth and deliberate. Landrey was a tall, pale man with white teeth and jet-black eyes that sparkled under the dome light.

Mallory and Macdonald sat in the back seat. Mallory said nothing; he stared out of the car window. Macdonald took a pull at his square bottle of Scotch, lost the cork on the floor of the car, and swore as he bent over to grope for it. When he found it he leaned back and looked morosely at Landrey's clear, pale face above the white silk scarf.

He said: "You still got that place on Highland Drive?"

Landrey said: "Yes, copper, I have. And it's not doin' so well."

Macdonald growled. He said: "That's a damn shame, Mr. Landrey."

Then he put his head back against the upholstery and closed his eyes.

The Cadillac turned off the highway. The driver seemed to know just where he was going. He circled around into a landscaped subdivision of rambling elaborate homes. Tree frogs sounded in the darkness, and there was a smell of orange blossoms.

Macdonald opened his eyes and leaned forward. "The house on the corner," he told the driver.

The house stood well back from a wide curve. It had a lot of tiled roof, an entrance like a Norman arch, and wrought-iron lanterns lit on either side of the door. By the sidewalk there was a pergola covered with climbing roses. The driver cut his lights and drifted expertly up to the pergola.

Mallory yawned and opened the car door. Cars were parked along the street around the corner. The cigarette tips of a couple of lounging chauffeurs spotted the soft bluish dark.

"Party," he said. "That makes it nice."

He got out, stood a moment looking across the lawn. Then he walked over soft grass to a pathway of dull bricks spaced so that the grass grew between them. He stood between the wrought-iron lanterns and rang the bell.

A maid in cap and apron opened the door. Mallory said:

"Sorry to disturb Mr. Atkinson, but it's important. Macdonald is the name."

The maid hesitated, then went back into the house, leaving the front door open a crack. Mallory pushed it open carelessly, looked into a roomy hallway with Indian rugs on the floor and walls. He went in.

A few yards down the hallway a doorway gave on a dim room lined with books, smelling of good cigars. Hats and coats were spread around on the chairs. From the back of the house a radio droned dance music.

Mallory took his Luger out and leaned against the jamb of the door, inside.

A man in evening dress came along the hall. He was a plump man with thick white hair above a shrewd, pink, irritable face. Beautifully tailored shoulders failed to divert attention from rather too much stomach. His heavy eyebrows were drawn together in a frown. He walked fast and looked mad.

Mallory stepped out of the doorway and put his gun in Atkinson's stomach.

"You're looking for me," he said.

Atkinson stopped, heaved a little, made a choked sound in his throat. His eyes were wide and startled. Mallory moved the Luger up, put the cold muzzle into the flesh at Atkinson's throat, just above the V of his wing collar. The lawyer partly lifted one arm, as though to make a sweep of the gun. Then he stood quite still, holding the arm up in the air.

Mallory said: "Don't talk. Just think. You're sold out. Macdonald has ratted on you. Costello and two other boys are taped up at Westwood. We want Rhonda Farr."

Atkinson's eyes were dull blue, opaque, without interior light. The mention of Rhonda Farr's name did not seem to make much impression on him. He squirmed against the gun and said:

"Why do you come to me?"

"We think you know where she is," Mallory said tonelessly. "But we won't talk about it here. Let's go outside."

Atkinson jerked, sputtered. "No . . . no, I have guests."

Mallory said coldly: "The guest we want isn't here." He pressed on the gun.

A sudden wave of emotion went over Atkinson's face. He took a short step back and snatched at the gun. Mallory's lips tightened. He twisted his wrist in a tight circle, and the gun sight flicked across Atkinson's mouth. Blood came out on his lips. His mouth began to puff. He got very pale.

Mallory said: "Keep your head, fat boy, and you may live through the night."

Atkinson turned and walked straight out of the open door, swiftly, blindly.

Mallory took his arm and jerked him to the left, onto the grass. "Make it slow," he said softly.

They rounded the pergola. Atkinson put his hands out in front of him and floundered at the car. A long arm came out of the open door and grabbed him. He went in, fell against the seat. Macdonald clapped a hand over his face and forced him back against the upholstery. Mallory got in and slammed the car door.

Tires squealed as the car circled rapidly and shot away. The driver drove a block before he switched the lights on again. Then he turned his head a little, said: "Where to, boss?"

Mallory said: "Anywhere. Back to town. Take it easy."

The Cadillac turned onto the highway again and began to drop down the long grade. Lights showed in the valley once more, little white lights that moved ever so slowly along the floor of the valley. Headlights.

Atkinson heaved up in the seat, got a handkerchief out and dabbed at his mouth. He peered at Macdonald and said in a composed voice:

"What's the frame, Mac? Shakedown?"

Macdonald laughed gruffly. Then he hiccoughed. He was a little drunk. He said thickly:

"Hell, no. The boys hung a snatch on the Farr girl tonight. Her friends here don't like it. But you wouldn't know anything about it, would you, big shot?" He laughed again, jeeringly.

Atkinson said slowly: "It's funny . . . but I wouldn't." He lifted his white head higher, went on: "Who are these men?"

Macdonald didn't answer him. Mallory lit a cigarette, guarding the match flame with cupped hands. He said slowly:

"That's not important, is it? Either you know where Rhonda Farr was taken, or you can give us a lead. Think it out. There's lots of time."

Landrey turned his head and looked back. His face was a pale blur in the dark.

"It's not much to ask, Mr. Atkinson," he said gravely. His voice was cool, suave, pleasant. He tapped on the seat back with his gloved fingers.

Atkinson stared towards him for a while, then put his head back against the upholstery. "Suppose I don't know anything about it," he said wearily.

Macdonald lifted his hand and hit him in the face. The lawyer's head jerked against the cushions. Mallory said in a cold, unpleasant voice:

"A little less of your crap, copper."

Macdonald swore at him, turned his head away. The car went on.

They were down in the valley now. A three-colored airport beacon swung through the sky not far away. There began to be wooded slopes and little beginnings of valley between dark hills. A train roared down from the Newhall tunnel, gathered speed and went by with a long shattering crash.

Landrey said something to his driver. The Cadillac turned off onto a dirt road. The driver switched the lights off and picked his way by moonlight. The dirt road ended in a spot of dead brown grass with low bushes around it. There were old cans and torn dis-colored newspapers faintly visible on the ground.

Macdonald got his bottle out, hefted it, and gurgled a drink. Atkinson said thickly:

"I'm a bit faint. Give me one."

Macdonald turned, held the bottle out, then growled: "Aw, go to hell!" and put it away in his coat. Mallory took a flash out of the door pocket, clicked it on, and put the beam on Atkinson's face. He said:

"Talk."

Atkinson put his hands on his knees and stared straight at the beacon of the flashlight. His eyes were glassy and there was blood on his chin. He spoke:

"This is a frame by Costello. I don't know what it's all about. But if it's Costello, a man named Slippy Morgan will be in on it. He has a shack on the mesa by Baldwin Hills. They might have taken Rhonda Farr there."

He closed his eyes, and a tear showed in the glare of the flash. Mallory said slowly:

"Macdonald should know that."

Atkinson kept his eyes shut, said: "I guess so." His voice was dull and without any feeling.

Macdonald balled his fist, lurched sideways and hit him in the face again. The lawyer groaned, sagged to one side. Mallory's hand jerked; jerked the flash. His voice shook with fury. He said:

"Do that again and I'll put a slug in your guts, copper. So help me, I will."

Macdonald rolled away, with a foolish laugh. Mallory snapped off the light. He said, more quietly:

"I think you're telling the truth, Atkinson. We'll case this shack of Slippy Morgan's."

The driver swung and backed the car, picked his way back to the highway again.

5

A WHITE PICKET FENCE showed up for a moment before the headlights went off. Behind it on a rise the gaunt shapes of a couple of derricks groped towards the sky. The darkened car went forward slowly, stopped across the street from a small frame house. There were no houses on that side of the street, nothing between the car and the oil field. The house showed no light.

Mallory got to the ground and went across. A gravel driveway led along to a shed without a door. There was a touring car parked under the shed. There was thin worn grass along the driveway and a dull patch of something that had once been a lawn at the back. There was a wire clothesline and a small stoop with a rusted screen door. The moon showed all this.

Beyond the stoop there was a single window with the blind drawn; two thin cracks of light showed along the edges of the blind. Mallory went back to the car, walking on the dry grass and the dirt road surface without sound.

He said: "Let's go, Atkinson."

Atkinson got out heavily, stumbled across the street like a man half-asleep. Mallory grabbed his arm. The two men went up the wooden steps, crossed the porch quietly. Atkinson fumbled and found the bell. He pressed it. There was a dull buzz inside the house. Mallory flattened himself against the wall, on the side where he would not be blocked by the opening screen door.

Then the house door came open without a sound, and a figure loomed behind the screen. There was no light behind the figure. The lawyer said mumblingly:

"It's Atkinson."

The screen hook was undone. The screen door came outward.

"What's the big idea?" said a lisping voice that Mallory had heard before.

Mallory moved, holding his Luger waist-high. The man in the doorway whirled at him. Mallory stepped in on him swiftly, making a clucking sound with tongue and teeth, shaking his head reprovingly.

"You wouldn't have a gun, would you, Slippy," he said, nudging the Luger forward. "Turn slow and easy, Slippy. When you feel something against your spine, go on in, Slippy. We'll be right with you."

The lanky man put his hands up and turned. He walked back into the darkness, Mallory's gun in his back. A small living room smelled of dust and casual cooking. A door had light under it. The lanky man put one hand down slowly and opened the door.

An unshaded light bulb hung from the middle of the ceiling. A thin woman in a dirty white smock stood under it, limp arms at her sides. Dull colorless eyes brooded under a mop of rusty hair. Her fingers fluttered and twitched in involuntary contractions of the muscles. She made a thin plaintive sound, like a starved cat.

The lanky man went and stood against the wall on the opposite

ide of the room, pressing the palms of his hands against wallpaper.
There was a fixed, meaningless smile on his face.

Landrey's voice said from behind: "I'll take care of Atkinson's
als."

He came into the room with a big automatic in his gloved hand.
Nice little home," he added pleasantly.

There was a metal bed in a corner of the room. Rhonda Farr was
ying on it, wrapped to the chin in a brown army blanket. Her white
vig was partly off her head and damp golden curls showed. Her
ace was bluish-white, a mask in which the rouge and lip paint
lared. She was snoring.

Mallory put his hand under the blanket, felt for her pulse. Then
e lifted an eyelid and looked closely at the upturned pupil.

He said: "Doped."

The woman in the smock wetted her lips. "A shot of M," she said
n a slack voice. "No harm done, mister."

Atkinson sat down on a hard chair that had a dirty towel on the
ack of it. His dress shirt was dazzling under the unshaded light.
The lower part of his face was smeared with dry blood. The lanky
nan looked at him contemptuously, and patted the stained wall-
aper with the flat of his hands. Then Macdonald came into the
oom.

His face was flushed and sweaty. He staggered a little and put a
and up along the doorframe. "Hi-ho, boys," he said vacantly. "I
ught to rate a promotion for this."

The lanky man stopped smiling. He ducked sideways very fast,
nd a gun jumped into his hand. Roar filled the room, a great
rashing roar. And again a roar.

The lanky man's duck became a slide and the slide degenerated
nto a fall. He spread himself out on the bare carpet in a leisurely
ort of way. He lay quite still, one half-open eye apparently looking
t Macdonald. The thin woman opened her mouth wide, but no
ound came out of it.

Macdonald put his other hand up to the doorframe, leaned for-
vard and began to cough. Bright red blood came out on his chin.
His hands came down the doorframe slowly. Then his shoulder
witched forward, he rolled like a swimmer in a breaking wave, and
rashed. He crashed on his face, his hat still on his head, the mouse-

colored hair at the nape of his neck showing below it in an untid
curl.

Mallory said: "Two down," and looked at Landrey with a di
gusted expression. Landrey looked down at his big automatic an
put it away out of sight, in the side pocket of his thin dark overcoa

Mallory stooped over Macdonald, put a finger to his templ
There was no heartbeat. He tried the jugular vein with the sam
result. Macdonald was dead, and he still smelled violently
whiskey.

There was a faint trace of smoke under the light bulb, an acri
fume of powder. The thin woman bent forward at the waist an
scrambled towards the door. Mallory jerked a hard hand again
her chest and threw her back.

"You're fine where you are."

Atkinson took his hands off his knees and rubbed them togethe
as if all the feeling had gone out of them. Landrey went over to th
bed, put his gloved hand down and touched Rhonda Farr's hai
"Hello, baby," he said lightly. "Long time no see." He went ou
of the room, saying: "I'll get the car over on this side of the street.

Mallory looked at Atkinson. He said casually: "Who has th
letters, Atkinson? The letters belonging to Rhonda Farr?"

Atkinson lifted his blank face slowly, squinted as though the ligh
hurt his eyes. He spoke in a vague, far-off sort of voice.

"I — I don't know. Costello, maybe. I never saw them."

Mallory let out a short harsh laugh which made no change i
the hard cold lines of his face. "Wouldn't it be funny as hell if that
true!"

He stooped over the bed in the corner and wrapped the brow
blanket closely around Rhonda Farr. When he lifted her she stoppe
snoring, but she did not wake.

6

A WINDOW OR TWO in front of the apartment house showed light. Mallory held his wrist up and looked at the curved watch on the inside of it. The faintly glowing hands were at half-past three. He spoke back into the car:

"Give me ten minutes or so. Then come on up. I'll fix the doors."

The street entrance to the apartment house was locked. Mallory unlocked it with a loose key, put it on the latch. There was a little light in the lobby, from one bulb in a floor lamp and from a hooded light above the switchboard. A wizened, white-haired little man was asleep in a chair by the switchboard, with his mouth open and his breath coming in long, wailing snores, like the sounds of an animal in pain.

Mallory walked up one flight of carpeted steps. On the second floor he pushed the button for the automatic elevator. When it came rumbling down from above he got in and pushed the button marked 7. He yawned. His eyes were dull with fatigue.

The elevator lurched to a stop, and Mallory went down the bright, silent corridor. He stopped at a gray olive-wood door and put his ear to the panel. Then he fitted the loose key slowly into the lock, turned it slowly, moved the door back an inch or two. He listened again, went in.

There was light from a lamp with a red shade that stood beside an easy chair. A man was sprawled in the chair and the light splashed on his face. He was bound at the wrists and ankles with strips of wide adhesive tape. There was a strip of adhesive across his mouth.

Mallory fixed the door latch and shut the door. He went across the room with quick silent steps. The man in the chair was Costello. His face was a purplish color above the white adhesive that plastered his lips together. His chest moved in jerks and his breath made a snorting noise in his big nose.

Mallory yanked the tape off Costello's mouth, put the heel of one hand on the man's chin, forced his mouth wide open. The cadence of the breathing changed a bit. Costello's chest stopped jerking and the purplish color of his face faded to pallor. He stirred, making a groaning sound.

Mallory took an unopened pint bottle of rye off the mantel and tore the metal strip from the cap with his teeth. He pushed Costello's head far back, poured some whiskey into his open mouth slapped his face hard. Costello choked, swallowed convulsively Some of the whiskey ran out of his nostrils. He opened his eyes focused them slowly. He mumbled something confused.

Mallory went through velour curtains that hung across a door way at the inner end of the room, into a short hall. The first doo led into a bedroom with twin beds. A light burned, and a man wa lying bound on each of the beds.

Jim, the gray-haired cop, was asleep or still unconscious. The side of his head was stiff with congealed blood. The skin of his face wa a dirty gray.

The eyes of the red-haired man were wide open, diamond bright angry. His mouth worked under the tape, trying to chew it. H had rolled over on his side and almost off the bed. Mallory pushed him back towards the middle, and said:

"It's all in the game."

He went back to the living room and switched on more light Costello had struggled up in the easy chair. Mallory took out pocket knife and reached behind him, sawed the tape that bound his wrists. Costello jerked his hands apart, grunted, and rubbed the backs of his wrists together where the tape had pulled hairs out Then he bent over and tore tape off his ankles. He said:

"That didn't do me any good. I'm a mouth breather." His voice was loose, flat and without cadence.

He got to his feet and poured two inches of rye into a glass, dran it at a gulp, sat down again and leaned his head against the high back of the chair. Life came into his face; glitter came into his washed-out eyes.

He said: "What's new?"

Mallory spooned at a bowl of water that had been ice, frowned and drank some whiskey straight. He rubbed the left side of hi head gently with his finger tips and winced. Then he sat down and lit a cigarette.

He said: "Several things. Rhonda Farr is home. Macdonald and Slippy Morgan got gunned. But that's not important. I'm after some letters you were trying to peddle to Rhonda Farr. Dig 'em up."

Costello lifted his head and grunted. He said: "I don't have the letters."

Mallory said: "Get the letters, Costello. Now." He sprinkled cigarette ash carefully in the middle of a green and yellow diamond in the carpet design.

Costello made an impatient movement. "I don't have them," he insisted. "I never saw them."

Mallory's eyes were slate-gray, very cold, and his voice was brittle. He said: "What you heels don't know about your racket is just pitiful . . . I'm tired, Costello. I don't feel like an argument. You'd look lousy with that big beezer smashed over on one side of your face with a gun barrel."

Costello put his bony hand up and rubbed the reddened skin around his mouth where the tape had chafed it. He glanced down the room. There was a slight movement of the velour curtains across the end door, as though a breeze had stirred them. But there was no breeze. Mallory was staring down at the carpet.

Costello stood up from the chair, slowly. He said: "I've got a wall safe. I'll open it up."

He went across the room to the wall in which the outside door was, lifted down a picture and worked the dial of a small inset circular safe. He swung the little round door open and thrust his arm into the safe.

Mallory said: "Stay just like that, Costello."

He stepped lazily across the room, and passed his left hand down Costello's arm, into the safe. It came out again holding a small pearl-handled automatic. He made a sibilant sound with his lips and put the little gun into his pocket.

"Just can't learn, can you, Costello?" he said in a tired voice.

Costello shrugged, went back across the room. Mallory plunged his hands into the safe and tumbled the contents out onto the floor. He dropped on one knee. There were some long white envelopes, a bunch of clippings fastened with a paperclip, a narrow, thick checkbook, a small photograph album, an address book, some loose papers, some yellow bank statements with checks inside. Mallory spread one of the long envelopes carelessly, without much interest.

The curtains over the end door moved again. Costello stood rigid in front of the mantel. A gun came through the curtains in a small hand that was very steady. A slim body followed the hand, a white face with blazing eyes — Erno.

Mallory came to his feet, his hands breast-high, empty.

"Higher, baby," Erno croaked. "Much higher, baby!"

Mallory raised his hands a little more. His forehead was wrinkled in a hard frown. Erno came forward into the room. His face glistened. A lock of oily black hair drooped over one eyebrow. His teeth showed in a stiff grin.

He said: "I think we'll give it to you right here, two-timer."

His voice had a questioning inflection, as if he waited Costello's confirmation.

Costello didn't say anything.

Mallory moved his head a little. His mouth felt very dry. He watched Erno's eyes, saw them tense. He said rather quickly:

"You've been crossed, mug, but not by me."

Erno's grin widened to a snarl, and his head went back. His trigger finger whitened at the first joint. Then there was a noise outside the door, and it came open.

Landrey came in. He shut the door with a jerk of his shoulder, and leaned against it, dramatically. Both his hands were in the side pockets of his thin dark overcoat. His eyes under the soft black hat were bright and devilish. He looked pleased. He moved his chin in the white silk evening scarf that was tucked carelessly about his neck. His handsome, pale face was like something carved out of old ivory.

Erno moved his gun slightly and waited. Landrey said cheerfully:

"Bet you a grand you hit the floor first!"

Erno's lips twitched under his shiny little mustache. Two guns went off at the same time. Landrey swayed like a tree hit by a gust of wind; the heavy roar of his .45 sounded again, muffled a little by cloth and the nearness to his body.

Mallory went down behind the davenport, rolled and came up with the Luger straight out in front of him. But Erno's face had already gone blank.

He went down slowly; his light body seemed to be drawn down by the weight of the gun in his right hand. He bent at the knees as he fell, and slid forward on the floor. His back arched once, and then went loose.

Landrey took his left hand out of his coat pocket and spread the fingers away from him as though pushing at something. Slowly and with difficulty he got the big automatic out of the other pocket and raised it inch by inch, turning on the balls of his feet. He swiveled his body towards Costello's rigid figure and squeezed the trigger again. Plaster jumped from the wall at Costello's shoulder.

Landrey smiled vaguely, said: "Damn!" in a soft voice. Then his eyes went up in his head and the gun plunged down from his nerveless fingers, bounded on the carpet. Landrey went down joint by joint, smoothly and gracefully, kneeled, swaying a moment before he melted over sideways, spread himself on the floor almost without sound. Mallory looked at Costello, and said in a strained, angry voice: "Boy, are you lucky!"

The buzzer droned insistently. Three little lights glowed red on the panel of the switchboard. The wizened, white-haired little man shut his mouth with a snap and struggled sleepily upright.

Mallory jerked past him with his head turned the other way, shot across the lobby, out of the front door of the apartment house, down the three marble-faced steps, across the sidewalk and the street. The driver of Landrey's car had already stepped on the starter. Mallory swung in beside him, breathing hard, and slammed the car door.

"Get goin' fast!" he rasped. "Stay off the boulevard. Cops here in five minutes!"

The driver looked at him and said: "Where's Landrey? . . . I heard shootin'."

Mallory held the Luger up, said swiftly and coldly: "Move, baby!"

The gears went in, the Cadillac jumped forward, the driver took a corner recklessly, the tail of his eye on the gun.

Mallory said: "Landrey stopped lead. He's cold." He held the Luger up, put the muzzle under the driver's nose. "But not from my gun. Smell that, friend. It hasn't been fired!"

The driver said: "Jeeze!" in a shattered voice, swung the big car wildly, missing the curb by inches.

It was getting to be daylight.

7

RHONDA FARR SAID: "Publicity, darling. Just publicity. Any kind is better than none at all. I'm not so sure my contract is going to be renewed and I'll probably need it."

She was sitting in a deep chair, in a large, long room. She looked at Mallory with lazy, indifferent, purplish blue eyes and moved her hand to a tall, misted glass. She took a drink.

The room was enormous. Mandarin rugs in soft colors swathed the floor. There was a lot of teakwood and red lacquer. Gold frames glinted high up on the walls, and the ceiling was remote and vague, like the dusk of a hot day. A huge carved radio gave forth muted and unreal strains.

Mallory wrinkled his nose and looked amused in a grim sort of way. He said:

"You're a nasty little rat. I don't like you."

Rhonda Farr said: "Oh, yes, you do, darling. You're crazy about me."

She smiled and fitted a cigarette into a jade-green holder that matched her jade-green lounging pajamas. Then she reached out her beautifully shaped hand and pushed the button of a bell that was set into the top of a low nacre and teakwood table at her side. A silent, white-coated Japanese butler drifted into the room and mixed more highballs.

"You're a pretty wise lad, aren't you, darling?" Rhonda Farr said, when he had gone out again. "And you have some letters in your pocket you think are body and soul to me. Nothing like it, mister, nothing like it." She took a sip of the fresh highball. "The letters you have are phony. They were written about a month ago. Landrey never had them. He gave *his* letters back a long time ago . . . What you have are just props." She put a hand to her beautifully waved hair. The experience of the previous night seemed to have left no trace on her.

Mallory looked at her carefully. He said: "How do you prove that?"

"The notepaper — if I have to prove it. There's a little man down at Fourth and Spring who makes a study of that kind of thing."

Mallory said: "The writing?"

Rhonda Farr smiled dimly. "Writing's easy to fake, if you have plenty of time. Or so I'm told. That's my story anyhow."

Mallory nodded, sipped at his own highball. He put his hand into his inside breast pocket and took out a flat manila envelope, legal size. He laid it on his knee.

"Four men got gunned out last night on account of these phony letters," he said carelessly.

Rhonda Farr looked at him mildly. "Two crooks, a double-crossing policeman, make three of them. I should lose my sleep over that trash! Of course, I'm sorry about Landrey."

Mallory said politely: "It's nice of you to be sorry about Landrey."

She said peacefully: "Landrey, as I told you once, was a pretty nice boy a few years ago, when he was trying to get into pictures. But he chose another business, and in that business he was bound to stop a bullet some time."

Mallory rubbed his chin. "It's funny he didn't remember he'd given you back your letters. Very funny."

"He wouldn't care, darling. He was that kind of actor, and he'd like the show. It gave him a chance for a swell pose. He'd like that terribly."

Mallory let his face get hard and disgusted. He said: "The job looked on the level to me. I didn't know much about Landrey, but he knew a good friend of mine in Chicago. He figured a way to the boys who were working on you, and I played his hunch. Things happened that made it easier — but a lot noisier."

Rhonda Farr tapped little bright nails against her little bright teeth. She said: "What are you back where you live, darling? One of those hoods they call private dicks?"

Mallory laughed harshly, made a vague movement and ran his fingers through his crisp dark hair. "Let it go, baby," he said softly. "Let it go."

Rhonda Farr looked at him with a surprised glance, then laughed rather shrilly. "It gets mad, doesn't it?" she cooed. She went on, in a dry voice: "Atkinson has been bleeding me for years, one way and another. I fixed the letters up and put them where he could get hold of them. They disappeared. A few days afterward a man with one of those tough voices called up and began to apply the pressure. I let it ride. I figured I'd hang a pinch on Atkinson somehow, and our two reputations put together would be good for a write-up that wouldn't hurt me too much. But the thing seemed to be spreading out, and I got scared. I thought of asking Landrey to help me out. I was sure he would like it."

Mallory said roughly: "Simple, straightforward kid, ain't you! Like hell!"

"You don't know much about this Hollywood racket, do you, darling?" Rhonda Farr said. She put her head on one side and hummed softly. The strains of a dance band floated idly through the quiet air. "That's a gorgeous melody . . . It's swiped from a Weber sonata . . . Publicity has to hurt a bit out here. Otherwise nobody believes it."

Mallory stood up, lifting the manila envelope off his knee. He dropped it in her lap.

"Five grand these are costing you," he said.

Rhonda Farr leaned back and crossed her jade-green legs. One little green slipper fell off her bare foot to the rug, and the manila envelope fell down beside it. She didn't stir towards either one.

She said: "Why?"

"I'm a businessman, baby. I get paid for my work. Landrey didn't pay me. Five grand was the price. The price to him, and now the price to you."

She looked at him almost casually, out of placid, cornflower-blue eyes, and said: "No deal . . . blackmailer. Just like I told you at the Bolivar. You have all my thanks, but I'm spending my money myself."

Mallory said curtly: "This might be a damn good way to spend some of it."

He leaned over and picked up her highball, drank a little of it. When he put the glass down he tapped the nails of two fingers against the side for a moment. A small tight smile wrinkled the corners of his mouth. He lit a cigarette and tossed the match into a bowl of hyacinths.

He said slowly: "Landrey's driver talked, of course. Landrey's friends want to see me. They want to know how come Landrey got rubbed out in Westwood. The cops will get around to me after a while. Someone is sure to tip them off. I was right beside four killings last night, and naturally I'm not going to run out on them. I'll probably have to spill the whole story. The cops will give you plenty of publicity, baby. Landrey's friends — I don't know what they'll do. Something that will hurt a lot, I should say."

Rhonda Farr jerked to her feet, fumbling with her toe for the green slipper. Her eyes had gone wide and startled.

"You'd . . . sell me out?" she breathed.

Mallory laughed. His eyes were bright and hard. He stared along the floor at a splash of light from one of the standing lamps. He said in a bored voice:

"Why the hell should I protect you? I don't owe you anything. And you're too damn tight with your dough to hire me. I haven't a record, but you know how the law boys love my sort. And Landrey's friends will just see a dirty plant that got a good lad killed. —— sake, why should I front for a chiseler like you?"

He snorted angrily. Red spots showed in his tanned cheeks.

Rhonda Farr stood quite still and shook her head slowly from side to side. She said: "No deal, blackmailer . . . no deal." Her voice was small and tired, but her chin stuck out hard and brave.

Mallory reached out and picked up his hat. "You're a hell of a guy," he said, grinning, "Christ! but you Hollywood frails must be hard to get on with!"

He leaned forward suddenly, put his left hand behind her head and kissed her on the mouth hard. Then he flipped the tips of his fingers across her cheek.

"You're a nice kid — in some ways," he said. "And a fair liar. Just fair. You didn't fake any letters, baby. Atkinson wouldn't fall for a trick like that."

Rhonda Farr stooped over, snatched the manila envelope off the rug, and tumbled out what was in it — a number of closely written gray pages, deckle-edged, with thin gold monograms. She stared down at them with quivering nostrils.

She said slowly: "I'll send you the money."

Mallory put his hand against her chin, and pushed her head back.

He said rather gently:

"I was kidding you, baby. I have that bad habit. But there are two funny things about these letters. They haven't any envelopes, and there's nothing to show who they were written to — nothing at all. The second thing is, Landrey had them in his pocket when he was killed."

He nodded and turned away. Rhonda Farr said sharply: "Wait!" Her voice was suddenly terrified.

Mallory said: "It gets you when it's over. Take a drink."

He went a little way down the room, turned his head. He said: "I have to go. Got a date with a big black spot . . . Send me some flowers. Wild, blue flowers, like your eyes."

He went out under an arch. A door opened and shut heavily. Rhonda Farr sat without moving for a long time.

8

CIGARETTE SMOKE LACED THE AIR. A group of people in evening clothes stood sipping cocktails at one side of a curtained opening that led to the gambling rooms. Beyond the curtains light blazed down on one end of a roulette table.

Mallory put his elbows on the bar, and the bartender left two young girls in party gowns and slid a white towel along the polished wood towards him. He said:

"What'll it be, chief?"

Mallory said: "A small beer."

The bartender gave it to him, smiled, went back to the two girls. Mallory sipped the beer, made a face, and looked into the long mirror that ran all the way behind the bar and slanted forward a little, so that it showed the floor all the way over to the far wall. A door opened in the wall and a man in dinner clothes came through. He had a wrinkled brown face and hair the color of steel wool. He met Mallory's glance in the mirror and came across the room nodding.

He said: "I'm Mardonne. Nice of you to come." He had a soft, husky voice, the voice of a fat man, but he was not fat.

Mallory said: "It's not a social call."

Mardonne said: "Let's go up to my office."

Mallory drank a little more of the beer, made another face, and pushed the glass away from him across the bar top. They went through the door, up a carpeted staircase that met another staircase halfway up. An open door shone light on the landing. They went in where the light was.

The room had been a bedroom, and no particular trouble had been taken to make it over into an office. It had gray walls, two or three prints in narrow frames. There was a big filing cabinet, a good safe, chairs. A parchment-shaded lamp stood on a walnut desk. A very blond young man sat on a corner of the desk swinging one leg over the other. He was wearing a soft hat with a gay band.

Mardonne said: "All right, Henry. I'll be busy."

The blond young man got off the desk, yawned, put his hand to his mouth with an affected flirt of the wrist. There was a large diamond on one of his fingers. He looked at Mallory, smiled, and went slowly out of the room, closing the door.

Mardonne sat down in a blue leather swivel chair. He lit a thin cigar and pushed a humidor across the grained top of the desk. Mallory took a chair at the end of the desk, between the door and a pair of open windows. There was another door, but the safe stood in front of it. He lit a cigarette, said:

"Landrey owed me some money. Five grand. Anybody here interested in paying it?"

Mardonne put his brown hands on the arms of his chair and rocked back and forth. "We haven't come to that," he said.

Mallory said: "Right. What have we come to?"

Mardonne narrowed his dull eyes. His voice was flat and without tone. "To how Landrey got killed."

Mallory put his cigarette in his mouth and clasped his hands together behind his head. He puffed smoke and talked through it at the wall above Mardonne's head.

"He crossed everybody up and then he crossed himself. He played too many parts and got his lines mixed. He was gun-drunk. When he got a rod in his hand he had to shoot somebody. Somebody shot back."

Mardonne went on rocking, said: "Maybe you could make it a little more definite."

"Sure . . . I could tell you a story . . . about a girl who wrote some letters once. She thought she was in love. They were reckless letters, the sort a girl would write who had more guts than was good for her. Time passed, and somehow the letters got on the blackmail market. Some workers started to shake the girl down. Not a high stake, nothing that would have bothered her, but it seems she liked to do things the hard way. Landrey thought he would help her out. He had a plan and the plan needed a man who could wear a tux, keep a spoon out of a coffee cup, and wasn't known in this town. He got me. I run a small agency in Chicago."

Mardonne swiveled towards the open windows and stared out at the tops of some trees. "Private dick, huh?" he grunted impassively. "From Chicago."

Mallory nodded, looked at him briefly, looked back at the same spot on the wall. "And supposed to be on the level, Mardonne. You wouldn't think it from some of the company I've been keeping lately."

Mardonne made a quick impatient gesture, said nothing.

Mallory went on: "Well, I gave the job a tumble, which was my first and worst mistake. I was making a little headway when the shakedown turned into a kidnaping. Not so good. I got in touch with Landrey and he decided to show with me. We found the girl without a lot of trouble. We took her home. We still had to get the letters. While I was trying to pry them loose from the guy I thought had them one of the bad boys got in the back way and wanted to play with his gun. Landrey made a swell entrance, struck a pose and shot it out with the hood, toe to toe. He stopped some lead. It was pretty, if you like that sort of thing, but it left me in a spot. So perhaps I'm prejudiced. I had to lam out and collect my ideas."

Mardonne's dull brown eyes showed a passing flicker of emotion. "The girl's story might be interesting, too," he said coolly.

Mallory blew a pale cloud of smoke. "She was doped and doesn't know anything. She wouldn't talk, if she did. And I don't know her name."

"I do," Mardonne said. "Landrey's driver also talked to me. So I won't have to bother you about that."

Mallory talked on, placidly. "That's the tale from the outside, without notes. The notes make it funnier — and a hell of a lot dirtier. The girl didn't ask Landrey for help, but he knew about the shakedown. He'd once had the letters, because they were written to him. His scheme to get on their trail was for me to make a wrong pass at the girl myself, make her think *I* had the letters, talk her into a meeting at a nightclub where we could be watched by the people who were working on her. She'd come, because she had that kind of guts. She'd be watched, because there would be an inside — maid, chauffeur or something. The boys would want to know about me. They'd pick me up, and if I didn't get conked out of hand, I might learn who was who in the racket. Sweet set-up, don't you think so?"

Mardonne said coldly: "A bit loose in places . . . Go on talking."

"When the decoy worked I knew it was fixed. I stayed with it, because for the time being I had to. After a while there was another sour play, unrehearsed this time. A big flattie who was taking graft money from the gang got cold feet and threw the boys for a loss. He didn't mind a little extortion, but a snatch was going off the deep end on a dark night. The break made things easier for me, and it didn't hurt Landrey any, because the flattie wasn't in on the clever stuff. The hood who got Landrey wasn't either, I guess. That one was just sore, thought he was being chiseled out of his cut."

Mardonne flipped his brown hands up and down on the chair arms, like a purchasing agent getting restless under a sales talk. "Were you supposed to figure things out this way?" he asked with a sneer.

"I used my head, Mardonne. Not soon enough, but I used it. Maybe I wasn't hired to think, but that wasn't explained to me,

either. If I got wise, it was Landrey's hard luck. He'd have to figure an out to that one. If I didn't, I was the nearest thing to an
honest stranger he could afford to have around."

Mardonne said smoothly: "Landrey had plenty of dough. He
had some brains. Not a lot, but some. He wouldn't go for a cheap
shake like that."

Mallory laughed harshly: "It wasn't so cheap to him, Mardonne. He wanted the girl. She'd got away from him, out of his
class. He couldn't pull himself up, but he could pull her down.
The letters were not enough to bring her into line. Add a kidnaping and a fake rescue by an old flame turned racketeer, and you have
a story no rag could be made to soft pedal. If it was spilled, it would
blast her right out of her job. *You* guess the price for not spilling it,
Mardonne."

Mardonne said: "Uh-huh," and kept on looking out of the window.

Mallory said: "But all that's on the cuff, now. I was hired to get
some letters, and I got them — out of Landrey's pocket when he
was bumped. I'd like to get paid for my time."

Mardonne turned in his chair and put his hands flat on the top
of the desk. "Pass them over," he said. "I'll see what they're worth
to me."

Mallory's eyes got sharp and bitter. "The trouble with you heels
is that you can't figure anybody to be on the up and up . . . The
letters are withdrawn from circulation. They passed around too
much and they wore out."

"It's a sweet thought," Mardonne sneered. "For somebody else.
Landrey was my partner, and I thought a lot of him . . . So you
give the letters away, and I pay you dough for letting Landrey get
gunned. I ought to write that one in my diary. My hunch is you've
been paid plenty already — by Miss Rhonda Farr."

Mallory said, sarcastically: "I figured it would look like that
to you. Maybe *you'd* like the story better this way . . . The girl
got tired of having Landrey trail her around. She faked some
letters and put them where her smart lawyer could lift them, pass
them along to a man who was running a strong-arm squad the
lawyer used in his business sometimes. The girl wrote to Landrey
for help and he got me. The girl got to me with a better bid. She

hired me to put Landrey on the spot. I played along with him until I got him under the gun of a wiper that was pretending to make a pass at me. The wiper let him have it, and I shot the wiper with Landrey's gun, to make it look good. Then I had a drink and went home to get some sleep."

Mardonne leaned over and pressed a buzzer on the side of his desk. He said: "I like that one a lot better. I'm wondering if I could make it stick."

"You could try," Mallory said lazily. "I don't guess it would be the first lead quarter you've tried to pass."

9

THE ROOM DOOR CAME OPEN and the blond boy strolled in. His lips were spread in a pleased grin and his tongue came out between them. He had an automatic in his hand.

Mardonne said: "I'm not busy any more, Henry."

The blond boy shut the door. Mallory stood up and backed slowly towards the wall. He said grimly:

"Now for the funny stuff, eh?"

Mardonne put brown fingers up and pinched the fat part of his chin. He said curtly:

"There won't be any shooting here. Nice people come to this house. Maybe you didn't spot Landrey, but I don't want you around. You're in my way."

Mallory kept on backing until he had his shoulders against the wall. The blond boy frowned, took a step towards him. Mallory said:

"Stay right where you are, Henry. I need room to think. You might get a slug into me, but you wouldn't stop my gun from talking a little. The noise wouldn't bother me at all."

Mardonne bent over his desk, looking sideways. The blond boy slowed up. His tongue still peeped out between his lips. Mardonne said:

"I've got some C notes in the desk here. I'm giving Henry ten of them. He'll go to your hotel with you. He'll even help you pack. When you get on the train east he'll pass you the dough. If you come back after that, it will be a new deal — from a cold deck." He put his hand down slowly and opened the desk drawer.

Mallory kept his eyes on the blond boy. "Henry might make a change in the continuity," he said pleasantly. "Henry looks kind of unstable to me."

Mardonne stood up, brought his hand from the drawer. He dropped a packet of notes on top of the desk. He said:

"I don't think so. Henry usually does what he is told."

Mallory grinned tightly. "Perhaps *that's* what I'm afraid of," he said. His grin got tighter still, and crookeder. His teeth glittered between his pale lips. "You said you thought a lot of Landrey, Mardonne. That's hooey. You don't care a thin dime about Landrey now he's dead. You probably stepped right into his half of the joint, and nobody around to ask questions. It's like that in the rackets. You want me out because you think you can still peddle your dirt — in the right place — for more than this small-time joint would net in a year. But you can't peddle it, Mardonne. The market's closed. Nobody's going to pay you a plugged nickel either to spill it or not to spill it."

Mardonne cleared his throat softly. He was standing in the same position, leaning forward a little over the desk, both hands on top of it, and the packet of notes between his hands. He licked his lips, said:

"All right, mastermind. Why not?"

Mallory made a quick but expressive gesture with his right thumb.

"I'm the sucker in this deal. *You're* the smart guy. I told you a straight story the first time and my hunch says Landrey wasn't in that sweet frame alone. *You* were in it up to your fat neck! . . . But you aced yourself backwards when you let Landrey pack those letters around with him. The girl can talk now. Not a whole lot, but enough to get backing from an outfit that isn't going to scrap a million-dollar reputation because some cheap gambler wants to get smart . . . If your money says different, you're going to get a jolt that'll have you picking your eye-teeth out of your socks. You're going to see the sweetest coverup even Hollywood ever fixed."

He paused, flashed a quick glance at the blond boy. "Something else, Mardonne. When you figure on gun play get yourself a loogan that knows what it's all about. The gay caballero here forgot to thumb back his safety."

Mardonne stood frozen. The blond boy's eyes flinched down to his gun for a split second of time. Mallory jumped fast along the wall, and his Luger snapped into his hand. The blond boy's face tensed, his gun crashed. Then the Luger cracked, and a slug went into the wall beside the blond boy's gay felt hat. Henry faded down gracefully, squeezed lead again. The shot knocked Mallory back against the wall. His left arm went dead.

His lips writhed angrily. He steadied himself; the Luger talked twice, very rapidly.

The blond boy's gun arm jerked up and the gun sailed against the wall high up. His eyes widened, his mouth came open in a yell of pain. Then he whirled, wrenched the door open and pitched straight out on the landing with a crash.

Light from the room streamed after him. Somebody shouted somewhere. A door banged. Mallory looked at Mardonne, saying evenly:

"Got me in the arm! ———— I could have killed the bastard four times!"

Mardonne's hand came up from the desk with a blued revolver in it. A bullet splashed into the floor at Mallory's feet. Mardonne lurched drunkenly, threw the gun away like something red hot. His hands groped high in the air. He looked scared stiff.

Mallory said: "Get in front of me, big shot! I'm moving out of here."

Mardonne came out from behind the desk. He moved jerkily, like a marionette. His eyes were as dead as stale oysters. Saliva drooled down his chin.

Something loomed in the doorway. Mallory heaved sideways, firing blindly at the door. But the sound of the Luger was overborne by the terrific flat booming of a shotgun. Searing flame stabbed down Mallory's right side. Mardonne got the rest of the load.

He plunged to the floor on his face, dead before he landed.

A sawed-off shotgun dumped itself in through the open door. A thick-bellied man in shirtsleeves eased himself down in the door-frame, clutching and rolling as he fell. A strangled sob came out of his mouth, and blood spread on the pleated front of a dress shirt.

Sudden noise flared out down below. Shouting, running feet, a shrilling off-key laugh, a high sound that might have been a shriek. Cars started outside, tires screeched on the driveway. The custom-ers were getting away. A pane of glass went out somewhere. There was a loose clatter of running feet on a sidewalk.

Across the lighted patch of landing nothing moved. The blond boy groaned softly, out there on the floor, behind the dead man in the doorway.

Mallory ploughed across the room, sank into the chair at the end of the desk. He wiped sweat from his eyes with the heel of his gun hand. He leaned his ribs against the desk, panting, watching the door.

His left arm was throbbing now, and his right leg felt like the plagues of Egypt. Blood ran down his sleeve inside, down on his hand, off the tips of two fingers.

After a while he looked away from the door, at the packet of notes lying on the desk under the lamp. Reaching across he pushed them into the open drawer with the muzzle of the Luger. Grinning with pain he leaned far enough over to pull the drawer shut. Then he opened and closed his eyes quickly, several times, squeezing them tight together, then snapping them open wide. That cleared his head a little. He drew the telephone towards him.

There was silence below stairs now. Mallory put the Luger down, lifted the phone off the prongs and put it down beside the Luger.

He said out loud: "Too bad, baby . . . Maybe I played it wrong after all . . . Maybe the louse hadn't the guts to hurt you at that . . . well . . . there's got to be talking done now."

As he began to dial, the wail of a siren got louder.

10

THE UNIFORMED OFFICER behind the typewriter desk talked into a Dictaphone, then looked at Mallory and jerked his thumb towards a glass-paneled door that said:

CAPTAIN OF DETECTIVES

PRIVATE

Mallory got up stiffly from a hard chair and went across the room, leaned against the wall to open the glass-paneled door, went on in.

The room he went into was paved with dirty brown linoleum, furnished with the peculiar sordid hideousness only municipalities can achieve. Cathcart, the captain of detectives, sat in the middle of it alone, between a littered roll-top desk that was not less than twenty years old and a flat oak table large enough to play Ping-Pong on.

Cathcart was a big shabby Irishman with a sweaty face and a loose-lipped grin. His white mustache was stained in the middle by nicotine. His hands had a lot of warts on them.

Mallory went towards him slowly, leaning on a heavy cane with a rubber tip. His right leg felt large and hot. His left arm was in a sling made from a black silk scarf. He was freshly shaved. His face was pale and his eyes were as dark as slate.

He sat down across the table from the captain of detectives, put his cane on the table, tapped a cigarette and lit it. Then he said casually:

"What's the verdict, Chief?"

Cathcart grinned. "How you feel, kid? You look kinda pulled down."

"Not bad. A bit stiff."

Cathcart nodded, cleared his throat, fumbled unnecessarily with some papers that were in front of him. He said:

"You're clear. It's a lulu, but you're clear. Chicago gives you a clean sheet — damn clean. Your Luger got Mike Corliss, a two-time loser. I'm keepin' the Luger for a souvenir. Okay?"

Mallory nodded. "Okay. I'm getting me a twenty-five with copper slugs. A sharpshooter's gun. No shock effect, but it goes better with evening clothes."

Cathcart looked at him closely for a minute, then went on: "Mike's prints are on the shotgun. The shotgun got Mardonne. Nobody's cryin' about that much. The blond kid ain't hurt bad. That automatic we found on the floor had his prints and that will take care of him for a while."

Mallory rubbed his chin wearily. "How about the others?"

The captain raised tangled eyebrows, and his eyes looked absent. He said: "I don't know of nothin' to connect you there. Do you?"

"Not a thing," Mallory said apologetically. "I was just wondering."

The captain said firmly: "Don't wonder. And don't get to guessin', if anybody should ask you . . . Take that Baldwin Hills thing. The way we figure it Macdonald got killed in the line of duty, takin' with him a dope peddler named Slippy Morgan. We have a tag out for Slippy's wife, but I don't guess we'll make her. Mac wasn't on the narcotic detail, but it was his night off and he was a great guy to gumshoe around on his night off. Mac loved his work."

Mallory smiled faintly, said politely: "Is that so?"

"Yeah," the captain said. "In the other one it seems this Landrey, a known gambler — he was Mardonne's partner too — that's kind of a funny coincidence — went down to Westwood to collect dough from a guy called Costello that ran a book on the eastern tracks. Jim Ralston, one of our boys, went with him. Hadn't ought to, but he knew Landrey pretty well. There was a little trouble about the money. Jim got beaned with a blackjack and Landrey and some little hood fogged each other. There was another guy there we don't trace. We got Costello, but he won't talk, and we don't like to beat up an old guy. He's got a rap comin' on account of the blackjack. He'll plead, I guess."

Mallory slumped down in his chair until the back of his neck rested on top of it. He blew smoke straight up towards the stained ceiling. He said:

"How about night before last? Or was that the time the roulette wheel backfired and the trick cigar blew a hole in the garage floor?"

The captain of detectives rubbed both his moist cheeks briskly, then hauled out a very large handkerchief and snorted into it.

"Oh that," he said negligently, "that wasn't nothin'. The blond kid — Henry Anson or something like that — says it was all his fault. He was Mardonne's bodyguard, but that didn't mean he could go shootin' anyone he might want to. That takes care of him, but we let him down easy for tellin' a straight story." The captain stopped short and stared at Mallory hard-eyed. Mallory was grinning. "Of course if you don't *like* his story . . ." the captain went on coldly.

Mallory said: "I haven't heard it yet. I'm sure I'll like it fine."

"Okay," Cathcart rumbled, mollified. "Well, this Anson says Mardonne buzzed him in where you and the boss were talkin'. You was makin' a kick about something, maybe a crooked wheel downstairs. There was some money on the desk and Anson got the idea it was a shake. You looked pretty fast to him, and not knowing you was a dick he gets kinda nervous. His gun went off. You didn't shoot right away, but the poor sap lets off another round and plugs you. Then, by ——— you drilled him in the shoulder, as who wouldn't, only if it had been me, I'd of pumped his guts. Then the shotgun boy comes bargin' in, lets go without asking any questions, fogs Mardonne and stops one from you. We kinda thought at first the guy might of got Mardonne on purpose, but the kid says no, he tripped in the door comin' in . . . Hell, we don't like for you to do all that shooting, you being a stranger and all that, but a man ought to have a right to protect himself against illegal weapons."

Mallory said gently: "There's the D.A. and the coroner. How about them? I'd kind of like to go back as clean as I came away."

Cathcart frowned down at the dirty linoleum and bit his thumb as if he liked hurting himself.

"The coroner don't give a damn about that trash. If the D.A. wants to get funny, I can tell him about a few cases his office didn't clean up so good."

Mallory lifted his cane off the table, pushed his chair back, put weight on the cane and stood up. "You have a swell police department here," he said. "I shouldn't think you'd have any crime at all."

He moved across towards the outer door. The captain said to his back:

"Goin' on to Chicago?"

Mallory shrugged carefully with his right shoulder, the good one. "I might stick around," he said. "One of the studios made me a proposition. Private extortion detail. Blackmail and so on."

The captain grinned heartily. "Swell," he said. "Eclipse Films is a swell outfit. They always been swell to me . . . Nice easy work, blackmail. Oughtn't to run into any rough stuff."

Mallory nodded solemnly. "Just light work, Chief. Almost effeminate, if you know what I mean."

He went on out, down the hall to the elevator, down to the street. He got into a taxi. It was hot in the taxi. He felt faint and dizzy going back to his hotel.

THE PENCIL

This is the first Marlowe short story in twenty years and was written especially for England. I have persistently refused to write short stories, because I think books are my natural element, but was persuaded to do this because people for whom I have a high regard seemed to want me to do it, and I have always wanted to write a story about the technique of the Syndicate's murders.

1959

Raymond Chandler

Publisher's Note:

"The Pencil" was Raymond Chandler's last published story. It was first printed in an abridged form in London's *Daily Mail* in 1959, shortly after his death; it appeared a year later, under the title "Wrong Pigeon," in the magazine *Manhunt*. This is the story's first appearance in book form in this country, and is prefaced by a note Mr. Chandler wrote for his English audience.

1

HE WAS A SLIGHTLY FAT MAN with a dishonest smile that pulled the corners of his mouth out half an inch leaving the thick lips tight and his eyes bleak. For a fattish man he had a slow walk. Most fat men are brisk and light on their feet. He wore a gray herringbone suit and a hand-painted tie with part of a diving girl visible on it. His shirt was clean, which comforted me, and his brown loafers, as wrong as the tie for his suit, shone from a recent polishing.

He sidled past me as I held the door between the waiting room and my thinking parlor. Once inside, he took a quick look around. I'd have placed him as a mobster, second grade, if I had been asked. For once I was right. If he carried a gun, it was inside his pants. His coat was too tight to hide the bulge of an underarm holster.

He sat down carefully and I sat opposite and we looked at each other. His face had a sort of foxy eagerness. He was sweating a little. The expression on my face was meant to be interested but not clubby. I reached for a pipe and the leather humidor in which I kept my Pearce's tobacco. I pushed cigarettes at him.

"I don't smoke." He had a rusty voice. I didn't like it any more than I liked his clothes, or his face. While I filled the pipe he reached inside his coat, prowled in a pocket, came out with a bill, glanced at it and dropped it across the desk in front of me. It was a nice bill and clean and new. One thousand dollars.

"Ever save a guy's life?"

"Once in a while, maybe."

"Save mine."

"What goes?"

"I heard you leveled with the customers, Marlowe."

"That's why I stay poor."

"I still got two friends. You make it three and you'll be out of the red. You got five grand coming if you pry me loose."

"From what?"

"You're talkative as hell this morning. Don't you pipe who I am?"

"Nope."

"Never been east, huh?"

"Sure — but I wasn't in your set."

"What set would that be?"

I was getting tired of it. "Stop being so goddam cagey or pick up your grand and be missing."

"I'm Ikky Rosenstein. I'll be missing but good unless you can figure some out. Guess."

"I've already guessed. You tell me and tell me quick. I don't have all day to watch you feeding me with an eyedropper."

"I ran out on the Outfit. The high boys don't go for that. To them it means you got info you figure you can peddle, or you got independent ideas, or you lost your moxie. Me, I lost my moxie. I had it up to here." He touched his Adam's apple with the fore-finger of a stretched hand. "I done bad things. I scared and hurt guys. I never killed nobody. That's nothing to the Outfit. I'm out of line. So they pick up the pencil and they draw a line. I got the word. The operators are on the way. I made a bad mistake. I tried to hole up in Vegas. I figured they'd never expect me to lie up in their own joint. They outfigured me. What I did's been done before, but I didn't know it. When I took the plane to L.A. there must have been somebody on it. They know where I live."

"Move."

"No good now. I'm covered." I knew he was right.

"Why haven't they taken care of you already?"

"They don't do it that way. Always specialists. Don't you know how it works?"

"More or less. A guy with a nice hardware store in Buffalo. A guy with a small dairy in K.C. Always a good front. They report back to New York or somewhere. When they mount the plane west or wherever they're going, they have guns in their briefcases. They're quiet and well-dressed and they don't sit together. They could be a couple of lawyers or income tax sharpies — anything at all that's well-mannered and inconspicuous. All sorts of people carry briefcases. Including women."

"Correct as hell. And when they land they'll be steered to me, but not from the airfield. They got ways. If I go to the cops, somebody will know about me. They could have a couple Mafia boys right on the City Council for all I know. It's been done. The cops will give me twenty-four hours to leave town. No use. Mexico? Worse than here. Canada? Better but still no good. Connections there too."

"Australia?"

"Can't get a passport. I been here twenty-five years — illegal. They can't deport me unless they can prove a crime on me. The Outfit would see they didn't. Suppose I got tossed into the freezer. I'm out on a writ in twenty-four hours. And my nice friends got a car waiting to take me home — only not home."

I had my pipe lit and going well. I frowned down at the grand note. I could use it very nicely. My checking account could kiss the sidewalk without stooping.

"Let's stop horsing," I said. "Suppose — just suppose — I could figure an out for you. What's your next move?"

"I know a place — if I could get there without bein' tailed. I'd leave my car here and take a rent car. I'd turn it in just short of the county line and buy a secondhand job. Halfway to where I'm going I trade it on a new last's model, a leftover. This is just the right time of year. Good discount, new models out soon. Not to save money — less show-off. Where I'd go is a good-sized place but still pretty clean."

"Uh-huh," I said. "Wichita, last I heard. But it may have changed."

He scowled at me. "Get smart, Marlowe, but not too damn smart."

"I'll get as smart as I want to. Don't try to make rules for me. If I take this on, there aren't any rules. I take it for this grand and the rest if I bring it off. Don't cross me. I might leak information. If I get knocked off, put just one red rose on my grave. I don't like cut flowers. I like to see them growing. But I could take one, because you're such a sweet character. When's the plane in?"

"Sometime today. It's nine hours from New York. Probably come in about five-thirty P.M."

"Might come by San Diego and switch or by San Francisco and switch. A lot of planes from Dago and Frisco. I need a helper."

"Goddam you, Marlowe —"

"Hold it. I know a girl. Daughter of a chief of police who got broken for honesty. She wouldn't leak under torture."

"You got no right to risk her," Ikky said angrily.

I was so astonished my jaw hung halfway to my waist. I closed it slowly and swallowed.

"Good God, the man's got a heart."

"Women ain't built for the rough stuff," he said grudgingly.

I picked up the thousand-dollar note and snapped it. "Sorry. No receipt," I said. "I can't have my name in your pocket. And there won't be any rough stuff if I'm lucky. They'd have me outclassed. There's only one way to work it. Now give me your address and all the dope you can think of, names, descriptions of any operators you have ever seen in the flesh."

He did. He was a pretty good observer. Trouble was the Outfit would know what he had seen. The operators would be strangers to him.

He got up silently and put his hand out. I had to shake it, but what he had said about women made it easier. His hand was moist. Mine would have been in his spot. He nodded and went out silently.

2

IT WAS A QUIET STREET in Bay City, if there are any quiet streets in this beatnik generation when you can't get through a meal without some male or female stomach singer belching out a kind of love that is as old-fashioned as a bustle or some Hammond organ jazzing it up in the customer's soup.

The little one-story house was as neat as a fresh pinafore. The front lawn was cut lovingly and very green. The smooth composition driveway was free of grease spots from standing cars, and the hedge that bordered it looked as though the barber came every day.

The white door had a knocker with a tiger's head, a go-to-hell window and a dingus that let someone inside talk to someone outside without even opening the little window.

I'd have given a mortgage on my left leg to live in a house like that. I didn't think I ever would.

The bell chimed inside and after a while she opened the door in a pale blue sports shirt and white shorts that were short enough to be friendly. She had gray-blue eyes, dark red hair and fine bones in her face. There was usually a trace of bitterness in the gray-blue eyes. She couldn't forget that her father's life had been destroyed by the crooked power of a gambling ship mobster, that her mother had died too. She was able to suppress the bitterness when she wrote nonsense about young love for the shiny magazines, but this wasn't her life. She didn't really have a life. She had an existence without much pain and enough oil money to make it safe. But in a tight spot she was as cool and resourceful as a good cop. Her name was Anne Riordan.

She stood to one side and I passed her pretty close. But I have rules too. She shut the door and parked herself on a davenport and went through the cigarette routine, and here was one doll who had the strength to light her own cigarette.

I stood looking around. There were a few changes, not many.

"I need your help," I said.

"That's the only time I ever see you."

"I've got a client who is an ex-hood; used to be a trouble-shooter for the Outfit, the Syndicate, the big mob, or whatever name you want to use for it. You know damn well it exists and is as rich as Rockefeller. You can't beat it because not enough people want to, especially the million-a-year lawyers that work for it, and the bar associations that seem more anxious to protect other lawyers than their own country."

"My God, are you running for office somewhere? I never knew you to sound so pure."

She moved her legs around, not provocatively — she wasn't the type — but it made it difficult for me to think straight just the same.

"Stop moving your legs around," I said. "Or else put a pair of slacks on."

"Damn you, Marlowe. Can't you think of anything else?"

"I'll try. I like to think that I know at least one pretty and charming female who doesn't have round heels." I swallowed and went on. "The man's name is Ikky Rosenstein. He's not beautiful and he's not anything that I like — except one. He got mad when I said I needed a girl helper. He said women were not made for the rough stuff. That's why I took the job. To a real mobster, a woman means no more than a sack of flour. They use women in the usual way, but if it's advisable to get rid of them, they do it without a second thought."

"So far you've told me a whole lot of nothing. Perhaps you need a cup of coffee or a drink."

"You're sweet but I don't in the morning — except sometimes and this isn't one of them. Coffee later. Ikky has been penciled."

"Now what's that?"

"You have a list. You draw a line through a name with a pencil. The guy is as good as dead. The Outfit has reasons. They don't do it just for kicks any more. They don't get any kick. It's bookkeeping to them."

"What on earth can I do? I might even have said, what can *you* do?"

"I can try. What you can do is help me spot their plane and see where they go — the operators assigned to the job."

"Yes, but how can you do anything?"

"I said I could try. If they took a night plane they are already here. If they took a morning plane they can't be here before five or so. Plenty of time to get set. You know what they look like."

"Oh sure. I meet killers every day. I have them in for whiskey sours and caviar on hot toast." She grinned. While she was grinning I took four long steps across the tan figured rug and lifted her and put a kiss on her mouth. She didn't fight me but she didn't go all trembly either. I went back and sat down.

"They'll look like anybody who's in a quiet well-run business or profession. They'll have quiet clothes and they'll be polite — when they want to be. They'll have briefcases with guns in them that have changed hands so often they can't possibly be traced. When and if they do the job, they'll drop the guns. They'll probably use revolvers, but they could use automatics. They won't use silencers because silencers can jam a gun and the weight makes it hard to shoot accurately. They won't sit together on the plane, but once off of it they may pretend to know each other and simply not have noticed during the flight. They may shake hands with appropriate smiles and walk away and get in the same taxi. I think they'll go to a hotel first. But very soon they will move into something from which they can watch Ikky's movements and get used to his schedule. They won't be in any hurry unless Ikky makes a move. That would tip them off that Ikky has been tipped off. He has a couple of friends left — he says."

"Will they shoot him from this room or apartment across the street — assuming there is one?"

"No. They'll shoot him from three feet away. They'll walk up behind him and say, 'Hello, Ikky.' He'll either freeze or turn. They'll fill him with lead, drop the guns, and hop into the car they have waiting. Then they'll follow the crash car off the scene."

"Who'll drive the crash car?"

"Some well-fixed and blameless citizen who hasn't been rapped. He'll drive his own car. He'll clear the way, even if he has to accidentally on purpose crash somebody, even a police car. He'll be so goddam sorry he'll cry all the way down his monogrammed shirt. And the killers will be long gone."

"Good heavens," Anne said. "How can you stand your life? If you did bring it off, they'll send operators to you."

"I don't think so. They don't kill a legit. The blame will go to the operators. Remember, these top mobsters are businessmen. They want lots and lots of money. They only get really tough when they figure they have to get rid of somebody, and they don't crave that. There's always a chance of a slip-up. Not much of a chance. No gang killing has ever been solved here or anywhere else except two or three times. Lepke Buchalter fried. Remember Anastasia? He was awful big and awful tough. Too big, too tough. Pencil."

She shuddered a little. "I think I need a drink myself."

I grinned at her. "You're right in the atmosphere, darling. I'll weaken."

She brought a couple of Scotch highballs. When we were drinking them I said: "If you spot them or think you spot them, follow to where they go — if you can do it safely. Not otherwise. If it's a hotel — and ten to one it will be — check in and keep calling me until you get me."

She knew my office number and I was still on Yucca Avenue. She knew that too.

"You're the damnedest guy," she said. "Women do anything you want them to. How come I'm still a virgin at twenty-eight?"

"We need a few like you. Why don't you get married?"

"To what? Some cynical chaser who has nothing left but technique? I don't know any really nice men — except you. I'm no pushover for white teeth and a gaudy smile."

I went over and pulled her to her feet. I kissed her long and hard. "I'm honest," I almost whispered. "That's something. But I'm too shop-soiled for a girl like you. I've thought of you, I've wanted you, but that sweet clear look in your eyes tells me to lay off."

"Take me," she said softly. "I have dreams too."

"I couldn't. It's not the first time it's happened to me. I've had too many women to deserve one like you. We have to save a man's life. I'm going."

She stood up and watched me leave with a grave face.

The women you get and the women you don't get — they live in different worlds. I don't sneer at either world. I live in both myself.

3

AT LOS ANGELES INTERNATIONAL AIRPORT you can't get close to the planes unless you're leaving on one. You see them land, if you happen to be in the right place, but you have to wait at a barrier to get a look at the passengers. The airport buildings don't make it any easier. They are strung out from here to breakfast time, and you can get callouses walking from TWA to American.

I copied an arrival schedule off the boards and prowled around like a dog that has forgotten where he put his bone. Planes came in, planes took off, porters carried luggage, passengers sweated and scurried, children whined, the loudspeaker overrode all the other noises.

I passed Anne a number of times. She took no notice of me.

At 5:45 they must have come. Anne disappeared. I gave it half an hour, just in case she had some other reason for fading. No. She was gone for good. I went out to my car and drove some long crowded miles to Hollywood and my office. I had a drink and sat. At 6:45 the phone rang.

"I think so," she said. "Beverly-Western Hotel. Room four-ten. I couldn't get any names. You know the clerks don't leave registration cards lying around these days. I didn't like to ask any questions. But I rode up in the elevator with them and spotted their room. I walked right on past them when the bellman put a key in their door, and walked down to the mezzanine and then downstairs with a bunch of women from the tearoom. I didn't bother to take a room."

"What were they like?"

"They came up the ramp together but I didn't hear them speak. Both had briefcases, both wore quiet suits, nothing flashy. White shirts, starched, one blue tie, one black striped with gray. Black shoes. A couple of businessmen from the east coast. They could be publishers, lawyers, doctors, account executives — no, cut the last; they weren't gaudy enough. You wouldn't look at them twice."

"Look at them twice. Faces."

"Both medium brown hair, one a bit darker than the other. Smooth faces, rather expressionless. One had gray eyes; the one with the lighter hair had blue eyes. Their eyes were interesting. Very quick to move, very observant, watching everything near them. That might have been wrong. They should have been a bit pre-occupied with what they came out for or interested in California. They seemed more occupied with faces. It's a good thing I spotted them and not you. You don't look like a cop, but you don't look like a man who is not a cop. You have marks on you."

"Phooey. I'm a damn good-looking heart wrecker."

"Their features were strictly assembly line. Neither looked Italian. Each picked up a flight suitcase. One suitcase was gray with two red and white stripes up and down, about six or seven inches from the ends, the other a blue and white tartan. I didn't know there was such a tartan."

"There is, but I forget the name of it."

"I thought you knew everything."

"Just almost everything. Run along home now."

"Do I get a dinner and maybe a kiss?"

"Later, and if you're not careful you'll get more than you want."

"A rapist, eh? I'll carry a gun. You'll take over and follow them?"

"If they're the right men, they'll follow me. I already took an apartment across the street from Ikky. That block on Poynter and the two on each side of it have about six lowlife apartment houses to the block. I'll bet the incidence of chippies is very high."

"It's high everywhere these days."

"So long, Anne. See you."

"When you need help."

She hung up. I hung up. She puzzled me. Too wise to be so nice. I guess all nice women are wise too. I called Ikky. He was out. I had a drink from the office bottle, smoked for half an hour and called again. This time I got him.

I told him the score up to then, and said I hoped Anne had picked the right men. I told him about the apartment I had taken.

"Do I get expenses?" I asked.

"Five grand ought to cover the lot."

"If I earn it and get it. I heard you had a quarter of a million," I said at a wild venture.

"Could be, pal; but how do I get at it? The high boys know where it is. It'll have to cool a long time."

I said that was all right. I had cooled a long time myself. Of course I didn't expect to get the four thousand, even if I brought the job off. Men like Ikky Rosenstein would steal their mother's gold teeth. There seemed to be a little good in him somewhere — but little was the operative word.

I spent the next half-hour trying to think of a plan. I couldn't think of one that looked promising. It was almost eight o'clock and I needed food. I didn't think the boys would move that night. Next morning they would drive past Ikky's place and scout the neighborhood.

I was ready to leave the office when the buzzer sounded from the door of my waiting room. I opened the communicating door. A small tight-looking man was standing in the middle of the floor rocking on his heels with his hands behind his back. He smiled at me, but he wasn't good at it. He walked towards me.

"You Marlowe?"

"Who else? What can I do for you?"

He was close now. He brought his right hand around fast with a gun in it. He stuck the gun in my stomach.

"You can lay off Ikky Rosenstein," he said in a voice that matched his face, "or you can get your belly full of lead."

4

HE WAS AN AMATEUR. If he had stayed four feet away, he might have had something. I reached up and took the cigarette out of my mouth and held it carelessly.

"What makes you think I know any Ikky Rosenstein?"

He laughed a high-pitched laugh and pushed his gun into my stomach.

"Wouldn't you like to know?" The cheap sneer, the empty triumph of that feeling of power when you hold a fat gun in a small hand.

"It would be fair to tell me."

As his mouth opened for another crack, I dropped the cigarette and swept a hand. I can be fast when I have to. There are boys that are faster, but they don't stick guns in your stomach. I got my thumb behind the trigger and my hand over his. I kneed him in the groin. He bent over with a whimper. I twisted his arm to the right and I had his gun. I hooked a heel behind his heel and he was on the floor. He lay there blinking with surprise and pain, his knees drawn up against his stomach. He rolled from side to side groaning. I reached down and grabbed his left hand and yanked him to his feet. I had six inches and forty pounds on him. They ought to have sent a bigger, better trained messenger.

"Let's go into my thinking parlor," I said. "We could have a chat and you could have a drink to pick you up. Next time don't get near enough to a prospect for him to get your gun hand. I'll just see if you have any more iron on you."

He hadn't. I pushed him through the door and into a chair. His breath wasn't quite so rasping. He grabbed out a handkerchief and mopped at his face.

"Next time," he said between his teeth. "Next time."

"Don't be an optimist. You don't look the part."

I poured him a drink of Scotch in a paper cup, set it down in front of him. I broke his .38 and dumped the cartridges into the desk drawer. I clicked the chamber back and laid the gun down.

"You can have it when you leave — if you leave."

"That's a dirty way to fight," he said, still gasping.

"Sure. Shooting a man is so much cleaner. Now, how did you get here?"

"Screw yourself."

"Don't be a crumb. I have friends. Not many, but some. I can get you for armed assault, and you know what would happen then. You'd be out on a writ or on bail and that's the last anyone would hear of you. The biggies don't go for failures. Now who sent you and how did you know where to come?"

"Ikky was covered," he said sullenly. "He's dumb. I trailed him here without no trouble at all. Why would he go see a private eye? People want to know."

"More."

"Go to hell."

"Come to think of it, I don't have to get you for armed assault. I can smash it out of you right here and now."

I got up from the chair and he put a flat hand out.

"If I get knocked about, a couple of real tough monkeys will drop around. If I don't report back, same thing. You ain't holding no real high cards. They just look high," he said.

"You haven't anything to tell. If this Ikky guy came to see me, you don't know why, nor whether I took him on. If he's a mobster, he's not my type of client."

"He come to get you to try to save his hide."

"Who from?"

"That'd be talking."

"Go right ahead. Your mouth seems to work fine. And tell the boys any time I front for a hood, that will be the day."

You have to lie a little once in a while in my business. I was lying a little. "What's Ikky done to get himself disliked? Or would that be talking?"

"You think you're a lot of man," he sneered, rubbing the place where I had kneed him. "In my league you wouldn't make pinch runner."

I laughed in his face. Then I grabbed his right wrist and twisted it behind his back. He began to squawk. I reached into his breast pocket with my left hand and hauled out a wallet. I let him go. He reached for his gun on the desk and I bisected his upper arm with a hard cut. He fell into the customer's chair and grunted.

"You can have your gun," I told him. "When I give it to you. Now be good or I'll have to bounce you just to amuse myself."

In the wallet I found a driver's licence made out to Charles Hickon. It did me no good at all. Punks of his type always have slangy pseudonyms. They probably called him Tiny, or Slim, or Marbles, or even just "you." I tossed the wallet back to him. It fell to the floor. He couldn't even catch it.

"Hell," I said, "there must be an economy campaign on, if they sent you to do more than pick up cigarette butts."

"Screw yourself."

"All right, mug. Beat it back to the laundry. Here's your gun."

He took it, made a business of shoving it into his waistband, stood up, gave me as dirty a look as he had in stock, and strolled to the door, nonchalant as a hustler with a new mink stole. He turned at the door and gave me the beady eye.

"Stay clean, tinhorn. Tin bends easy."

With this blinding piece of repartee he opened the door and drifted out.

After a little while I locked my other door, cut the buzzer, made the office dark, and left. I saw no one who looked like a life-taker. I drove to my house, packed a suitcase, drove to a service station where they were almost fond of me, stored my car and picked up a Hertz Chevrolet. I drove this to Poynter Street, dumped my suitcase in the sleazy apartment I had rented early in the afternoon, and went to dinner at Victor's. It was nine o'clock, too late to drive to Bay City and take Anne to dinner. She'd have cooked her own long ago.

I ordered a double Gibson with fresh limes and drank it, and I was as hungry as a schoolboy.

5

ON THE WAY BACK TO POYNTER STREET I did a good deal of weaving in and out and circling blocks and stopping, with a gun on the seat beside me. As far as I could tell, no one was trying to tail me.

I stopped on Sunset at a service station and made two calls from the box. I caught Bernie Ohls just as he was leaving to go home.

"This is Marlowe, Bernie. We haven't had a fight in years. I'm getting lonely."

"Well, get married. I'm chief investigator for the Sheriff's Office now. I rank Acting Captain until I pass the exam. I don't hardly speak to private eyes."

"Speak to this one. I could need help. I'm on a ticklish job where I could get killed."

"And you expect me to interfere with the course of nature?"

"Come off it, Bernie. I haven't been a bad guy. I'm trying to save an ex-mobster from a couple of executioners."

"The more they mow each other down, the better I like it."

"Yeah. If I call you, come running or send a couple of good boys. You'll have had time to teach them."

We exchanged a couple of mild insults and hung up. I dialed Ikky Rosenstein's number. His rather unpleasant voice said: "Okay, talk."

"Marlowe. Be ready to move out about midnight. We've spotted your boy friends and they are holed up at the Beverly-Western. They won't move to your street tonight. Remember, they don't know you've been tipped."

"Sounds chancy."

"Good God, it wasn't meant to be a Sunday School picnic. You've been careless, Ikky. You were followed to my office. That cuts the time we have."

He was silent for a moment. I heard him breathing. "Who by?" he asked.

"Some little tweezer who stuck a gun in my belly and gave me the trouble of taking it away from him. I can only figure why they sent a punk on the theory that they don't want me to know too much, in case I don't know it already."

"You're in for trouble, friend."

"When not? I'll come over to your place about midnight. Be ready. Where's your car?"

"Out front."

"Get it on a side street and make a business of locking it up. Where's the back door of your flop?"

"In back. Where would it be? On the alley."

"Leave your suitcase there. We walk out together and go to your car. We drive the alley and pick up the suitcase or cases."

"Suppose some guy steals them?"

"Yeah. Suppose you get dead. Which do you like better?"

"Okay," he grunted. "I'm waiting. But we're taking big chances."

"So do race drivers. Does that stop them? There's no way to get out but fast. Douse your lights about ten and rumple the bed well. It would be good if you could leave some baggage behind. Wouldn't look so planned."

He grunted another okay and I hung up. The telephone box was well-lighted outside. They usually are, at service stations. I took a good long gander around while I pawed over the collection of give-away maps inside the station. I saw nothing to worry me. I took a map of San Diego just for the hell of it and got into my rent car.

On Poynter I parked around the corner and went up to my second-floor sleazy apartment and sat in the dark watching from my window. I saw nothing to worry about. A couple of medium-class chippies came out of Ikky's apartment house and were picked up in a late model car. A man about Ikky's height and build went into the apartment house. Various people came and went. The street was fairly quiet. Since they put in the Hollywood Freeway nobody much uses the off-the-boulevard streets unless they live in the neighborhood.

It was a nice fall night — or as nice as they get in Los Angeles' spoiled climate — clearish but not even crisp. I don't know what's happened to the weather in our overcrowded city, but it's not the weather I knew when I came to it.

It seemed like a long time to midnight. I couldn't spot anybody watching anything, and no couple of quiet-suited men paged any of the six apartment houses available. I was pretty sure they'd try mine first when they came, if Anne had picked the right men, and if anybody had come at all, and if the tweezer's message back to his bosses had done me any good or otherwise. In spite of the hundred ways Anne could be wrong, I had a hunch she was right. The killers had no reason to be cagey if they didn't know Ikky had been warned. No reason but one. He had come to my office and been tailed there. But the Outfit, with all its arrogance of power, might laugh at the idea he had been tipped off or come to me for help. I was so small they would hardly be able to see me.

At midnight I left the apartment, walked two blocks watching for a tail, crossed the street and went into Ikky's dive. There was no locked door, and no elevator. I climbed steps to the third floor and looked for his apartment. I knocked lightly. He opened the door with a gun in his hand. He probably looked scared.

There were two suitcases by the door and another against the far wall. I went over and lifted it. It was heavy enough. I opened it. It was unlocked.

"You don't have to worry," he said. "It's got everything a guy could need for three-four nights, and nothing except some clothes that I couldn't glom off in any ready-to-wear place."

I picked up one of the other suitcases. "Let's stash this by the back door."

"We can leave by the alley too."

"We leave by the front door. Just in case we're covered — though I don't think so — we're just two guys going out together. Just one thing. Keep both hands in your coat pockets and the gun in your right. If anybody calls out your name behind you, turn fast and shoot. Nobody but a life-taker will do it. I'll do the same."

"I'm scared," he said in his rusty voice.

"Me too, if it helps any. But we have to do it. If you're braced, they'll have guns in their hands. Don't bother asking them questions. They wouldn't answer in words. If it's just my small friend, we'll cool him and dump him inside the door. Got it?"

He nodded, licking his lips. We carried the suitcases down and put them outside the back door. I looked along the alley. Nobody, and only a short distance to the side street. We went back in and along the hall to the front. We walked out on Poynter Street with all the casualness of a wife buying her husband a birthday tie.

Nobody made a move. The street was empty. We walked around the corner to Ikky's rent car. He unlocked it. I went back with him for the suitcases. Not a stir. We put the suitcases in the car and started up and drove to the next street.

A traffic light not working, a boulevard stop or two, the entrance to the freeway. There was plenty of traffic on it even at midnight. California is loaded with people going places and making speed to get there. If you don't drive eighty miles an hour, everybody passes you. If you do, you have to watch the rear-view mirror for highway patrol cars. It's the rat race of rat races.

Ikky did a quiet seventy. We reached the junction to Route 66 and he took it. So far nothing. I stayed with him to Pomona.

"This is far enough for me," I said. "I'll grab a bus back if there is one, or park myself in a motor court. Drive to a service station and we'll ask for the bus stop. It should be close to the freeway. Take us towards the business section."

He did that and stopped midway of a block. He reached out his pocketbook, and held out four thousand-dollar bills to me.

"I don't really feel I've earned all that. It was too easy."

He laughed with a kind of wry amusement on his pudgy face. "Don't be a sap. I have it made. You didn't know what you was walking into. What's more, your troubles are just beginning. The Outfit has eyes and ears everywhere. Perhaps I'm safe if I'm damn careful. Perhaps I ain't as safe as I think I am. Either way, you did what I asked. Take the dough. I got plenty."

I took it and put it away. He drove to an all-night service station and we were told where to find the bus stop. "There's a cross-country Greyhound at two-twenty-five A.M.," the attendant said, looking at a schedule. "They'll take you, if they got room."

Ikky drove to the bus stop. We shook hands and he went gunning down the road towards the freeway. I looked at my watch and found a liquor store still open and bought a pint of Scotch. Then I found a bar and ordered a double with water.

My troubles were just beginning, Ikky had said. He was so right.

I got off at the Hollywood bus station, grabbed a taxi and drove to my office. I asked the driver to wait a few moments. At that time of night he was glad to. The colored night man let me into the building.

"You work late, Mr. Marlowe. But you always did, didn't you?"

"It's that sort of a business," I said. "Thanks, Jasper."

Up in my office I pawed the floor for mail and found nothing but a longish narrowish box, special delivery, with a Glendale postmark.

It contained nothing at all but a new freshly sharpened pencil, the mobster's mark of death.

6

I DIDN'T TAKE IT TOO HARD. When they mean it, they don't send it to you. I took it as a sharp warning to lay off. There might be a beating arranged. From their point of view, that would be good discipline. "When we pencil a guy, any guy that tries to help him is in for a smashing." That could be the message.

I thought of going to my house on Yucca Avenue. Too lonely. I thought of going to Anne's place in Bay City. Worse. If they got wise to her, real hoods would think nothing of raping her and then beating her up.

It was the Poynter Street flop for me. Easily the safest place now. I went down to the waiting taxi and had him drive me to within three blocks of the so-called apartment house. I went upstairs, undressed and slept raw. Nothing bothered me but a broken spring. That bothered my back. I lay until 3:30 pondering the situation with my massive brain. I went to sleep with a gun under the pillow, which is a bad place to keep a gun when you have one pillow as thick and soft as a typewriter pad. It bothered me, so I transferred it to my right hand. Practice had taught me to keep it there even in sleep.

I woke up with the sun shining. I felt like a piece of spoiled meat. I struggled into the bathroom and doused myself with cold water and wiped off with a towel you couldn't have seen if you held it sideways. This was a really gorgeous apartment. All it needed was a set of Chippendale furniture to graduate it into the slum class.

There was nothing to eat and if I went out, Miss-Nothing Marlowe might miss something. I had a pint of whiskey. I looked at it and smelled it, but I couldn't take it for breakfast, on an empty stomach, even if I could reach my stomach, which was floating around near the ceiling. I looked into the closets in case a previous tenant might have left a crust of bread in a hasty departure. Nope. I wouldn't have liked it anyhow, not even with whiskey on it. So I sat in the window. An hour of that and I was ready to bite a piece off a bellhop.

I dressed and went around the corner to the rent car and drove to an eatery. The waitress was sore too. She swept a cloth over the counter in front of me and let me have the last customer's crumbs in my lap.

"Look, sweetness," I said, "don't be so generous. Save the crumbs for a rainy day. All I want is two eggs three minutes — no more — a slice of your famous concrete toast, a tall glass tomato juice with a dash of Lea and Perrins, a big happy smile, and don't give anybody else any coffee. I might need it all."

"I got a cold," she said. "Don't push me around. I might crack you one on the kisser."

"Let's be pals. I had a rough night too."

She gave me a half-smile and went through the swing door sidewise. It showed more of her curves, which were ample, even excessive. But I got the eggs the way I liked them. The toast had been painted with melted butter past its bloom.

"No Lea and Perrins," she said, putting down the tomato juice. "How about a little Tabasco? We're fresh out of arsenic too."

I used two drops of Tabasco, swallowed the eggs, drank two cups of coffee and was about to leave the toast for a tip, but I went soft and left a quarter instead. That really brightened her. It was a joint where you left a dime or nothing. Mostly nothing.

Back on Poynter nothing had changed. I got to my window again and sat. At about 8:30 the man I had seen go into the apartment house across the way — the one with the same sort of height and build as Ikky — came out with a small briefcase and turned east. Two men got out of a dark blue sedan. They were of the same height and very quietly dressed and had soft hats pulled low over their foreheads. Each jerked out a revolver.

"Hey, Ikky!" one of them called out.

The man turned. "So long, Ikky," the other man said. Gunfire racketed between the houses. The man crumpled and lay motionless. The two men rushed for their car and were off, going west. Halfway down the block I saw a Caddy pull out and start ahead of them.

In no time at all they were completely gone.

It was a nice swift clean job. The only thing wrong with it was that they hadn't given it enough time for preparation.

They had shot the wrong man.

7

I GOT OUT OF THERE FAST, almost as fast as the two killers. There was a smallish crowd grouped around the dead man. I didn't have to look at him to know he was dead — the boys were pros. Where he lay on the sidewalk on the other side of the street I couldn't see him; people were in the way. But I knew just how he would look and I already heard sirens in the distance. It could have been just the routine shrieking from Sunset, but it wasn't. So somebody had telephoned. It was too early for the cops to be going to lunch.

I strolled around the corner with my suitcase and jammed into the rent car and went away from there. The neighborhood was not my piece of shortcake any more. I could imagine the questions.

"Just what took you over there, Marlowe? You got a flop of your own, ain't you?"

"I was hired by an ex-mobster in trouble with the Outfit. They'd sent killers after him."

"Don't tell us he was trying to go straight."

"I don't know. But I liked his money."

"Didn't do much to earn it, did you?"

"I got him away last night. I don't know where he is now. I don't want to know."

"You got him away?"

"That's what I said."

"Yeah — only he's in the morgue with multiple bullet wounds. Try something better. Or somebody's in the morgue."

And on and on. Policeman's dialogue. It comes out of an old shoe box. What they say doesn't mean anything, what they ask doesn't mean anything. They just keep boring in until you are so exhausted you flip on some detail. Then they smile happily and rub their hands, and say: "Kind of careless there, weren't you? Let's start all over again."

The less I had of that, the better. I parked in my usual parking slot and went up to the office. It was full of nothing but stale air. Every time I went into the dump it felt more and more tired. Why the hell hadn't I got myself a government job ten years ago? Make it fifteen years. I had brains enough to get a mail-order law degree. The country's full of lawyers that couldn't write a complaint without the book.

So I sat in my office chair and disadmired myself. After a while I remembered the pencil. I made certain arrangements with a forty-five gun, more gun than I ever carry — too much weight. I dialed the Sheriff's Office and asked for Bernie Ohls. I got him. His voice was sour.

"Marlowe. I'm in trouble — real trouble."

"Why tell me?" he growled. "You must be used to it by now."

"This kind of trouble you don't get used to. I'd like to come over and tell you."

"You in the same office?"

"The same."

"Have to go over that way. I'll drop in."

He hung up. I opened two windows. The gentle breeze wafted a smell of coffee and stale fat to me from Joe's Eats next door. I hated it, I hated myself, I hated everything.

Ohls didn't bother with my elegant waiting room. He rapped on my own door and I let him in. He scowled his way to the customer's chair.

"Okay. Give."

"Ever hear of a character named Ikky Rosenstein?"

"Why would I? Record?"

"An ex-mobster who got disliked by the mob. They put a pencil through his name and sent the usual two tough boys on a plane. He got tipped and hired me to help him get away."

"Nice clean work."

"Cut it out, Bernie." I lit a cigarette and blew smoke in his face. In retaliation he began to chew a cigarette. He never lit one, but he certainly mangled them.

"Look," I went on. "Suppose the man wants to go straight and suppose he doesn't. He's entitled to his life as long as he hasn't killed anyone. He told me he hadn't."

"And you believed the hood, huh? When do you start teaching Sunday School?"

"I neither believed him nor disbelieved him. I took him on. There was no reason not to. A girl I know and I watched the planes yesterday. She spotted the boys and tailed them to a hotel. She was sure of what they were. They looked it right down to their black shoes. They got off the plane separately and then pretended to know each other and not to have noticed on the plane. This girl — "

"Would she have a name?"

"Only for you."

"I'll buy, if she hasn't cracked any laws."

"Her name is Anne Riordan. She lives in Bay City. Her father was once Chief of Police there. And don't say that makes him a crook, because he wasn't."

"Uh-huh. Let's have the rest. Make a little time too."

"I took an apartment opposite Ikky. The killers were still at the hotel. At midnight I got Ikky out and drove with him as far as Pomona. He went on in his rent car and I came back by Greyhound. I moved into the apartment on Poynter Street, right across from his dump."

"Why — if he was already gone?"

I opened the middle desk drawer and took out the nice sharp pencil. I wrote my name on a piece of paper and ran the pencil through it.

"Because someone sent me this. I didn't think they'd kill me, but I thought they planned to give me enough of a beating to warn me off any more pranks."

"They knew you were in on it?"

"Ikky was tailed here by a little squirt who later came around and stuck a gun in my stomach. I knocked him around a bit, but I had to let him go. I thought Poynter Street was safer after that. I live lonely."

"I get around," Bernie Ohls said. "I hear reports. So they gunned the wrong guy."

"Same height, same build, same general appearance. I saw them gun him. I couldn't tell if it was the two guys from the Beverly-Western. I'd never seen them. It was just two guys in dark suits with hats pulled down. They jumped into a blue Pontiac sedan, about two years old, and lammed off, with a big Caddy running crash for them."

Bernie stood up and stared at me for a long moment. "I don't think they'll bother with you now," he said. "They've hit the wrong guy. The mob will be very quiet for a while. You know something? This town is getting to be almost as lousy as New York, Brooklyn and Chicago. We could end up real corrupt."

"We've made a hell of a good start."

"You haven't told me anything that makes me take action, Phil. I'll talk to the city homicide boys. I don't guess you're in any trouble. But you saw the shooting. They'll want that."

"I couldn't identify anybody, Bernie. I didn't know the man who was shot. How did *you* know it was the wrong man?"

"You told me, stupid."

"I thought perhaps the city boys had a make on him."

"They wouldn't tell me, if they had. Besides, they ain't hardly had time to go out for breakfast. He's just a stiff in the morgue to them until the ID comes up with something. But they'll want to talk to you, Phil. They just love their tape recorders."

He went out and the door whooshed shut behind him. I sat there wondering whether I had been a dope to talk to him. Or to take Ikky's troubles on. Five thousand green men said no. But they can be wrong too.

Somebody banged on my door. It was a uniform holding a telegram. I receipted for it and tore it loose.

It said: ON MY WAY TO FLAGSTAFF. MIRADOR MOTOR COURT. THINK I'VE BEEN SPOTTED. COME FAST.

I tore the wire into small pieces and burned them in my big ashtray.

8

I CALLED ANNE RIORDAN.

"Funny thing happened," I told her, and told her about the funny thing.

"I don't like the pencil," she said. "And I don't like the wrong man being killed, probably some poor bookkeeper in a cheap business or he wouldn't be living in that neighborhood. You should never have touched it, Phil."

"Ikky had a life. Where he's going he might make himself decent. He can change his name. He must be loaded or he wouldn't have paid me so much."

"I said I didn't like the pencil. You'd better come down here for a while. You can have your mail re-addressed — if you get any mail. You don't have to work right away anyhow. And L.A. is oozing with private eyes."

"You don't get the point. I'm not through with the job. The city dicks have to know where I am, and if they do, all the crime beat reporters will know too. The cops might even decide to make me a suspect. Nobody who saw the shooting is going to put out a description that means anything. The American people know better than to be witnesses to gang killings."

"All right, loud brain. But my offer stands."

The buzzer sounded in the outside room. I told Anne I had to hang up. I opened the communicating door and a well-dressed — I might say elegantly dressed — middle-aged man stood six feet inside the outer door. He had a pleasantly dishonest smile on his face. He wore a white Stetson and one of those narrow ties that go through an ornamental buckle. His cream-colored flannel suit was beautifully tailored.

He lit a cigarette with a gold lighter and looked at me over the first puff of smoke.

"Mr. Marlowe?"

I nodded.

"I'm Foster Grimes from Las Vegas. I run the Rancho Esperanza on South Fifth. I hear you got a little involved with a man named Ikky Rosenstein."

"Won't you come in?"

He strolled past me into my office. His appearance told me nothing. A prosperous man who liked or felt it good business to look a bit western. You see them by the dozen in the Palm Springs winter season. His accent told me he was an easterner, but not New England. New York or Baltimore, likely. Long Island, the Berkshires — no, too far from the city.

I showed him the customer's chair with a flick of the wrist and sat down in my antique swivel-squeaker. I waited.

"Where is Ikky now, if you know?"

"I don't know, Mr. Grimes."

"How come you messed with him?"

"Money."

"A damned good reason." He smiled. "How far did it go?"

"I helped him leave town. I'm telling you this, although I don't know who the hell you are, because I've already told an old friend-enemy of mine, a top man in the Sheriff's Office."

"What's a friend-enemy?"

"Law men don't go around kissing me, but I've known him for years, and we are as much friends as a private star can be with a law man."

"I told you who I was. We have a unique set-up in Vegas. We own the place except for one lousy newspaper editor who keeps climbing our backs and the backs of our friends. We let him live because letting him live makes us look better than knocking him off. Killings are not good business any more."

"Like Ikky Rosenstein."

"That's not a killing. It's an execution. Ikky got out of line."

"So your gun boys had to rub the wrong guy. They could have hung around a little to make sure."

"They would have, if you'd kept your nose where it belonged. They hurried. We don't appreciate that. We want cool efficiency."

"Who's this great big fat 'we' you keep talking about?"

"Don't go juvenile on me, Marlowe."

"Okay. Let's say I know."

"Here's what we want." He reached into his pocket and drew out a loose bill. He put it on the desk on his side. "Find Ikky and tell him to get back in line and everything is oke. With an innocent bystander gunned, we don't want any trouble or any extra publicity. It's that simple. You get this now," he nodded at the bill. It was a grand. Probably the smallest bill they had. "And another when you find Ikky and give him the message. If he holds out — curtains."

"Suppose I say take your goddam grand and blow your nose with it?"

"That would be unwise." He flipped out a Colt Woodsman with a short silencer on it. A Colt Woodsman will take one without jamming. He was fast too, fast and smooth. The genial expression on his face didn't change.

"I never left Vegas," he said calmly. "I can prove it. You're dead in your office chair and nobody knows anything. Just another private eye that tried the wrong pitch. Put your hands on the desk and think a little. Incidentally, I'm a crack shot even with this damned silencer."

"Just to sink a little lower in the social scale, Mr. Grimes, I ain't putting no hands on no desk. But tell me about this."

I flipped the nicely sharpened pencil across to him. He grabbed for it after a swift change of the gun to his left hand — very swift. He held the pencil up so that he could look at it without taking his eyes off me.

I said: "It came to me by special delivery mail. No message, no return address. Just the pencil. Think I've never heard about the pencil, Mr. Grimes?"

He frowned and tossed the pencil down. Before he could shift his long lithe gun back to his right hand I dropped mine under the desk and grabbed the butt of the .45 and put my finger hard on the trigger.

"Look under the desk, Mr. Grimes. You'll see a .45 in an open-end holster. It's fixed there and it's pointing at your belly. Even if you could shoot me through the heart the .45 would still go off from a convulsive movement of my hand. And your belly would be hanging by a shred and you would be knocked out of that chair. A .45 slug can throw you back six feet. Even the movies learned that at last."

"Looks like a Mexican stand-off," he said quietly. He holstered his gun. He grinned. "Nice smooth work, Marlowe. We could use you. But it's a long time for you and no time at all to us. Find Ikky and don't be a drip. He'll listen to reason. He doesn't really want to be on the run for the rest of his life. We'd trace him eventually."

"Tell me something, Mr. Grimes. Why pick on me? Apart from Ikky, what did I ever do to make you dislike me?"

Not moving, he thought a moment, or pretended to. "The Larsen case. You helped send one of our boys to the gas chamber. That we don't forget. We had you in mind as a fall guy for Ikky. You'll always be a fall guy, unless you play it our way. Something will hit you when you least expect it."

"A man in my business is always a fall guy, Mr. Grimes. Pick up your grand and drift out quietly. I might decide to do it your way, but I have to think. As for the Larsen case, the cops did all the work. I just happened to know where he was. I don't guess you miss him terribly."

"We don't like interference." He stood up. He put the grand note casually back in his pocket. While he was doing it I let go of the .45 and jerked out my Smith & Wesson five-inch .38.

He looked at it contemptuously. "I'll be in Vegas, Marlowe. In fact I never left Vegas. You can catch me at the Esperanza. No, we don't give a damn about Larsen personally. Just another gun handler. They come in gross lots. We *do* give a damn that some punk private eye fingered him."

He nodded and went out by my office door.

I did some pondering. I knew Ikky wouldn't go back to the Outfit. He wouldn't trust them enough if he got the chance. But there was another reason now. I called Anne Riordan again.

"I'm going to look for Ikky. I have to. If I don't call you in three days, get hold of Bernie Ohls. I'm going to Flagstaff, Arizona. Ikky says he will be there."

"You're a fool," she wailed. "It's some sort of trap."

"A Mr. Grimes of Vegas visited me with a silenced gun. I beat him to the punch, but I won't always be that lucky. If I find Ikky and report to Grimes, the mob will let me alone."

"You'd condemn a man to death?" Her voice was sharp and incredulous.

"No. He won't be there when I report. He'll have to hop a plane to Montreal, buy forged papers — Montreal is almost as crooked as we are — and plane to Europe. He may be fairly safe there. But the Outfit has long arms and Ikky will have a damned dull life staying alive. He hasn't any choice. For him it's either hide or get the pencil."

"So clever of you, darling. What about your own pencil?"

"If they meant it, they wouldn't have sent it. Just a bit of scare technique."

"And you don't scare, you wonderful handsome brute."

"I scare. But it doesn't paralyze me. So long. Don't take any lovers until I get back."

"Damn you, Marlowe!"

She hung up on me. I hung up on myself.

Saying the wrong thing is one of my specialities.

I beat it out of town before the homicide boys could hear about me. It would take them quite a while to get a lead. And Bernie Ohls wouldn't give a city dick a used paper bag. The Sheriff's men and the City Police co-operate about as much as two tomcats on a fence.

9

I MADE PHOENIX BY EVENING and parked myself in a motor court on the outskirts. Phoenix was damned hot. The motor court had a dining room, so I had dinner. I collected some quarters and dimes from the cashier and shut myself in a phone booth and started to call the Mirador in Flagstaff. How silly could I get? Ikky might be registered under any name from Cohen to Cordileone, from Watson to Woichehovski. I called anyway and got nothing but as much of a smile as you can get on the phone. So I asked for a room the following night. Not a chance unless someone checked out, but they would put me down for a cancellation or something. Flagstaff is too near the Grand Canyon. Ikky must have arranged in advance. That was something to ponder too.

I bought a paperback and read it. I set my alarm watch for 6:30. The paperback scared me so badly that I put two guns under my pillow. It was about a guy who bucked the hoodlum boss of Milwaukee and got beaten up every fifteen minutes. I figured that his head and face would be nothing but a piece of bone with a strip of skin hanging from it. But in the next chapter he was as gay as a meadowlark. Then I asked myself why I was reading this drivel when I could have been memorizing *The Brothers Karamazov*. Not knowing any good answers, I turned the light out and went to sleep. At 6:30 I shaved and showered and had breakfast and took off for Flagstaff. I got there by lunchtime, and there was Ikky in the restaurant eating mountain trout. I sat down across from him. He looked surprised to see me.

I ordered mountain trout and ate it from the outside in, which is the proper way. Boning spoils it a little.

"What gives?" he asked me with his mouth full. A delicate eater.

"You read the papers?"

"Just the sporting section."

"Let's go to your room and talk about it. There's more than that."

We paid for our lunches and went along to a nice double. The motor courts are getting so good that they make a lot of hotels look cheap. We sat down and lit cigarettes.

"The two hoods got up too early and went over to Poynter Street. They parked outside your apartment house. They hadn't been briefed carefully enough. They shot a guy who looked a little like you."

"That's a hot one." He grinned. "But the cops will find out, and the Outfit will find out. So the tag for me stays on."

"You must think I'm dumb," I said. "I am."

"I thought you did a first-class job, Marlowe. What's dumb about that?"

"What job did I do?"

"You got me out of there pretty slick."

"Anything about it you couldn't have done yourself?"

"With luck — no. But it's nice to have a helper."

"You mean sucker."

His face tightened. And his rusty voice growled. "I don't catch. And give me back some of that five grand, will you? I'm shorter than I thought."

"I'll give it back to you when you find a hummingbird in a salt shaker."

"Don't be like that." He almost sighed, and flicked a gun into his hand. I didn't have to flick. I was holding one in my side pocket.

"I oughtn't to have boobed off," I said. "Put the heater away. It doesn't pay any more than a Vegas slot machine."

"Wrong. Them machines pay the jackpot every so often. Otherwise — no customers."

"Every so seldom, you mean. Listen, and listen good."

He grinned. His dentist was tired waiting for him.

"The set-up intrigued me," I went on, debonair as Milo Vance in a Van Dyne story and a lot brighter in the head. "First off, could it be done? Second, if it could be done, where would I be? But gradually I saw the little touches that flaw the picture. Why would you come to me at all? The Outfit isn't that naive. Why would they send a little punk like this Charles Hickon or whatever name he uses on Thursdays? Why would an old hand like you let anybody trail you to a dangerous connection?"

"You slay me, Marlowe. You're so bright I could find you in the dark. You're so dumb you couldn't see a red, white and blue giraffe. I bet you were back there in your unbrain emporium playing with that five grand like a cat with a bag of catnip. I bet you were kissing the notes."

"Not after you handled them. Then why the pencil that was sent to me? Big dangerous threat. It reinforced the rest. But like I told your choir boy from Vegas, they don't send them when they mean them. By the way, he had a gun too. A Woodsman twenty-two with a silencer. I had to make him put it away. He was nice about that. He started waving grands at me to find out where you were and tell him. A well-dressed, nice-looking front man for a pack of dirty rats. The Women's Christian Temperance Association and some bootlicking politicians gave them the money to be big, and they learned how to use it and make it grow. Now they're pretty well unstoppable. But they're still a pack of dirty rats. And they're always where they can't make a mistake. That's inhuman. Any man has a right to a few mistakes. Not the rats. They have to be perfect all the time. Or else they get stuck with *you*."

"I don't know what the hell you're talking about. I just know it's too long."

"Well, allow me to put it in English. Some poor jerk from the East Side gets involved with the lower echelons of a mob. You know what an echelon is, Ikky?"

"I been in the Army," he sneered.

"He grows up in the mob, but he's not all rotten. He's not rotten enough. So he tries to break loose. He comes out here and gets himself a cheap job of some sort and changes his name or names and lives quietly in a cheap apartment house. But the mob by now has agents in many places. Somebody spots him and recognizes him. It might be a pusher, a front man for a bookie joint, a night girl, even a cop that's on the take. So the mob, or call them the Outfit, say through their cigar smoke: 'Ikky can't do this to us. It's a small operation because he's small. But it annoys us. Bad for discipline. Call a couple of boys and have them pencil him.' But what boys do they call? A couple they're tired of. Been around too long. Might make a mistake or get chilly toes. Perhaps they like killing. That's bad too. That makes recklessness. The best boys are the ones that don't care either way. So although they don't know it, the boys they call are on their way out. But it would be kind of cute to frame a guy they already don't like, for fingering a hood named Larsen. One of these puny little jokes the Outfit takes big. 'Look guys, we even got time to play footies with a private eye. Jesus, we can do anything. We could even suck our thumbs.' So they send a ringer."

"The Torri brothers ain't ringers. They're real hard boys. They proved it — even if they did make a mistake."

"Mistake nothing. They got Ikky Rosenstein. You're just a singing commercial in this deal. And as of now you're under arrest for murder. You're worse off than that. The Outfit will habeas corpus you out of the clink and blow you down. You've served your purpose and you failed to finger me into a patsy."

His finger tightened on the trigger. I shot the gun out of his hand. My gun in my coat pocket was small, but at that distance accurate. And it was one of my days to be accurate myself.

He made a faint moaning sound and sucked at his hand. I went over and kicked him hard in the chest. Being nice to killers is not part of my repertoire. He went over backwards and sidewise and stumbled four or five steps. I picked up his gun and held it on him while I tapped all the places — not just pockets or holsters — where a man could stash a second gun. He was clean — that way anyhow.

"What are you trying to do to me?" he said whiningly. "I paid you. You're clear. I paid you damn well."

"We both have problems there. Yours is to stay alive." I took a pair of cuffs out of my pocket and wrestled his hands behind him and snapped them on. His hand was bleeding. I tied his show handkerchief around it. I went to the telephone.

Flagstaff was big enough to have a police force. The D.A. might even have his office there. This was Arizona, a poor state, relatively. The cops might even be honest.

10

I HAD TO STICK AROUND FOR A FEW DAYS, but I didn't mind that as long as I could have trout caught eight or nine thousand feet up. I called Anne and Bernie Ohls. I called my answering service. The Arizona D.A. was a young keen-eyed man and the Chief of Police was one of the biggest men I ever saw.

I got back to L.A. in time and took Anne to Romanoff's for dinner and champagne.

"What I can't see," she said over a third glass of bubbly, "is why they dragged you into it, why they set up the fake Ikky Rosenstein. Why didn't they just let the two life-takers do their job?"

"I couldn't really say. Unless the big boys feel so safe they're developing a sense of humor. And unless this Larsen guy that went to the gas chamber was bigger than he seemed to be. Only three or four important mobsters have made the electric chair or the rope or the gas chamber. None that I know of in the life-imprisonment states like Michigan. If Larsen was bigger than anyone thought, they might have had my name on a waiting list."

"But why wait?" she asked me. "They'd go after you quickly."

"They can afford to wait. Who's going to bother them — Kefauver? He did his best, but do you notice any change in the set-up — except when they make one themselves?"

"Costello?"

"Income tax rap — like Capone. Capone may have had several hundred men killed, and killed a few of them himself, personally. But it took the Internal Revenue boys to get him. The Outfit won't make that mistake often."

"What I like about you, apart from your enormous personal charm, is that when you don't know an answer you make one up."

"The money worries me," I said. "Five grand of their dirty money. What do I do with it?"

"Don't be a jerk all your life. You earned the money and you risked your life for it. You can buy Series E Bonds. They'll make the money clean. And to me that would be part of the joke."

"*You* tell *me* one good reason why they pulled the switch."

"You have more of a reputation than you realize. And how would it be if the false Ikky pulled the switch? He sounds like one of these over-clever types that can't do anything simple."

"The Outfit will get him for making his own plans — if you're right."

"If the D.A. doesn't. And I couldn't care less about what happens to him. More champagne, please."

11

THEY EXTRADITED "IKKY" and he broke under pressure and named the two gunmen — after I had already named them, the Torri brothers. But nobody could find them. They never went home. And you can't prove conspiracy on one man. The law couldn't even get him for accessory after the fact. They couldn't prove he knew the real Ikky had been gunned.

They could have got him for some trifle, but they had a better idea. They left him to his friends. They turned him loose.

Where is he now? My hunch says nowhere.

Anne Riordan was glad it was all over and I was safe. Safe — that isn't a word you use in my trade.

II

THE LITTLE SISTER

1

THE PEBBLED GLASS DOOR PANEL is lettered in flaked black paint: PHILIP MARLOWE — INVESTIGATIONS. It is a reasonably shabby door at the end of a reasonably shabby corridor in the sort of building that was new about the year the all-tile bathroom became the basis of civilization. The door is locked, but next to it is another door with the same legend which is not locked. Come on in — there's nobody in here but me and a big bluebottle fly. But not if you're from Manhattan, Kansas.

It was one of those clear, bright summer mornings we get in the early spring in California before the high fog sets in. The rains are over. The hills are still green and in the valley across the Hollywood hills you can see snow on the high mountains. The fur stores are advertising their annual sales. The call houses that specialize in sixteen-year-old virgins are doing a land-office business. And in Beverly Hills the jacaranda trees are beginning to bloom.

I had been stalking the bluebottle fly for five minutes, waiting for him to sit down. He didn't want to sit down. He just wanted to do wing-overs and sing the Prologue to *Pagliacci*. I had the fly swatter poised in midair and I was all set. There was a patch of bright sunlight on the corner of the desk and I knew that sooner or later that was where he was going to light. But when he did, I didn't even see him at first. The buzzing stopped and there he was. And then the phone rang.

I reached for it inch by inch with a slow and patient left hand.

I lifted the phone slowly and spoke into it softly: "Hold the line a moment, please."

I laid the phone down gently on the brown blotter. He was still there, shining and blue-green and full of sin. I took a deep breath and swung. What was left of him sailed halfway across the room and dropped to the carpet. I went over and picked him up by his good wing and dropped him into the wastebasket.

"Thanks for waiting," I said into the phone.

"Is this Mr. Marlowe, the detective?" It was a small, rather hurried, little-girlish voice. I said it was Mr. Marlowe, the detective.

"How much do you charge for your services, Mr. Marlowe?"

"What was it you wanted done?"

The voice sharpened a little. "I can't very well tell you that over the phone. It's — it's very confidential. Before I'd waste time coming to your office I'd have to have some idea — "

"Forty bucks a day and expenses. Unless it's the kind of job that can be done for a flat fee."

"That's far too much," the little voice said. "Why, it might cost hundreds of dollars and I only get a small salary and — "

"Where are you now?"

"Why, I'm in a drugstore. It's right next to the building where your office is."

"You could have saved a nickel. The elevator's free."

"I — I beg your pardon?"

I said it all over again. "Come on up and let's have a look at you," I added. "If you're in my kind of trouble, I can give you a pretty good idea — "

"I have to know something about you," the small voice said very firmly. "This is a very delicate matter, very personal. I couldn't talk to just anybody."

"If it's that delicate," I said, "maybe you need a lady detective."

"Goodness, I didn't know there were any." Pause. "But I don't think a lady detective would do at all. You see, Orrin was living in a very tough neighborhood, Mr. Marlowe. At least I thought it was tough. The manager of the rooming house is a most unpleasant person. He smelled of liquor. Do you drink, Mr. Marlowe?"

"Well, now that you mention it — "

"I don't think I'd care to employ a detective that uses liquor in any form. I don't even approve of tobacco."

"Would it be all right if I peeled an orange?"

I caught the sharp intake of breath at the far end of the line. "You might at least talk like a gentleman," she said.

"Better try the University Club," I told her. "I heard they had a couple left over there, but I'm not sure they'll let you handle them." I hung up.

It was a step in the right direction, but it didn't go far enough. I ought to have locked the door and hid under the desk.

2

FIVE MINUTES LATER the buzzer sounded on the outer door of the half-office I use for a reception room. I heard the door close again. Then I didn't hear anything more. The door between me and there was half-open. I listened and decided somebody had just looked in at the wrong office and left without entering. Then there was a small knocking on wood. Then the kind of cough you use for the same purpose. I got my feet off the desk, stood up and looked out. There she was. She didn't have to open her mouth for me to know who she was. And nobody ever looked less like Lady Macbeth. She was a small, neat, rather prissy-looking girl with primly smooth brown hair and rimless glasses. She was wearing a brown tailor-made and from a strap over her shoulder hung one of those awkward-looking square bags that make you think of a Sister of Mercy taking first aid to the wounded. On the smooth brown hair was a hat that had been taken from its mother too young. She had no make-up, no lipstick and no jewelry. The rimless glasses gave her that librarian's look.

"That's no way to talk to people over the telephone," she said sharply. "You ought to be ashamed of yourself."

"I'm just too proud to show it," I said. "Come on in." I held the door for her. Then I held the chair for her.

She sat down on about two inches of the edge. "If I talked like that to one of Dr. Zugsmith's patients," she said, "I'd lose my position. He's most particular how I speak to the patients — even the difficult ones."

"How is the old boy? I haven't seen him since that time I fell off the garage roof."

She looked surprised and quite serious. "Why surely you can't know Dr. Zugsmith." The tip of a rather anemic tongue came out between her lips and searched furtively for nothing.

"I know a Dr. George Zugsmith," I said, "in Santa Rosa."

"Oh no. This is Dr. Alfred Zugsmith, in Manhattan. Manhattan, Kansas, you know, not Manhattan, New York."

"Must be a different Dr. Zugsmith," I said. "And your name?"

"I'm not sure I'd care to tell you."

"Just window shopping, huh?"

"I suppose you could call it that. If I have to tell my family affairs to a total stranger, I at least have the right to decide whether he's the kind of person I could trust."

"Anybody ever tell you you're a cute little trick?"

The eyes behind the rimless cheaters flashed. "I should hope not."

I reached for a pipe and started to fill it. "Hope isn't exactly the word," I said. "Get rid of that hat and get yourself a pair of those slinky glasses with colored rims. You know, the ones that are all cock-eyed and oriental —"

"Dr. Zugsmith wouldn't permit anything like that," she said quickly. Then, "Do you really think so?" she asked, and blushed ever so slightly.

I put a match to the pipe and puffed smoke across the desk. She winced back.

"If you hire me," I said, "I'm the guy you hire. Me. Just as I am. If you think you're going to find any lay readers in this business you're crazy. I hung up on you, but you came up here all the same. So you need help. What's your name and trouble?"

She just stared at me.

"Look," I said. "You come from Manhattan, Kansas. The last

time I memorized the *World Almanac* that was a little town not far from Topeka. Population around twelve thousand. You work for Dr. Alfred Zugsmith and you're looking for somebody named Orrin. Manhattan is a small town. It has to be. Only half a dozen places in Kansas are anything else. I already have enough information about you to find out your whole family history."

"But why should you want to?" she asked, troubled.

"Me?" I said. "I don't want to. I'm fed up with people telling me histories. I'm just sitting here because I don't have any place to go. I don't want to work. I don't want anything."

"You talk too much."

"Yes," I said, "I talk too much. Lonely men always talk too much. Either that or they don't talk at all. Shall we get down to business? You don't look like the type that goes to see private detectives, and especially private detectives you don't know."

"I know that," she said quietly. "And Orrin would be absolutely livid. Mother would be furious too. I just picked your name out of the phone book —"

"What principle?" I asked. "And with the eyes closed or open?"

She stared at me for a moment as if I were some kind of freak. "Seven and thirteen," she said quietly.

"How?"

"Marlowe has seven letters," she said, "and Philip Marlowe has thirteen. Seven together with thirteen —"

"What's *your* name?" I almost snarled.

"Orfamay Quest." She crinkled her eyes as if she could cry. She spelled the first name out for me, all one word. "I live with my mother," she went on, her voice getting rapid now as if my time were costing her. "My father died four years ago. He was a doctor. My brother Orrin was going to be a surgeon, too, but he changed into engineering after two years of medical. Then a year ago Orrin came out to work for the Cal-Western Aircraft Company in Bay City. He didn't have to. He had a good job in Wichita. I guess he just sort of wanted to come out here to California. Most everybody does."

"*Al*-most everybody," I said. "If you're going to wear those rimless glasses, you might at least try to live up to them."

She giggled and drew a line along the desk with her finger tip, looking down. "Did you mean those slanting kind of glasses that make you look kind of oriental?"

"Uh-huh. Now about Orrin. We've got him to California, and we've got him to Bay City. What do we do with him?"

She thought a moment and frowned. Then she studied my face as if making up her mind. Then her words came with a burst: "It wasn't like Orrin not to write to us regularly. He only wrote twice to mother and three times to me in the last six months. And the last letter was several months ago. Mother and I got worried. So it was my vacation and I came out to see him. He'd never been away from Kansas before." She stopped. "Aren't you going to take any notes?" she asked.

I grunted.

"I thought detectives always wrote things down in little notebooks."

"I'll make the gags," I said. "You tell the story. You came out on your vacation. Then what?"

"I'd written to Orrin that I was coming but I didn't get any answer. Then I sent a wire to him from Salt Lake City but he didn't answer that either. So all I could do was go down where he lived. It's an awful long way. I went in a bus. It's in Bay City. Number four forty-nine Idaho Street."

She stopped again, then repeated the address, and I still didn't write it down. I just sat there looking at her glasses and her smooth brown hair and the silly little hat and the fingernails with no color and her mouth with no lipstick and the tip of the little tongue that came and went between the pale lips.

"Maybe you don't know Bay City, Mr. Marlowe."

"Ha," I said. "All I know about Bay City is that every time I go there I have to buy a new head. You want me to finish your story for you?"

"Wha-a-at?" Her eyes opened so wide that the glasses made them look like something you see in the deep-sea fish tanks.

"He's moved," I said. "And you don't know where he's moved to. And you're afraid he's living a life of sin in a penthouse on top of the Regency Towers with something in a long mink coat and an interesting perfume."

"Well for goodness' sakes!"

"Or am I being coarse?" I asked.

"Please, Mr. Marlowe," she said at last. "I don't think anything of the sort about Orrin. And if Orrin heard you say that you'd be sorry. He can be awfully mean. But I know something has happened. It was just a cheap rooming house, and I didn't like the manager at all. A horrid kind of man. He said Orrin had moved away a couple of weeks before and he didn't know where to and he didn't care, and all he wanted was a good slug of gin. I don't know why Orrin would even live in a place like that."

"Did you say slug of gin?" I asked.

She blushed. "That's what the manager said. I'm just telling you."

"All right," I said. "Go on."

"Well, I called the place where he worked. The Cal-Western Company, you know. And they said he'd been laid off like a lot of others and that was all they knew. So then I went to the post office and asked if Orrin had put in a change of address to anywhere. And they said they couldn't give me any information. It was against the regulations. So I told them how it was and the man said, well if I was his sister he'd go look. So he went and looked and came back and said no. Orrin hadn't put in any change of address. So then I began to get a little frightened. He might have had an accident or something."

"Did it occur to you to ask the police about that?"

"I wouldn't dare ask the police. Orrin would never forgive me. He's difficult enough at the best of times. Our family —" She hesitated and there was something behind her eyes she tried not to have there. So she went on breathlessly: "Our family's not the kind of family —"

"Look," I said wearily, "I'm not talking about the guy lifting a wallet. I'm talking about him getting knocked down by a car and losing his memory or being too badly hurt to talk."

She gave me a level look which was not too admiring. "If it was anything like that, we'd know," she said. "Everybody has things in their pockets to tell who they are."

"Sometimes all they have left is the pockets."

"Are you trying to scare me, Mr. Marlowe?"

"If I am, I'm certainly getting nowhere fast. Just what do you think might have happened?"

She put her slim forefinger to her lips and touched it very carefully with the tip of that tongue. "I guess if I knew that I wouldn't have to come and see you. How much would you charge to find him?"

I didn't answer for a long moment, then I said: "You mean alone, without telling anybody?"

"Yes. I mean alone, without telling anybody."

"Uh-huh. Well that depends. I told you what my rates were."

She clasped her hands on the edge of the desk and squeezed them together hard. She had about the most meaningless set of gestures I had ever laid eyes on. "I thought you being a detective and all you could find him right away," she said. "I couldn't possibly afford more than twenty dollars. I've got to buy my meals here and my hotel and the train going back and you know the hotel is so terribly expensive and the food on the train —"

"Which one are you staying at?"

"I — I'd rather not tell you, if you don't mind."

"Why?"

"I'd just rather not. I'm terribly afraid of Orrin's temper. And, well I can always call you up, can't I?"

"Uh-huh. Just what is it you're scared of, besides Orrin's temper, Miss Quest?" I had let my pipe go out. I struck a match and held it to the bowl, watching her over it.

"Isn't pipe-smoking a very dirty habit?" she asked.

"Probably," I said. "But it would take more than twenty bucks to have me drop it. And don't try to sidestep my questions."

"You can't talk to me like that," she flared up. "Pipe-smoking is a dirty habit. Mother never let Father smoke in the house, even the last two years after he had his stroke. He used to sit with that empty pipe in his mouth sometimes. But she didn't like him to do that really. We owed a lot of money too and she said she couldn't afford to give him money for useless things like tobacco. The church needed it much more than he did."

"I'm beginning to get it," I said slowly. "Take a family like yours and somebody in it has to be the dark meat."

She stood up sharply and clasped the first-aid kit to her body. "I don't like you," she said. "I don't think I'm going to employ you. If you're insinuating that Orrin has done something wrong, well I can assure you that it's not Orrin who's the black sheep of our family."

I didn't move an eyelash. She swung around and marched to the door and put her hand on the knob and then she swung around again and marched back and suddenly began to cry. I reacted to that just the way a stuffed fish reacts to cut bait. She got out her little handkerchief and tickled the corners of her eyes.

"And now I suppose you'll call the p-police," she said with a catch in her voice. "And the Manhattan p-paper will hear all about it and they'll print something n-nasty about us."

"You don't suppose anything of the sort. Stop chipping at my emotions. Let's see a photo of him."

She put the handkerchief away in a hurry and dug something else out of her bag. She passed it across the desk. An envelope. Thin, but there could be a couple of snapshots in it. I didn't look inside.

"Describe him the way you see him," I said.

She concentrated. That gave her a chance to do something with her eyebrows. "He was twenty-eight years old last March. He has light brown hair, much lighter than mine, and lighter blue eyes, and he brushes his hair straight back. He's very tall, over six feet. But he only weighs about a hundred and forty pounds. He's sort of bony. He used to wear a little blond mustache but Mother made him cut it off. She said — "

"Don't tell me. The minister needed it to stuff a cushion."

"You can't talk like that about my mother," she yelped, getting pale with rage.

"Oh stop being silly. There's a lot of things about you I don't know. But you can stop pretending to be an Easter lily right now. Does Orrin have any distinguishing marks on him, like moles or scars, or a tattoo of the Twenty-third Psalm on his chest? And don't bother to blush."

"Well, you don't have to yell at me. Why don't you look at the photograph?"

"He probably has his clothes on. After all, you're his sister. You ought to know."

"No, he hasn't," she said tightly. "He has a little scar on his left hand where he had a wen removed."

"What about his habits? What does he do for fun — besides not smoking or drinking or going out with girls?"

"Why — how did you know that?"

"Your mother told me."

She smiled. I was beginning to wonder if she had one in her. She had very white teeth and she didn't wave her gums. That was something. "Aren't you silly," she said. "He studies a lot and he has a very expensive camera he likes to snap people with when they don't know. Sometimes it makes them mad. But Orrin says people ought to see themselves as they really are."

"Let's hope it never happens to him," I said. "What kind of camera is it?"

"One of those little cameras with a very fine lens. You can take snaps in almost any kind of light. A Leica."

I opened the envelope and took out a couple of small prints, very clear. "These weren't taken with anything like that," I said.

"Oh no. Philip took those, Philip Anderson. A boy I was going with for a while." She paused and sighed. "And I guess that's really why I came here, Mr. Marlowe. Just because your name's Philip too."

I just said: "Uh-huh," but I felt touched in some vague sort of way. "What happened to Philip Anderson?"

"But it's about Orrin — "

"I know," I interrupted. "But what happened to Philip Anderson?"

"He's still there in Manhattan." She looked away. "Mother doesn't like him very much. I guess you know how it is."

"Yes," I said, "I know how it is. You can cry if you want to. I won't hold it against you. I'm just a big soft slob myself."

I looked at the two prints. One of them was looking down and was no good to me. The other was a fairly good shot of a tall angular bird with narrow-set eyes and a thin straight mouth and a pointed chin. He had the expression I expected to see. If you forgot to wipe the mud off your shoes, he was the boy who would tell you. I laid the photos aside and looked at Orfamay Quest, trying to find something in her face even remotely like his. I couldn't. Not the slightest trace of family resemblance, which of course meant absolutely nothing. It never has.

"All right," I said. "I'll go down there and take a look. But you ought to be able to guess what's happened. He's in a strange city. He's making good money for a while. More than he's ever made in his life, perhaps. He's meeting a kind of people he never met before. And it's not the kind of town — believe me it isn't, I know Bay City — that Manhattan, Kansas, is. So he just broke training and he doesn't want his family to know about it. He'll straighten out."

She just stared at me for a moment in silence, then she shook her head. "No. Orrin's not the type to do that, Mr. Marlowe."

"Anyone is," I said. "Especially a fellow like Orrin. The small-town sanctimonious type of guy who's lived his entire life with his mother on his neck and the minister holding his hand. Out here he's lonely. He's got dough. He'd like to buy a little sweetness and light, and not the kind that comes through the east window of a church. Not that I have anything against that. I mean he already had enough of that, didn't he?"

She nodded her head silently.

"So he starts to play," I went on, "and he doesn't know how to play. That takes experience too. He's got himself all jammed up with some floozy and a bottle of hootch and what he's done looks to him as if he'd stolen the bishop's pants. After all, the guy's going on twenty-nine years old and if he wants to roll in the gutter that's his business. He'll find somebody to blame it on after a while."

"I hate to believe you, Mr. Marlowe," she said slowly. "I'd hate for Mother — "

"Something was said about twenty dollars," I cut in.

She looked shocked. "Do I have to pay you now?"

"What would be the custom in Manhattan, Kansas?"

"We don't have any private detectives in Manhattan. Just the regular police. That is, I don't think we do."

She probed in the inside of her tool kit again and dragged out a red change purse and from that she took a number of bills, all neatly folded and separate. Three fives and five ones. There didn't seem to be much left. She kind of held the purse so I could see how empty it was. Then she straightened the bills out on the desk and put one on top of the other and pushed them across. Very slowly, very sadly, as if she was drowning a favorite kitten.

"I'll give you a receipt," I said.

"I don't need a receipt, Mr. Marlowe."

"I do. You won't give me your name and address, so I want something with your name on it."

"What for?"

"To show I'm representing you." I got the receipt book out and made the receipt and held the book for her to sign the duplicate. She didn't want to. After a moment, reluctantly she took the hard pencil and wrote *Orfamay Quest* in a neat secretary's writing across the face of the duplicate.

"Still no address?" I asked.

"I'd rather not."

"Call me any time then. My home number is in the phone book, too. Bristol Apartments, apartment four twenty-eight."

"I shan't be very likely to visit you," she said coldly.

"I haven't asked you yet," I said. "Call me around four if you like. I might have something. And then again I might not."

She stood up. "I hope Mother won't think I've done wrong," she said, picking at her lip now with the pale fingernail. "Coming here, I mean."

"Just don't tell me any more of the things your mother won't like," I said. "Just leave that part out."

"Well really!"

"And stop saying 'well really.' "

"I think you are a very offensive person," she said.

"No, you don't. You think I'm cute. And I think you're a fascinating little liar. You don't think I'm doing this for any twenty bucks, do you?"

She gave me a level, suddenly cool stare. "Then why?" Then when I didn't answer, she added: "Because spring is in the air?"

I still didn't answer. She blushed a little. Then she giggled.

I didn't have the heart to tell her I was just plain bored with doing nothing. Perhaps it *was* the spring too. And something in her eyes that was much older than Manhattan, Kansas.

"I think you're very nice — really," she said softly. Then she turned quickly and almost ran out of the office. Her steps along the corridor outside made tiny, sharp pecky sounds, kind of like Mother drumming on the edge of the dinner table when Father tried to promote himself a second piece of pie. And him with no money any more. No nothing. Just sitting in a rocker on the front porch back there in Manhattan, Kansas, with his empty pipe in his mouth. Rocking on the front porch, slow and easy, because when you've had a stroke you have to take it slow and easy. And wait for the next one. And the empty pipe in his mouth. No tobacco. Nothing to do but wait.

I put Orfamay Quest's twenty hard-earned dollars in an envelope and wrote her name on it and dropped it in the desk drawer. I didn't like the idea of running around loose with that much currency on me.

3

YOU COULD KNOW BAY CITY a long time without knowing Idaho Street. And you could know a lot of Idaho Street without knowing number 449. The block in front of it had a broken paving that had almost gone back to dirt. The warped fence of a lumberyard bordered the cracked sidewalk on the opposite side of the street. Halfway up the block the rusted rails of a spur track turned into a pair of high, chained wooden gates that seemed not to have been opened for twenty years. Little boys with chalk had been writing and drawing pictures on the gates and all along the fence.

Number 449 had a shallow, paintless front porch on which five wood-and-cane rockers loafed dissolutely, held together with wire and the moisture of the beach air. The green shades over the lower windows of the house were two-thirds down and full of cracks. Beside the front door there was a large printed sign: NO VACANCIES. That had been there a long time too. It had got faded and fly-specked. The door opened on a long hall from which stairs went up a third of the way back. To the right there was a narrow shelf with a chained, indelible pencil hanging beside it. There was a push button and a yellow and black sign above which read MANAGER, and was held up by three thumbtacks no two of which matched. There was a pay phone on the opposite wall.

I pushed the bell. It rang somewhere nearby but nothing happened. I rang it again. The same nothing happened. I prowled along to a door with a black-and-white metal sign on it — MANAGER. I knocked on that. Then I kicked it. Nobody seemed to mind my kicking it.

I went back out of the house and down around the side where a narrow concrete walk led to the service entrance. It looked as if it was in the right place to belong to the manager's apartment. The rest of the house would be just rooms. There was a dirty garbage pail on the small porch and a wooden box full of liquor bottles. Behind the screen the back door of the house was open. It was gloomy inside. I put my face against the screen and peered in. Through the open inner door beyond the service porch I could see a straight chair with a man's coat hanging over it and in the chair a man in shirtsleeves with his hat on. He was a small man. I couldn't see what he was doing, but he seemed to be sitting at the end of the built-in breakfast table in the breakfast nook.

I banged on the screen door. The man paid no attention. I banged again, harder. This time he tilted his chair back and showed me a small pale face with a cigarette in it. "Whatcha want?" he barked.

"Manager."

"Not in, bub."

"Who are you?"

"What's it to you?"

"I want a room."

"No vacancies, bub. Can't you read large print?"

"I happen to have different information," I said.

"Yeah?" He shook ash from his cigarette by flicking it with a nail without removing it from his small sad mouth. "Go fry your head in it."

He tilted his chair forward again and went on doing whatever it was he was doing.

I made noise getting down off the porch and none whatever coming back up on it. I felt the screen door carefully. It was hooked. With the open blade of a penknife I lifted the hook and eased it out of the eye. It made a small tinkle but louder tinkling sounds were being made beyond, in the kitchen.

I stepped into the house, crossed the service porch, went through the door into the kitchen. The little man was too busy to notice me. The kitchen had a three-burner gas stove, a few shelves of greasy dishes, a chipped icebox and the breakfast nook. The table in the breakfast nook was covered with money. Most of it was paper, but there was silver also, in all sizes up to dollars. The little man was counting and stacking it and making entries in a small book. He wetted his pencil without bothering the cigarette that lived in his face.

There must have been several hundred dollars on that table.

"Rent day?" I asked genially.

The small man turned very suddenly. For a moment he smiled and said nothing. It was the smile of a man whose mind is not smiling. He removed the stub of cigarette from his mouth, dropped it on the floor and stepped on it. He reached a fresh one out of his shirt and put it in the same hole in his face and started fumbling for a match.

"You came in nice," he said pleasantly.

Finding no match, he turned casually in his chair and reached into a pocket of his coat. Something heavy knocked against the wood of the chair. I got hold of his wrist before the heavy thing came out of the pocket. He threw his weight backwards and the pocket of the coat started to lift towards me. I yanked the chair out from under him.

He sat down hard on the floor and knocked his head against the end of the breakfast table. That didn't keep him from trying to kick me in the groin. I stepped back with his coat and took a .38 out of the pocket he had been playing with.

"Don't sit on the floor just to be chummy," I said.

He got up slowly, pretending to be groggier than he was. His hand fumbled at the back of his collar and light winked on metal as his arm swept towards me. He was a game little rooster.

I sideswiped his jaw with his own gun and he sat down on the floor again. I stepped on the hand that held the knife. His face twisted with pain but he didn't make a sound. So I kicked the knife into a corner. It was a long thin knife and it looked very sharp.

"You ought to be ashamed of yourself," I said. "Pulling guns and knives on people that are just looking for a place to live. Even for these times that's out of line."

He held his hurt hand between his knees and squeezed it and began to whistle through his teeth. The slap on the jaw didn't seem to have hurt him. "Okay," he said, "okay. I ain't supposed to be perfect. Take the dough and beat it. But don't ever think we won't catch up with you."

I looked at the collection of small bills and medium bills and silver on the table. "You must meet a lot of sales resistance, the weapons you carry," I told him. I walked across to the inner door and tried it. It was not locked. I turned back.

"I'll leave your gun in the mailbox," I said. "Next time ask to see the buzzer."

He was still whistling gently between his teeth and holding his hand. He gave me a narrow, thoughtful eye, then shoveled the money into a shabby briefcase and slipped its catch. He took his hat off, straightened it around, put it back jauntily on the back of his head and gave me a quiet efficient smile.

"Never mind about the heater," he said. "The town's full of old iron. But you could leave the skiv with Clausen. I've done quite a bit of work on it to get it in shape."

"And with it?" I said.

"Could be." He flicked a finger at me airily. "Maybe we meet again some day soon. When I got a friend with me."

"Tell him to wear a clean shirt," I said. "And lend you one."

"My, my," the little man said chidingly. "How tough we get how quick once we get that badge pinned on."

He went softly past me and down the wooden steps from the back porch. His footsteps tapped to the street and faded. They sounded very much like Orfamay's heels clicking along the corridor in my office building. And for some reason I had that empty feeling of having miscounted the trumps. No reason for it at all. Maybe it was the steely quality about the little man. No whimper, no bluster, just the smile, the whistling between the teeth, the light voice and the unforgetting eyes.

I went over and picked up the knife. The blade was long and round and thin, like a rattailed file that has been ground smooth. The handle and the guard were lightweight plastic and seemed all one piece. I held the knife by the handle and gave it a quick flip at the table. The blade came loose and quivered in the wood.

I took a deep breath and slid the handle down over the end again and worked the blade loose from the table. A curious knife, with design and purpose in it, and neither of them agreeable.

I opened the door beyond the kitchen and went through it with the gun and knife in one hand.

It was a wall-bed living room, with the wall bed down and rumpled. There was an overstuffed chair with a hole burned in the arm. A high oak desk with tilted doors like old-fashioned cellar doors stood against the wall by the front window. Near this there was a studio couch and on the studio couch lay a man. His feet hung over the end of the couch in knobby gray socks. His head had missed the pillow by two feet. It was nothing much to miss from the color of the slip on it. The upper part of him was contained in a colorless shirt and a threadbare gray coat-sweater. His mouth was open and his face was shining with sweat and he breathed like an old Ford with a leaky head gasket. On a table beside him was a plate full of cigarette stubs, some of which had a homemade look. On the floor a near full gin bottle and a cup that seemed to have contained coffee but not at all recently. The room was full mostly of gin and bad air, but there was also a reminiscence of marijuana smoke.

I opened a window and leaned my forehead against the screen to get a little cleaner air into my lungs and looked out into the street. Two kids were wheeling bicycles along the lumberyard fence, stopping from time to time to study the examples of restroom art on the boarding. Nothing else moved in the neighborhood. Not even a dog. Down at the corner was dust in the air as though a car had passed that way.

I went over to the desk. Inside it was the house register, so I leafed back until I came to the name *Orrin P. Quest,* written in a sharp meticulous handwriting, and the number 214 added in pencil by another hand that was by no means sharp or meticulous. I followed on through to the end of the register but found no new registration for room 214. A party named G. W. Hicks had room 215. I shut the register in the desk and crossed to the couch. The man stopped his snoring and bubbling and threw his right arm across his body as if he thought he was making a speech. I leaned down and gripped his nose tight between my first and second fingers and stuffed a handful of his sweater into his mouth. He stopped snoring and jerked his eyes open. They were glazed and bloodshot. He struggled against my hand. When I was sure he was fully awake I let go of him, picked the bottle full of gin off the floor and poured some into a glass that lay on its side near the bottle. I showed the glass to the man.

His hand came out to it with the beautiful anxiety of a mother welcoming a lost child.

I moved it out of his reach and said: "You the manager?"

He licked his lips stickily and said: "Gr-r-r-r."

He made a grab for the glass. I put it on the table in front of him. He grasped it carefully in both hands and poured the gin into his face. Then he laughed heartily and threw the glass at me. I managed to catch it and up-end it on the table again. The man looked me over with a studied but unsuccessful attempt at sternness.

"What gives?" he croaked in an annoyed tone.

"Manager?"

He nodded and almost fell off the couch. "Must be I'm drunky," he said. "Kind of a bit of a little bit drunky."

"You're not bad," I said. "You're still breathing."

He put his feet on the ground and pushed himself upright. He cackled with sudden amusement, took three uneven steps, went down on his hands and knees and tried to bite the leg of a chair.

I pulled him up on his feet again, set him down in the overstuffed chair with the burned arm and poured him another slug of his medicine. He drank it, shuddered violently and all at once his eyes seemed to get sane and cunning. Drunks of his type have a certain balanced moment of reality. You never know when it will come or how long it will last.

"Who the hell are you?" he growled.

"I'm looking for a man named Orrin P. Quest."

"Huh?"

I said it again. He smeared his face with his hands and said tersely: "Moved away."

"Moved away when?"

He waved his hand, almost fell out of his chair and waved it again the other way to restore his balance. "Gimme a drink," he said.

I poured another slug of the gin and held it out of his reach.

"Gimme," the man said urgently. "I'm not happy."

"All I want is the present address of Orrin P. Quest."

"Just think of that," he said wittily, and made a loose pass at the glass I was holding.

I put the glass down on the floor and got one of my business cards out for him. "This might help you to concentrate," I told him.

He peered at the card closely, sneered, bent it in half and bent it again. He held it on the flat of his hand, spit on it, and tossed it over his shoulder.

I handed him the glass of gin. He drank it to my health, nodded solemnly, and threw the glass over his shoulder too. It rolled along the floor and thumped the baseboard. The man stood up with surprising ease, jerked a thumb towards the ceiling, doubled the fingers of his hand under it and made a sharp noise with his tongue and teeth.

"Beat it," he said. "I got friends." He looked at the telephone on the wall and back at me with cunning. "A couple of boys to take care of you," he sneered. I said nothing. "Don't believe me, huh?" he snarled, suddenly angry. I shook my head.

He started for the telephone, clawed the receiver off the hook, and dialed the five digits of a number. I watched him. One-three-five-seven-two.

That took all he had for the time being. He let the receiver fall and bang against the wall and he sat down on the floor beside it. He put it to his ear and growled at the wall: "Lemme talk to the Doc." I listened silently. "Vince! The Doc!" he shouted angrily.

He shook the receiver and threw it away from him. He put his hands down on the floor and started to crawl in a circle. When he saw me he looked surprised and annoyed. He got shakily to his feet again and held his hand out. "Gimme a drink."

I retrieved the fallen glass and milked the gin bottle into it. He accepted it with the dignity of an intoxicated dowager, drank it down with an airy flourish, walked calmly over to the couch and lay down, putting the glass under his head for a pillow. He went to sleep instantly.

I put the telephone receiver back on its hook, glanced out in the kitchen again, felt the man on the couch over and dug some keys out of his pocket. One of them was a passkey. The door to the hall-way had a spring lock and I fixed it so that I could come in again and started up the stairs. I paused on the way to write "Doc — Vince, 13572" on an envelope. Maybe it was a clue.

The house was quite silent as I went on up.

4

THE MANAGER'S MUCH-FILED PASSKEY turned the lock of room 214 without noise. I pushed the door open. The room was not empty. A chunky, strongly built man was bending over a suitcase on the bed, with his back to the door. Shirts and socks and underwear were laid out on the bed cover, and he was packing them leisurely and carefully, whistling between his teeth in a low monotone.

He stiffened as the door hinge creaked. His hand moved fast for the pillow on the bed.

"I beg your pardon," I said. "The manager told me this room was vacant."

He was as bald as a grapefruit. He wore dark gray flannel slacks and transparent plastic suspenders over a blue shirt. His hands came up from the pillow, went to his head, and down again. He turned and he had hair.

It looked as natural as hair ever looked, smooth, brown, not parted. He glared at me from under it.

"You can always try knocking," he said.

He had a thick voice and a broad careful face that had been around.

"Why would I? If the manager said the room was empty?"

He nodded, satisfied. The glare went out of his eyes.

I came further into the room without invitation. An open love-pulp magazine lay face down on the bed near the suitcase. A cigar smoked in a green glass ashtray. The room was careful and orderly, and, for that house, clean.

"He must have thought you had already moved out," I said, trying to look like a well-meaning party with some talent for the truth.

"Have it in half an hour," the man said.

"Okay if I look around?"

He smiled mirthlessly. "Ain't been in town long, have you?"

"Why?"

"New around here, ain't you?"

"Why?"

"Like the house and the neighborhood?"

"Not much," I said. "The room looks all right."

He grinned, showing a porcelain jacket crown that was too white for his other teeth. "How long you been looking?"

"Just started," I said. "Why all the questions?"

"You make me laugh," the man said, not laughing. "You don't look at rooms in this town. You grab them sight unseen. This burg's so jam-packed even now that I could get ten bucks just for telling there's a vacancy here."

"That's too bad," I said. "A man named Orrin P. Quest told me about the room. So there's one sawbuck you don't get to spend."

"That so?" Not a flicker of an eye. Not a movement of a muscle. I might as well have been talking to a turtle. "Don't get tough with me," the man said. "I'm a bad man to get tough with."

He picked his cigar out of the green glass ashtray and blew a little smoke. Through it he gave me the cold gray eye. I got a cigarette out and scratched my chin with it.

"What happens to people that get tough with you?" I asked him. "You make them hold your toupee?"

"You lay off my toupee," he said savagely.

"So sorry," I said.

"There's a 'No Vacancy' sign on the house," the man said. "So what makes you come here and find one?"

"You didn't catch the name," I said. "Orrin P. Quest." I spelled it for him. Even that didn't make him happy. There was a dead-air pause.

He turned abruptly and put a pile of handkerchiefs into his suit-case. I moved a little closer to him. When he turned back there was what might have been a watchful look on his face. But it had been a watchful face to start with.

"Friend of yours?" he asked casually.

"We grew up together," I said.

"Quiet sort of guy," the man said easily. "I used to pass the time of day with him. Works for Cal-Western, don't he?"

"He did," I said.

"Oh. He quit?"

"Let out."

We went on staring at each other. It didn't get either of us any-where. We both had done too much of it in our lives to expect mir-acles.

The man put the cigar back in his face and sat down on the side of the bed beside the open suitcase. Glancing into it I saw the square butt of an automatic peeping out from under a pair of badly folded shorts.

"This Quest party's been out of here ten days," the man said thoughtfully. "So he still thinks the room is vacant, huh?"

"According to the register it *is* vacant," I said.

He made a contemptuous noise. "That rummy downstairs prob-ably ain't looked at the register in a month. Say — wait a minute." His eyes sharpened and his hand wandered idly over the open suit-case and gave an idle pat to something that was close to the gun. When the hand moved away, the gun was no longer visible.

"I've been kind of dreamy all morning or I'd have wised up," he said. "You're a dick."

"All right. Say I'm a dick."

"What's the beef?"

"No beef at all. I just wondered why you had the room."

"I moved from two fifteen across the hall. This here is a better room. That's all. Simple. Satisfied?"

"Perfectly," I said, watching the hand that could be near the gun if it wanted to.

"What kind of dick? City? Let's see the buzzer."

I didn't say anything.

"I don't believe you got no buzzer."

"If I showed it to you, you're the type of guy would say it was counterfeit. So you're Hicks."

He looked surprised.

"George W. Hicks," I said. "It's in the register. Room two fifteen. You just got through telling me you moved from two fifteen." I glanced around the room. "If you had a blackboard here, I'd write it out for you."

"Strictly speaking, we don't have to get into no snarling match," he said. "Sure I'm Hicks. Pleased to meetcha. What's yours?"

He held his hand out. I shook hands with him, but not as if I had been longing for the moment to arrive.

"My name's Marlowe," I said. "Philip Marlowe."

"You know something," Hicks said politely, "you're a goddam liar."

I laughed in his face.

"You ain't getting no place with that breezy manner, bub. What's your connection?"

I got my wallet out and handed him one of my business cards. He read it thoughtfully and tapped the edge against his porcelain crown.

"He coulda went somewhere without telling me," he mused.

"Your grammar," I said, "is almost as loose as your toupee."

"You lay off my toupee, if you know what's good for you," he shouted.

"I wasn't going to eat it," I said. "I'm not that hungry."

He took a step towards me, and dropped his right shoulder. A scowl of fury dropped his lip almost as far.

"Don't hit me. I'm insured," I told him.

"Oh hell. Just another screwball." He shrugged and put his lip back up on his face. "What's the lay?"

"I have to find this Orrin P. Quest," I said.

"Why?"

I didn't answer that.

After a moment he said: "Okay, I'm a careful guy myself. That's why I'm movin' out."

"Maybe you don't like the reefer smoke."

"That," he said emptily, "and other things. That's why Quest left. Respectable type. Like me. I think a couple of hard boys threw a scare into him."

"I see," I said. "That would be why he left no forwarding address. And why did they throw a scare into him?"

"You just mentioned reefer smoke, didn't you? Wouldn't he be the type to go to headquarters about that?"

"In Bay City?" I asked. "Why would he bother? Well, thanks a lot, Mr. Hicks. Going far?"

"Not far," he said. "No. Not very far. Just far enough."

"What's your racket?" I asked him.

"Racket?" He looked hurt.

"Sure. What do you shake them for? How do you make your dibs?"

"You got me wrong, brother. I'm a retired optometrist."

"That why you have the .45 gun in there?" I pointed to the suitcase.

"Nothing to get cute about," he said sourly. "It's been in the family for years." He looked down at the card again. "Private investigator, huh?" he said thoughtfully. "What kind of work do you do mostly?"

"Anything that's reasonably honest," I said.

He nodded. "Reasonably is a word you could stretch. So is honest."

I gave him a shady leer. "You're so right," I agreed. "Let's get together some quiet afternoon and stretch them." I reached out and slipped the card from between his fingers and dropped it into my pocket. "Thanks for the time," I said.

I went out and closed the door, then stood against it listening. I don't know what I expected to hear. Whatever it was I didn't hear it. I had a feeling he was standing exactly where I had left him and looking at the spot where I had made my exit. I made noise going along the hall and stood at the head of the stairs.

A car drove away from in front of the house. Somewhere a door closed. I went quietly back to room 215 and used the passkey to enter. I closed and locked its door silently, and waited just inside.

5

NOT MORE THAN TWO MINUTES PASSED before Mr. George W. Hicks was on his way. He came out so quietly that I wouldn't have heard him if I hadn't been listening for precisely that kind of movement. I heard the slight metallic sound of the doorknob turning. Then slow steps. Then very gently the door was closed. The steps moved off. The faint distant creak of the stairs. Then nothing. I waited for the sound of the front door. It didn't come. I opened the door of 215 and moved along the hall to the stairhead again. Below there was the careful sound of a door being tried. I looked down to see Hicks going into the manager's apartment. The door closed behind him. I waited for the sound of voices. No voices.

I shrugged and went back to 215.

The room showed signs of occupancy. There was a small radio on a night table, an unmade bed with shoes under it, and an old bathrobe hung over the cracked, pull-down green shade to keep the glare out.

I looked at all this as if it meant something, then stepped back into the hall and relocked the door. Then I made another pilgrimage into room 214. Its door was now unlocked. I searched the room with care and patience and found nothing that connected it in any way with Orrin P. Quest. I didn't expect to. There was no reason why I should. But you always have to look.

I went downstairs, listened outside the manager's door, heard nothing, went in and crossed to put the keys on the desk. Lester B. Clausen lay on his side on the couch with his face to the wall, dead to the world. I went through the desk, found an old account book that seemed to be concerned with rent taken in and expenses paid out and nothing else. I looked at the register again. It wasn't up to date but the party on the couch seemed enough explanation for that. Orrin P. Quest had moved away. Somebody had taken over his room. Somebody else had the room registered to Hicks. The little man counting money in the kitchen went nicely with the neighborhood. The fact that he carried a gun and a knife was a social eccentricity that would cause no comment at all on Idaho Street.

I reached the small Bay City telephone book off the hook beside the desk. I didn't think it would be much of a job to sift out the party that went by the name of "Doc" or "Vince" and the phone number one-three-five-seven-two. First of all I leafed back through the register. Something which I ought to have done first. The page with Orrin Quest's registration had been torn out. A careful man, Mr. George W. Hicks. Very careful.

I closed the register, glanced over at Lester B. Clausen again, wrinkled my nose at the stale air and the sickly sweetish smell of gin and of something else, and started back to the entrance door. As I reached it, something for the first time penetrated my mind. A drunk like Clausen ought to be snoring very loudly. He ought to be snoring his head off with a nice assortment of checks and gurgles and snorts. He wasn't making any sound at all. A brown army blanket was pulled up around his shoulders and the lower part of his head. He looked very comfortable, very calm. I stood over him and looked down. Something which was not an accidental fold held the army blanket away from the back of his neck. I moved it. A square yellow wooden handle was attached to the back of Lester B. Clausen's neck. On the side of the yellow handle were printed the words COMPLIMENTS OF THE CRUMSEN HARDWARE COMPANY. The position of the handle was just below the occipital bulge.

It was the handle of an ice pick . . .

I did a nice quiet thirty-five getting away from the neighborhood. On the edge of the city, a frog's jump from the line, I shut myself in an outdoor telephone booth and called the Police Department.

"Bay City Police. Moot talking," a furry voice said.

I said: "Number four forty-nine Idaho Street. In the apartment of the manager. His name's Clausen."

"Yeah?" the voice said. "What do we do?"

"I don't know," I said. "It's a bit of a puzzle to me. But the man's name is Lester B. Clausen. Got that?"

"What makes it important?" the furry voice said without suspicion.

"The coroner will want to know," I said, and hung up.

6

I DROVE BACK TO HOLLYWOOD and locked myself in the office with the Bay City telephone book. It took me a quarter-hour to find out that the party who went with the telephone number one-three-five-seven-two in Bay City was a Dr. Vincent Lagardie, who called himself a neurologist and had his home and offices on Wyoming Street, which according to my map was not quite in the best residential neighborhood and not quite out of it. I locked the Bay City telephone book up in my desk and went down to the corner drugstore for a sandwich and a cup of coffee and used a pay booth to call Dr. Vincent Lagardie. A woman answered and I had some trouble getting through to Dr. Lagardie himself. When I did his voice was impatient. He was very busy, in the middle of an examination he said. I never knew a Doctor who wasn't. Did he know Lester B. Clausen? He never heard of him. What was the purpose of my inquiry?

"Mr. Clausen tried to telephone you this morning," I said. "He was too drunk to talk properly."

"But I don't know Mr. Clausen," the doctor's cool voice answered. He didn't seem to be in quite such a hurry now.

"Well that's all right then," I said. "Just wanted to make sure. Somebody stuck an ice pick into the back of his neck."

There was a quiet pause. Dr. Lagardie's voice was now almost unctuously polite. "Has this been reported to the police?"

"Naturally," I said. "But it shouldn't bother you — unless of course it was your ice pick."

He passed that one up. "And who is this speaking?" he inquired suavely.

"The name is Hicks," I said. "George W. Hicks. I just moved out of there. I don't want to get mixed up with that sort of thing. I just figured when Clausen tried to call you — this was before he was dead, you understand — that you might be interested."

"I'm sorry, Mr. Hicks," Dr. Lagardie's voice said, "but I don't *know* Mr. Clausen. I have never *heard* of Mr. Clausen or had any contact with him whatsoever. And I have an excellent memory for names."

"Well, that's fine," I said. "And you won't meet him now. But somebody *may* want to know why he tried to telephone you — unless I forgot to pass the information along."

There was a dead pause. Dr. Lagardie said: "I can't think of any comment to make on that."

I said: "Neither can I. I may call you again. Don't get me wrong, Dr. Lagardie. This isn't any kind of a shake. I'm just a mixed-up little man who needs a friend. I kind of felt that a doctor — like a clergyman — "

"I'm at your entire disposal," Dr. Lagardie said. "Please feel free to consult me."

"Thank you, Doctor," I said fervently. "Thank you very very much."

I hung up. If Dr. Vincent Lagardie was on the level, he would now telephone the Bay City Police Department and tell them the story. If he didn't telephone the police, he wasn't on the level. Which might or might not be useful to know.

7

THE PHONE ON MY DESK rang at four o'clock sharp.

"Did you find Orrin yet, Mr. Marlowe?"

"Not yet. Where are you?"

"Why I'm in the drugstore next to —"

"Come on up and stop acting like Mata Hari," I said.

"Aren't you ever polite to anybody?" she snapped.

I hung up and fed myself a slug of Old Forester to brace my nerves for the interview. As I was inhaling it I heard her steps tripping along the corridor. I moved across and opened the door.

"Come in this way and miss the crowd," I said.

She seated herself demurely and waited.

"All I could find out," I told her, "is that the dump on Idaho Street is peddling reefers. That's marijuana cigarettes."

"Why, how disgusting," she said.

"We have to take the bad with the good in this life," I said. "Orrin must have got wise and threatened to report it to the police."

"You mean," she said in her little-girl manner, "that they might hurt him for doing that?"

"Well, most likely they'd just throw a scare into him first."

"Oh, they couldn't scare Orrin, Mr. Marlowe," she said decisively. "He just gets mean when people try to run him."

"Yeah," I said. "But we're not talking about the same things. You can scare anybody — with the right technique."

She set her mouth stubbornly. "No, Mr. Marlowe. They couldn't scare Orrin."

"Okay," I said. "So they didn't scare him. Say they just cut off one of his legs and beat him over the head with it. What would he do then — write to the Better Business Bureau?"

"You're making fun of me," she said politely. Her voice was as cool as boarding-house soup. "Is that all you did all day? Just find Orrin had moved and it was a bad neighborhood? Why I found that out for myself, Mr. Marlowe. I thought you being a detective and all —" She trailed off, leaving the rest of it in the air.

"I did a little more than that," I said. "I gave the landlord a little gin and went through the register and talked to a man named Hicks. George W. Hicks. He wears a toupee. I guess maybe you didn't meet him. He has, or had, Orrin's room. So I thought maybe — " It was my turn to do a little trailing in the air.

She fixed me with her pale blue eyes enlarged by the glasses. Her mouth was small and firm and tight, her hands clasped on the desk in front of her over her large square bag, her whole body stiff and erect and formal and disapproving.

"I paid you twenty dollars, Mr. Marlowe," she said coldly. "I understood that was in payment of a day's work. It doesn't seem to me that you've done a day's work."

"No," I said. "That's true. But the day isn't over yet. And don't bother about the twenty bucks. You can have it back if you like. I didn't even bruise it."

I opened the desk drawer and got out her money. I pushed it across the desk. She looked at it but didn't touch it. Her eyes came up slowly to meet mine.

"I didn't mean it like that. I know you're doing the best you can, Mr. Marlowe."

"With the facts I have."

"But I've told you all I know."

"I don't think so," I said.

"Well I'm sure I can't help what you think," she said tartly. "After all, if I knew what I wanted to know already, I wouldn't have come here and asked you to find it out, would I?"

"I'm not saying you know all you want to know," I answered. "The point is I don't know all I want to know in order to do a job for you. And what you tell me doesn't add up."

"What doesn't add up? I've told you the truth. I'm Orrin's sister. I guess I know what kind of person he is."

"How long did he work for Cal-Western?"

"I've told you that. He came out to California just about a year ago. He got work right away because he practically had the job before he left."

"He wrote home how often? Before he stopped writing."

"Every week. Sometimes oftener. He'd take turns writing to Mother and me. Of course the letters were for both of us."

"About what?"

"You mean what did he write about?"

"What did you think I meant?"

"Well, you don't have to snap at me. He wrote about his work nd the plant and the people there and sometimes about a show e'd been to. Or it was about California. He'd write about church oo."

"Nothing about girls?"

"I don't think Orrin cared much for girls."

"And lived at the same address all this time?"

She nodded, looking puzzled.

"And he stopped writing how long ago?"

That took thought. She pressed her lips and pushed a finger tip round the middle of the lower one. "About three or four months," he said at last.

"What was the date of his last letter?"

"I — I'm afraid I can't tell you exactly the date. But it was like said, three or four — "

I waved a hand at her. "Anything out of the ordinary in it? Anyhing unusual said or anything unusual unsaid?"

"Why no. It seemed just like all the rest."

"Don't you have any friends or relatives in this part of the counry?"

She gave me a funny stare, started to say something, then shook er head sharply. "No."

"Okay. Now I'll tell you what's wrong. I'll skip over your not elling me where you're staying, because it might be just that you're fraid I'll show up with a quart of hooch under my arm and make pass at you."

"That's not a very nice way to talk," she said.

"Nothing I say is nice. I'm not nice. By your standards nobody with less than three prayerbooks could be nice. But I *am* inquisiive. What's wrong with this picture is that you're not scared. Neiher you personally nor your mother. And you ought to be scared s hell."

She clutched her bag to her bosom with tight little fingers. "You nean something has happened to him?" Her voice faded off into sort of sad whisper, like a mortician asking for a down payment.

"I don't know that anything has. But in your position, knowing the kind of guy Orrin was, the way his letters came through and then didn't, I can't see myself waiting for my summer vacation to come around before I start asking questions. I can't see myself by-passing the police who have an organization for finding people. And going to a lone-wolf operator you never heard of, asking him to root around for you in the rubble. And I can't see your dear old mother just sitting there in Manhattan, Kansas, week after week darning the minister's winter underwear. No letter from Orrin. No news. And all she does about it is take a long breath and mend up another pair of pants."

She came to her feet with a lunge. "You're a horrid, disgusting person," she said angrily. "I think you're vile. Don't you dare say Mother and I weren't worried. Just don't you dare."

I pushed the twenty dollars' worth of currency a little closer to the other side of the desk. "You were worried twenty dollars' worth, honey," I said. "But about what I wouldn't know. I guess I don't really want to know. Just put this hunk of the folding back in your saddlebag and forget you ever met me. You might want to lend it to another detective tomorrow."

She snapped her bag shut viciously on the money. "I'm not very likely to forget your rudeness," she said between her teeth. "Nobody in the world's ever talked to me the way you have."

I stood up and wandered around the end of the desk. "Don't think about it too much. You might get to like it."

I reached up and twitched her glasses off. She took half a step back, almost stumbled, and I reached an arm around her by pure instinct. Her eyes widened and she put her hands against my chest and pushed. I've been pushed harder by a kitten.

"Without the cheaters those eyes are really something," I said in an awed voice.

She relaxed and let her head go back and her lips open a little. "I suppose you do this to all the clients," she said softly. Her hands now had dropped to her sides. The bag whacked against my leg. She leaned her weight on my arm. If she wanted me to let go of her, she had her signals mixed.

"I just didn't want you to lose your balance," I said.

"I knew you were the thoughtful type." She relaxed still more. Her head went back now. Her upper lids drooped, fluttered a bit and her lips came open a little farther. On them appeared the faint provocative smile that nobody ever has to teach them. "I suppose you thought I did it on purpose," she said.

"Did what on purpose?"

"Stumbled, sort of."

"Wel-l-l-l."

She reached a quick arm around my neck and started to pull. So I kissed her. It was either that or slug her. She pushed her mouth hard at me for a long moment, then quietly and very comfortably wriggled around in my arms and nestled. She let out a long easy sigh.

"In Manhattan, Kansas, you could be arrested for this," she said.

"If there was any justice, I could be arrested just for being there," I said.

She giggled and poked the end of my nose with a finger tip. "I suppose you really prefer fast girls," she said, looking up at me sideways. "At least you won't have to wipe off any lip rouge. Maybe I'll wear some next time."

"Maybe we'd better sit down on the floor," I said. "My arm's getting tired."

She giggled again and disengaged herself gracefully. "I guess you think I've been kissed lots of times," she said.

"What girl hasn't?"

She nodded, gave me the up-from-under look that made her eyelashes cut across the iris. "Even at the church socials they play kissing games," she said.

"Or there wouldn't be any church socials," I said.

We looked at each other with no particular expression.

"Well-l-l —" she began at last. I handed her back her glasses. She put them on. She opened her bag, looked at herself in a small mirror, rooted around in her bag and came out with her hand clenched.

"I'm sorry I was mean," she said, and pushed something under the blotter of my desk. She gave me another little frail smile and marched to the door and opened it.

"I'll call you," she said intimately. And out she went, tap, tap, tap down the hall.

I went over and lifted the blotter and smoothed out the crumpled currency that lay under it. It hadn't been much of a kiss, but it looked like I had another chance at the twenty dollars.

The phone rang before I had quite started to worry about Mr. Lester B. Clausen. I reached for it absently. The voice I heard was an abrupt voice, but thick and clogged, as if it was being strained through a curtain or somebody's long white beard.

"You Marlowe?" it said.

"Speaking."

"You got a safe-deposit box, Marlowe?"

I had enough of being polite for one afternoon. "Stop asking and start telling," I said.

"I asked you a question, Marlowe."

"I didn't answer it," I said. "Like this." I reached over and pressed down the riser on the phone. Held it that way while I fumbled around for a cigarette. I knew he would call right back. They always do when they think they're tough. They haven't used their exit line. When it rang I started right in.

"If you have a proposition, state it. And I get called 'mister' until you give me some money."

"Don't let that temper ride you so hard, friend. I'm in a jam. I need help. I need something kept in a safe place. For a few days. Not longer. And for that you make a little quick money."

"How little?" I asked. "And how quick?"

"A C note. Right here and waiting. I'm warming it for you."

"I can hear it purr," I said. "Right where and waiting?" I was listening to the voice twice, once when I heard it and once when it echoed in my mind.

"Room three thirty-two, Van Nuys Hotel. Knock two quick ones and two slow ones. Not too loud. I got to have live action. How fast can you —"

"What is it you want me to keep?"

"That'll wait till you get here. I said I was in a hurry."

"What's your name?"

"Just room three thirty-two."

"Thanks for the time," I said. "Goodbye."

"Hey. Wait a minute, dope. It's nothing hot like you think. No ice. No emerald pendants. It just happens to be worth a lot of money to me — and nothing at all to anybody else."

"The hotel has a safe."

"Do you want to die poor, Marlowe?"

"Why not? Rockefeller did. Goodbye again."

The voice changed. The furriness went out of it. It said sharply and swiftly: "How's every little thing in Bay City?"

I didn't speak. Just waited. There was a dim chuckle over the wire. "Thought that might interest you, Marlowe. Room three thirty-two it is. Tramp on it, friend. Make speed."

The phone clicked in my ear. I hung up. For no reason a pencil rolled off the desk and broke its point on the glass doohickey under one of the desk legs. I picked it up and slowly and carefully sharpened it in the Boston sharpener screwed to the edge of the window frame, turning the pencil around to get it nice and even. I laid it down in the tray on the desk and dusted off my hands. I had all the time in the world. I looked out of the window. I didn't see anything. I didn't hear anything.

And then, for even less reason, I saw Orfamay Quest's face without the glasses, and polished and painted and with blond hair piled high on the forehead with a braid around the middle of it. And bedroom eyes. They all have to have bedroom eyes. I tried to imagine this face in a vast close-up being gnawed by some virile character from the wide-open spaces of Romanoff's bar.

It took me twenty-nine minutes to get to the Van Nuys Hotel.

8

ONCE, LONG AGO, it must have had a certain elegance. But no more. The memories of old cigars clung to its lobby like the dirty gilt on its ceiling and the sagging springs of its leather lounging chairs. The marble of the desk had turned a yellowish brown with age. But the floor carpet was new and had a hard look, like the room clerk. I passed him up and strolled over to the cigar counter in the corner and put down a quarter for a package of Camels. The girl behind the counter was a straw blonde with a long neck and tired eyes. She put the cigarettes in front of me, added a packet of matches, dropped my change into a slotted box market THE COMMUNITY CHEST THANKS YOU.

"You'd want me to do that, wouldn't you," she said, smiling patiently. "You'd want to give your change to the poor little underprivileged kids with bent legs and stuff, wouldn't you?"

"Suppose I didn't," I said.

"I dig up seven cents," the girl said, "and it would be very painful." She had a low lingering voice with a sort of moist caress in it like a damp bath towel. I put a quarter after the seven cents. She gave me her big smile then. It showed more of her tonsils.

"You're nice," she said. "I can see you're nice. A lot of fellows would have come in here and made a pass at a girl. Just think. Over seven cents. A pass."

"Who's the house peeper here now?" I asked her, without taking up the option.

"There's two of them." She did something slow and elegant to the back of her head, exhibiting what seemed like more than one handful of blood-red fingernails in the process. "Mr. Hady is on nights and Mr. Flack is on days. It's day now so it would be Mr. Flack would be on."

"Where could I find him?"

She leaned over the counter and let me smell her hair, pointing with a half-inch fingernail towards the elevator bank. "It's down along that corridor there, next to the porter's room. You can't miss the porter's room on account of it has a half-door and says PORTER on the upper part in gold letters. Only that half is folded back like, so I guess maybe you can't see it."

"I'll see it," I said. "Even if I have to get a hinge screwed to my neck. What does this Flack look like?"

"Well," she said, "he's a little squatty number, with a bit of a mustache. A sort of chunky type. Thick-set like, only not tall." Her fingers moved languidly along the counter to where I could have touched them without jumping. "He's not interesting," she said. "Why bother?"

"Business," I said, and made off before she threw a half-nelson on me.

I looked back at her from the elevators. She was staring after me with an expression she probably would have said was thoughtful.

The porter's room was halfway down the corridor to the Spring Street entrance. The door beyond it was half-open. I looked around its edge, then went in and closed it behind me.

A man was sitting at a small desk which had dust on it, a very large ashtray and very little else. He was short and thick-set. He had something dark and bristly under his nose about an inch long. I sat down across from him and put a card on the desk.

He reached for the card without excitement, read it, turned it over and read the back with as much care as the front. There was nothing on the back to read. He picked half of a cigar out of his ashtray and burned his nose lighting it.

"What's the gripe?" he growled at me.

"No gripe. You Flack?"

He didn't bother to answer. He gave me a steady look which may or may not have concealed his thoughts, depending on whether he had any to conceal.

"Like to get a line on one of the customers," I said.

"What name?" Flack asked, with no enthusiasm.

"I don't know what name he's using here. He's in room three thirty-two."

"What name was he using before he came here?" Flack asked.

"I don't know that either."

"Well, what did he look like?" Flack was suspicious now. He reread my card but it added nothing to his knowledge.

"I never saw him, so far as I know."

Flack said: "I must be overworked. I don't get it."

"I had a call from him," I said. "He wanted to see me."

"Am I stopping you?"

"Look, Flack. A man in my business makes enemies at times. You ought to know that. This party wants something done. Tells me to come on over, forgets to give his name, and hangs up. I figured I'd do a little checking before I went up there."

Flack took the cigar out of his mouth and said patiently: "I'm in terrible shape. I still don't get it. Nothing makes sense to me any more."

I leaned over the desk and spoke to him slowly and distinctly: "The whole thing could be a nice way to get me into a hotel room and knock me off and then quietly check out. You wouldn't want anything like that to happen in your hotel, would you, Flack?"

"Supposing I cared," he said, "you figure you're that important?"

"Do you smoke that piece of rope because you like it or because you think it makes you look tough?"

"For forty-five bucks a week," Flack said, "would I smoke anything better?" He eyed me steadily.

"No expense account yet," I told him. "No deal yet."

He made a sad sound and got up wearily and went out of the room. I lit one of my cigarettes and waited. He came back in a short time and dropped a registration card on the desk. *Dr. G. W. Hambleton, El Centro, California* was written on it in a firm round hand in ink. The clerk had written other things on it, including the room number and daily rate. Flack pointed a finger that needed a manicure or failing that a nailbrush.

"Came in at two forty-seven P.M.," he said. "Just today, that is. Nothing on his bill. One day's rent. No phone calls. No nothing. That what you want?"

"What does he look like?" I asked.

"I didn't see him. You think I stand out there by the desk and take pictures of them while they register?"

"Thanks," I said. "Dr. G. W. Hambleton, El Centro. Much obliged." I handed him back the registration card.

"Anything I ought to know," Flack said as I went out, "don't forget where I live. That is, if you call it living."

I nodded and went out. There are days like that. Everybody you meet is a dope. You begin to look at yourself in the glass and wonder.

9

ROOM 332 WAS AT THE BACK of the building near the door to the fire escape. The corridor which led to it had a smell of old carpet and furniture oil and the drab anonymity of a thousand shabby lives. The sand bucket under the racked fire hose was full of cigarette and cigar stubs, an accumulation of several days. A radio pounded brassy music through an open transom. Through another transom people were laughing fit to kill themselves. Down at the end by room 332 it was quieter.

I knocked the two longs and two shorts as instructed. Nothing happened. I felt jaded and old. I felt as if I had spent my life knocking at doors in cheap hotels that nobody bothered to open. I tried again. Then turned the knob and walked in. A key with a red fiber tag hung in the inside keyhole.

There was a short hall with a bathroom on the right. Beyond the hall the upper half of a bed was in view and a man lay on it in shirt and pants.

I said: "Dr. Hambleton?"

The man didn't answer. I went past the bathroom door towards him. A whiff of perfume reached me and I started to turn, but not quickly enough. A woman who had been in the bathroom was standing there holding a towel in front of the lower part of her face. Dark glasses showed above the towel. And then the brim of a wide-brimmed straw hat in a sort of dusty delphinium blue. Under that was fluffed-out pale blond hair. Blue ear buttons lurked somewhere back in the shadows. The sunglasses were in white frames with broad flat sidebows. Her dress matched her hat. An embroidered silk or rayon coat was open over the dress. She wore gauntleted gloves and there was an automatic in her right hand. White bone grip. Looked like a .32.

"Turn around and put your hands behind you," she said through the towel. The voice muffled by the towel meant as little to me as the dark glasses. It was not the voice which had talked to me on the telephone. I didn't move.

"Don't ever think I'm fooling," she said. "I'll give you exactly three seconds to do what I say."

"Couldn't you make it a minute? I like looking at you."

She made a threatening gesture with the little gun. "Turn around," she snapped. "But fast."

"I like the sound of your voice too."

"All right," she said, in a tight dangerous tone. "If that's the way you want it, that's the way you want it."

"Don't forget you're a lady," I said, and turned around and put my hands up to my shoulders. A gun muzzle poked into the back of my neck. Breath almost tickled my skin. The perfume was an elegant something or other, not strong, not decisive. The gun against my neck went away and a white flame burned for an instant behind my eyes. I grunted and fell forward on my hands and knees and reached back quickly. My hand touched a leg in a nylon stocking but slipped off, which seemed a pity. It felt like a nice leg. The jar of another blow on the head took the pleasure out of this and I made the hoarse sound of a man in desperate shape. I collapsed on the floor. The door opened. A key rattled. The door closed. The key turned. Silence.

I climbed up to my feet and went into the bathroom. I bathed my head with a towel from the rack soaked with cold water. It felt as if the heel of a shoe had hit me. Certainly it was not a gun butt. There was a little blood, not much. I rinsed the towel out and stood there patting the bruise and wondering why I didn't run after her screaming. But what I was doing was staring into the open medicine cabinet over the basin. The upper part of a can of talcum had been pried off the shoulder. There was talcum all over the shelf. A toothpaste tube had been cut open. Someone had been looking for something.

I went back to the little hallway and tried the room door. Locked from the outside. I bent down and looked through the keyhole. But it was an up-and-down lock, with the outer and inner keyholes on different levels. The girl in the dark glasses with the white rims didn't know much about hotels. I twisted the night latch, which opened the outside lock, opened the door, looked along the empty corridor, and closed the door again.

Then I went towards the man on the bed. He had not moved during all this time, for a somewhat obvious reason.

Beyond the little hallway the room widened towards a pair of windows through which the evening sun slanted in a shaft that reached almost across the bed and came to a stop under the neck of the man that lay there. What it stopped on was blue and white and shining and round. He lay quite comfortably half on his face with his hands down at his sides and his shoes off. The side of his face was on the pillow and he seemed relaxed. He was wearing a toupee. The last time I talked to him his name had been George W. Hicks. Now it was Dr. G. W. Hambleton. Same initials. Not that it mattered any more. I wasn't going to be talking to him again. There was no blood. None at all, which is one of the few nice things about an expert ice-pick job.

I touched his neck. It was still warm. While I was doing it the shaft of sunlight moved away from the knob of the ice pick towards his left ear. I turned away and looked the room over. The telephone bell box had been opened and left open. The Gideon Bible was thrown in the corner. The desk had been searched. I went to a closet and looked into that. There were clothes in it and a suit-case I had seen before. I found nothing that seemed important. I picked a snap-brim hat off the floor and put it on the desk and went back to the bathroom. The point of interest now was whether the people who had ice-picked Dr. Hambleton had found what they came for. They had had very little time.

I searched the bathroom carefully. I moved the top of the toilet tank and drained it. There was nothing in it. I peered down the overflow pipe. No thread hung there with a small object at the end of it. I searched the bureau. It was empty except for an old envelope. I unhooked the window screens and felt under the sills outside. I picked the Gideon Bible off the floor and leafed through it again.

I examined the backs of three pictures and studied the edge of the carpet. It was tacked close to the wall and there were little pockets of dust in the depressions made by the tacks. I got down on the floor and examined the part under the bed. Just the same. I stood on a chair, looked into the bowl of the light fixture. It contained dust and dead moths. I looked the bed over. It had been made up by a professional and not touched since. I felt the pillow under the dead man's head, then got the extra pillow out of the closet and examined its edges. Nothing.

Dr. Hambleton's coat hung over a chair back. I went through that, knowing it was the least likely place to find anything. Somebody with a knife had worked on the lining and the shoulder padding. There were matches, a couple of cigars, a pair of dark glasses, a cheap handkerchief not used, a Bay City movie theater ticket stub, a small comb, an unopened package of cigarettes. I looked at it in the light. It showed no sign of having been disturbed. I disturbed it. I tore off the cover, went through it, found nothing but cigarettes.

That left Dr. Hambleton himself. I eased him over and got into his trouser pockets. Loose change, another handkerchief, a small tube of dental floss, more matches, a bunch of keys, a folder of bus schedules. In a pigskin wallet was a book of stamps, a second comb (here was a man who really took care of his toupee), three flat packages of white powder, seven printed cards reading *Dr. G. W. Hambleton, O. D. Tustin Building, El Centro, California, Hours 9–12 and 2–4, and by appointment. Telephone El Centro 5–0406.* There was no driver's license, no social-security card, no insurance cards, no real identification at all. There was $164 in currency in the wallet. I put the wallet back where I found it.

I lifted Dr. Hambleton's hat off the desk and examined the sweatband and the ribbon. The ribbon bow had been picked loose with a knife point, leaving hanging threads. There was nothing hidden inside the bow. No evidence of any previous ripping and restitching.

This was the take. If the killers knew what they were looking for, it was something that could be hidden in a book, a telephone box, a tube of toothpaste, or a hatband. I went back into the bathroom and looked at my head again. It was still oozing a tiny trickle of blood. I gave it more cold water and dried the cut with toilet paper and flushed that down the bowl. I went back and stood a moment looking down on Dr. Hambleton, wondering what his mistake had been. He had seemed a fairly wise bird. The sunlight had moved over to the far edge of the room now, off the bed and down into a sad dusty corner.

I grinned suddenly, bent over and quickly and with the grin still on my face, out of place as it was, pulled off Dr. Hambleton's toupee and turned it inside out. As simple as all that. To the lining of the toupee a piece of orange-colored paper was fastened by Scotch tape, protected by a square of cellophane. I pulled it loose, turned it over, and saw that it was a numbered claim check belonging to the Bay City Camera Shop. I put it in my wallet and put the toupee carefully back on the dead egg-bald head.

I left the room unlocked because I had no way to lock it.

Down the hall the radio still blared through the transom and the exaggerated alcoholic laughter accompanied it from across the corridor.

10

OVER THE TELEPHONE the Bay City Camera Shop man said: "Yes, Mr. Hicks. We have them for you. Six enlarged prints on glossy from your negative."

"What time do you close?" I asked.

"Oh, in about five minutes. We open at nine in the morning."

"I'll pick them up in the morning. Thanks."

I hung up, reached mechanically into the slot and found somebody's else's nickel. I walked over to the lunch counter and bought myself a cup of coffee with it, and sat there sipping and listening to the auto horns complaining on the street outside. It was time to go home. Whistles blew. Motors raced. Old brake linings squeaked.

There was a dull steady mutter of feet on the sidewalk outside. It was just after five-thirty. I finished the coffee, stuffed a pipe, and strolled a half-block back to the Van Nuys Hotel. In the writing room I folded the orange camera-shop check into a sheet of hotel stationery and addressed an envelope to myself. I put a special-delivery stamp on it and dropped it in the mail chute by the elevator bank. Then I went along to Flack's office again.

Again I closed his door and sat down across from him. Flack didn't seem to have moved an inch. He was chewing morosely on the same cigar butt and his eyes were still full of nothing. I relit my pipe by striking a match on the side of his desk. He frowned.

"Dr. Hambleton doesn't answer his door," I said.

"Huh?" Flack looked at me vacantly.

"Party in three thirty-two. Remember? He doesn't answer his door."

"What should I do — bust my girdle?" Flack asked.

"I knocked several times," I said. "No answer. Thought he might be taking a bath or something, although I couldn't hear anything. Went away for a while, then tried again. Same no answer again."

Flack looked at a turnip watch he got from his vest. "I'm off at seven," he said. "Jesus. A whole hour to go, and more. Boy, am I hungry."

"Working the way you do," I said, "you must be. You have to keep your strength up. Do I interest you at all in room three thirty-two?"

"You said he wasn't in," Flack said irritably. "So what? He wasn't in."

"I didn't say he wasn't in. I said he didn't answer his door."

Flack leaned forward. Very slowly he removed the débris of the cigar from his mouth and put it in the glass tray. "Go on. Make me like it," he said carefully.

"Maybe you'd like to run up and look," I said. "Maybe you didn't see a first-class ice-pick job lately."

Flack put his hands on the arms of his chair and squeezed the wood hard. "Aw," he said painfully, "aw." He got to his feet and opened the desk drawer. He took out a large black gun, flicked the gate open, studied the cartridges, squinted down the barrel, snapped the cylinder back into place. He unbuttoned his vest and tucked the gun down inside his waistband. In an emergency he could probably have got to it in less than a minute. He put his hat on firmly and jerked a thumb at the door.

We went up to the third floor in silence. We went down the corridor. Nothing had changed. No sound had increased or diminished. Flack hurried along to 332 and knocked from force of habit. Then tried the door. He looked back at me with a twisted mouth.

"You said the door wasn't locked," he complained.

"I didn't exactly say that. It *was* unlocked, though."

"It ain't now," Flack said, and unshipped a key on a long chain. He unlocked the door and glanced up and down the hall. He twisted the knob slowly without sound and eased the door a couple of times. He listened. No sounds came from within. Flack stepped back, took the black gun out of his waistband. He removed the key from the door, kicked it wide open, and brought the gun up hard and straight, like the wicked foreman of the Lazy Q. "Let's go," he said out of the corner of his mouth.

Over his shoulder I could see that Dr. Hambleton lay exactly as before, but the ice-pick handle didn't show from the entrance. Flack leaned forward and edged cautiously into the room. He reached the bathroom door and put his eye to the crack, then pushed the door open until it bounced against the tub. He went in and came out, stepped down into the room, a tense and wary man who was taking no chances.

He tried the closet door, leveled his gun and jerked it wide open. No suspects in the closet.

"Look under the bed," I said.

Flack bent swiftly and looked under the bed.

"Look under the carpet," I said.

"You kidding me?" Flack asked nastily.

"I just like to watch you work."

He bent over the dead man and studied the ice pick.

"Somebody locked that door," he sneered. "Unless you're lying about it's being unlocked."

I said nothing.

"Well I guess it's the cops," he said slowly. "No chance to cover up on this one."

"It's not your fault," I told him. "It happens even in good hotels."

11

THE RED-HEADED INTERN filled out a DOA form and clipped his stylus to the outside pocket of his white jacket. He snapped the book shut with a faint grin on his face.

"Punctured spinal cord just below the occipital bulge, I'd say," he said carelessly. "A very vulnerable spot. If you know how to find it. And I suppose you do."

Detective Lieutenant Christy French growled. "Think it's the first time I've seen one?"

"No, I guess not," the intern said. He gave a last quick look at the dead man, turned and walked out of the room. "I'll call the coroner," he said over his shoulder. The door closed behind him.

"What a stiff means to those birds is what a plate of wormed-up cabbage means to me," Christy French said sourly to the closed door. His partner, a cop named Fred Beifus, was down on one knee by the telephone box. He had dusted it for fingerprints and blown off the loose powder. He was looking at the smudge through a small magnifiying glass. He shook his head, then picked something off the screw with which the box had been fastened shut.

"Gray cotton undertaker's gloves," he said disgustedly. "Cost about four cents a pair wholesale. Fat lot of good printing this joint. They were looking for something in the telephone box, huh?"

"Evidently something that could be there," French said. "I didn't expect prints. These ice-pick jobs are a specialty. We'll get the experts after a while. This is just a quick-over."

He was stripping the dead man's pockets and laying what had been in them out on the bed beside the quiet and already waxy corpse. Flack was sitting in a chair by the window, looking out morosely. The assistant manager had been up, said nothing with a worried expression, and gone away. I was leaning against the bathroom wall and sorting out my fingers.

Flack said suddenly: "I figure an ice-pick job's a dame's work. You can buy them anywhere. Ten cents. If you want one fast, you can slip it down inside a garter and let it hang there."

Christy French gave him a brief glance which had a kind of wonder in it. Beifus said: "What kind of dames you been running around with, honey? The way stockings cost nowadays a dame would as soon stick a saw down her sock."

"I never thought of that," Flack said.

Beifus said: "Leave us do the thinking, sweetheart. It takes equipment."

"No need to get tough," Flack said.

Beifus took his hat off and bowed. "You mustn't deny us our little pleasures, Mr. Flack."

Christy French said: "Besides, a woman would keep on jabbing. She wouldn't even know how much was enough. Lots of the punks don't. Whoever did this one was a performer. He got the spinal cord the first try. And another thing — you have to have the guy quiet to do it. That means more than one guy, unless he was doped, or the killer was a friend of his."

I said: "I don't see how he could have been doped, if he's the party that called me on the phone."

French and Beifus both looked at me with the same expression of patient boredom. "If," French said, "and since you didn't know the guy — according to you — there's always the faint possibility that you wouldn't know his voice. Or am I being too subtle?"

"I don't know," I said. "I haven't read your fan mail."

French grinned.

"Don't waste it on him," Beifus told French. "Save it for when you talk to the Friday Morning Club. Some of them old ladies in the shiny-nose league go big for the nicer angles of murder."

French rolled himself a cigarette and lit it with a kitchen match he struck on the back of a chair. He sighed.

"They worked the technique out in Brooklyn," he explained. "Sunny Moe Stein's boys specialized in it, but they run it into the ground. It got so you couldn't walk across a vacant lot without finding some of their work. Then they came out here, what was left of them. I wonder why did they do that."

"Maybe we just got more vacant lots," Beifus said.

"Funny thing, though," French said, almost dreamily. "When Weepy Moyer had the chill put on Sunny Moe Stein over on Franklin Avenue last February, the killer used a gun. Moe wouldn't have liked that at all."

"I betcha that was why his face had that disappointed look, after they washed the blood off," Beifus remarked.

"Who's Weepy Moyer?" Flack asked.

"He was next to Moe in the organization," French told him. "This could easily be his work. Not that he'd have done it personal."

"Why not?" Flack asked sourly.

"Don't you guys ever read a paper? Moyer's a gentleman now. He knows the nicest people. Even has another name. And as for the Sunny Moe Stein job, it just happened we had him in jail on a gambling rap. We didn't get anywhere. But we did make him a very sweet alibi. Anyhow he's a gentleman, like I said, and gentlemen don't go around sticking ice picks into people. They hire it done."

"Did you ever have anything on Moyer?" I asked.

French looked at me sharply. "Why?"

"I just had an idea. But it's very fragile," I said.

French eyed me slowly. "Just between us girls in the powder room," he said, "we never even proved the guy we had *was* Moyer. But don't broadcast it. Nobody's supposed to know but him and his lawyer and the D.A. and the police beat and the City Hall and maybe two or three hundred other people."

He slapped the dead man's empty wallet against his thigh and sat down on the bed. He leaned casually against the corpse's leg, lit a cigarette and pointed with it.

"That's enough time on the vaudeville circuit. Here's what we got, Fred. First off, the customer here was not too bright. He was going by the name of Dr. G. W. Hambleton and had the cards printed with an El Centro address and a phone number. It took just two minutes to find out there ain't any such address or any such phone number. A bright boy doesn't lay open that easy. Next, the guy is definitely not in the chips. He has fourteen smackeroos folding in here and about two bucks loose change. On his key ring he don't have any car key or any safe-deposit key or any house key. All he's got is a suitcase key and seven filed Yale master keys. Filed fairly recently at that. I figure he was planning to sneak the hotel a little. Do you think these keys would work in your dump, Flack?"

Flack went over and stared at the keys. "Two of them are the right size," he said. "I couldn't tell if they'd work by just looking. If I want a master key I have to get it from the office. All I carry is a passkey. I can only use that if the guest is out." He took a key out of his pocket, a key on a long chain, and compared it. He shook his head. "They're no good without more work," he said. "Far too much metal on them."

French flicked ash into the palm of his hand and blew it off as dust. Flack went back to his chair by the window.

"Next point," Christy French announced. "He don't have a driver's license or any identification. None of his outside clothes were bought in El Centro. He had some kind of a grift, but he don't have the looks or personality to bounce checks."

"You didn't really see him at his best," Beifus put in.

"And this hotel is the wrong dump for that anyway," French went on. "It's got a crummy reputation."

"Now wait a minute!" Flack began.

French cut him short with a gesture. "I know every hotel in the metropolitan district, Flack. It's my business to know. For fifty bucks I could organize a double-strip act with French trimmings inside of an hour in any room in this hotel. Don't kid me. You earn your living and I'll earn mine. Just don't kid me. All right. The customer had something he was afraid to keep around. That means he knew somebody was after him and getting close. So he offers Marlowe a hundred bucks to keep it for him. But he doesn't have that much money on him. So what he must have been planning on was getting Marlowe to gamble with him. It couldn't have been hot jewelry then. It had to be something semi-legitimate. That right, Marlowe?"

"You could leave out the semi," I said.

French grinned faintly. "So what he had was something that could be kept flat or rolled up — in a phone box, a hatband, a Bible, a can of talcum. We don't know whether it was found or not. But we do know there was very little time. Not much more than half an hour."

"If Dr. Hambleton did the phoning," I said. "You opened that can of beans yourself."

"It's kind of pointless any other way. The killers wouldn't be in a hurry to have him found. Why should they ask anybody to come over to his room?" He turned to Flack. "Any chance to check his visitors?"

Flack shook his head gloomily. "You don't even have to pass the desk to get to the elevators."

Beifus said: "Maybe that was one reason he came here. That, and the homey atmosphere."

"All right," French said. "Whoever knocked him off could come and go without any questions asked. All he had to know was his room number. And that's about all we know. Okay, Fred?"

Beifus nodded.

I said: "Not quite all. It's a nice toupee, but it's still a toupee."

French and Beifus both swung around quickly. French reached, carefully removed the dead man's hair, and whistled. "I wondered what that damn intern was grinning at," he said. "The bastard didn't even mention it. See what I see, Fred?"

"All I see is a guy without no hair," Beifus answered.

"Maybe you never knew him at that. Mileaway Marston. Used to be a runner for Ace Devore."

"Why sure enough." Beifus chuckled. He leaned over and patted the dead bald head gently. "How you been all this time, Mileaway? I didn't see you in so long I forgot. But you know me, pal. Once a softy always a softy."

The man on the bed looked old and hard and shrunken without his toupee. The yellow mask of death was beginning to set his face into rigid lines.

French said calmly: "Well, that takes a load off my mind. This punk ain't going to be no twenty-four-hour-a-day job. The hell with him." He replaced the toupee over one eye and stood up off the bed. "That's all for you two," he said to Flack and me.

Flack stood up.

"Thanks for the murder, honey," Beifus told him. "You get any more in your nice hotel, don't forget our service. Even when it ain't good, it's quick."

Flack went down the short hall and yanked the door open. I followed him out. On the way to the elevator we didn't speak. Nor on the way down. I walked with him along to his little office, followed him in and shut the door. He seemed surprised.

He sat down at his desk and reached for his telephone. "I got to make a report to the assistant manager," he said. "Something you want?"

I rolled a cigarette around on my fingers, put a match to it and blew smoke softly across the desk. "One hundred and fifty dollars," I said.

Flack's small, intent eyes became round holes in a face washed clean of expression. "Don't get funny in the wrong place," he said.

"After those two comedians upstairs, you could hardly blame me if I did. But I'm not being funny." I beat a tattoo on the edge of the desk and waited.

Tiny beads of sweat showed on Flack's lip above his little mustache. "I got business to attend to," he said, more throatily this time. "Beat it and keep going."

"Such a tough little man," I said. "Dr. Hambleton had $164 currency in his wallet when I searched him. He promised me a hundred as retainer, remember? Now, in the same wallet, he has fourteen dollars. And I *did* leave the door of his room unlocked. And somebody else locked it. You locked it, Flack."

Flack took hold of the arms of his chair and squeezed. His voice came from the bottom of a well saying: "You can't prove a damn thing."

"Do I have to try?"

He took the gun out of his waistband and laid it on the desk in front of him. He stared down at it. It didn't have any message for him. He looked up at me again. "Fifty-fifty, huh?" he said brokenly.

There was a moment of silence between us. He got his old shabby wallet out and rooted in it. He came up with a handful of currency and spread bills out on the desk, sorted them into two piles and pushed one pile my way.

I said: "I want the whole hundred and fifty."

He hunched down in his chair and stared at a corner of the desk. After a long time, he sighed. He put the two piles together and pushed them over — to my side of the desk.

"It wasn't doing him any good," Flack said. "Take the dough and breeze. I'll remember you, buddy. All you guys make me sick to my stomach. How do I know you didn't take half a grand off him."

"I'd take it all. So would the killer. Why leave fourteen dollars?"

"So why did I leave fourteen dollars?" Flack asked, in a tired voice, making vague movements along the desk edge with his fingers. I picked up the money, counted it and threw it back at him.

"Because you're in the business and could size him up. You knew he'd at least have room rent, and a few dollars for loose change. The cops would expect the same thing. Here, I don't want the money. I want something else."

He stared at me with his mouth open.

"Put that dough out of sight," I said.

He reached for it and crammed it back in his wallet. "What something else?" His eyes were small and thoughtful. His tongue pushed out his lower lip. "It don't seem to me *you're* in a very hot trading position either."

"You could be a little wrong about that. If I have to go back up there and tell Christy French and Beifus I was up there before and searched the body, I'd get a tongue-lashing all right. But he'd understand that I haven't been holding out just to be smart. He'd know somewhere in the background I had a client I was trying to protect. I'd get tough talk and bluster. But that's not what *you'd* get." I stopped and watched the faint glisten of moisture forming on his forehead now. He swallowed hard. His eyes were sick.

"Cut out the wise talk and lay your deal on the deck," he said. He grinned suddenly, rather wolfishly. "Got here a little late to protect her, didn't you?" The fat sneer he lived with was coming home again, but slowly, but gladly.

I killed my cigarette and got another one out and went through all the slow futile face-saving motions of lighting it, getting rid of the match, blowing smoke off to one side, inhaling deeply as though that scrubby little office was a hilltop overlooking the bouncing ocean — all the tired clichéd mannerisms of my trade.

"All right," I said. "I'll admit it was a woman. I'll admit she must have been up there while he was dead, if that makes you happy. I guess it was just shock that made her run away."

"Oh sure," Flack said nastily. The fat sneer was all the way home now. "Or maybe she hadn't ice-picked a guy in a month. Kind of lost touch."

"But why would she take his key?" I said, talking to myself. "And why leave it at the desk? Why not just walk away and leave the whole thing? What if she did think she had to lock the door? Why not drop the key in a sand jar and cover it up? Or take it away with her and lose it? Why do anything with that key that would connect her with that room?" I brought my eyes down and gave Flack a thick leaden stare. "Unless of course she was seen to leave the room — with the key in her hand — and followed out of the hotel."

"What for would anybody do that?" Flack asked.

"Because whoever saw her could have got into that room at once. He had a passkey."

Flack's eyes flicked up at me and dropped all in one motion.

"So he must have followed her," I said. "He must have seen her dump the key at the desk and stroll out of the hotel and he must have followed her a little further than that."

Flack said derisively: "What makes you so wonderful?"

I leaned down and pulled the telephone towards me. "I'd better call Christy and get this over with," I said. "The more I think about it the scareder I get. Maybe she did kill him. I can't cover up for a murderer."

I took the receiver off the hook. Flack slammed his moist paw down hard on top of my hand. The phone jumped on the desk. "Lay off." His voice was almost a sob. "I followed her to a car parked down the street. Got the number. Crissake, pal, give me some kind of a break." He was fumbling wildly in his pockets. "Know what I make on this job? Cigarette and cigar money and hardly a dime more. Wait a minute now. I think — " He looked down and played solitaire with some dirty envelopes, finally selected one and tossed it over to me. "License number," he said wearily, "and if it's any satisfaction to you, I can't even remember what it was."

I looked down at the envelope. There was a scrawled license number on it all right. Ill-written and faint and oblique, the way it would be written hastily on a paper held in a man's hand on the street. 6N333. California 1947.

"Satisfied?" This was Flack's voice. Or it came out of his mouth. I tore the number off and tossed the envelope back to him.

"Four-P-three-two-seven," I said, watching his eyes. Nothing flicked in them. No trace of derision or concealment. "But how do I know this isn't just some license number you had already?"

"You just got to take my word for it."

"Describe the car," I said.

"Caddy convertible, not new, top up. About 1942 model. Sort of dusty blue color."

"Describe the woman."

"Want a lot for your dough, don't you, peeper?"

"Dr. Hambleton's dough."

He winced. "All right. Blonde. White coat with some colored stitching on it. Wide blue straw hat. Dark glasses. Height about five-two. Built like a Conover model."

"Would you know her again — without the glasses?" I asked carefully.

He pretended to think. Then shook his head, no.

"What was that license number again, Flackie?" I caught him off guard.

"Which one?" he said.

I leaned across the desk and dropped some cigarette ash on his gun. I did some more staring into his eyes. But I knew he was licked now. He seemed to know too. He reached for his gun, blew off the ash and put it back in the drawer of his desk.

"Go on. Beat it," he said between his teeth. "Tell the cops I frisked the stiff. So what? Maybe I lose a job. Maybe I get tossed in the fishbowl. So what? When I come out I'm solid. Little Flackie don't have to worry about coffee and crullers. Don't think for a minute those dark cheaters fool little Flackie. I've seen too many movies to miss that lovely puss. And if you ask me that babe'll be around for a long time. She's a comer — and who knows" — he leered at me triumphantly — "she'd need a bodyguard one of these days. A guy to have around, watch things, keep her out of jams. Somebody that knows the ropes and ain't unreasonable about dough . . . What's the matter?"

I had put my head on one side and was leaning forward. I was listening. "I thought I heard a church bell," I said.

"There ain't any church around here," he said contemptuously. "It's that platinum brain of yours getting cracks in it."

"Just one bell," I said. "Very slow. Tolling is the word, I believe."

Flack listened with me. "I don't hear anything," he said sharply.

"Oh you wouldn't hear it," I said. "You'd be the one guy in the whole world who wouldn't hear it."

He just sat there and stared at me with his nasty little eyes half-closed and his nasty little mustache shining. One of his hands twitched on the desk, an aimless movement.

I left him to his thoughts, which were probably as small, ugly and frightened as the man himself.

12

THE APARTMENT HOUSE was over on Doheny Drive, just down the hill from the Strip. It was really two buildings, one behind the other, loosely connected by a floored patio with a fountain, and a room built over the arch. There were mailboxes and bells in the imitation-marble foyer. Three out of the sixteen had no names over them. The names that I read meant nothing to me. The job needed a little more work. I tried the front door, found it unlocked, and the job still needed more work.

Outside stood two Cadillacs, a Lincoln Continental and a Packard Clipper. Neither of the Cadillacs had the right color or license. Across the way a guy in riding breeches was sprawled with his legs over the door of a low-cut Lancia. He was smoking and looking up at the pale stars which know enough to keep their distance from Hollywood. I walked up the steep hill to the boulevard and a block east and smothered myself in an outdoor sweat-box phone booth. I dialed a man named Peoria Smith, who was so-called because he stuttered — another little mystery I hadn't had time to work out.

"Mavis Weld," I said. "Phone number. This is Marlowe."

"S-s-s-sure," he said. "M-M-Mavis Weld, huh? You want h-h-her ph-ph-phone number?"

"How much?"

"Be-b-b-be ten b-b-b-bucks," he said.

"Just forget I called," I said.

"W-w-wait a minute! I ain't supposed to give out with them b-b-babes' phone numbers. An assistant prop man is taking a hell of a chance."

I waited and breathed back my own breath.

"The address goes with it naturally," Peoria whined, forgetting to stutter.

"Five bucks," I said. "I've got the address already. And don't haggle. If you think you're the only studio grifter in the business of selling unlisted telephone numbers — "

"Hold it," he said wearily, and went to get his little red book. A left-handed stutterer. He only stuttered when he wasn't excited. He came back and gave it to me. A Crestview number of course. If you don't have a Crestview number in Hollywood you're a bum.

I opened up the steel-and-glass cell to let in some air while I dialed again. After two rings a drawling sexy voice answered. I pulled the door shut.

"Ye-e-e-s," the voice cooed.

"Miss Weld, please."

"And who is calling Miss Weld, if you please?"

"I have some stills Whitey wants me to deliver tonight."

"Whitey? And who is Whitey, amigo?"

"The head still-photographer at the studio," I said. "Don't you know that much? I'll come up if you'll tell me which apartment. I'm only a couple of blocks away."

"Miss Weld is taking a bath." She laughed. I guess it was a silvery tinkle where she was. It sounded like somebody putting away saucepans where I was. "But of course bring up the photographs. I am sure she is dying to see them. The apartment number is fourteen."

"Will you be there too?"

"But of course. But naturally. Why do you ask that?"

I hung up and staggered out into the fresh air. I went down the hill. The guy in the riding breeches was still hanging out of the Lancia but one of the Cadillacs was gone and two Buick convertibles had joined the cars in front. I pushed the bell to number fourteen, went on through the patio where scarlet Chinese honeysuckle was lit by a peanut spotlight. Another light glowed down on the big ornamental pool full of fat goldfish and silent lily pads, the lilies folded tight for the night. There were a couple of stone seats and a lawn swing. The place didn't look very expensive except that every place was expensive that year. The apartment was on the second floor, one of two doors facing across a wide landing.

The bell chimed and a tall dark girl in jodhpurs opened the door. Sexy was very faint praise for her. The jodhpurs, like her hair, were coal black. She wore a white silk shirt with a scarlet scarf loose around her throat. It was not as vivid as her mouth. She held a long brown cigarette in a pair of tiny golden tweezers. The fingers holding it were more than adequately jeweled. Her black hair was parted in the middle and a line of scalp as white as snow went over the top of her head and dropped out of sight behind. Two thick braids of her shining black hair lay one on each side of her slim brown neck. Each was tied with a small scarlet bow. But it was a long time since she was a little girl.

She looked sharply down at my empty hands. Studio stills are usually a little too big to put in your pocket.

I said: "Miss Weld, please."

"You can give me the stills." The voice was cool, drawling and insolent, but the eyes were something else. She looked almost as hard to get as a haircut.

"For Miss Weld personally. Sorry."

"I told you she was taking a bath."

"I'll wait."

"Are you quite sure you have the stills, amigo?"

"As sure as I'll ever be. Why?"

"Your name?" Her voice froze on the second word, like a feather taking off in a sudden draft. Then it cooed and hovered and soared and eddied and the silent invitation of a smile picked delicately at the corners of her lips, very slowly, like a child trying to pick up a snowflake.

"Your last picture was wonderful, Miss Gonzales."

The smile flashed like lightning and changed her whole face. The body came erect and vibrant with delight. "But it was stinking," she glowed. "Positively goddamned stinking, you sweet lovely man. You know but positively goddam well it was stinking."

"Nothing with you in it stinks for me, Miss Gonzales."

She stood away from the door and waved me in. "We will have a drink," she said. "The goddamest drink we will have. I adore flattery, however dishonest."

I went in. A gun in the kidney wouldn't have surprised me a bit. She stood so that I had to practically push her mammaries out of the way to get through the door. She smelled the way the Taj Mahal looks by moonlight. She closed the door and danced over to a small portable bar.

"Scotch? Or would you prefer a mixed drink? I mix a perfectly loathsome Martini," she said.

"Scotch is fine, thanks."

She made a couple of drinks in a couple of glasses you could almost have stood umbrellas in. I sat down in a chintz chair and looked around. The place was old-fashioned. It had a false fireplace with gas logs and a marble mantel, cracks in the plaster, a couple of vigorously colored daubs on the walls that looked lousy enough to have cost money, an old black chipped Steinway and for once no Spanish shawl on it. There were a lot of new-looking books in bright jackets scattered around and a double-barreled shotgun with a handsomely carved stock stood in the corner with a white satin bow tied around the barrels. Hollywood wit.

The dark lady in the jodhpurs handed me a glass and perched on the arm of my chair. "You may call me Dolores if you wish," she said, taking a hearty swig out of her own tumbler.

"Thanks."

"And what may I call you?"

I grinned.

"Of course," she said, "I am most fully aware that you are a god-dam liar and that you have no stills in your pockets. Not that I wish to inquire into your no doubt very private business."

"Yeah?" I inhaled a couple of inches of my liquor. "Just what kind of bath is Miss Weld taking? An old-fashioned soap or something with Arabian spices in it?"

She waved the remains of the brown cigarette in the small gold clasp. "Perhaps you would like to help her. The bathroom is over there — through the arch and to the right. Most probably the door is not locked."

"Not if it's that easy," I said.

"Oh." She gave me the brilliant smile again. "You like to do the difficult things in life. I must remember to be less approachable, must I not?" She removed herself elegantly from the arm of my chair and ditched her cigarette, bending over enough so that I could trace the outline of her hips.

"Don't bother, Miss Gonzales. I'm just a guy who came here on business. I don't have any idea of raping anybody."

"No?" The smile became soft, lazy and, if you can't think of a better word, provocative.

"But I'm sure as hell working up to it," I said.

"You are an amusing son-of-a-bitch," she said with a shrug and went off through the arch, carrying her half-quart of Scotch and water with her. I heard a gentle tapping on a door and her voice: "Darling, there's a man here who says he has some stills from the studio. He says. Muy simpàtico. Muy guapo tambièn. Con co-jones."

A voice I had heard before said sharply: "Shut up, you little bitch. I'll be out in a second."

The Gonzales came back through the archway humming. Her glass was empty. She went to the bar again. "But you are not drinking," she cried, looking at my glass.

"I ate dinner. I only have a two-quart stomach anyway. I understand a little Spanish."

She tossed her head. "You are shocked?" Her eyes rolled. Her shoulders did a fan dance.

"I'm pretty hard to shock."

"But you heard what I said? Madre de Dios. I'm so terribly sorry."

"I'll bet," I said.

She finished making herself another highball.

"Yes. I am so sorry," she sighed. "That is, I think I am. Sometimes I am not sure. Sometimes I do not give a good goddam. It is so confusing. All my friends tell me I am far too outspoken. I do shock you, don't I?" She was on the arm of my chair again.

"No. But if I wanted to be shocked I'd know right where to come." She reached her glass behind her indolently and leaned towards me.

"But I do not live here," she said. "I live at the Chateau Bercy."

"Alone?"

She slapped me delicately across the tip of my nose. The next thing I knew I had her in my lap and she was trying to bite a piece off my tongue. "You are a very sweet son-of-a-bitch," she said. Her mouth was as hot as ever a mouth was. Her lips burned like dry ice. Her tongue was driving hard against my teeth. Her eyes looked enormous and black and the whites showed under them.

"I am so tired," she whispered into my mouth. "I am so worn, so incredibly tired."

I felt her hand in my breast pocket. I shoved her off hard, but she had my wallet. She danced away with it laughing, flicked it open and went through it with fingers that darted like little snakes.

"So glad you two got acquainted," a voice off to one side said coolly. Mavis Weld stood in the archway.

Her hair was fluffed out carelessly and she hadn't bothered with make-up. She wore a hostess gown and very little else. Her legs ended in little green and silver slippers. Her eyes were empty, her lips contemptuous. But she was the same girl all right, dark glasses on or off.

The Gonzales gave her a quick darting glance, closed my wallet and tossed it. I caught it and put it away. She strolled to a table and picked up a black bag with a long strap, hooked it over her shoulder and moved towards the door.

Mavis Weld didn't move, didn't look at her. She looked at me. But there was no emotion of any kind in her face. The Gonzales opened the door and glanced outside and almost closed it and turned.

"The name is Philip Marlowe," she said to Mavis Weld. "Nice, don't you think?"

"I didn't know you bothered to ask them their names," Mavis Weld said. "You so seldom know them long enough."

"I see," the Gonzales answered gently. She turned and smiled at me faintly. "Such a charming way to call a girl a whore, don't you think?"

Mavis Weld said nothing. Her face had no expression.

"At least," the Gonzales said smoothly as she pulled the door open again, "I haven't been sleeping with any gunmen lately."

"Are you sure you can remember?" Mavis Weld asked her in exactly the same tone. "Open the door, honey. This is the day we put the garbage out."

The Gonzales looked back at her slowly, levelly, and with a knife in her eyes. Then she made a faint sound with her lips and teeth and yanked the door wide. It closed behind her with a jarring smash. The noise didn't even flicker the steady dark-blue glare in Mavis Weld's eyes.

"Now suppose you do the same — but more quietly," she said.

I got out a handkerchief and scrubbed the lipstick over my face. It looked exactly the color of blood, fresh blood. "That could happen to anybody," I said. "I wasn't petting her. She was petting me."

She marched to the door and heaved it open. "On your way, dreamboat. Make with the feet."

"I came here on business, Miss Weld."

"Yes. I can imagine. Out. I don't know you. I don't want to know you. And if I did, this wouldn't be either the day or the hour."

"Never the time and place and the loved one all together," I said.

"What's that?" She tried to throw me out with the point of her chin, but even she wasn't that good.

"Browning. The poet, not the automatic. I feel sure you'd prefer the automatic."

"Look, little man, do I have to call the manager to bounce you downstairs like a basketball?"

I went over and pushed the door shut. She held on to the last moment. She didn't quite kick me, but it cost her an effort not to. I tried to ease her away from the door without appearing to. She didn't ease worth a darn. She stood her ground, one hand still reaching for the doorknob, her eyes full of dark-blue rage.

"If you're going to stand that close to me," I said, "maybe you'd better put some clothes on."

She took her hand back and swung it hard. The slap sounded like Miss Gonzales slamming the door, but it stung. And it reminded me of the sore place on the back of my head.

"Did I hurt you?" she said softly.

I nodded.

"That's fine." She hauled off and slapped me again, harder if anything. "I think you'd better kiss me," she breathed. Her eyes were clear and limpid and melting. I glanced down casually. Her right hand was balled into a very businesslike fist. It wasn't too small to work with, either.

"Believe me," I said. "There's only one reason I don't. Even if you had your little black gun with you. Or the brass knuckles you probably keep on your night table."

She smiled politely.

"I might just happen to be working for you," I said. "And I don't go whoring around after every pair of legs I see." I looked down at hers. I could see them all right and the flag that marked the goal line was no larger than it had to be. She pulled the hostess gown together and turned and walked over to the little bar shaking her head.

"I'm free, white and twenty-one," she said. "I've seen all the approaches there are. I think I have. If I can't scare you, lick you, or seduce you, what the hell can I buy you with?"

"Well—"

"Don't tell me," she interrupted sharply and turned with a glass in her hand. She drank and tossed the loose hair around and smiled a thin little smile. "Money, of course. How damned stupid of me to overlook that."

"Money would help," I said.

Her mouth twisted in wry disgust but the voice was almost affectionate. "How much money?"

"Oh a hundred bucks would do to start with."

"You're cheap. It's a cheap little bastard, isn't it? A hundred bucks it says. Is a hundred bucks money in your circle, darling?"

"Make it two hundred then. I could retire on that."

"Still cheap. Every week of course. In a nice clean envelope?"

"You could skip the envelope. I'd only get it dirty."

"And just what would I get for this money, my charming little gumshoe? I'm quite sure of what you are, of course."

"You'd get a receipt. Who told you I was a gumshoe?"

She stared out of her own eyes for a brief instant before the act dropped over her again. "It must have been the smell." She sipped her drink and stared at me over it with a faint smile of contempt.

"I'm beginning to think you write your own dialogue," I said. "I've been wondering just what was the matter with it."

I ducked. A few drops splattered me. The glass splintered on the wall behind me. The broken pieces fell soundlessly.

"And with that," she said, completely calm, "I believe I must have used up my entire stock of girlish charm."

I went over and picked up my hat. "I never thought *you* killed him," I said. "But it would help to have some sort of reason for not telling you were there. It's a help to have enough money for a retainer just to establish myself. And enough information to justify my accepting the retainer."

She picked a cigarette out of a box, tossed it in the air, caught it between her lips effortlessly and lit it with a match that came from nowhere.

"My goodness. Am I supposed to have killed somebody?" she asked. I was still holding the hat. It made me feel foolish. I don't know why. I put it on and started for the door.

"I trust you have carfare home," the contemptuous voice said behind me.

I didn't answer. I just kept going. When I had the door ready to open she said: "I also trust Miss Gonzales gave you her address and phone number. You should be able to get almost anything out of her — including, I am told, money."

I let go of the doorknob and went back across the room fast. She stood her ground and the smile on her lips didn't slip a millimeter.

"Look," I said. "You're going to find this hard to believe. But

I came over here with the quaint idea that you might be a girl who needed some help — and would find it rather hard to get anyone you could bank on. I figured you went to that hotel room to make some kind of a pay-off. And the fact that you went by yourself and took chances on being recognized — and *were* recognized by a house dick whose standard of ethics would take about as much strain as a very tired old cobweb — all this made me think you might be in one of those Hollywood jams that really mean curtains. But you're not in any jam. You're right up front under the baby spot pulling every tired ham gesture you ever used in the most tired B-picture you ever acted in — if acting is the word — "

"Shut up," she said, between teeth so tight they grated. "Shut up, you slimy, blackmailing keyhole peeper."

"You don't need me," I said. "You don't need anybody. You're so goddam smart you could talk your way out of a safe-deposit box. Okay. Go ahead and talk your way out. I won't stop you. Just don't make me listen to it. I'd burst out crying to think a mere slip of an innocent little girl like you should be so clever. You do things to me, honey. Just like Margaret O'Brien."

She didn't move or breathe when I reached the door, nor when I opened it. I don't know why. The stuff wasn't *that* good.

I went down the stairs and across the court and out of the front door, almost bumping into a slim dark-eyed man who was standing there lighting a cigarette.

"Excuse me," he said quietly. "I'm afraid I'm in your way."

I started to go around him, then I noticed that his lifted right hand held a key. I reached out and snapped it out of his hand for no reason at all. I looked at the number stamped on it. No. 14. Mavis Weld's apartment. I threw it off behind some bushes.

"You don't need that," I said. "The door isn't locked."

"Of course," he said. There was a peculiar smile on his face. "How stupid of me."

"Yeah," I said. "We're both stupid. Anybody's stupid that bothers with that tramp."

"I wouldn't quite say that," he answered quietly, his small sad eyes watching me without any particular expression.

"You don't have to," I said. "I just said it for you. I beg your

ardon. I'll get your key." I went over behind the bushes, picked
t up and handed it to him.

"Thank you very much," he said. "And by the way ——" He
topped. I stopped. "I hope I don't interrupt an interesting
quarrel," he said. "I should hate to do that. No?" He smiled.
Well, since Miss Weld is a friend in common, may I introduce
ıyself. My name is Steelgrave. Haven't I seen you somewhere?"

"No you haven't seen me anywhere, Mr. Steelgrave," I said. "My
ame's Marlowe, Philip Marlowe. It's extremely unlikely that
ve've met. And strange to relate I never heard of you, Mr. Steel-
rave. And I wouldn't give a damn, even if your name was Weepy
Moyer." I never knew quite why I said that. There was nothing
o make me say it, except that the name had been mentioned. A
eculiar stillness came over his face. A peculiar fixed look in his
ilent black eyes. He took the cigarette out of his mouth, looked at
he tip, flicked a little ash off it, although there was no ash to flick
ff, looking down as he said: "Weepy Moyer? Peculiar name. I
on't think I ever heard that. Is he somebody I should know?"

"Not unless you're unusually fond of ice picks," I said, and left
im. I went on down the steps, crossed to my car, looked back be-
ore I got in. He was standing there looking down at me, the cig-
rette between his lips. From that distance I couldn't see whether
here was any expression on his face. He didn't move or make any
ind of gesture when I looked back at him. He didn't even turn
way. He just stood there. I got in and drove off.

13

DROVE EAST ON SUNSET but I didn't go home. At La Brea I turned
orth and swung over to Highland, out over Cahuenga Pass and
own onto Ventura Boulevard, past Studio City and Sherman
)aks and Encino. There was nothing lonely about the trip. There

never is on that road. Fast boys in stripped-down Fords shot in and out of the traffic streams, missing fenders by a sixteenth of an inch, but somehow always missing them. Tired men in dusty coupés and sedans winced and tightened their grip on the wheel and ploughed on north and west towards home and dinner, an evening with the sports page, the blatting of the radio, the whining of their spoiled children and the gabble of their silly wives. I drove on past the gaudy neons and the false fronts behind them, the sleazy hamburger joints that look like palaces under the colors, the circular drive-ins as gay as circuses with the chipper hard-eyed carhops, the brilliant counters, and the sweaty greasy kitchens that would have poisoned a toad. Great double trucks rumbled down over Sepulveda from Wilmington and San Pedro and crossed towards the Ridge Route, starting up in low-low from the traffic lights with a growl of lions in the zoo.

Behind Encino an occasional light winked from the hills through thick trees. The homes of screen stars. Screen stars, phooey. The veterans of a thousand beds. Hold it, Marlowe, you're not human tonight.

The air got cooler. The highway narrowed. The cars were so few now that the headlights hurt. The grade rose against chalk walls and at the top a breeze, unbroken from the ocean, danced casually across the night.

I ate dinner at a place near Thousand Oaks. Bad but quick. Feed 'em and throw 'em out. Lots of business. We can't bother with you sitting over your second cup of coffee, mister. You're using money space. See those people over there behind the rope. They want to eat. Anyway they think they have to. God knows why they want to eat here. They could do better home out of a can. They're just restless. Like you. They have to get the car out and go somewhere. Sucker-bait for the racketeers that have taken over the restaurants. Here we go again. You're not human tonight, Marlowe.

I paid off and stopped in a bar to drop a brandy on top of the New York cut. Why New York, I thought. It was Detroit where they made machine tools. I stepped out into the night air that nobody had yet found out how to option. But a lot of people were probably trying. They'd get around to it.

I drove on to the Oxnard cut-off and turned back along the ocean. The big eight-wheelers and sixteen-wheelers were streaming north, all hung over with orange lights. On the right the great fat solid Pacific trudging into shore like a scrubwoman going home. No moon, no fuss, hardly a sound of the surf. No smell. None of the marsh wild smell of the sea. A California ocean. California, the department-store state. The most of everything and the best of nothing. Here we go again. You're not human tonight, Marlowe.

All right. Why would I be? I'm sitting in that office, playing with a dead fly and in pops this dowdy little item from Manhattan, Kansas, and chisels me down to a shop-worn twenty to find her brother. He sounds like a creep but she wants to find him. So with his fortune clasped to my chest, I trundle down to Bay City and the routine I go through is so tired I'm half asleep on my feet. I meet nice people, with and without ice picks in their necks. I leave, and I leave myself wide-open too. Then she comes in and takes the twenty away from me and gives me a kiss and gives it back to me because I didn't do a full day's work.

So I go see Dr. Hambleton, retired (and how) optometrist from El Centro, and meet again the new style in neckwear. And I don't tell the cops. I just frisk the customer's toupee and put on an act. Why? Who am I cutting my throat for this time? A blonde with sexy eyes and too many door keys? A girl from Manhattan, Kansas? I don't know. All I know is that something isn't what it seems and the old tired but always reliable hunch tells me that if the hand is played the way it is dealt the wrong person is going to lose the pot. Is that my business? Well, what is my business? Do I know? Did I ever know? Let's not go into that. You're not human tonight, Marlowe. Maybe I never was or ever will be. Maybe I'm an ecto-plasm with a private license. Maybe we all get like this in the cold half-lit world where always the wrong thing happens and never the right.

Malibu. More movie stars. More pink and blue bathtubs. More tufted beds. More Chanel No. 5. More Lincoln Continentals and Cadillacs. More wind-blown hair and sunglasses and attitudes and pseudo-refined voices and waterfront morals. Now, wait a minute. Lots of nice people work in pictures. You've got the wrong attitude, Marlowe. You're not human tonight.

I smelled Los Angeles before I got to it. It smelled stale and old like a living room that had been closed too long. But the colored lights fooled you. The lights were wonderful. There ought to be a monument to the man who invented neon lights. Fifteen stories high, solid marble. There's a boy who really made something out of nothing.

So I went to a picture show and it had to have Mavis Weld in it. One of those glass-and-chromium deals where everybody smiled too much and talked too much and knew it. The women were always going up a long curving staircase to change their clothes. The men were always taking monogrammed cigarettes out of expensive cases and snapping expensive lighters at each other. And the help was round-shouldered from carrying trays with drinks across the terrace to a swimming pool about the size of Lake Huron but a lot neater.

The leading man was an amiable ham with a lot of charm, some of it turning a little yellow at the edges. The star was a bad-tempered brunette with contemptuous eyes and a couple of bad close-ups that showed her pushing forty-five backwards almost hard enough to break a wrist. Mavis Weld played second lead and she played it with wraps on. She was good, but she could have been ten times better. But if she had been ten times better half her scenes would have been yanked out to protect the star. It was as neat a bit of tightrope walking as I ever saw. Well it wouldn't be a tightrope she'd be walking from now on. It would be a piano wire. It would be very high. And there wouldn't be any net under it.

14

I HAD A REASON for going back to the office. A special-delivery letter with an orange claim check ought to have arrived there by now. Most of the windows were dark in the building, but not all. People work nights in other businesses than mine. The elevator man said "howdy" from the depths of his throat and trundled me up. The corridor had lighted open doors where the scrubwomen were still cleaning up the débris of the wasted hours. I turned a corner past the slobbery hum of a vacuum cleaner, let myself into my dark office and opened the windows. I sat there at the desk doing nothing, not even thinking. No special-delivery letter. All the noise of the building, except the vacuum cleaner, seemed to have flowed out into the street and lost itself among the turning wheels of innumerable cars. Then somewhere along the hall outside a man started whistling "Lili Marlene" with elegance and virtuosity. I knew who that was. The night man checking office doors. I switched the desk lamp on and he passed without trying mine. His steps went away, then came back with a different sound, more of a shuffle. The buzzer sounded in the other office which was still unlocked. That would be special delivery. I went out to get it, only it wasn't.

A fat man in sky-blue pants was closing the door with that beautiful leisure only fat men ever achieve. He wasn't alone, but I looked at him first. He was a large man and wide. Not young nor handsome, but he looked durable. Above the sky-blue gabardine slacks he wore a two-tone leisure jacket which would have been revolting on a zebra. The neck of his canary-yellow shirt was open wide, which it had to be if his neck was going to get out. He was hatless and his large head was decorated with a reasonable amount of pale salmon-colored hair. His nose had been broken but well set and it hadn't been a collector's item in the first place.

The creature with him was a weedy number with red eyes and sniffles. Age about twenty, five feet nine, thin as a broom straw. His nose twitched and his mouth twitched and his hands twitched and he looked very unhappy.

The big man smiled genially. "Mr. Marlowe, no doubt?"

I said: "Who else?"

"It's a little late for a business call," the big man said, and hid half the office by spreading out his hands. "I hope you don't mind. Or do you already have all the business you can handle?"

"Don't kid me. My nerves are frayed," I said. "Who's the junky?"

"Come along, Alfred," the big man said to his companion. "And stop acting girlish."

"In a pig's valise," Alfred told him.

The big man turned to me placidly. "Why do all these punks keep saying that? It isn't funny. It isn't witty. It doesn't mean anything. Quite a problem, this Alfred. I got him off the stuff, you know, temporarily at least. Say 'how do you do' to Mr. Marlowe, Alfred."

"Screw him," Alfred said.

The big man sighed. "My name's Toad," he said. "Joseph P. Toad."

I didn't say anything.

"Go ahead and laugh," the big man said. "I'm used to it. Had the name all my life." He came towards me with his hand out. I took it. The big man smiled pleasantly into my eyes. "Okay, Alfred," he said without looking back.

Alfred made what seemed to be a very slight and unimportant movement at the end of which a heavy automatic was pointing at me.

"Careful, Alfred," the big man said, holding my hand with a grip that would have bent a girder. "Not yet."

"In a pig's valise," Alfred said. The gun pointed at my chest. His finger tightened around the trigger. I watched it tighten. I knew at precisely what moment that tightening would release the hammer. It didn't seem to make any difference. This was happening somewhere else in a cheesy program picture. It wasn't happening to me.

The hammer of the automatic clicked dryly on nothing. Alfred lowered the gun with a grunt of annoyance and it disappeared whence it had come. He started to twitch again. There was nothing nervous about his movements with the gun. I wondered just what junk he was off of.

The big man let go of my hand, the genial smile still over his large healthy face.

He patted a pocket. "I got the magazine," he said. "Alfred ain't reliable lately. The little bastard might have shot you."

Alfred sat down in a chair and tilted it against the wall and breathed through his mouth.

I let my heels down on the floor again.

"I bet he scared you," Joseph P. Toad said.

I tasted salt on my tongue.

"You ain't so tough," Toad said, poking me in the stomach with a fat finger.

I stepped away from the finger and watched his eyes.

"What does it cost?" he asked almost gently.

"Let's go into my parlor," I said.

I turned my back on him and walked through the door into the other office. It was hard work but I made it. I sweated all the way. I went around behind the desk and stood there waiting. Mr. Toad followed me in placidly. The junky came twitching in behind him.

"You don't have a comic book around, do you?" Toad asked. "Keeps him quiet."

"Sit down," I said. "I'll look."

He reached for the chair arms. I jerked a drawer open and got my hand around the butt of a Luger. I brought it up slowly, looking at Alfred. Alfred didn't even look at me. He was studying the corner of the ceiling and trying to keep his mouth out of his eye.

"This is as comic as I get," I said.

"You won't need that," the big man said genially.

"That's fine," I said, like somebody else talking, far away behind a wall. I could just barely hear the words. "But if I do, here it is. And this one's loaded. Want me to prove it to you?"

The big man looked as near worried as he would ever look. "I'm sorry you take it like that," he said. "I'm so used to Alfred I hardly notice him. Maybe you're right. Maybe I ought to do something about him."

"Yeah," I said. "Do it this afternoon before you come up here. It's too late now."

"Now wait a minute, Mr. Marlowe." He put his hand out. I slashed at it with the Luger. He was fast, but not fast enough. I cut the back of his hand open with the sight on the gun. He grabbed at it and sucked at the cut. "Hey, please! Alfred's my nephew. My sister's kid. I kind of look after him. He wouldn't hurt a fly, really."

"Next time you come up I'll have one for him not to hurt," I said.

"Now don't be like that, mister. Please don't be like that. I've got quite a nice little proposition — "

"Shut up," I said. I sat down very slowly. My face burned. I had difficulty speaking clearly at all. I felt a little drunk. I said, slowly and thickly: "A friend of mine told me about a fellow that had something like this pulled on him. He was at a desk the way I am. He had a gun, just the way I have. There were two men on the other side of the desk, like you and Alfred. The man on my side began to get mad. He couldn't help himself. He began to shake. He couldn't speak a word. He just had this gun in his hand. So without a word he shot twice under the desk, right where your belly is."

The big man turned a sallow green color and started to get up. But he changed his mind. He got a violent-looking handkerchief out of his pocket and mopped his face. "You seen that in a picture," he said.

"That's right," I said. "But the man who made the picture told me where he got the idea. *That* wasn't in any picture." I put the Luger down on the desk in front of me and said in a more natural voice: "You've got to be careful about firearms, Mr. Toad. You never know but what it may upset a man to have an Army .45 snapped in his face — especially when he doesn't know it's not loaded. It made me kind of nervous for a minute. I haven't had a shot of morphine since lunch time."

Toad studied me carefully with narrow eyes. The junky got up and went to another chair and kicked it around and sat down and tilted his greasy head against the wall. But his nose and hands kept on twitching.

"I heard you were kind of hard-boiled," Toad said slowly, his eyes cool and watchful.

"You heard wrong. I'm a very sensitive guy. I go all to pieces over nothing."

"Yeah. I understand." He stared at me a long time without speaking. "Maybe we played this wrong. Mind if I put my hand in my pocket? I don't wear a gun."

"Go ahead," I said. "It would give me the greatest possible pleasure to see you try to pull a gun."

He frowned, then very slowly got out a flat pigskin wallet and drew out a crisp new one-hundred-dollar bill. He laid it on the edge of the glass top, drew out another just like it, then one by one three more. He laid them carefully in a row along the desk, end

end. Alfred let his chair settle to the floor and stared at the
money with his mouth quivering.

"Five C's," the big man said. He folded his wallet and put it away.
watched every movement he made. "For nothing at all but keep-
ng the nose clean. Check?"

I just looked at him.

"You ain't looking for nobody," the big man said. "You couldn't
nd nobody. You don't have time to work for nobody. You didn't
ear a thing or see a thing. You're clean. Five C's clean. Okay?"

There was no sound in the office but Alfred's sniffling. The big
nan half turned his head. "Quiet, Alfred. I'll give you a shot when
ve leave," the big man told him. "Try to act nice." He sucked
gain at the cut on the back of his hand.

"With you for a model that ought to be easy," I said.

"Screw you," Alfred said.

"Limited vocabulary," the big man told me. "Very limited. Get
he idea, chum?" He indicated the money. I fingered the butt of
he Luger. He leaned forward a little. "Relax, can't you? It's sim-
le. This is a retainer. You don't do a thing for it. Nothing is what
ou do. If you keep on doing nothing for a reasonable length of
ime you get the same amount later on. That's simple, isn't it?"

"And who am I doing this nothing for?" I asked.

"Me. Joseph P. Toad."

"What's your racket?"

"Business representative, you might call me."

"What else could I call you? Besides what I could think up my-
elf?"

"You could call me a guy that wants to help out a guy that don't
vant to make trouble for a guy."

"And what could I call that lovable character?" I asked.

Joseph P. Toad gathered the five hundred-dollar bills together,
ined up the edges neatly and pushed the packet across the desk.
"You can call him a guy that would rather spill money than blood,"
he said. "But he don't mind spilling blood if it looks like that's
what he's got to do."

"How is he with an ice pick?" I asked. "I can see how lousy he is
with a .45."

The big man chewed his lower lip, then pulled it out with a

blunt forefinger and thumb and nibbled on the inside of it softly, like a milch cow chewing her cud. "We're not talking about ice picks," he said at length. "All we're talking about is how you might get off on the wrong foot and do yourself a lot of harm. Whereas if you don't get off on no foot at all, you're sitting pretty and money coming in."

"Who is the blonde?" I asked.

He thought about that and nodded. "Maybe you're into this too far already," he sighed. "Maybe it's too late to do business."

After a moment he leaned forward and said gently: "Okay. I'll check back with my principal and see how far out he wants to come. Maybe we can still do business. Everything stands as it is until you hear from me. Check?"

I let him have that one. He put his hands on the desk and very slowly stood up, watching the gun I was pushing around on the blotter.

"You can keep the dough," he said. "Come on, Alfred." He turned and walked solidly out of the office.

Alfred's eyes crawled sideways watching him, then jerked to the money on the desk. The big automatic appeared with the same magic in his thin right hand. Dartingly as an eel he moved over to the desk. He kept the gun on me and reached for the money with his left hand. It disappeared into his pocket. He gave me a smooth cool empty grin, nodded and moved away, apparently not realizing for a moment that I was holding a gun too.

"Come on, Alfred," the big man called sharply from outside the door. Alfred slipped through the door and was gone.

The outer door opened and closed. Steps went along the hall. Then silence. I sat there thinking back over it, trying to make up my mind whether it was pure idiocy or just a new way to toss a scare.

Five minutes later the telephone rang.

A thick pleasant voice said: "Oh by the way, Mr. Marlowe, I guess you know Sherry Ballou, don't you?"

"Nope."

"Sheridan Ballou, Incorporated. The big agent? You ought to look him up sometime."

I held the phone silently for a moment. Then I said: "Is he her agent?"

"He might be," Joseph P. Toad said, and paused a moment. "I suppose you realize we're just a couple of bit players, Mr. Marlowe. That's all. Just a couple of bit players. Somebody wanted to find out a little something about you. It seemed the simplest way to do it. Now, I'm not so sure."

I didn't answer. He hung up. Almost at once the phone rang again.

A seductive voice said: "You do not like me so well, do you, amigo?"

"Sure I do. Just don't keep biting me."

"I am at home at the Chateau Bercy. I am lonely."

"Call an escort bureau."

"But please. That is no way to talk. This is business of a great importance."

"I bet. But not the business I'm in."

"That slut — what does she say about me?" she hissed.

"Nothing. Oh, she might have called you a Tijuana hooker in riding pants. Would you mind?"

That amused her. The silvery giggle went on for a little while. "Always the wisecrack with you. Is it not so? But you see I did not then know you were a detective. That makes a very big difference."

I could have told her how wrong she was. I just said: "Miss Gonzales, you said something about business. What kind of business, if you're not kidding me?"

"Would you like to make a great deal of money? A very great deal of money?"

"You mean without getting shot?" I asked.

Her incaught breath came over the wire. "Sí," she said thoughtfully. "There is also that to consider. But you are so brave, so big, so — "

"I'll be at my office at nine in the morning, Miss Gonzales. I'll be a lot braver then. Now if you'll excuse me — "

"You have a date? Is she beautiful? More beautiful than I am?"

"For Crissake," I said. "Don't you ever think of anything but one thing?"

"The hell with you, darling," she said, and hung up in my face.

I turned the lights out and left. Halfway down the hall I met a man looking at numbers. He had a special delivery in his hand. So I had to go back to the office and put it in the safe. And the phone rang again while I was doing this.

I let it ring. I had had enough for one day. I just didn't care. It could have been the Queen of Sheba with her cellophane pajamas on — or off — I was too tired to bother. My brain felt like a bucket of wet sand.

It was still ringing as I reached the door. No use. I had to go back. Instinct was stronger than weariness. I lifted the receiver.

Orfamay Quest's twittery little voice said: "Oh, Mr. Marlowe, I've been trying to get you for just the longest time. I'm so upset. I'm — "

"In the morning," I said. "The office is closed."

"Please, Mr. Marlowe — just because I lost my temper for a moment — "

"In the morning."

"But I tell you I have to see you." The voice didn't quite rise to a yell. "It's terribly important."

"Un-huh."

She sniffled. "You — you kissed me."

"I've kissed better since," I said. To hell with her. To hell with all women.

"I've heard from Orrin," she said.

That stopped me for a moment, then I laughed. "You're a nice little liar," I said. "Goodbye."

"But really I have. He called me. On the telephone. Right here where I'm staying."

"Fine," I said. "Then you don't need a detective at all. And if you did, you've got a better one than I am right in the family. I couldn't even find out where you were staying."

There was a little pause. She still had me talking to her anyway. She'd kept me from hanging up. I had to give her that much.

"I wrote to him where I'd be staying," she said at last.

"Un-huh. Only he didn't get the letter because he had moved and he didn't leave any forwarding address. Remember? Try again some time when I'm not so tired. Goodnight, Miss Quest. And you don't have to tell me where you are staying now. I'm not working for you."

"Very well, Mr. Marlowe. I'm ready to call the police now. But I don't think you'll like it. I don't think you'll like it at all."

"Why?"

"Because there's murder in it, Mr. Marlowe, and murder is a very nasty word — don't you think?"

"Come on up," I said. "I'll wait."

I hung up. I got the bottle of Old Forester out. There was nothing slow about the way I poured myself a drink and dropped it down my throat.

15

SHE CAME IN BRISKLY ENOUGH this time. Her motions were small and quick and determined. There was one of those thin little, bright little smiles on her face. She put her bag down firmly, settled herself in the customer's chair and went on smiling.

"It's nice of you to wait for me," she said. "I bet you haven't had your dinner yet, either."

"Wrong," I said. "I have had my dinner. I am now drinking whiskey. You don't approve of whiskey drinking do you?"

"I certainly do not."

"That's just dandy," I said. "I hoped you hadn't changed your mind." I put the bottle up on the desk and poured myself another slug. I drank a little of it and gave her a leer above the glass.

"If you keep on with that you won't be in any condition to listen to what I have to say," she snapped.

"About this murder," I said. "Anybody I know? I can see you're not murdered — yet."

"Please don't be unnecessarily horrid. It's not my fault. You doubted me over the telephone so I had to convince you. Orrin did call me up. But he wouldn't tell me where he was or what he was doing. I don't know why."

"He wanted you to find out for yourself," I said. "He's building your character."

"That's not funny. It's not even smart."

"But you've got to admit it's nasty," I said. "Who was murdered? Or is that a secret too?"

She fiddled a little with her bag, not enough to overcome her embarrassment, because she wasn't embarrassed. But enough to needle me into taking another drink.

"That horrid man in the rooming house was murdered. Mr. — Mr. — I forget his name."

"Let's both forget it," I said. "Let's do something together for once." I dropped the whiskey bottle into the desk drawer and stood up. "Look, Orfamay, I'm not asking you how you know all this. Or rather how Orrin knows it all. Or if he *does* know it. You've found him. That's what you wanted me to do. Or he's found you, which comes to the same thing."

"It's not the same thing," she cried. "I haven't really found him. He wouldn't tell me where he was living."

"Well if it is anything like the last place, I don't blame him."

She set her lips in a firm line of distaste. "He wouldn't tell me anything really."

"Just about murders," I said. "Trifles like that."

She laughed bubblingly. "I just said that to scare you. I don't really mean anybody was murdered, Mr. Marlowe. You sounded so cold and distant. I thought you wouldn't help any more. And — well, I just made it up."

I took a couple of deep breaths and looked down at my hands. I straightened out the fingers slowly. Then I stood up. I didn't say anything.

"Are you mad at me?" she asked timidly, making a little circle on the desk with the point of a finger.

"I ought to slap your face off," I said. "And quit acting innocent. Or it mightn't be your face I'd slap."

Her breath caught with a jerk. "Why, how dare you!"

"You used that line," I said. "You used it too often. Shut up and get the hell out of here. Do you think I enjoy being scared to death?

Oh — there's this." I yanked a drawer open, got out her twenty dollars and threw them down in front of her. "Take this money away. Endow a hospital or a research laboratory with it. It makes me nervous having it around."

Her hand reached automatically for the money. Her eyes behind the cheaters were round and wondering. "Goodness," she said, assembling her handbag with a nice dignity. "I'm sure I didn't know you scared that easy. I thought you were tough."

"That's just an act," I growled, moving around the desk. She leaned back in her chair away from me. "I'm only tough with little girls like you that don't let their fingernails grow too long. I'm all mush inside." I took hold of her arm and yanked her to her feet. Her head went back. Her lips parted. I was hell with the women that day.

"But you will find Orrin for me, won't you?" she whispered. "It was all a lie. Everything I've told you was a lie. He didn't call me up. I — I don't know anything."

"Perfume," I said sniffing. "Why, you little darling. You put perfume behind your ears — and all for me!"

She nodded her little chin half an inch. Her eyes were melting. "Take my glasses off," she whispered. "Philip, I don't mind if you take a little whiskey once in a while. Really I don't."

Our faces were about six inches apart. I was afraid to take her glasses off. I might have socked her on the nose.

"Yes," I said in a voice that sounded like Orson Welles with his mouth full of crackers. "I'll find him for you, honey, if he's still alive. And for free. Not a dime of expense involved. I only ask one thing."

"What, Philip?" she asked softly, and opened her lips a little wider.

"Who was the black sheep in your family?"

She jerked away from me like a startled fawn might, if I had a startled fawn and it jerked away from me. She stared at me stony-faced.

"You said Orrin wasn't the black sheep in your family. Remember? With a very peculiar emphasis. And when you mentioned your sister Leila, you sort of passed on quickly as if the subject was distasteful."

"I — I don't remember saying anything like that," she said very slowly.

"So I was wondering," I said. "What name does your sister Leila use in pictures?"

"Pictures?" She sounded vague. "Oh, you mean motion pictures? Why I never said she was in pictures. I never said anything about her like that."

I gave her my big homely lopsided grin. She suddenly flew into a rage.

"Mind your own business about my sister Leila," she spit at me. "You leave my sister Leila out of your dirty remarks."

"What dirty remarks?" I asked. "Or should I try to guess?"

"All you think about is liquor and women," she screamed. "I hate you!" She rushed to the door and yanked it open and went out. She practically ran down the hall.

I went back around my desk and slumped into the chair. A very strange little girl. Very strange indeed. After a while the phone started ringing again, as it would. On the fourth ring I leaned my head on my hand and groped for it, fumbled it to my face.

"Utter McKinley Funeral Parlors," I said.

A female voice said: "Wha-a-t?" and went off into a shriek of laughter. That one was a riot at the Police Smoker in 1921. What a wit. Like a hummingbird's beak. I put the lights out and went home.

16

EIGHT FORTY-FIVE the next morning found me parked a couple of doors from the Bay City Camera Shop, breakfasted and peaceful and reading the local paper through a pair of sunglasses. I had already chewed my way through the Los Angeles paper, which contained no item about ice picks in the Van Nuys or any other hotel.

Not even MYSTERIOUS DEATH IN DOWNTOWN HOTEL, with no names or weapons specified. The Bay City *News* wasn't too busy to write up a murder. They put it on the first page, right next to the price of meat.

LOCAL MAN FOUND STABBED
IN IDAHO STREET ROOMING HOUSE

An anonymous telephone call late yesterday sent police speeding to an address on Idaho Street opposite the Seamans and Jansing Company's lumberyard. Entering the unlocked door of his apartment, officers found Lester B. Clausen, 45, manager of the rooming house, dead on the couch. Clausen had been stabbed in the neck with an ice pick which was still in his body. After a preliminary examination, Coroner Frank L. Crowdy announced that Clausen had been drinking heavily and may have been unconscious at the time of his death. No signs of struggle were observed by the police.

Detective Lieutenant Moses Maglashan immediately took charge and questioned tenants of the rooming house on their return from work, but no light has so far been thrown on the circumstances of the crime. Interviewed by this reporter, Coroner Crowdy stated that Clausen's death might have been suicide but that the position of the wound made this unlikely. Examination of the rooming-house register disclosed that a page had recently been torn out. Lieutenant Maglashan, after questioning the tenants at length, stated that a thick-set middle-aged man with brown hair and heavy features had been noticed in the hallway of the rooming house on several occasions, but that none of the tenants knew his name or occupation. After carefully checking all rooms, Maglashan further gave it as his opinion that one of the roomers had left recently and in some haste. The mutilation of the register, however, the character of the neighborhood, the lack of an accurate description of the missing man, made the job of tracing him extremely difficult.

"I have no idea at present why Clausen was murdered," Maglashan announced at a late hour last night. "But I have had my eye on this man for some time. Many of his associates are known to me. It's a tough case, but we'll crack it."

It was a nice piece and only mentioned Maglashan's name twelve times in the text and twice more in picture captions. There was a photo of him on page three holding an ice pick and looking at it with profound thought wrinkling his brows. There was a photo of

449 Idaho Street which did it more than justice and a photo of something with a sheet over it on a couch and Lieutenant Maglashan pointing at it sternly. There was also a close-up of the mayor looking as executive as hell behind his official desk and an interview with him on the subject of post-war crime. He said just what you would expect a mayor to say — a watered-down shot of J. Edgar Hoover with some extra bad grammar thrown in.

At three minutes to nine the door of the Bay City Camera Shop opened and an elderly Negro began to sweep dirt across the sidewalk into the gutter. At nine A.M. a neat-appearing young guy in glasses fixed the lock on the door and I went in there with the black-and-orange check Dr. G. W. Hambleton had pasted to the inside of his toupee.

The neat-appearing young man gave me a searching glance as I exchanged the check and some money for an envelope containing a tiny negative and half a dozen shiny prints blown up to eight times the size of the negative. He didn't say anything, but the way he looked at me gave me the impression that he remembered I was not the man who had left the negative.

I went out and sat in my car and looked over the catch. The prints showed a man and a blond girl sitting in a rounded booth in a restaurant with food in front of them. They were looking up as though their attention had suddenly been attracted and they had only just had time to react before the camera had clicked. It was clear from the lighting that no flashbulb had been used.

The girl was Mavis Weld. The man was rather small, rather dark, rather expressionless. I didn't recognize him. There was no reason why I should. The padded leather seat was covered with tiny figures of dancing couples. That made the restaurant The Dancers. This added to the confusion. Any amateur camera hound that tried to flash a lens in there without getting an okay from the management would have been thrown out so hard that he would have bounced all the way down to Hollywood and Vine. I figured it must have been the hidden-camera trick, the way they took Ruth Snyder in the electric chair. He would have the little camera up hanging by a strap under his coat collar, the lens just peeping out from his open jacket, and he would have rigged a bulb release that he could hold in his pocket. It wasn't too hard for me to guess who had taken the picture. Mr. Orrin P. Quest must have moved fast and smooth to get out of there with his face still in front of his head. I put the pictures in my vest pocket and my fingers touched a crumpled piece of paper. I got it out and read: "Doctor Vincent Lagardie, 965 Wyoming Street, Bay City." That was the Vince I had talked to on the phone, the one Lester B. Clausen might have been trying to call.

An elderly flatfoot was strolling down the line of parked cars, marking tires with yellow chalk. He told me where Wyoming Street was. I drove out there. It was a cross-town street well out beyond the business district, parallel with two numbered streets. Number 965, a gray-white frame house, was on a corner. On its door a brass plate said VINCENT LAGARDIE, M.D., HOURS 10:00 TO 12:00 AND 2:30 to 4:00.

The house looked quiet and decent. A woman with an unwilling small boy was going up the steps. She read the plate, looked at a watch pinned to her lapel and chewed irresolutely on her lip. The small boy looked around carefully, then kicked her on the ankle. She winced but her voice was patient. "Now, Johnny, you mustn't do that to Aunty Fern," she said mildly.

She opened the door and dragged the little ape in with her. Diagonally across the intersection was a big white colonial mansion with a portico which was roofed and much too small for the house. Floodlight reflectors were set into the front lawn. The walk was bordered by tree roses in bloom. A large black and silver sign over the portico said: THE GARLAND HOME OF PEACE. I wondered how Dr. Lagardie liked looking out of his front windows at a funeral parlor. Maybe it made him careful.

I turned around at the intersection and drove back to Los Angeles, and went up to the office to look at my mail and lock my catch from the Bay City Camera Shop up in the battered green safe — all but one print. I sat down at the desk and studied this through a magnifying glass. Even with that and the camera shop blow-up the detail was still clear. There was an evening paper, a *News-Chronicle*, lying on the table in front of the dark, thin, expressionless man who sat beside Mavis Weld. I could just read the headline. LIGHT HEAVYWEIGHT CONTENDER SUCCUMBS TO RING INJURIES. Only a noon or late sports edition would use a headline like that. I pulled the phone towards me. It rang just as I got my hand on it.

"Marlowe? This is Christy French downtown. Any ideas this morning?"

"Not if your teletype's working. I've seen a Bay City paper."

"Yeah, we got that," he said casually. "Sounds like the same guy, don't it? Same initials, same description, same method of murder, and the time element seems to check. I hope to Christ this doesn't mean Sunny Moe Stein's mob have started in business again."

"If they have, they've changed their technique," I said. "I was reading up on it last night. The Stein mob used to jab their victims full of holes. One of them had over a hundred stab wounds in him."

"They could learn better," French said a little evasively, as if he didn't want to talk about it. "What I called you about was Flack. Seen anything of him since yesterday afternoon?"

"No."

"He skipped out. Didn't come to work. Hotel called his landlady. Packed up and left last night. Destination unknown."

"I haven't seen him or heard from him," I said.

"Didn't it strike you as kind of funny our stiff only had fourteen bucks in his kick?"

"It did a little. You answered that yourself."

"I was just talking. I don't buy that any more. Flack's either scared out or come into money. Either he saw something he didn't tell and got paid to breeze, or else he lifted the customer's case dough, leaving the fourteen bucks to make it look better."

I said: "I'll buy either one. Or both at the same time. Whoever searched that room so thoroughly wasn't looking for money."

"Why not?"

"Because when this Dr. Hambleton called me up I suggested the hotel safe to him. He wasn't interested."

"A type like that wouldn't have hired you to hold his dough anyway," French said. "He wouldn't have hired you to keep anything for him. He wanted protection or he wanted a sidekick — or maybe just a messenger."

"Sorry," I said. "He told me just what I told you."

"And seeing he was dead when you got over there," French said with a too-casual drawl, "you couldn't hardly have given him one of your business cards."

I held the phone too tight and thought back rapidly over my talk with Hicks in the Idaho Street rooming house. I saw him holding my card between his fingers, looking down at it. And then I saw myself taking it out of his hand quickly, before he froze to it. I took a deep breath and let it out slowly.

"Hardly," I said. "And stop trying to scare me to death."

"He had one, chum. Folded twice across in his pants watch pocket. We missed it the first time."

"I gave Flack a card," I said, stiff-lipped.

There was silence. I could hear voices in the background and the clack of a typewriter. Finally French said dryly: "Fair enough. See you later." He hung up abruptly.

I put the phone down very slowly in its cradle and flexed my cramped fingers. I stared down at the photo lying on the desk in front of me. All it told me was that two people, one of whom I knew, were having lunch at The Dancers. The paper on the table told me the date, or would.

I dialed the *News-Chronicle* and asked for the sports section. Four minutes later I wrote on a pad: "Ritchy Belleau, popular young light heavyweight contender, died in the Sister Hospital just before midnight February 19 as a result of ring injuries sustained the previous evening in the main event at the Hollywood Legion Stadium. The *News-Chronicle* Noon Sports Edition for February 20 carried the headlines."

I dialed the same number again and asked for Kenny Haste in the City Room. He was an ex-crime reporter I had known for years. We chatted around for a minute and then I said:

"Who covered the Sunny Moe Stein killing for you?"

"Tod Barrow. He's on the *Post-Despatch* now. Why?"

"I'd like the details, if any."

He said he would send to the morgue for the file and call me, which he did ten minutes later. "He was shot twice in the head, in his car, about two blocks from the Chateau Bercy on Franklin. Time, about eleven-fifteen P.M."

"Date, February twentieth," I said, "or was it?"

"Check, it was. No witnesses, no arrests except the usual police stock company of book-handlers, out-of-work fight managers and other professional suspects. What's in it?"

"Wasn't a pal of his supposed to be in town about that time?"

"Nothing here says so. What name?"

"Weepy Moyer. A cop friend of mine said something about a Hollywood money man being held on suspicion and then released for lack of evidence."

Kenny said: "Wait a minute. Something's coming back to me — yeah. Fellow named Steelgrave, owns The Dancers, supposed to be a gambler and so on. Nice guy. I've met him. That was a bust."

"How do you mean, a bust?"

"Some smart monkey tipped the cops he was Weepy Moyer and they held him for ten days on an open charge for Cleveland. Cleveland brushed it off. That didn't have anything to do with the Stein killing. Steelgrave was under glass all that week. No connection at all. Your cop friend has been reading pulp magazines."

"They all do," I said. "That's why they talk so tough. Thanks, Kenny."

We said goodbye and hung up and I sat leaning back in my chair and looking at my photograph. After a while I took scissors and cut out the piece that contained the folded newspaper with the headline. I put the two pieces in separate envelopes and put them in my pocket with the sheet from the pad.

I dialed Miss Mavis Weld's Crestview number. A woman's voice answered after several rings. It was a remote and formal voice that I might or might not have heard before. All it said was, "Hello?"

"This is Philip Marlowe. Is Miss Weld in?"

"Miss Weld will not be in until late this evening. Do you care to leave a message?"

"Very important. Where could I reach her?"

"I'm sorry. I have no information."

"Would her agent know?"

"Possibly."

"You're quite sure you're not Miss Weld?"

"Miss Weld is not in." She hung up.

I sat there and listened to the voice. At first I thought yes, then I thought no. The longer I thought the less I knew. I went down to the parking lot and got my car out.

17

ON THE TERRACE at The Dancers a few early birds were getting ready to drink their lunch. The glass-fronted upstairs room had the awning let down in front of it. I drove on past the curve that goes down into the Strip and stopped across the street from a square building of two stories of rose-red brick with small white leaded bay windows and a Greek porch over the front door and what looked, from across the street, like an antique pewter doorknob. Over the door was a fanlight and the name SHERIDAN BALLOU, INC. in black wooden letters severely stylized. I locked my car and crossed to the front door. It was white and tall and wide and had a keyhole big enough for a mouse to crawl through. Inside this keyhole was the real lock. I went for the knocker, but they had thought of that too. It was all in one piece and didn't knock.

So I patted one of the slim fluted white pillars and opened the door and walked directly into the reception room which filled the entire front of the building. It was furnished in dark antique-looking furniture and many chairs and settees of quilted chintz-like material. There were lace curtains at the windows and chintz boxes around them that matched the chintz of the furniture. There was a flowered carpet and a lot of people waiting to see Mr. Sheridan Ballou.

Some of them were bright and cheerful and full of hope. Some looked as if they had been there for days. One small dark girl was sniffling into her handkerchief in the corner. Nobody paid any attention to her. I got a couple of profiles at nice angles before the company decided I wasn't buying anything and didn't work there.

A dangerous-looking redhead sat languidly at an Adam desk talking into a pure-white telephone. I went over there and she put a couple of cold blue bullets into me with her eyes and then stared at the cornice that ran around the room.

"No," she said into the phone. "No. So sorry. I'm afraid it's no use. Far, far too busy." She hung up and ticked off something on a list and gave me some more of her steely glance.

"Good morning. I'd like to see Mr. Ballou," I said. I put my plain card on her desk. She lifted it by one corner, smiled at it amusedly.

"Today?" she inquired amiably. "This week?"

"How long does it usually take?"

"It *has* taken six months," she said cheerfully. "Can't somebody else help you?"

"No."

"So sorry. Not a chance. Drop in again won't you? Somewhere about Thanksgiving." She was wearing a white wool skirt, a burgundy silk blouse and a black velvet over-jacket with short sleeves. Her hair was a hot sunset. She wore a golden topaz bracelet and topaz earrings and a topaz dinner ring in the shape of a shield. Her fingernails matched her blouse exactly. She looked as if it would take a couple of weeks to get her dressed.

"I've got to see him," I said.

She read my card again. She smiled beautifully. "Everyone has," she said. "Why — er — Mr. Marlowe. Look at all these lovely people. Every one of them has been here since the office opened two hours ago."

"This is important."

"No doubt. In what way if I may ask?"

"I want to peddle a little dirt."

She picked a cigarette out of a crystal box and lit it with a crystal lighter. "Peddle? You mean for money — in Hollywood?"

"Could be."

"What kind of dirt? Don't be afraid to shock me."

"It's a bit obscene, Miss — Miss — " I screwed my head around to read the plaque on her desk.

"Helen Grady," she said. "Well, a little well-bred obscenity never did any harm, did it?"

"I didn't say it was well-bred."

She leaned back carefully and puffed smoke in my face.

"Blackmail in short." She sighed. "Why the hell don't you lam out of here, bud? Before I throw a handful of fat coppers in your lap?"

I sat on the corner of her desk, grabbed a double handful of her cigarette smoke and blew it into her hair. She dodged angrily.

"Beat it, lug," she said in a voice that could have been used for paint remover.

"Oh-oh. What happened to the Bryn Mawr accent?"

Without turning her head she said sharply: "Miss Vane."

A tall slim elegant dark girl with supercilious eyebrows looked up. She had just come through an inner door camouflaged as a stained-glass window. The dark girl came over. Miss Grady handed her my card: "Spink."

Miss Vane went back through the stained-glass window with the card.

"Sit down and rest your ankles, big stuff," Miss Grady informed me. "You may be here all week."

I sat down in a chintz winged chair, the back of which came eight inches above my head. It made me feel shrunken. Miss Grady gave me her smile again, the one with the hand-honed edge, and bent to the telephone once more.

I looked around. The little girl in the corner had stopped crying and was making up her face with calm unconcern. A very tall distinguished-looking party swung up a graceful arm to stare at his elegant wrist watch and oozed gently to his feet. He set a pearl-gray homburg at a rakish angle on the side of his head, checked his yellow chamois gloves and his silver-knobbed cane, and strolled languidly over to the red-headed receptionist.

"I have been waiting two hours to see Mr. Ballou," he said icily in a rich sweet voice that had been modulated by a lot of training. "I'm not accustomed to waiting two hours to see anybody."

"So sorry, Mr. Fortescue. Mr. Ballou is just too busy for words this A.M."

"I'm sorry I cannot leave him a check," the elegant tall party remarked with a weary contempt. "Probably the only thing that would interest him. But in default of that — "

"Just a minute, kid." The redhead picked up a phone and said into it: "Yes? . . . Who says so besides Goldwyn? Can't you reach somebody that's not crazy? . . . Well try again." She slammed the telephone down. The tall party had not moved.

"In default of that," he resumed, as if he had never stopped speaking, "I should like to leave a short personal message."

"Please do," Miss Grady told him. "I'll get it to him somehow."

"Tell him with my love that he is a dirty polecat."

"Make it skunk, darling," she said. "He doesn't know any English words."

"Make it skunk and double skunk," Fortescue told her. "With a slight added nuance of sulphurated hydrogen and a very cheap grade of whorehouse perfume." He adjusted his hat and gave his profile the once-over in a mirror. "I now bid you good morning and to hell with Sheridan Ballou, Incorporated."

The tall actor stalked out elegantly, using his cane to open the door.

"What's the matter with him?" I asked.

She looked at me pityingly. "Billy Fortescue? Nothing's the matter with him. He isn't getting any parts so he comes in every day and goes through that routine. He figures somebody might see him and like it."

I shut my mouth slowly. You can live a long time in Hollywood and never see the part they use in pictures.

Miss Vane appeared through the inner door and made a chin-jerk at me. I went in past her. "This way. Second on the right." She watched me while I went down the corridor to the second door which was open. I went in and closed the door.

A plump white-haired Jew sat at the desk smiling at me tenderly. "Greetings," he said. "I'm Moss Spink. What's on the thinker, pal? Park the body. Cigarette?" He opened a thing that looked like a trunk and presented me with a cigarette which was not more than a foot long. It was in an individual glass tube.

"No thanks," I said. "I smoke tobacco."

He sighed. "All right. Give. Let's see. Your name's Marlowe. Huh? Marlowe. Marlowe. Have I ever heard of anybody named Marlowe?"

"Probably not," I said. "I never heard of anybody named Spink. I asked to see a man named Ballou. Does that sound like Spink? I'm not looking for anybody named Spink. And just between you and me, the hell with people named Spink."

"Anti-Semitic, huh?" Spink said. He waved a generous hand on which a canary-yellow diamond looked like an amber traffic light. "Don't be like that," he said. "Sit down and dust off the brains. You don't know me. You don't want to know me. Okay. I ain't offended. In a business like this you got to have somebody around that don't get offended."

"Ballou," I said.

"Now be reasonable, pal. Sherry Ballou's a very busy guy. He works twenty hours a day and even then he's way behind schedule. Sit down and talk it out with little Spinky."

"You're what around here?" I asked him.

"I'm his protection, pal. I gotta protect him. A guy like Sherry can't see everybody. I see people for him. I'm the same as him — up to a point you understand."

"Could be I'm past the point you're up to," I said.

"Could be," Spink agreed pleasantly. He peeled a thick tape off an aluminum individual cigar container, reached the cigar out tenderly and looked it over for birthmarks. "I don't say not. Why not demonstrate a little? Then we'll know. Up to now all you're doing is throwing a line. We get so much of that in here it don't mean a thing to us."

I watched him clip and light the expensive-looking cigar. "How do I know you wouldn't double-cross him?" I asked cunningly.

Spink's small tight eyes blinked and I wasn't sure but that there were tears in them. "Me cross Sherry Ballou?" he asked brokenly in a hushed voice, like a six-hundred-dollar funeral. "Me? I'd sooner double-cross my own mother."

"That doesn't mean anything to me either," I said. "I never met your mother."

Spink laid his cigar aside in an ashtray the size of a bird bath. He waved both his arms. Sorrow was eating into him. "Oh, pal. What a way to talk," he wailed. "I love Sherry Ballou like he was my own father. Better. My father — well, skip it. Come on, pal. Be human. Give with a little of the old trust and friendliness. Spill the dirt to little Spinky, huh?"

I drew an envelope from my pocket and tossed it across the desk to him. He pulled the single photograph from it and stared at it solemnly. He laid it down on the desk. He looked up at me, down at the photo, up at me. "Well," he said woodenly, in a voice suddenly empty of the old trust and friendliness he had been talking about. "What's it got that's so wonderful?"

"Do I have to tell you who the girl is?"

"Who's the guy?" Spink snapped.

I said nothing.

"I said who's the guy?" Spink almost yelled at me. "Cough up, mug. Cough up."

I still didn't say anything. Spink reached slowly for his telephone, keeping his hard bright eyes on my face.

"Go on. Call them," I said. "Call downtown and ask for Lieutenant Christy French in the homicide bureau. There's another boy that's hard to convince."

Spink took his hand off the phone. He got up slowly and went out with the photograph. I waited. Outside on Sunset Boulevard traffic went by distantly, monotonously. The minutes dropped silently down a well. The smoke of Spink's freshly lit cigar played in the air for a moment, then was sucked through the vent of the air-conditioning apparatus. I looked at the innumerable inscribed photos on the walls, all inscribed to Sherry Ballou with somebody's eternal love. I figured they were back numbers if they were in Spink's office.

18

AFTER A WHILE Spink came back and gestured to me. I followed him along the corridor through double doors into an anteroom with two secretaries. Past them towards more double doors of heavy black glass with silver peacocks etched into the panels. As we neared the doors they opened of themselves.

We went down three carpeted steps into an office that had everything in it but a swimming pool. It was two stories high, surrounded by a balcony loaded with book shelves. There was a concert grand Steinway in the corner and a lot of glass and bleached-wood furniture and a desk about the size of a badminton court and chairs and couches and tables and a man lying on one of the couches with his coat off and his shirt open over a Charvet scarf you could have found in the dark by listening to it purr. A white cloth was over his eyes and forehead and a lissome blond girl was wringing out another in a silver bowl of ice water at a table beside him.

The man was a big shapely guy with wavy dark hair and a strong brown face below the white cloth. An arm dropped to the carpet and a cigarette hung between fingers, wisping a tiny thread of smoke.

The blond girl changed the cloth deftly. The man on the couch groaned. Spink said: "This is the boy, Sherry. Name of Marlowe."

The man on the couch groaned. "What does he want?"

Spink said: "Won't spill."

The man on the couch said: "What did you bring him in for then? I'm tired."

Spink said: "Well you know how it is, Sherry. Sometimes you kind of got to."

The man on the couch said: "What did you say his beautiful name was?"

Spink turned to me. "You can tell us what you want now. And make it snappy, Marlowe."

I said nothing.

After a moment the man on the couch slowly raised the arm with the cigarette at the end of it. He got the cigarette wearily into his mouth and drew on it with the infinite languor of a decadent aristocrat moldering in a ruined château.

"I'm talking to you, pal," Spink said harshly. The blonde changed the cloth again, looking at nobody. The silence hung in the room as acrid as the smoke of the cigarette. "Come on, lug. Snap it up."

I got one of my Camels out and lit it and picked out a chair and sat down. I stretched my hand out and looked at it. The thumb twitched up and down slowly every few seconds.

Spink's voice cut into this furiously: "Sherry don't have all day, you."

"What would he do with the rest of the day?" I heard myself asking. "Sit on a white satin couch and have his toenails gilded?"

The blonde turned suddenly and stared at me. Spink's mouth fell open. He blinked. The man on the couch lifted a slow hand to the corner of the towel over his eyes. He removed enough so that one seal-brown eye looked at me. The towel fell softly back into place.

"You can't talk like that in here," Spink said in a tough voice.

I stood up. I said: "I forgot to bring my prayer book. This is the first time I knew God worked on commission."

Nobody said anything for a minute. The blonde changed the towel again.

From under it the man on the couch said calmly: "Get the Jesus out of here, darlings. All but the new chum."

Spink gave me a narrow glare of hate. The blonde left silently.

Spink said: "Why don't I just toss him out on his can?"

The tired voice under the towel said: "I've been wondering about that so long I've lost interest in the problem. Beat it."

"Okay, boss," Spink said. He withdrew reluctantly. He paused at the door, gave me one more silent snarl and disappeared.

The man on the couch listened to the door close and then said: "How much?"

"You don't want to buy anything."

He pushed the towel off his head, tossed it to one side and sat up slowly. He put his bench-made pebble-grain brogues on the carpet and passed a hand across his forehead. He looked tired but not dissipated. He fumbled another cigarette from somewhere, lit it and stared morosely through the smoke at the floor.

"Go on," he said.

"I don't know why you wasted all the build-up on me," I said. "But I credit you with enough brains to know you couldn't buy anything, and know it would stay bought."

Ballou picked up the photo that Spink had put down near him on a long low table. He reached out a languid hand. "The piece that's cut out would be the punch line, no doubt," he said.

I got the envelope out of my pocket and gave him the cut out corner, watched him fit the two pieces together.

"With a glass you can read the headline," I said.

"There's one on my desk. Please."

I went over and got the magnifying glass off his desk. "You're used to a lot of service, aren't you, Mr. Ballou?"

"I pay for it." He studied the photograph through the glass and sighed. "Seems to me I saw that fight. They ought to take more care of these boys."

"Like you do of your clients," I said.

He laid down the magnifying glass and leaned back to stare at me with cool untroubled eyes.

"That's the chap that owns The Dancers. Name's Steelgrave. The girl is a client of mine, of course." He made a vague gesture towards a chair. I sat down in it. "What were you thinking of asking, Mr. Marlowe?"

"For what?"

"All the prints and the negative. The works."

"Ten grand," I said, and watched his mouth. The mouth smiled, rather pleasantly.

"It needs a little more explanation, doesn't it? All I see is two people having lunch in a public place. Hardly disastrous to the reputation of my client. I assume that was what you had in mind."

I grinned. "You can't buy anything, Mr. Ballou. I could have had a positive made from the negative and another negative from the positive. If that snap is evidence of something, you could never know you had suppressed it."

"Not much of a sales talk for a blackmailer," he said, still smiling.

"I always wonder why people pay blackmailers. They can't buy anything. Yet they do pay them, sometimes over and over and over again. And in the end are just where they started."

"The fear of today," he said, "always overrides the fear of tomorrow. It's a basic fact of the dramatic emotions that the part is greater than the whole. If you see a glamour star on the screen in a position of great danger, you fear for her with one part of your mind, the emotional part. Notwithstanding that your reasoning mind knows that she is the star of the picture and nothing very bad is going to happen to her. If suspense and menace didn't defeat reason, there would be very little drama."

I said: "Very true, I guess," and puffed some of my Camel smoke around.

His eyes narrowed a little. "As to really being able to buy anything, if I paid you a substantial price and didn't get what I bought,

I'd have you taken care of. Beaten to a pulp. And when you got out of the hospital, if you felt aggressive enough, you could try to get me arrested."

"It's happened to me," I said. "I'm a private eye. I know what you mean. Why are you talking to me?"

He laughed. He had a deep pleasant effortless laugh. "I'm an agent, sonny. I always tend to think traders have a little something in reserve. But we won't talk about any ten grand. She hasn't got it. She only makes a grand a week so far. I admit she's very close to the big money, though."

"That would stop her cold," I said, pointing to the photo. "No big money, no swimming pool with underwater lights, no platinum mink, no name in neons, no nothing. All blown away like dust."

He laughed contemptuously.

"Okay if I show this to the johns downtown, then?" I said.

He stopped laughing. His eyes narrowed. Very quietly he asked:

"Why would they be interested?"

I stood up. "I don't think we're going to do any business, Mr. Ballou. And you're a busy man. I'll take myself off."

He got up off the couch and stretched, all six feet two of him. He was a very fine hunk of man. He came over and stood close to me. His seal-brown eyes had little gold flecks in them. "Let's see who you are, sonny."

He put his hand out. I dropped my open wallet into it. He read the photostat of my license, poked a few more things out of the wallet and glanced at them. He handed it back.

"What would happen, if you did show your little picture to the cops?"

"I'd first of all have to connect it up with something they're working on — something that happened in the Van Nuys Hotel yesterday afternoon. I'd connect it up through the girl — who won't talk to me — that's why I'm talking to you."

"She told me about it last night." He sighed.

"Told you how much?" I asked.

"That a private detective named Marlowe had tried to force her to hire him, on the ground that she was seen in a downtown hotel inconveniently close to where a murder was committed."

"How close?" I asked.

"She didn't say."

"Nuts she didn't."

He walked away from me to a tall cylindrical jar in the corner. From this he took one of a number of short thin Malacca canes. He began to walk up and down the carpet, swinging the cane deftly past his right shoe.

I sat down again and killed my cigarette and took a deep breath. "It could only happen in Hollywood," I grunted.

He made a neat about-turn and glanced at me. "I beg your pardon."

"That an apparently sane man could walk up and down inside the house with a Piccadilly stroll and a monkey stick in his hand."

He nodded. "I caught the disease from a producer at MGM. Charming fellow. Or so I've been told." He stopped and pointed the cane at me. "You amuse the hell out of me, Marlowe. Really you do. You're so transparent. You're trying to use me for a shovel to dig yourself out of a jam."

"There's some truth in that. But the jam I'm in is nothing to the jam your client would be in if I hadn't done the thing that put me in the jam."

He stood quite still for a moment. Then he threw the cane away from him and walked over to a liquor cabinet and swung the two halves of it open. He poured something into a couple of pot-bellied glasses. He carried one of them over to me. Then went back and got his own. He sat down with it on the couch.

"Armagnac," he said. "If you knew me, you'd appreciate the compliment. This stuff is pretty scarce. The Krauts cleaned most of it out. Our brass got the rest. Here's to you."

He lifted the glass, sniffed and sipped a tiny sip. I put mine down in a lump. It tasted like good French brandy.

Ballou looked shocked. "My God, you sip that stuff, you don't swallow it whole."

"I swallow it whole," I said. "Sorry. She also told you that if somebody didn't shut my mouth, she would be in a lot of trouble."

He nodded.

"Did she suggest how to go about shutting my mouth?"

"I got the impression she was in favor of doing it with some kind of heavy blunt instrument. So I tried out a mixture of threat and bribery. We have an outfit down the street that specializes in protecting picture people. Apparently they didn't scare you and the bribe wasn't big enough."

"They scared me plenty," I said. "I damn near fanned a Luger at them. That junky with the .45 puts on a terrific act. And as for the money not being big enough, it's all a question of how it's offered to me."

He sipped a little more of his Armagnac. He pointed at the photograph lying in front of him with the two pieces fitted together.

"We got to where you were taking that to the cops. What then?"

"I don't think we got that far. We got to why she took this up with you instead of with her boy friend. He arrived just as I left. He has his own key."

"Apparently she just didn't." He frowned and looked down into his Armagnac.

"I like that fine," I said. "I'd like it still better if the guy didn't have her doorkey."

He looked up rather sadly. "So would I. So would we all. But show business has always been like that — any kind of show business. If these people didn't live intense and rather disordered lives, if their emotions didn't ride them too hard — well, they wouldn't be able to catch those emotions in flight and imprint them on a few feet of celluloid or project them across the footlights."

"I'm not talking about her love life," I said. "She doesn't have to shack up with a redhot."

"There's no proof of that, Marlowe."

I pointed to the photograph. "The man that took that is missing and can't be found. He's probably dead. Two other men who lived at the same address are dead. One of them was trying to peddle those pictures just before he got dead. She went to his hotel in person to take delivery. So did whoever killed him. She didn't get delivery and neither did the killer. They didn't know where to look."

"And you did?"

"I was lucky. I'd seen him without his toupee. None of this is what I call proof, maybe. You could build an argument against it. Why bother? Two men have been killed, perhaps three. She took an awful chance. Why? She wanted that picture. Getting it was worth an awful chance. Why, again? It's just two people having lunch on a certain day. The day Moe Stein was shot to death on Franklin Avenue. The day a character named Steelgrave was in jail because the cops got a tip he was a Cleveland redhot named Weepy Moyer. That's what the record shows. But the photo says he was out of jail. And by saying that about him on that particular day it says who is he. And she knows it. And he still has her doorkey."

I paused and we eyed each other solidly for a while. I said: "You don't really want the cops to have that picture, do you? Win, lose or draw, they'd crucify her. And when it was all over it wouldn't make a damn bit of difference whether Steelgrave was Moyer or whether Moyer killed Stein or had him killed or just happened to be out on a jail pass the day he was killed. If he got away with it, there'd always be enough people to think it was a fix. She wouldn't get away with anything. She's a gangster's girl in the public mind. And as far as your business is concerned, she's definitely and completely through."

Ballou was silent for a moment, staring at me without expression. "And where are you all this time?" he asked softly.

"That depends a good deal on you, Mr. Ballou."

"What do you really want?" His voice was thin and bitter now.

"What I wanted from her and couldn't get. Something that gives me a colorable right to act in her interests up to the point where I decided I can't go any farther."

"By suppressing evidence?" he asked tightly.

"If it *is* evidence. The cops couldn't find out without smearing Miss Weld. Maybe I can. They wouldn't be bothered to try; they don't care enough. I do."

"Why?"

"Let's say it's the way I earn my living. I might have other motives, but that one's enough."

"What's your price?"

"You sent it to me last night. I wouldn't take it then. I'll take it now. With a signed letter employing my services to investigate an attempt to blackmail one of your clients."

I got up with my empty glass and went over and put it down on the desk. As I bent down I heard a soft whirring noise. I went around behind the desk and yanked upon a drawer. A wire recorder slid out on a hinged shelf. The motor was running and the fine steel wire was moving steadily from one spool to the other. I looked across at Ballou.

"You can shut it off and take the record with you," he said. "You can't blame me for using it."

I moved the switch over to rewind and the wire reversed direction and picked up speed until the wire was winding so fast I couldn't see it. It made a sort of high keening noise, like a couple of pansies fighting for a piece of silk. The wire came loose and the machine stopped. I took the spool off and dropped it into my pocket.

"You might have another one," I said. "I'll have to chance that."

"Pretty sure of yourself, aren't you, Marlowe?"

"I only wish I was."

"Press that button on the end of the desk, will you?"

I pressed it. The black glass doors opened and a dark girl came in with a stenographer's notebook.

Without looking at her Ballou began to dictate. "Letter to Mr. Philip Marlowe, with his address. Dear Mr. Marlowe: This agency herewith employs you to investigate an attempt to blackmail one of its clients, particulars of which have been given to you verbally. Your fee is to be one hundred dollars a day with a retainer of five hundred dollars, receipt of which you acknowledge on the copy of this letter. Blah, blah, blah. That's all, Eileen. Right away, please."

I gave the girl my address and she went out.

I took the wire spool out of my pocket and put it back in the drawer.

Ballou crossed his knees and danced the shiny tip of his shoe up and down staring at it. He ran his hand through crisp dark hair.

"One of these days," he said, "I'm going to make the mistake which a man in my business dreads above all other mistakes. I'm going to find myself doing business with a man I can trust and I'm going to be just too goddam smart to trust him. Here, you'd better keep this." He held out the two pieces of the photograph.

Five minutes later I left. The glass doors opened when I was three feet from them. I went past the two secretaries and down the corridor past the open door of Spink's office. There was no sound in there, but I could smell his cigar smoke. In the reception room exactly the same people seemed to be sitting around in the chintzy chairs. Miss Helen Grady gave me her Saturday-night smile. Miss Vane beamed at me.

I had been forty minutes with the boss. That made me as gaudy as a chiropractor's chart.

19

THE STUDIO COP at the semicircular glassed-in desk put down his telephone and scribbled on a pad. He tore off the sheet and pushed in through the narrow slit not more than three quarters of an inch wide where the glass did not quite meet the top of his desk. His voice coming through the speaking device set into the glass panel had a metallic ring.

"Straight through to the end of the corridor," he said. "You'll find a drinking fountain in the middle of the patio. George Wilson will pick up there."

I said: "Thanks. Is this bullet-proof glass?"

"Sure. Why?"

"I just wondered," I said. "I never heard of anybody shooting his way into the picture business."

Behind me somebody snickered. I turned to look at a girl in slacks with a red carnation behind her ear. She was grinning.

"Oh, brother, if a gun was all it took."

I went over to an olive-green door that didn't have any handle. It made a buzzing sound and let me push it open. Beyond was an olive-green corridor with bare walls and a door at the far end. A rat trap. If you got into that and something was wrong, they could still stop you. The far door made the same buzz and click. I wondered how the cop knew I was at it. So I looked up and found his eyes staring at me in a tilted mirror. As I touched the door the mirror went blank. They thought of everything.

Outside in the hot midday sun flowers rioted in a small patio with tiled walks and a pool in the middle and a marble seat. The drinking fountain was beside the marble seat. An elderly and beautifully dressed man was lounging on the marble seat watching three tan-colored boxers root up some tea-rose begonias. There was an expression of intense but quiet satisfaction on his face. He didn't glance at me as I came up. One of the boxers, the biggest one, came over and made a wet on the marble seat beside his pants leg. He leaned down and patted the dog's hard short-haired head.

"You Mr. Wilson?" I asked.

He looked up at me vaguely. The middle-sized boxer trotted up and sniffed and wet after the first one.

"Wilson?" He had a lazy voice with a touch of drawl to it. "Oh no. My name's not Wilson. Should it be?"

"Sorry." I went over to the drinking fountain and hit myself in the face with a stream of water. While I was wiping it off with a handkerchief the smallest boxer did his duty on the marble bench.

The man whose name was not Wilson said lovingly, "Always do it in the exact same order. Fascinates me."

"Do what?" I asked.

"Pee," he said. "Question of seniority it seems. Very orderly. First Maisie. She's the mother. Then Mac. Year older than Jock, the baby. Always the same. Even in my office."

"In your office?" I said, and nobody ever looked stupider saying anything.

He lifted his whitish eyebrows at me, took a plain brown cigar out of his mouth, bit the end off and spit it into the pool.

"That won't do the fish any good," I said.

He gave me an up-from-under look. "I raise boxers. The hell with fish."

I figured it was just Hollywood. I lit a cigarette and sat down on the bench. "In your office," I said. "Well, every day has its new idea, hasn't it."

"Up against the corner of the desk. Do it all the time. Drives my secretaries crazy. Gets into the carpet, they say. What's the matter with women nowadays? Never bothers me. Rather like it. You get fond of dogs, you even like to watch them pee."

One of the dogs heaved a full-blown begonia plant into the middle of the tiled walk at his feet. He picked it up and threw it into the pool.

"Bothers the gardeners, I suppose," he remarked as he sat down again. "Oh well, if they're not satisfied, they can always — " He stopped dead and watched a slim mail girl in yellow slacks deliberately detour in order to pass through the patio. She gave him a quick side glance and went off making music with her hips.

"You know what's the matter with this business?" he asked me.

"Nobody does," I said.

"Too much sex," he said. "All right in its proper time and place. But we get it in carload lots. Wade through it. Stand up to our necks in it. Gets to be like flypaper." He stood up. "We have too many flies too. Nice to have met you, Mr. — "

"Marlowe," I said. "I'm afraid you don't know me."

"Don't know anybody," he said. "Memory's going. Meet too many people. Name's Oppenheimer."

"Jules Oppenheimer?"

He nodded. "Right. Have a cigar." He held one out to me. I showed my cigarette. He threw the cigar into the pool, then frowned. "Memory's going," he said sadly. "Wasted fifty cents. Oughtn't to do that."

"You run this studio," I said.

He nodded absently. "Ought to have saved that cigar. Save fifty cents and what have you got?"

"Fifty cents," I said, wondering what the hell he was talking about.

"Not in this business. Save fifty cents in this business and all you have is five dollars' worth of bookkeeping." He paused and made a motion to the three boxers. They stopped whatever they were rooting at and watched him. "Just run the financial end," he said. "That's easy. Come on, children, back to the brothel." He sighed. "Fifteen hundred theaters," he added.

I must have been wearing my stupid expression again. He waved a hand around the patio. "Fifteen hundred theaters is all you need.

A damn sight easier than raising purebred boxers. The motion-picture business is the only business in the world in which you can make all the mistakes there are and still make money."

"Must be the only business in the world where you can have three dogs pee up against your office desk," I said.

"You have to have the fifteen hundred theaters."

"That makes it a little harder to get a start," I said.

He looked pleased. "Yes. That *is* the hard part." He looked across the green clipped lawn at a four-story building which made one side of the open square. "All offices over there," he said. "I never go there. Always redecorating. Makes me sick to look at the stuff some of these people put in their suites. Most expensive talent in the world. Give them anything they like, all the money they want. Why? No reason at all. Just habit. Doesn't matter a damn what they do or how they do it. Just give me fifteen hundred theaters."

"You wouldn't want to be quoted on that, Mr. Oppenheimer?"

"You a newspaper man?"

"No."

"Too bad. Just for the hell of it I'd like to see somebody try to get that simple elementary fact of life into the papers." He paused and snorted. "Nobody'd print it. Afraid to. Come on, children!"

The big one, Maisie, came over and stood beside him. The middle-sized one paused to ruin another begonia and then trotted up beside Maisie. The little one, Jock, lined up in order, then with a sudden inspiration, lifted a hind leg at the cuff of Oppenheimer's pants. Maisie blocked him off casually.

"See that?" Oppenheimer beamed. "Jock tried to get out of turn. Maisie wouldn't stand for it." He leaned down and patted Maisie's head. She looked up at him adoringly.

"The eyes of your dog," Oppenheimer mused. "The most unforgettable thing in the world."

He strolled off down the tiled path towards the executive building, the three boxers trotting sedately beside him.

"Mr. Marlowe?"

I turned to find that a tall sandy-haired man with a nose like a straphanger's elbow had sneaked up on me.

"I'm George Wilson. Glad to know you. I see you know Mr. Oppenheimer."

"Been talking to him. He told me how to run the picture business. Seems all it takes is fifteen hundred theaters."

"I've been working here five years. I've never even spoken to him."

"You just don't get peed on by the right dogs."

"You could be right. Just what can I do for you, Mr. Marlowe?"

"I want to see Mavis Weld."

"She's on the set. She's in a picture that's shooting."

"Could I see her on the set for a minute?"

He looked doubtful. "What kind of pass did they give you?"

"Just a pass, I guess." I held it out to him. He looked it over.

"Ballou sent you. He's her agent. I guess we can manage. Stage twelve. Want to go over there now?"

"If you have time."

"I'm the unit publicity man. That's what my time is for." We walked along the tiled path towards the corners of two buildings. A concrete roadway went between them towards the back lot and the stages.

"You in Ballou's office?" Wilson asked.

"Just came from there."

"Quite an organization, I hear. I've thought of trying that business myself. There's nothing in this but a lot of grief."

We passed a couple of uniformed cops, then turned into a narrow alley between two stages. A red wigwag was swinging in the middle of the alley, a red light was on over a door marked 12, and a bell was ringing steadily above the red light. Wilson stopped beside the door. Another cop in a tilted-back chair nodded to him, and looked me over with that dead gray expression that grows on them like scum on a water tank.

The bell and the wigwag stopped and the red light went off. Wilson pulled a heavy door open and I went in past him. Inside was another door. Inside that what seemed after the sunlight to be pitch darkness. Then I saw a concentration of lights in the far corner. The rest of the enormous sound stage seemed to be empty.

We went towards the lights. As we drew near, the floor seemed to be covered with thick black cables. There were rows of folding chairs, a cluster of portable dressing rooms with names on the doors. We were wrong way on to the set and all I could see was the wooden backing and on either side a big screen. A couple of back-projection machines sizzled off to the side.

A voice shouted: "Roll 'em." A bell rang loudly. The two screens came alive with tossing waves. Another calmer voice said: "Watch your positions, please, we may have to end up matching this little vignette. All right, action."

Wilson stopped dead and touched my arm. The voices of the actors came out of nowhere, neither loud nor distinct, an unimportant murmur with no meaning.

One of the screens suddenly went blank. The smooth voice, without change of tone, said: "Cut."

The bell rang again and there was a general sound of movement. Wilson and I went on. He whispered in my ear: "If Ned Gammon doesn't get this take before lunch, he'll bust Torrance on the nose."

"Oh. Torrance in this?" Dick Torrance at the time was a ranking star of the second grade, a not uncommon type of Hollywood actor that nobody really wants but a lot of people in the end have to take for lack of better.

"Care to run over the scene again, Dick?" the calm voice asked, as we came around the corner of the set and saw what it was — the deck of a pleasure yacht near the stern. There were two girls and three men in the scene. One of the men was middle-aged, in sport clothes, lounging in a deck chair. One wore whites and had red hair and looked like the yacht's captain. The third was the amateur yachtsman, with the handsome cap, the blue jacket with gold buttons, the white shoes and slacks and the supercilious charm. This was Torrance. One of the girls was a dark beauty who had been younger: Susan Crawley. The other was Mavis Weld. She wore a wet white sharkskin swimsuit, and had evidently just come aboard. A make-up man was spraying water on her face and arms and the edges of her blond hair.

Torrance hadn't answered. He turned suddenly and stared at the camera. "You think I don't know my lines?"

A gray-haired man in gray clothes came forward into the light from the shadowy background. He had hot black eyes, but there was no heat in his voice.

"Unless you changed them intentionally," he said, his eyes steady on Torrance.

"It's just possible that I'm not used to playing in front of a back-projection screen that has a habit of running out of film only in the middle of a take."

"That's a fair complaint," Ned Gammon said. "Trouble is he only has two hundred and twelve feet of film, and that's my fault. If you could take the scene just a little faster — "

"Huh." Torrance snorted. "If *I* could take it a little faster. Perhaps Miss Weld could be prevailed upon to climb aboard this yacht in rather less time than it would take to build the damn boat."

Mavis Weld gave him a quick, contemptuous look.

"Weld's timing is just right," Gammon said. "Her performance is just right too."

Susan Crawley shrugged elegantly. "I had the impression she could speed it up a trifle, Ned. It's good, but it *could* be better."

"If it was any better, darling," Mavis Weld told her smoothly, "somebody might call it acting. You wouldn't want anything like that to happen in *your* picture, would you?"

Torrance laughed. Susan Crawley turned and glared at him. "What's funny, Mister Thirteen?"

Torrance's face settled into an icy mask. "The name again?" he almost hissed.

"Good heavens, you mean you didn't know," Susan Crawley said wonderingly. "They call you Mister Thirteen because any time you play a part it means twelve other guys have turned it down."

"I see," Torrance said coolly, then burst out laughing again. He turned to Ned Gammon. "Okay, Ned. Now everybody's got the rat poison out of their system, maybe we can give it to you the way you want it."

Ned Gammon nodded. "Nothing like a little hamming to clear the air. All right here we go."

He went back beside the camera. The assistant shouted, "Roll 'em," and the scene went through without a hitch.

"Cut," Gammon said. "Print that one. Break for lunch everybody."

The actors came down a flight of rough wooden steps and nodded to Wilson. Mavis Weld came last, having stopped to put on a terry-cloth robe and a pair of beach sandals. She stopped dead when she saw me. Wilson stepped forward.

"Hello, George," Mavis Weld said, staring at me. "Want something from me?"

"Mr. Marlowe would like a few words with you. Okay?"

"Mr. Marlowe?"

Wilson gave me a quick sharp look. "From Ballou's office. I supposed you knew him."

"I may have seen him." She was still staring at me. "What is it?"

I didn't speak.

After a moment she said, "Thanks, George. Better come along to my dressing room, Mr. Marlowe."

She turned and walked off around the far side of the set. A green and white dressing room stood against the wall. The name on the door was Miss Weld. At the door she turned and looked around carefully. Then she fixed her lovely blue eyes on my face.

"And now, Mr. Marlowe?"

"You *do* remember me?"

"I believe so."

"Do we take up where we left off — or have a new deal with a clean deck?"

"Somebody let you in here. Who? Why? That takes explaining."

"I'm working for you. I've been paid a retainer and Ballou has the receipt."

"How very thoughtful. And suppose I don't want you to work for me? Whatever your work is."

"All right, be fancy," I said. I took the Dancers photo out of my pocket and held it out. She looked at me a long steady moment before she dropped her eyes. Then she looked at the snapshot of herself and Steelgrave in the booth. She looked at it gravely without movement. Then very slowly she reached up and touched the tendrils of damp hair at the side of her face. Ever so slightly she shivered. Her hand came out and she took the photograph. She stared at it. Her eyes came up again slowly, slowly.

"Well?" she asked.

"I have the negative and some other prints. You would have had them, if you had had more time and known where to look. Or if he had stayed alive to sell them to you."

"I'm a little chilly," she said. "And I have to eat some lunch." She held the photo out to me.

"You're a little chilly and you have to eat some lunch," I said.

I thought a pulse beat in her throat. But the light was not too good. She smiled very faintly. The bored-aristocrat touch.

"The significance of all this escapes me," she said.

"You're spending too much time on yachts. What you mean is, I know you and I know Steelgrave, so what has this photo got that makes anybody give me a diamond dog collar?"

"All right," she said. "What?"

"I don't know," I said. "But if finding out is what it takes to shake you out of this duchess routine, I'll find out. And in the meantime you're still chilly and you still have to eat some lunch."

"And you've waited too long," she said quietly. "You haven't anything to sell. Except perhaps your life."

"I'd sell that cheap. For love of a pair of dark glasses and a delphinium-blue hat and a crack on the head from a high-heeled slipper."

Her mouth twitched as if she was going to laugh. But there was no laughter in her eyes.

"Not to mention three slaps in the face," she said. "Goodbye, Mr. Marlowe. You came too late. Much, much too late."

"For me — or for you?" She reached back and opened the door of the dressing room.

"I think for both of us." She went in quickly, leaving the door open.

"Come in and shut the door," her voice said from the dressing room.

I went in and shut the door. It was no fancy custom-built star's dressing room. Strictly utility only. There was a shabby couch, one easy chair, a small dressing table with mirror and two lights, a straight chair in front of it, a tray that had held coffee.

Mavis Weld reached down and plugged in a round electric heater. Then she grabbed up a towel and rubbed the damp edges of her hair. I sat down on the couch and waited.

"Give me a cigarette." She tossed the towel to one side. Her eyes came close to my face as I lit the cigarette for her. "How did you like that little scene we ad-libbed on the yacht?"

"Bitchy."

"We're all bitches. Some smile more than others, that's all. Show business. There's something cheap about it. There always has been. There was a time when actors went in at the back door. Most of them still should. Great strain, great urgency, great hatred, and it comes out in nasty little scenes. They don't mean a thing."

"Cat talk," I said.

She reached up and pulled a finger tip down the side of my cheek. It burned like a hot iron. "How much money do you make, Marlowe?"

"Forty bucks a day and expenses. That's the asking price. I take twenty-five. I've taken less." I thought about Orfamay's worn twenty.

She did that with her finger again and I just didn't grab hold of her. She moved away from me and sat in the chair, drawing the robe close. The electric heater was making the little room warm.

"Twenty-five dollars a day," she said wonderingly.

"Little lonely dollars."

"Are they very lonely?"

"Lonely as lighthouses."

She crossed her legs and the pale glow of her skin in the light seemed to fill the room.

"So ask me the questions," she said, making no attempt to cover her thighs.

"Who's Steelgrave?"

"A man I've known for years. And liked. He owns things. A restaurant or two. Where he comes from — that I don't know."

"But you know him very well."

"Why don't you ask me if I sleep with him?"

"I don't ask that kind of question."

She laughed and snapped ash from her cigarette. "Miss Gonzales would be glad to tell you."

"The hell with Miss Gonzales."

"She's dark and lovely and passionate. And very, very kind."

"And exclusive as a mailbox," I said. "The hell with her. About Steelgrave — has he ever been in trouble?"

"Who hasn't?"

"With the police."

Her eyes widened a little too innocently. Her laugh was a little too silvery. "Don't be ridiculous. The man is worth a couple of million dollars."

"How did he get it?"

"How would I know?"

"All right. You wouldn't. That cigarette's going to burn your fingers." I leaned across and took the stub out of her hand. Her hand lay open on her bare leg. I touched the palm with a finger tip. She drew away from me and tightened the hand into a fist.

"Don't do that," she said sharply.

"Why? I used to do that to girls when I was a kid."

"I know." She was breathing a little fast. "It makes me feel very young and innocent and kind of naughty. And I'm far from being young and innocent any more."

"Then you don't really know anything about Steelgrave."

"I wish you'd make up your mind whether you are giving me a third degree or making love to me."

"My mind has nothing to do with it," I said.

After a silence she said: "I really do have to eat something, Marlowe. I'm working this afternoon. You wouldn't want me to collapse on the set, would you?"

"Only stars do that." I stood up. "Okay, I'll leave. Don't forget I'm working for you. I wouldn't be if I thought you'd killed anybody. But you were there. You took a big chance. There was something you wanted very badly."

She reached the photo out from somewhere and stared at it, biting her lip. Her eyes came up without her head moving.

"It could hardly have been this."

"That was the one thing he had so well hidden that it was not found. But what good is it? You and a man called Steelgrave in a booth at The Dancers. Nothing in that."

"Nothing at all," she said.

"So it has to be something about Steelgrave — or something about the date."

Her eyes snapped down to the picture again. "There's nothing to tell the date," she said quickly. "Even if it meant something. Unless the cut-out piece —"

"Here." I gave her the cut-out piece. "But you'll need a magnifier. Show it to Steelgrave. Ask *him* if it means anything. Or ask Ballou."

I started towards the exit of the dressing room. "Don't kid yourself, the date can't be fixed," I said over my shoulder. "Steelgrave won't."

"You're just building a sand castle, Marlowe."

"Really?" I looked back at her, not grinning. "You really think that? Oh no you don't. You went there. The man was murdered. You had a gun. He was a known crook. And I found something the police would love to have me hide from them. Because it must be as full of motive as the ocean is full of salt. As long as the cops don't find it I have a license. And as long as somebody else doesn't find it I don't have an ice pick in the back of my neck. Would you say I was in an overpaid profession?"

She just sat there and looked at me, one hand on her kneecap, squeezing it. The other moving restlessly, finger by finger, on the arm of the chair.

All I had to do was turn the knob and go on out. I don't know why it had to be so hard to do.

20

There was the usual coming and going in the corridor outside my office and when I opened the door and walked into the musty silence of the little waiting room there was the usual feeling of having been dropped down a well dried up twenty years ago to which no one would come back ever. The smell of old dust hung in the air as flat and stale as a football interview.

I opened the inner door and inside there it was the same dead air, the same dust along the veneer, the same broken promise of a life of ease. I opened the windows and turned on the radio. It came up too loud and when I had it tuned down to normal the phone sounded as if it had been ringing for some time. I took my hat off it and lifted the receiver.

It was high time I heard from her again. Her cool compact voice said: "This time I really mean it."

"Go on."

"I lied before. I'm not lying now. I really have heard from Orrin."

"Go on."

"You're not believing me. I can tell by your voice."

"You can't tell anything by my voice. I'm a detective. Heard from him how?"

"By phone from Bay City."

"Wait a minute." I put the receiver down on the stained brown blotter and lit my pipe. No hurry. Lies are always patient. I took it up again.

"We've been through that routine," I said. "You're pretty forgetful for your age. I don't think Dr. Zugsmith would like it."

"Please don't tease me. This is very serious. He got my letter. He went to the post office and asked for his mail. He knew where I'd be staying. And about when I'd be here. So he called up. He's staying with a doctor he got to know down there. Doing some kind of work for him. I told you he had two years medical."

"Doctor have a name?"

"Yes. A funny name. Dr. Vincent Lagardie."

"Just a minute. There's somebody at the door."

I laid the phone down very carefully. It might be brittle. It might be made of spun glass. I got a handkerchief out and wiped the palm of my hand, the one that had been holding it. I got up and went to the built-in wardrobe and looked at my face in the flawed mirror. It was me all right. I had a strained look. I'd been living too fast.

Dr. Vincent Lagardie, 965 Wyoming Street. Catty-corners from The Garland Home of Peace. Frame house on the corner. Quiet. Nice neighborhood. Friend of the extinct Clausen. Maybe. Not according to him. But still maybe.

I went back to the telephone and squeezed the jerks out of my voice. "How would you spell that?" I asked.

She spelled it — with ease and precision. "Nothing to do then, is there?" I said. "All jake to the angels — or whatever they say in Manhattan, Kansas."

"Stop sneering at me. Orrin's in a lot of trouble. Some" — her voice quivered a little and her breath came quickly — "some gangsters are after him."

"Don't be silly, Orfamay. They don't have gangsters in Bay City. They're all working in pictures. What's Dr. Lagardie's phone number?"

She gave it to me. It was right. I won't say the pieces were beginning to fall into place, but at least they were getting to look like parts of the same puzzle. Which is all I ever get or ask.

"Please go down there and see him and help him. He's afraid to leave the house. After all I did pay you."

"I gave it back."

"Well, I offered it to you again."

"You more or less offered me other things that are more than I'd care to take."

There was silence.

"All right," I said. "All right. If I can stay free that long. I'm in a lot of trouble myself."

"Why?"

"Telling lies and not telling the truth. It always catches up with me. I'm not as lucky as some people."

"But I'm not lying, Philip. I'm not lying. I'm frantic."

"Take a deep breath and get frantic so I can hear it."

"They might kill him," she said quietly.

"And what is Dr. Vincent Lagardie doing all this time?"

"He doesn't know, of course. Please, please go at once. I have the address here. Just a moment."

And the little bell rang, the one that rings far back at the end of the corridor, and is not loud, but you'd better hear it. No matter what other noises there are you'd better hear it.

"He'll be in the phone book," I said. "And by an odd coincidence I have a Bay City phone book. Call me around four. Or five. Better make it five."

I hung up quickly. I stood up and turned the radio off, not having heard a thing it said. I closed the windows again. I opened the drawer of my desk and took out the Luger and strapped it on. I fitted my hat on my head. On the way out I had another look at the face in the mirror.

I looked as if I had made up my mind to drive off a cliff.

21

THEY WERE JUST FINISHING a funeral service at The Garland Home of Peace. A big gray hearse was waiting at the side entrance. Cars were clotted along both sides of the street, three black sedans in a row at the side of Dr. Vincent Lagardie's establishment. People were coming sedately down the walk from the funeral chapel to the corner and getting into their cars. I stopped a third of a block away and waited. The cars didn't move. Then three people came out with a woman heavily veiled and all in black. They half carried her down to a big limousine. The boss mortician fluttered around making elegant little gestures and body movements as graceful as a Chopin ending. His composed gray face was long enough to wrap twice around his neck.

The amateur pallbearers carried the coffin out the side door and professionals eased the weight from them and slid it into the back of the hearse as smoothly as if it had no more weight than a pan of butter rolls. Flowers began to grow into a mound over it. The glass doors were closed and motors started all over the block.

A few moments later nothing was left but one sedan across the way and the boss mortician sniffing a tree rose on his way back to count the take. With a beaming smile he faded into his neat colonial doorway and the world was still and empty again. The sedan that was left hadn't moved. I drove along and made a U-turn and came up behind it. The driver wore blue serge and a soft cap with a shiny peak. He was doing a crossword puzzle from the morning paper. I stuck a pair of those diaphanous mirror sunglasses on my nose and strolled past him towards Dr. Lagardie's place. He didn't look up. When I was a few yards ahead I took the glasses off and pretended to polish them on my handkerchief. I caught him in one of the mirror lenses. He still didn't look up. He was just a guy doing a crossword puzzle. I put the mirror glasses back on my nose, and went around to Dr. Lagardie's front door.

The sign over the door said: RING AND ENTER. I rang, but the door wouldn't let me enter. I waited. I rang again. I waited again. There was silence inside. Then the door opened a crack very slowly, and the thin expressionless face over a white uniform looked out at me.

"I'm sorry. Doctor is not seeing any patients today." She blinked at the mirror glasses. She didn't like them. Her tongue moved restlessly inside her lips.

"I'm looking for a Mr. Quest. Orrin P. Quest."

"Who?" There was a dim reflection of shock behind her eyes.

"Quest. Q as in quintessential, U as in uninhibited, E as in Extrasensory, S as in Subliminal, T as in Toots. Put them all together and they spell Brother."

She looked at me as if I had just come up from the floor of the ocean with a drowned mermaid under my arm.

"I beg your pardon. Dr. Lagardie is not — "

She was pushed out of the way by invisible hands and a thin dark haunted man stood in the half-open doorway.

"I am Dr. Lagardie. What is it, please?"

I gave him a card. He read it. He looked at me. He had the white pinched look of a man who is waiting for a disaster to happen.

"We talked over the phone," I said. "About a man named Clausen."

"Please come in," he said quickly. "I don't remember, but come in."

I went in. The room was dark, the blinds drawn, the windows closed. It was dark, and it was cold.

The nurse backed away and sat down behind a small desk. It was an ordinary living room with light painted woodwork which had once been dark, judging by the probable age of the house. A square arch divided the living room from the dining room. There were easy chairs and a center table with magazines. It looked like what it was — the reception room of a doctor practicing in what had been a private home.

The telephone rang on the desk in front of the nurse. She started and her hand went out and then stopped. She stared at the telephone. After a while it stopped ringing.

"What was the name you mentioned?" Dr. Lagardie asked me softly.

"Orrin Quest. His sister told me he was doing some kind of work for you, Doctor. I've been looking for him for days. Last night he called her up. From here, she said."

"There is no one of that name here," Dr. Lagardie said politely. "There hasn't been."

"You don't know him at all?"

"I have never heard of him."

"I can't figure why he would say that to his sister."

The nurse dabbed at her eyes furtively. The telephone on her desk burred and made her jump again. "Don't answer it," Dr. Lagardie said without turning his head.

We waited while it rang. Everybody waits while a telephone rings. After a while it stopped.

"Why don't you go home, Miss Watson? There's nothing for you to do here."

"Thank you, Doctor." She sat without moving, looking down at the desk. She squeezed her eyes shut and blinked them open. She shook her head hopelessly.

Dr. Lagardie turned back to me. "Shall we go into my office?"

We went across through another door leading to a hallway. I walked on eggs. The atmosphere of the house was charged with foreboding. He opened a door and ushered me into what must have once been a bedroom, but nothing suggested a bedroom. It was a small compact doctor's office. An open door showed a part of an examination room. A sterilizer was working in the corner. There were a lot of needles cooking in it.

"That's a lot of needles," I said, always quick with an idea.

"Sit down, Mr. Marlowe."

He went behind the desk and sat down and picked up a long thin letter-opening knife.

He looked at me levelly from his sorrowful eyes. "No, I don't know anyone named Orrin Quest, Mr. Marlowe. I can't imagine any reason in the world why a person of that name should say he was in my house."

"Hiding out," I said.

His eyebrows went up. "From what?"

"From some guys that might want to stick an ice pick in the back of his neck. On account of he is a little too quick with his little Leica. Taking people's photographs when they want to be private. Or it could be something else, like peddling reefers and he got wise. Am I talking in riddles?"

"It was you who sent the police here," he said coldly.

I didn't say anything.

"It was you who called up and reported Clausen's death."

I said the same as before.

"It was you who called me up and asked me if I knew Clausen. I said I did not."

"But it wasn't true."

"I was under no obligation to give you information, Mr. Marlowe."

I nodded and got a cigarette out and lit it. Dr. Lagardie glanced at his watch. He turned in his chair and switched off the sterilizer. I looked at the needles. A lot of needles. Once before I had had trouble in Bay City with a guy who cooked a lot of needles.

"What makes it?" I asked him. "The yacht harbor?"

He picked up the wicked-looking paper knife with a silver handle in the shape of a nude woman. He pricked the ball of his thumb. A pearl of dark blood showed on it. He put it to his mouth and licked it. "I like the taste of blood," he said softly.

There was a distant sound as of the front door opening and closing. We both listened to it carefully. We listened to retreating steps on the front steps of the house. We listened hard.

"Miss Watson has gone home," Dr. Lagardie said. "We are all alone in the house." He mulled that over and licked his thumb again. He laid the knife down carefully on the desk blotter. "Ah, the question of the yacht harbor," he added. "The proximity of Mexico you are thinking of, no doubt. The ease with which marijuana —"

"I wasn't thinking so much of marijuana any more." I stared again at the needles. He followed my stare. He shrugged.

I said: "Why so many of them?"

"Is it any of your business?"

"Nothing's any of my business."

"But you seem to expect your questions to be answered."

"I'm just talking," I said. "Waiting for something to happen. Something's going to happen in this house. It's leering at me from corners."

Dr. Lagardie licked another pearl of blood off his thumb.

I looked hard at him. It didn't buy me a way into his soul. He was quiet, dark and shuttered and all the misery of life was in his eyes. But he was still gentle.

"Let me tell you about the needles," I said.

"By all means." He picked the long thin knife up again.

"Don't do that," I said sharply. "It gives me the creeps. Like petting snakes."

He put the knife down again gently and smiled. "We do seem to talk in circles," he suggested.

"We'll get there. About the needles. A couple of years back I had a case that brought me down here and mixed me up with a doctor named Almore. Lived over on Altair Street. He had a funny practice. Went out nights with a big case of hypodermic needles — all ready to go. Loaded with the stuff. He had a peculiar practice. Drunks, rich junkies, of whom there are far more than people think, overstimulated people who had driven themselves beyond the possibility of relaxing. Insomniacs — all the neurotic types that can't take it cold. Have to have their little pills and little shots in the arm. Have to have help over the humps. It gets to be all humps after a while. Good business for the doctor. Almore was the doctor for them. It's all right to say it now. He died a year or so back. Of his own medicine."

"And you think I may have inherited his practice?"

"Somebody would. As long as there are the patients, there will be the doctor."

He looked even more exhausted than before. "I think you are an ass, my friend. I did not know Dr. Almore. And I do not have the sort of practice you attribute to him. As for the needles — just to get that trifle out of the way — they are in somewhat constant use in the medical profession today, often for such innocent medicaments as vitamin injections. And needles get dull. And when they are dull they are painful. Therefore in the course of the day one may use a dozen or more. Without narcotics in a single one."

He raised his head slowly and stared at me with a fixed contempt.

"I can be wrong," I said. "Smelling that reefer smoke over at Clausen's place yesterday, and having him call your number on the telephone — and call you by your first name — all this probably made me jump to wrong conclusions."

"I have dealt with addicts," he said. "What doctor has not? It is a complete waste of time."

"They get cured sometimes."

"They can be deprived of their drug. Eventually after great suffering they can do without it. That is not curing them, my friend. That is not removing the nervous or emotional flaw which made them become addicts. It is making them dull negative people who sit in the sun and twirl their thumbs and die of sheer boredom and inanition."

"That's a pretty raw theory, Doctor."

"You raised the subject. I have disposed of it. I will raise another subject. You may have noticed a certain atmosphere and strain about this house. Even with those silly mirror glasses on. Which you may now remove. They don't make you look in the least like Cary Grant."

I took them off. I'd forgotten all about them.

"The police have been here, Mr. Marlowe. A certain Lieutenant Maglashan, who is investigating Clausen's death. He would be pleased to meet you. Shall I call him? I'm sure he would come back."

"Go ahead, call him," I said. "I just stopped off here on my way to commit suicide."

His hand went towards the telephone but was pulled to one side by the magnetism of the paper knife. He picked it up again. Couldn't leave it alone, it seemed.

"You could kill a man with that," I said.

"Very easily." And he smiled a little.

"An inch and a half in the back of the neck, square in the center, just under the occipital bulge."

"An ice pick would be better," he said. "Especially a short one, filed down very sharp. It would not bend. If you miss the spinal cord, you do no great damage."

"Takes a bit of medical knowledge then?" I got out a poor old package of Camels and untangled one from the cellophane.

He just kept on smiling. Very faintly, rather sadly. It was not the smile of a man in fear. "That would help," he said softly. "But any reasonably dexterous person could acquire the technique in ten minutes."

"Orrin Quest had a couple of years medical," I said.

"I told you I did not know anybody of that name."

"Yeah, I know you did. I didn't quite believe you."

He shrugged his shoulders. But his eyes as always went to the knife in the end.

"We're a couple of sweethearts," I said. "We just sit here making with the old over-the-desk dialogue. As though we hadn't a care in the world. Because both of us are going to be in the clink by nightfall."

He raised his eyebrows again. I went on:

"You, because Clausen knew you by your first name. And you may have been the last man he talked to. Me, because I've been doing all the things a P.I. never gets away with. Hiding evidence, hiding information, finding bodies and not coming in with my hat in my hand to these lovely incorruptible Bay City cops. Oh, I'm through. Very much through. But there's a wild perfume in the air this afternoon. I don't seem to care. Or I'm in love. I just don't seem to care."

"You have been drinking," he said slowly.

"Only Chanel No. 5, and kisses, and the pale glow of lovely legs, and the mocking invitation in deep blue eyes. Innocent things like that."

He just looked sadder than ever. "Women can weaken a man terribly, can they not?" he said.

"Clausen."

"A hopeless alcoholic. You probably know how they are. They

drink and drink and don't eat. And little by little the vitamin deficiency brings on the symptoms of delirium. There is only one thing to do for them." He turned and looked at the sterilizer. "Needles, and more needles. It makes me feel dirty. I am a graduate of the Sorbonne. But I practice among dirty little people in a dirty little town."

"Why?"

"Because of something that happened years ago — in another city. Don't ask me too much, Mr. Marlowe."

"He used your first name."

"It is a habit with people of a certain class. One-time actors especially. And one-time crooks."

"Oh," I said. "That all there is to it?"

"All."

"Then the cops coming here doesn't bother you on account of Clausen. You're just afraid of this other thing that happened somewhere else long gone. Or it could even be love."

"Love?" He dropped the word slowly off the end of his tongue, tasting it to the last. A bitter little smile stayed after the word, like powder smell in the air after a gun is fired. He shrugged and pushed a desk cigarette box from behind a filing tray and over to my side of the desk.

"Not love then," I said. "I'm trying to read your mind. Here you are a guy with a Sorbonne degree and a cheap little practice in a cheap and nasty little town. I know it well. So what are you doing here? What are you doing with people like Clausen? What was the rap, Doctor? Narcotics, abortions, or were you by any chance a medic for the gang boys in some hot eastern city?"

"As for instance?" he smiled thinly.

"As for instance Cleveland."

"A very wild suggestion, my friend." His voice was like ice now.

"Wild as all hell," I said. "But a fellow like me with very limited brains tends to try to fit the things he knows into a pattern. It's often wrong, but it's an occupational disease with me. It goes like this, if you want to listen."

"I am listening." He picked the knife up again and pricked lightly at the blotter on his desk.

"You knew Clausen. Clausen was killed very skillfully with an ice pick, killed while I was in the house, upstairs talking to a grifter named Hicks. Hicks moved out fast taking a page of the register with him, the page that had Orrin Quest's name on it. Later that afternoon Hicks was killed with an ice pick in L.A. His room had been searched. There was a woman there who had come to buy something from him. She didn't get it. I had more time to search. I did get it. Presumption A: Clausen and Hicks killed by same man, not necessarily for same reason. Hicks killed because he muscled in on another guy's racket and muscled the other guy out. Clausen killed because he was a babbling drunk and might know who would be likely to kill Hicks. Any good so far?"

"Not the slightest interest to me," Dr. Lagardie said.

"But you *are* listening. Sheer good manners, I suppose. Okay. Now what did I find? A photo of a movie queen and an ex-Cleveland gangster, maybe, now a Hollywood restaurant owner, et cetera, having lunch on a particular day. Day when this ex-Cleveland gangster was supposed to be in hock at the County Jail, also day when ex-Cleveland gangster's one-time sidekick was shot dead on Franklin Avenue in Los Angeles. Why was he in hock? Tip-off that he was who he was, and say what you like against the L.A. cops they do try to run back-east hot shots out of town. Who gave them the tip? The guy they pinched gave it to them himself, because his ex-partner was being troublesome and had to be rubbed out, and being in jail was a first-class alibi when it happened."

"All fantastic," Dr. Lagardie smiled wearily. "Utterly fantastic."

"Sure. It gets worse. Cops couldn't prove anything on ex-gangster. Cleveland police not interested. The L.A. cops turn him loose. But they wouldn't have turned him loose if they'd seen that photo. Photo therefore strong blackmail material, first against ex-Cleveland character, if he really is the guy; secondly against movie queen for being seen around with him in public. A good man could make a fortune out of that photo. Hicks not good enough. Paragraph. Presumption B: Orrin Quest, the boy I'm trying to find, took that photo. Taken with Contax or Leica, without flashbulb, without subjects knowing they were being photographed. Quest had a Leica and liked to do things like that. In this case of course he had a more commercial motive. Question, how did he get a chance to take photo? Answer, the movie queen was his sister. She would let him come up and speak to her. He was out of work, needed money. Likely enough she gave him some and made it a condition he stay away from her. She wants no part of her family. Is it still utterly fantastic, Doctor?"

He stared at me moodily. "I don't know," he said slowly. "It begins to have possibilities. But why are you telling this rather dangerous story to me?"

He reached a cigarette out of the box and tossed me one casually. I caught it and looked it over. Egyptian, oval and fat, a little rich for my blood. I didn't light it, just sat holding it between my fingers, watching his dark unhappy eyes. He lit his own cigarette and puffed nervously.

"I'll tie you in on it now," I said. "You knew Clausen. Professionally, you said. I showed him I was a dick. He tried at once to call you up; he was too drunk to talk to you. I caught the number and later told you he was dead. Why? If you were on the level, you would call the cops. You didn't. Why? You knew Clausen, you could have known some of his roomers. No proof either way. Paragraph. Presumption C: you knew Hicks or Orrin Quest or both. The L.A. cops couldn't or didn't establish identity of ex-Cleveland character — let's give him his new name, call him Steelgrave. But *somebody* had to be able to — if that photo was worth killing people over. Did you ever practice medicine in Cleveland, Doctor?"

"Certainly not." His voice seemed to come from far off. His eyes were remote too. His lips opened barely enough to admit his cigarette. He was very still.

I said: "They have a whole roomful of directories over at the telephone office. From all over the country. I checked you up.

"A suite in a downtown office building," I said. "And now this — an almost furtive practice in a little beach town. You'd have liked to change your name — but you couldn't and keep your license. Somebody had to mastermind this deal, Doctor. Clausen was a bum, Hicks a stupid lout, Orrin Quest a nasty-minded creep. But they could be used. You couldn't go up against Steelgrave directly. You wouldn't have stayed alive long enough to brush your teeth. You had to work through pawns — expendable pawns. Well — are we getting anywhere?"

He smiled faintly and leaned back in his chair with a sigh. "Presumption D, Mr. Marlowe," he almost whispered. "You are an unmitigated idiot."

I grinned and reached for a match to light his fat Egyptian cigarette.

"Added to all the rest," I said, "Orrin's sister calls me up and tells me he is in your house. There are a lot of weak arguments taken one at a time, I admit. But they do seem to sort of focus on you." I puffed peacefully on the cigarette.

He watched me. His face seemed to fluctuate and become vague, to move far off and come back. I felt a tightness in my chest. My mind had slowed to a turtle's gallop.

"What's going on here?" I heard myself mumble.

I put my hands on the arms of the chair and pushed myself up. "Been dumb, haven't I?" I said, with the cigarette still in my mouth and me still smoking it. Dumb was hardly the word. Have to coin a new word.

I was out of the chair and my feet were stuck in two barrels of cement. When I spoke my voice seemed to come through cotton-wool.

I let go of the arms of the chair and reached for the cigarette. I missed it clean a couple of times, then got my hand around it. It didn't feel like a cigarette. It felt like the hind leg of an elephant. With sharp toenails. They stuck into my hand. I shook my hand and the elephant took his leg away.

A vague but enormously tall figure swung around in front of me and a mule kicked me in the chest. I sat down on the floor.

"A little potassium hydrocyanide," a voice said, over the transatlantic telephone. "Not fatal, not even dangerous. Merely relaxing . . ."

I started to get up off the floor. You ought to try it sometime. But have somebody nail the floor down first. This one looped the loop. After a while it steadied a little. I settled for an angle of forty-five degrees. I took hold of myself and started to go somewhere.

There was a thing that might have been Napoleon's tomb on the horizon. That was a good enough objective. I started that way. My heart beat fast and thick and I was having trouble opening my lungs. Like after being winded at football. You think your breath will never come back. Never, never, never.

Then it wasn't Napoleon's tomb any more. It was a raft on a swell. There was a man on it. I'd seen him somewhere. Nice fellow. We'd got on fine. I started towards him and hit a wall with my shoulder. That spun me around. I started clawing for something to hold on to. There was nothing but the carpet. How did I get down there? No use asking. It's a secret. Every time you ask a question they just push the floor in your face. Okay, I started to crawl along the carpet. I was on what formerly had been my hands and knees. No sensation proved it. I crawled towards a dark wooden wall. Or it could have been black marble. Napoleon's tomb again. What did I ever do to Napoleon? What for should he keep shoving his tomb at me?

"Need a drink of water," I said.

I listened for the echo. No echo. Nobody said anything. Maybe I didn't say it. Maybe it was just an idea I thought better of. Potassium cyanide. That's a couple of long words to be worrying about when you're crawling through tunnels. Nothing fatal, he said. Okay, this is just fun. What you might call semi-fatal. Philip Marlowe, 38, a private license operator of shady reputation, was apprehended by police last night while crawling through the Ballona Storm Drain with a grand piano on his back. Questioned at the University Heights Police Station Marlowe declared he was taking the piano to the Maharajah of Coot-Berar. Asked why he was wearing spurs Marlowe declared that a client's confidence was sacred. Marlowe is being held for investigation. Chief Hornside said police were not yet ready to say more. Asked if the piano was in tune Chief Hornside declared that he had played the Minute Waltz on it in thirty-five seconds and so far as he could tell there were no strings in the piano. He intimated that something else was. A complete statement to the press will be made within twelve hours, Chief Hornside said abruptly. Speculation is rife that Marlowe was attempting to dispose of a body.

A face swam towards me out of the darkness. I changed direction and started for the face. But it was too late in the afternoon. The sun was setting. It was getting dark rapidly. There was no face. There was no wall, no desk. Then there was no floor. There was nothing at all.

I wasn't even there.

22

A BIG BLACK GORILLA with a big black paw had his big black paw over my face and was trying to push it through the back of my neck. I pushed back. Taking the weak side of an argument is my specialty. Then I realized that he was trying to keep me from opening my eyes.

I decided to open my eyes just the same. Others have done it, why not me? I gathered my strength and very slowly, keeping the back straight, flexing the thighs and knees, using the arms as ropes, I lifted the enormous weight of my eyelids.

I was looking at the ceiling, lying on my back on the floor, a position in which my calling has occasionally placed me. I rolled my head. My lungs felt stiff and my mouth felt dry. The room was just Dr. Lagardie's consulting room. Same chair, same desk, same walls and window. There was a shuttered silence hanging around.

I got up on my haunches and braced myself on the floor and shook my head. It went into a flat spin. It spun down about five thousand feet and then I dragged it out and leveled off. I blinked. Same floor, same desk, same walls. But no Dr. Lagardie.

I wet my lips and made some kind of a vague noise to which nobody paid any attention. I got up on my feet. I was as dizzy as a dervish, as weak as a worn-out washer, as low as a badger's belly, as timid as a titmouse, and as unlikely to succeed as a ballet dancer with a wooden leg.

I groped my way over behind the desk and slumped into Lagardie's chair and began to paw fitfully through his equipment for a likely-looking bottle of liquid fertilizer. Nothing doing. I got up again. I was as hard to lift as a dead elephant. I staggered around looking into cabinets of shining white enamel which contained everything somebody else was in a hurry for. Finally, after what seemed like four years on the road gang, my little hand closed around six ounces of ethyl alcohol. I got the top off the bottle and sniffed. Grain alcohol. Just what the label said. All I needed now was a glass and some water. A good man ought to be able to get that far. I started through the door to the examination room. The air still had the aromatic perfume of overripe peaches. I hit both sides of the doorway going through and paused to take a fresh sighting.

At that moment I was aware that steps were coming down the hall. I leaned against the wall wearily and listened.

Slow, dragging steps, with a long pause between each. At first they seemed furtive. Then they just seemed very, very tired. An old man trying to make it to his last armchair. That made two of us. And then I thought, for no reason at all, of Orfamay's father back there on the porch in Manhattan, Kansas, moving quietly along to his rocking chair with his cold pipe in his hand, to sit down and look out over the front lawn and have himself a nice economical smoke that required no matches and no tobacco and didn't mess up the living-room carpet. I arranged his chair for him. In the shade at the end of the porch where the bougainvillaea was thick I helped him sit down. He looked up and thanked me with the good side of his face. His fingernails scratched on the arms of the chair as he leaned back.

The fingernails scratched, but it wasn't on the arm of any chair. It was a real sound. It was close by, on the outside of a closed door that led from the examination room to the hallway. A thin feeble scratch, possibly a young kitten wanting to be let in. Okay, Marlowe, you're an old animal lover. Go over and let the kitten in. I started. I made it with the help of the nice examination couch with the rings on the end and the nice clean towels. The scratching had stopped. Poor little kitten, outside and wanting in. A tear formed itself in my eye and trickled down my furrowed cheek. I let go of the examination table and made a smooth four yards to the door. The heart was bumping inside me. And the lungs still had that feeling of having been in storage for a couple of years.

I took a deep breath and got hold of the doorknob and opened it. Just at the last moment it occurred to me to reach for a gun. It occurred to me but that's as far as I got. I'm a fellow that likes to take an idea over by the light and have a good look at it. I'd have had to let go of the doorknob. It seemed like too big an operation. I just twisted the knob and opened the door instead.

He was braced to the doorframe by four hooked fingers made of white wax. He had eyes an eighth of an inch deep, pale gray-blue, wide open. They looked at me but they didn't see me. Our faces were inches apart. Our breathing met in midair. Mine was quick and harsh, his was the far-off whisper which has not yet begun to rattle. Blood bubbled from his mouth and ran down his chin. Something made me look down. Blood drained slowly down the inside of his trouser leg and out on his shoe and from his shoe it flowed without haste to the floor. It was already a small pool.

I couldn't see where he had been shot. His teeth clicked and I thought he was going to speak, or try to speak. But that was the only sound from him. He had stopped breathing. His jaw fell slack. Then the rattle started. It isn't a rattle at all, of course. It isn't anything like a rattle.

Rubber heels squeaked on the linoleum between the rug and the door sill. The white fingers slid away from the doorframe. The man's body started to wind up on the legs. The legs refused to hold it. They scissored. His torso turned in midair, like a swimmer in a wave, and jumped at me.

In the same moment his other arm, the one that had been out of sight, came up and over in a galvanic sweep that seemed not to have any possible living impetus behind it. It fell across my left shoulder as I reached for him. A bee stung me between the shoulder blades. Something besides the bottle of alcohol I had been holding thumped to the floor and rattled against the bottom of the wall.

I clamped my teeth hard and spread my feet and caught him under the arms. He weighed like five men. I took a step back and tried to hold him up. It was like trying to lift one end of a fallen tree. I went down with him. His head bumped the floor. I couldn't help it. There wasn't enough of me working to stop it. I straightened him out a bit and got away from him. I climbed up on my knees, and bent down and listened. The rattle stopped. There was a long silence. Then there was a muted sigh, very quiet and indolent and without urgency. Another silence. Another still slower sigh, languid and peaceful as a summer breeze drifting past the nodding roses.

Something happened to his face and behind his face, the indefinable thing that happens in that always baffling and inscrutable moment, the smoothing out, the going back over the years to the age of innocence. The face now had a vague inner amusement, an almost roguish lift at the corners of the mouth. All of which was very silly, because I knew damn well, if I ever knew anything at all, that Orrin P. Quest had not been that kind of boy.

In the distance a siren wailed. I stayed kneeling and listened. It wailed and went away. I got to my feet and went over and looked out of the side window. In front of The Garland Home of Peace another funeral was forming up. The street was thick with cars again. People walked slowly up the path past the tree roses. Very slowly, the men with their hats in their hands long before they reached the little colonial porch.

I dropped the curtain and went over and picked up the bottle of ethyl alcohol and wiped it off with my handkerchief and laid it aside. I was no longer interested in alcohol. I bent down again and the bee sting between my shoulder blades reminded me that there was something else to pick up. A thing with a round white wooden handle that lay against the baseboard. An ice pick with a filed-down blade not more than three inches long. I held it against the light and looked at the needle-sharp tip. There might or might not have been a faint stain of my blood on it. I pulled a finger gently beside the point. No blood. The point was very sharp.

I did some more work with my handkerchief and then bent down and put the ice pick on the palm of his right hand, white and waxy against the dull nap of the carpet. It looked too arranged. I shook his arm enough to make it roll off his hand to the floor. I thought about going through his pockets, but a more ruthless hand than mine would have done that already.

In a flash of sudden panic I went through mine instead. Nothing had been taken. Even the Luger under my arm had been left. I dragged it out and sniffed at it. It had not been fired, something I should have known without looking. You don't walk around much after being shot with a Luger.

I stepped over the dark red pool in the doorway and looked along the hall. The house was still silent and waiting. The blood trail led me back and across to a room furnished like a den. There was a studio couch and a desk, some books and medical journals, an ashtray with five fat oval stubs in it. A metallic glitter near the leg of the studio couch turned out to be a used shell from an automatic — .32 caliber. I found another under the desk. I put them in my pocket.

I went back out and up the stairs. There were two bedrooms both in use, one pretty thoroughly stripped of clothes. In an ashtray more of Dr. Lagardie's oval stubs. The other room contained Orrin Quest's meager wardrobe, his spare suit and overcoat neatly hung in the closet, his shirts and socks and underwear equally neat in the drawers of a chest. Under the shirts at the back I found a Leica with an F.2 lens.

I left all these things as they were and went back downstairs into the room where the dead man lay indifferent to these trifles. I wiped off a few more doorknobs out of sheer perverseness, hesitated over the phone in the front room, and left without touching it. The fact that I was still walking around was a pretty good indication that the good Dr. Lagardie hadn't killed anybody.

People were still crawling up the walk to the oddly undersized colonial porch of the funeral parlor across the street. An organ was moaning inside.

I went around the corner of the house and got into my car and left. I drove slowly and breathed deeply from the bottom of my lungs, but I still couldn't seem to get enough oxygen.

Bay City ends about four miles from the ocean. I stopped in front of the last drugstore. It was time for me to make one more of my anonymous phone calls. Come and pick up the body, fellows. Who am I? Just a lucky boy who keeps finding them for you. Modest too. Don't even want my name mentioned.

I looked at the drugstore and in through the plate-glass front. A girl with slanted cheaters was reading at a magazine. She looked something like Orfamay Quest. Something tightened up my throat.

I let the clutch in and drove on. She had a right to know first, law or no law. And I was far outside the law already.

23

I STOPPED AT THE OFFICE DOOR with the key in my hand. Then I went noiselessly along to the other door, the one that was always unlocked, and stood there and listened. She might be in there already, waiting, with her eyes shining behind the slanted cheaters and the small moist mouth willing to be kissed. I would have to tell her a harder thing than she dreamed of, and then after a while she would go and I would never see her again.

I didn't hear anything. I went back and unlocked the other door and picked the mail up and carried it over and dumped it on the desk. Nothing in it made me feel any taller. I left it and crossed to turn the latch in the other door and after a long slow moment I opened it and looked out. Silence and emptiness. A folded piece of paper lay at my feet. It had been pushed under the door. I picked it up and unfolded it.

"Please call me at the apartment house. Most urgent. I must see you." It was signed D.

I dialed the number of the Chateau Bercy and asked for Miss Gonzales. Who was calling, please? One moment please, Mr. Marlowe. Buzz, buzz. Buzz, buzz.

"Allo?"

"The accent's a bit thick this afternoon."

"Ah, it is you, amigo. I waited so long in your funny little office. Can you come over here and talk to me?"

"Impossible. I'm waiting for a call."

"Well, may I come there?"

"What's it all about?"

"Nothing I could discuss on the telephone, amigo."

"Come ahead."

I sat there and waited for the telephone to ring. It didn't ring. I looked out of the window. The crowd was seething on the boulevard, the kitchen of the coffee shop next door was pouring the smell of Blue Plate Specials out of its ventilator shaft. Time passed and I sat there hunched over the desk, my chin in a hand, staring at the mustard-yellow plaster of the end wall, seeing on it the vague figure of a dying man with a short ice pick in his hand, and feeling the sting of its point between my shoulder blades. Wonderful what Hollywood will do to a nobody. It will make a radiant glamour queen out of a drab little wench who ought to be ironing a truck driver's shirts, a he-man hero with shining eyes and brilliant smile reeking of sexual charm out of some overgrown kid who was meant to go to work with a lunchbox. Out of a Texas carhop with the literacy of a character in a comic strip it will make an international courtesan, married six times to six millionaires and so blasé and decadent at the end of it that her idea of a thrill is to seduce a furniture mover in a sweaty undershirt.

And by remote control it might even take a small-town prig like Orrin Quest and make an ice-pick murderer out of him in a matter of months, elevating his simple meanness into the classic sadism of the multiple killer.

It took her a little over ten minutes to get there. I heard the door open and close and I went through to the waiting room and there she was, the All-American Gardenia. She hit me right between the eyes. Her own were deep and dark and unsmiling.

She was all in black, like the night before, but a tailor-made outfit this time, a wide black straw hat set at a rakish angle, the collar of a white silk shirt folded out over the collar of her jacket, and her throat brown and supple and her mouth as red as a new fire engine.

"I waited a long time," she said. "I have not had any lunch."

"I had mine," I said. "Cyanide. Very satisfying. I've only just stopped looking blue."

"I am not in an amusing mood this morning, amigo."

"You don't have to amuse me," I said. "I amuse myself. I do a brother act that has me rolling in the aisle. Let's go inside."

We went into my private thinking parlor and sat down.

"You always wear black?" I asked.

"But yes. It is more exciting when I take my clothes off."

"Do you have to talk like a whore?"

"You do not know much about whores, amigo. They are always most respectable. Except of course the very cheap ones."

"Yeah," I said. "Thanks for telling me. What is the urgent

matter we have to talk about? Going to bed with you is not urgent. It can be done any day."

"You are in a nasty mood."

"Okay. I'm in a nasty mood."

She got one of her long brown cigarettes out of her bag and fitted it carefully into the golden tweezers. She waited for me to light it for her. I didn't so she lit it herself with a golden lighter.

She held this doohickey in a black gauntleted glove and stared at me out of depthless black eyes that had no laughter in them now.

"Would you like to go to bed with me?"

"Most anyone would. But let's leave sex out of it for now."

"I do not draw a very sharp line between business and sex," she said evenly. "And you cannot humiliate me. Sex is a net with which I catch fools. Some of these fools are useful and generous. Occasionally one is dangerous."

She paused thoughtfully.

I said: "If you're waiting for me to say something that lets on I know who a certain party is — okay, I know who he is."

"Can you prove it?"

"Probably not. The cops couldn't."

"The cops," she said contemptuously, "do not always tell all they know. They do not always prove everything they could prove. I suppose you know he was in jail for ten days last February."

"Yes."

"Did it not occur to you as strange that he did not get bail?"

"I don't know what charge they had him on. If it was as a material witness —"

"Do you not think he could get the charge changed to something bailable — if he really wanted to?"

"I haven't thought much about it," I lied. "I don't know the man."

"You have never spoken to him?" she asked idly, a little too idly. I didn't answer.

She laughed shortly. "Last night, amigo. Outside Mavis Weld's apartment. I was sitting in a car across the street."

"I may have bumped into him accidentally. Was that the guy?"

"You do not fool me at all."

"Okay. Miss Weld was pretty rough with me. I went away sore. Then I meet this ginzo with her doorkey in his hand. I yank it out of his hand and toss it behind some bushes. Then I apologize and go get it for him. He seemed like a nice little guy too."

"Ver-ry nice," she drawled. "He was *my* boy friend also."

I grunted.

"Strange as it may seem I'm not a hell of a lot interested in your love life, Miss Gonzales. I assume it covers a wide field — all the way from Stein to Steelgrave."

"Stein?" she asked softly. "Who is Stein?"

"A Cleveland hot shot that got himself gunned in front of your apartment house last February. He had an apartment there. I thought perhaps you might have met him."

She let out a silvery little laugh. "Amigo, there are men I do not know. Even at the Chateau Bercy."

"Reports say he was gunned two blocks away," I said. "I like it better that it happened right in front. And you were looking out of the window and saw it happen. And saw the killer run away and just under a streetlight he turned back and the light caught his face and darned if it wasn't old man Steelgrave. You recognized him by his rubber nose and the fact that he was wearing his tall hat with the pigeons on it."

She didn't laugh.

"You like it better that way." She purred.

"We could make more money that way."

"But Steelgrave was in jail." She smiled. "And even if he was not in jail — even if, for example, I happened to be friendly with a certain Dr. Chalmers who was county jail physician at the time and he told me, in an intimate moment, that he had given Steelgrave a pass to go to the dentist — with a guard of course, but the guard was a reasonable man — on the very day Stein was shot — even if this happened to be true, would it not be a very poor way to use the information by blackmailing Steelgrave?"

"I hate to talk big," I said, "but I'm not afraid of Steelgrave — or a dozen like him in one package."

"But I am, amigo. A witness to a gang murder is not in a very safe position in this country. No, we will not blackmail Steelgrave.

And we will not say anything about Mr. Stein, whom I may or may not have known. It is enough that Mavis Weld is a close friend of a known gangster and is seen in public with him."

"We'd have to prove he was a known gangster," I said.

"Can we not do that?"

"How?"

She made a disappointed mouth. "But I felt sure that was what you had been doing these last couple of days."

"Why?"

"I have private reasons."

"They mean nothing to me while you keep them private."

She got rid of the brown cigarette stub in my ashtray. I leaned over and squashed it out with the stub of a pencil. She touched my hand lightly with a gauntleted finger. Her smile was the reverse of anesthetic. She leaned back and crossed her legs. The little lights began to dance in her eyes. It was a long time between passes — for her.

"Love is such a dull word," she mused. "It amazes me that the English language so rich in the poetry of love can accept such a feeble word for it. It has no life, no resonance. It suggests to me little girls in ruffled summer dresses, with little pink smiles, and little shy voices, and probably the most unbecoming underwear."

I said nothing. With an effortless change of pace she became businesslike again.

"Mavis will get seventy-five thousand dollars a picture from now on, and eventually one hundred fifty thousand. She has started to climb and nothing will stop her. Except possibly a bad scandal."

"Then somebody ought to tell her who Steelgrave is," I said. "Why don't you? And incidentally, suppose we did have all this proof, what's Steelgrave doing all the time we're putting the bite on Weld?"

"Does he have to know? I hardly think she would tell him. In fact, I hardly think she would go on having anything to do with him. But that would not matter to us — if we had our proof. And if she knew we had it."

Her black gauntleted hand moved towards her black bag, stopped, drummed lightly on the edge of the desk, and so got back

to where she could drop it in her lap. She hadn't looked at the bag.
I hadn't either.

I stood up. "I might happen to be under some obligation to Miss
Weld. Ever think of that?"

She just smiled.

"And if that was so," I said, "don't you think it's about time you
got the hell out of my office?"

She put her hands on the arms of her chair and started to get up,
still smiling. I scooped the bag before she could change direction.
Her eyes filled with glare. She made a spitting sound.

I opened the bag and went through and found a white envelope
that looked a little familiar. Out of it I shook the photo at The
Dancers, the two pieces fitted together and pasted on another piece
of paper.

I closed the bag and tossed it across to her.

She was on her feet now, her lips drawn back over her teeth.
She was very silent.

"Interesting," I said, and snapped a digit at the glazed surface of
the print. "If it's not a fake. Is that Steelgrave?"

The silvery laugh bubbled up again. "You are a ridiculous character, amigo. You really are. I did not know they made such people
any more."

"Pre-war stock," I said. "We're getting scarcer every day. Where
did you get this?"

"From Mavis Weld's purse in Mavis Weld's dressing room. While
she was on the set."

"She know?"

"She does not know."

"I wonder where she got it."

"From you."

"Nonsense." I raised my eyebrows a few inches. "Where would
I get it?"

She reached the gauntleted hand across the desk. Her voice was
cold. "Give it back to me, please."

"I'll give it back to Mavis Weld. And I hate to tell you this, Miss
Gonzales, but I'd never get anywhere as a blackmailer. I just don't
have the engaging personality."

"Give it back to me!" she said sharply. "If you do not — "

She cut herself off. I waited for her to finish. A look of contempt showed on her smooth features.

"Very well," she said. "It is my mistake. I thought you were smart, I can see that you are just another dumb private eye. This shabby little office" — she waved a black gloved hand at it — "and the shabby little life that goes on here — they ought to tell me what sort of idiot you are."

"They do," I said.

She turned slowly and walked to the door. I got around the desk and she let me open it for her.

She went out slowly. The way she did it hadn't been learned at business college.

She went on down the hall without looking back. She had a beautiful walk.

The door bumped against the pneumatic door closer and very softly clicked shut. It seemed to take a long time to do that. I stood there watching it as if I had never seen it happen before. Then I turned and started back towards my desk and the phone rang.

I picked it up and answered it. It was Christy French. "Marlowe? We'd like to see you down at headquarters."

"Right away?"

"If not sooner," he said, and hung up.

I slipped the pasted-together print from under the blotter and went over to put it in the safe with the others. I put my hat on and closed the window. There was nothing to wait for. I looked at the green tip on the sweep hand of my watch. It was a long time until five o'clock. The sweep hand went around and around the dial like a door-to-door salesman. The hands stood at four-ten. You'd think she'd have called up by now. I peeled my coat off and unstrapped the shoulder harness and locked it with the Luger in the desk drawer. The cops don't like you to be wearing a gun in their territory. Even if you have the right to wear one. They like you to come in properly humble, with your hat in your hand, and your voice low and polite, and your eyes full of nothing.

I looked at the watch again. I listened. The building seemed quiet this afternoon. After a while it would be silent and then the madonna of the dark-gray mop would come shuffling along the hall, trying doorknobs.

I put my coat back on and locked the communicating door and switched off the buzzer and let myself out into the hallway. And then the phone rang. I nearly took the door off its hinges getting back to it. It was her voice all right, but it had a tone I had never heard before. A cool balanced tone, not flat or empty or dead, or even childish. Just the voice of a girl I didn't know and yet did know. What was in that voice I knew before she said more than three words.

"I called you up because you told me to," she said. "But you don't have to tell me anything. I went down there."

I was holding the phone with both hands.

"You went down there," I said. "Yes. I heard that. So?"

"I — borrowed a car," she said. "I parked across the street. There were so many cars you would never have noticed me. There's a funeral home there. I wasn't following you. I tried to go after you when you came out but I don't know the streets down there at all. I lost you. So I went back."

"What did you go back for?"

"I don't really know. I thought you looked kind of funny when you came out of the house. Or maybe I just had a feeling. He being my brother and all. So I went back and rang the bell. And nobody answered the door. I thought that was funny too. Maybe I'm psychic or something. All of a sudden I seemed to have to get into that house. And I didn't know how to do it, but I had to."

"That's happened to me," I said, and it was my voice, but somebody had been using my tongue for sandpaper.

"I called the police and told them I had heard shots," she said. "They came and one of them got into the house through a window. And then he let the other one in. And after a while they let me in. And then they wouldn't let me go. I had to tell them all about it, who he was, and that I had lied about the shots, but I was afraid something had happened to Orrin. And I had to tell them about you too."

"That's all right," I said. "I'd have told them myself as soon as I could get a chance to tell *you*."

"It's kind of awkward for you, isn't it?"

"Yes."

"Will they arrest you or something?"

"They could."

"You left him lying there on the floor. Dead. You had to, I guess."

"I had my reasons," I said. "They won't sound too good, but I had them. It made no difference to him."

"Oh you'd have your reasons all right," she said. "You're very smart. You'd always have reasons for things. Well, I guess you'll have to tell the police your reasons too."

"Not necessarily."

"Oh yes, you will," the voice said, and there was a ring of pleasure in it I couldn't account for. "You certainly will. They'll make you."

"We won't argue about that," I said. "In my business a fellow does what he can to protect a client. Sometimes he goes a little too far. That's what I did. I've put myself where they can hurt me. But not entirely for you."

"You left him lying on the floor, dead," she said. "And I don't care what they do to you. If they put you in prison, I think I would like that. I bet you'll be awfully brave about it."

"Sure," I said. "Always a gay smile. Did you see what he had in his hand?"

"He didn't have anything in his hand."

"Well, lying near his hand."

"There wasn't anything. There wasn't anything at all. What sort of thing?"

"That's fine," I said. "I'm glad of that. Well, goodbye. I'm going down to headquarters now. They want to see me. Good luck, if I don't see you again."

"You'd better keep your good luck," she said. "You might need it. And I wouldn't want it."

"I did my best for you," I said. "Perhaps if you'd given me a little more information in the beginning — "

She hung up while I was saying it.

I put the phone down in its cradle as gently as if it was a baby. I got out a handkerchief and wiped the palms of my hands. I went over to the washbasin and washed my hands and face. I sloshed cold water on my face and dried it off hard with the towel and looked at it in the mirror.

"You drove off a cliff all right," I said to the face.

24

In the center of the room was a long yellow oak table. Its edges were unevenly grooved with cigarette burns. Behind it was a window with wire over the stippled glass. Also behind it with a mess of papers spread out untidily in front of him was Detective Lieutenant Fred Beifus. At the end of the table leaning back on two legs of an armchair was a big burly man whose face had for me the vague familiarity of a face previously seen in a halftone on newsprint. He had a jaw like a park bench. He had the butt end of a carpenter's pencil between his teeth. He seemed to be awake and breathing, but apart from that he just sat.

There were two roll-top desks at the other side of the table and there was another window. One of the roll-top desks was backed to the window. A woman with orange-colored hair was typing out a report on a typewriter stand beside the desk. At the other desk, which was endways to the window, Christy French sat in a tilted-back swivel chair with his feet on the corner of the desk. He was looking out of the window, which was open and afforded a magnificent view of the police parking lot and the back of a billboard.

"Sit down there," Beifus said, pointing.

I sat down across from him in a straight oak chair without arms. It was far from new and when new had not been beautiful.

"This is Lieutenant Moses Maglashan of the Bay City police," Beifus said. "He don't like you any better than we do."

Lieutenant Moses Maglashan took the carpenter's pencil out of his mouth and looked at the teeth marks in the fat octagonal pencil butt. Then he looked at me. His eyes went over me slowly exploring me, noting me, cataloguing me. He said nothing. He put the pencil back in his mouth.

Beifus said: "Maybe I'm a queer, but for me you don't have no more sex appeal than a turtle." He half turned to the typing woman in the corner. "Millie."

She swung around from the typewriter to a shorthand notebook. "Name's Philip Marlowe," Beifus said. "With an 'e' on the end, if you're fussy. License number?"

He looked back at me. I told him. The orange queen wrote without looking up. To say she had a face that would have stopped a clock would have been to insult her. It would have stopped a runaway horse.

"Now if you're in the mood," Beifus told me, "you could start in at the beginning and give us all the stuff you left out yesterday. Don't try to sort it out. Just let it flow natural. We got enough stuff to check you as you go along."

"You want me to make a statement?"

"A very full statement," Beifus said. "Fun, huh?"

"This statement is to be voluntary and without coercion?"

"Yeah. They all are." Beifus grinned.

Maglashan looked at me steadily for a moment. The orange queen turned back to her typing. Nothing for her yet. Thirty years of it had perfected her timing.

Maglashan took a heavy worn pigskin glove out of his pocket and put it on his right hand and flexed his fingers.

"What's that for?" Beifus asked him.

"I bite my nails times," Maglashan said. "Funny. Only bite 'em on my right hand." He raised his slow eyes to stare at me. "Some guys are more voluntary than others," he said idly. "Something to do with the kidneys, they tell me. I've known guys of the not so voluntary type that had to go to the can every fifteen minutes for weeks after they got voluntary. Couldn't seem to hold water."

"Just think of that," Beifus said wonderingly.

"Then there's the guys can't talk above a husky whisper," Maglashan went on. "Like punch-drunk fighters that have stopped too many with their necks."

Maglashan looked at me. It seemed to be my turn.

"Then there's the type that won't go to the can at all," I said. "They try too hard. Sit in a chair like this for thirty hours straight. Then they fall down and rupture a spleen or burst a bladder. They overco-operate. And after sunrise court, when the tank is empty, you find them dead in a dark corner. Maybe they ought to have seen a doctor, but you can't figure everything, can you, Lieutenant?"

"We figure pretty close down in Bay City," he said. "When we got anything to figure with."

There were hard lumps of muscle at the corners of his jaws. His eyes had a reddish glare behind them.

"I could do lovely business with you," he said, staring at me. "Just lovely."

"I'm sure you could, Lieutenant. I've always had a swell time in Bay City — while I stayed conscious."

"I'd keep you conscious a long, long time, baby. I'd make a point of it. I'd give it my personal attention."

Christy French turned his head slowly and yawned. "What makes you Bay City cops so tough?" he asked. "You pickle your nuts in salt water or something?"

Beifus put his tongue out so that the tip showed and ran it along his lips.

"We've always been tough," Maglashan said, not looking at him. "We like to be tough. Jokers like this character here keep us tuned up." He turned back to me. "So you're the sweetheart that phoned in about Clausen. You're right handy with a pay phone, ain't you, sweetheart?"

I didn't say anything.

"I'm talking to you, sweetheart," Maglashan said. "I asked you a question, sweetheart. When I ask a question I get answered. Get that, sweetheart?"

"Keep on talking and you'll answer yourself," Christy French said. "And maybe you won't like the answer, and maybe you'll be so damn tough you'll have to knock yourself out with that glove. Just to prove it."

Maglashan straightened up. Red spots the size of half-dollars glowed dully on his cheeks.

"I come up here to get co-operation," he told French slowly.

"The big razzoo I can get at home. From my wife. Here I don't expect the wise numbers to work out on me."

"You'll get co-operation," French said. "Just don't try to steal the picture with that nineteen-thirty dialogue." He swung his chair around and looked at me. "Let's take out a clean sheet of paper and play like we're just starting this investigation. I know all your arguments. I'm no judge of them. The point is do you want to talk or get booked as a material witness?"

"Ask the questions," I said. "If you don't like the answers, you can book me. If you book me, I get to make a phone call."

"Correct," French said, "*if* we book you. But we don't have to. We can ride the circuit with you. It might take days."

"And canned corn-beef hash to eat," Breifus put in cheerfully.

"Strictly speaking, it wouldn't be legal," French said. "But we do it all the time. Like you do a few things which you hadn't ought to do maybe. Would you say you were legal in this picture?"

"No."

Maglashan let out a deep-throated "Ha!"

I looked across at the orange queen who was back to her notebook, silent and indifferent.

"You got a client to protect," French said.

"Maybe."

"You mean you did have a client. She ratted on you."

I said nothing.

"Name's Orfamay Quest," French said, watching me.

"Ask your questions," I said.

"What happened down there on Idaho Street?"

"I went there looking for her brother. He'd moved away, she said, and she'd come out here to see him. She was worried. The manager, Clausen, was too drunk to talk sense. I looked at the register and saw another man had moved into Quest's room. I talked to this man. He told me nothing that helped."

French reached around and picked a pencil off the desk and tapped it against his teeth. "Ever see this man again?"

"Yes. I told him who I was. When I went back downstairs Clausen was dead. And somebody had torn a page out of the register. The page with Quest's name on it. I called the police."

"But you didn't stick around?"

"I had no information about Clausen's death."

"But you didn't stick around," French repeated. Maglashan made a savage noise in his throat and threw the carpenter's pencil clear across the room. I watched it bounce against the wall and floor and come to a stop.

"That's correct," I said.

"In Bay City," Maglashan said, "we could murder you for that."

"In Bay City you could murder me for wearing a blue tie," I said.

He started to get up. Beifus looked sideways at him and said: "Leave Christy handle it. There's always a second show."

"We could break you for that," French said to me without inflection.

"Consider me broke," I said. "I never liked the business anyway."

"So you came back to your office. What then?"

"I reported to the client. Then a guy called me up and asked me over to the Van Nuys Hotel. He was the same guy I had talked to down on Idaho Street, but with a different name."

"You could have told us that, couldn't you?"

"If I had, I'd have had to tell you everything. That would have violated the conditions of my employment."

French nodded and tapped his pencil. He said slowly: "A murder wipes out agreements like that. Two murders ought to do it double. And two murders by the same method, treble. You don't look good, Marlowe. You don't look good at all."

"I don't even look good to the client," I said, "after today."

"What happened today?"

"She told me her brother had called her up from this doctor's house. Dr. Lagardie. The brother was in danger. I was to hurry on down and take care of him. I hurried on down. Dr. Lagardie and his nurse had the office closed. They acted scared. The police had been there." I looked at Maglashan.

"Another of his phone calls," Maglashan snarled.

"Not me this time," I said.

"All right. Go on," French said, after a pause.

"Lagardie denied knowing anything about Orrin Quest. He sent his nurse home. Then he slipped me a doped cigarette and I went away from there for a while. When I came to I was alone in the house. Then I wasn't. Orrin Quest, or what was left of him, was scratching at the door. He fell through it and died as I opened it. With his last ounce of strength he tried to stick me with an ice pick." I moved my shoulders. The place between them was a little stiff and sore, nothing more.

French looked hard at Maglashan. Maglashan shook his head, but French kept on looking at him. Beifus began to whistle under his breath. I couldn't make out the tune at first, and then I could. It was "Old Man Mose Is Dead."

French turned his head and said slowly: "No ice pick was found by the body."

"I left it where it fell," I said.

Maglashan said: "Looks like I ought to be putting on my glove again." He stretched it between his fingers. "Somebody's a goddam liar and it ain't me."

"All right," French said. "All right. Let's not be theatrical. Suppose the kid did have an ice pick in his hand, that doesn't prove he was born holding one."

"Filed down," I said. "Short. Three inches from the handle to the tip of the point. That's not the way they come from the hardware store."

"Why would he want to stick you?" Beifus asked with his derisive grin. "You were his pal. You were down there to keep him safe for his sister."

"I was just something between him and the light," I said. "Something that moved and could have been a man and could have been the man that hurt him. He was dying on his feet. I'd never seen him before. If he ever saw me, I didn't know it."

"It could have been a beautiful friendship," Beifus said with a sigh. "Except for the ice pick, of course."

"And the fact that he had it in his hand and tried to stick me with it could mean something."

"For instance what?"

"A man in his condition acts from instinct. He doesn't invent new techniques. He got me between the shoulder blades, a sting, the feeble last effort of a dying man. Maybe it would have been a different place and a much deeper penetration if he had had his health."

Maglashan said: "How much longer we have to barber round with this monkey? You talk to him like he was human. Leave me talk to him my way."

"The captain doesn't like it," French said casually.

"Hell with the captain."

"The captain doesn't like small-town cops saying the hell with him," French said.

Maglashan clamped his teeth tight and the line of his jaw showed white. His eyes narrowed and glistened. He took a deep breath through his nose.

"Thanks for the co-operation," he said, and stood up. "I'll be on my way." He rounded the corner of the table and stopped beside me. He put his left hand out and tilted my chin up again.

"See you again, sweetheart. In *my* town."

He lashed me across the face twice with the wrist end of the glove. The buttons stung sharply. I put my hand up and rubbed my lower lip.

French said: "For Crissake, Maglashan, sit down and let the guy speak his piece. And keep your hands off him."

Maglashan looked back at him and said: "Think you can make me?"

French just shrugged. After a moment Maglashan rubbed his big hand across his mouth and strolled back to his chair. French said:

"Let's have your ideas about all this, Marlowe."

"Among other things Clausen was probably pushing reefers," I said. "I sniffed marijuana smoke in his apartment. A tough little guy was counting money in the kitchen when I got there. He had a gun and a sharpened rattail file, both of which he tried to use on me. I took them away from him and he left. He would be the runner. But Clausen was liquored to a point where you wouldn't want to trust him any more. They don't go for that in the organizations. The runner thought I was a dick. Those people wouldn't want Clausen picked up. He would be too easy to milk. The minute they smelled dick around the house Clausen would be missing."

French looked at Maglashan. "That make any sense to you?"

"It could happen," Maglashan said grudgingly.

French said: "Suppose it was so, what's it got to do with this Orrin Quest?"

"Anybody can smoke reefers," I said. "If you're dull and lonely and depressed and out of a job, they might be very attractive. But when you smoke them you get warped ideas and calloused emotions. And marijuana affects different people different ways. Some it makes very tough and some it just makes never-no-mind. Suppose Quest tried to put the bite on somebody and threatened to go to the police. Quite possibly all three murders are connected with the reefer gang."

"That don't jibe with Quest having a filed-down ice pick," Beifus said.

I said: "According to the lieutenant here he didn't have one. So I must have imagined that. Anyhow, he might just have picked it up. They might be standard equipment around Dr. Lagardie's house. Get anything on him?"

He shook his head. "Not so far."

"He didn't kill me, probably he didn't kill anybody," I said. "Quest told his sister — according to her — that he was working for Dr. Lagardie, but that some gangsters were after him."

"This Lagardie," French said, prodding at his blotter with a pen point, "what do you make of him?"

"He used to practice in Cleveland. Downtown in a large way. He must have had his reasons for hiding out in Bay City."

"Cleveland, huh?" French drawled and looked at a corner of the ceiling. Beifus looked down at his papers. Maglashan said:

"Probably an abortionist. I've had my eye on him for some time."

"Which eye?" Beifus asked him mildly.

Maglashan flushed.

French said: "Probably the one he didn't have on Idaho Street."

Maglashan stood up violently. "You boys think you're so goddam smart it might interest you to know that we're just a small-town police force. We got to double in brass once in a while. Just the same I like that reefer angle. It might cut down my work considerable. I'm looking into it right now."

He marched solidly to the door and left. French looked after him. Beifus did the same. When the door closed they looked at each other.

"I betcha they pull that raid again tonight," Beifus said.

French nodded.

Beifus said: "In a flat over a laundry. They'll go down on the beach and pull in three or four vagrants and stash them in the flat and then they'll line them up for the camera boys after they pull the raid."

French said: "You're talking too much, Fred."

Beifus grinned and was silent. French said to me: "If you were guessing, what would you guess they were looking for in that room at the Van Nuys?"

"A claim check for a suitcase full of weed."

"Not bad," French said. "And, still guessing, where would it have been?"

"I thought about that. When I talked to Hicks down at Bay City he wasn't wearing his muff. A man doesn't around the house. But he was wearing it on the bed at the Van Nuys. Maybe he didn't put it on himself."

French said: "So?"

I said: "Wouldn't be a bad place to stash a claim check."

French said: "You could pin it down with a piece of Scotch tape. Quite an idea."

There was a silence. The orange queen went back to her typing. I looked at my nails. They weren't as clean as they might be. After the pause French said slowly:

"Don't think for a minute you're in the clear, Marlowe. Still guessing, how came Dr. Lagardie to mention Cleveland to you?"

"I took the trouble to look him up. A doctor can't change his name if he wants to go on practicing. The ice pick made you think of Weepy Moyer. Weepy Moyer operated in Cleveland. Sunny Moe Stein operated in Cleveland. It's true the ice-pick technique was different, but it was an ice pick. You said yourself the boys might have learned. And always with these gangs there's a doctor somewhere in the background."

"Pretty wild," French said. "Pretty loose connection."

"Would I do myself any good if I tightened it up?"

"Can you?"

"I can try."

French sighed. "The little Quest girl is okay," he said. "I talked to her mother back in Kansas. She really did come out here to look for her brother. And she really did hire you to do it. She gives you a good write-up. Up to a point. She really did suspect her brother was mixed up in something wrong. You make any money on the deal?"

"Not much," I said. "I gave her back the fee. She didn't have much."

"That way you don't have to pay income tax on it," Beifus said.

French said, "Let's break this off. The next move is up to the D.A. And if I know Endicott, it will be a week from Tuesday before he decides how to play it." He made a gesture towards the door.

I stood up. "Will it be all right if I don't leave town?" I asked. They didn't bother to answer that one.

I just stood there and looked at them. The ice-pick wound between my shoulders had a dry sting, and the flesh around the place was stiff. The side of my face and mouth smarted where Maglashan had sideswiped me with his well-used pigskin glove. I was in the deep water. It was dark and unclear and the taste of the salt was in my mouth.

They just sat there and looked back at me. The orange queen was clacking her typewriter. Cop talk was no more treat to her than legs to a dance director. They had the calm weathered faces of healthy men in hard condition. They had the eyes they always have, cloudy and gray like freezing water. The firm-set mouth, the hard little wrinkles at the corners of the eyes, the hard hollow meaningless stare, not quite cruel and a thousand miles from kind. The dull ready-made clothes, worn without style, with a sort of contempt; the look of men who are poor and yet proud of their power, watching always for ways to make it felt, to shove it into you and twist it and grin and watch you squirm, ruthless without malice, cruel and yet not always unkind. What would you expect them to be? Civilization had no meaning for them. All they saw of it was the failures, the dirt, the dregs, the aberrations and the disgust.

"What you standing there for?" Beifus asked sharply. "You

want us to give you a great big spitty kiss? No snappy comeback, huh? Too bad." His voice fell away into a dull drone. He frowned and reached a pencil off the desk. With a quick motion of his fingers he snapped it in half and held the two halves out on his palm.

"We're giving you that much break," he said thinly, the smile all gone. "Go on out and square things up. What the hell you think we're turning you loose for? Maglashan bought you a rain check. Use it."

I put my hand up and rubbed my lip. My mouth had too many teeth in it.

Beifus lowered his eyes to the table, picked up a paper and began to read it. Christy French swung around in his chair and put his feet on the desk and stared out of the open window at the parking lot. The orange queen stopped typing. The room was suddenly full of heavy silence, like a fallen cake.

I went on out, parting the silence as if I was pushing my way through water.

25

THE OFFICE WAS EMPTY AGAIN. No leggy brunettes, no little girls with slanted glasses, no neat dark men with gangster's eyes.

I sat down at the desk and watched the light fade. The going-home sounds had died away. Outside the neon signs began to glare at one another across the boulevard. There was something to be done, but I didn't know what. Whatever it was it would be useless. I tidied up my desk, listening to the scrape of a bucket on the tiling of the corridor. I put my papers away in the drawer, straightened the pen stand, got out a duster and wiped off the glass and then the telephone. It was dark and sleek in the fading light. It wouldn't ring tonight. Nobody would call me again. Not now, not this time. Perhaps not ever.

I put the duster away folded with the dust in it, leaned back and just sat, not smoking, not even thinking. I was a blank man. I had no face, no meaning, no personality, hardly a name. I didn't want to eat. I didn't even want a drink. I was the page from yesterday's calendar crumpled at the bottom of the waste basket.

So I pulled the phone towards me and dialed Mavis Weld's number. It rang and rang and rang. Nine times. That's a lot of ringing, Marlowe. I guess there's nobody home. Nobody home to you. I hung up. Who would you like to call now? You got a friend somewhere that might like to hear your voice? No. Nobody.

Let the telephone ring, please. Let there be somebody to call up and plug me into the human race again. Even a cop. Even a Maglashan. Nobody has to like me. I just want to get off this frozen star.

The telephone rang.

"Amigo," her voice said. "There is trouble. Bad trouble. She wants to see you. She likes you. She thinks you are an honest man."

"Where?" I asked. It wasn't really a question, just a sound I made. I sucked on a cold pipe and leaned my head on my hand, brooding at the telephone. It was a voice to talk to anyway.

"You will come?"

"I'd sit up with a sick parrot tonight. Where do I go?"

"I will come for you. I will be before your building in fifteen minutes. It is not easy to get where we go."

"How is it coming back," I asked, "or don't we care?"

But she had already hung up.

Down at the drugstore lunch counter I had time to inhale two cups of coffee and a melted-cheese sandwich with two slivers of ersatz bacon imbedded in it, like dead fish in the silt at the bottom of a drained pool.

I was crazy. I liked it.

26

IT WAS A BLACK MERCURY CONVERTIBLE with a light top. The top was up. When I leaned in at the door Dolores Gonzales slid over towards me along the leather seat.

"You drive please, amigo. I do not really ever like to drive."

The light from the drugstore caught her face. She had changed her clothes again, but it was still all black, save for a flame-colored shirt. Slacks and a kind of loose coat like a man's leisure jacket.

I leaned on the door of the car. "Why didn't she call me?"

"She couldn't. She did not have the number and she had very little time."

"Why?"

"It seemed to be while someone was out of the room for just a moment."

"And where is this place she called from?"

"I do not know the name of the street. But I can find the house. That is why I come. Please get into the car and let us hurry."

"Maybe," I said. "And again maybe I am not getting into the car. Old age and arthritis have made me cautious."

"Always the wisecrack," she said. "It is a very strange man."

"Always the wisecrack where possible," I said, "and it is a very ordinary guy with only one head — which has been rather harshly used at times. The times usually started out like this."

"Will you make love to me tonight?" she asked softly.

"That again is an open question. Probably not."

"You would not waste your time. I am not one of these synthetic blondes with a skin you could strike matches on. These ex-laundresses with large bony hands and sharp knees and unsuccessful breasts."

"Just for half an hour," I said, "Let's leave the sex to one side. It's great stuff, like chocolate sundaes. But there comes a time you would rather cut your throat. I guess maybe I'd better cut mine."

I went around the car and slid under the wheel and started the motor.

"We go west," she said, "through the Beverly Hills and then farther on."

I let the clutch in and drifted around the corner to go south to Sunset. Dolores got one of her long brown cigarettes out.

"Did you bring a gun?" she asked.

"No. What would I want a gun for?" The inside of my left arm pressed against the Luger in the shoulder harness.

"It is better not perhaps." She fitted the cigarette into the little golden tweezer thing and lit it with the golden lighter. The light flaring in her face seemed to be swallowed up by her depthless black eyes.

I turned west on Sunset and swallowed myself up in three lanes of racetrack drivers who were pushing their mounts hard to get nowhere and do nothing.

"What kind of trouble is Miss Weld in?"

"I do not know. She just said that it was trouble and she was much afraid and she needed you."

"You ought to be able to think up a better story than that."

She didn't answer. I stopped for a traffic signal and turned to look at her. She was crying softly in the dark.

"I would not hurt a hair of Mavis Weld's head," she said. "I do not quite expect that you would believe me."

"On the other hand," I said, "maybe the fact that you don't have a story helps."

She started to slide along the seat towards me.

"Keep to your own side of the car," I said. "I've got to drive this heap."

"You do not want my head on your shoulder?"

"Not in this traffic."

I stopped at Fairfax with the green light to let a man make a left turn. Horns blew violently behind. When I started again the car that had been right behind swung out and pulled level and a fat guy in a sweatshirt yelled:

"Aw go get yourself a hammock!"

He went on, cutting in so hard that I had to brake.

"I used to like this town," I said, just to be saying something and not to be thinking too hard. "A long time ago. There were trees along Wilshire Boulevard. Beverly Hills was a country town. Westwood was bare hills and lots offering at eleven hundred dollars and no takers. Hollywood was a bunch of frame houses on the interurban line. Los Angeles was just a big dry sunny place with ugly homes and no style, but goodhearted and peaceful. It had the climate they just yap about now. People used to sleep out on porches. Little groups who thought they were intellectual used to call it the Athens of America. It wasn't that, but it wasn't a neon-lighted slum either."

We crossed La Cienega and went into the curve of the Strip. The Dancers was a blaze of light. The terrace was packed. The parking lot was like ants on a piece of overripe fruit.

"Now we get characters like this Steelgrave owning restaurants. We get guys like that fat boy that bawled me out back there. We've got the big money, the sharpshooters, the percentage workers, the fast-dollar boys, the hoodlums out of New York and Chicago and Detroit — and Cleveland. We've got the flash restaurants and nightclubs they run, and the hotels and apartment houses they own, and the grifters and con men and female bandits that live in them. The luxury trades, the pansy decorators, the Lesbian dress designers, the riffraff of a big hard-boiled city with no more personality than a paper cup. Out in the fancy suburbs dear old Dad is reading the sports page in front of a picture window, with his shoes off, thinking he is high class because he has a three-car garage. Mom is in front of her princess dresser trying to paint the suitcases out from under her eyes. And Junior is clamped onto the telephone calling up a succession of high school girls that talk pidgin English and carry contraceptives in their make-up kit."

"It is the same in all big cities, amigo."

"Real cities have something else, some individual bony structure under the muck. Los Angeles has Hollywood — and hates it. It ought to consider itself damn lucky. Without Hollywood it would be a mail-order city. Everything in the catalogue you could get better somewhere else."

"You are bitter tonight, amigo."

"I've got a few troubles. The only reason I'm driving this car with you beside me is that I've got so much trouble a little more will seem like icing."

"You have done something wrong?" she asked, and came close to me along the seat.

"Well, just collecting a few bodies," I said. "Depends on the point of view. The cops don't like the work done by us amateurs. They have their own service."

"What will they do to you?"

"They might run me out of town and I couldn't care less. Don't push me so hard. I need this arm to shift gears with."

She pulled away in a huff. "I think you are very nasty to get along with," she said. "Turn right at the Lost Canyon Road."

After a while we passed the University. All the lights of the city were on now, a vast carpet of them stretching down the slope to the south and on into the almost infinite distance. A plane droned overhead losing altitude, its two signal lights winking on and off alternately. At Lost Canyon I swung right skirting the big gates that led into Bel-Air. The road began to twist and climb. There were too many cars; the headlights glared angrily down the twisting white concrete. A little breeze blew down over the pass. There was the odor of wild sage, the acrid tang of eucalyptus, and the quiet smell of dust. Windows glowed on the hillside. We passed a big white two-storied Monterey house that must have cost $70,000 and had a cut-out illuminated sign in front: CAIRN TERRIERS.

"The next to the right," Dolores said.

I made the turn. The road got steeper and narrower. There were houses behind walls and masses of shrubbery but you couldn't see anything. Then we came to the fork and there was a police car with a red spotlight parked at it and across the right side of the fork two cars parked at right angles. A torch waved up and down. I slowed the car and stopped level with the police car. Two cops sat in it smoking. They didn't move.

"What goes on?"

"Amigo, I have no idea at all." Her voice had a hushed withdrawn sound. She might have been a little scared. I didn't know what of.

A tall man, the one with the torch, came around the side of the car and poke the flash at me, then lowered it.

"We're not using this road tonight," he said. "Going anywhere in particular?"

I set the brake, reached for a flash which Dolores got out of
the glove compartment. I snapped the light onto the tall man.
He wore expensive-looking slacks, a sport shirt with initials on the
pocket and a polka-dot scarf knotted around his neck. He had horn-
rimmed glasses and glossy wavy black hair. He looked as Hollywood as all hell.

I said: "Any explanation — or are you just making law?"

"The law is over there, if you want to talk to them." His voice
held a tone of contempt. "We are merely private citizens. We live
around here. This is a residential neighborhood. We mean to keep
it that way."

A man with a sporting gun came out of the shadows and stood
beside the tall man. He held the gun in the crook of his left arm,
muzzle pointed down. But he didn't look as if he just had it for
ballast.

"That's jake with me," I said. "I didn't have any other plans.
We just want to go to a place."

"What place?" the tall man asked coolly.

I turned to Dolores. "What place?"

"It is a white house on the hill, high up," she said.

"And what did you plan to do up there?" the tall man asked.

"The man who lives there is my friend," she said tartly.

He shone the flash in her face for a moment. "You look swell,"
he said. "But we don't like your friend. We don't like characters
that try to run gambling joints in this kind of neighborhood."

"I know nothing about a gambling joint," Dolores told him
sharply.

"Neither do the cops," the tall man said. "They don't even want
to find out. What's your friend's name, darling?"

"That is not of your business," Dolores spit at him.

"Go on home and knit socks, darling," the tall man said. He
turned to me.

"The road's not in use tonight," he said. "Now you know why."

"Think you can make it stick?" I asked him.

"It will take more than you to change our plans. You ought to
see our tax assessments. And those monkeys in the prowl car — and
a lot more like them down at the City Hall — just sit on their hands
when we ask for the law to be enforced."

I unlatched the car door and swung it open. He stepped back and let me get out. I walked over to the prowl car. The two cops in it were leaning back lazily. Their loudspeaker was turned low, just audibly muttering. One of them was chewing gum rhythmically.

"How's to break up this road block and let the citizens through?" I asked him.

"No orders, buddy. We're just here to keep the peace. Anybody starts anything, we finish it."

"They say there's a gambling house up the line."

"They say," the cop said.

"You don't believe them?"

"I don't even try, buddy," he said, and spat past my shoulder.

"Suppose I have urgent business up there."

He looked at me without expression and yawned.

"Thanks a lot, buddy," I said.

I went back to the Mercury, got my wallet out and handed the tall man a card. He put his flash on it, and said: "Well?"

He snapped the flash off and stood silent. His face began to take form palely in the darkness.

"I'm on business. To me it's important business. Let me through and perhaps you won't need this block tomorrow."

"You talk large, friend."

"Would I have the kind of money it takes to patronize a private gambling club?"

"*She* might." He flicked an eye at Dolores. "She might have brought you along for protection."

He turned to the shotgun man. "What do you think?"

"Chance it. Just two of them and both sober."

The tall one snapped his flash on again and made a sidesweep with it back and forth. A car motor started. One of the block cars backed around onto the shoulder. I got in and started the Mercury, went on through the gap and watched the block car in the mirror as it took up position again, then cut its high beam lights.

"Is this the only way in and out of here?"

"They think it is, amigo. There is another way, but it is a private road through an estate. We would have had to go around by the valley side."

"We nearly didn't get through," I told her. "This can't be very bad trouble anybody is in."

"I knew you would find a way, amigo."

"Something stinks," I said nastily. "And it isn't wild lilac."

"Such a suspicious man. Do you not even want to kiss me?"

"You ought to have used a little of that back at the road block. That tall guy looked lonely. You could have taken him off in the bushes."

She hit me across the mouth with the back of her hand. "You son of a bitch," she said casually. "The next driveway on the left, if you please."

We topped a rise and the road ended suddenly in a wide black circle edged with whitewashed stones. Directly ahead was a wire fence with a wide gate in it, and a sign on the gate: PRIVATE ROAD NO TRESPASSING. The gate was open and a padlock hung from one end of a loose chain on the posts. I turned the car around a white oleander bush and was in the motor yard of a long, low white house with a tile roof and a four-car garage in the corner, under a walled balcony. Both the wide garage doors were closed. There was no light in the house. A high moon made a bluish radiance on the white stucco walls. Some of the lower windows were shuttered. Four packing cases full of trash stood in a row at the foot of the steps. There was a big garbage can upended and empty. There were two steel drums with papers in them.

There was no sound from the house, no sign of life. I stopped the Mercury, cut the lights and the motor, and just sat. Dolores moved in the corner. The seat seemed to be shaking. I reached across and touched her. She was shivering.

"What's the matter?"

"Get — get out, please," she said as if her teeth chattered.

"How about you?"

She opened the door on her side and jumped out. I got out my side and left the door hanging open, the keys in the lock. She came around the back of the car and as she got close to me I could almost feel her shaking before she touched me. Then she leaned up against me hard thigh to thigh and breast to breast. Her arms went around my neck.

"I am being very foolish," she said softly. "He will kill me for this — just as he killed Stein. Kiss me."

I kissed her. Her lips were hot and dry. "Is he in there?"

"Yes."

"Who else?"

"Nobody else — except Mavis. He will kill her too."

"Listen——"

"Kiss me again. I have not very long to live, amigo. When you are the finger for a man like that — you die young."

I pushed her away from me, but gently.

She stepped back and lifted her right hand quickly. There was a gun in it now.

I looked at the gun. There was a dull shine on it from the high moon. She held it level and her hand wasn't shaking now.

"What a friend I would make if I pulled this trigger," she said. "They'd hear the shot down the road."

She shook her head. "No, there is a little hill between. I do not think they would hear, amigo."

I thought the gun would jump when she pulled the trigger. If I dropped just at the right moment —

I wasn't that good. I didn't say anything. My tongue felt large in my mouth.

She went on slowly, in a soft tired voice: "With Stein it did not matter. I would have killed him myself, gladly. That filth. To die is not much, to kill is not much. But to entice people to their deaths — " She broke off with what might have been a sob. "Amigo, I liked you for some strange reason. I should be far beyond such nonsense. Mavis took him away from me, but I did not not want him to kill her. The world is full of men who have enough money."

"He seems like a nice little guy," I said, still watching the hand that held the gun. Not a quiver in it now.

She laughed contemptuously. "Of course he does. That is why he is what he is. You think you are tough, amigo. You are a very soft peach compared with Steelgrave." She lowered the gun and now it was my time to jump. I still wasn't good enough.

"He has killed a dozen men," she said. "With a smile for each one. I have known him for a long time. I knew him in Cleveland."

"With ice picks?" I asked.

"If I give you the gun, will you kill him for me?"

"Would you believe me if I promised?"

"Yes." Somewhere down the hill there was the sound of a car. But it seemed as remote as Mars, as meaningless as the chattering of monkeys in the Brazilian jungle. It had nothing to do with me.

"I'd kill him if I had to," I said, licking along my lips.

I was leaning a little, knees bent, all set for a jump again.

"Goodnight, amigo. I wear black because I am beautiful and wicked — and lost."

She held the gun out to me. I took it. I just stood there holding it. For another silent moment neither of us moved. Then she smiled and tossed her head and jumped into the car. She started the motor and slammed the door shut. She idled the motor down and sat looking out at me. There was a smile on her face now.

"I was pretty good in there, no?" she said softly.

Then the car backed violently with a harsh tearing of the tires on the asphalt paving. The lights jumped on. The car curved away and was gone past the oleander bush. The lights turned left, into the private road. The lights drifted off among the trees and the sound faded into the long-drawn *whee* of tree frogs. Then that stopped and for a moment there was no sound at all. And no light except the tired old moon.

I broke the magazine from the gun. It had seven shells in it. There was another in the breach. Two less than a full load. I sniffed the muzzle. It had been fired since it was cleaned. Fired twice, perhaps.

I pushed the magazine into place again and held the gun on the flat of my hand. It had a white bone grip. .32 caliber.

Orrin Quest had been shot twice. The two exploded shells I picked up on the floor of the room were .32 caliber.

And yesterday afternoon, in room 332 of the Hotel Van Nuys, a blond girl with a towel in front of her face had pointed a .32-caliber automatic with a white bone grip at me.

You can get too fancy about these things. You can also not get fancy enough.

27

I WALKED ON RUBBER HEELS across to the garage and tried to open one of the two wide doors. There were no handles, so it must have been operated by a switch. I played a tiny pencil flash on the frame, but no switch looked at me.

I left that and prowled over to the trash barrels. Wooden steps went up to a service entrance. I didn't think the door would be unlocked for my convenience. Under the porch was another door. This was unlocked and gave on darkness and the smell of corded eucalyptus wood. I closed the door behind me and put the little flash on again. In the corner there was another staircase, with a thing like a dumb-waiter beside it. It wasn't dumb enough to let me work it. I started up the steps.

Somewhere remotely something buzzed. I stopped. The buzzing stopped. I started again. The buzzing didn't. I went on up to a door with no knob, set flush. Another gadget.

But I found the switch to this one. It was an oblong movable plate set into the door frame. Too many dusty hands had touched it. I pressed it and the door clicked and fell back off the latch. I pushed it open, with the tenderness of a young intern delivering his first baby.

Inside was a hallway. Through shuttered windows moonlight caught the white corner of a stove and the chromed griddle on top of it. The kitchen was big enough for a dancing class. An open arch led to a butler's pantry tiled to the ceiling. A sink, a huge ice-box set into the wall, a lot of electrical stuff for making drinks without trying. You pick your poison, press a button, and four days later you wake up on the rubbing table in a reconditioning parlor.

Beyond the butler's pantry a swing door. Beyond the swing door a dark dining room with an open end to a glassed-in lounge into which the moonlight poured like water through the floodgates of a dam.

A carpeted hall led off somewhere. From another flat arch a

flying buttress of a staircase went up into more darkness, but shimmered as it went, in what might have been glass, brick, and stainless steel.

At last I came to what should be the living room. It was curtained and quite dark, but it had the feel of great size. The darkness was heavy in it and my nose twitched at a lingering odor that said somebody had been there not too long ago. I stopped breathing and listened. Tigers could be in the darkness watching me. Or guys with large guns, standing flat-footed, breathing softly with their mouths open. Or nothing and nobody and too much imagination in the wrong place.

I edged back to the wall and felt around for a light switch. There's always a light switch. Everybody has light switches. Usually on the right side as you go in. You go into a dark room and you want light. Okay, you have a light switch in a natural place at a natural height. This room hadn't. This was a different kind of house. They had odd ways of handling doors and lights. The gadget this time might be something fancy like having to sing A above high C, or stepping on a flat button under the carpet, or maybe you just spoke and said: "Let there be light," and a mike picked it up and turned the voice vibration into a low-power electrical impulse and a transformer built that up to enough voltage to throw a silent mercury switch.

I was psychic that night. I was a fellow who wanted company in a dark place and was willing to pay a high price for it. The Luger under my arm and the .32 in my hand made me tough. Two-gun Marlowe, the kid from Cyanide Gulch.

I took the wrinkles out of my lips and said aloud:

"Hello again. Anybody here needing a detective?"

Nothing answered me, not even a stand-in for an echo. The sound of my voice fell on silence like a tired head on a swan's-down pillow.

And then amber light began to grow high up behind the cornice that circumnavigated the huge room. It brightened very slowly, as if controlled by a rheostat panel in a theater. Heavy apricot-colored curtains covered the windows.

The walls were apricot too. At the far end was a bar off to one side, a little catty-corner, reaching back into the space by the butler's pantry. There was an alcove with small tables and padded seats. There were floor lamps and soft chairs and love seats and the usual paraphernalia of a living room, and there were long shrouded tables in the middle of the floor space.

The boys back at the road block had something after all. But the joint was dead. The room was empty of life. It was almost empty. Not quite empty.

A blonde in a pale cocoa fur coat stood leaning against the side of a grandfather's chair. Her hands were in the pockets of the coat. Her hair was fluffed out carelessly and her face was not chalk-white because the light was not white.

"Hello again yourself," she said in a dead voice. "I still think you came too late."

"Too late for what?"

I walked towards her, a movement which was always a pleasure. Even then, even in that too silent house.

"You're kind of cute," she said. "I didn't think you were cute. You found a way in. You — " Her voice clicked off and strangled itself in her throat.

"I need a drink," she said after a thick pause. "Or maybe I'll fall down."

"That's a lovely coat," I said. I was up to her now. I reached out and touched it. She didn't move. Her mouth moved in and out, trembling.

"Stone marten," she whispered. "Forty thousand dollars. Rented. For the picture."

"Is this part of the picture?" I gestured around the room.

"This is the picture to end all pictures — for me. I — I do need that drink. If I try to walk — " the clear voice whispered away into nothing. Her eyelids fluttered up and down.

"Go ahead and faint," I said. "I'll catch you on the first bounce."

A smile struggled to arrange her face for smiling. She pressed her lips together, fighting hard to stay on her feet.

"Why did I come too late?" I asked. "Too late for what?"

"Too late to be shot."

"Shucks, I've been looking forward to it all evening. Miss Gonzales brought me."

"I know."

I reached out and touched the fur again. Forty thousand dollars is nice to touch, even rented.

"Dolores will be disappointed as hell," she said, her mouth edged with white.

"No."

"She put you on the spot — just as she did Stein."

"She may have started out to. But she changed her mind."

She laughed. It was a silly pooped-out little laugh like a child trying to be supercilious at a playroom tea party.

"What a way you have with the girls," she whispered. "How the hell do you do it, wonderful? With doped cigarettes? It can't be your clothes or your money or your personality. You don't have any. You're not too young, nor too beautiful. You've seen your best days and — "

Her voice had been coming faster and faster, like a motor with a broken governor. At the end she was chattering. When she stopped a spent sigh drifted along the silence and she caved at the knees and fell straight forward into my arms.

If it was an act it worked perfectly. I might have had guns in all nine pockets and they would have been as much use to me as nine little pink candles on a birthday cake.

But nothing happened. No hard characters peeked at me with automatics in their hands. No Steelgrave smiled at me with the faint dry remote killer's smile. No stealthy footsteps crept up behind me.

She hung in my arms as limp as a wet tea towel and not as heavy as Orrin Quest, being less dead, but heavy enough to make the tendons in my knee joints ache. Her eyes were closed when I pushed her head away from my chest. Her breath was inaudible and she had that bluish look on the parted lips.

I got my right hand under her knees and carried her over to a gold couch and spread her out on it. I straightened up and went along to the bar. There was a telephone on the corner of it but I couldn't find the way through to the bottles. So I had to swing over the top. I got a likely-looking bottle with a blue and silver label and five stars on it. The cork had been loosened. I poured dark and pungent brandy into the wrong kind of glass and went back over the bar top, taking the bottle with me.

She was lying as I had left her, but her eyes were open.

"Can you hold a glass?"

She could with a little help. She drank the brandy and pressed the edge of the glass hard against her lips as if she wanted to hold them still. I watched her breathe into the glass and cloud it. A slow smile formed itself on her mouth.

"It's cold tonight," she said.

She swung her legs over the edge of the couch and put her feet on the floor.

"More," she said, holding the glass out. I poured into it. "Where's yours?"

"Not drinking. My emotions are being worked on enough without that."

The second drink made her shudder. But the blue look had gone away from her mouth and her lips didn't glare like stoplights and the little etched lines at the corners of her eyes were not in relief any more.

"Who's working on your emotions?"

"Oh, a lot of women that keep throwing their arms around my neck and fainting on me and getting kissed and so forth. Quite a full couple of days for a beat-up gumshoe with no yacht."

"No yacht," she said. "I'd hate that. I was brought up rich."

"Yeah," I said. "You were born with a Cadillac in your mouth. And I could guess where."

Her eyes narrowed. "Could you?"

"Didn't think it was a very tight secret, did you?"

"I — I — " She broke off and made a helpless gesture. "I can't think of any lines tonight."

"It's the technicolor dialogue," I said. "It freezes up on you."

"Aren't we talking like a couple of nuts?"

"We could get sensible. Where's Steelgrave?"

She just looked at me. She held the empty glass out and I took it and put it somewhere or other without taking my eyes off her. Nor she hers off me. It seemed as if a long long minute went by.

"He was here," she said at last, as slowly as if she had to invent the words one at a time. "May I have a cigarette?"

"The old cigarette stall," I said. I got a couple out and put them in my mouth and lit them. I leaned across and tucked one between her ruby lips.

"Nothing's cornier than that," she said. "Except maybe butterfly kisses."

"Sex is a wonderful thing," I said. "When you don't want to answer questions."

She puffed loosely and blinked, then put her hand up to adjust the cigarette. After all these years I can never put a cigarette in a girl's mouth where she wants it.

She gave her head a toss and swung the soft loose hair around her cheeks and watched me to see how hard that hit me. All the whiteness had gone now. Her cheeks were a little flushed. But behind her eyes things watched and waited.

"You're rather nice," she said, when I didn't do anything sensational. "For the kind of guy you are."

I stood that well too.

"But I don't really know what kind of guy you are, do I?" She laughed suddenly and a tear came from nowhere and slid down her cheek. "For all I know you might be nice for any kind of guy." She snatched the cigarette loose and put her hand to her mouth and bit on it. "What's the matter with me? Am I drunk?"

"You're stalling for time," I said. "But I can't make up my mind whether it's to give someone time to get here — or to give somebody time to get far away from here. And again it could just be brandy on top of shock. You're a little girl and you want to cry into your mother's apron."

"Not my mother," she said. "I could get as far crying into a rain barrel."

"Dealt and passed. So where is Steelgrave?"

"You ought to be glad wherever he is. He had to kill you. Or thought he had."

"You wanted me here, didn't you? Were you that fond of him?"

She blew cigarette ash off the back of her hand. A flake of it went into my eye and made me blink.

"I must have been," she said, "once." She put a hand down on her knee and spread the fingers out, studying the nails. She brought her eyes up slowly without moving her head. "It seems like about a thousand years ago I met a nice quiet little guy who knew how to behave in public and didn't shoot his charm around every bistro in town. Yes, I liked him. I liked him a lot."

She put her hand up to her mouth and bit a knuckle. Then she put the same hand into the pocket of the fur coat and brought out a white-handled automatic, the brother of the one I had myself.

"And in the end I liked him with this," she said.

I went over and took it out of her hand. I sniffed the muzzle. Yes. That made two of them fired around.

"Are you going to wrap it up in a handkerchief, the way they do in the movies?"

I just dropped it into my other pocket, where it could pick up a few interesting crumbs of tobacco and some seeds that grow only on the southeast slope of the Beverly Hills City Hall. It might amuse a police chemist for a while.

28

I WATCHED HER FOR A MINUTE, biting at the end of my lip. She watched me. I saw no change of expression. Then I started prowling the room with my eyes. I lifted up the dust cover on one of the long tables. Under it was a roulette layout but no wheel. Under the table was nothing.

"Try that chair with the magnolias on it," she said.

She didn't look towards it so I had to find it myself. Surprising how long it took me. It was a high-backed wing chair, covered in flowered chintz, the kind of chair that a long time ago was intended to keep the draft off while you sat crouched over a fire of cannel coal.

It was turned away from me. I went over there walking softly, in low gear. It almost faced the wall. Even at that it seemed ridiculous that I hadn't spotted him on my way back from the bar. He leaned in the corner of the chair with his head tilted back. His carnation was red and white and looked as fresh as though the flower girl had just pinned it into his lapel. His eyes were half-open as such eyes usually are. They stared at a point in the corner of the ceiling. The bullet had gone through the outside pocket of his double-breasted jacket. It had been fired by someone who knew where the heart was.

I touched his cheek and it was still warm. I lifted his hand and let it fall. It was quite limp. It felt like the back of somebody's hand. I reached for the big artery in his neck. No blood moved in him and very little had stained his jacket. I wiped my hands off on my handkerchief and stood for a little longer looking down at his quiet little face. Everything I had done or not done, everything wrong and everything right — all wasted.

I went back and sat down near her and squeezed my kneecaps.

"What did you expect me to do?" she asked. "He killed my brother."

"Your brother was no angel."

"He didn't have to kill him."

"Somebody had to — and quick."

Her eyes widened suddenly.

I said: "Didn't you ever wonder why Steelgrave never went after me and why he let you go to the Van Nuys yesterday instead of going himself? Didn't you ever wonder why a fellow with his resources and experience never tried to get hold of those photographs, no matter what he had to do to get them?"

She didn't answer.

"How long have you known the photographs existed?" I asked.

"Weeks, nearly two months. I got one in the mail a couple of days after — after that time we had lunch together."

"After Stein was killed."

"Yes, of course."

"Did you think Steelgrave had killed Stein?"

"No. Why should I? Until tonight, that is."

"What happened after you got the photo?"

"My brother Orrin called me up and said he had lost his job and was broke. He wanted money. He didn't say anything about the photo. He didn't have to. There was only one time it could have been taken."

"How did he get your number?"

"Telephone? How did you?"

"Bought it."

"Well — " She made a vague movement with her hand. "Why not call the police and get it over with?"

"Wait a minute. Then what? More prints of the photo?"

"One every week. I showed them to *him*." She gestured toward the chintzy chair. "He didn't like it. I didn't tell him about Orrin."

"He must have known. His kind find things out."

"I suppose so."

"But not where Orrin was hiding out," I said. "Or he wouldn't have waited this long. *When* did you tell Steelgrave?"

She looked away from me. Her fingers kneaded her arm. "Today," she said in a distant voice.

"Why today?"

Her breath caught in her throat. "Please," she said. "Don't ask me a lot of useless questions. Don't torment me. There's nothing you can do. I thought there was — when I called Dolores. There isn't now."

I said: "All right. There's something you don't seem to understand. Steelgrave knew that whoever was behind that photograph wanted money — a lot of money. He knew that sooner or later the blackmailer would have to show himself. That was what Steelgrave was waiting for. He didn't care anything about the photo itself, except for your sake."

"He certainly proved that," she said wearily.

"In his own way," I said.

Her voice came to me with glacial calm. "He killed my brother. He told me so himself. The gangster showed through then all right. Funny people you meet in Hollywood, don't you — including me."

"You were fond of him once," I said brutally.

Red spots flared on her cheeks.

"I'm not fond of anybody," she said. "I'm all through being fond of people." She glanced briefly towards the high-backed chair. "I stopped being fond of him last night. He asked me about you, who you were and so on. I told him. I told him that I would have to admit that I was at the Van Nuys Hotel when that man was lying there dead "

"You were going to tell the police that?"

"I was going to tell Julius Oppenheimer. He would know how to handle it."

"If he didn't one of his dogs would," I said.

She didn't smile. I didn't either.

"If Oppenheimer couldn't handle it, I'd be through in pictures," she added without interest. "Now I'm through everywhere else as well."

I got a cigarette out and lit it. I offered her one. She didn't want one. I wasn't in any hurry. Time seemed to have lost its grip on me. And almost everything else. I was flat out.

"You're going too fast for me," I said, after a moment. "You didn't know when you went to the Van Nuys that Steelgrave was Weepy Moyer?"

"No."

"Then what did you go there for?"

"To buy back those photographs."

"That doesn't check. The photographs didn't mean anything to you then. They were just you and him having lunch."

She stared at me and winked her eyes tight, then opened them wide. "I'm not going to cry," she said. "I said I didn't *know*. But when he was in jail that time, I had to know there was something about him that he didn't care to have known. I knew he had been in some kind of racket, I guess. But not killing people."

I said: "Uh-huh." I got up and walked around the high-backed chair again. Her eyes traveled slowly to watch me. I leaned over the dead Steelgrave and felt under his arm on the left side. There was a gun there in the holster. I didn't touch it. I went back and sat down opposite her again.

"It's going to cost a lot of money to fix this," I said.

For the first time she smiled. It was a very small smile, but it was a smile. "I don't have a lot of money," she said. "So that's out."

"Oppenheimer has. You're worth millions to him by now."

"He wouldn't chance it. Too many people have their knives into the picture business these days. He'll take his loss and forget it in six months."

"You said you'd go to him."

"I said if I got into a jam and hadn't really done anything, I'd go to him. But I have done something now."

"How about Ballou? You're worth a lot to him too."

"I'm not worth a plugged nickel to anybody. Forget it, Marlowe. You mean well, but I know these people."

"That puts it up to me," I said. "That would be why you sent for me."

"Wonderful," she said. "You fix it, darling. For free." Her voice was brittle and shallow again.

I went and sat beside her on the davenport. I took hold of her arm and pulled her hand out of the fur pocket and took hold of that. It was almost ice cold, in spite of the fur.

She turned her head and looked at me squarely. She shook her head a little. "Believe me, darling, I'm not worth it — even to sleep with."

I turned the hand over and opened the fingers out. They were stiff and resisted. I opened them out one by one. I smoothed the palm of her hand.

"Tell me why you had the gun with you."

"The gun?"

"Don't take time to think. Just tell me. Did you mean to kill him?"

"Why not, darling? I thought I meant something to him. I guess I'm a little vain. He fooled me. Nobody means anything to the Steelgraves of this world. And nobody means anything to the Mavis Welds of this world any more."

She pulled away from me and smiled thinly. "I oughtn't to have given you that gun. If I killed you I might get clear yet."

I took it out and held it towards her. She took it and stood up quickly. The gun pointed at me. The small tired smile moved her lips again. Her finger was very firm on the trigger.

"Shoot high," I said. "I'm wearing my bullet-proof underwear."

She dropped the gun to her side and for a moment she just stood staring at me. Then she tossed the gun down on the davenport.

"I guess I don't like the script," she said. "I don't like the lines. It just isn't me, if you know what I mean."

She laughed and looked down at the floor. The point of her shoe moved back and forth on the carpeting. "We've had a nice chat, darling. The phone's over there at the end of the bar."

"Thanks, do you remember Dolores's number?"

"Why Dolores?"

When I didn't answer she told me. I went along the room to the corner of the bar and dialed. The same routine as before. Good evening, the Chateau Bercy, who is calling Miss Gonzales please. One moment, please, buzz, buzz, and then a sultry voice saying: "Hello?"

"This is Marlowe. Did you really mean to put me on a spot?"

I could almost hear her breath catch. Not quite. You can't really hear it over the phone. Sometimes you think you can.

"Amigo, but I am glad to hear your voice," she said. "I am so very very glad."

"Did you or didn't you?"

"I — I don't know. I am very sad to think that I might have. I like you very much."

"I'm in a little trouble here."

"Is he —" Long pause. Apartment house phone. Careful. "Is he there?"

"Well — in a way. He is and yet he isn't."

I really did hear her breath this time. A long indrawn sigh that was almost a whistle.

"Who else is there?"

"Nobody. Just me and my homework. I want to ask you something. It is deadly important. Tell me the truth. Where did you get that thing you gave me tonight?"

"Why, from him. He gave it to me."

"When?"

"Early this evening. Why?"

"How early?"

"About six o'clock, I think."

"*Why* did he give it to you?"

"He asked me to keep it. He always carried one."

"Asked you to keep it why?"

"He did not say, amigo. He was a man that did things like that. He did not often explain himself."

"Notice anything unusual about it? About what he gave you?"

"Why — no, I did not."

"Yes, you did. You noticed that it had been fired and that it smelled of burned powder."

"But I did not — "

"Yes, you did. Just like that. You wondered about it. You didn't like to keep it. You didn't keep it. You gave it back to him. You don't like them around anyhow."

There was a long silence. She said at last, "But of course. But why did he want me to have it? I mean, if that was what happened."

"He didn't tell you why. He just tried to ditch a gun on you and you weren't having any. Remember?"

"That is something I have to tell?"

"Sí."

"Will it be safe for me to do that?"

"When did you ever try to be safe?"

She laughed softly. "Amigo, you understand me very well."

"Goodnight," I said.

"One moment, you have not told me what happened."

"I haven't even telephoned you."

I hung up and turned.

Mavis Weld was standing in the middle of the floor watching me.

"You have your car here?" I asked.

"Yes."

"Get going."

"And do what?"

"Just go home. That's all."

"You can't get away with it," she said softly.

"You're my client."

"I can't let you. I killed him. Why should you be dragged into it?"

"Don't stall. And when you leave go the back way. Not the way Dolores brought me."

She stared me straight in the eyes and repeated in a tense voice, "But I killed him."

"I can't hear a word you say."

Her teeth took hold of her lower lip and held it cruelly. She seemed hardly to breathe. She stood rigid. I went over close to her and touched her cheek with a finger tip. I pressed it hard and watched the white spot turn red.

"If you want to know my motive," I said, "it has nothing to do with you. I owe it to the johns. I haven't played clean cards in this game. They know. I know. I'm just giving them a chance to use the loud pedal."

"As if anyone ever had to give them that," she said, and turned abruptly and walked away. I watched her to the arch and waited for her to look back. She went on through without turning. After a long time I heard a whirring noise. Then the bump of something heavy — the garage door going up. A car started a long way off. It idled down and after another pause the whirring noise again.

When that stopped the motor faded off into the distance. I heard nothing now. The silence of the house hung around me in thick loose folds like that fur coat around the shoulders of Mavis Weld.

I carried the glass and bottle of brandy over to the bar and climbed over it. I rinsed the glass in a little sink and set the bottle back on the shelf. I found the trick catch this time and swung the door open at the end opposite the telephone. I went back to Steelgrave.

I took out the gun Dolores had given me and wiped it off and put his small limp hand around the butt, held it there and let go. The gun thudded to the carpet. The position looked natural. I wasn't thinking about fingerprints. He would have learned long ago not to leave them on any gun.

That left me with three guns. The weapon in his holster I took out and went and put it on the bar shelf under the counter, wrapped in a towel. The Luger I didn't touch. The other white-handled automatic was left. I tried to decide about how far away from him it had been fired. Beyond scorching distance, but probably very close beyond. I stood about three feet from him and fired two shots past him. They nicked peacefully into the wall. I dragged the chair around until it faced into the room. I laid the small automatic down on the dust cover of one of the roulette tables. I touched the big muscle in the side of his neck, usually the first to harden. I couldn't tell whether it had begun to set or not. But his skin was colder than it had been.

There was not a hell of a lot of time to play around with.

I went to the telephone and dialed the number of the Los Angeles Police Department. I asked the police operator for Christy French. A voice from homicide came on, said he had gone home and what was it. I said it was a personal call he was expecting. They gave me his phone number at home, reluctantly, not because they cared, but because they hate to give anybody anything any time.

I dialed and a woman answered and screamed his name. He sounded rested and calm.

"This is Marlowe. What were you doing?"

"Reading the funnies to my kid. He ought to be in bed. What's doing?"

"Remember over at the Van Nuys yesterday you said a man could make a friend if he got you something on Weepy Moyer?"

"Yeah."

"I need a friend."

He didn't sound very interested. "What you got on him?"

"I'm assuming it's the same guy. Steelgrave."

"Too much assuming, kid. We had him in the fishbowl because we thought the same. It didn't pan any gold."

"You got a tip. He set that tip up himself. So the night Stein was squibbed off he would be where you knew."

"You just making this up — or got evidence?" He sounded a little less relaxed.

"If a man got out of jail on a pass from the jail doctor, could you prove that?"

There was a silence. I heard a child's voice complaining and a woman's voice speaking to the child.

"It's happened," French said heavily. "I dunno. That's a tough order to fill. They'd send him under guard. Did he get to the guard?"

"That's my theory."

"Better sleep on it. Anything else?"

"I'm out at Stillwood Heights. In a big house where they were setting up for gambling and the local residents didn't like it."

"Read about it. Steelgrave there?"

"He's here. I'm here alone with him."

Another silence. The kid yelled and I thought I heard a slap. The kid yelled louder. French yelled at somebody.

"Put him on the phone," French said at last.

"You're not bright tonight, Christy. Why would I call *you?*"

"Yeah," he said. "Stupid of me. What's the address there?"

"I don't know. But it's up at the end of Tower Road in Stillwood Heights and the phone number is Halldale nine-five-zero-three-three. I'll be waiting for you."

He repeated the number and said slowly: "This time you wait, huh?"

"It had to come sometime."

The phone clicked and I hung up.

I went back through the house putting on lights as I found them and came out at the back door at the top of the stairs. There was a floodlight for the motor yard. I put that on. I went down the steps and walked along to the oleander bush. The private gate stood open as before. I swung it shut, hooked up the chain and clicked the padlock. I went back, walking slowly, looking up at the moon, sniffing the night air, listening to the tree frogs and the crickets. I went into the house and found the front door and put the light on over that. There was a big parking space in front and a circular lawn with roses. But you had to slide back around the house to the rear to get away.

The place was a dead end except for the driveway through the neighboring grounds. I wondered who lived there. A long way off through trees I could see the lights of a big house. Some Hollywood big shot, probably, some wizard of the slobbery kiss, and the pornographic dissolve.

I went back in and felt the gun I had just fired. It was cold enough. And Mr. Steelgrave was beginning to look as if he meant to stay dead.

No siren. But the sound of a car coming up the hill at last. I went out to meet it, me and my beautiful dream.

29

THEY CAME IN AS THEY SHOULD, big, tough and quiet, their eyes flickering with watchfulness and cautious with disbelief.

"Nice place," French said. "Where's the customer?"

"In there," Beifus said, without waiting for me to answer.

They went along the room without haste and stood in front of him looking down solemnly.

"Dead, wouldn't you say?" Beifus remarked, opening up the act.

French leaned down and took the gun that lay on the floor with thumb and finger on the trigger guard. His eyes flicked sideways and he jerked his chin. Beifus took the other white-handled gun by sliding a pencil into the end of the barrel.

"Fingerprints all in the right places, I hope," Beifus said. He sniffed. "Oh yeah, this baby's been working. How's yours, Christy?"

"Fired," French said. He sniffed again. "But not recently." He took a clip flash from his pocket and shone it into the barrel of the black gun. "Hours ago."

"Down at Bay City, in a house on Wyoming Street," I said.

Their heads swung around to me in unison.

"Guessing?" French asked slowly.

"Yes."

He walked over to the covered table and laid the gun down some distance from the other. "Better tag them right away, Fred. They're twins. We'll both sign the tags."

Beifus nodded and rooted around in his pockets. He came up with a couple of tie-on tags. The things cops carry around with them.

French moved back to me. "Let's stop guessing and get to the part you know."

"A girl I know called me this evening and said a client of mine was in danger up here — from him." I pointed with my chin at the dead man in the chair. "This girl rode me up here. We passed the road block. A number of people saw us both. She left me in back of the house and went home."

"Somebody with a name?" French asked.

"Dolores Gonzales, Chateau Bercy Apartments. On Franklin. She's in pictures."

"Oh-ho," Beifus said and rolled his eyes.

"Who's your client? Same one?" French asked.

"No. This is another party altogether."

"She have a name?"

"Not yet."

They stared at me with hard bright faces. French's jaw moved almost with a jerk. Knots of muscles showed at the sides of his jaw bone.

"New rules, huh?" he said softly.

I said, "There has to be some agreement about publicity. The D.A. ought to be willing."

Beifus said, "You don't know the D.A. good, Marlowe. He eats publicity like I eat tender young garden peas."

French said, "We don't give you any undertaking whatsoever."

"She hasn't any name," I said.

"There's a dozen ways we can find out, kid," Beifus said. "Why go into this routine that makes it tough for all of us?"

"No publicity," I said, "unless charges are actually filed."

"You can't get away with it, Marlowe."

"Goddam it," I said, "this man killed Orrin Quest. You take that gun downtown and check it against the bullets in Quest. Give me that much at least, before you force me into an impossible position."

"I wouldn't give you the dirty end of a burnt match," French said.

I didn't say anything. He stared at me with cold hate in his eyes. His lips moved slowly and his voice was thick saying, "You here when he got it?"

"No."

"Who was?"

"He was," I said, looking across at the dead Steelgrave.

"Who else?"

"I won't lie to you," I said. "And I won't tell you anything I don't want to tell — except on the terms I stated. I don't know who was here when he got it."

"Who was here when you got here?"

I didn't answer. He turned his head slowly and said to Beifus: "Put the cuffs on him. Behind."

Beifus hesitated. Then he took a pair of steel handcuffs out of his left hip pocket and came over to me. "Put your hands behind you," he said in an uncomfortable voice.

I did. He clicked the cuffs on. French walked over slowly and stood in front of me. His eyes were half-closed. The skin around them was grayish with fatigue.

"I'm going to make a little speech," he said. "You're not going to like it."

I didn't say anything.

French said: "It's like this with us, baby. We're coppers and everybody hates our guts. And as if we didn't have enough trouble, we have to have you. As if we didn't get pushed around enough by the guys in the corner offices, the City Hall gang, the day chief, the night chief, the Chamber of Commerce, His Honor the Mayor in his paneled office four times as big as the three lousy rooms the whole homicide staff has to work out of. As if we didn't have to handle one hundred and fourteen homicides last year out of three rooms that don't have enough chairs for the whole duty squad to sit down in at once. We spend our lives turning over dirty underwear and sniffing rotten teeth. We go up dark stairways to get a gun punk with a skinful of hop and sometimes we don't get all the way up, and our wives wait dinner that night and all the other nights. We don't come home any more. And nights we do come home, we come home so goddam tired we can't eat or sleep or even read the lies the papers print about us. So we lie awake in the dark in a cheap house on a cheap street and listen to the drunks down the block having fun. And just about the time we drop off the phone rings and we get up and start all over again. Nothing we do is right, not ever. Not once. If we get a confession, we beat it out of the guy, they say, and some shyster calls us Gestapo in court and sneers at us when we muddle our grammar. If we make a mistake they put us back in uniform on Skid Row and we spend the nice cool summer evenings picking drunks out of the gutter and being yelled at by whores and taking knives away from greaseballs in zoot suits. But all that ain't enough to make us entirely happy. We got to have you."

He stopped and drew in his breath. His face glistened a little as if with sweat. He leaned forward from his hips.

"We got to have you," he repeated. "We got to have sharpers with private licenses hiding information and dodging around corners and stirring up dust for us to breathe in. We got to have you suppressing evidence and framing set-ups that wouldn't fool a sick baby. You wouldn't mind me calling you a goddam cheap double-crossing keyhole peeper, would you, baby?"

"You want me to mind?" I asked him.

He straightened up. "I'd love it," he said. "In spades redoubled."

"Some of what you say is true," I said. "Not all. Any private eye wants to play ball with the police. Sometimes it's a little hard to find out who's making the rules of the ball game. Sometimes he doesn't trust the police, and with cause. Sometimes he just gets in a jam without meaning to and has to play his hand out the way it's dealt. He'd usually rather have a new deal. He'd like to keep on earning a living."

"Your license is dead," French said. "As of now. That problem won't bother you any more."

"It's dead when the commission that gave it to me says so. Not before."

Beifus said quietly, "Let's get on with it, Christy. This could wait."

"I'm getting on with it," French said. "My way. This bird hasn't cracked wise yet. I'm waiting for him to crack wise. The bright repartee. Don't tell me you're all out of the quick stuff, Marlowe."

"Just what is it you want me to say?" I asked him.

"Guess," he said.

"You're a man eater tonight," I said. "You want to break me in half. But you want an excuse. And you want me to give it to you?"

"That might help," he said between his teeth.

"What would you have done in my place?" I asked him.

"I couldn't imagine myself getting that low."

He licked at the point of his upper lip. His right hand was hanging loose at his side. He was clenching and unclenching the fingers without knowing it.

"Take it easy, Christy," Beifus said. "Lay off."

French didn't move. Beifus came over and stepped between us. French said, "Get out of there, Fred."

"No."

French doubled his fist and slugged him hard on the point of the jaw. Beifus stumbled back and knocked me out of the way. His knees wobbled. He bent forward and coughed. He shook his head slowly in a bent-over position. After a while he straightened up with a grunt. He turned and looked at me. He grinned.

"It's a new kind of third degree," he said. "The cops beat hell out of each other and the suspect cracks up from the agony of watching."

His hand went up and felt the angle of his jaw. It already showed swelling. His mouth grinned but his eyes were still a little vague. French stood rooted and silent.

Beifus got out a pack of cigarettes and shook one loose and held the pack out to French. French looked at the cigarette, looked at Beifus.

"Seventeen years of it," he said. "Even my wife hates me."

He lifted his open hand and slapped Beifus across the cheek with it lightly. Beifus kept on grinning.

French said: "Was it you I hit, Fred?"

Beifus said: "Nobody hit me, Christy. Nobody that I can remember."

French said: "Take the cuffs off him and take him out to the car. He's under arrest. Cuff him to the rail if you think it's necessary."

"Okay." Beifus went around behind me. The cuffs came loose. "Come along, baby," Beifus said.

I stared hard at French. He looked at me as if I was the wallpaper. His eyes didn't seem to see me at all.

I went out under the archway and out of the house.

30

NEVER KNEW HIS NAME, but he was rather short and thin for a cop, which was what he must have been, partly because he was there, and partly because when he leaned across the table to reach a card I could see the leather underarm holster and the butt end of a police .38.

He didn't speak much, but when he did he had a nice voice, a soft-water voice. And he had a smile that warmed the whole room.

"Wonderful casting," I said, looking at him across the cards.

We were playing double Canfield. Or he was. I was just there, watching him, watching his small and very neat and very clean hands go out across the table and touch a card and lift it delicately and put it somewhere else. When he did this he pursed his lips a little and whistled without tune, a low soft whistle, like a very young engine that is not yet sure of itself.

He smiled and put a red nine on a black ten.

"What do you do in your spare time?" I asked him.

"I play the piano a good deal," he said. "I have a seven-foot Steinway. Mozart and Bach mostly. I'm a bit old-fashioned. Most people find it dull stuff. I don't."

"Perfect casting," I said, and put a card somewhere.

"You'd be surprised how difficult some of that Mozart is," he said. "It sounds so simple when you hear it played well."

"Who can play it well?" I asked.

"Schnabel."

"Rubinstein?"

He shook his head. "Too heavy. Too emotional. Mozart is just music. No comment needed from the performer."

"I bet you get a lot of them in the confession mood," I said. "Like the job?"

He moved another card and flexed his fingers lightly. His nails were bright but short. You could see he was a man who loved to move his hands, to make little neat inconspicuous motions with them, motions without any special meaning, but smooth and flowing and light as swan's-down. They gave him a feel of delicate things delicately done, but not weak. Mozart, all right. I could see that.

It was about five-thirty, and the sky behind the screened window was getting light. The roll-top desk in the corner was rolled shut. The room was the same room I had been in the afternoon before. Down at the end of the table the square carpenter's pencil was lying where somebody had picked it up and put it back after Lieutenant Maglashan of Bay City threw it against the wall. The flat desk at which Christy French had sat was littered with ash. An old cigar butt clung to the extreme edge of a glass ashtray. A moth circled around the overhead light on a drop cord that had one of those green-and-white glass shades they still have in country hotels.

"Tired?" he asked.

"Pooped."

"You oughtn't to get yourself involved in these elaborate messes. No point in it that I can see."

"No point in shooting a man?"

He smiled the warm smile. "You never shot anybody."

"What makes you say that?"

"Common sense — and a lot of experience sitting here with people."

"I guess you do like the job," I said.

"It's night work. Gives me the days to practice. I've had it for twelve years now. Seen a lot of funny ones come and go."

He got another ace out, just in time. We were almost blocked.

"Get many confessions?"

"I don't take confessions," he said. "I just establish a mood."

"Why give it all away?"

He leaned back and tapped lightly with the edge of a card on the edge of the table. The smile came again. "I'm not giving anything away. We got you figured long ago."

"Then what are they holding me for?"

He wouldn't answer that. He looked around at the clock on the wall. "I think we could get some food now." He got up and went to the door. He half opened it and spoke softly to someone out side. Then he came back and sat down again and looked at what we had in the way of cards.

"No use," he said. "Three more up and we're blocked. Okay with you to start over?"

"Okay with me if we never started at all. I don't play cards. Chess."

He looked up at me quickly. "Why didn't you say so? I'd rather have played chess too."

"I'd rather drink some hot black coffee as bitter as sin."

"Any minute now. But I won't promise the coffee's what you're used to."

"Hell, I eat anywhere . . . Well, if I didn't shoot him, who did?"

"Guess that's what is annoying them."

"They ought to be glad to have him shot."

"They probably are," he said. "But they don't like the way it was done."

"Personally I thought it was as neat a job as you could find."

He looked at me in silence. He had the cards between his hands, all in a lump. He smoothed them out and flicked them over on their faces and dealt them rapidly into the two decks. The cards seemed to pour from his hands in a stream, in a blur.

"If you were that fast with a gun—" I began.

The stream of cards stopped. Without apparent motion a gun took their place. He held it lightly in his right hand pointed at a distant corner of the room. It went away and the cards started flowing again.

"You're wasted in here," I said. "You ought to be in Las Vegas."

He picked up one of the packs and shuffled it slightly and quickly, cut it, and dealt me a king high flush in spades.

"I'm safer with a Steinway," he said.

The door opened and a uniformed man came in with a tray.

We ate canned corn-beef hash and drank hot but weak coffee. By that time it was full morning.

At eight-fifteen Christy French came in and stood with his hat on the back of his head and dark smudges under his eyes.

I looked from him to the little man across the table. But he wasn't there any more. The cards weren't there either. Nothing was there but a chair pushed in neatly to the table and the dishes we had eaten off gathered on a tray. For a moment I had that creepy feeling.

Then Christy French walked around the table and jerked the chair out and sat down and leaned his chin on his hand. He took his hat off and rumpled his hair. He stared at me with hard morose eyes. I was back in coptown again.

31

"THE D.A. WANTS TO SEE YOU at nine o'clock," he said. "After that I guess you can go on home. That is, if he doesn't hang a pinch on you. I'm sorry you had to sit up in that chair all night."

"It's all right," I said. "I needed the exercise."

"Yeah, back in the groove again," he said. He stared moodily at the dishes on the tray.

"Got Lagardie?" I asked him.

"No. He's a doctor all right, though." His eyes moved to mine. "He practiced in Cleveland."

I said: "I hate it to be that tidy."

"How do you mean?"

"Young Quest wants to put the bite on Steelgrave. So he just by pure accident runs into the one guy in Bay City that could prove who Steelgrave was. *That's* too tidy."

"Aren't you forgetting something?"

"I'm tired enough to forget my name. What?"

"Me too," French said. "*Somebody* had to tell him who Steelgrave was. When that photo was taken Moe Stein hadn't been squibbed off. So what good was the photo unless somebody knew who Steelgrave was?"

"I guess Miss Weld knew," I said. "And Quest was her brother."

"You're not making much sense, chum." He grinned a tired grin. "Would she help her brother put the bite on her boy friend and on her too?"

"I give up. Maybe the photo was just a fluke. His other sister — my client that was — said he liked to take candid camera shots. The candider the better. If he lived long enough you'd have had him up for mopery."

"For murder," French said indifferently.

"Oh?"

"Maglashan found that ice pick all right. He just wouldn't give out to you."

"There'd have to be more than that."

"There is, but it's a dead issue. Clausen and Mileaway Marston both had records. The kid's dead. His family's respectable. He had an off-streak in him and he got in with the wrong people. No point in smearing his family just to prove the police can solve a case."

"That's white of you. How about Steelgrave?"

"That's out of my hands." He started to get up. "When a gangster gets his, how long does the investigation last?"

"Just as long as it's front-page stuff," I said. "But there's a question of identity involved here."

"No."

I stared at him. "How do you mean, no?"

"Just no. We're sure." He was on his feet now. He combed his hair with his fingers and rearranged his tie and hat. Out of the corner of his mouth he said in a low voice: "Off the record — we were always sure. We just didn't have a thing on him."

"Thanks," I said, "I'll keep it to myself. How about the guns?"

He stopped and stared down at the table. His eyes came up to mine rather slowly. "They both belonged to Steelgrave. What's more he had a permit to carry a gun. From the sheriff's office in another county. Don't ask me why. One of them" — he paused and looked up at the wall over my head — "one of them killed Quest . . . The same gun killed Stein."

"Which one?"

He smiled faintly. "It would be hell if the ballistics man got them mixed up and we didn't know," he said.

He waited for me to say something. I didn't have anything to say. He made a gesture with his hand.

"Well, so long. Nothing personal you know, but I hope the D.A. takes your hide off — in long thin strips."

He turned and went out.

I could have done the same, but I just sat there and stared across the table at the wall, as if I had forgotten how to get up. After a while the door opened and the orange queen came in. She unlocked her roll-top desk and took her hat off of her impossible hair and hung her jacket on a bare hook in the bare wall. She opened the window near her and uncovered her typewriter and put paper in it. Then she looked across at me.

"Waiting for somebody?"

"I room here," I said. "Been here all night."

She looked at me steadily for a moment. "You were here yesterday afternoon. I remember."

She turned to her typewriter and her fingers began to fly. From the open window behind her came the growl of cars filling up the parking lot. The sky had a white glare and there was not much smog. It was going to be a hot day.

The telephone rang on the orange queen's desk. She talked into it inaudibly, and hung up. She looked across at me again.

"Mr. Endicott's in his office," she said. "Know the way?"

"I worked there once. Not for him, though. I got fired."

She looked at me with that City Hall look they have. A voice that seemed to come from anywhere but her mouth said:

"Hit him in the face with a wet glove."

I went over near her and stood looking down at the orange hair. There was plenty of gray at the roots.

"Who said that?"

"It's the wall," she said. "It talks. The voices of the dead men who have passed through on the way to hell."

I went out of the room walking softly and shut the door against the closer so that it wouldn't make any noise.

32

YOU GO IN THROUGH DOUBLE SWING DOORS. Inside the double doors there is a combination PBX and information desk at which sits one of those ageless women you see around municipal offices everywhere in the world. They were never young and will never be old. They have no beauty, no charm, no style. They don't have to please anybody. They are safe. They are civil without ever quite being polite and intelligent and knowledgeable without any real interest in anything. They are what human beings turn into when they trade life for existence and ambition for security.

Beyond this desk there is a row of glassed-in cubicles stretching along one side of a very long room. On the other side is the waiting room, a row of hard chairs all facing one way, towards the cubicles.

About half of the chairs were filled with people waiting and the look of long waiting on their faces and the expectation of still longer waiting to come. Most of them were shabby. One was from the jail, in denim, with a guard. A white-faced kid built like a tackle, with sick, empty eyes.

At the back of the line of cubicles a door was lettered SEWELL EN-DICOTT DISTRICT ATTORNEY. I knocked and went on into a big airy corner room. A nice enough room, old-fashioned with padded black leather chairs and pictures of former D.A.'s and governors on the walls. Breeze fluttered the net curtains at four windows. A fan on a high shelf purred and swung slowly in a languid arc.

Sewell Endicott sat behind a flat dark desk and watched me come. He pointed to a chair across from him. I sat down. He was tall, thin and dark with loose black hair and long delicate fingers.

"You're Marlowe?" he said in a voice that had a touch of the soft South.

I didn't think he really needed an answer to that. I just waited.

"You're in a bad spot, Marlowe. You don't look good at all. You've been caught suppressing evidence helpful to the solution of a murder. That is obstructing justice. You could go up for it."

"Suppressing what evidence?" I asked.

He picked a photo off his desk and frowned at it. I looked across at the other two people in the room. They sat in chairs side by side. One of them was Mavis Weld. She wore the dark glasses with the wide white bows. I couldn't see her eyes, but I thought she was looking at me. She didn't smile. She sat very still.

By her side sat a man in an angelic pale-gray flannel suit with a carnation the size of a dahlia in his lapel. He was smoking a mono-grammed cigarette and flicking the ashes on the floor, ignoring the smoking stand at his elbow. I knew him by pictures I had seen in the papers. Lee Farrell, one of the hottest trouble-shooting lawyers in the country. His hair was white but his eyes were bright and young. He had a deep outdoor tan. He looked as if it would cost a thousand dollars to shake hands with him.

Endicott leaned back and tapped the arm of his chair with his long fingers. He turned with polite deference to Mavis Weld.

"And how well did you know Steelgrave, Miss Weld?"

"Intimately. He was very charming in some ways. I can hardly believe — " She broke off and shrugged.

"And you are prepared to take the stand and swear as to the time and place when this photograph was taken?" He turned the photograph over and showed it to her.

Farrell said indifferently, "Just a moment. Is that the evidence Mr. Marlowe is supposed to have suppressed?"

"I ask the questions," Endicott said sharply.

Farrell smiled. "Well, in case the answer is yes, that photo isn't evidence of anything."

Endicott said softly: "Will you answer my question, Miss Weld?"

She said quietly and easily: "No, Mr. Endicott, I couldn't swear when that picture was taken or where. I didn't know it was being taken."

"All you have to do is look at it," Endicott suggested.

"And all I know is what I get from looking at it," she told him.

I grinned. Farrell looked at me with a twinkle. Endicott caught the grin out of the corner of his eye. "Something you find amusing?" he snapped at me.

"I've been up all night. My face keeps slipping," I said.

He gave me a stern look and turned to Mavis Weld again.

"Will you amplify that, Miss Weld?"

"I've had a lot of photos taken of me, Mr. Endicott. In a lot of different places and with a lot of different people. I have had lunch and dinner at The Dancers with Mr. Steelgrave and with various other men. I don't know what you want me to say."

Farrell put in smoothly, "If I understand your point, you would like Miss Weld to be your witness to connect this photo up. In what kind of proceeding?"

"That's my business," Endicott said shortly. "Somebody shot Steelgrave to death last night. It could have been a woman. It could even have been Miss Weld. I'm sorry to say that, but it seems to be in the cards."

Mavis Weld looked down at her hands. She twisted a white glove between her fingers.

"Well, let's assume a proceeding," Farrell said. "One in which that photo is part of your evidence — if you can get it in. But you can't get it in. Miss Weld won't get it in for you. All she knows about the photo is what she sees by looking at it. What anybody can see. You'd have to connect it up with a witness who could swear as to when, how and where it was taken. Otherwise I'd object — if I happened to be on the other side. I could even introduce experts to swear the photo was faked."

"I'm sure you could," Endicott said dryly.

"The only man who could connect it up for you is the man who took it," Farrell went on without haste or heat. "I understand he's dead. I suspect that was why he was killed."

Endicott said: "This photo is clear evidence of itself that at a certain time and place Steelgrave was not in jail and therefore had no alibi for the killing of Stein."

Farrell said: "It's evidence when and if you get it introduced in evidence, Endicott. For Pete's sake, I'm not trying to tell you the law. You know it. Forget that picture. It proves nothing whatsoever. No paper would dare print it. No judge would admit it in evidence, because no competent witness can connect it up. And if that's the evidence Marlowe suppressed, then he didn't in a legal sense suppress evidence at all."

"I wasn't thinking of trying Steelgrave for murder," Endicott said dryly. "But I *am* a little interested in who killed him. The police department, fantastically enough, also has an interest in that. I hope our interest doesn't offend you."

Farrell said: "Nothing offends me. That's why I'm where I am. Are you sure Steelgrave was murdered?"

Endicott just stared at him. Farrell said easily: "I understand two guns were found, both the property of Steelgrave."

"Who told you?" Endicott asked sharply. He leaned forward frowning.

Farrell dropped his cigarette into the smoking stand and shrugged. "Hell, these things come out. One of these guns had killed Quest and also Stein. The other had killed Steelgrave. Fired at close quarters too. I admit those boys don't as a rule take that way out. But it could happen."

Endicott said gravely: "No doubt. Thanks for the suggestion. It happens to be wrong."

Farrell smiled a little and was silent. Endicott turned slowly to Mavis Weld.

"Miss Weld, this office — or the present incumbent of it at least — doesn't believe in seeking publicity at the expense of people to whom a certain kind of publicity might be fatal. It is my duty to determine whether anyone should be brought to trial for any of these murders, and to prosecute them, if the evidence warrants it. It is not my duty to ruin your career by exploiting the fact that you had the bad luck or bad judgment to be the friend of a man who, although never convicted or even indicted for any crime, was undoubtedly a member of a criminal mob at one time. I don't think you have been quite candid with me about this photograph, but I won't press the matter now. There is not much point in my asking you whether you shot Steelgrave. But I do ask you whether you have any knowledge that would point to who may have or might have killed him."

Farrell said quickly: "Knowledge, Miss Weld — not mere suspicion."

She faced Endicott squarely. "No."

He stood up and bowed. "That will be all for now then. Thanks for coming in."

Farrell and Mavis Weld stood up. I didn't move. Farrell said: "Are you calling a press conference?"

"I think I'll leave that to you, Mr. Farrell. You have always been very skillful in handling the press."

Farrell nodded and went to open the door. They went out. She didn't seem to look at me when she went out, but something touched the back of my neck lightly. Probably accidental. Her sleeve.

Endicott watched the door close. He looked across the desk at me. "Is Farrell representing you? I forgot to ask him."

"I can't afford him. So I'm vulnerable."

He smiled thinly. "I let them take all the tricks and then salve my dignity by working out on you, eh?"

"I couldn't stop you."

"You're not exactly proud of the way you have handled things, are you, Marlowe?"

"I got off on the wrong foot. After that I just had to take my lumps."

"Don't you think you owe a certain obligation to the law?"

"I would — if the law was like you."

He ran his long pale fingers through his tousled black hair.

"I could make a lot of answers to that," he said. "They'd all sound about the same. The citizen is the law. In this country we haven't got around to understanding that. We think of the law as an enemy. We're a nation of cop-haters."

"It'll take a lot to change that," I said. "On both sides."

He leaned forward and pressed a buzzer. "Yes," he said quietly. "It will. But somebody has to make a beginning. Thanks for coming in."

As I went out a secretary came in at another door with a fat file in her hand.

33

A SHAVE AND A SECOND BREAKFAST made me feel a little less like the box of shavings the cat had had kittens in. I went up to the office and unlocked the door and sniffed in the twice-breathed air and the smell of dust. I opened a window and inhaled the fry-cook smell from the coffee shop next door. I sat down at my desk and felt the grit on it with my finger tips. I filled a pipe and lit it and leaned back and looked around.

"Hello," I said.

I was just talking to the office equipment, the three green filing cases, the threadbare piece of carpet, the customer's chair across from me, and the light fixture in the ceiling with three dead moths in it that had been there for at least six months. I was talking to the pebbled glass panel and the grimy woodwork and the pen set on the desk and the tired, tired telephone. I was talking to the scales on an alligator, the name of the alligator being Marlowe, a private detective in our thriving little community. Not the brainiest guy in the world, but cheap. He started out cheap and he ended cheaper still.

I reached down and put the bottle of Old Forester up on the desk. It was about a third full. Old Forester. Now who gave you that, pal? That's green-label stuff. Out of your class entirely. Must have been a client. I had a client once.

And that got me thinking about her, and maybe I have stronger thoughts than I know. The telephone rang, and the funny little precise voice sounded just as it had the first time she called me up.

"I'm in that telephone booth," she said. "If you're alone, I'm coming up."

"Uh-huh."

"I suppose you're mad at me," she said.

"I'm not mad at anybody. Just tired."

"Oh yes you are," her tight little voice said. "But I'm coming up anyway. I don't care if you *are* mad at me."

She hung up. I took the cork out of the bottle of Old Forester and gave a sniff at it. I shuddered. That settled it. Any time I couldn't smell whiskey without shuddering I was through.

I put the bottle away and got up to unlock the communicating door. Then I heard her tripping along the hall. I'd know those tight little footsteps anywhere. I opened the door and she came up to me and looked at me shyly.

It was all gone. The slanted cheaters, and the new hair-do and the smart little hat and the perfume and the prettied-up touch. The costume jewelry, the rouge, the everything. All gone. She was right back where she started that first morning. Same brown tailor-made, same square bag, same rimless glasses, same prim little narrow-minded smile.

"It's me," she said. "I'm going home."

She followed me into my private thinking parlor and sat down primly and I sat down just any old way and stared at her.

"Back to Manhattan," I said. "I'm surprised they let you."

"I may have to come back."

"Can you afford it?"

She gave a quick little half-embarrassed laugh. "It won't cost me anything," she said. She reached up and touched the rimless glasses. "These feel all wrong now," she said. "I liked the others. But Dr. Zugsmith wouldn't like them at all." She put her bag on the desk and drew a line along the desk with her finger tip. That was just like the first time too.

"I can't remember whether I gave you back your twenty dollars or not," I said. "We kept passing it back and forth until I lost count."

"Oh, you gave it to me," she said. "Thank you."

"Sure?"

"I never make mistakes about money. Are you all right? Did they hurt you?"

"The police? No. And it was as tough a job as they ever didn't do."

She looked innocently surprised. Then her eyes glowed. "You must be awfully brave," she said.

"Just luck," I said. I picked up a pencil and felt the point. It was a good sharp point, if anybody wanted to write anything. I didn't. I reached across and slipped the pencil through the strap of her bag and pulled it towards me.

"Don't touch my bag," she said quickly and reached for it.

I grinned and drew it out of her reach. "All right. But it's such a cute little bag. It's so like you."

She leaned back. There was a vague worry behind her eyes, but she smiled. "You think I'm cute — Philip? I'm so ordinary."

"I wouldn't say so."

"You wouldn't?"

"Hell no, I think you're one of the most unusual girls I ever met." I swung the bag by its strap and set it down on the corner of the desk. Her eyes fastened on it quickly, but she licked her lip and kept on smiling at me.

"And I bet you've known an awful lot of girls," she said. "Why" — she looked down and did that with her finger tip on the desk again — "why didn't you ever get married?"

I thought of all the ways you answer that. I thought of all the women I had liked that much. No, not all. But some of them.

"I suppose I know the answer," I said. "But it would just sound corny. The ones I'd maybe like to marry — well, I haven't what they need. The others you don't have to marry. You just seduce them — if they don't beat you to it."

She flushed to the roots of her mousy hair.

"You're horrid when you talk like that."

"That goes for some of the nice ones too," I said. "Not what you said. What I said. You wouldn't have been so hard to take yourself."

"Don't talk like that, please!"

"Well, would you?"

She looked down at the desk. "I wish you'd tell me," she said slowly, "what happened to Orrin. I'm all confused."

"I told you he probably went off the rails. The first time you came in. Remember?"

She nodded slowly, still blushing.

"Abnormal sort of home life," I said. "Very inhibited sort of guy and with a very highly developed sense of his own importance. It looked at you out of the picture you gave me. I don't want to go psychological on you, but I figure he was just the type to go very completely haywire, if he went haywire at all. Then there's that awful money hunger that runs in your family — all except one."

She smiled at me now. If she thought I meant her, that was jake with me.

"There's one question I want to ask you," I said. "Was your father married before?"

She nodded, yes.

"That helps. Leila had another mother. That suits me fine. Tell me some more. After all I did a lot of work for you, for a very low fee of no dollars net."

"You got paid," she said sharply. "Well paid. By Leila. And don't expect me to call her Mavis Weld. I won't do it."

"You didn't know I was going to get paid."

"Well" — there was a long pause, during which her eyes went to her bag again — "you did get paid."

"Okay, pass that. Why wouldn't you tell me who she was?"

"I was ashamed. Mother and I were both ashamed."

"Orrin wasn't. He loved it."

"Orrin?" There was a tidy little silence while she looked at her bag again. I was beginning to get curious about that bag. "But he had been out here and I suppose he'd got used to it."

"Being in pictures isn't that bad, surely."

"It wasn't just that," she said swiftly, and her tooth came down on the outer edge of her lower lip and something flared in her eyes and very slowly died away. I just put another match to my pipe. I was too tired to show emotions, even if I felt any.

"I know. Or anyway I kind of guessed. How did Orrin find out something about Steelgrave that the cops didn't know?"

"I — I don't know," she said slowly, picking her way among her words like a cat on a fence. "Could it have been that doctor?"

"Oh sure," I said, with a big warm smile. "He and Orrin got to be friends somehow. A common interest in sharp tools maybe."

She leaned back in her chair. Her little face was thin and angular now. Her eyes had a watchful look.

"Now you're just being nasty," she said. "Every so often you have to be that way."

"Such a pity," I said. "I'd be a lovable character if I'd let myself alone. Nice bag." I reached for it and pulled it in front of me and snapped it open.

She came up out of her chair and lunged.

"You let my bag alone!"

I looked her straight in the rimless glasses. "You want to go home to Manhattan, Kansas, don't you? Today? You got your ticket and everything?"

She worked her lips and slowly sat down again.

"Okay," I said. "I'm not stopping you. I just wondered how much dough you squeezed out of the deal."

She began to cry. I opened the bag and went through it. Nothing until I came to the zipper pocket at the back. I unzipped and reached in. There was a flat packet of new bills in there. I took them out and riffled them. Ten centuries. All new. All nice. An even thousand dollars. Nice traveling money.

I leaned back and tapped the edge of the packet on my desk. She sat silent now, staring at me with wet eyes. I got a handkerchief out of her bag and tossed it across to her. She dabbed at her eyes. She watched me around the handkerchief. Once in a while she made a nice little appealing sob in her throat.

"Leila gave the money to me," she said softly.

"What size chisel did you use?"

She just opened her mouth and a tear ran down her cheek into it.

"Skip it," I said. I dropped the pack of money back into the bag, snapped the bag shut and pushed it across the desk to her. "I guess you and Orrin belong to that class of people that can convince themselves that everything they do is right. He can blackmail his sister and then when a couple of small-time crooks get wise to his racket and take it away from him, he can sneak up on them and knock them off with an ice pick in the back of the neck. Probably didn't even keep him awake that night. You can do much the same. Leila didn't give you that money. Steelgrave gave it to you. For what?"

"You're filthy," she said. "You're vile. How dare you say such things to me?"

"Who tipped off the law that Dr. Lagardie knew Clausen? Lagardie thought I did. I didn't. So you did. Why? To smoke out your brother who was not cutting you in — because right then he had lost his deck of cards and was hiding out. I'd like to see some of those letters he wrote home. I bet they're meaty. I can see him working at it, watching his sister, trying to get her lined up for his Leica, with the good Dr. Lagardie waiting quietly in the background for his share of the take. What did you hire me for?"

"I didn't know," she said evenly. She wiped her eyes again and put the handkerchief away in the bag and got herself all collected and ready to leave. "Orrin never mentioned any names. I didn't even know Orrin had lost his pictures. But I knew he had taken them and that they were very valuable. I came out to make sure."

"Sure of what?"

"That Orrin treated me right. He could be awfully mean sometimes. He might have kept all the money himself."

"Why did he call you up night before last?"

"He was scared. Dr. Lagardie wasn't pleased with him any more. He didn't have the pictures. Somebody else had them. Orrin didn't know who. But he was scared."

"I had them. I still have," I said. "They're in that safe."

She turned her head very slowly to look at the safe. She ran a finger tip questioningly along her lip. She turned back.

"I don't believe you," she said, and her eyes watched me like a cat watching a mousehole.

"How's to split that grand with me. You get the pictures."

She thought about it. "I could hardly give you all that money for something that doesn't belong to you," she said, and smiled. "Please give them to me. Please, Philip. Leila ought to have them back."

"For how much dough?"

She frowned and looked hurt.

"She's my client now," I said. "But double-crossing her wouldn't be bad business — at the right price."

"I don't believe you have them."

"Okay." I got up and went to the safe. In a moment I was back with the envelope. I poured the prints and the negative out on the desk — my side of the desk. She looked down at them and started to reach.

I picked them up and shuffled them together and held one so

that she could look at it. When she reached for it I moved it back.

"But I can't see it so far away," she complained.

"It costs money to get closer."

"I never thought you were a crook," she said with dignity.

I didn't say anything. I relit my pipe.

"I could make you give them to the police," she said.

"You could try."

Suddenly she spoke rapidly. "I couldn't give you this money I have, really I couldn't. We — well Mother and I owe money still on account of Father and the house isn't clear and — "

"What did you sell Steelgrave for the grand?"

Her mouth fell open and she looked ugly. She closed her lips and pressed them together. It was a tight hard little face that I was looking at.

"You had one thing to sell," I said. "You knew where Orrin was. To Steelgrave that information was worth a grand. Easy. It's a question of connecting up evidence. You wouldn't understand. Steelgrave went down there and killed him. He paid you the money for the address."

"Leila told him," she said in a faraway voice.

"Leila told me she told him," I said. "If necessary Leila would tell the world she told him. Just as she would tell the world she killed Steelgrave — if that was the only way out. Leila is a sort of free-and-easy Hollywood babe that doesn't have very good morals. But when it comes to bedrock guts — she has what it takes. She's not the ice-pick type. And she's not the blood-money type."

The color flowed away from her face and left her as pale as ice. Her mouth quivered, then tightened up hard into a little knot. She pushed her chair back and leaned forward to get up.

"Blood money," I said quietly. "Your own brother. And you set him up so they could kill him. A thousand dollars blood money. I hope you'll be happy with it."

She stood away from the chair and took a couple of steps backward. Then suddenly she giggled.

"Who could prove it?" she half squealed. "Who's alive to prove it? You? Who are you? A cheap shyster, a nobody." She went off into a shrill peal of laughter. "Why even twenty dollars buys you."

I was still holding the packet of photos. I struck a match and dropped the negative into the ash tray and watched it flare up.

She stopped dead, frozen in a kind of horror. I started to tear the pictures up into strips. I grinned at her.

"A cheap shyster," I said. "Well, what would you expect? I don't have any brothers or sisters to sell out. So I sell out my clients."

She stood rigid and glaring. I finished my tearing-up job and lit the scraps of paper in the tray.

"One thing I regret," I said. "Not seeing your meeting back in Manhattan, Kansas, with dear old Mom. Not seeing the fight over how to split that grand. I bet that would be something to watch."

I poked at the paper with a pencil to keep it burning. She came slowly, step by step, to the desk and her eyes were fixed on the little smoldering heap of torn prints.

"I could tell the police," she whispered. "I could tell them a lot of things. They'd believe me."

"I could tell them who shot Steelgrave," I said. "Because I know who didn't. They might believe *me*."

The small head jerked up. The light glinted on the glasses. There were no eyes behind them.

"Don't worry," I said. "I'm not going to. It wouldn't cost me enough. And it would cost somebody else too much."

The telephone rang and she jumped a foot. I turned and reached for it and put my face against it and said, "Hello."

"Amigo, are you all right?"

There was a sound in the background. I swung around and saw the door click shut. I was alone in the room.

"Are you all right, amigo?"

"I'm tired. I've been up all night. Apart from — "

"Has the little one called you up?"

"The little sister? She was just in here. She's on her way back to Manhattan with the swag."

"The swag?"

"The pocket money she got from Steelgrave for fingering her brother."

There was a silence, then she said gravely, "You cannot know that, amigo."

"Like I know I'm sitting leaning on this desk holding on to this telephone. Like I know I hear your voice. And not quite so certainly, but certainly enough like I know who shot Steelgrave."

"You are somewhat foolish to say that to me, amigo. I am not above reproach. You should not trust me too much."

"I make mistakes, but this won't be one. I've burned all the photographs. I tried to sell them to Orfamay. She wouldn't bid high enough."

"Surely you are making fun, amigo."

"Am I? Who of?"

She tinkled her laugh over the wire. "Would you like to take me to lunch?"

"I might. Are you home?"

"Sí."

"I'll come over in a little while."

"But I shall be delighted."

I hung up.

The play was over. I was sitting in the empty theater. The curtain was down and projected on it dimly I could see the action. But already some of the actors were getting vague and unreal. The little sister above all. In a couple of days I would forget what she looked like. Because in a way she *was* so unreal. I thought of her tripping back to Manhattan, Kansas, and dear old Mom, with that fat little new little thousand dollars in her purse. A few people had been killed so she could get it, but I didn't think that would bother her for long. I thought of her getting down to the office in the morning — what was the man's name? Oh yes. Dr. Zugsmith — and dusting off his desk before he arrived and arranging the magazines in the waiting room. She'd have her rimless cheaters on and a plain dress and her face would be without make-up and her manners to the patients would be most correct.

"Dr. Zugsmith will see you now, Mrs. Whoosis."

She would hold the door open with a little smile and Mrs. Whoosis would go in past her and Dr. Zugsmith would be sitting behind his desk as professional as hell with a white coat on and his stethoscope hanging around his neck. A case file would be in front of him and his note pad and prescription pad would be neatly squared off.

Nothing that Dr. Zugsmith didn't know. You couldn't fool him. He had it all at his finger tips. When he looked at a patient he knew the answers to all the questions he was going to ask just as a matter of form.

When he looked at his receptionist, Miss Orfamay Quest, he saw a nice quiet young lady, properly dressed for a doctor's office, no red nails, no loud make-up, nothing to offend the old-fashioned type of customer. An ideal receptionist, Miss Quest.

Dr. Zugsmith, when he thought about her at all, thought of her with self-satisfaction. He had made her what she was. She was just what the doctor ordered.

Most probably he hadn't made a pass at her yet. Maybe they don't in those small towns. Ha, ha! I grew up in one.

I changed position and looked at my watch and got that bottle of Old Forester up out of the drawer after all. I sniffed it. It smelled good. I poured myself a good stiff jolt and held it up against the light.

"Well, Dr. Zugsmith," I said out loud, just as if he was sitting there on the other side of the desk with a drink in his hand, "I don't know you very well and you don't know me at all. Ordinarily I don't believe in giving advice to strangers, but I've had a short intensive course of Miss Orfamay Quest and I'm breaking my rule. If ever that little girl wants anything from you, give it to her quick. Don't stall around or gobble about your income tax and your overhead. Just wrap yourself in a smile and shell out. Don't get involved in any discussions about what belongs to who. Keep the little girl happy, that's the main thing. Good luck to you, Doctor, and don't leave any harpoons lying around the office."

I drank off half of my drink and waited for it to warm me up. When it did that I drank the rest and put the bottle away.

I knocked the cold ashes out of my pipe and refilled it from the leather humidor an admirer had given me for Christmas, the admirer by an odd coincidence having the same name as mine.

When I had the pipe filled I lit it carefully, without haste, and went on out and down the hall, as breezy as a Britisher coming in from a tiger hunt.

34

THE CHATEAU BERCY was old but made over. It had the sort of lobby that asks for plush and India-rubber plants, but gets glass brick, cornice lighting, three-cornered glass tables, and a general air of having been redecorated by a parolee from a nut hatch. Its color scheme was bile green, linseed-poultice brown, sidewalk gray and monkey-bottom blue. It was as restful as a split lip.

The small desk was empty but the mirror behind it could be diaphanous, so I didn't try to sneak up the stairs. I rang a bell and a large soft man oozed out from behind a wall and smiled at me with moist soft lips and bluish white teeth and unnaturally bright eyes.

"Miss Gonzales," I said. "Name's Marlowe. She's expecting me."

"Why, yes, of course," he said, fluttering his hands. "Yes, of course. I'll telephone up at once." He had a voice that fluttered too. He picked up the telephone and gurgled into it and put it down.

"Yes, Mr. Marlowe. Miss Gonzales says to come right up. Apartment four twelve." He giggled. "But I suppose you know."

"I know now," I said. "By the way were you here last February?"

"Last February? Last February? Oh yes, I was here last February." He pronounced it exactly as spelled.

"Remember the night Stein got chilled out front?"

The smile went away from the fat face in a hurry. "Are you a police officer?" His voice was now thin and reedy.

"No. But your pants are unzipped, if you care."

He looked down with horror and zipped them up with hands that almost trembled.

"Why, thank you," he said. "Thank you." He leaned across the low desk. "It was not exactly out front," he said. "That is not exactly. It was almost to the next corner."

"Living here, wasn't he?"

"I'd really rather not talk about it. Really I'd rather not talk about it." He paused and ran his pinkie along his lower lip. "Why do you ask?"

"Just to keep you talking. You want to be more careful, bud. I can smell it on your breath."

The pink flowed all over him right down to his neck. "If you suggest I have been drinking—"

"Only tea," I said. "And not from a cup."

I turned away. He was silent. As I reached the elevator I looked back. He stood with his hands flat on the desk and his head strained around to watch me. Even from a distance he seemed to be trembling.

The elevator was self-service. The fourth floor was cool gray, the carpet thick. There was a small bell push beside apartment 412. It chimed softly inside. The door was swung open instantly. The beautiful deep dark eyes looked at me and the red, red mouth smiled at me. Black slacks and the flame-colored shirt, just like last night.

"Amigo," she said softly. She put her arms out. I took hold of her wrists and brought them together and made her palms touch. I played patacake with her for a moment. The expression in her eyes was languorous and fiery at the same time.

I let go of her wrists, closed the door with my elbow and slid past her. It was like the first time.

"You ought to carry insurance on those," I said touching one. It was real enough. The nipple was as hard as a ruby.

She went into her joyous laugh. I went on in and looked the place over. It was French gray and dusty blue. Not her colors, but very nice. There was a false fireplace with gas logs, and enough chairs and tables and lamps, but not too many. There was a neat little cellaret in the corner.

"You like my little apartment, amigo?"

"Don't say little apartment. That sounds like a whore too."

I didn't look at her. I didn't want to look at her. I sat down on a davenport and rubbed a hand across my forehead.

"Four hours sleep and a couple of drinks," I said. "And I'd be able to talk nonsense to you again. Right now I've barely strength to talk sense. But I've got to."

She came to sit close to me. I shook my head. "Over there. I really do have to talk sense."

She sat down opposite and looked at me with grave dark eyes. "But yes, amigo, whatever you wish. I am your girl — at least I would gladly be your girl."

"Where did you live in Cleveland?"

"In Cleveland?" Her voice was very soft, almost cooing. "Did I say I had lived in Cleveland?"

"You said you knew him there."

She thought back and then nodded. "I was married then, amigo. What is the matter?"

"You did live in Cleveland then?"

"Yes," she said softly.

"You got to know Steelgrave how?"

"It was just that in those days it was fun to know a gangster. A form of inverted snobbery, I suppose. One went to the places where they were said to go and if one was lucky, perhaps some evening — "

"You let him pick you up."

She nodded brightly. "Let us say *I* picked *him* up. He was a very nice little man. Really, he was."

"What about the husband? *Your* husband. Or don't you remember?"

She smiled. "The streets of the world are paved with discarded husbands," she said.

"Isn't it the truth? You find them everywhere. Even in Bay City."

That bought me nothing. She shrugged politely. "I would not doubt it."

"Might even be a graduate of the Sorbonne. Might even be mooning away in a measly small-town practice. Waiting and hoping. That's one coincidence I'd like to eat. It has a touch of poetry."

The polite smile stayed in place on her lovely face.

"We've slipped far apart," I said. "Ever so far. And we got to be pretty clubby there for a while."

I looked down at my fingers. My head ached. I wasn't even forty per cent of what I ought to be. She reached me a crystal cigarette box and I took one. She fitted one for herself into the golden tweezers. She took it from a different box.

"I'd like to try one of yours," I said.

"But Mexican tobacco is so harsh to most people."

"As long as it's tobacco," I said, watching her. I made up my mind. "No, you're right. I wouldn't like it."

"What," she asked carefully, "is the meaning of this by-play?"

"Desk clerk's a muggle-smoker."

She nodded slowly. "I have warned him," she said. "Several times."

"Amigo," I said.

"What?"

"You don't use much Spanish do you? Perhaps you don't know much Spanish. Amigo gets worn to shreds."

"We are not going to be like yesterday afternoon, I hope," she said slowly.

"We're not. The only thing Mexican about you is a few words and a careful way of talking that's supposed to give the impression of a person speaking a language they had to learn. Like saying 'do not' instead of 'don't.' That sort of thing."

She didn't answer. She puffed gently on her cigarette and smiled.

"I'm in bad trouble downtown," I went on. "Apparently Miss Weld had the good sense to tell it to her boss — Julius Oppenheimer — and he came through. Got Lee Farrell for her. I don't think they think she shot Steelgrave. But they think I know who did, and they don't love me any more."

"And do you know, amigo?"

"Told you over the phone I did."

She looked at me steadily for a longish moment. "I was there." Her voice had a dry, serious sound for once.

"It was very curious, really. The little girl wanted to see the gambling house. She had never seen anything like that and there had been in the papers — "

"She was staying here — with you?"

"Not in my apartment, amigo. In a room I got for her here."

"No wonder she wouldn't tell me," I said. "But I guess you didn't have time to teach her the business."

She frowned very slightly and made a motion in the air with the brown cigarette. I watched its smoke write something unreadable in the still air.

"Please. As I was saying, she wanted to go to that house. So I called him up and he said to come along. When we got there he was drunk. I have never seen him drunk before. He laughed and put his arm around little Orfamay and told her she had earned her money well. He said he had something for her, then he took from his pocket a billfold wrapped in a cloth of some kind and gave it to her. When she unwrapped it there was a hole in the middle of it and the hole was stained with blood."

"That wasn't nice," I said. "I wouldn't even call it characteristic."

"You did not know him very well."

"True. Go on."

"Little Orfamay took the billfold and stared at it and then stared at him and her white little face was very still. Then she thanked him and opened her bag to put the billfold in it, as I thought — it was all very curious — "

"A scream," I said. "It would have had me gasping on the floor."

" — but instead she took a gun out of her bag. It was a gun he had given Mavis, I think. It was like the one — "

"I know exactly what it was like," I said. "I played with it some."

"She turned around and shot him dead with one shot. It was very dramatic."

She put the brown cigarette back in her mouth and smiled at me. A curious, rather distant smile, as if she was thinking of something far away.

"You made her confess to Mavis Weld," I said.

She nodded.

"Mavis wouldn't have believed *you*, I guess."

"I did not care to risk it."

"It wasn't you gave Orfamay the thousand bucks, was it, darling? To make her tell? She's a little girl who would go a long way for a thousand bucks."

"I do not care to answer that," she said with dignity.

"No. So last night when you rushed me out there, you already knew he was dead and there wasn't anything to be afraid of and all that act with the gun was just an act."

"I do not like to play God," she said softly. "There was a situation and I knew that somehow or other you would get Mavis out of it. There was no one else who would. Mavis was determined to take the blame."

"I better have a drink," I said. "I'm sunk."

She jumped up and went to the little cellaret. She came back with a couple of huge glasses of Scotch and water. She handed me one and watched me over her glass as I tried it out. It was wonderful. I drank some more. She sank down into her chair again, and reached for the golden tweezers.

"I chased her out," I said finally. "Mavis, I'm talking about. She told me she had shot him. She had the gun. The twin of the one you gave me. You didn't probably notice that yours had been fired."

"I know very little about guns," she said softly.

"Sure. I counted the shells in it, and assuming it had been full to start with, two had been fired. Quest was killed with two shots from a .32 automatic. Same caliber. I picked up the empty shells in the den down there."

"Down where, amigo?"

It was beginning to grate. Too much amigo, far too much.

"Of course I couldn't know it was the same gun, but it seemed worth trying out. Only confuse things up a little anyhow, and give Mavis that much break. So I switched guns on him, and put his behind the bar. His was a black .38. More like what he would carry, if he carried one at all. Even with a checked grip you can leave prints, but with an ivory grip you're apt to leave a fair set of finger marks on the left side. Steelgrave wouldn't carry that kind of gun."

Her eyes were round and empty and puzzled. "I am afraid I am not following you too well."

"And if he killed a man he would kill him dead, and be sure of it. This guy got up and walked a bit."

A flash of something showed in her eyes and was gone.

"I'd like to say he talked a bit," I went on. "But he didn't. His lungs were full of blood. He died at my feet. Down there."

"But down where? You have not told me where it was that this — "

"Do I have to?"

She sipped from her glass. She smiled. She put the glass down. I said:

"You were present when little Orfamay told him where to go."

"Oh yes, of course." Nice recovery. Fast and clean. But her smile looked a little more tired.

"Only he didn't go," I said.

Her cigarette stopped in midair. That was all. Nothing else. It went on slowly to her lips. She puffed elegantly.

"That's what's been the matter all along," I said. "I just wouldn't buy what was staring me in the face. Steelgrave is Weepy Moyer. That's solid, isn't it?"

"Most certainly. And it can be proved."

"Steelgrave is a reformed character and doing fine. Then this Stein comes out bothering him, wanting to cut in. I'm guessing, but that's about how it would happen. Okay, Stein has to go. Steelgrave doesn't want to kill anybody — and he has never been accused of killing anybody. The Cleveland cops wouldn't come out and get him. No charges pending. No mystery — except that he had been connected with a mob in some capacity. But he has to get rid of Stein. So he gets himself pinched. And then he gets out of jail by bribing the jail doctor, and he kills Stein and goes back into jail at once. When the killing shows up whoever let him out of jail is going to run like hell and destroy any records there might be of his going out. Because the cops will come over and ask questions."

"Very naturally, amigo."

I looked her over for cracks, but there weren't any yet.

"So far so good. But we've got to give this lad credit for a few brains. Why did he let them hold him in jail for ten days? Answer one: to make himself an alibi. Answer two: because he knew that sooner or later this question of him being Moyer was going to get aired, so why not give them the time and get it over with? That way any time a racket boy gets blown down around here they're not going to keep pulling Steelgrave in and trying to hang the rap on him."

"You like that idea, amigo?"

"Yes. Look at it this way. Why would he have lunch in a public place the very day he was out of the cooler to knock Stein off? And if he did, why would young Quest happen around to snap that picture? Stein hadn't been killed, so the picture wasn't evidence of anything. I like people to be lucky, but that's *too* lucky. Again, even if Steelgrave didn't know his picture had been taken, he knew who Quest was. Must have. Quest had been tapping his sister for eating money since he lost his job, maybe before. Steelgrave had a key to her apartment. He must have known something about this brother of hers. Which simply adds up to the result, that *that* night of all nights Steelgrave would *not* have shot Stein — even if he had planned to."

"It is now for me to ask you who did," she said politely.

"Somebody who knew Stein and could get close to him. Somebody who already knew that photo had been taken, knew who Steelgrave was, knew that Mavis Weld was on the edge of becoming a big star, knew that her association with Steelgrave was dangerous, but would be a thousand times more dangerous if Steelgrave could be framed for the murder of Stein. Knew Quest, because he had been to Mavis Weld's apartment, and had met him there and given him the works, and he was a boy that could be knocked clean out of his mind by that sort of treatment. Knew that those bone-handled .32's were registered to Steelgrave, although he had only bought them to give to a couple of girls, and if he carried a gun himself, it would be one that was not registered and could not be traced to him. Knew — "

"Stop!" Her voice was a sharp stab of sound, but neither frightened nor even angry. "You will stop at once, please! I will not tolerate this another minute. You will now go!"

I stood up. She leaned back and a pulse beat in her throat. She was exquisite, she was dark, she was deadly. And nothing would ever touch her, not even the law.

"Why did you kill Quest?" I asked her.

She stood up and came close to me, smiling again. "For two reasons, amigo. He was more than a little crazy and in the end he would have killed me. And the other reason is that none of this — absolutely none of it — was for money. It was for love."

I started to laugh in her face. I didn't. She was dead serious. It was out of this world.

"No matter how many lovers a woman may have," she said softly, "there is always one she cannot bear to lose to another woman. Steelgrave was the one."

I just stared into her lovely dark eyes. "I believe you," I said at last.

"Kiss me, amigo."

"Good God!"

"I must have men, amigo. But the man I loved is dead. I killed him. That man I would not share."

"You waited a long time."

"I can be patient — as long as there is hope."

"Oh, nuts."

She smiled a free, beautiful and perfectly natural smile. "And you cannot do a damn thing about all this, darling, unless you destroy Mavis Weld utterly and finally."

"Last night she proved she was willing to destroy herself."

"If she was not acting." She looked at me sharply and laughed. "That hurt, did it not? You are in love with her."

I said slowly: "That would be kind of silly. I could sit in the dark with her and hold hands, but for how long? In a little while she will drift off into a haze of glamour and expensive clothes and froth and unreality and muted sex. She won't be a real person any more. Just a voice from a sound track, a face on a screen. I'd want more than that."

I moved towards the door without putting my back to her. I didn't really expect a slug. I thought she liked better having me the way I was — and not being able to do a damn thing about any of it.

I looked back as I opened the door. Slim, dark and lovely and smiling. Reeking with sex. Utterly beyond the moral laws of this or any world I could imagine.

She was one for the book all right. I went out quietly. Very softly her voice came to me as I closed the door.

"Querido — I have liked you very much. It is too bad."

I shut the door.

35

As THE ELEVATOR OPENED at the lobby a man stood there waiting for it. He was tall and thin and his hat was pulled low over his eyes. It was a warm day but he wore a thin topcoat with the collar up. He kept his chin low.

"Dr. Lagardie," I said softly.

He glanced at me with no trace of recognition. He moved into the elevator. It started up.

I went across to the desk and banged the bell. The large fat soft man came out and stood with a pained smile on his loose mouth. His eyes were not quite so bright.

"Give me the phone."

He reached down and put it on the desk. I dialed Madison 7911. The voice said: "Police." This was the Emergency Board.

"Chateau Bercy Apartments, Franklin and Girard in Hollywood. A man named Dr. Vincent Lagardie wanted for questioning by Homicide, Lieutenants French and Beifus, has just gone up to apartment four twelve. This is Philip Marlowe, a private detective."

"Franklin and Girard. Wait there please. Are you armed?"

"Yes."

"Hold him if he tries to leave."

I hung up and wiped my mouth off. The fat softy was leaning against the counter, white around the eyes.

They came fast — but not fast enough. Perhaps I ought to have stopped him. Perhaps I had a hunch what he would do, and deliberately let him do it. Sometimes when I'm low I try to reason it out. But it gets too complicated. The whole damn case was that way. There was never a point where I could do the natural obvious thing without stopping to rack my head dizzy with figuring how it would affect somebody I owed something to.

When they cracked the door he was sitting on the couch holding her pressed against his heart. His eyes were blind and there was bloody foam on his lips. He had bitten through his tongue.

Under her left breast and tight against the flame-colored shirt lay the silver handle of a knife I had seen before. The handle was in the shape of a naked woman. The eyes of Miss Dolores Gonzales were half-open and on her lips there was the dim ghost of a provocative smile.

"The Hippocrates smile," the ambulance intern said, and sighed. "On her it looks good."

He glanced across at Dr. Lagardie who saw nothing and heard nothing, if you could judge by his face.

"I guess somebody lost a dream," the intern said. He bent over and closed her eyes.

THE LONG GOODBYE

1

THE FIRST TIME I laid eyes on Terry Lennox he was drunk in a
Rolls-Royce Silver Wraith outside the terrace of The Dancers. The
parking lot attendant had brought the car out and he was still
holding the door open because Terry Lennox's left foot was still
dangling outside, as if he had forgotten he had one. He had a
young-looking face but his hair was bone white. You could tell
by his eyes that he was plastered to the hairline, but otherwise
he looked like any other nice young guy in a dinner jacket who
had been spending too much money in a joint that exists for that
purpose and for no other.

There was a girl beside him. Her hair was a lovely shade of
dark red and she had a distant smile on her lips and over her
shoulders she had a blue mink that almost made the Rolls-Royce
look like just another automobile. It didn't quite. Nothing can.

The attendant was the usual half-tough character in a white
coat with the name of the restaurant stitched across the front of
it in red. He was getting fed up.

"Look, mister," he said with an edge to his voice, "would you
mind a whole lot pulling your leg into the car so I can kind of
shut the door? Or should I open it all the way so you can fall
out?"

The girl gave him a look which ought to have stuck at least
four inches out of his back. It didn't bother him enough to give
him the shakes. At The Dancers they get the sort of people that
disillusion you about what a lot of golfing money can do for the
personality.

A low-swung foreign speedster with no top drifted into the parking lot and a man got out of it and used the dash lighter on a long cigarette. He was wearing a pullover check shirt, yellow slacks, and riding boots. He strolled off trailing clouds of incense, not even bothering to look towards the Rolls-Royce. He probably thought it was corny. At the foot of the steps up to the terrace he paused to stick a monocle in his eye.

The girl said with a nice burst of charm: "I have a wonderful idea, darling. Why don't we just take a cab to your place and get your convertible out? It's such a wonderful night for a run up the coast to Montecito. I know some people there who are throwing a dance around the pool."

The white-haired lad said politely: "Awfully sorry, but I don't have it any more. I was compelled to sell it." From his voice and articulation you wouldn't have known he had had anything stronger than orange juice to drink.

"Sold it, darling? How do you mean?" She slid away from him along the seat but her voice slid away a lot farther than that.

"I mean I had to," he said. "For eating money."

"Oh, I see." A slice of spumoni wouldn't have melted on her now.

The attendant had the white-haired boy right where he could reach him — in a low-income bracket. "Look, buster," he said, "I've got to put a car away. See you some more some other time — maybe."

He let the door swing open. The drunk promptly slid off the seat and landed on the blacktop on the seat of his pants. So I went over and dropped my nickel. I guess it's always a mistake to interfere with a drunk. Even if he knows and likes you he is always liable to haul off and poke you in the teeth. I got him under the arms and got him up on his feet.

"Thank you so very much," he said politely.

The girl slid under the wheel. "He gets so goddam English when he's loaded," she said in a stainless-steel voice. "Thanks for catching him."

"I'll get him in the back of the car," I said.

"I'm terribly sorry. I'm late for an engagement." She let the clutch in and the Rolls started to glide. "He's just a lost dog," she added with a cool smile. "Perhaps you can find a home for him. He's housebroken — more or less."

And the Rolls ticked down the entrance driveway on to Sunset Boulevard, made a right turn, and was gone. I was looking after her when the attendant came back. And I was still holding the man up and he was now sound asleep.

"Well, that's one way of doing it," I told the white coat.

"Sure," he said cynically. "Why waste it on a lush? Them curves and all."

"You know him?"

"I heard the dame call him Terry. Otherwise I don't know him from a cow's caboose. But I only been here two weeks."

"Get my car, will you?" I gave him the ticket.

By the time he brought my Olds over I felt as if I was holding up a sack of lead. The white coat helped me get him into the front seat. The customer opened an eye and thanked us and went to sleep again.

"He's the politest drunk I ever met," I said to the white coat.

"They come all sizes and shapes and all kinds of manners," he said. "And they're all bums. Looks like this one had a plastic job one time."

"Yeah." I gave him a dollar and he thanked me. He was right about the plastic job. The right side of my new friend's face was frozen and whitish and seamed with thin fine scars. The skin had a glossy look along the scars. A plastic job and a pretty drastic one.

"Whatcha aim to do with him?"

"Take him home and sober him up enough to tell me where he lives."

The white coat grinned at me. "Okay, sucker. If it was me, I'd just drop him in the gutter and keep going. Them booze hounds just make a man a lot of trouble for no fun. I got a philosophy about them things. The way the competition is nowadays a guy has to save his strength to protect hisself in the clinches."

"I can see you've made a big success out of it," I said.

He looked puzzled and then he started to get mad, but by that time I was in the car and moving.

He was partly right of course. Terry Lennox made me plenty of trouble. But after all that's my line of work.

I was living that year in a house on Yucca Avenue in the Laurel Canyon district. It was a small hillside house on a dead-end street with a long flight of redwood steps to the front door and a grove of eucalyptus trees across the way. It was furnished, and it belonged to a woman who had gone to Idaho to live with her widowed daughter for a while. The rent was low, partly because the owner wanted to be able to come back on short notice, and partly because of the steps. She was getting too old to face them every time she came home.

I got the drunk up them somehow. He was eager to help but his legs were rubber and he kept falling asleep in the middle of an apologetic sentence. I got the door unlocked and dragged him inside and spread him on the long couch, threw a rug over him and let him go back to sleep. He snored like a grampus for an hour. Then he came awake all of a sudden and wanted to go to the bathroom. When he came back he looked at me peeringly, squinting his eyes, and wanted to know where the hell he was. I told him. He said his name was Terry Lennox and that he lived in an apartment in Westwood and no one was waiting up for him. His voice was clear and unslurred.

He said he could handle a cup of black coffee. When I brought it he sipped it carefully holding the saucer close under the cup.

"How come I'm here?" he asked, looking around.

"You squiffed out at The Dancers in a Rolls. Your girl friend ditched you."

"Quite," he said. "No doubt she was entirely justified."

"You English?"

"I've lived there. I wasn't born there. If I might call a taxi, I'll take myself off."

"You've got one waiting."

He made the steps on his own going down. He didn't say much on the way to Westwood, except that it was very kind of me and he was sorry to be such a nuisance. He had probably said it so often and to so many people that it was automatic.

His apartment was small and stuffy and impersonal. He might

have moved in that afternoon. On a coffee table in front of a hard green davenport there was a half empty Scotch bottle and melted ice in a bowl and three empty fizzwater bottles and two glasses and a glass ash tray loaded with stubs with and without lipstick. There wasn't a photograph or a personal article of any kind in the place. It might have been a hotel room rented for a meeting or a farewell, for a few drinks and a talk, for a roll in the hay. It didn't look like a place where anyone lived.

He offered me a drink. I said no thanks. I didn't sit down. When I left he thanked me some more, but not as if I had climbed a mountain for him, nor as if it was nothing at all. He was a little shaky and a little shy but polite as hell. He stood in the open door until the automatic elevator came up and I got into it. Whatever he didn't have he had manners.

He hadn't mentioned the girl again. Also, he hadn't mentioned that he had no job and no prospects and that almost his last dollar had gone into paying the check at The Dancers for a bit of high class fluff that couldn't stick around long enough to make sure he didn't get tossed in the sneezer by some prowl car boys, or rolled by a tough hackie and dumped out in a vacant lot.

On the way down in the elevator I had an impulse to go back up and take the Scotch bottle away from him. But it wasn't any of my business and it never does any good anyway. They always find a way to get it if they have to have it.

I drove home chewing my lip. I'm supposed to be tough but there was something about the guy that got me. I didn't know what it was unless it was the white hair and the scarred face and the clear voice and the politeness. Maybe that was enough. There was no reason why I should ever see him again. He was just a lost dog, like the girl said.

2

IT WAS THE WEEK after Thanksgiving when I saw him again. The stores along Hollywood Boulevard were already beginning to fill up with overpriced Christmas junk, and the daily papers were beginning to scream about how terrible it would be if you didn't get your Christmas shopping done early. It would be terrible anyway; it always is.

It was about three blocks from my office building that I saw a cop car double-parked and the two buttons in it staring at something over by a shop window on the sidewalk. The something was Terry Lennox — or what was left of him — and that little was not too attractive.

He was leaning against a store front. He had to lean against something. His shirt was dirty and open at the neck and partly outside his jacket and partly not. He hadn't shaved for four or five days. His nose was pinched. His skin was so pale that the long thin scars hardly showed. And his eyes were like holes poked in a snowbank. It was pretty obvious that the buttons in the prowl car were about ready to drop the hook on him, so I went over there fast and took hold of his arm.

"Straighten up and walk," I said, putting on the tough. I winked at him from the side. "Can you make it? Are you stinko?"

He looked me over vaguely and then smiled his little one-sided smile. "I have been," he breathed. "Right now I guess I'm just a little — empty."

"Okay, but make with the feet. You're halfway into the drunk tank already."

He made the effort and let me walk him through the sidewalk loafers to the edge of the curb. There was a taxi stand there and I yanked open the door.

"He goes first," the hackie said, jerking a thumb at the cab ahead. He swung his head around and saw Terry. "If at all," he added.

THE LONG GOODBYE 425

"This is an emergency. My friend is sick."

"Yeah," the hackie said. "He could get sick somewheres else."

"Five bucks," I said, "and let's see that beautiful smile."

"Oh well," he said, and stuck a magazine with a Martian on the cover behind his mirror. I reached in and got the door open. I got Terry Lennox in and the shadow of the prowl car blocked the far window. A gray-haired cop got out and came over. I went around the taxi and met him.

"Just a minute, Mac. What have we got here? Is the gentleman in the soiled laundry a real close friend of yours?"

"Close enough for me to know he needs a friend. He's not drunk."

"For financial reasons, no doubt," the cop said. He put his hand out and I put my license in it. He looked at it and handed it back. "Oh-oh," he said. "A P.I. picking up a client." His voice changed and got tough. "That tells a little something about you, Mr. Marlowe. What about him?"

"His name's Terry Lennox. He works in pictures."

"That's nice." He leaned into the taxi and stared at Terry back in the corner. "I'd say he didn't work too lately. I'd say he didn't sleep indoors too lately. I'd even say he was a vag and so maybe we ought to take him in."

"Your arrest record can't be that low," I said. "Not in Hollywood."

He was still looking in at Terry. "What's your friend's name, buddy?"

"Philip Marlowe," Terry said slowly. "He lives on Yucca Avenue, Laurel Canyon."

The cop pulled his head out of the window space. He turned, and made a gesture with his hand. "You could of just told him."

"I could have, but I didn't."

He stared at me for a second or two. "I'll buy it this time," he said. "But get him off the street." He got into the police car and the police car went away.

I got into the taxi and we went the three-odd blocks to my parking lot and shifted to my car. I held out the five-spot to the hackie. He gave me a stiff look and shook his head.

"Just what's on the meter, Jack, or an even buck if you feel like it. I been down and out myself. In Frisco. Nobody picked me up in no taxi either. There's one stony-hearted town."

"San Francisco," I said mechanically.

"I call it Frisco," he said. "The hell with them minority groups. Thanks." He took the dollar and went away.

We went to a drive-in where they made hamburgers that didn't taste like something the dog wouldn't eat. I fed Terry Lennox a couple and a bottle of beer and drove him home. The steps were still tough on him but he grinned and panted and made the climb. An hour later he was shaved and bathed and he looked human again. We sat down over a couple of very mild drinks.

"Lucky you remembered my name," I said.

"I made a point of it," he said. "I looked you up too. Could I do less?"

"So why not give me a ring? I live here all the time. I have an office as well."

"Why should I bother you?"

"Looks like you had to bother somebody. Looks like you don't have many friends."

"Oh I have friends," he said, "of a sort." He turned his glass on the table top. "Asking for help doesn't come easy — especially when it's all your own fault." He looked up with a tired smile. "Maybe I can quit drinking one of these days. They all say that, don't they?"

"It takes about three years."

"Three years?" He looked shocked.

"Usually it does. It's a different world. You have to get used to a paler set of colors, a quieter lot of sounds. You have to allow for relapses. All the people you used to know well will get to be just a little strange. You won't even like most of them, and they won't like you too well."

"That wouldn't be much of a change," he said. He turned and looked at the clock. "I have a two-hundred-dollar suitcase checked at the Hollywood bus station. If I could bail it out I could buy a cheap one and pawn the one that's checked for enough to get to Vegas on the bus. I can get a job there."

I didn't say anything. I just nodded and sat there nursing my drink.

"You're thinking that idea might have come to me a little sooner," he said quietly.

"I'm thinking there's something behind all this that's none of my business. Is the job for sure or just a hope?"

"It's for sure. Fellow I knew very well in the army runs a big club there, the Terrapin Club. He's part racketeer, of course, they all are — but the other part is a nice guy."

"I can manage the bus fare and something over. But I'd just as soon it bought something that would stay bought for a while. Better talk to him on the phone."

"Thank you, but it's not necessary. Randy Starr won't let me down. He never has. And the suitcase will pawn for fifty dollars. I know from experience."

"Look," I said, "I'd put up what you need. I'm no big soft-hearted slob. So you take what's offered and be good. I want you out of my hair because I've got a feeling about you."

"Really?" He looked down into his glass. He was only sipping the stuff. "We've only met twice and you've been more than white to me both times. What sort of feeling?"

"A feeling that next time I'll find you in worse trouble than I can get you out of. I don't know just why I have the feeling, but I have it."

He touched the right side of his face gently with two finger-tips. "Maybe it's this. It does make me look a little sinister, I suppose. But it's an honorable wound — or anyhow the result of one."

"It's not that. That doesn't bother me at all. I'm a private dick. You're a problem that I don't have to solve. But the problem is there. Call it a hunch. If you want to be extra polite, call it a sense of character. Maybe that girl didn't walk out on you at The Dancers just because you were drunk. Maybe she had a feeling too."

He smiled faintly. "I was married to her once. Her name is Sylvia Lennox. I married her for her money."

I stood up scowling at him. "I'll fix you some scrambled eggs. You need food."

"Wait a minute, Marlowe. You're wondering why if I was down and out and Sylvia had plenty I couldn't ask her for a few bucks. Did you ever hear of pride?"

"You're killing me, Lennox."

"Am I? My kind of pride is different. It's the pride of a man who has nothing else. I'm sorry if I annoy you."

I went out to my kitchen and cooked up some Canadian bacon and scrambled eggs and coffee and toast. We ate in the breakfast nook. The house belonged to the period that always had one.

I said I had to go to the office and would pick up his suitcase on the way back. He gave me the check ticket. His face now had a little color and the eyes were not so far back in his head that you had to grope for them.

Before I went out I put the whiskey bottle on the table in front of the couch. "Use your pride on that," I said. "And call Vegas, if only as a favor to me."

He just smiled and shrugged his shoulders. I was still sore going down the steps. I didn't know why, any more than I knew why a man would starve and walk the streets rather than pawn his wardrobe. Whatever his rules were he played by them.

The suitcase was the damndest thing you ever saw. It was bleached pigskin and when new had been a pale cream color. The fittings were gold. It was English made and if you could buy it here at all, it would cost more like eight hundred than two.

I planked it down in front of him. I looked at the bottle on the cocktail table. He hadn't touched it. He was as sober as I was. He was smoking, but not liking that very well.

"I called Randy," he said. "He was sore because I hadn't called him before."

"It takes a stranger to help you," I said. "A present from Sylvia?" I pointed at the suitcase.

He looked out of the window. "No. That was given to me in England, long before I met her. Very long ago indeed. I'd like to leave it with you, if you could lend me an old one."

I got five double sawbucks out of my wallet and dropped them in front of him. "I don't need security."

"That wasn't the idea at all. You're no pawnbroker. I just don't want it with me in Vegas. And I don't need this much money."

"Okay. You keep the money and I'll keep the suitcase. But this house is easy to burgle."

"It wouldn't matter," he said indifferently. "It wouldn't matter at all."

He changed his clothes and we ate dinner at Musso's about five-thirty. No drinks. He caught the bus on Cahuenga and I drove home thinking about this and that. His empty suitcase was on my bed where he had unpacked it and put his stuff in a light-weight job of mine. His had a gold key which was in one of the locks. I locked the suitcase up empty and tied the key to the handle and put it on the high shelf on my clothes closet. It didn't feel quite empty, but what was in it was no business of mine.

It was a quiet night and the house seemed emptier than usual. I set out the chessmen and played a French defense against Steinitz. He beat me in forty-four moves, but I had him sweating a couple of times.

The phone rang at nine-thirty and the voice that spoke was one I had heard before.

"Is this Mr. Philip Marlowe?"

"Yeah. I'm Marlowe."

"This is Sylvia Lennox, Mr. Marlowe. We met very briefly in front of The Dancers one night last month. I heard afterwards that you had been kind enough to see that Terry got home."

"I did that."

"I suppose you know that we are not married any more, but I've been a little worried about him. He gave up the apartment he had in Westwood and nobody seems to know where he is."

"I noticed how worried you were the night we met."

"Look, Mr. Marlowe, I've been married to the man. I'm not very sympathetic to drunks. Perhaps I was a little unfeeling and perhaps I had something rather important to do. You're a private detective and this can be put on a professional basis, if you prefer it."

"It doesn't have to be put on any basis at all, Mrs. Lennox. He's on a bus going to Las Vegas. He has a friend there who will give him a job."

She brightened up very suddenly. "Oh — to Las Vegas? How sentimental of him. That's where we were married."

"I guess he forgot," I said, "or he would have gone somewhere else."

Instead of hanging up on me she laughed. It was a cute little laugh. "Are you always as rude as this to your clients?"

"You're not a client, Mrs. Lennox."

"I might be someday. Who knows? Let's say to your lady friends, then."

"Same answer. The guy was down and out, starving, dirty, without a bean. You could have found him if it had been worth your time. He didn't want anything from you then and he probably doesn't want anything from you now."

"That," she said coolly, "is something you couldn't possibly know anything about. Good night." And she hung up.

She was dead right, of course, and I was dead wrong. But I didn't feel wrong. I just felt sore. If she had called up half an hour earlier I might have been sore enough to beat the hell out of Steinitz — except that he had been dead for fifty years and the chess game was out of a book.

3

THREE DAYS BEFORE CHRISTMAS I got a cashier's check on a Las Vegas bank for $100. A note written on hotel paper came with it. He thanked me, wished me a Merry Christmas and all kinds of luck and said he hoped to see me again soon. The kick was in a postscript. "Sylvia and I are starting a second honeymoon. She says please don't be sore at her for wanting to try again."

I caught the rest of it in one of those snob columns in the society section of the paper. I don't read them often, only when I run out of things to dislike.

"Your correspondent is all fluttery at the news that Terry and Sylvia Lennox have rehitched at Las Vegas, the dears. She's the younger daughter of multimillionaire Harlan Potter of San Francisco and Pebble Beach, of course. Sylvia is having Marcel and Jeanne Duhaux redecorate the entire mansion in Encino from basement to roof in the most *devastatingly* dernier cri. Curt Westerheym, Sylvia's last but one, my dears, gave her the little eighteen-room shack for a wedding present, you may remember. And whatever happened to Curt, you ask? Or do you? St. Tropez has the answer, and permanently I hear. Also a certain very, *very* blue-blooded French duchess with two perfectly adorable children. And what does Harlan Potter think of the remarriage, you may also ask? One can only guess. Mr. Potter is one person who but *never* gives an interview. How exclusive can you get, darlings?"

I threw the paper into the corner and turned on the TV set. After the society page dog vomit even the wrestlers looked good. But the facts were probably right. On the society page they better be.

I had a mental picture of the kind of eighteen-room shack that would go with a few of the Potter millions, not to mention decorations by Duhaux in the latest subphallic symbolism. But I had no mental picture at all of Terry Lennox loafing around one of the swimming pools in Bermuda shorts and phoning the butler by R/T to ice the champagne and get the grouse atoasting. There was no reason why I should have. If the guy wanted to be somebody's woolly bear, it was no skin off my teeth. I just didn't want to see him again. But I knew I would — if only on account of his goddam gold-plated pigskin suitcase.

It was five o'clock of a wet March evening when he walked into my down-at-heels brain emporium. He looked changed. Older, very sober and severe and beautifully calm. He looked like a guy who had learned to roll with a punch. He wore an oyster-white raincoat and gloves and no hat and his white hair was as smooth as a bird's breast.

"Let's go to some quiet bar and have a drink," he said, as if he had been in ten minutes before. "If you have the time, that is."

We didn't shake hands. We never did. Englishmen don't shake hands all the time like Americans and although he wasn't English he had some of the mannerisms.

I said: "Let's go by my place and pick up your fancy suitcase. It kind of worries me."

He shook his head. "It would be kind of you to keep it for me."

"Why?"

"I just feel that way. Do you mind? It's a sort of link with a time when I wasn't a no-good waster."

"Nuts to that," I said. "But it's your business."

"If it bothers you because you think it might be stolen — "

"That's your business too. Let's go get that drink."

We went to Victor's. He drove me in a rust-colored Jupiter-Jowett with a flimsy canvas rain top under which there was only just room for the two of us. It had pale leather upholstery and what looked like silver fittings. I'm not too fussy about cars, but the damn thing did make my mouth water a little. He said it would do sixty-five in second. It had a squatty little gear shift that barely came up to his knee.

"Four speeds," he said. "They haven't invented an automatic shift that will work for one of these jobs yet. You don't really need one. You can start it in third even uphill and that's as high as you can shift in traffic anyway."

"Wedding present?"

"Just a casual 'I happened to see this gadget in a window' sort of present. I'm a very pampered guy."

"Nice," I said. "If there's no price tag."

He glanced at me quickly and then put his eyes back on the wet pavement. Double wipers swished gently over the little windscreen. "Price tag? There's always a price tag, chum. You think I'm not happy maybe?"

"Sorry. I was out of line."

"I'm rich. Who the hell wants to be happy?" There was a bitterness in his voice that was new to me.

"How's your drinking?"

"Perfectly elegant, old top. For some strange reason I seem to be able to handle the stuff. But you never know, do you?"

"Perhaps you were never really a drunk."

We sat in a corner of the bar at Victor's and drank gimlets. "They don't know how to make them here," he said. "What they call a gimlet is just some lime or lemon juice and gin with a dash of sugar and bitters. A real gimlet is half gin and half Rose's Lime Juice and nothing else. It beats martinis hollow."

"I was never fussy about drinks. How did you get on with Randy Starr? Down my street he's called a tough number."

He leaned back and looked thoughtful. "I guess he is. I guess they all are. But it doesn't show on him. I could name you a couple of lads in the same racket in Hollywood that act the part. Randy doesn't bother. In Las Vegas he's a legitimate businessman. You look him up next time you're there. He'll be your pal."

"Not too likely. I don't like hoodlums."

"That's just a word, Marlowe. We have that kind of world. Two wars gave it to us and we are going to keep it. Randy and I and another fellow were in a jam once. It made a sort of bond between us."

"Then why didn't you ask him for help when you needed it?"

He drank up his drink and signaled the waiter. "Because he couldn't refuse."

The waiter brought fresh drinks and I said: "That's just talk to me. If by any chance the guy owed you something, think of *his* end. He'd like a chance to pay something back."

He shook his head slowly. "I know you're right. Of course I did ask him for a job. But I worked at it while I had it. As for asking favors or handouts, no."

"But you'll take them from a stranger."

He looked me straight in the eye. "The stranger can keep going and pretend not to hear."

We had three gimlets, not doubles, and it didn't do a thing to him. That much would just get a real souse started. So I guess maybe he was cured at that.

Then he drove me back to the office.

"We have dinner at eight-fifteen," he said. "Only millionaires can afford it. Only millionaires' servants will stand for it nowadays. Lots of lovely people coming."

From then on it got to be a sort of habit with him to drop in around five o'clock. We didn't always go to the same bar, but oftener to Victor's than anywhere else. It may have had some association for him that I didn't know about. He never drank too much, and that surprised him.

"It must be something like the tertian ague," he said. "When it hits you it's bad. When you don't have it, it's as though you never did have it."

"What I don't get is why a guy with your privileges would want to drink with a private eye."

"Are you being modest?"

"Nope. I'm just puzzled. I'm a reasonably friendly type but we don't live in the same world. I don't even know where you hang out except that it's Encino. I should guess your home life is adequate."

"I don't have any home life."

We were drinking gimlets again. The place was almost empty. There was the usual light scattering of compulsive drinkers getting tuned up at the bar on the stools, the kind that reach very slowly for the first one and watch their hands so they won't knock anything over.

"I don't get that. Am I supposed to?"

"Big production, no story, as they say around the movie lots. I guess Sylvia is happy enough, though not necessarily with me. In our circle that's not too important. There's always something to do if you don't have to work or consider the cost. It's no real fun but the rich don't know that. They never had any. They never want anything very hard except maybe somebody else's wife and that's a pretty pale desire compared with the way a plumber's wife wants new curtains for the living room."

I didn't say anything. I let him carry the ball.

"Mostly I just kill time," he said, "and it dies hard. A little tennis, a little golf, a little swimming and horseback riding, and the exquisite pleasure of watching Sylvia's friends trying to hold out to lunch time before they start killing their hangovers."

"The night you went to Vegas she said she didn't like drunks."

He grinned crookedly. I was getting so used to his scarred face that I only noticed it when some change of expression emphasized its one-sided woodenness.

"She meant drunks without money. With money they are just heavy drinkers. If they vomit in the lanai, that's for the butler to handle."

"You didn't have to have it the way it is."

He finished his drink at a gulp and stood up. "I've got to run, Marlowe. Besides I'm boring you and God knows I'm boring myself."

"You're not boring me. I'm a trained listener. Sooner or later I may figure out why you like being a kept poodle."

He touched his scars gently with a fingertip. He had a remote little smile. "You should wonder why she wants me around, not why I want to be there, waiting patiently on my satin cushion to have my head patted."

"You like satin cushions," I said, as I stood up to leave with him. "You like silk sheets and bells to ring and the butler to come with his deferential smile."

"Could be. I was raised in an orphanage in Salt Lake City."

We went out into the tired evening and he said he wanted to walk. We had come in my car, and for once I had been fast enough to grab the check. I watched him out of sight. The light from a store window caught the gleam of his white hair for a moment as he faded into the light mist.

I liked him better drunk, down and out, hungry and beaten and proud. Or did I? Maybe I just liked being top man. His reasons for things were hard to figure. In my business there's a time to ask questions and a time to let your man simmer until he boils over. Every good cop knows that. It's a good deal like chess or boxing. Some people you have to crowd and keep off balance. Some you just box and they will end up beating themselves.

He would have told me the story of his life if I had asked him. But I never even asked him how he got his face smashed. If I had and he told me, it just possibly might have saved a couple of lives. Just possibly, no more.

4

THE LAST TIME we had a drink in a bar was in May and it was earlier than usual, just after four o'clock. He looked tired and thinner but he looked around with a slow smile of pleasure.

"I like bars just after they open for the evening. When the air inside is still cool and clean and everything is shiny and the barkeep is giving himself that last look in the mirror to see if his tie is straight and his hair is smooth. I like the neat bottles on the bar back and the lovely shining glasses and the anticipation. I like to watch the man mix the first one of the evening and put it down on a crisp mat and put the little folded napkin beside it. I like to taste it slowly. The first quiet drink of the evening in a quiet bar — that's wonderful."

I agreed with him.

"Alcohol is like love," he said. "The first kiss is magic, the second is intimate, the third is routine. After that you take the girl's clothes off."

"Is that bad?" I asked him.

"It's excitement of a high order, but it's an impure emotion — impure in the aesthetic sense. I'm not sneering at sex. It's necessary and it doesn't have to be ugly. But it always has to be managed. Making it glamorous is a billion-dollar industry and it costs every cent of it."

He looked around and yawned. "I haven't been sleeping well. It's nice in here. But after a while the lushes will fill the place up and talk loud and laugh and the goddam women will start waving their hands and screwing up their faces and tinkling their goddam bracelets and making with the packaged charm which will later on in the evening have a slight but unmistakable odor of sweat."

"Take it easy," I said. "So they're human, they sweat, they get dirty, they have to go to the bathroom. What did you expect — golden butterflies hovering in a rosy mist?"

He emptied his glass and held it upside down and watched a

slow drop form on the rim and then tremble and fall.

"I'm sorry for her," he said slowly. "She's such an absolute bitch. Could be I'm fond of her too in a remote sort of way. Some day she'll need me and I'll be the only guy around not holding a chisel. Likely enough then I'll flunk out."

I just looked at him. "You do a great job of selling yourself," I said after a moment.

"Yeah, I know. I'm a weak character, without guts or ambition. I caught the brass ring and it shocked me to find out it wasn't gold. A guy like me has one big moment in his life, one perfect swing on the high trapeze. Then he spends the rest of his time trying not to fall off the sidewalk into the gutter."

"What's this in favor of?" I got out a pipe and started to fill it.

"She's scared. She's scared stiff."

"What of?"

"I don't know. We don't talk much any more. Maybe of the old man. Harlan Potter is a coldhearted son of a bitch. All Victorian dignity on the outside. Inside he's as ruthless as a Gestapo thug. Sylvia is a tramp. He knows it and he hates it and there's nothing he can do about it. But he waits and he watches and if Sylvia ever gets into a big mess of scandal he'll break her in half and bury the two halves a thousand miles apart."

"You're her husband."

He lifted the empty glass and brought it down hard on the edge of the table. It smashed with a sharp ping. The barman stared, but didn't say anything.

"Like that, chum. Like that. Oh sure, I'm her husband. That's what the record says. I'm the three white steps and the big green front door and the brass knocker you rap one long and two short and the maid lets you into the hundred-dollar whorehouse."

I stood up and dropped some money on the table. "You talk too damn much," I said, "and it's too damn much about you. See you later."

I walked out leaving him sitting there shocked and white-faced as well as I could tell by the kind of light they have in bars. He called something after me, but I kept going.

Ten minutes later I was sorry. But ten minutes later I was somewhere else. He didn't come to the office any more. Not at all, not once. I had got to him where it hurt.

I didn't see him again for a month. When I did it was five o'clock in the morning and just beginning to get light. The persistent ringing of the doorbell yanked me out of bed. I plowed down the hall and across the living room and opened up. He stood there looking as if he hadn't slept for a week. He had a light topcoat on with the collar turned up and he seemed to be shivering. A dark felt hat was pulled down over his eyes.

He had a gun in his hand.

5

THE GUN WASN'T POINTED at me, he was just holding it. It was a medium-caliber automatic, foreign made, certainly not a Colt or a Savage. With the white tired face and the scars and the turned-up collar and the pulled-down hat and the gun he could have stepped right out of an old-fashioned kick-em-in-the-teeth gangster movie.

"You're driving me to Tijuana to get a plane at ten-fifteen," he said. "I have a passport and visa and I'm all set except for transportation. For certain reasons I can't take a train or a bus or a plane from L.A. Would five hundred bucks be a reasonable taxi fare?"

I stood in the doorway and didn't move to let him in. "Five hundred plus the gat?" I asked.

He looked down at it rather absently. Then he dropped it into his pocket.

"It might be a protection," he said, "for you. Not for me."

"Come on in then." I stood to one side and he came in with an exhausted lunge and fell into a chair.

The living room was still dark, because of the heavy growth of shrubbery the owner had allowed to mask the windows. I put a lamp on and mooched a cigarette. I lit it. I stared down at him. I rumpled my hair which was already rumpled. I put the old tired grin on my face.

"What the hell's the matter with me sleeping such a lovely morning away? Ten-fifteen, huh? Well, there's plenty of time. Let's go out to the kitchen and I'll brew some coffee."

"I'm in a great deal of trouble, shamus." Shamus, it was the first time he had called me that. But it kind of went with his style of entry, the way he was dressed, the gun and all.

"It's going to be a peach of a day. Light breeze. You can hear those tough old eucalyptus trees across the street whispering to each other. Talking about old times in Australia when the walla-bies hopped about underneath the branches and the koala bears rode piggyback on each other. Yes, I got the general idea you were in some trouble. Let's talk about it after I've had a couple of cups of coffee. I'm always a little lightheaded when I first wake up. Let us confer with Mr. Huggins and Mr. Young."

"Look, Marlowe, this is not the time — "

"Fear nothing, old boy. Mr. Huggins and Mr. Young are two of the best. They make Huggins-Young coffee. It's their life work, their pride and joy. One of these days I'm going to see that they get the recognition they deserve. So far all they're mak-ing is money. You couldn't expect that to satisfy them."

I left him with that bright chatter and went out to the kitchen at the back. I turned the hot water on and got the coffee maker down off the shelf. I wet the rod and measured the stuff into the top and by that time the water was steaming. I filled the lower half of the dingus and set it on the flame. I set the upper part on top and gave it a twist so it would bind.

By that time he had come in after me. He leaned in the door-way a moment and then edged across to the breakfast nook and slid into the seat. He was still shaking. I got a bottle of Old Grand-Dad off the shelf and poured him a shot in a big glass. I knew he would need a big glass. Even with that he had to use both hands to get it to his mouth. He swallowed, put the glass down with a thud, and hit the back of the seat with a jar.

"Almost passed out," he muttered. "Seems like I've been up for a week. Didn't sleep at all last night."

The coffee maker was almost ready to bubble. I turned the flame low and watched the water rise. It hung a little at the bottom of the glass tube. I turned the flame up just enough to get it over the hump and then turned it low again quickly. I stirred the coffee and covered it. I set my timer for three minutes. Very methodical guy, Marlowe. Nothing must interfere with his coffee technique. Not even a gun in the hand of a desperate character.

I poured him another slug. "Just sit there," I said. "Don't say a word. Just sit."

He handled the second slug with one hand. I did a fast wash-up in the bathroom and the bell of the timer went just as I got back. I cut the flame and set the coffee maker on a straw mat on the table. Why do I go into such detail? Because the charged atmosphere made every little thing stand out as a performance, a movement distinct and vastly important. It was one of those hypersensitive moments when all your automatic movements, however long established, however habitual, become separate acts of will. You are like a man learning to walk after polio. You take nothing for granted, absolutely nothing at all.

The coffee was all down and the air rushed in with its usual fuss and the coffee bubbled and then became quiet. I removed the top of the maker and set it on the drainboard in the socket of the cover.

I poured two cups and added a slug to his. "Black for you, Terry." I added two lumps of sugar and some cream to mine. I was coming out of it by now. I wasn't conscious of how I opened the Frig and got the cream carton.

I sat down across from him. He hadn't moved. He was propped in the corner of the nook, rigid. Then without warning his head came down on the table and he was sobbing.

He didn't pay any attention when I reached across and dug the gun out of his pocket. It was a Mauser 7.65, a beauty. I sniffed it. I sprang the magazine loose. It was full. Nothing in the breach.

He lifted his head and saw the coffee and drank some slowly, not looking at me. "I didn't shoot anybody," he said.

"Well — not recently anyhow And the gun would have had

to be cleaned. I hardly think you shot anybody with this."

"I'll tell you about it," he said.

"Wait just a minute." I drank my coffee as quickly as the heat would let me. I refilled my cup. "It's like this," I said. "Be very careful what you tell me. If you really want me to ride you down to Tijuana, there are two things I must not be told. One — are you listening?"

He nodded very slightly. He was looking blank-eyed at the wall over my head. The scars were very livid this morning. His skin was almost dead white but the scars seemed to shine out of it just the same.

"One," I repeated slowly, "if you have committed a crime or anything the law calls a crime — a serious crime, I mean — I can't be told about it. Two, if you have essential knowledge that such a crime has been committed, I can't be told about that either. Not if you want me to drive you to Tijuana. That clear?"

He looked me in the eye. His eyes focused, but they were lifeless. He had the coffee inside him. He had no color, but he was steady. I poured him some more and loaded it the same way.

"I told you I was in a jam," he said.

"I heard you. I don't want to know what kind of jam. I have a living to earn, a license to protect."

"I could hold the gun on you," he said.

I grinned and pushed the gun across the table. He looked down at it but didn't touch it.

"Not to Tijuana you couldn't hold it on me, Terry. Not across the border, not up the steps into a plane. I'm a man who occasionally has business with guns. We'll forget about the gun. I'd look great telling the cops I was so scared I just had to do what you told me to. Supposing, of course, which I don't know, that there was anything to tell the cops."

"Listen," he said, "it will be noon or even later before anybody knocks at the door. The help knows better than to disturb her when she sleeps late. But by about noon her maid would knock and go in. She wouldn't be in her room."

I sipped my coffee and said nothing.

"The maid would see that her bed hadn't been slept in," he

went on. "Then she would think of another place to look. There's a big guest house pretty far back from the main house. It has its own driveway and garage and so on. Sylvia spent the night there. The maid would eventually find her there."

I frowned. "I've got to be very careful what questions I ask you, Terry. Couldn't she have spent the night away from home?"

"Her clothes would be thrown all over her room. She never hangs anything up. The maid would know she had put a robe over her pajamas and gone out that way. So it would only be to the guest house."

"Not necessarily," I said.

"It would be to the guest house. Hell, do you think they don't know what goes on in the guest house? Servants always know."

"Pass it," I said.

He ran a finger down the side of his good cheek hard enough to leave a red streak. "And in the guest house," he went on slowly, "the maid would find — "

"Sylvia dead drunk, paralyzed, spifflicated, iced to the eyebrows," I said harshly.

"Oh." He thought about it. Big think. "Of course," he added, "that's how it would be. Sylvia is not a souse. When she does get over the edge it's pretty drastic."

"That's the end of the story," I said. "Or almost. Let me improvise. The last time we drank together I was a bit rough with you, walked out if you recall. You irritated the hell out of me. Thinking it over afterwards I could see that you were just trying to sneer yourself out of a feeling of disaster. You say you have a passport and a visa. It takes a little time to get a visa to Mexico. They don't let just anybody in. So you've been planning to blow for some time. I was wondering how long you would stick."

"I guess I felt some vague kind of obligation to be around, some idea she might need me for something more than a front to keep the old man from nosing around too hard. By the way, I tried to call you in the middle of the night."

"I sleep hard. I didn't hear."

"Then I went to a Turkish bath place. I stayed a couple of hours, had a steam bath, a plunge, a needle shower, a rubdown and made a couple of phone calls from there. I left the car at La

Brea and Fountain. I walked from there. Nobody saw me turn into your street."

"Do these phone calls concern me?"

"One was to Harlan Potter. The old man flew down to Pasadena yesterday, some business. He hadn't been to the house. I had a lot of trouble getting him. But he finally talked to me. I told him I was sorry, but I was leaving." He was looking a little sideways when he said this, towards the window over the sink and the tecoma bush that fretted against the screen.

"How did he take it?"

"He was sorry. He wished me luck. Asked if I needed any money." Terry laughed harshly. "Money. Those are the first five letters of his alphabet. I said I had plenty. Then I called Sylvia's sister. Much the same story there. That's all."

"I want to ask this," I said. "Did you ever find her with a man in that guest house?"

He shook his head. "I never tried. It would not have been difficult. It never has been."

"Your coffee's getting cold."

"I don't want any more."

"Lots of men, huh? But you went back and married her again. I realize that she's quite a dish, but all the same — "

"I told you I was no good. Hell, why did I leave her the first time? Why after that did I get stinking every time I saw her? Why did I roll in the gutter rather than ask her for money? She's been married five times, not including me. Any one of them would go back at the crook of her finger. And not just for a million bucks."

"She's quite a dish," I said. I looked at my watch. "Just why does it have to be ten-fifteen at Tijuana?"

"There's always space on that flight. Nobody from L.A. wants to ride a DC-3 over mountains when he can take a Connie and make it in seven hours to Mexico City. And the Connies don't stop where I want to go."

I stood up and leaned against the sink. "Now let's add it up and don't interrupt me. You came to me this morning in a highly emotional condition and wanted to be driven to Tijuana to catch an early plane. You had a gun in your pocket, but I needn't have seen it. You told me you had stood things as long as you could but last night you blew up. You found your wife **dead** drunk and a man had been with her. You got out and went to a Turkish bath to pass the time until morning and you phoned your wife's two closest relatives and told them what you were doing. Where you went was none of my business. You had the necessary documents to enter Mexico. How you went was none of my business either. We are friends and I did what you asked me without much thought. Why wouldn't I? You're not paying me anything. You had your car but you felt too upset to drive yourself. That's your business too. You're an emotional guy and you got yourself a bad wound in the war. I think I ought to pick up your car and shove it in a garage somewhere for storage."

He reached into his clothes and pushed a leather keyholder across the table.

"How does it sound?" he asked.

"Depends who's listening. I haven't finished. You took nothing but the clothes you stood up in and some money you had from your father-in-law. You left everything she had given you including that beautiful piece of machinery you parked at La Brea and Fountain. You wanted to go away as clean as it was possible for you to go and still go. All right. I'll buy it. Now I shave and get dressed."

"Why are you doing it, Marlowe?"

"Buy yourself a drink while I shave."

I walked out and left him sitting there hunched in the corner of the nook. He still had his hat and light topcoat on. But he looked a lot more alive.

I went into the bathroom and shaved. I was back in the bedroom knotting my tie when he came and stood in the doorway. "I washed the cups just in case," he said. "But I got thinking. Maybe it would be better if you called the police."

"Call them yourself. I haven't anything to tell them."

"You want me to?"

I turned around sharply and gave him a hard stare. "God damn it!" I almost yelled at him. "Can't you for Chrissake just leave it lay?"

"I'm sorry."

"Sure you're sorry. Guys like you are always sorry, and always too late."

He turned and walked back along the hall to the living room. I finished dressing and locked up the back part of the house. When I got to the living room he had fallen asleep in a chair, his head on one side, his face drained of color, his whole body slack with exhaustion. He looked pitiful. When I touched his shoulder he came awake slowly as if it was a long way from where he was to where I was.

When I had his attention I said, "What about a suitcase? I still got that white pigskin job on the top shelf in my closet."

"It's empty," he said without interest. "Also it's too conspicuous."

"You'd be more conspicuous without any baggage."

I walked back to the bedroom and stood up on the steps in the clothes closet and pulled the white pigskin job down off the high shelf. The square ceiling trap was right over my head, so I pushed that up and reached in as far as I could and dropped his leather keyholder behind one of the dusty tie beams or whatever they were.

I climbed down with the suitcase, dusted it off, and shoved some things into it, a pair of pajamas never worn, toothpaste, an extra toothbrush, a couple of cheap towels and washcloths, a package of cotton handkerchiefs, a fifteen-cent tube of shaving cream, and one of the razors they give away with a package of blades. Nothing used, nothing marked, nothing conspicuous, except that his own stuff would be better. I added a pint of bourbon still in its wrapping paper. I locked the suitcase and left the key in one of the locks and carried it up front. He had gone to sleep again. I opened the door without waking him and carried the suitcase down to the garage and put it in the convertible behind the front seat. I got the car out and locked the garage and went back up the steps to wake him. I finished locking up and we left.

I drove fast but not fast enough to get tagged. We hardly spoke on the way down. We didn't stop to eat either. There wasn't that much time.

The border people had nothing to say to us. Up on the windy mesa where the Tijuana Airport is I parked close to the office and just sat while Terry got his ticket. The propellers of the DC-3 were already turning over slowly, just enough to keep warm. A tall dreamboat of a pilot in a gray uniform was chatting with a group of four people. One was about six feet four and carried a gun case. There was a girl in slacks beside him, and a smallish middle-aged man and a gray-haired woman so tall that she made him look puny. Three or four obvious Mexicans were standing around as well. That seemed to be the load. The steps were at the door but nobody seemed anxious to get in. Then a Mexican flight steward came down the steps and stood waiting. There didn't seem to be any loudspeaker equipment. The Mexicans climbed into the plane but the pilot was still chatting with the Americans.

There was a big Packard parked next to me. I got out and took a gander at the license on the post. Maybe someday I'll learn to mind my own business. As I pulled my head out I saw the tall woman staring in my direction.

Then Terry came across the dusty gravel.

"I'm all set," he said. "This is where I say goodbye."

He put his hand out. I shook it. He looked pretty good now, just tired, just tired as all hell.

I lifted the pigskin suitcase out of the Olds and put it down on the gravel. He stared at it angrily.

"I told you I didn't want it," he said snappishly.

"There's a nice pint of hooch in it, Terry. Also some pajamas and stuff. And it's all anonymous. If you don't want it, check it. Or throw it away."

"I have reasons," he said stiffly.

"So have I."

He smiled suddenly. He picked up the suitcase and squeezed my arm with his free hand. "Okay, pal. You're the boss. And remember, if things get tough, you have a blank check. You don't owe me a thing. We had a few drinks together and got to be friendly and I talked too much about me. I left five C notes in your coffee can. Don't be sore at me."

"I'd rather you hadn't."

"I'll never spend half of what I have."

"Good luck, Terry."

The two Americans were going up the steps into the plane. A

squatty guy with a wide dark face came out of the door of the office building and waved and pointed.

"Climb aboard," I said. "I know you didn't kill her. That's why I'm here."

He braced himself. His whole body got stiff. He turned slowly, then looked back.

"I'm sorry," he said quietly. "But you're wrong about that. I'm going to walk quite slowly to the plane. You have plenty of time to stop me."

He walked. I watched him. The guy in the doorway of the office was waiting, but not too impatient. Mexicans seldom are. He reached down and patted the pigskin suitcase and grinned at Terry. Then he stood aside and Terry went through the door. In a little while Terry came out through the door on the other side, where the customs people are when you're coming in. He walked, still slowly, across the gravel to the steps. He stopped there and looked towards me. He didn't signal or wave. Neither did I. Then he went up into the plane, and the steps were pulled back.

I got into the Olds and started it and backed and turned and moved halfway across the parking space. The tall woman and the short man were still out on the field. The woman had a handkerchief out to wave. The plane began to taxi down to the end of the field raising plenty of dust. It turned at the far end and the motors revved up in a thundering roar. It began to move forward picking up speed slowly.

The dust rose in clouds behind it. Then it was airborne. I watched it lift slowly into the gusty air and fade off into the naked blue sky to the southeast.

Then I left. Nobody at the border gate looked at me as if my face meant as much as the hands on a clock.

6

IT'S A LONG DRAG back from Tijuana and one of the dullest drives in the state. Tijuana is nothing; all they want there is the buck. The kid who sidles over to your car and looks at you with big wistful eyes and says, "One dime, please, mister," will try to sell you his sister in the next sentence. Tijuana is not Mexico. No border town is anything but a border town, just as no waterfront is anything but a waterfront. San Diego? One of the most beautiful harbors in the world and nothing in it but navy and a few fishing boats. At night it is fairyland. The swell is as gentle as an old lady singing hymns. But Marlowe has to get home and count the spoons.

The road north is as monotonous as a sailor's chantey. You go through a town, down a hill, along a stretch of beach, through a town, down a hill, along a stretch of beach.

It was two o'clock when I got back and they were waiting for me in a dark sedan with no police tags, no red light, only the double antenna, and not only police cars have those. I was halfway up the steps before they came out of it and yelled at me, the usual couple in the usual suits, with the usual stony leisure of movement, as if the world was waiting hushed and silent for them to tell it what to do.

"Your name Marlowe? We want to talk to you."

He let me see the glint of a badge. For all I caught of it he might have been Pest Control. He was gray blond and looked sticky. His partner was tall, good-looking, neat, and had a precise nastiness about him, a goon with an education. They had watching and waiting eyes, patient and careful eyes, cool disdainful eyes, cops' eyes. They get them at the passing-out parade at the police school.

"Sergeant Green, Central Homicide. This is Detective Dayton."

I went on up and unlocked the door. You don't shake hands with big city cops. That close is too close.

They sat in the living room. I opened the windows and the

breeze whispered. Green did the talking.

"Man named Terry Lennox. Know him, huh?"

"We have a drink together once in a while. He lives in Encino, married money. I've never been where he lives."

"Once in a while," Green said. "How often would that be?"

"It's a vague expression. I meant it that way. It could be once a week or once in two months."

"Met his wife?"

"Once, very briefly, before they were married."

"You saw him last when and where?"

I took a pipe off the end table and filled it. Green leaned forward close to me. The tall lad sat farther back holding a ballpoint poised over a red-edged pad.

"This is where I say, 'What's this all about?' and you say, 'We ask the questions.'"

"So you just answer them, huh?"

I lit the pipe. The tobacco was a little too moist. It took me some time to light it properly and three matches.

"I got time," Green said, "but I already used up a lot of it waiting around. So snap it up, mister. We know who you are. And you know we ain't here to work up an appetite."

"I was just thinking," I said. "We used to go to Victor's fairly often, and not so often to The Green Lantern and The Bull and Bear — that's the place down at the end of the Strip that tries to look like an English inn — "

"Quit stalling."

"Who's dead?" I asked.

Detective Dayton spoke up. He had a hard, mature, don't-try-to-fool-with-me voice. "Just answer the questions, Marlowe. We are conducting a routine investigation. That's all you need to know."

Maybe I was tired and irritable. Maybe I felt a little guilty. I could learn to hate this guy without even knowing him. I could just look at him across the width of a cafeteria and want to kick his teeth in.

"Shove it, Jack," I said. "Keep that guff for the juvenile bureau. It's a horse laugh even to them."

Green chuckled. Nothing changed in Dayton's face that you

could put a finger on but he suddenly looked ten years older and twenty years nastier. The breath going through his nose whistled faintly.

"He passed the bar examination," Green said. "You can't fool around with Dayton."

I got up slowly and went over to the bookshelves. I took down the bound copy of the California Penal Code. I held it out to Dayton.

"Would you kindly find me the section that says I have to answer the questions?"

He was holding himself very still. He was going to slug me and we both knew it. But he was going to wait for the break. Which meant that he didn't trust Green to back him up if he got out of line.

He said: "Every citizen has to co-operate with the police. In all ways, even by physical action, and especially by answering any questions of a non-incriminating nature the police think it necessary to ask." His voice saying this was hard and bright and smooth.

"It works out that way," I said. "Mostly by a process of direct or indirect intimidation. In law no such obligation exists. Nobody has to tell the police anything, any time, anywhere."

"Aw shut up," Green said impatiently. "You're crawfishing and you know it. Sit down. Lennox's wife has been murdered. In a guest house at their place in Encino. Lennox has skipped out. Anyway he can't be found. So we're looking for a suspect in a murder case. That satisfy you?"

I threw the book in a chair and went back to the couch across the table from Green. "So why come to me?" I asked. "I've never been near the house. I told you that."

Green patted his thighs, up and down, up and down. He grinned at me quietly. Dayton was motionless in the chair. His eyes ate me.

"On account of your phone number was written on a pad in his room during the past twenty-four hours," Green said. "It's a date pad and yesterday was torn off but you could see the impression on today's page. We don't know when he called you up. We don't know where he went or why or when. But we got to ask, natch."

"Why in the guest house?" I asked, not expecting him to answer, but he did.

He blushed a little. "Seems she went there pretty often. At night. Had visitors. The help can see down through the trees where the lights show. Cars come and go, sometimes late, sometimes very late. Too much is enough, huh? Don't kid yourself. Lennox is our boy. He went down that way about one in the A.M. The butler happened to see. He come back alone, maybe twenty minutes later. After that nothing. The lights stayed on. This morning no Lennox. The butler goes down by the guest house. The dame is as naked as a mermaid on the bed and let me tell you he don't recognize her by her face. She practically ain't got one. Beat to pieces with a bronze statuette of a monkey."

"Terry Lennox wouldn't do anything like that," I said. "Sure she cheated on him. Old stuff. She always had. They'd been divorced and remarried. I don't suppose it made him happy but why should he go crazy over it now?"

"Nobody knows that answer," Green said patiently. "It happens all the time. Men and women both. A guy takes it and takes it and takes it. Then he don't. He probably don't know why himself, why at that particular instant he goes berserk. Only he does, and somebody's dead. So we got business to do. So we ask you one simple question. So quit horsing around or we take you in."

"He's not going to tell you, Sergeant," Dayton said acidly. "He read that law book. Like a lot of people that read a law book he thinks the law is in it."

"You make the notes," Green said, "and leave your brains alone. If you're real good we'll let you sing 'Mother Machree' at the police smoker."

"The hell with you, Sarge, if I may say so with proper respect for your rank."

"Let's you and him fight," I said to Green. "I'll catch him when he drops."

Dayton laid his note pad and ball-point aside very carefully. He stood up with a bright gleam in his eyes. He walked over and stood in front of me.

"On your feet, bright boy. Just because I went to college don't make me take any guff from a nit like you."

I started to get up. I was still off balance when he hit me. He hooked me with a neat left and crossed it. Bells rang, but not for dinner. I sat down hard and shook my head. Dayton was still there. He was smiling now.

"Let's try again," he said. "You weren't set that time. It wasn't really kosher."

I looked at Green. He was looking at his thumb as if studying a hangnail. I didn't move or speak, waiting for him to look up. If I stood up again, Dayton would slug me again. He might slug me again anyhow. But if I stood up and he slugged me, I would take him to pieces, because the blows proved he was strictly a boxer. He put them in the right place but it would take a lot of them to wear me down.

Green said almost absently: "Smart work, Billy boy. You gave the man exactly what he wanted. Clam juice."

Then he looked up and said mildly: "Once more, for the record, Marlowe. Last time you saw Terry Lennox, where and how and what was talked about, and where did you come from just now. Yes — or no?"

Dayton was standing loosely, nicely balanced. There was a soft sweet sheen in his eyes.

"How about the other guy?" I asked, ignoring him.

"What other guy was that?"

"In the hay, in the guest house. No clothes on. You're not saying she had to go down there to play solitaire."

"That comes later — when we get the husband."

"Fine. If it's not too much trouble when you already have a patsy."

"You don't talk, we take you in, Marlowe."

"As a material witness?"

"As a material my foot. As a suspect. Suspicion of accessory after the fact of murder. Helping a suspect escape. My guess is you took the guy somewhere. And right now a guess is all I need. The skipper is tough these days. He knows the rule book but he gets absent-minded. This could be a misery for you. One way or another we get a statement from you. The harder it is to get, the surer we are we need it."

"That's a lot of crap to him," Dayton said. "He knows the book."

"It's a lot of crap to everybody," Green said calmly. "But it still works. Come on, Marlowe. I'm blowing the whistle on you."

"Okay," I said. "Blow it. Terry Lennox was my friend. I've got a reasonable amount of sentiment invested in him. Enough not to spoil it just because a cop says come through. You've got a case against him, maybe far more than I hear from you. Motive, opportunity, and the fact that he skipped out. The motive is old stuff, long neutralized, almost part of the deal. I don't admire that kind of deal, but that's the kind of guy he is — a little weak and very gentle. The rest of it means nothing except that if he knew she was dead he knew he was a sitting duck for you. At the inquest if they have one and if they call me, I'll have to answer questions. I don't have to answer yours. I can see you're a nice guy, Green. Just as I can see your partner is just another goddam badge flasher with a power complex. If you want to get me in a real jam, let him hit me again. I'll break his goddam pencil for him."

Green stood up and looked at me sadly. Dayton hadn't moved. He was a one-shot tough guy. He had to have time out to pat his back.

"I'll use the phone," Green said. "But I know what answer I'll get. You're a sick chicken, Marlowe. A very sick chicken. Get the hell outa my way." This last to Dayton. Dayton turned and went back and picked up his pad.

Green crossed to the phone and lifted it slowly, his plain face creased with the long slow thankless grind. That's the trouble with cops. You're all set to hate their guts and then you meet one that goes human on you.

The Captain said to bring me in, and rough.

They put handcuffs on me. They didn't search the house, which seemed careless of them. Possibly they figured I would be too experienced to have anything there that could be dangerous to me. In which they were wrong. Because if they had made any kind of job of it they would have found Terry Lennox's car keys. And when the car was found, as it would be sooner or later, they would fit the keys to it and know he had been in my company.

Actually, as it turned out, that meant nothing. The car was never found by any police. It was stolen sometime in the night, driven most probably to El Paso, fitted with new keys and forged papers, and put on the market eventually in Mexico City. The procedure is routine. Mostly the money comes back in the form of heroin. Part of the good-neighbor policy, as the hoodlums see it.

7

THE HOMICIDE SKIPPER that year was a Captain Gregorius, a type of copper that is getting rarer but by no means extinct, the kind that solves crimes with the bright light, the soft sap, the kick to the kidneys, the knee to the groin, the fist to the solar plexus, the night stick to the base of the spine. Six months later he was indicted for perjury before a grand jury, booted without trial, and later stamped to death by a big stallion on his ranch in Wyoming.

Right now I was his raw meat. He sat behind his desk with his coat off and his sleeves rolled almost to his shoulders. He was as bald as a brick and getting heavy around the waist like all hard-muscled men in middle age. His eyes were fish gray. His big nose was a network of burst capillaries. He was drinking coffee and not quietly. His blunt strong hands had hairs thick on their backs. Grizzled tufts stuck out of his ears. He pawed something on his desk and looked at Green.

Green said: "All we got on him is he won't tell us nothing, skipper. The phone number makes us look him up. He's out riding and don't say where. He knows Lennox pretty well and don't say when he saw him last."

"Thinks he's tough," Gregorius said indifferently. "We could change that." He said it as if he didn't care one way or another. He probably didn't. Nobody was tough to him. "Point is the D.A. smells a lot of headlines on this one. Can't blame him, seeing who the girl's old man is. I guess we better pick this fellow's nose for him."

He looked at me as if I was a cigarette stub, or an empty chair. Just something in his line of vision, without interest for him.

Dayton said respectfully: "It's pretty obvious that his whole attitude was designed to create a situation where he could refuse to talk. He quoted law at us and needled me into socking him. I was out of line there, Captain."

Gregorius eyed him bleakly. "You must needle easy if this punk can do it. Who took the cuffs off?"

Green said he did. "Put them back on," Gregorius said. "Tight. Give him something to brace him up."

Green put the cuffs back on or started to. "Behind the back," Gregorius barked. Green cuffed my hands behind my back. I was sitting in a hard chair.

"Tighter," Gregorius said. "Make them bite."

Green made them tighter. My hands started to feel numb.

Gregorius looked at me finally. "You can talk now. Make it snappy."

I didn't answer him. He leaned back and grinned. His hand went out slowly for his coffee cup and went around it. He leaned forward a little. The cup jerked but I beat it by going sideways out of the chair. I landed hard on my shoulder, rolled over and got up slowly. My hands were quite numb now. They didn't feel anything. The arms above the cuffs were beginning to ache.

Green helped me back into the chair. The wet smear of the coffee was over the back and some of the seat, but most of it was on the floor.

"He don't like coffee," Gregorius said. "He's a swifty. He moves fast. Good reflexes."

Nobody said anything. Gregorius looked me over with fish eyes.

"In here, mister, a dick license don't mean any more than a calling card. Now let's have your statement, verbal at first. We'll take it down later. Make it complete. Let's have, say, a full account of your movements since ten P.M. last night. I mean full. This office is investigating a murder and the prime suspect is missing. You connect with him. Guy catches his wife cheating and beats her head to raw flesh and bone and bloodsoaked hair. Our old friend the bronze statuette. Not original but it works. You think any goddam private eye is going to quote law at me over this, mister, you got a hell of a tough time coming your way. There ain't a police force in the country could do its job with a law book. You got information and I want it. You could of said no and I could of not believed you. But you didn't even say no. You're not dummying up on me, my friend. Not six cents worth. Let's go."

"Would you take the cuffs off, Captain?" I asked. "I mean if I made a statement?"

"I might. Make it short."

"If I told you I hadn't seen Lennox within the last twenty-four hours, hadn't talked to him and had no idea where he might be — would that satisfy you, Captain?"

"It might — if I believed it."

"If I told you I had seen him and where and when, but had no idea he had murdered anyone or that any crime had been committed, and further had no idea where he might be at this moment, that wouldn't satisfy you at all, would it?"

"With more detail I might listen. Things like where, when, what he looked like, what was talked about, where he was headed. It might grow into something."

"With your treatment," I said, "it would probably grow into making me an accessory."

His jaw muscles bulged. His eyes were dirty ice. "So?"

"I don't know," I said. "I need legal advice. I'd like to co-operate. How would it be if we had somebody from the D.A.'s office here?"

He let out a short raucous laugh. It was over very soon. He got up slowly and walked around the desk. He leaned down close to me, one big hand on the wood, and smiled. Then without change of expression he hit me on the side of the neck with a fist like a piece of iron.

The blow traveled eight or ten inches, no more. It nearly took my head off. Bile seeped into my mouth. I tasted blood mixed with it. I heard nothing but a roaring in my head. He leaned over me still smiling, his left hand still on the desk. His voice seemed to come from a long way off.

"I used to be tough but I'm getting old. You take a good punch, mister, and that's all you get from me. We got boys over at the City Jail that ought to be working in the stockyards. Maybe we hadn't ought to have them because they ain't nice clean powder-puff punchers like Dayton here. They don't have four kids and a rose garden like Green. They live for different amusements. It takes all kinds and labor's scarce. You got any more funny little ideas about what you might say, if you bothered to say it?"

"Not with the cuffs on, Captain." It hurt even to say that much.

He leaned farther towards me and I smelled his sweat and the gas of corruption. Then he straightened and went back around the desk and planted his solid buttocks in his chair. He picked up a three-cornered ruler and ran his thumb along one edge as if it was a knife. He looked at Green.

"What are you waiting for, Sergeant?"

"Orders." Green ground out the word as if he hated the sound of his own voice.

"You got to be told? You're an experienced man, it says in the records. I want a detailed statement of this man's movements for the past twenty-four hours. Maybe longer, but that much at first. I want to know what he did every minute of the time. I want it signed and witnessed and checked. I want it in two hours. Then I want him back here clean, tidy, and unmarked. And one thing more, Sergeant."

He paused and gave Green a stare that would have frozen a fresh-baked potato.

" — next time I ask a suspect a few civil questions I don't want you standing there looking as if I had torn his ear off."

"Yes, sir." Green turned to me. "Let's go," he said gruffly.

Gregorius bared his teeth at me. They needed cleaning — badly. "Let's have the exit line, chum."

"Yes, sir," I said politely. "You probably didn't intend it, but you've done me a favor. With an assist from Detective Dayton. You've solved a problem for me. No man likes to betray a friend but I wouldn't betray an enemy into your hands. You're not only a gorilla, you're an incompetent. You don't know how to operate a simple investigation. I was balanced on a knife edge and you could have swung me either way. But you had to abuse me, throw coffee in my face, and use your fists on me when I was in a spot where all I could do was take it. From now on I wouldn't tell you the time by the clock on your own wall."

For some strange reason he sat there perfectly still and let me say it. Then he grinned. "You're just a little old cop-hater, friend. That's all you are, shamus, just a little old cop-hater."

"There are places where cops are not hated, Captain. But in those places you wouldn't be a cop."

He took that too. I guess he could afford it. He'd probably taken worse many times. Then the phone rang on his desk. He looked at it and gestured. Dayton stepped smartly around the desk and lifted the receiver.

"Captain Gregorius' office. Detective Dayton speaking."

He listened. A tiny frown drew his handsome eyebrows together. He said softly: "One moment, please, sir."

He held the phone out to Gregorius. "Commissioner Allbright, sir."

Gregorius scowled. "Yeah? What's that snotty bastard want?" He took the phone, held it a moment and smoothed his face out. "Gregorius, Commissioner."

He listened. "Yeah, he's here in my office, Commissioner. I been asking him a few questions. Not co-operative. Not co-operative at all . . . How's that again?" A sudden ferocious scowl twisted his face into dark knots. The blood darkened his forehead. But his voice didn't change in tone by a fraction. "If that's a direct order it ought to come through the Chief of Detectives, Commissioner . . . Sure, I'll act on it until it's confirmed. Sure . . . Hell, no. Nobody laid a glove on him . . . Yes, sir. Right away."

He put the phone back in its cradle. I thought his hand shook a little. His eyes moved up and across my face and then to Green. "Take the cuffs off," he said tonelessly.

Green unlocked the cuffs. I rubbed my hands together, waiting for the pins and needles of circulation.

"Book him in the county jail," Gregorius said slowly. "Suspicion of murder. The D.A. has glommed the case right out of our hands. Lovely system we got around here."

Nobody moved. Green was close to me, breathing hard. Gregorius looked up at Dayton.

"Whatcha waiting for, cream puff? An ice-cream cone maybe?"

Dayton almost choked. "You didn't give me any orders, skipper."

"Say sir to me, damn you! I'm skipper to sergeants and better. Not to you, kiddo. Not to you. Out."

"Yes, sir." Dayton walked quickly to the door and went out. Gregorius heaved himself to his feet and moved to the window and stood with his back to the room.

"Come on, let's drift," Green muttered in my ear.

"Get him out of here before I kick his face in," Gregorius said to the window.

Green went to the door and opened it. I started through. Gregorius barked suddenly: "Hold it! Shut that door!"

Green shut it and leaned his back to it.

"Come here, you!" Gregorius barked at me.

I didn't move. I stood and looked at him. Green didn't move either. There was a grim pause. Then very slowly Gregorius walked across the room and stood facing me toe to toe. He put his big hard hands in his pockets. He rocked on his heels.

"Never laid a glove on him," he said under his breath, as if talking to himself. His eyes were remote and expressionless. His mouth worked convulsively.

Then he spat in my face.

He stepped back. "That will be all, thank you."

He turned and went back to the window. Green opened the door again.

I went through it reaching for my handkerchief.

8

CELL No. 3 in the felony tank has two bunks, Pullman style, but the tank was not very full and I had the cell to myself. In the felony tank they treat you pretty well. You get two blankets, neither dirty nor clean, and a lumpy mattress two inches thick which goes over crisscrossed metal slats. There is a flush toilet, a washbasin, paper towels and gritty gray soap. The cell block is clean and doesn't smell of disinfectant. The trusties do the work. The supply of trusties is always ample.

The jail deputies look you over and they have wise eyes. Unless you are a drunk or a psycho or act like one you get to keep your matches and cigarettes. Until preliminary you wear your own clothes. After that you wear the jail denim, no tie, no belt, no shoelaces. You sit on the bunk and wait. There is nothing else to do.

In the drunk tank it is not so good. No bunk, no chair, no blankets, no nothing. You lie on the concrete floor. You sit on the toilet and vomit in your own lap. That is the depth of misery. I've seen it.

Although it was still daylight the lights were on in the ceiling. Inside the steel door of the cell block was a basket of steel bars around the Judas window. The lights were controlled from outside the steel door. They went out at nine P.M. Nobody came through the door or said anything. You might be in the middle of a sentence in a newspaper or magazine. Without any sound of a click or any warning — darkness. And there you were until the summer dawn with nothing to do but sleep if you could, smoke if you had anything to smoke, and think if you had anything to think about that didn't make you feel worse than not thinking at all.

In jail a man has no personality. He is a minor disposal problem and a few entries on reports. Nobody cares who loves or hates him, what he looks like, what he did with his life. Nobody reacts to him unless he gives trouble. Nobody abuses him. All that is asked of him is that he go quietly to the right cell and remain quiet when he gets there. There is nothing to fight against, nothing to be mad at. The jailers are quiet men without animosity or sadism. All this stuff you read about men yelling and screaming, beating against the bars, running spoons along them, guards rushing in with clubs — all that is for the big house. A good jail is one of the quietest places in the world. You could walk through the average cell block at night and look in through the bars and see a huddle of brown blanket, or a head of hair, or a pair of eyes looking at nothing. You might hear a snore. Once in a long while you might hear a nightmare. The life in a jail is in suspension, without purpose or meaning. In another cell you might see a man who cannot sleep or even try to sleep. He is sitting on the edge of his bunk doing nothing. He looks at you or doesn't. You look at him. He says nothing and you say nothing. There is nothing to communicate.

In the corner of the cell block there may be a second steel door that leads to the show-up box. One of its walls is wire mesh painted black. On the back wall are ruled lines for height. Overhead are floodlights. You go in there in the morning as a rule, just before the night captain goes off duty. You stand against the measuring lines and the lights glare at you and there is no light behind the wire mesh. But plenty of people are out there: cops, detectives, citizens who have been robbed or assaulted or swindled or kicked out of their cars at gun point or conned out of their life savings. You don't see or hear them. You hear the voice of the night captain. You receive him loud and clear. He puts you through your paces as if you were a performing dog. He is tired and cynical and competent. He is the stage manager of a play that has had the longest run in history, but it no longer interests him.

"All right, you. Stand straight. Pull your belly in. Pull your chin in. Keep your shoulders back. Hold your head level. Look straight front. Turn left. Turn right. Face front again and hold your hands out. Palms up. Palms down. Pull your sleeves back. No visible scars. Hair dark brown, some gray. Eyes brown. Height six feet, one half inch. Weight about one ninety. Name, Philip Marlowe. Occupation private detective. Well, well, nice to see you, Marlowe. That's all. Next man."

Much obliged, Captain. Thanks for the time. You forgot to have me open my mouth. I have some nice inlays and one very high-class porcelain jacket crown. Eighty-seven dollars worth of porcelain jacket crown. You forgot to look inside my nose too, Captain. A lot of scar tissue in there for you. Septum operation and was that guy a butcher! Two hours of it in those days. I hear they do it in twenty minutes now. I got it playing football, Captain, a slight miscalculation in an attempt to block a punt. I blocked the guy's foot instead — after he kicked the ball. Fifteen yards penalty, and that's about how much stiff bloody tape they pulled out of my nose an inch at a time the day after the operation. I'm not bragging, Captain. I'm just telling you. It's the little things that count.

On the third day a deputy unlocked my cell in the middle of the morning.

"Your lawyer's here. Kill the butt — and not on the floor."

I flushed it down the toilet. He took me to the conference room. A tall pale dark-haired man was standing there looking out of the window. There was a fat brown briefcase on the table. He turned. He waited for the door to close. Then he sat down near his briefcase on the far side of a scarred oak table that came out of the Ark. Noah bought it secondhand. The lawyer opened a hammered silver cigarette case and put it in front of him and looked me over.

"Sit down, Marlowe. Care for a cigarette? My name is Endicott. Sewell Endicott. I've been instructed to represent you without cost or expense to you. I guess you'd like to get out of here, wouldn't you?"

I sat down and took one of the cigarettes. He held a lighter for me.

"Nice to see you again, Mr. Endicott. We've met before — while you were D.A."

He nodded. "I don't remember, but it's quite possible." He smiled faintly. "That position was not quite in my line. I guess I don't have enough tiger in me."

"Who sent you?"

"I'm not at liberty to say. If you accept me as your attorney, the fee will be taken care of."

"I guess that means they've got him."

He just stared at me. I puffed at the cigarette. It was one of those things with filters in them. It tasted like a high fog strained through cotton wool.

"If you mean Lennox," he said, "and of course you do, no — they haven't got him."

"Why the mystery, Mr. Endicott? About who sent you."

"My principal wishes to remain anonymous. That is the privilege of my principal. Do you accept me?"

"I don't know," I said. "If they haven't got Terry, why are they holding me? Nobody has asked me anything, nobody has been near me."

He frowned and looked down at his long white delicate fingers. "District Attorney Springer has taken personal charge of this matter. He may have been too busy to question you yet. But you are entitled to arraignment and a preliminary hearing. I can get you out on bail on a habeas corpus proceeding. You probably know what the law is."

"I'm booked on suspicion of murder."

He shrugged impatiently. "That's just a catch-all. You could have been booked in transit to Pittsburgh, or any one of a dozen charges. What they probably mean is accessory after the fact. You took Lennox somewhere, didn't you?"

I didn't answer. I dropped the tasteless cigarette on the floor and stepped on it. Endicott shrugged again and frowned.

"Assume you did then, just for the sake of argument. To make you an accessory they have to prove intent. In this case that would mean knowledge that a crime had been committed and that Lennox was a fugitive. It's bailable in any case. Of course what you really are is a material witness. But a man can't be held in prison as a material witness in this state except by court order. He's not a material witness unless a judge so declares. But the law enforcement people can always find a way to do what they want to do."

"Yeah," I said. "A detective named Dayton slugged me. A homicide captain named Gregorius threw a cup of coffee at me, hit me in the neck hard enough to bust an artery — you can see it's still swollen, and when a call from Police Commissioner Allbright kept him from turning me over to the wrecking crew, he spat in my face. You're quite right, Mr. Endicott. The law boys can always do what they want to do."

He looked at his wrist watch rather pointedly. "You want out on bail or don't you?"

"Thanks. I don't think I do. A guy out on bail is already half guilty in the public mind. If he gets off later on, he had a smart lawyer."

"That's silly," he said impatiently.

"Okay, it's silly. I'm silly. Otherwise I wouldn't be here. If you're in touch with Lennox, tell him to quit bothering about me. I'm not in here for him. I'm in here for me. No complaints. It's part of the deal. I'm in a business where people come to me with troubles. Big troubles, little troubles, but always troubles they don't want to take to the cops. How long would they come if any bruiser with a police shield could hold me upside down and drain my guts?"

"I see your point," he said slowly. "But let me correct you on one thing. I am not in touch with Lennox. I scarcely know him. I'm an officer of the court, as all lawyers are. If I knew where Lennox was, I couldn't conceal the information from the District Attorney. The most I could do would be to agree to surrender him at a specified time and place after I had had an interview with him."

"Nobody else would bother to send you here to help me."

"Are you calling me a liar?" He reached down to rub out his cigarette stub on the underside of the table.

"I seem to remember that you're a Virginian, Mr. Endicott. In this country we have a sort of historical fixation about Virginians. We think of them as the flower of southern chivalry and honor."

He smiled. "That was nicely said. I only wish it was true. But we're wasting time. If you had had a grain of sense you'd have told the police you hadn't seen Lennox for a week. It didn't have to be true. Under oath you could always have told the real story. There's no law against lying to the cops. They expect it. They feel much happier when you lie to them than when you refuse to talk to them. That's a direct challenge to their authority. What do you expect to gain by it?"

I didn't answer. I didn't really have an answer. He stood up and reached for his hat and snapped his cigarette case shut and put it in his pocket.

"You had to play the big scene," he said coldly. "Stand on your rights, talk about the law. How ingenuous can a man get, Marlowe? A man like you who is supposed to know his way around. The law isn't justice. It's a very imperfect mechanism. If you press exactly the right buttons and are also lucky, justice may show up in the answer. A mechanism is all the law was ever intended to be. I guess you're not in any mood to be helped. So I'll take myself off. You can reach me if you change your mind."

"I'll stick it out for a day or two longer. If they catch Terry they won't care how he got away. All they'll care about is the circus they can make of the trial. The murder of Mr. Harlan Potter's daughter is headline material all over the country. A crowd-pleaser like Springer could ride himself right into Attorney General on that show, and from there into the governor's chair and from there — " I stopped talking and let the rest of it float in the air.

Endicott smiled a slow derisive smile. "I don't think you know very much about Mr. Harlan Potter," he said.

"And if they don't get Lennox, they won't *want* to know how he got away, Mr. Endicott. They'll just want to forget the whole thing fast."

"Got it all figured out, haven't you, Marlowe?"

"I've had the time. All I know about Mr. Harlan Potter is that he is supposed to be worth a hundred million bucks, and that he owns nine or ten newspapers. How's the publicity going?"

"The publicity?" His voice was ice cold saying it.

"Yeah. Nobody's interviewed me from the press. I expected to make a big noise in the papers out of this. Get lots of business. Private eye goes to jail rather than split on a pal."

He walked to the door and turned with his hand on the knob. "You amuse me, Marlowe. You're childish in some ways. True, a hundred million dollars can buy a great deal of publicity. It can also, my friend, if shrewdly employed, buy a great deal of silence."

He opened the door and went out. Then a deputy came in and took me back to Cell No. 3 in the felony block.

"Guess you won't be with us long, if you've got Endicott," he said pleasantly as he locked me in. I said I hoped he was right.

9

THE DEPUTY on the early night shift was a big blond guy with meaty shoulders and a friendly grin. He was middle-aged and had long since outlived both pity and anger. He wanted to put in eight easy hours and he looked as if almost anything would be easy down his street. He unlocked my door.

"Company for you. Guy from the D.A.'s office. No sleep, huh?"

"It's a little early for me. What time is it?"

"Ten-fourteen." He stood in the doorway and looked over the cell. One blanket was spread on the lower bunk, one was folded for a pillow. There were a couple of used paper towels in the trash bucket and a small wad of toilet paper on the edge of the washbasin. He nodded approval. "Anything personal in here?"

"Just me."

He left the cell door open. We walked along a quiet corridor to the elevator and rode down to the booking desk. A fat man in a gray suit stood by the desk smoking a corncob. His fingernails were dirty and he smelled.

"I'm Spranklin from the D.A.'s office," he told me in a tough voice. "Mr. Grenz wants you upstairs." He reached behind his hip and came up with a pair of bracelets. "Let's try these for size."

The jail deputy and the booking clerk grinned at him with deep enjoyment. "What's the matter, Sprank? Afraid he'll mug you in the elevator?"

"I don't want no trouble," he growled. "Had a guy break from me once. They ate my ass off. Let's go, boy."

The booking clerk pushed a form at him and he signed it with a flourish. "I never take no unnecessary chances," he said. "Man never knows what he's up against in this town."

A prowl car cop brought in a drunk with a bloody ear. We went towards the elevator. "You're in trouble, boy," Spranklin told me in the elevator. "Heap bad trouble." It seemed to give him a vague satisfaction. "A guy can get hisself in a lot of trouble in this town."

The elevator man turned his head and winked at me. I grinned.

"Don't try nothing, boy," Spranklin told me severely. "I shot a man once. Tried to break. They ate my ass off."

"You get it coming and going, don't you?"

He thought it over. "Yeah," he said. "Either way they eat your ass off. It's a tough town. No respect."

We got out and went in through the double doors of the D.A.'s office. The switchboard was dead, with lines plugged in for the night. There was nobody in the waiting chairs. Lights were on in a couple of offices. Spranklin opened the door of a small lighted room which contained a desk, a filing case, a hard chair or two, and a thick-set man with a hard chin and stupid eyes. His face was red and he was just pushing something into the drawer of his desk.

"You could knock," he barked at Spranklin.

"Sorry, Mr. Grenz," Spranklin bumbled. "I was thinkin' about the prisoner."

He pushed me into the office. "Should I take the cuffs off, Mr. Grenz?"

"I don't know what the hell you put them on for," Grenz said sourly. He watched Spranklin unlock the cuffs on my wrist. He had the key on a bunch the size of a grapefruit and it troubled him to find it.

"Okay, scram," Grenz said. "Wait outside to take him back."

"I'm kind of off duty, Mr. Grenz."

"You're off duty when I say you're off duty."

Spranklin flushed and edged his fat bottom out through the door. Grenz looked after him savagely, then when the door closed he moved the same look to me. I pulled a chair over and sat down.

"I didn't tell you to sit down," Grenz barked.

I got a loose cigarette out of my pocket and stuck it in my mouth. "And I didn't say you could smoke," Grenz roared.

"I'm allowed to smoke in the cell block. Why not here?"

"Because this is my office. *I* make the rules here." A raw smell of whiskey floated across the desk.

"Take another quick one," I said. "It'll calm you down. You got kind of interrupted when we came in."

His back hit the back of the chair hard. His face went dark red. I struck a match and lit my cigarette.

After a long minute Grenz said softly. "Okay, tough boy. Quite a man, aren't you? You know something? They're all sizes and shapes when they come in here, but they all go out the same size — small. And the same shape — bent."

"What did you want to see me about, Mr. Grenz? And don't mind me if you feel like hitting that bottle. I'm a fellow that will take a snort myself, if I'm tired and nervous and overworked."

"You don't seem much impressed by the jam you're in."

"I don't figure I'm in any jam."

"We'll see about that. Meantime I want a very full statement from you." He flicked a finger at a recording set on a stand beside his desk. "We'll take it now and have it transcribed tomorrow. If the Chief Deputy is satisfied with your statement, he may release you on your own undertaking not to leave town. Let's go." He switched on the recorder. His voice was cold, decisive, and as nasty as he knew how to make it. But his right hand kept edging towards the desk drawer. He was too young to have veins in his nose, but he had them, and the whites of his eyes were a bad color.

"I get so tired of it," I said.

"Tired of what?" he snapped.

"Hard little men in hard little offices talking hard little words that don't mean a goddam thing. I've had fifty-six hours in the felony block. Nobody pushed me around, nobody tried to prove he was tough. They didn't have to. They had it on ice for when they needed it. And why was I in there? I was booked on suspicion. What the hell kind of legal system lets a man be shoved in a felony tank because some cop didn't get an answer to some questions? What evidence did he have? A telephone number on a pad. And what was he trying to prove by locking me up? Not a damn thing except that he had the power to do it. Now you're on the same pitch — trying to make me feel what a lot of power you generate in this cigar box you call your office. You send this scared baby sitter over late at night to bring me in here. You think maybe sitting alone with my thoughts for fifty-six hours has made gruel out of my brains? You think I'm going to cry in your lap and ask you to stroke my head because I'm so awful goddam lonely in the great big jail? Come off it, Grenz. Take your drink and get human; I'm willing to assume you are just doing your job. But take the brass knuckles off before you start. If you're big enough you don't need them, and if you need them you're not big enough to push me around."

He sat there and listened and looked at me. Then he grinned sourly. "Nice speech," he said. "Now you've got the crap out of your system, let's get that statement. You want to answer specific questions or just tell it your own way?"

"I was talking to the birds," I said. "Just to hear the breeze blow. I'm not making any statement. You're a lawyer and you know I don't have to."

"That's right," he said coolly. "I know the law. I know police work. I'm offering you a chance to clear yourself. If you don't want it, that's jake with me too. I can arraign you tomorrow morning at ten A.M. and have you set for a preliminary hearing. You may get bail, although I'll fight it, but if you do, it will be stiff. It'll cost you plenty. That's one way we can do it."

He looked down at a paper on his desk, read it, and turned it face down.

"On what charge?" I asked him.

"Section thirty-two. Accessory after the fact. A felony. It rates up to a five-spot in Quentin."

"Better catch Lennox first," I said carefully. Grenz had something and I sensed it in his manner. I didn't know how much, but he had something all right.

He leaned back in his chair and picked up a pen and twirled it slowly between his palms. Then he smiled. He was enjoying himself.

"Lennox is a hard man to hide, Marlowe. With most people you need a photo and a good clear photo. Not with a guy that has scars all over one side of his face. Not to mention white hair, and not over thirty-five years old. We got four witnesses, maybe more."

"Witnesses to what?" I was tasting something bitter in my mouth, like the bile I had tasted after Captain Gregorius slugged me. That reminded me that my neck was still sore and swollen. I rubbed it gently.

"Don't be a chump, Marlowe. A San Diego superior court judge and his wife happened to be seeing their son and daughter-in-law off on that plane. All four saw Lennox and the judge's wife saw the car he came in and who came with him. You don't have a prayer."

"That's nice," I said. "How did you get to them?"

"Special bulletin on radio and TV. A full description was all it took. The judge called in."

"Sounds good," I said judicially. "But it takes a little more than that, Grenz. You have to catch him and prove he committed a murder. Then you have to prove I knew it."

He snapped a finger at the back of the telegram. "I think I will take that drink," he said. "Been working nights too much." He opened the drawer and put a bottle and a shot glass on the desk. He poured it full to the brim and knocked it back in a lump. "Better," he said. "Much better. Sorry I can't offer you one while you're in custody." He corked the bottle and pushed it away from him, but not out of reach. "Oh yeah, we got to prove something, you said. Well, it could be we already got a confession, chum. Too bad, huh?"

A small but very cold finger moved the whole length of my spine, like an icy insect crawling.

"So why do you need a statement from me?"

He grinned. "We like a tidy record. Lennox will be brought back and tried. We need everything we can get. It's not so much what we want from you as what we might be willing to let you get away with — if you co-operate."

I stared at him. He did a little paper-fiddling. He moved around in his chair, looked at his bottle, and had to use up a lot of will power not grabbing for it. "Maybe you'd like the whole libretto," he said suddenly with an off-key leer. "Well, smart guy, just to show you I'm not kidding, here it is."

I leaned across his desk and he thought I was reaching for his bottle. He grabbed it away and put it back in the drawer. I just wanted to drop a stub in his ash tray. I leaned back again and lit another pill. He spoke rapidly.

"Lennox got off the plane at Mazatlán, an airline junction point and a town of about thirty-five thousand. He disappeared for two or three hours. Then a tall man with black hair and a dark skin and what might have been a lot of knife scars booked to Torreón under the name of Silvano Rodriguez. His Spanish was good but not good enough for a man of his name. He was too tall for a Mexican with such a dark skin. The pilot turned in a report on him. The cops were too slow at Torreón. Mex cops are no balls of fire. What they do best is shoot people. By the time they got going the man had chartered a plane and gone on to a little mountain town called Otatoclán, a small time summer resort with a lake. The pilot of the charter plane had trained as a combat pilot in Texas. He spoke good English. Lennox pretended not to catch what he said."

"If it *was* Lennox," I put in.

"Wait a while, chum. It was Lennox all right. Okay, he gets off at Otatoclán and registers at the hotel there, this time as Mario de Cerva. He was wearing a gun, a Mauser 7.65, which doesn't mean too much in Mexico, of course. But the charter pilot thought the guy didn't seem kosher, so he had a word with the local law. They put Lennox under surveillance. They did some checking with Mexico City and then they moved in."

Grenz picked up a ruler and sighted along it, a meaningless gesture which kept him from looking at me.

I said, "Uh-huh. Smart boy, your charter pilot, and nice to his customers. The story stinks."

He looked up at me suddenly. "What we want," he said dryly, "is a quick trial, a plea of second degree which we will accept. There are some angles we'd rather not go into. After all, the family is pretty influential."

"Meaning Harlan Potter."

He nodded briefly. "For my money the whole idea is all wet. Springer could have a field day with it. It's got everything. Sex, scandal, money, beautiful unfaithful wife, wounded war hero husband — I suppose that's where he got the scars — hell, it would be front page stuff for weeks. Every rag in the country would eat it up. So we shuffle it off to a fast fade." He shrugged. "Okay, if the chief wants it that way, it's up to him. Do I get that statement?" He turned to the recording machine which had been humming away softly all this time, with the light showing in front.

"Turn it off," I said.

He swung around and gave me a vicious look. "You like it in jail?"

"It's not too bad. You don't meet the best people, but who the hell wants to? Be reasonable, Grenz. You're trying to make a fink out of me. Maybe I'm obstinate, or even sentimental, but I'm practical too. Suppose you had to hire a private eye — yeah, yeah, I know how you would hate the idea — but just suppose you were where it was your only out. Would you want one that finked on his friends?"

He stared at me with hate.

"A couple more points. Doesn't it strike you that Lennox's evasion tactics were just a little too transparent? If he wanted to be caught, he didn't have to go to all that trouble. If he didn't want to be caught, he had brains enough not to disguise himself as a Mexican in Mexico."

"Meaning what?" Grenz was snarling at me now.

"Meaning you could just be filling me up with a lot of hooey you made up, that there wasn't any Rodriguez with dyed hair and there wasn't any Mario de Cerva at Otatoclán, and you don't know any more about where Lennox is than where Black Beard the Pirate buried his treasure."

He got his bottle out again. He poured himself a shot and drank it down quickly, as before. He relaxed slowly. He turned in his chair and switched off the recording machine.

"I'd like to have tried you," he said gratingly. "You're the kind of wise guy I like to work over. This rap will be hanging over you for a long long time, cutie. You'll walk with it and eat with it and sleep with it. And next time you step out of line we'll murder you with it. Right now I got to do something that turns my guts inside out."

He pawed on his desk and pulled the face-down paper to him, turned it over and signed it. You can always tell when a man is writing his own name. He has a special way of moving. Then he stood up and marched around the desk and threw the door of his shoe box open and yelled for Spranklin.

The fat man came in with his B.O. Grenz gave him the paper.

"I've just signed your release order," he said. "I'm a public servant and sometimes I have unpleasant duties. Would you care to know why I signed it?"

I stood up. "If you want to tell me."

"The Lennox case is closed, mister. There ain't any Lennox case. He wrote out a full confession this afternoon in his hotel room and shot himself. In Otatoclán, just like I said."

I stood there looking at nothing. Out of the corner of my eye I saw Grenz back away slowly as if he thought I might be going to slug him. I must have looked pretty nasty for a moment. Then he was behind his desk again and Spranklin had grabbed onto my arm.

"Come on, move," he said in a whining kind of voice. "Man likes to get to home nights once in a while."

I went out with him and closed the door. I closed it quietly as if on a room where someone had just died.

10

I DUG OUT THE CARBON of my property slip and turned it over and receipted on the original. I put my belongings back in my pockets. There was a man draped over the end of the booking desk and as I turned away he straightened up and spoke to me. He was about six feet four inches tall and as thin as a wire.

"Need a ride home?"

In the bleak light he looked young-old, tired and cynical, but he didn't look like a grifter. "For how much?"

"For free. I'm Lonnie Morgan of the *Journal*. I'm knocking off."

"Oh, police beat," I said.

"Just this week. The City Hall is my regular beat."

We walked out of the building and found his car in the parking lot. I looked up at the sky. There were stars but there was too much glare. It was a cool pleasant night. I breathed it in. Then I got into his car and he drove away from there.

"I live way out in Laurel Canyon," I said. "Just drop me anywhere."

"They ride you in," he said, "but they don't worry how you get home. This case interests me, in a repulsive sort of way."

"It seems there isn't any case," I said. "Terry Lennox shot himself this afternoon. So they say. So they say."

"Very convenient," Lonnie Morgan said, staring ahead through the windshield. His car drifted quietly along quiet streets. "It helps them build their wall."

"What wall?"

"Somebody's building a wall around the Lennox case, Marlowe. You're smart enough to see that, aren't you? It's not getting the kind of play it rates. The D.A. left town tonight for Washington. Some kind of convention. He walked out on the sweetest hunk of publicity he's had in years. Why?"

"No use to ask me. I've been in cold storage."

"Because somebody made it worth his while, that's why. I don't mean anything crude like a wad of dough. Somebody promised him something important to him and there's only one man connected with the case in a position to do that. The girl's father."

I leaned my head back in a corner of the car. "Sounds a little unlikely," I said. "What about the press? Harlan Potter owns a few papers, but what about the competition?"

He gave me a brief amused glance and then concentrated on his driving. "Ever been a newspaperman?"

"No."

"Newspapers are owned and published by rich men. Rich men all belong to the same club. Sure, there's competition — hard tough competition for circulation, for newsbeats, for exclusive stories. Just so long as it doesn't damage the prestige and privilege and position of the owners. If it does, down comes the lid. The lid, my friend, is down on the Lennox case. The Lennox case, my friend, properly built up, could have sold a hell of a lot of papers.

It has everything. The trial would have drawn feature writers from all over the country. But there ain't going to be no trial. On account of Lennox checked out before it could get moving. Like I said — very convenient — for Harlan Potter and his family."

I straightened up and gave him a hard stare.

"You calling the whole thing a fix?"

He twisted his mouth sardonically. "Could just be Lennox had some help committing suicide. Resisting arrest a little. Mexican cops have very itchy trigger fingers. If you want to lay a little bet, I'll give you nice odds that nobody gets to count the bullet holes."

"I think you're wrong," I said. "I knew Terry Lennox pretty well. He wrote himself off a long time ago. If they brought him back alive, he would have let them have it their way. He'd have copped a manslaughter plea."

Lonnie Morgan shook his head. I knew what he was going to say and he said it. "Not a chance. If he had shot her or cracked her skull, maybe yes. But there was too much brutality. Her face was beaten to a pulp. Second degree murder would be the best he could get, and even that would raise a stink."

I said: "You could be right."

He looked at me again. "You say you knew the guy. Do you go for the setup?"

"I'm tired. I'm not in a thinking mood tonight."

There was a long pause. Then Lonnie Morgan said quietly: "If I was a real bright guy instead of a hack newspaperman, I'd think maybe he didn't kill her at all."

"It's a thought."

He stuck a cigarette in his mouth and lit it by scratching a match on the dashboard. He smoked silently with a fixed frown on his thin face. We reached Laurel Canyon and I told him where to turn off the boulevard and where to turn again into my street. His car churned up the hill and stopped at the foot of my redwood steps.

I got out. "Thanks for the ride, Morgan. Care for a drink?"

"I'll take a rain check. I figure you'd rather be alone."

"I've got lots of time to be alone. Too damn much."

"You've got a friend to say goodbye to," he said. "He must have been that if you let them toss you into the can on his account."

"Who said I did that?"

He smiled faintly. "Just because I can't print it don't mean I didn't know it, chum. So long. See you around."

I shut the car door and he turned and drove off down the hill. When his tail lights vanished around the corner I climbed the steps, picked up newspapers, and let myself into the empty house. I put all the lamps on and opened all the windows. The place was stuffy.

I made some coffee and drank it and took the five C notes out of the coffee can. They were rolled tight and pushed down into the coffee at the side. I walked up and down with a cup of coffee in my hand, turned the TV on, turned it off, sat, stood, and sat again. I read through the papers that had piled up on the front steps. The Lennox case started out big, but by that morning it was a Part Two item. There was a photo of Sylvia, but none of Terry. There was a snap of me that I didn't know existed. "L.A. Private Detective Held for Questioning." There was a large photo of the Lennox home in Encino. It was pseudo English with a lot of peaked roof and it would have cost a hundred bucks to wash the windows. It stood on a knoll in a big two acres, which is a lot of real estate for the Los Angeles area. There was a photo of the guest house, which was a miniature of the main building. It was hedged in with trees. Both photos had obviously been taken from some distance off and then blown up and trimmed. There was no photo of what the papers called the "death room."

I had seen all this stuff before, in jail, but I read it and looked at it again with different eyes. It told me nothing except that a rich and beautiful girl had been murdered and the press had been pretty thoroughly excluded. So the influence had started to work very early. The crime beat boys must have gnashed their teeth and gnashed them in vain. It figured. If Terry talked to his father-in-law in Pasadena the very night she was killed, there would have been a dozen guards on the estate before the police were even notified.

But there was something that didn't figure at all — the way she had been beaten up. Nobody could sell me that Terry had done that.

I put the lamps out and sat by an open window. Outside in a

bush a mockingbird ran through a few trills and admired himself before settling down for the night.

My neck itched, so I shaved and showered and went to bed and lay on my back listening, as if far off in the dark I might hear a voice, the kind of calm and patient voice that makes everything clear. I didn't hear it and I knew I wasn't going to. Nobody was going to explain the Lennox case to me. No explanation was necessary. The murderer had confessed and he was dead. There wouldn't even be an inquest.

As Lonnie Morgan of the *Journal* had remarked — very convenient. If Terry Lennox had killed his wife, that was fine. There was no need to try him and bring out all the unpleasant details. If he hadn't killed her, that was fine too. A dead man is the best fall guy in the world. He never talks back.

11

IN THE MORNING I shaved again and dressed and drove downtown in the usual way and parked in the usual place and if the parking lot attendant happened to know that I was an important public character he did a top job in hiding it. I went upstairs and along the corridor and got keys out to unlock my door. A dark smooth-looking guy watched me.

"You Marlowe?"

"So?"

"Stick around," he said. "A guy wants to see you." He unplastered his back from the wall and strolled off languidly.

I stepped inside the office and picked up the mail. There was more of it on the desk where the night cleaning woman had put it. I slit the envelopes after I opened windows, and threw away what I didn't want, which was practically all of it. I switched on the buzzer to the other door and filled a pipe and lit it and then just sat there waiting for somebody to scream for help.

I thought about Terry Lennox in a detached sort of way. He was already receding into the distance, white hair and scarred face and weak charm and his peculiar brand of pride. I didn't judge him or analyze him, just as I had never asked him questions about how he got wounded or how he ever happened to get himself married to anyone like Sylvia. He was like somebody you meet on board ship and get to know very well and never really know at all. He was gone like the same fellow when he says goodbye at the pier and let's keep in touch, old man, and you know you won't and he won't. Likely enough you'll never even see the guy again. If you do he will be an entirely different person, just another Rotarian in a club car. How's business? Oh, not too bad. You look good. So do you. I've put on too much weight. Don't we all? Remember that trip in the *Franconia* (or whatever it was)? Oh sure, swell trip, wasn't it?

The hell it was a swell trip. You were bored stiff. You only talked to the guy because there wasn't anybody around that interested you. Maybe it was like that with Terry Lennox and me. No, not quite. I owned a piece of him. I had invested time and money in him, and three days in the icehouse, not to mention a slug on the jaw and a punch in the neck that I felt every time I swallowed. Now he was dead and I couldn't even give him back his five hundred bucks. That made me sore. It is always the little things that make you sore.

The door buzzer and the telephone rang at the same time. I answered the phone first because the buzzer meant only that somebody had walked into my pint-size waiting room.

"Is this Mr. Marlowe? Mr. Endicott is calling you. One moment please."

He came on the line. "This is Sewell Endicott," he said, as if he didn't know his goddam secretary had already fed me his name.

"Good morning, Mr. Endicott."

"Glad to hear they turned you loose. I think possibly you had the right idea not to build any resistance."

"It wasn't an idea. It was just mulishness."

"I doubt if you'll hear any more about it. But if you do and need help, let me hear from you."

"Why would I? The man is dead. They'd have a hell of a time proving he ever came near me. Then they'd have to prove I had guilty knowledge. And then they'd have to prove he had committed a crime or was a fugitive."

He cleared his throat. "Perhaps," he said carefully, "you haven't been told he left a full confession."

"I was told, Mr. Endicott. I'm talking to a lawyer. Would I be out of line in suggesting that the confession would have to be proved too, both as to genuineness and as to veracity?"

"I'm afraid I have no time for a legal discussion," he said sharply. "I'm flying to Mexico with a rather melancholy duty to perform. You can probably guess what it is?"

"Uh-huh. Depends who you're representing. You didn't tell me, remember."

"I remember very well. Well, goodbye, Marlowe. My offer of help is still good. But let me also offer you a little advice Don't be too certain you're in the clear. You're in a pretty vulnerable business."

He hung up. I put the phone back in its cradle carefully. I sat for a moment with my hand on it, scowling. Then I wiped the scowl off my face and got up to open the communicating door into my waiting room.

A man was sitting by the window ruffling a magazine. He wore a bluish-gray suit with an almost invisible pale blue check. On his crossed feet were black moccasin-type ties, the kind with two eyelets that are almost as comfortable as strollers and don't wear your socks out every time you walk a block. His white handkerchief was folded square and the end of a pair of sunglasses showed behind it. He had thick dark wavy hair. He was tanned very dark. He looked up with bird-bright eyes and smiled under a hairline mustache. His tie was a dark maroon tied in a pointed bow over a sparkling white shirt.

He threw the magazine aside. "The crap these rags go for," he said. "I been reading a piece about Costello. Yeah, they know all about Costello. Like I know all about Helen of Troy."

"What can I do for you?"

He looked me over unhurriedly. "Tarzan on a big red scooter," he said.

"What?"

"You. Marlowe. Tarzan on a big red scooter. They rough you up much?"

"Here and there. What makes it your business?"

"After Allbright talked to Gregorius?"

"No. Not after that."

He nodded shortly. "You got a crust asking Allbright to use ammunition on that slob."

"I asked you what made it your business. Incidentally I don't know Commissioner Allbright and I didn't ask him to do anything. Why would he do anything for me?"

He stared at me morosely. He stood up slowly, graceful as a panther. He walked across the room and looked into my office. He jerked his head at me and went in. He was a guy who owned the place where he happened to be. I went in after him and shut the door. He stood by the desk looking around, amused.

"You're small time," he said. "Very small time."

I went behind my desk and waited.

"How much you make in a month, Marlowe?"

I let it ride, and lit my pipe.

"Seven-fifty would be tops," he said.

I dropped a burnt match into a tray and puffed tobacco smoke.

"You're a piker, Marlowe. You're a peanut grifter. You're so little it takes a magnifying glass to see you."

I didn't say anything at all.

"You got cheap emotions. You're cheap all over. You pal around with a guy, eat a few drinks, talk a few gags, slip him a little dough when he's strapped, and you're sold out to him. Just like some school kid that read *Frank Merriwell*. You got no guts, no brains, no connections, no savvy, so you throw out a phony attitude and expect people to cry over you. Tarzan on a big red scooter." He smiled a small weary smile. "In my book you're a nickel's worth of nothing."

He leaned across the desk and flicked me across the face backhanded, casually and contemptuously, not meaning to hurt me, and the small smile stayed on his face. Then when I didn't even move for that he sat down slowly and leaned an elbow on the desk and cupped his brown chin in his brown hand. The bird-bright eyes stared at me without anything in them but brightness.

"Know who I am, cheapie?"

"Your name's Menendez. The boys call you Mendy. You operate on the Strip."

"Yeah? How did I get so big?"

"I wouldn't know. You probably started out as a pimp in a Mexican whorehouse."

He took a gold cigarette case out of his pocket and lit a brown cigarette with a gold lighter. He blew acrid smoke and nodded. He put the gold cigarette case on the desk and caressed it with his fingertips.

"I'm a big bad man, Marlowe. I make lots of dough. I got to make lots of dough to juice the guys I got to juice in order to make lots of dough to juice the guys I got to juice. I got a place in Bel-Air that cost ninety grand and I already spent more than that to fix it up. I got a lovely platinum-blond wife and two kids in private schools back east. My wife's got a hundred and fifty grand in rocks and another seventy-five in furs and clothes. I got a butler, two maids, a cook, a chauffeur, not counting the monkey that walks behind me. Everywhere I go I'm a darling. The best of everything, the best food, the best drinks, the best hotel suites. I got a place in Florida and a seagoing yacht with a crew of five men. I got a Bentley, two Cadillacs, a Chrysler station wagon, and an MG for my boy. Couple of years my girl gets one too. What you got?"

"Not much," I said. "This year I have a house to live in — all to myself."

"No woman?"

"Just me. In addition to that I have what you see here and twelve hundred dollars in the bank and and a few thousand in bonds. That answer your question?"

"What's the most you ever made on a single job?"

"Eight-fifty."

"Jesus, how cheap can a guy get?"

"Stop hamming and tell me what you want."

He killed his cigarette half smoked and immediately lit another. He leaned back in his chair. His lip curled at me.

"We were three guys in a foxhole eating," he said. "It was cold as hell, snow all around. We eat out of cans. Cold food. A little shelling, more mortar fire. We are blue with the cold, and I mean blue, Randy Starr and me and this Terry Lennox. A mortar shell plops right in the middle of us and for some reason it don't go off. Those jerries have a lot of tricks. They got a twisted sense of humor. Sometimes you think it's a dud and three seconds later it ain't a dud. Terry grabs it and he's out of the foxhole before Randy and me can even start to get unstuck. But I mean quick, brother. Like a good ball handler. He throws himself face down and throws the thing away from him and it goes off in the air. Most of it goes over his head but a hunk gets the side of his face. Right then the krauts mount an attack and the next thing we know we ain't there any more."

Menendez stopped talking and gave me the bright steady glare of his dark eyes.

"Thanks for telling me," I said.

"You take a good ribbing, Marlowe. You're okay. Randy and me talked things over and we decided that what happened to Terry Lennox was enough to screw up any guy's brains. For a long time we figured he was dead but he wasn't. The krauts got him. They worked him over for about a year and a half. They did a good job but they hurt him too much. It cost us money to find out, and it cost us money to find him. But we made plenty in the black market after the war. We could afford it. All Terry gets out of saving our lives is half of a new face, white hair, and a bad case of nerves. Back east he hits the bottle, gets picked up here and there, kind of goes to pieces. There's something on his mind but we never know what. The next thing we know he's married to this rich dame and riding high. He unmarries her, hits bottom again, marries her again, and she gets dead. Randy and me can't do a thing for him. He won't let us except for that short job in Vegas. And when he gets in a real jam he don't come to us, he goes to a cheapie like you, a guy that cops can push around. So then *he* gets dead, and without telling us goodbye, and without giving us a chance to pay off. I got connections in Mexico that could have buried him forever. I could have got him out of the country faster than a card sharp can stack a deck. But he goes crying to you. It makes me sore. A cheapie, a guy cops can push around."

"The cops can push anybody around. What do you want me to do about it?"

"Just lay off," Menendez said tightly.

"Lay off what?"

"Trying to make yourself dough or publicity out of the Lennox case. It's finished, wrapped up. Terry's dead and we don't want him bothered any more. The guy suffered too much."

"A hoodlum with sentiment," I said. "That slays me."

"Watch your lip, cheapie. Watch your lip. Mendy Menendez don't argue with guys. He tells them. Find yourself another way to grab a buck. Get me?"

He stood up. The interview was finished. He picked up his gloves. They were snow-white pigskin. They didn't look as if he ever had them on. A dressy type, Mr. Menendez. But very tough behind it all.

"I'm not looking for publicity," I said. "And nobody's offered me any dough. Why would they and for what?"

"Don't kid me, Marlowe. You didn't spend three days in the freezer just because you're a sweetheart. You got paid off. I ain't saying who by but I got a notion. And the party I'm thinking about has plenty more of the stuff. The Lennox case is closed and it stays closed even if —" He stopped dead and flipped his gloves at the desk edge.

"Even if Terry didn't kill her," I said.

His surprise was as thin as the gold on a weekend wedding ring. "I'd like to go along with you on that, cheapie. But it don't make any sense. But if it did make sense — and Terry wanted it the way it is — then that's how it stays."

I didn't say anything. After a moment he grinned slowly. "Tarzan on a big red scooter," he drawled. "A tough guy. Lets me come in here and walk all over him. A guy that gets hired for nickels and dimes and gets pushed around by anybody. No dough, no family, no prospects, no nothing. See you around, cheapie."

I sat still with my jaws clamped, staring at the glitter of his gold cigarette case on the desk corner. I felt old and tired. I got up slowly and reached for the case.

"You forgot this," I said, going around the desk.

"I got half a dozen of them," he sneered.

When I was near enough to him I held it out. His hand reached for it casually. "How about half a dozen of these?" I asked him and hit him as hard as I could in the middle of his belly.

He doubled up mewling. The cigarette case fell to the floor. He backed against the wall and his hands jerked back and forth convulsively. His breath fought to get into his lungs. He was sweating. Very slowly and with an intense effort he straightened up and we were eye to eye again. I reached out and ran a finger along the bone of his jaw. He held still for it. Finally he worked a smile onto his brown face.

"I didn't think you had it in you," he said.

"Next time bring a gun — or don't call me cheapie."

"I got a guy to carry the gun."

"Bring him with you. You'll need him."

"You're a hard guy to get sore, Marlowe."

I moved the gold cigarette case to one side with my foot and bent and picked it up and handed it to him. He took it and dropped it into his pocket.

"I couldn't figure you," I said. "Why it was worth your time to come up here and ride me. Then it got monotonous. All tough guys are monotonous. Like playing cards with a deck that's all aces. You've got everything and you've got nothing. You're just sitting there looking at yourself. No wonder Terry didn't come to you for help. It would be like borrowing money from a whore."

He pressed delicately on his stomach with two fingers. "I'm sorry you said that, cheapie. You could crack wise once too often."

He walked to the door and opened it. Outside the bodyguard straightened from the opposite wall and turned. Menendez jerked his head. The bodyguard came into the office and stood there looking me over without expression.

"Take a good look at him, Chick," Menendez said. "Make sure you know him just in case. You and him might have business one of these days."

"I already saw him, Chief," the smooth dark tight-lipped guy said in the tight-lipped voice they all affect. "He wouldn't bother me none."

"Don't let him hit you in the guts," Menendez said with a sour grin. "His right hook ain't funny."

The bodyguard just sneered at me. "He wouldn't get that close."

"Well, so long, cheapie," Menendez told me and went out.

"See you around," the bodyguard told me coolly. "The name's Chick Agostino. I guess you'll know me."

"Like a dirty newspaper," I said. "Remind me not to step on your face."

His jaw muscles bulged. Then he turned suddenly and went out after his boss.

The door closed slowly on the pneumatic gadget. I listened but I didn't hear their steps going down the hall. They walked as softly as cats. Just to make sure, I opened the door again after a minute and looked out. But the hall was quite empty.

I went back to my desk and sat down and spent a little time wondering why a fairly important local racketeer like Menendez would think it worth his time to come in person to my office and warn me to keep my nose clean, just minutes after I had received a similar though differently expressed warning from Sewell Endicott.

I didn't get anywhere with that, so I thought I might as well make it a perfect score. I lifted the phone and put in a call to the Terrapin Club at Las Vegas, person to person, Philip Marlowe calling Mr. Randy Starr. No soap. Mr. Starr was out of town, and would I talk to anyone else? I would not. I didn't even want to talk to Starr very badly. It was just a passing fancy. He was too far away to hit me.

After that nothing happened for three days. Nobody slugged me or shot at me or called me up on the phone and warned me to keep my nose clean. Nobody hired me to find the wandering daughter, the erring wife, the lost pearl necklace, or the missing will. I just sat there and looked at the wall. The Lennox case died almost as suddenly as it had been born. There was a brief inquest to which I was not summoned. It was held at an odd hour, without previous announcement and without a jury. The coroner entered his own verdict, which was that the death of Sylvia Potter Westerheym di Giorgio Lennox had been caused with homicidal intent by her husband, Terence William Lennox, since deceased outside the jurisdiction of the coroner's office. Presumably a confession was read into the record. Presumably it was verified enough to satisfy the coroner.

The body was released for burial. It was flown north and buried in the family vault. The press was not invited. Nobody gave any interviews, least of all Mr. Harlan Potter, who never gave interviews. He was about as hard to see as the Dalai Lama. Guys with a hundred million dollars live a peculiar life, behind a screen of servants, bodyguards, secretaries, lawyers, and tame executives. Presumably they eat, sleep, get their hair cut, and wear clothes. But you never know for sure. Everything you read or hear about them has been processed by a public relations gang of guys who are paid big money to create and maintain a usable personality, something simple and clean and sharp, like a sterilized needle. It doesn't have to be true. It just has to be consistent with the known facts, and the known facts you could count on your fingers.

Late afternoon of the third day the telephone rang and I was talking to a man who said his name was Howard Spencer, that he was a representative of a New York publishing house in California on a brief business trip, that he had a problem he would like to discuss with me and would I meet him in the bar of the Ritz-Beverly Hotel at eleven A.M. the next morning.

I asked him what sort of problem.

"Rather a delicate one," he said, "but entirely ethical. If we don't agree, I shall expect to pay you for your time, naturally."

"Thank you, Mr. Spencer, but that won't be necessary. Did someone I know recommend me to you?"

"Someone who knows about you — including your recent brush with the law, Mr. Marlowe. I might say that that was what interested me. My business, however, has nothing to do with that tragic affair. It's just that — well, let's discuss it over a drink, rather than over the telephone."

"You sure you want to mix it with a guy who has been in the cooler?"

He laughed. His laugh and his voice were both pleasant. He talked the way New Yorkers used to talk before they learned to talk Flatbush.

"From my point of view, Mr. Marlowe, that is a recommendation. Not, let me add, the fact that you were, as you put it in the cooler, but the fact, shall I say, that you appear to be extremely reticent, even under pressure."

He was a guy who talked with commas, like a heavy novel. Over the phone anyway.

"Okay, Mr. Spencer, I'll be there in the morning."

He thanked me and hung up. I wondered who could have given me the plug. I thought it might be Sewell Endicott and called him to find out. But he had been out of town all week, and still was. It didn't matter much. Even in my business you occasionally get a satisfied customer. And I needed a job because I needed the money — or thought I did, until I got home that night and found the letter with a portrait of Madison in it.

12

THE LETTER was in the red and white birdhouse mailbox at the foot of my steps. A woodpecker on top of the box attached to the swing arm was raised and even at that I might not have looked inside because I never got mail at the house. But the woodpecker had lost the point of his beak quite recently. The wood was fresh broken. Some smart kid shooting off his atom gun.

The letter had Correo Aéreo on it and a flock of Mexican stamps and writing that I might or might not have recognized if Mexico hadn't been on my mind pretty constantly lately. I couldn't read the postmark. It was hand-stamped and the ink pad was pretty far gone. The letter was thick. I climbed my steps and sat down in the living room to read it. The evening seemed very silent. Perhaps a letter from a dead man brings its own silence with it.

It began without date and without preamble.

I'm sitting beside a second-floor window in a room in a not too clean hotel in a town called Otatoclán, a mountain town with a lake. There's a mailbox just below the window and when the mozo comes in with some coffee I've ordered he is going to mail the letter for me and hold it up so that I can see it before he puts it in the slot. When he does that he gets a hundred-peso note, which is a hell of a lot of money for him.

Why all the finagling? There's a swarthy character with pointed shoes and a dirty shirt outside the door watching it. He's waiting for something, I don't know what, but he won't let me out. It doesn't matter too much as long as the letter gets posted. I want you to have this money because I don't need it and the local gendarmerie would swipe it for sure. It is not intended to buy anything. Call it an apology for making you so much trouble and a token of esteem for a pretty decent guy. I've done everything wrong as usual, but I still have the gun. My hunch is that you have probably made up your mind on a certain point. I might have killed her and perhaps I did, but I never could have done the other thing. That kind of brutality is not in my line. So something is very sour. But it doesn't matter, not in the least. The main thing now is to save an unnecessary and useless scandal. Her father and her sister never did me any harm. They have their lives to live and I'm up to here in disgust with mine. Sylv· didn't make a bum out of me, I was one already. I can't give you any very clear answer about why she married me. I suppose it was just a whim. At least she died young and beautiful. They say lust makes a man old, but keeps a woman young. They say a lot of nonsense. They say the rich can always protect themselves and that in their world it is always summer. I've lived with them and they are bored and lonely people.

I have written a confession. I feel a little sick and more than a little scared. You read about these situations in books, but you don't read the truth. When it happens to you, when all you have left is the gun in your pocket, when you are cornered in a dirty little hotel in a strange country, and have only one way out — believe me, pal, there is nothing elevating or dramatic about it. It is just plain nasty and sordid and gray and grim.

So forget it and me. But first drink a gimlet for me at Victor's. And the next time you make coffee, pour me a cup and put some bourbon in it and light me a cigarette and put it beside the cup. And after that forget the whole thing. Terry Lennox over and out. And so goodbye.

A knock at the door. I guess it will be the mozo with the coffee. If it isn't, there will be some shooting. I like Mexicans, as a rule, but I don't like their jails. So long.

TERRY

That was all. I refolded the letter and put it back in the envelope. It had been the mozo with the coffee all right. Otherwise I would never have had the letter. Not with a portrait of Madison in it. A portrait of Madison is a $5000 bill.

It lay in front of me green and crisp on the table top. I had never even seen one before. Lots of people who work in banks haven't either. Very likely characters like Randy Starr and Menendez wear them for folding money. If you went to a bank and asked for one, they wouldn't have it. They'd have to get it for you from the Federal Reserve. It might take several days. There are only about a thousand of them in circulation in the whole U.S.A. Mine had a nice glow around it. It created a little private sunshine all its own.

I sat there and looked at it for a long time. At last I put it away in my letter case and went out to the kitchen to make that coffee. I did what he asked me to, sentimental or not. I poured two cups and added some bourbon to his and set it down on the side of the table where he had sat the morning I took him to the plane. I lit a cigarette for him and set it in an ash tray beside the cup. I watched the steam rise from the coffee and the thin thread of smoke rise from the cigarette. Outside in the tecoma a bird was gussing around, talking to himself in low chirps, with an occasional brief flutter of wings.

Then the coffee didn't steam any more and the cigarette stopped smoking and was just a dead butt on the edge of an ash tray. I dropped it into the garbage can under the sink. I poured the coffee out and washed the cup and put it away.

That was that. It didn't seem quite enough to do for five thousand dollars.

I went to a late movie after a while. It meant nothing. I hardly saw what went on. It was just noise and big faces. When I got home again I set out a very dull Ruy Lopez and that didn't mean anything either. So I went to bed.

But not to sleep. At three A.M. I was walking the floor and listening to Khachaturyan working in a tractor factory. He called it a violin concerto. I called it a loose fan belt and the hell with it.

A white night for me is as rare as a fat postman. If it hadn't been for Mr. Howard Spencer at the Ritz-Beverly I would have killed a bottle and knocked myself out. And the next time I saw a polite character drunk in a Rolls-Royce Silver Wraith, I would depart rapidly in several directions. There is no trap so deadly as the trap you set for yourself.

13

AT ELEVEN O'CLOCK I was sitting in the third booth on the right-hand side as you go in from the dining-room annex. I had my back against the wall and I could see anyone who came in or went out. It was a clear morning, no smog, no high fog even, and the sun dazzled the surface of the swimming pool which began just outside the plate-glass wall of the bar and stretched to the far end of the dining room. A girl in a white sharkskin suit and a luscious figure was climbing the ladder to the high board. I watched the band of white that showed between the tan of her thighs and the suit. I watched it carnally. Then she was out of sight, cut off by the deep overhang of the roof. A moment later I saw her flash down in a one and a half. Spray came high enough to catch the sun and make rainbows that were almost as pretty as the girl. Then she came up the ladder and unstrapped her white helmet and shook her bleach job loose. She wobbled her bottom over to a small white table and sat down beside a lumberjack in white drill pants and dark glasses and a tan so evenly dark that he couldn't have been anything but the hired man around the pool. He reached over and patted her thigh. She opened a mouth like a firebucket and laughed. That terminated my interest in her. I couldn't hear the laugh but the hole in her face when she unzippered her teeth was all I needed.

The bar was pretty empty. Three booths down a couple of sharpies were selling each other pieces of Twentieth Century-Fox, using double-arm gestures instead of money. They had a telephone on the table between them and every two or three minutes they would play the match game to see who called Zanuck with a hot idea. They were young, dark, eager and full of vitality. They put as much muscular activity into a telephone conversation as I would put into carrying a fat man up four flights of stairs.

There was a sad fellow over on a bar stool talking to the bartender, who was polishing a glass and listening with that plastic smile people wear when they are trying not to scream. The customer was middle-aged, handsomely dressed, and drunk. He wanted to talk and he couldn't have stopped even if he hadn't really wanted to talk. He was polite and friendly and when I heard him he didn't seem to slur his words much, but you knew that he got up on the bottle and only let go of it when he fell asleep at night. He would be like that for the rest of his life and that was what his life was. You would never know how he got that way because even if he told you it would not be the truth. At the very best a distorted memory of the truth as he knew it. There is a sad man like that in every quiet bar in the world.

I looked at my watch and this high-powered publisher man was already twenty minutes late. I would wait half an hour and then I would leave. It never pays to let the customer make all the rules. If he can push you around, he will assume other people can too, and that is not what he hires you for. And right now I didn't need the work badly enough to let some fathead from back east use me for a horse-holder, some executive character in a paneled office on the eighty-fifth floor, with a row of pushbuttons and an intercom and a secretary in a Hattie Carnegie Career Girl's Special and a pair of those big beautiful promising eyes. This was the kind of operator who would tell you to be there at nine sharp and if you weren't sitting quietly with a pleased smile on your pan when he floated in two hours later on a double Gibson, he would have a paroxysm of outraged executive ability which would necessitate five weeks at

Acapulco before he got back the hop on his high hard one.

The old bar waiter came drifting by and glanced softly at my weak Scotch and water. I shook my head and he bobbed his white thatch, and right then a dream walked in. It seemed to me for an instant that there was no sound in the bar, that the sharpies stopped sharping and the drunk on the stool stopped burbling away, and it was like just after the conductor taps on his music stand and raises his arms and holds them poised.

She was slim and quite tall in a white linen tailormade with a black and white polka-dotted scarf around her throat. Her hair was the pale gold of a fairy princess. There was a small hat on it into which the pale gold hair nestled like a bird in its nest. Her eyes were cornflower blue, a rare color, and the lashes were long and almost too pale. She reached the table across the way and was pulling off a white gauntleted glove and the old waiter had the table pulled out in a way no waiter ever will pull a table out for me. She sat down and slipped the gloves under the strap of her bag and thanked him with a smile so gentle, so exquisitely pure, that he was damn near paralyzed by it. She said something to him in a very low voice. He hurried away, bending forward. There was a guy who really had a mission in life.

I stared. She caught me staring. She lifted her glance half an inch and I wasn't there any more. But wherever I was I was holding my breath.

There are blondes and blondes and it is almost a joke word nowadays. All blondes have their points, except perhaps the metallic ones who are as blond as a Zulu under the bleach and as to disposition as soft as a sidewalk. There is the small cute blonde who cheeps and twitters, and the big statuesque blonde who straight-arms you with an ice-blue glare. There is the blonde who gives you the up-from-under look and smells lovely and shimmers and hangs on your arm and is always very very tired when you take her home. She makes that helpless gesture and has that goddamned headache and you would like to slug her except that you are glad you found out about the headache before you invested too much time and money and hope in her. Because the headache will always be there, a weapon that never wears out and is as deadly as the bravo's rapier or Lucrezia's poison vial.

There is the soft and willing and alcoholic blonde who doesn't care what she wears as long as it is mink or where she goes as long as it is the Starlight Roof and there is plenty of dry champagne. There is the small perky blonde who is a little pal and wants to pay her own way and is full of sunshine and common sense and knows judo from the ground up and can toss a truck driver over her shoulder without missing more than one sentence out of the editorial in the *Saturday Review*. There is the pale, pale blonde with anemia of some non-fatal but incurable type. She is very languid and very shadowy and she speaks softly out of nowhere and you can't lay a finger on her because in the first place you don't want to and in the second place she is reading *The Waste Land* or Dante in the original, or Kafka or Kierkegaard or studying Provençal. She adores music and when the New York Philharmonic is playing Hindemith she can tell you which one of the six bass viols came in a quarter of a beat too late. I hear Toscanini can also. That makes two of them.

And lastly there is the gorgeous show piece who will outlast three kingpin racketeers and then marry a couple of millionaires at a million a head and end up with a pale rose villa at Cap Antibes, an Alfa-Romeo town car complete with pilot and co-pilot, and a stable of shopworn aristocrats, all of whom she will treat with the affectionate absent-mindedness of an elderly duke saying goodnight to his butler.

The dream across the way was none of these, not even of that kind of world. She was unclassifiable, as remote and clear as mountain water, as elusive as its color. I was still staring when a voice close to my elbow said:

"I'm shockingly late. I apologize. You must blame it on this. My name's Howard Spencer. You're Marlowe, of course."

I turned my head and looked at him. He was middle-aged, rather plump, dressed as if he didn't give any thought to it, but well shaved and with thin hair smoothed back carefully over a head that was wide between the ears. He wore a flashy double-breasted vest, the sort of thing you hardly ever see in California except perhaps on a visiting Bostonian. His glasses were rimless and he was patting a shabby old dog of a briefcase which was evidently the "this."

"Three brand new book-length manuscripts. Fiction. It would be embarrassing to lose them before we have a chance to reject them."

He made a signal to the old waiter who had just stepped back from placing a tall green something or other in front of the dream. "I have a weakness for gin and orange. A silly sort of drink really. Will you join me? Good."

I nodded and the old waiter drifted away.

Pointing to the briefcase I said: "How do you know you are going to reject them?"

"If they were any good, they wouldn't be dropped at my hotel by the writers in person. Some New York agent would have them."

"Then why take them at all?"

"Partly not to hurt feelings. Partly the thousand-to-one chance all publishers live for. But mostly you're at a cocktail party and get introduced to all sorts of people, and some of them have novels written and you are just liquored up enough to be benevolent and full of love for the human race, so you say you'd love to see the script. It is then dropped at your hotel with such sickening speed that you are forced to go through the motions of reading it. But I don't suppose you are much interested in publishers and their problems."

The waiter brought the drinks. Spencer grabbed for his and took a healthy swig. He wasn't noticing the golden girl across the way. I had all his attention. He was a good contact man.

"If it's part of the job," I said. "I can read a book once in a while."

"One of our most important authors lives around here," he said casually. "Maybe you've read his stuff. Roger Wade."

"Uh-huh."

"I see your point." He smiled sadly. "You don't care for historical romances. But they sell brutally."

"I don't have any point, Mr. Spencer. I looked at one of his books once. I thought it was tripe. Is that the wrong thing for me to say?"

He grinned. "Oh no. There are many people who agree with you. But the point is at the moment that he's an automatic best seller. And every publisher has to have a couple with the way costs are now."

I looked across at the golden girl. She had finished her limeade or whatever it was and was glancing at a microscopic wrist watch. The bar was filling up a little, but not yet noisy. The two sharpies were still waving their hands and the solo drinker on the bar stool had a couple of pals with him. I looked back at Howard Spencer.

"Something to do with your problem?" I asked him. "This fellow Wade, I mean."

He nodded. He was giving me a careful once over. "Tell me a little about yourself, Mr. Marlowe. That is, if you don't find the request objectionable."

"What sort of thing? I'm a licensed private investigator and have been for quite a while. I'm a lone wolf, unmarried, getting middle-aged, and not rich. I've been in jail more than once and I don't do divorce business. I like liquor and women and chess and a few other things. The cops don't like me too well, but I know a couple I get along with. I'm a native son, born in Santa Rosa, both parents dead, no brothers or sisters, and when I get knocked off in a dark alley sometime, if it happens, as it could to anyone in my business, and to plenty of people in any business or no business at all these days, nobody will feel that the bottom has dropped out of his or her life."

"I see," he said. "But all that doesn't exactly tell me what I want to know."

I finished the gin and orange. I didn't like it. I grinned at him. "I left out one item, Mr. Spencer. I have a portrait of Madison in my pocket."

"A portrait of Madison? I'm afraid I don't — "

"A five-thousand-dollar bill," I said. "Always carry it. My lucky piece."

"Good God," he said in a hushed voice. "Isn't that terribly dangerous?"

"Who was it said that beyond a certain point all dangers are equal?"

"I think it was Walter Bagehot. He was talking about a steeple-jack." Then he grinned. "Sorry, but I *am* a publisher. You're all right, Marlowe. I'll take a chance on you. If I didn't you would tell me to go to hell. Right?"

I grinned back at him. He called the waiter and ordered another pair of drinks.

"Here it is," he said carefully. "We are in bad trouble over Roger Wade. He can't finish a book. He's losing his grip and there's something behind it. The man seems to be going to pieces. Wild fits of drinking and temper. Every once in a while he disappears for days on end. Not very long ago he threw his wife downstairs and put her in the hospital with five broken ribs. There's no trouble between them in the usual sense, none at all. The man just goes nuts when he drinks." Spencer leaned back and looked at me gloomily. "We have to have that book finished. We need it badly. To a certain extent my job depends on it. But we need more than that. We want to save a very able writer who is capable of much better things than he has ever done. Something is very wrong. This trip he won't even see me. I realize this sounds like a job for a psychiatrist. Mrs. Wade disagrees. She is convinced that he is perfectly sane but that something is worrying him to death. A blackmailer, for instance. The Wades have been married five years. Something from his past may have caught up with him. It might even be — just as a wild guess — a fatal hit-and-run accident and someone has the goods on him. We don't know what it is. We want to know. And we are willing to pay well to correct the trouble. If it turns out to be a medical matter, well — that's that. If not, there has to be an answer. And in the meantime Mrs. Wade has to be protected. He might kill her the next time. You never know."

The second round of drinks came. I left mine untouched and watched him gobble half of his in one swallow. I lit a cigarette and just stared at him.

"You don't want a detective," I said. "You want a magician. What the hell could I do? If I happened to be there at exactly the right time, and if he isn't too tough for me to handle, I might knock him out and put him to bed. But I'd have to *be* there. It's a hundred to one against. You know that."

"He's about your size," Spencer said, "but he's not in your condition. And you could be there all the time."

"Hardly. And drunks are cunning. He'd be certain to pick a time when I wasn't around to throw his wingding. I'm not in the market for a job as a male nurse."

"A male nurse wouldn't be any use. Roger Wade is not the kind of man to accept one. He is a very talented guy who has been jarred loose from his self-control. He has made too much money writing junk for halfwits. But the only salvation for a writer is to write. If there is anything good in him, it will come out."

"Okay, I'm sold on him," I said wearily. "He's terrific. Also he's damn dangerous. He has a guilty secret and he tries to drown it in alcohol. It's not my kind of problem, Mr. Spencer."

"I see." He looked at his wrist watch with a worried frown that knotted his face and made it look older and smaller. "Well, you can't blame me for trying."

He reached for his fat briefcase. I looked across at the golden girl. She was getting ready to leave. The white-haired waiter was hovering over her with the check. She gave him some money and a lovely smile and he looked as if he had shaken hands with God. She touched up her lips and put her white gauntlets on and the waiter pulled the table halfway across the room for her to stroll out.

I glanced at Spencer. He was frowning down at the empty glass on the table edge. He had the briefcase on his knees.

"Look," I said. "I'll go see the man and try to size him up, if you want me to. I'll talk to his wife. But my guess is he'll throw me out of the house."

A voice that was not Spencer's said: "No, Mr. Marlowe, I don't think he would do that. On the contrary I think he might like you."

I looked up into the pair of violet eyes. She was standing at the end of the table. I got up and canted myself against the back of the booth in that awkward way you have to stand when you can't slide out.

"Please don't get up," she said in a voice like the stuff they use to line summer clouds with. "I know I owe you an apology, but it seemed important for me to have a chance to observe you before I introduced myself. I am Eileen Wade."

Spencer said grumpily: "He's not interested, Eileen."

She smiled gently. "I disagree."

I pulled myself together. I had been standing there off balance with my mouth open and me breathing through it like a sweet girl graduate. This was really a dish. Seen close up she was almost paralyzing.

"I didn't say I wasn't interested, Mrs. Wade. What I said or meant to say was that I didn't think I could do any good, and it might be a hell of a mistake for me to try. It might do a lot of harm."

She was very serious now. The smile had gone. "You are deciding too soon. You can't judge people by what they do. If you judge them at all, it must be by what they are."

I nodded vaguely. Because that was exactly the way I had thought about Terry Lennox. On the facts he was no bargain, except for that one brief flash of glory in the foxhole — if Menendez told the truth about that — but the facts didn't tell the whole story by any means. He had been a man it was impossible to dislike. How many do you meet in a lifetime that you can say that about?

"And you have to know them for that," she added gently. "Good-bye, Mr. Marlowe. If you should change your mind — " She opened her bag quickly and gave me a card — "and thank you for being here."

She nodded to Spencer and walked away. I watched her out of the bar, down the glassed-in annex to the dining room. She carried herself beautifully. I watched her turn under the archway that led to the lobby. I saw the last flicker of her white linen skirt as she turned the corner. Then I eased myself down into the booth and grabbed the gin and orange.

Spencer was watching me. There was something hard in his eyes.

"Nice work," I said, "but you ought to have looked at her once in a while. A dream like that doesn't sit across the room from you for twenty minutes without your even noticing."

"Stupid of me, wasn't it?" He was trying to smile, but he didn't really want to. He didn't like the way I had looked at her. "People have such queer ideas about private detectives. When you think of having one in your home — "

"Don't think of having this one in your home," I said. "Anyhow, think up another story first. You can do better than trying to make me believe anybody, drunk or sober, would throw that gorgeous downstairs and break five ribs for her."

He reddened. His hands tightened on the briefcase. "You think I'm a liar?"

"What's the difference? You've made your play. You're a little hot for the lady yourself, maybe."

He stood up suddenly. "I don't like your tone," he said. "I'm not sure I like *you*. Do me a favor and forget the whole idea. I think this ought to pay you for your time."

He threw a twenty on the table, and then added some ones for the waiter. He stood a moment staring down at me. His eyes were bright and his face was still red. "I'm married and have four children," he said abruptly.

"Congratulations."

He made a swift noise in his throat and turned and went. He went pretty fast. I watched him for a while and then I didn't. I drank the rest of my drink and got out my cigarettes and shook one loose and stuck it in my mouth and lit it. The old waiter came up and looked at the money.

"Can I get you anything else, sir?"

"Nope. The dough is all yours."

He picked it up slowly. "This is a twenty-dollar bill, sir. The gentleman made a mistake."

"He can read. The dough is all yours, I said."

"I'm sure I'm very grateful. If you are quite sure, sir — "

"Quite sure."

He bobbed his head and went away, still looking worried. The bar was filling up. A couple of streamlined demi-virgins went by caroling and waving. They knew the two hotshots in the booth farther on. The air began to be spattered with darlings and crimson fingernails.

I smoked half of my cigarette, scowling at nothing, and then got up to leave. I turned to reach back for my cigarettes and something bumped into me hard from behind. It was just what I needed. I swung around and I was looking at the profile of a broad-beamed crowd-pleaser in an overdraped Oxford flannel. He had the outstretched arm of the popular character and the two-by-six grin of the guy who never loses a sale.

I took hold of the outstretched arm and spun him around. "What's the matter, Jack? Don't they make the aisles wide enough for your personality?"

He shook his arm loose and got tough. "Don't get fancy, buster. I might loosen your jaw for you."

"Ha, ha," I said. "You might play center field for the Yankees and hit a home run with a breadstick."

He doubled a meaty fist.

"Darling, think of your manicure," I told him.

He controlled his emotions. "Nuts to you, wise guy," he sneered.

"Some other time, when I have less on my mind."

"Could there be less?"

"G'wan, beat it," he snarled. "One more crack and you'll need new bridgework."

I grinned at him. "Call me up, Jack. But with better dialogue."

His expression changed. He laughed. "You in pictures, chum?"

"Only the kind they pin up in the post office."

"See you in the mug book," he said, and walked away, still grinning.

It was all very silly, but it got rid of the feeling. I went along the annex and across the lobby of the hotel to the main entrance. I paused inside to put on my sunglasses. It wasn't until I got into my car that I remembered to look at the card Eileen Wade had given me. It was an engraved card, but not a formal calling card, because it had an address and a telephone number on it. Mrs. Roger Stearns Wade, 1247 Idle Valley Road. Tel. Idle Valley 5-6324.

I knew a good deal about Idle Valley, and I knew it had changed a great deal from the days when they had the gatehouse at the entrance and the private police force, and the gambling casino on the lake, and the fifty-dollar joy girls. Quiet money had taken over the tract after the casino was closed out. Quiet money had made it a subdivider's dream. A club owned the lake and the lake frontage and if they didn't want you in the club, you didn't get to play in the water. It was exclusive in the only remaining sense of the word that doesn't mean merely expensive.

I belonged in Idle Valley like a pearl onion on a banana split.

Howard Spencer called me up late in the afternoon. He had got over his mad and wanted to say he was sorry and he hadn't handled the situation very well, and had I perhaps any second thoughts.

"I'll go see him if he asks me to. Not otherwise."

"I see. There would be a substantial bonus —"

"Look, Mr. Spencer," I said impatiently, "you can't hire destiny. If Mrs. Wade is afraid of the guy, she can move out. That's *her* problem. Nobody could protect her twenty-four hours a day from her own husband. There isn't that much protection in the world. But that's not all you want. You want to know why and how and when the guy jumped the rails, and then fix it so that he doesn't do it again — at least until he finishes that book. And that's up to him.

If he wants to write the damn book bad enough, he'll lay off the hooch until he does it. You want too damn much."

"They all go together," he said. "It's all one problem. But I guess I understand. It's a little oversubtle for your kind of operation. Well, goodbye. I'm flying back to New York tonight."

"Have a smooth trip."

He thanked me and hung up. I forgot to tell him I had given his twenty to the waiter. I thought of calling back to tell him, then I thought he was miserable enough already.

I closed the office and started off in the direction of Victor's to drink a gimlet, as Terry had asked me to in his letter. I changed my mind. I wasn't feeling sentimental enough. I went to Lowry's and had a martini and some prime ribs and Yorkshire pudding instead.

When I got home I turned on the TV set and looked at the fights. They were no good, just a bunch of dancing masters who ought to have been working for Arthur Murray. All they did was jab and bob up and down and feint one another off balance. Not one of them could hit hard enough to wake his grandmother out of a light doze. The crowd was booing and the referee kept clapping his hands for action, but they went right on swaying and jittering and jabbing long lefts. I turned to another channel and looked at a crime show. The action took place in a clothes closet and the faces were tired and over familiar and not beautiful. The dialogue was stuff even Monogram wouldn't have used. The dick had a colored houseboy for comic relief. He didn't need it, he was plenty comical all by himself. And the commercials would have sickened a goat raised on barbed wire and broken beer bottles.

I cut it off and smoked a long cool tightly packed cigarette. It was kind to my throat. It was made of fine tobacco. I forgot to notice what brand it was. I was about ready to hit the hay when Detective-Sergeant Green of homicide called me up.

"Thought you might like to know they buried your friend Lennox a couple of days ago right in that Mexican town where he died. A lawyer representing the family went down there and attended to it. You were pretty lucky this time, Marlowe. Next time you think of helping a pal skip the country, don't."

"How many bullet holes did he have in him?"

"What's that?" he barked. Then he was silent for a space. Then he said rather too carefully: "One, I should say. It's usually enough when it blows a guy's head off. The lawyer is bringing back a set of prints and whatever was in his pockets. Anything more you'd like to know?"

"Yeah, but you can't tell me. I'd like to know who killed Lennox's wife."

"Cripes, didn't Grenz tell you he left a full confession? It was in the papers, anyway. Don't you read the papers any more?"

"Thanks for calling me, Sergeant. It was real kind of you."

"Look, Marlowe," he said raspingly. "You got any funny ideas about this case, you could buy yourself a lot of grief talking about them. The case is closed, finalized, and laid away in mothballs. Damn lucky for you it is. Accessory after the fact is good for five years in this state. And let me tell you something else. I've been a cop a long time and one thing I've learned for sure is it ain't always what you do that gets you sent up. It's what it can be made to look like when it comes in to court. Goodnight."

He hung up in my ear. I replaced the phone thinking that an honest cop with a bad conscience always acts tough. So does a dishonest cop. So does almost anyone, including me.

14

NEXT MORNING THE BELL RANG as I was wiping the talcum off an earlobe. When I got to the door and opened up I looked into a pair of violet-blue eyes. She was in brown linen this time, with a pimento-colored scarf, and no earrings or hat. She looked a little pale, but not as though anyone had been throwing her downstairs. She gave me a hesitant little smile.

"I know I shouldn't have come here to bother you, Mr. Marlowe. You probably haven't even had breakfast. But I had a reluctance to go to your office and I hate telephoning about personal matters."

"Sure. Come in, Mrs. Wade. Would you go for a cup of coffee?"

She came into the living room and sat on the davenport without looking at anything. She balanced her bag on her lap and sat with her feet close together. She looked rather prim. I opened windows and pulled up venetian blinds and lifted a dirty ash tray off the cocktail table in front of her.

"Thank you. Black coffee, please. No sugar."

I went out to the kitchen and spread a paper napkin on a green metal tray. It looked as cheesy as a celluloid collar. I crumpled it up and got out one of those fringed things that come in sets with little triangular napkins. They came with the house, like most of the furniture. I set out two Desert Rose coffee cups and filled them and carried the tray in.

She sipped. "This is very nice," she said. "You make good coffee."

"Last time anyone drank coffee with me was just before I went to jail," I said. "I guess you knew I'd been in the cooler, Mrs. Wade."

She nodded. "Of course. You were suspected of having helped him escape, wasn't it?"

"They didn't say. They found my telephone number on a pad in his room. They asked me questions I didn't answer — mostly because of the way they were asked. But I don't suppose you are interested in that."

She put her cup down carefully and leaned back and smiled at me. I offered her a cigarette.

"I don't smoke, thank you. Of course I'm interested. A neighbor of ours knew the Lennoxes. He must have been insane. He doesn't sound at all like that kind of man."

I filled a bulldog pipe and lit it. "I guess so," I said. "He must have been. He was badly wounded in the war. But he's dead and it's all done with. And I don't think you came here to talk about that."

She shook her head slowly. "He was a friend of yours, Mr. Marlowe. You must have a pretty strong opinion. And I think you are a pretty determined man."

I tamped the tobacco in my pipe and lit it again. I took my time and stared at her over the pipe bowl while I was doing it.

"Look, Mrs. Wade," I said finally. "My opinion means nothing. It happens every day. The most unlikely people commit the most unlikely crimes. Nice old ladies poison whole families. Clean-cut kids commit multiple holdups and shootings. Bank managers with spotless records going back twenty years are found out to be long-term embezzlers. And successful and popular and supposedly happy novelists get drunk and put their wives in the hospital. We know damn little about what makes even our best friends tick."

I thought it would burn her up, but she didn't do much more than press her lips together and narrow her eyes.

"Howard Spencer shouldn't have told you that," she said. "It was my own fault. I didn't know enough to keep away from him. I've learned since that the one thing you can never do to a man who is drinking too much is to try to stop him. You probably know that much better than I do."

"You certainly can't stop him with words," I said. "If you're lucky, and *if* you have the strength, you can sometimes keep him from hurting himself or someone else. Even that takes luck."

She reached quietly for her coffee cup and saucer. Her hands were lovely, like the rest of her. The nails were beautifully shaped and polished and only very slightly tinted.

"Did Howard tell you he hadn't seen my husband this time?"

"Yeah."

She finished her coffee and put the cup carefully back on the tray. She fiddled with the spoon for a few seconds. Then she spoke without looking up at me.

"He didn't tell you why, because he didn't know. I am very fond of Howard but he is the managing type, wants to take charge of everything. He thinks he is very executive."

I waited, not saying anything. There was another silence. She looked at me quickly then looked away again. Very softly she said: "My husband has been missing for three days. I don't know where he is. I came here to ask you to find him and bring him home. Oh, it has happened before. One time he drove himself all the way to Portland and got sick in a hotel there and had to get a doctor to sober him up. It's a wonder how he ever got that far without getting into trouble. He hadn't eaten anything for three days. Another time he was in a Turkish bath in Long Beach, one of those Swedish places where they give high colonics. And the last time it was some sort of small private and probably not very reputable sanitarium. This was less than three weeks ago. He wouldn't tell me the name of it or where it was, just said he had been taking a cure and was all right. But he looked deadly pale and weak. I got a brief glimpse of the man who brought him home. A tall young man dressed in the sort of overelaborate cowboy outfit you would only see on the stage or in a technicolor musical film. He let Roger out in the driveway and backed out and drove away at once."

"Could have been a dude ranch," I said. "Some of these tame cowpunchers spend every dime they make on a fancy outfit like that. The women go crazy over them. That's what they're there for."

She opened her bag and took out a folded paper. "I've brought you a check for five hundred dollars, Mr. Marlowe. Will you accept it as a retainer?"

She put the folded check down on the table. I looked at it, but didn't touch it. "Why?" I asked her. "You say he has been gone three days. It takes three or four to sober a man up and get some food into him. Won't he come back the way he did before? Or does something make this time different?"

"He can't stand much more of it, Mr. Marlowe. It will kill him. The intervals are getting shorter. I'm badly worried. I'm more than worried, I'm scared. It's unnatural. We've been married for five years. Roger was always a drinker, but not a psychopathic drinker. Something is all wrong. I want him found. I didn't sleep more than an hour last night."

"Any idea *why* he drinks?"

The violet eyes were looking at me steadily. She seemed a bit fragile this morning, but certainly not helpless. She bit her lower lip and shook her head. "Unless it's me," she said at last, almost in a whisper. "Men fall out of love with their wives."

"I'm only an amateur psychologist, Mrs. Wade. A man in my racket has to be a little of that. I'd say it's more likely he has fallen out of love with the kind of stuff he writes."

"It's quite possible," she said quietly. "I imagine all writers have spells like that. It's true that he can't seem to finish a book he is working on. But it isn't as if he had to finish it for the rent money. I don't think that is quite enough reason."

"What sort of guy is he sober?"

She smiled. "Well, I'm rather prejudiced. *I* think he is a very nice guy indeed."

"And how is he drunk?"

"Horrible. Bright and hard and cruel. He thinks he is being witty when he is only being nasty."

"You left out violent."

She raised her tawny eyebrows. "Just once, Mr. Marlowe. And too much has been made of that. I'd never have told Howard Spencer. Roger told him himself."

I got up and walked around in the room. It was going to be a hot day. It already was hot. I turned the blinds on one of the windows to keep the sun out. Then I gave it to her straight.

"I looked him up in *Who's Who* yesterday afternoon. He's forty-two years old, yours is his only marriage, no children. His people are New Englanders, he went to Andover and Princeton. He has a war record and a good one. He has written twelve of these fat sex-and-swordplay historical novels and every damn one of them has been on the best-seller lists. He must have made plenty of the folding. If he had fallen out of love with his wife, he sounds like the type who would say so and get a divorce. If he was haring around with another woman, you would probably know about it, and anyway he wouldn't have to get drunk just to prove he felt bad. If you've been married five years, then he was thirty-seven when that happened. I'd say he knew most of what there is to know about women by that time. I say most, because nobody ever knows all of it."

I stopped and looked at her and she smiled at me. I wasn't hurting her feelings. I went on.

"Howard Spencer suggested — on what grounds I have no idea — that what's the matter with Roger Wade is something that happened a long time ago before you were married and that it has caught up with him now, and is hitting him harder than he can take. Spencer thought of blackmail. Would you know?"

She shook her head slowly. "If you mean would I know if Roger had been paying out a lot of money to someone — no, I wouldn't know that. I don't meddle with his bookkeeping affairs. He could give away a lot of money without my knowing it."

"Okay then. Not knowing Mr. Wade I can't have much idea how he would react to having the bite put on him. If he has a violent temper, he might break somebody's neck. If the secret, whatever it is, might damage his social or professional standing or even, to take an extreme case, made the law boys drop around, he might pay off — for a while anyhow. But none of this gets us anywhere. You want him found, you're worried, you're more than worried. So how do I go about finding him? I don't want your money, Mrs. Wade. Not now anyway."

She reached into her bag again and came up with a couple of pieces of yellow paper. They looked like second sheets, folded, and one of them looked crumpled. She smoothed them out and handed them to me.

"One I found on his desk," she said. "It was very late, or rather early in the morning. I knew he had been drinking and I knew he hadn't come upstairs. About two o'clock I went down to see if he was all right — or comparatively all right, passed out on the floor or the couch or something. He was gone. The other paper was in the wastebasket or rather caught on the edge, so that it hadn't fallen in."

I looked at the first piece, the one not crumpled. There was a short typewritten paragraph on it, no more. It read: "I do not care to be in love with myself and there is no longer anyone else for me to be in love with. Signed: Roger (F. Scott Fitzgerald) Wade. P.S. This is why I never finished *The Last Tycoon*."

"That mean anything to you, Mrs. Wade?"

"Just attitudinizing. He has always been a great admirer of Scott Fitzgerald. He says Fitzgerald is the best drunken writer since Coleridge, who took dope. Notice the typing, Mr. Marlowe. Clear, even, and no mistakes."

"I did. Most people can't even write their names properly when soused." I opened the crumpled paper. More typing, also without any errors or unevenness. This one read: "I do not like you, Dr. V. But right now you're the man for me."

She spoke while I was still looking at it. "I have no idea who Dr. V. is. We don't know any doctor with a name beginning that way. I suppose he is the one who has that place where Roger was the last time."

"When the cowpoke brought him home? Your husband didn't mention any names at all — even place names?"

She shook her head. "Nothing. I've looked in the directory. There are dozens of doctors of one sort or another whose names begin with V. Also, it may not be his surname."

"Quite likely he's not even a doctor," I said. "That brings up the question of ready cash. A legitimate man would take a check, but a quack wouldn't. It might turn into evidence. And a guy like that wouldn't be cheap. Room and board at his house would come high. Not to mention the needle."

She looked puzzled. "The needle?"

"All the shady ones use dope on their clients. Easiest way to handle them. Knock them out for ten or twelve hours and when they come out of it, they're good boys. But using narcotics without a license can get you room and board with Uncle Sam. And that comes very high indeed."

"I see. Roger probably would have several hundred dollars. He always keeps that much in his desk. I don't know why. I suppose it's just a whim. There's none there now."

"Okay," I said. "I'll try to find Dr. V. I don't know just how, but I'll do my best. Take the check with you, Mrs. Wade."

"But why? Aren't you entitled —"

"Later on, thanks. And I'd rather have it from Mr. Wade. He's not going to like what I do in any case."

"But if he's sick and helpless —"

"He could have called his own doctor or asked you to. He didn't. That means he didn't want to."

She put the check back in her bag and stood up. She looked very forlorn. "Our doctor refused to treat him," she said bitterly.

"There are hundreds of doctors, Mrs. Wade. Any one of them would handle him once. Most of them would stay with him for some time. Medicine is a pretty competitive affair nowadays."

"I see. Of course you must be right." She walked slowly to the door and I walked with her. I opened it.

"You could have called a doctor on your own. Why didn't you?"

She faced me squarely. Her eyes were bright. There might have been a hint of tears in them. A lovely dish and no mistake.

"Because I love my husband, Mr. Marlowe. I'd do anything in the world to help him. But I know what sort of man he is too. If I called a doctor every time he took too many drinks, I wouldn't have a husband very long. You can't treat a grown man like a child with a sore throat."

"You can if he's a drunk. Often you damn well have to."

She was standing close to me. I smelled her perfume. Or thought I did. It hadn't been put on with a spray gun. Perhaps it was just the summer day.

"Suppose there *is* something shameful in his past," she said, dragging the words out one by one as if each of them had a bitter taste. "Even something criminal. It would make no difference to me. But I'm not going to be the means of its being found out."

"But it's all right if Howard Spencer hires me to find out?"

She smiled very slowly. "Do you really think I expected you to give Howard any answer but the one you did — a man who went to jail rather than betray a friend?"

"Thanks for the plug, but that wasn't why I got jugged."

She nodded after a moment of silence, said goodbye, and started down the redwood steps. I watched her into her car, a slim gray Jaguar, very new looking. She drove it up to the end of the street and swung around in the turning circle there. Her glove waved at me as she went by down the hill. The little car whisked around the corner and was gone.

There was a red oleander bush against part of the front wall of the house. I heard a flutter in it and a baby mockingbird started cheeping anxiously. I spotted him hanging on to one of the top branches, flapping his wings as if he was having trouble keeping his balance. From the cypress trees at the corner of the wall there was a single harsh warning chirp. The cheeping stopped at once and the little fat bird was silent.

I went inside and shut the door and left him to his flying lesson. Birds have to learn too.

15

No MATTER HOW SMART you think you are, you have to have a place to start from: a name, an address, a neighborhood, a background, an atmosphere, a point of reference of some sort. All I had was typing on a crumpled yellow page that said, "I do not like you, Dr. V. But right now you're the man for me." With that I could pinpoint the Pacific Ocean, spend a month wading through the lists of half a dozen county medical associations, and end up with the big round 0. In our town quacks breed like guinea pigs. There are eight counties within a hundred miles of the City Hall and in every town in every single one of them there are doctors, some genuine medical men, some just mail-order mechanics with a license to cut corns or jump up and down on your spine. Of the real doctors some are prosperous and some poor, some ethical, others not sure they can afford it. A well-heeled patient with incipient D.T.'s could be money from home to plenty of old geezers who have fallen behind in the vitamin and antibiotic trade. But without a clue there was no place to start. I didn't have the clue and Eileen Wade either didn't have it or didn't know she had it. And even if I found somebody that fitted and had the right initial, he might turn out to be a myth, so far as Roger Wade was concerned. The jingle might be something that just happened to run through his head while he was getting himself stewed up. Just as the Scott Fitzgerald allusion might be merely an off-beat way of saying goodbye.

In a situation like that the small man tries to pick the big man's brains. So I called up a man I knew in The Carne Organization, a flossy agency in Beverly Hills that specialized in protection for the carriage trade — protection meaning almost anything with one foot inside the law. The man's name was George Peters and he said he could give me ten minutes if I made it fast.

They had half the second floor of one of these candy-pink four-storied buildings where the elevator doors open all by themselves with an electric eye, where the corridors are cool and quiet, and the parking lot has a name on every stall, and the druggist off the front lobby has a sprained wrist from filling bottles of sleeping pills.

The door was French gray outside with raised metal lettering, as clean and sharp as a new knife. THE CARNE ORGANIZATION, INC. GERALD C. CARNE, PRESIDENT. Below and smaller: *Entrance.* It might have been an investment trust.

Inside was a small and ugly reception room, but the ugliness was deliberate and expensive. The furniture was scarlet and dark green, the walls were a flat Brunswick green, and the pictures hung on them were framed in a green about three shades darker than that. The pictures were guys in red coats on big horses that were just crazy to jump over high fences. There were two frameless mirrors tinted a slight but disgusting shade of rose pink. The magazines on the table of polished primavera were of the latest issue and each one was enclosed in a clear plastic cover. The fellow who decorated that room was not a man to let colors scare him. He probably wore a pimento shirt, mulberry slacks, zebra shoes, and vermilion drawers with his initials on them in a nice Mandarin orange.

The whole thing was just window-dressing. The clients of The Carne Organization were charged a minimum of one hundred fish *per diem* and they expected service in their homes. They didn't go sit in no waiting rooms. Carne was an ex-colonel of military police, a big pink and white guy as hard as a board. He had offered me a job once, but I never got desperate enough to take it. There are one hundred and ninety ways of being a bastard and Carne knew all of them.

A rubbed glass partition slid open and a receptionist looked out at me. She had an iron smile and eyes that could count the money in your hip wallet.

"Good morning. May I help you?"

"George Peters, please. My name is Marlowe."

She put a green leather book on the ledge. "Is he expecting you, Mr. Marlowe? I don't see your name on the appointment list."

"It's a personal matter. I just talked to him on the phone."

"I see. How do you spell your name, Mr. Marlowe? And your first name, please?"

I told her. She wrote it down on a long narrow form, then slipped the edge under a clock punch.

"Who's that supposed to impress?" I asked her.

"We are very particular about details here," she said coldly. "Colonel Carne says you never know when the most trivial fact may turn out to be vital."

"Or the other way around," I said, but she didn't get it. When she had finished her book work she looked up and said:

"I will announce you to Mr. Peters."

I told her that made me very happy. A minute later a door in the paneling opened and Peters beckoned me into a battleship-gray corridor lined with little offices that looked like cells. His office had soundproofing on the ceiling, a gray steel desk with two matching chairs, a gray dictating machine on a gray stand, a telephone and pen set of the same color as the walls and floor. There were a couple of framed photographs on the walls, one of Carne in uniform, with his snowdrop helmet on, and one of Carne as a civilian seated behind a desk and looking inscrutable. Also framed on the wall was a small inspirational legend in steely letters on a gray background. It read:

A CARNE OPERATIVE DRESSES, SPEAKS AND BEHAVES LIKE A GENTLE-MAN AT ALL TIMES AND IN ALL PLACES. THERE ARE NO EXCEPTIONS TO THIS RULE.

Peters crossed the room in two long steps and pushed one of the pictures aside. Set into the gray wall behind it was a gray microphone pickup. He pulled it out, unclipped a wire, and pushed it back in place. He moved the picture in front of it again.

"Right now I'd be out of a job," he said, "except that the son of a bitch is out fixing a drunk-driving rap for some actor. All the mike switches are in his office. He has the whole joint wired. The other morning I suggested to him that he have a microfilm camera installed with infra red light behind a diaphanous mirror in the reception room. He didn't like the idea too well. Maybe because somebody else had it."

He sat down in one of the hard gray chairs. I stared at him. He was a gawky long-legged man with a bony face and receding hair. His skin had the worn weathered look of a man who has been out of doors a great deal, in all kinds of weather. He had deep-set eyes and an upper lip almost as long as his nose. When he grinned the bottom half of his face disappeared into two enormous ditches that ran from his nostrils to the ends of his wide mouth.

"How can you take it?" I asked him.

"Sit down, pal. Breathe quietly, keep your voice down, and remember that a Carne operative is to a cheap shamus like you what Toscanini is to an organ grinder's monkey." He paused and grinned. "I take it because I don't give a damn. It's good money and any time Carne starts acting like he thought I was doing time in that maximum-security prison he ran in England during the war, I'll pick up my check and blow. What's your trouble? I hear you had it rough a while back."

"No complaints about that. I'd like to look at your file on the barred-window boys. I know you have one. Eddie Dowst told me after he quit here."

He nodded. "Eddie was just a mite too sensitive for The Carne Organization. The file you mention is top secret. In no circumstances must any confidential information be disclosed to outsiders. I'll get it at once."

He went out and I stared at the gray wastebasket and the gray linoleum and the gray leather corners of the desk blotter. Peters came back with a gray cardboard file in his hand. He put it down and opened it.

"For Chrissake, haven't you got anything in this place that isn't gray?"

"The school colors, my lad. The spirit of the organization. Yeah, I have something that isn't gray."

He pulled a desk drawer open and took out a cigar about eight inches long.

"An Upman Thirty," he said. "Presented to me by an elderly gent from England who has been forty years in California and still says 'wireless.' Sober he is just an old swish with a good deal of superficial charm, which is all right with me, because most people don't have any, superficial or otherwise, including Carne. He has as much charm as a steel puddler's underpants. Not sober, the client has a strange habit of writing checks on banks which never heard of him. He always makes good and with my fond help he has so far stayed out of the icebox. He gave me this. Should we smoke it together, like a couple of Indian chiefs planning a massacre?"

"I can't smoke cigars."

Peters looked at the huge cigar sadly. "Same here," he said. "I thought of giving it to Carne. But it's not really a one-man cigar, even when the one man is Carne." He frowned. "You know something? I'm talking too much about Carne. I must be edgy." He dropped the cigar back in the drawer and looked at the open file. "Just what do we want from this?"

"I'm looking for a well-heeled alcoholic with expensive tastes and money to gratify them. So far he hasn't gone in for check-bouncing. I haven't heard so anyway. He has a streak of violence and his wife is worried about him. She thinks he's hid out in some sobering-up joint but she can't be sure. The only clue we have is a jingle mentioning a Dr. V. Just the initial. My man is gone three days now."

Peters stared at me thoughtfully. "That's not too long," he said. "What's to worry about?"

"If I find him first, I get paid."

He looked at me some more and shook his head. "I don't get it, but that's okay. We'll see." He began to turn the pages of the file. "It's not too easy," he said. "These people come and go. A single letter ain't much of a lead." He pulled a page out of the folder, turned some more pages, pulled another, and finally a third. "Three of them here," he said. "Dr. Amos Varley, an osteopath. Big place in Altadena. Makes or used to make night calls for fifty bucks. Two registered nurses. Was in a hassle with the State Narcotics people a couple of years back, and turned in his prescription book. This information is not really up to date."

I wrote down the name and address in Altadena.

"Then we have Dr. Lester Vukanich. Ear, Nose, and Throat, Stockwell Building, on Hollywood Boulevard. This one's a dilly. Office practice mostly, and seems to sort of specialize in chronic sinus infections. Rather a neat routine. You go in and complain of a sinus headache and he washes out your antrums for you. First of course he has to anesthetize with Novocain. But if he likes your looks it don't have to be Novocain. Catch?"

"Sure." I wrote that one down.

"This is good," Peters went on, reading some more. "Obviously his trouble would be supplies. So our Dr. Vukanich does a lot of fishing off Ensenada and flies down in his own plane."

"I wouldn't think he'd last long if he brings the dope in himself," I said.

Peters thought about that and shook his head. "I don't think I agree. He could last forever if he's not too greedy. His only real danger is a discontented customer — pardon me, I mean patient — but he probably knows how to handle that. He's had fifteen years in the same office."

"Where the hell do you get this stuff?" I asked him.

"We're an organization, my boy. Not a lone wolf like you. Some we get from the clients themselves, some we get from the inside. Carne's not afraid to spend money. He's a good mixer when he wants to be."

"He'd love this conversation."

"Screw him. Our last offering today is a man named Verringer. The operative who filed on him is long gone. Seems a lady poet suicided at Verringer's ranch in Sepulveda Canyon one time. He runs a sort of art colony for writers and such who want seclusion and a congenial atmosphere. Rates moderate. He sounds legit. He calls himself doctor, but doesn't practice medicine. Could be a Ph.D. Frankly, I don't know why he's in here. Unless there was something about this suicide." He picked up a newspaper clipping pasted to a blank sheet. "Yeah, overdose of morphine. No suggestion Verringer knew anything about it."

"I like Verringer," I said. "I like him very much."

Peters closed the file and slapped it. "You haven't seen this," he said. He got up and left the room. When he came back I was standing up to leave. I started to thank him, but he shook it off.

"Look," he said, "there must be hundreds of places where your man could be."

I said I knew that.

"And by the way, I heard something about your friend Lennox that might interest you. One of our boys ran across a fellow in

New York five or six years ago that answers the description exactly. But the guy's name was not Lennox, he says. It was Marston. Of course he could be wrong. The guy was drunk all the time, so you couldn't really be sure."

I said: "I doubt if it was the same man. Why would he change his name? He had a war record that could be checked."

"I didn't know that. Our man's in Seattle right now. You can talk to him when he gets back, if it means anything to you. His name is Ashterfelt."

"Thanks for everything, George. It was a pretty long ten minutes."

"I might need *your* help some day."

"The Carne Organization," I said, "never needs anything from anybody."

He made a rude gesture with his thumb. I left him in his metallic gray cell and departed through the waiting room. It looked fine now. The loud colors made sense after the cell block.

16

BACK FROM THE HIGHWAY at the bottom of Sepulveda Canyon were two square yellow gateposts. A five-barred gate hung open from one of them. Over the entrance was a sign hung on wire: PRIVATE ROAD. NO ADMITTANCE. The air was warm and quiet and full of the tomcat smell of eucalyptus trees.

I turned in and followed a graveled road around the shoulder of a hill, up a gentle slope, over a ridge and down the other side into a shallow valley. It was hot in the valley, ten or fifteen degrees hotter than on the highway. I could see now that the graveled road ended in a loop around some grass edged with stones that had been lime-washed. Off to my left there was an empty swimming pool, and nothing ever looks emptier than an empty swimming pool. Around three sides of it there was what remained of a lawn dotted with redwood lounging chairs with badly faded pads on them. The pads had been of many colors, blue, green, yellow, orange, rust red. Their edge bindings had come loose in spots, the buttons had popped, and the pads were bloated where this had happened. On the fourth side there was the high wire fence of a tennis court. The diving board over the empty pool looked knee-sprung and tired. Its matting covering hung in shreds and its metal fittings were flaked with rust.

I came to the turning loop and stopped in front of a redwood building with a shake roof and a wide front porch. The entrance had double screen doors. Large black flies dozed on the screens. Paths led off among the ever green and always dusty California oaks and among the oaks there were rustic cabins scattered loosely over the side of the hill, some almost completely hidden. Those I could see had that desolate out-of-season look. Their doors were shut, their windows were blanked by drawn curtains of monk's cloth or something on that order. You could almost feel the thick dust on their sills.

I switched off the ignition and sat there with my hands on the wheel listening. There was no sound. The place seemed to be as dead as Pharaoh, except that the doors behind the double screens were open and something moved in the dimness of the room beyond. Then I heard a light accurate whistling and a man's figure showed against the screen, pushed it open and strolled down the steps. He was something to see.

He wore a flat black gaucho hat with the woven strap under his chin. He wore a white silk shirt, spotlessly clean, open at the throat, with tight wristlets and loose puffed sleeves above. Around his neck a black fringed scarf was knotted unevenly so that one end was short and the other dropped almost to his waist. He wore a wide black sash and black pants, skin-tight at the hips, coal black, and stitched with gold thread down the side to where they were slashed and belled out loosely with gold buttons along both sides of the slash. On his feet he wore patent-leather dancing pumps.

He stopped at the foot of the steps and looked at me, still whistling. He was as lithe as a whip. He had the largest and emptiest smoke-colored eyes I had ever seen, under long silky lashes. His features were delicate and perfect without being weak. His nose was straight and almost but not quite thin, his mouth was a handsome pout, there was a dimple in his chin, and his small ears nestled gracefully against his head. His skin had that heavy pallor which the sun never touches.

He struck an attitude with his left hand on a hip and his right made a graceful curve in the air.

"Greetings," he said. "Lovely day, isn't it?"

"Pretty hot in here for me."

"I like it hot." The statement was flat and final and closed the discussion. What I liked was beneath his notice. He sat down on a step, produced a long file from somewhere, and began to file his fingernails. "You from the bank?" he asked without looking up.

"I'm looking for Dr. Verringer."

He stopped working with the file and looked off into the warm distance. "Who's he?" he asked with no possible interest.

"He owns the place. Laconic as hell, aren't you? As if you didn't know."

He went back to his file and fingernails. "You got told wrong, sweetie. The bank owns the place. They done foreclosed it or it's in escrow or something. I forget the details."

He looked up at me with the expression of a man to whom details mean nothing. I got out of the Olds and leaned against the hot door, then I moved away from that to where there was some air.

"Which bank would that be?"

"You don't know, you don't come from there. You don't come from there, you don't have any business here. Hit the trail, sweetie. Buzz off but fast."

"I have to find Dr. Verringer."

"The joint's not operating, sweetie. Like it says on the sign, this is a private road. Some gopher forgot to lock the gate."

"You the caretaker?"

"Sort of. Don't ask any more questions, sweetie. My temper's not reliable."

"What do you do when you get mad — dance a tango with a ground squirrel?"

He stood up suddenly and gracefully. He smiled a minute, an empty smile. "Looks like I got to toss you back in your little old convertible," he said.

"Later. Where would I find Dr. Verringer about now?"

He pocketed his file in his shirt and something else took its place in his right hand. A brief motion and he had a fist with shining brass knuckles on it. The skin over his cheekbones was tighter and there was a flame deep in his large smoky eyes.

He strolled towards me. I stepped back to get more room. He went on whistling but the whistle was high and shrill.

"We don't have to fight," I told him. "We don't have anything to fight about. And you might split those lovely britches."

He was as quick as a flash. He came at me with a smooth leap and his left hand snaked out very fast. I expected a jab and moved my head well enough but what he wanted was my right wrist and he got it. He had a grip too. He jerked me off balance and the hand with the brass knucks came around in a looping bolo punch. A crack on the back of the head with those and I would be a sick man. If I pulled he would catch me on the side of the face or on the upper arm below the point of the shoulder. It would have been a dead arm or a dead face, whichever it happened to be. In a spot like that there is only one thing to do.

I went with the pull. In passing I blocked his left foot from behind, grabbed his shirt and heard it tear. Something hit me on the back of the neck, but it wasn't the metal. I spun to the left and he went over sideways and landed catlike and was on his feet again before I had any kind of balance. He was grinning now. He was delighted with everything. He loved his work. He came for me fast.

A strong beefy voice yelled from somewhere: "Earl! Stop that at once! At once, do you hear me?"

The gaucho boy stopped. There was a sort of sick grin on his face. He made a quick motion and the brass knucks disappeared into the wide sash around the top of his pants.

I turned and looked at a solid chunk of man in a Hawaiian shirt hurrying towards us down one of the paths waving his arms. He came up breathing a little fast.

"Are you crazy, Earl?"

"Don't ever say that, Doc," Earl said softly. Then he smiled, turned away, and went to sit on the steps of the house. He took off the flat-crowned hat, produced a comb, and began to comb his thick dark hair with an absent expression. In a second or two he started to whistle softly.

The heavy man in the loud shirt stood and looked at me. I stood and looked at him.

"What's going on here?" he growled. "Who are you, sir?"

"Name's Marlowe. I was asking for Dr. Verringer. The lad you call Earl wanted to play games. I figure it's too hot."

"I am Dr. Verringer," he said with dignity. He turned his head. "Go in the house, Earl."

Earl stood up slowly. He gave Dr. Verringer a thoughtful studying look, his large smoky eyes blank of expression. Then he went up the steps and pulled the screen door open. A cloud of flies buzzed angrily and then settled on the screen again as the door closed.

"Marlowe?" Dr. Verringer gave me his attention again. "And what can I do for you, Mr. Marlowe?"

"Earl says you are out of business here."

"That is correct. I am just waiting for certain legal formalities before moving out. Earl and I are alone here."

"I'm disappointed," I said, looking disappointed. "I thought you had a man named Wade staying with you."

He hoisted a couple of eyebrows that would have interested a Fuller Brush man. "Wade? I might possibly know somebody of that name — it's a common enough name — but why should he be staying with me?"

"Taking the cure."

He frowned. When a guy has eyebrows like that he can really do you a frown. "I am a medical man, sir, but no longer in practice. What sort of cure did you have in mind?"

"The guy's a wino. He goes off his rocker from time to time and disappears. Sometimes he comes home under his own power, sometimes he gets brought home, and sometimes he takes a bit of finding." I got a business card out and handed it to him.

He read it with no pleasure.

"What goes with Earl?" I asked him. "He think he's Valentino or something?"

He made with the eyebrows again. They fascinated me. Parts of them curled off all by themselves as much as an inch and a half. He shrugged his meaty shoulders.

"Earl is quite harmless, Mr. Marlowe. He is — at times — a little dreamy. Lives in a play world, shall we say?"

"You say it, Doc. From where I stand he plays rough."

"Tut, tut, Mr. Marlowe. You exaggerate surely. Earl likes to dress himself up. He is childlike in that respect."

"You mean he's a nut," I said. "This place some kind of sanitarium, isn't it? Or was?"

"Certainly not. When it was in operation it was an artists' colony. I provided meals, lodging, facilities for exercise and entertainment, and above all seclusion. And for moderate fees. Artists, as you probably know, are seldom wealthy people. In the term artists I of course include writers, musicians, and so on. It was a rewarding occupation for me — while it lasted."

He looked sad when he said this. The eyebrows drooped at the outer corners to match his mouth. Give them a little more growth and they would be *in* his mouth.

"I know that," I said. "It's in the file. Also the suicide you had here a while back. A dope case, wasn't it?"

He stopped drooping and bristled. "What file?" he asked sharply.

"We've got a file on what we call the barred-window boys, Doctor. Places where you can't jump out of when the French fits take over. Small private sanitariums or what have you that treat alcoholics and dopers and mild cases of mania."

"Such places must be licensed by law," Dr. Verringer said harshly.

"Yeah. In theory anyway. Sometimes they kind of forget about that."

He drew himself up stiffly. The guy had a kind of dignity, at that. "The suggestion is insulting, Mr. Marlowe. I have no knowledge of why my name should be on any such list as you mention. I must ask you to leave."

"Let's get back to Wade. Could he be here under another name, maybe?"

"There is no one here but Earl and myself. We are quite alone. Now if you will excuse me — "

"I'd like to look around."

Sometimes you can get them mad enough to say something off key. But not Dr. Verringer. He remained dignified. His eyebrows went all the way with him. I looked towards the house. From inside there came a sound of music, dance music. And very faintly the snapping of fingers.

"I bet he's in there dancing," I said. "That's a tango. I bet you he's dancing all by himself in there. Some kid."

"Are you going to leave, Mr. Marlowe? Or shall I have to ask Earl to assist me in putting you off my property?"

"Okay, I'll leave. No hard feelings, Doctor. There were only three names beginning with V and you seemed the most promising of them. That's the only real clue we had — Dr. V. He scrawled it on a piece of paper before he left: Dr. V."

"There must be dozens," Dr. Verringer said evenly.

"Oh sure. But not dozens in our file of the barred-window boys. Thanks for the time, Doctor. Earl bothers me a little."

I turned and went over to my car and got into it. By the time I had the door shut Dr. Verringer was beside me. He leaned in with a pleasant expression.

"We need not quarrel, Mr. Marlowe. I realize that in your occupation you often have to be rather intrusive. Just what bothers you about Earl?"

"He's so obviously a phony. Where you find one thing phony you're apt to expect others. The guy's a manic-depressive, isn't he? Right now he's on the upswing."

He stared at me in silence. He looked grave and polite. "Many interesting and talented people have stayed with me, Mr. Marlowe. Not all of them were as level-headed as you may be. Talented people are often neurotic. But I have no facilities for the care of lunatics or alcoholics, even if I had the taste for that sort of work. I have no staff except Earl, and he is hardly the type to care for the sick."

"Just what would say he is the type for, Doctor? Apart from bubble-dancing and stuff?"

He leaned on the door. His voice got low and confidential.

"Earl's parents were dear friends of mine, Mr. Marlowe. Someone has to look after Earl and they are no longer with us. Earl has to live a quiet life, away from the noise and temptations of the city. He is unstable but fundamentally harmless. I control him with absolute ease, as you saw."

"You've got a lot of courage," I said.

He sighed. His eyebrows waved gently, like the antennae of some suspicious insect. "It has been a sacrifice," he said. "A rather heavy one. I thought Earl could help me with my work here. He plays beautiful tennis, swims and dives like a champion, and can dance all night. Almost always he is amiability itself. But from time to time there were — incidents." He waved a broad hand as if pushing painful memories into the background. "In the end it was either give up Earl or give up my place here."

He held both hands palms up, spread them apart, turned them over and let them fall to his sides. His eyes looked moist with unshed tears.

"I sold out," he said. "This peaceful little valley will become a real estate development. There will be sidewalks and lampposts and children with scooters and blatting radios. There will even" — he heaved a forlorn sigh — "be Television." He waved his hand in a sweeping gesture. "I hope they will spare the trees," he said, "but I'm afraid they won't. Along the ridges there will be television aerials instead. But Earl and I will be far away, I trust."

"Goodbye, Doctor. My heart bleeds for you."

He put out his hand. It was moist but very firm. "I appreciate your sympathy and understanding, Mr. Marlowe. And I regret I am unable to help you in your quest for Mr. Slade."

"Wade," I said.

"Pardon me, Wade, of course. Goodbye and good luck, sir."

I started up and drove back along the graveled road by the way I had come. I felt sad, but not quite as sad as Dr. Verringer would have liked me to feel.

I came out through the gates and drove far enough around the curve of the highway to park out of sight of the entrance. I got out and walked back along the edge of the paving to where I could just see the gates from the barbed-wire boundary fence. I stood there under a eucalyptus and waited.

Five minutes or so passed. Then a car came down the private road churning gravel. It stopped out of sight from where I was. I pulled back still farther into the brush. I heard a creaking noise, then the click of a heavy catch and the rattle of a chain. The car motor revved up and the car went back up the road.

When the sound of it had died I went back to my Olds and did a U turn to face back towards town. As I drove past the entrance to Dr. Verringer's private road I saw that the gate was fastened with a padlocked chain. No more visitors today, thank you.

17

I DROVE THE TWENTY-ODD MILES back to town and ate lunch. While I ate I felt more and more silly over the whole deal. You just don't find people the way I was going about it. You meet interesting characters like Earl and Dr. Verringer, but you don't meet the man you are looking for. You waste tires, gasoline, words, and nervous energy in a game with no pay-off. You're not even betting table limit four ways on Black 28. With three names that started with V, I had as much chance of paging my man as I had of breaking Nick the Greek in a crap game.

Anyway the first one is always wrong, a dead end, a promising lead that blows up in your face with no music. But he shouldn't have said Slade instead of Wade. He was an intelligent man. He wouldn't forget that easy, and if he did he would just forget.

Maybe, and maybe not. It had not been a long acquaintance. Over my coffee I thought about Drs. Vukanich and Varley. Yes or no? They would kill most of the afternoon. By then I could call the Wade mansion in Idle Valley and be told the head of the household had returned to his domicile and all was gleaming bright for the time being.

Dr. Vukanich was easy. He was only half a dozen blocks down

the line. But Dr. Varley was away to hell and gone in the Altadena hills, a long, hot, boring drive. Yes or no?

The final answer was yes. For three good reasons. One was that you can never know too much about the shadow line and the people who walk it. The second was that anything I could add to the file Peters had got out for me was just that much thanks and goodwill. The third reason was that I didn't have anything else to do.

I paid my check, left my car where it was, and walked the north side of the street to the Stockwell Building. It was an antique with a cigar counter in the entrance and a manually operated elevator that lurched and hated to level off. The corridor of the sixth floor was narrow and the doors had frosted glass panels. It was older and much dirtier than my own building. It was loaded with doctors, dentists, Christian Science practitioners not doing too good, the kind of lawyers you hope the other fellow has, the kind of doctors and dentists who just scrape along. Not too skillful, not too clean, not too much on the ball, three dollars and please pay the nurse; tired, discouraged men who know just exactly where they stand, what kind of patients they can get and how much money they can be squeezed into paying. Please Do Not Ask For Credit. Doctor is In, Doctor is Out. That's a pretty shaky molar you have there, Mrs. Kazinski. Now if you want this new acrylic filling, every bit as good as a gold inlay, I can do it for you for $14. Novocain will be two dollars extra, if you wish it. Doctor is In, Doctor is Out. That will be Three Dollars. Please Pay the Nurse.

In a building like that there will always be a few guys making real money, but they don't look it. They fit into the shabby background, which is protective coloring for them. Shyster lawyers who are partners in a bail-bond racket on the side (only about two per cent of all forfeited bail bonds are ever collected). Abortionists posing as anything you like that explains their funishings. Dope pushers posing as urologists, dermatologists, or any branch of medicine in which the treatment can be frequent, and the regular use of local anesthetics is normal.

Dr. Lester Vukanich had a small and ill-furnished waiting room in which there were a dozen people, all uncomfortable. They looked like anybody else. They had no signs on them. Anyway you can't tell a doper well under control from a vegetarian book-keeper. I had to wait three quarters of an hour. The patients went in through two doors. An active ear, nose, and throat man can handle four sufferers at once, if he has enough room.

Finally I got in. I got to sit in a brown leather chair beside a table covered with a white towel on which was a set of tools. A sterilizing cabinet bubbled against the wall. Dr. Vukanich came in briskly with his white smock and his round mirror strapped to his forehead. He sat down in front of me on a stool.

"A sinus headache, is it? Very severe?" He looked at a folder the nurse had given him.

I said it was awful. Blinding. Especially when I first got up in the morning. He nodded sagely.

"Characteristic," he said, and fitted a glass cap over a thing that looked like a fountain pen.

He pushed it into my mouth. "Close the lips but not the teeth, please." While he said it he reached out and switched off the light. There was no window. A ventilating fan purred somewhere.

Dr. Vukanich withdrew his glass tube and put the lights back up. He looked at me carefully.

"No congestion at all, Mr. Marlowe. If you have a headache, it is not from a sinus condition. I'd hazard a guess that you never had sinus trouble in your life. You had a septum operation some-time in the past, I see."

"Yes, Doctor. Got a kick playing football."

He nodded. "There is a slight shelf of bone which should have been cut away. Hardly enough to interfere with breathing, how-ever."

He leaned back on the stool and held his knee. "Just what did you expect me to do for you?" he asked. He was a thin-faced man with an uninteresting pallor. He looked like a tubercular white rat.

"I wanted to talk to you about a friend of mine. He's in bad shape. He's a writer. Plenty of dough, but bad nerves. Needs help. He lives on the sauce for days on end. He needs that little extra something. His own doctor won't co-operate any more."

"Exactly what do you mean by co-operate?" Dr. Vukanich asked.

"All the guy needs is an occasional shot to calm him down. I thought maybe we could work something out. The money would be solid."

"Sorry, Mr. Marlowe. It is not my sort of problem." He stood up. "Rather a crude approach, if I may say so. Your friend may consult me, if he chooses. But he'd better have something wrong with him that requires treatment. That will be ten dollars, Mr. Marlowe."

"Come off it, Doc. You're on the list."

Dr. Vukanich leaned against the wall and lit a cigarette. He was giving me time. He blew smoke and looked at it. I gave him one of my cards to look at instead. He looked at it.

"What list would that be?" he inquired.

"The barred-window boys. I figure you might know my friend already. His name's Wade. I figure you might have him stashed away somewhere in a little white room. The guy is missing from home."

"You are an ass," Dr. Vukanich told me. "I don't go in for penny ante stuff like four-day liquor cures. They cure nothing in any case. I have no little white rooms and I am not acquainted with the friend you mention — even if he exists. That will be ten dollars — cash — right now. Or would you rather I called the police and make a complaint that you solicited me for narcotics?"

"That would be dandy," I said. "Let's."

"Get out of here, you cheap grifter."

I stood up off the chair. "I guess I made a mistake, Doctor. The last time the guy broke parole he holed up with a doctor whose name began with V. It was strictly an undercover operation. They fetched him late at night and brought him back the same way when he was over the jumps. Didn't even wait long enough to see him go in the house. So when he hops the coop again and don't come back for quite a piece, naturally we check over our files for a lead. We come up with three doctors whose names begin with V."

"Interesting," he said with a bleak smile. He was still giving me time. "What is the basis of your selection?"

I stared at him. His right hand was moving softly up and down the upper part of his left arm on the inside of it. His face was covered with a light sweat.

"Sorry, Doctor. We operate very confidential."

"Excuse me a moment. I have another patient that — "

He left the rest of it hanging in the air and went out. While he was gone a nurse poked her head through the doorway, looked at me briefly and withdrew.

Then Dr. Vukanich came back in strolling happily. He was smiling and relaxed. His eyes were bright.

"What? Are you still here?" He looked very surprised or pretended to. "I thought our little visit had been brought to an end."

"I'm leaving. I thought you wanted me to wait."

He chuckled. "You know something, Mr. Marlowe? We live in extraordinary times. For a mere five hundred dollars I could have you put in the hospital with several broken bones. Comical, isn't it?"

"Hilarious," I said. "Shoot yourself in the vein, don't you, Doc? Boy, do you brighten up!"

I started out. "Hasta luego, amigo," he chirped. "Don't forget my ten bucks. Pay the nurse."

He moved to an intercom and was speaking into it as I left. In the waiting room the same twelve people or twelve just like them were being uncomfortable. The nurse was right on the job.

"That will be ten dollars, please, Mr. Marlowe. This office requires immediate cash payment."

I stepped among the crowded feet to the door. She bounded out of her chair and ran around the desk. I pulled the door open.

"What happens when you don't get it?" I asked her.

"You'll find out what happens," she said angrily.

"Sure. You're just doing your job. So am I. Take a gander at the card I left and you'll see what my job is."

I went on out. The waiting patients looked at me with disapproving eyes. That was no way to treat Doctor.

18

DR. AMOS VARLEY was a very different proposition. He had a big old house in a big old garden with big old oak trees shading it. It was a massive frame structure with elaborate scrollwork along the overhang of the porches and the white porch railings had turned and fluted uprights like the legs of an old-fashioned grand piano. A few frail elderly people sat in long chairs on the porches with rugs tucked around them.

The entrance doors were double and had stained-glass panels. The hall inside was wide and cool and the parquetry floor was polished and without a single rug. Altadena is a hot place in summer. It is pushed back against the hills and the breeze jumps clear over it. Eighty years ago people knew how to build houses for this climate.

A nurse in crisp white took my card and after a wait Dr. Amos Varley condescended to see me. He was a big bald-headed guy with a cheery smile. His long white coat was spotless, he walked noiselessly on crepe rubber soles.

"What can I do for you, Mr. Marlowe?" He had a rich soft voice to soothe the pain and comfort the anxious heart. Doctor is here, there is nothing to worry about, everything will be fine. He had that bedside manner, thick, honeyed layers of it. He was wonderful — and he was as tough as armor plate.

"Doctor, I am looking for a man named Wade, a well-to-do alcoholic who has disappeared from his home. His past history suggests that he is holed up in some discreet joint than can handle him with skill. My only lead is a reference to a Dr. V. You're my third Dr. V. and I'm getting discouraged."

He smiled benignly. "Only your third, Mr. Marlowe? Surely there must be a hundred doctors in and around the Los Angeles area whose names begin with V."

"Sure, but not many of them would have rooms with barred windows. I noticed a few upstairs here, on the side of the house."

"Old people," Dr. Varley said sadly, but it was a rich full sadness. "Lonely old people, depressed and unhappy old people, Mr. Marlowe. Sometimes—" He made an expressive gesture with his hand, a curving motion outwards, a pause, then a gentle falling, like a dead leaf fluttering to the ground. "I don't treat alcoholics here," he added precisely. "Now if you will excuse me—,"

"Sorry, Doctor. You just happened to be on our list. Probably a mistake. Something about a run-in with the narcotics people a couple of years ago."

"Is that so?" He looked puzzled, then the light broke. "Ah, yes, an assistant I was unwise enough to employ. For a very short time. He abused my confidence badly. Yes, indeed."

"Not the way I heard it," I said. "I guess I heard it wrong."

"And how did you hear it, Mr. Marlowe?" He was still giving me the full treatment with his smile and his mellow tones.

"That you had to turn in your narcotic prescription book."

That got to him a little. He didn't quite scowl but he peeled off a few layers of the charm. His blue eyes had a chilly glint. "And the source of this fantastic information?"

"A large detective agency that has facilities for building files on that sort of thing."

"A collection of cheap blackmailers, no doubt."

"Not cheap, Doctor. Their base rate is a hundred dollars a day. It's run by a former colonel of military police. No nickel grabber, Doctor. He rates way up."

"I shall give him a piece of my mind," Dr. Varley said with cool distaste. "His name?" The sun had set in Dr. Varley's manner. It was getting to be a chilly evening.

"Confidential, Doctor. But don't give it a thought. All in the day's work. Name of Wade doesn't ring a bell at all, huh?"

"I believe you know your way out, Mr. Marlowe."

The door of a small elevator opened behind him. A nurse pushed a wheel chair out. The chair contained what was left of a broken old man. His eyes were closed, his skin had a bluish tinge. He was well wrapped up. The nurse wheeled him silently across the polished floor and out of a side door. Dr. Varley said softly:

"Old people. Sick old people. Lonely old people. Do not come back, Mr. Marlowe. You might annoy me. When annoyed

I can be rather unpleasant. I might even say *very* unpleasant."

"Okay by me, Doctor. Thanks for the time. Nice little dying-in home you got here."

"What was that?" He took a step towards me and peeled off the remaining layers of honey. The soft lines of his face set themselves into hard ridges.

"What's the matter?" I asked him. "I can see my man wouldn't be here. I wouldn't look for anybody here that wasn't too frail to fight back. Sick old people. Lonely old people. You said it yourself, Doctor. Unwanted old people, but with money and hungry heirs. Most of them probably judged incompetent by the court."

"I am getting annoyed," Dr. Varley said.

"Light food, light sedation, firm treatment. Put them out in the sun, put them back in the bed. Bar some of the windows in case there's a little spunk left. They love you, Doctor, one and all. They die holding your hand and seeing the sadness in your eyes. It's genuine too."

"It certainly is," he said in a low throaty growl. His hands were fists now. I ought to knock it off. But he had begun to nauseate me.

"Sure it is," I said. "Nobody likes to lose a good paying customer. Especially one you don't even have to please."

"Somebody has to do it," he said. "Somebody has to care for these sad old people, Mr. Marlowe."

"Somebody has to clean out cesspools. Come to think of it that's a clean honest job. So long, Dr. Varley. When my job makes me feel dirty I'll think of you. It will cheer me up no end."

"You filthy louse," Dr. Varley said between his wide white teeth. "I ought to break your back. Mine is an honorable branch of an honorable profession."

"Yeah." I looked at him wearily. "I know it is. Only it smells of death."

He didn't slug me, so I walked away from him and out. I looked back from the wide double doors. He hadn't moved. He had a job to do, putting back the layers of honey.

19

I DROVE BACK TO HOLLYWOOD feeling like a short length of chewed string. It was too early to eat, and too hot. I turned on the fan in my office. It didn't make the air any cooler, just a little more lively. Outside on the boulevard the traffic brawled endlessly. Inside my head thoughts stuck together like flies on flypaper.

Three shots, three misses. All I had been doing was seeing too many doctors.

I called the Wade home. A Mexican sort of accent answered and said that Mrs. Wade was not at home. I asked for Mr. Wade. The voice said Mr. Wade was not home either. I left my name. He seemed to catch it without any trouble. He said he was the houseboy.

I called George Peters at The Carne Organization. Maybe he knew some more doctors. He wasn't in. I left a phony name and a right telephone number. An hour crawled by like a sick cockroach. I was a grain of sand on the desert of oblivion. I was a two-gun cowpoke fresh out of bullets. Three shots, three misses. I hate it when they come in threes. You call on Mr. A. Nothing. You call on Mr. B. Nothing. You call on Mr. C. More of the same. A week later you find out it should have been Mr. D. Only you didn't know he existed and by the time you found out, the client had changed his mind and killed the investigation.

Drs. Vukanich and Varley were scratched. Varley had it too rich to fool with hooch cases. Vukanich was a punk, a high-wire performer who hit the main line in his own office. The help must know. At least some of the patients must know. All it took to finish him was one sorehead and one telephone call. Wade wouldn't have gone within blocks of him, drunk or sober. He might not be the brightest guy in the world — plenty of successful people are far from mental giants — but he couldn't be dumb enough to fool with Vukanich.

The only possible was Dr. Verringer. He had the space and the seclusion. He probably had the patience. But Sepulveda Canyon was a long way from Idle Valley. Where was the point of contact, how did they know each other, and if Verringer owned that property and had a buyer for it, he was halfway to being pretty well heeled. That gave me an idea. I called a man I knew in a title company to find out the status of the property. No answer. The title company had closed for the day.

I closed for the day too, and drove over to La Cienaga to Rudy's Bar-B-Q, gave my name to the master of ceremonies, and waited for the big moment on a bar stool with a whiskey sour in front of me and Marek Weber's waltz music in my ears. After a while I got in past the velvet rope and ate one of Rudy's "world-famous" Salisbury steaks, which is hamburger on a slab of burnt wood, ringed with browned-over mashed potato, supported by fried onion rings and one of those mixed up salads which men will eat with complete docility in restaurants, although they would probably start yelling if their wives tried to feed them one at home.

After that I drove home. As I opened the front door the phone started to ring.

"This is Eileen Wade, Mr. Marlowe. You wanted me to call you."

"Just to find out if anything had happened at your end. I have been seeing doctors all day and have made no friends."

"No, I'm sorry. He still hasn't showed up. I can't help being rather anxious. Then you have nothing to tell me, I suppose." Her voice was low and dispirited.

"It's a big crowded county, Mrs. Wade."

"It will be four whole days tonight."

"Sure, but that's not too long."

"For me it is." She was silent for a while. "I've been doing a lot of thinking, trying to remember something," she went on. "There must be something, some kind of hint or memory. Roger talks a great deal about all sorts of things."

"Does the name Verringer mean anything to you, Mrs. Wade?"

"No, I'm afraid not. Should it?"

"You mentioned that Mr. Wade was brought home one time by a tall young man dressed in a cowboy outfit. Would you recognize this tall young man if you saw him again, Mrs. Wade?"

"I suppose I might," she said hesitantly, "if the conditions were the same. But I only caught the merest glimpse of him. Was his name Verringer?"

"No, Mrs. Wade. Verringer is a heavily built, middle-aged man who runs, or more accurately has run, some kind of guest ranch in Sepulveda Canyon. He has a dressed up fancy boy named Earl working for him. And Verringer calls himself a doctor."

"That's wonderful," she said warmly. "Don't you feel that you're on the right track?"

"I could be wetter than a drowned kitten. I'll call you when I know. I just wanted to make sure Roger hadn't come home and that you hadn't recalled anything definite."

"I'm afraid I haven't been of much help to you," she said sadly. "Please call me at any time, no matter how late it is."

I said I would do that and we hung up. I took a gun and a three-cell flashlight with me this time. The gun was a tough little short-barreled .32 with flat-point cartridges. Dr. Verringer's boy Earl might have other toys than brass knuckles. If he had, he was plenty goofy enough to play with them.

I hit the highway again and drove as fast as I dared. It was a moonless night, and would be getting dark by the time I reached the entrance to Dr. Verringer's estate. Darkness was what I needed.

The gates were still locked with the chain and padlock. I drove on past and parked well off the highway. There was still some light under the trees but it wouldn't last long. I climbed the gate and went up the side of the hill looking for a hiking path. Far back in the valley I thought I heard a quail. A mourning dove exclaimed against the miseries of life. There wasn't any hiking path or I couldn't find one, so I went back to the road and walked along the edge of the gravel. The eucalyptus trees gave way to the oaks and I crossed the ridge and far off I could see a few lights. It took me three quarters of an hour to work up behind the swimming pool and the tennis courts to a spot where I could look down on the main building at the end of the road. It was lighted up and I could hear music coming from it. And farther off in the trees another cabin showed light. There were small dark cabins dotted all over the place in the trees. I went along a path now and suddenly a floodlight went on at the back of the main cabin. I stopped dead. The floodlight was not looking for anything. It pointed straight down and made a wide pool of light on the back porch and the ground beyond. Then a door banged open and Earl came out. Then I knew I was in the right place.

Earl was a cowpoke tonight, and it had been a cowpoke who brought Roger Wade home the time before. Earl was spinning a rope. He wore a dark shirt stitched with white and a polka-dot scarf knotted loosely around his neck. He wore a wide leather belt with a load of silver on it and a pair of tooled leather holsters with ivory-handled guns in them. He wore elegant riding pants and boots cross-stitched in white and glistening new. On the back of his head was a white sombrero and what looked like a woven silver cord hanging loosely down his shirt, the ends not fastened.

He stood there alone under the white floodlight, spinning his rope around him, stepping in and out of it, an actor without an audience, a tall, slender, handsome dude wrangler putting on a show all by himself and loving every minute of it. Two-Gun Earl, the Terror of Cochise County. He belonged on one of those guest ranches that are so all-fired horsy the telephone girl wears riding boots to work.

All at once he heard a sound, or pretended to. The rope dropped, his hands swept the two guns from the holsters, and the crook of his thumbs was over the hammers as they came level. He peered into the darkness. I didn't dare move. The damn guns could be loaded. But the floodlight had blinded him and he didn't see anything. He slipped his guns back in the holsters, picked up the rope and gathered it loosely, went back into the house. The light went off, and so did I.

I moved around through the trees and got close to the small lighted cabin on the slope. No sound came from it. I reached a screened window and looked in. The light came from a lamp on a night table beside a bed. A man lay flat on his back in the bed, his body relaxed, his arms in pajama sleeves outside the covers, his eyes wide open and staring at the ceiling. He looked big. His face was partly shadowed, but I could see that he was pale and that he needed a shave and had needed one for just about the right length of time. The spread fingers of his hands lay motionless on the outside of the bed. He looked as if he hadn't moved for hours.

I heard steps coming along the path at the far side of the cabin. A screen door creaked and then the solid shape of Dr. Verringer showed in the doorway. He was carrying what looked like a large glass of tomato juice. He switched on a standing lamp. His Hawaiian shirt gleamed yellowly. The man in the bed didn't even look at him.

Dr. Verringer put the glass down on the night table and pulled a chair close and sat down. He reached for one of the wrists and felt a pulse. "How are you feeling now, Mr. Wade?" His voice was kindly and solicitous.

The man on the bed didn't answer him or look at him. He went on staring at the ceiling.

"Come, come, Mr. Wade. Let us not be moody. Your pulse is only slightly faster than normal. You are weak, but otherwise — "

"Tejjy," the man on the bed said suddenly, "tell the man that if he knows how I am, the son of a bitch needn't bother to ask me." He had a nice clear voice, but the tone was bitter.

"Who is Tejjy?" Dr. Verringer asked patiently.

"My mouthpiece. She's up there in the corner."

Dr. Verringer looked up. "I see a small spider," he said. "Stop acting, Mr. Wade. It is not necessary with me."

"*Tegenaria domestica,* the common jumping spider, pal. I like spiders. They practically never wear Hawaiian shirts."

Dr. Verringer moistened his lips. "I have no time for playfulness, Mr. Wade."

"Nothing playful about Tejjy." Wade turned his head slowly, as if it weighed very heavy, and stared at Dr. Verringer contemptuously. "Tejjy is dead serious. She creeps up on you. When you're not looking she makes a quick silent hop. After a while she's near enough. She makes the last jump. You get sucked dry, Doctor. Very dry. Tejjy doesn't eat you. She just sucks the juice until there's nothing left but the skin. If you plan to wear that shirt much longer, Doctor, I'd say it couldn't happen too soon."

Dr. Verringer leaned back in the chair. "I need five thousand dollars," he said calmly. "How soon could that happen?"

"You got six hundred and fifty bucks," Wade said nastily. "As well as my loose change. How the hell much does it cost in this bordello?"

"Chicken feed," Dr. Verringer said. "I told you my rates had gone up."

"You didn't say they had moved to Mount Wilson."

"Don't fence with me, Wade," Dr. Verringer said curtly. "You are in no position to get funny. Also you have betrayed my confidence."

"I didn't know you had any."

Dr. Verringer tapped slowly on the arms of the chair. "You called me up in the middle of the night," he said. "You were in a desperate condition. You said you would kill yourself if I didn't come. I didn't want to do it and you know why. I have no license to practice medicine in this state. I am trying to get rid of this property without losing it all. I have Earl to look after and he was about due for a bad spell. I told you it would cost you a lot of money. You still insisted and I went. I want five thousand dollars."

"I was foul with strong drink," Wade said. "You can't hold a man to that kind of bargain. You're damn well paid already."

"Also," Dr. Verringer said slowly, "you mentioned my name to your wife. You told her I was coming for you."

Wade looked surprised. "I didn't do anything of the sort," he said. "I didn't even see her. She was asleep."

"Some other time then. A private detective has been here asking about you. He couldn't possibly have known where to come, unless he was told. I stalled him off, but he may come back. You have to go home, Mr. Wade. But first I want my five thousand dollars."

"You're not the brightest guy in the world, are you, Doc? If my wife knew where I was, why would she need a detective? She could have come herself — supposing she cared that much. She could have brought Candy, our houseboy. Candy would cut your Blue Boy into thin strips while Blue Boy was making up his mind what picture he was starring in today."

"You have a nasty tongue, Wade. And a nasty mind."

"I have a nasty five thousand bucks too, Doc. Try and get it."

"You will write me a check," Dr. Verringer said firmly. "Now, at once. Then you will get dressed and Earl will take you home."

"A check?" Wade was almost laughing. "Sure I'll give you a check. Fine. How will you cash it?"

Dr. Verringer smiled quietly. "You think you will stop payment, Mr. Wade. But you won't. I assure you that you won't."

"You fat crook!" Wade yelled at him.

Dr. Verringer shook his head. "In some things, yes. Not in all. I am a mixed character like most people. Earl will drive you home."

"Nix. That lad makes my skin crawl," Wade said.

Dr. Verringer stood up gently and reached over and patted the shoulder of the man on the bed. "To me Earl is quite harmless, Mr. Wade. I have ways of controlling him."

"Name one," a new voice said, and Earl came through the door in his Roy Rogers outfit. Dr. Verringer turned smiling.

"Keep that psycho away from me," Wade yelled, showing fear for the first time.

Earl put his hands on his ornamented belt. His face was deadpan. A light whistling noise came from between his teeth. He moved slowly into the room.

"You shouldn't have said that," Dr. Verringer said quickly, and turned towards Earl. "All right, Earl. I'll handle Mr. Wade myself. I'll help him get dressed while you bring the car up here as close to the cabin as possible. Mr. Wade is quite weak."

"And he's going to be a lot weaker," Earl said in a whistling kind of voice. "Out of my way, fatso."

"Now, Earl — " he reached out and grabbed the handsome young man's arm — "you don't want to go back to Camarillo, do you? One word from me and — "

That was as far as he got. Earl jerked his arm loose and his right hand came up with a flash of metal. The armored fist crashed against Dr. Verringer's jaw. He went down as if shot through the heart. The fall shook the cabin. I started running.

I reached the door and yanked it open. Earl spun around, leaning forward a little, staring at me without recognition. There was a bubbling sound behind his lips. He started for me fast.

I jerked the gun out and showed it to him. It meant nothing. Either his own guns were not loaded or he had forgotten all about them. The brass knuckles were all he needed. He kept coming.

I fired through the open window across the bed. The crash of the gun in the small room seemed much louder than it should have been. Earl stopped dead. His head slewed around and he looked at the hole in the window screen. He looked back at me. Slowly his face came alive and he grinned.

"Wha' happen?" he asked brightly.

"Get rid of the knucks," I said, watching his eyes.

He looked surprisingly down at his hand. He slipped the mauler off and threw it casually in the corner.

"Now the gun belt," I said. "Don't touch the guns, just the buckle."

"They're not loaded," he said smiling. "Hell, they're not even guns, just stage money."

"The belt. Hurry it."

He looked at the short-barreled .32. "That a real one? Oh sure it is. The screen. Yeah, the screen."

The man on the bed wasn't on the bed any more. He was behind Earl. He reached swiftly and pulled one of the bright guns loose. Earl didn't like this. His face showed it.

"Lay off him," I said angrily. "Put that back where you got it."

"He's right," Wade said. "They're cap guns." He backed away and put the shiny pistol on the table. "Christ, I'm as weak as a broken arm."

"Take the belt off," I said for the third time. When you start something with a type like Earl you have to finish it. Keep it simple and don't change your mind.

He did it at last, quite amiably. Then, holding the belt, he walked over to the table and got his other gun and put it in the holster and put the belt right back on again. I let him do it. It wasn't until then that he saw Dr. Verringer crumpled on the floor against the wall. He made a sound of concern, went quickly across the room into the bathroom, and came back with a glass jug of water. He dumped the water on Dr. Verringer's head. Dr. Verringer sputtered and rolled over. Then he groaned. Then he clapped a hand to his jaw. Then he started to get up. Earl helped him.

"Sorry, Doc. I must have just let fly without seeing who it was."

"It's all right, nothing broken," Verringer said, waving him away.

"Get the car up here, Earl. And don't forget the key for the padlock down below."

"Car up here, sure. Right away. Key for the padlock. I got it. Right away, Doc."

He went out of the room whistling.

Wade was sitting on the side of the bed, looking shaky. "You the dick he was talking about?" he asked me. "How did you find me?"

"Just asking around from people who know about these things," I said. "If you want to get home, you might get clothes on."

Dr. Verringer was leaning against the wall, massaging his jaw. "I'll help him," he said thickly. "All I do is help people and all they do is kick me in the teeth."

"I know just how you feel," I said.

I went out and left them to work at it.

20

THE CAR WAS CLOSE BY when they came out, but Earl was gone. He had stopped the car, cut the lights, and walked back towards the big cabin without saying anything to me. He was still whistling, groping for some half-remembered tune.

Wade climbed carefully into the back seat and I got in beside him. Dr. Verringer drove. If his jaw hurt badly and his head ached, he didn't show it or mention it. We went over the ridge and down to the end of the graveled drive. Earl had already been down and unlocked the gate and pulled it open. I told Verringer where my car was and he pulled up close to it. Wade got into it and sat silent, staring at nothing. Verringer got out and went round beside him. He spoke to Wade gently.

"About my five thousand dollars, Mr. Wade. The check you promised me."

Wade slid down and rested his head on the back of the seat. "I'll think about it."

"You promised it. I need it."

"Duress, the word is, Verringer, a threat of harm. I have protection now."

"I fed and washed you," Verringer persisted. "I came in the night. I protected you, I cured you — for the time being, at least."

"Not five grand worth," Wade sneered. "You got plenty out of my pockets."

Verringer wouldn't let go. "I have a promise of a connection in Cuba, Mr. Wade. You are a rich man. You should help others in their need. I have Earl to look after. To avail myself of this opportunity I need the money. I will pay it back in full."

I began to squirm. I wanted to smoke, but I was afraid it would make Wade sick.

"Like hell you'd pay it back," Wade said wearily. "You won't live long enough. One of these nights Blue Boy will kill you in your sleep."

Verringer stepped back. I couldn't see his expression, but his voice hardened. "There are more unpleasant ways to die," he said. "I think yours will be one of them."

He walked back to his car and got into it. He drove in through his gates and was gone. I backed and turned and headed towards the city. After a mile or two Wade muttered: "Why should I give that fat slob five thousand dollars?"

"No reason at all."

"Then why do I feel like a bastard for not giving it to him?"

"No reason at all."

He turned his head just enough to look at me. "He handled me like a baby," Wade said. "He hardly left me alone for fear Earl would come in and beat me up. He took every dime I had in my pockets."

"You probably told him to."

"You on his side?"

"Skip it," I said. "This is just a job to me."

Silence for a couple of miles more. We went past the fringe of one of the outlying suburbs. Wade spoke again.

"Maybe I'll give it to him. He's broke. The property is foreclosed. He won't get a dime out of it. All on account of that psycho. Why does he do it?"

"I wouldn't know."

"I'm a writer," Wade said. "I'm supposed to understand what makes people tick. I don't understand one damn thing about anybody."

I turned over the pass and after a climb the lights of the valley spread out endlessly in front of us. We dipped down to the highway north and west that goes to Ventura. After a while we passed through Encino. I stopped for a light and looked up towards the lights high on the hill where the big houses were. In one of them the Lennoxes had lived. We went on.

"The turn-off is pretty close now," Wade said. "Or do you know it?"

"I know it."

"By the way, you haven't told me your name."

"Philip Marlowe."

"Nice name." His voice changed sharply, saying: "Wait a minute. You the guy that was mixed up with Lennox?"

"Yeah."

He was staring at me in the darkness of the car. We passed the last buildings on the main drag of Encino.

"I knew her," Wade said. "A little. Him I never saw. Queer business, that. The law boys gave you the rough edge, didn't they?"

I didn't answer him.

"Maybe you don't like to talk about it," he said.

"Could be. Why would it interest you?"

"Hell, I'm a writer. It must be quite a story."

"Take tonight off. You must be feeling pretty weak."

"Okay, Marlowe. Okay. You don't like me. I get it."

We reached the turn-off and I swung the car into it and towards the low hills and the gap between them that was Idle Valley.

"I don't either like you or dislike you," I said. "I don't know you. Your wife asked me to find you and bring you home. When I deliver you at your house I'm through. Why she picked on me I couldn't say. Like I said, it's just a job."

We turned the flank of a hill and hit a wider, more firmly paved road. He said his house was a mile farther on, on the right side. He told me the number, which I already knew. For a guy in his shape he was a pretty persistent talker.

"How much is she paying you?" he asked.

"We didn't discuss it."

"Whatever it is, it's not enough. I owe you a lot of thanks. You did a great job, chum. I wasn't worth the trouble."

"That's just the way you feel tonight."

He laughed. "You know something, Marlowe? I could get to like you. You're a bit of a bastard — like me."

We reached the house. It was a two-story over-all shingle house with a small pillared portico and a long lawn from the entrance to a thick row of shrubs inside the white fence. There was a light in the portico. I pulled into the driveway and stopped close to the garage.

"Can you make it without help?"

"Of course." He got out of the car. "Aren't you coming in for a drink or something?"

"Not tonight, thanks; I'll wait here until you're in the house."

He stood there breathing hard. "Okay," he said shortly.

He turned and walked carefully along a flagged path to the front door. He held on to a white pillar for a moment, then tried the door. It opened, he went in. The door stayed open and light washed across the green lawn. There was a sudden flutter of voices. I started backing from the driveway, following the back-up light. Somebody called out.

I looked and saw Eileen Wade standing in the open doorway. I kept going and she started to run. So I had to stop. I cut the lights and got out of the car. When she came up I said:

"I ought to have called you, but I was afraid to leave him."

"Of course. Did you have a lot of trouble?"

"Well — a little more than ringing a doorbell."

"Please come in the house and tell me all about it."

"He should be in bed. By tomorrow he'll be as good as new."

"Candy will put him to bed," she said. "He won't drink tonight, if that's what you are thinking of."

"Never occurred to me. Goodnight, Mrs. Wade."

"You must be tired. Don't you want a drink yourself?"

I lit a cigarette. It seemed like a couple of weeks since I had tasted tobacco. I drank in the smoke.

"May I have just one puff?"

She came close to me and I handed her the cigarette. She drew on it and coughed. She handed it back laughing. "Strictly an amateur, as you see."

"So you knew Sylvia Lennox," I said. "Was that why you wanted to hire me?"

"I knew who?" She sounded puzzled.

"Sylvia Lennox." I had the cigarette back now. I was eating it pretty fast.

"Oh," she said, startled. "That girl that was — murdered. No, I didn't know her personally. I knew who she was. Didn't I tell you that?"

"Sorry, I'd forgotten just what you did tell me."

She was still standing there quietly, close to me, slim and tall in a white dress of some sort. The light from the open door touched the fringe of her hair and made it glow softly.

"Why did you ask me if that had anything to do with my wanting to, as you put it, hire you?" When I didn't answer at once she added, "Did Roger tell you he knew her?"

"He said something about the case when I told him my name. He didn't connect me with it immediately, then he did. He talked so damn much I don't remember half of what he said."

"I see. I must go in, Mr. Marlowe, and see if my husband needs anything. And if you won't come in — "

"I'll leave this with you," I said.

I took hold of her and pulled her towards me and tilted her head back. I kissed her hard on the lips. She didn't fight me and she didn't respond. She pulled herself away quietly and stood there looking at me.

"You shouldn't have done that," she said. "That was wrong. You're too nice a person."

"Sure. Very wrong," I agreed. "But I've been such a nice faithful well-behaved gun dog all day long, I got charmed into one of the silliest ventures I ever tackled, and damned if it didn't turn out just as though somebody had written a script for it. You know something? I believe you knew where he was all along — or at least knew the name of Dr. Verringer. You just wanted to get me involved with him, tangled up with him so I'd feel a sense of responsibility to look after him. Or am I crazy?"

"Of course you're crazy," she said coldly. "That is the most outrageous nonsense I ever listened to." She started to turn away.

"Wait a minute," I said. "That kiss won't leave a scar. You just think it will. And don't tell me I'm too nice a person. I'd rather be a heel."

She looked back. "Why?"

"If I hadn't been a nice guy to Terry Lennox, he would still be alive."

"Yes?" she said quietly. "How can you be so sure? Goodnight, Mr. Marlowe. And thank you so very much for almost everything."

She walked back along the edge of the grass. I watched her into the house. The door closed. The porch light went off. I waved at nothing and drove away.

21

NEXT MORNING I GOT UP LATE on account of the big fee I had earned the night before. I drank an extra cup of coffee, smoked an extra cigarette, ate an extra slice of Canadian bacon, and for the three hundredth time I swore I would never again use an electric razor. That made the day normal. I hit the office about ten, picked up some odds and ends of mail, slit the envelopes and let the stuff lie on the desk. I opened the windows wide to let out the smell of dust and dinginess that collected in the night and hung in the still air, in the corners of the room, in the slats of the venetian blinds. A dead moth was spread-eagled on a corner of the desk. On the window sill a bee with tattered wings was crawling along the woodwork, buzzing in a tired remote sort of way, as if she knew it wasn't any use, she was finished, she had flown too many missions and would never get back to the hive again.

I knew it was going to be one of those crazy days. Everyone has them. Days when nobody rolls in but the loose wheels, the dingoes who park their brains with their gum, the squirrels who can't find their nuts, the mechanics who always have a gear wheel left over.

The first was a big blond roughneck named Kuissenen or something Finnish like that. He jammed his massive bottom in the customer's chair and planted two wide horny hands on my desk and said he was a power-shovel operator, that he lived in Culver City, and the goddam woman who lived next door to him was trying to poison his dog. Every morning before he let the dog out for a run in the back yard he had to search the place from fence to fence for meatballs thrown over the potato vine from next door. He'd found nine of them so far and they were loaded with a greenish powder he knew was an arsenic weed killer.

"How much to watch out and catch her at it?" He stared at me as unblinkingly as a fish in a tank.

"Why not do it yourself?"

"I got to work for a living, mister. I'm losing four twentyfive an hour just coming up here to ask."

"Try the police?"

"I try the police. They might get around to it some time next year. Right now they're busy sucking up to MGM."

"S.P.C.A.? The Tailwaggers?"

"What's them?"

I told him about the Tailwaggers. He was far from interested. He knew about the S.P.C.A. The S.P.C.A. could take a running jump. They couldn't see nothing smaller than a horse.

"It says on the door you're an investigator," he said truculently. "Okay, go the hell out and investigate. Fifty bucks if you catch her."

"Sorry," I said. "I'm tied up. Spending a couple of weeks hiding in a gopher hole in your back yard would be out of my line anyway — even for fifty bucks."

He stood up glowering. "Big shot," he said. "Don't need the dough, huh? Can't be bothered saving the life of a itty-bitty dog. Nuts to you, big shot."

"I've got troubles too, Mr. Kuissenen."

"I'll twist her goddam neck if I catch her," he said, and I didn't doubt he could have done it. He could have twisted the hind leg off of an elephant. "That's what makes it I want somebody else. Just because the little tike barks when a car goes by the house.

Sour-faced old bitch."

He started for the door. "Are you sure it's the dog she's trying to poison?" I asked his back.

"Sure I'm sure." He was halfway to the door before the nickel dropped. He swung around fast then. "Say that again, buster."

I just shook my head. I didn't want to fight him. He might hit me on the head with my desk. He snorted and went out, almost taking the door with him.

The next cookie in the dish was a woman, not old, not young, not clean, not too dirty, obviously poor, shabby, querulous and stupid. The girl she roomed with — in her set any woman who works out is a girl — was taking money out of her purse. A dollar here, four bits there, but it added up. She figured she was out close to twenty dollars in all. She couldn't afford it. She couldn't afford to move either. She couldn't afford a detective. She thought I ought to be willing to throw a scare into the roommate just on the telephone like, not mentioning any names.

It took her twenty minutes or more to tell me this. She kneaded her bag incessantly while telling it.

"Anybody you know could do that," I said.

"Yeah, but you bein' a dick and all."

"I don't have a license to threaten people I know nothing about."

"I'm goin' to tell her I been in to see you. I don't have to say it's her. Just that you're workin' on it."

"I wouldn't if I were you. If you mention my name she may call me up. If she does that, I'll tell her the facts."

She stood up and slammed her shabby bag against her stomach. "You're no gentleman," she said shrilly.

"Where does it say I have to be?"

She went out mumbling.

After lunch I had Mr. Simpson W. Edelweiss. He had a card to prove it. He was manager of a sewing machine agency. He was a small tired-looking man about forty-eight to fifty, small hands and feet, wearing a brown suit with sleeves too long, and a stiff white collar behind a purple tie with black diamonds on it. He sat on the edge of the chair without fidgeting and looked at me out of sad black eyes. His hair was black too and thick and rough without a sign of gray in it that I could see. He had a clipped mustache with a reddish tone. He could have passed for thirty-five if you didn't look at the backs of his hands.

"Call me Simp," he said. "Everybody else does. I got it coming. I'm a Jewish man married to a Gentile woman, twenty-four years of age, beautiful. She run away a couple of times before."

He got out a photo of her and showed it to me. She might have been beautiful to him. To me she was a big sloppy-looking cow of a woman with a weak mouth.

"What's your trouble, Mr. Edelweiss? I don't do divorce business." I tried to give him back the photo. He waved it away. "The client is always mister to me," I added. "Until he has told me a few dozen lies anyway."

He smiled. "Lies I got no use for. It's not a divorce matter. I just want Mabel back again. But she don't come back until I find her. Maybe it's a kind of game with her."

He told me about her, patiently, without rancor. She drank, she played around, she wasn't a very good wife by his standards, but he could have been brought up too strict. She had a heart as big as a house, he said, and he loved her. He didn't kid himself he was any dreamboat, just a steady worker bringing home the pay check. They had a joint bank account. She had drawn it all out, but he was prepared for that. He had a pretty good idea who she had lit out with, and if he was right the man would clean her out and leave her stranded.

"Name of Kerrigan," he said. "Monroe Kerrigan. I don't aim to knock the Catholics. There is plenty of bad Jews too. This Kerrigan is a barber when he works. I ain't knocking barbers either. But a lot of them are drifters and horse players. Not real steady."

"Won't you hear from her when she is cleaned out?"

"She gets awful ashamed. She might hurt herself."

"It's a Missing Persons job, Mr. Edelweiss. You should go down and make a report."

"No. I'm not knocking the police, but I don't want it that way. Mabel would be humiliated."

The world seemed to be full of people Mr. Edelweiss was not knocking. He put some money on the desk.

"Two hundred dollars," he said. "Down payment. I'd rather do it my way."

"It will happen again," I said.

"Sure." He shrugged and spread his hands gently. "But twenty-four years old and me almost fifty. How could it be different? She'll settle down after a while. Trouble is, no kids. She can't have kids. A Jew likes to have a family. So Mabel knows that. She's humiliated."

"You're a very forgiving man, Mr. Edelweiss."

"Well I ain't a Christian," he said. "And I'm not knocking Christians, you understand. But with me it's real. I don't just say it. I do it. Oh, I almost forgot the most important."

He got out a picture postcard and pushed it across the desk after the money. "From Honolulu she sends it. Money goes fast in Honolulu. One of my uncles had a jewelry business there. Retired now. Lives in Seattle."

I picked the photo up again. "I'll have to farm this one out," I told him. "And I'll have to have this copied."

"I could hear you saying that, Mr. Marlowe, before I got here. So I come prepared." He took out an envelope and it contained five more prints. "I got Kerrigan too, but only a snapshot." He went into another pocket and gave me another envelope. I looked at Kerrigan. He had a smooth dishonest face that did not surprise me. Three copies of Kerrigan.

Mr. Simpson W. Edelweiss gave me another card which had on it his name, his residence, his telephone number. He said he hoped it would not cost too much but that he would respond at once to any demand for further funds and he hoped to hear from me.

"Two hundred ought to pretty near do it if she's still in Honolulu," I said. "What I need now is a detailed physical description of both parties that I can put into a telegram. Height, weight, age, coloring, any noticeable scars or other identifying marks, what clothes she was wearing and had with her, and how much money was in the account she cleaned out. If you've been through this before, Mr. Edelweiss, you will know what I want."

"I got a peculiar feeling about this Kerrigan. Uneasy."

I spent another half hour milking him and writing things down. Then he stood up quietly, shook hands quietly, bowed and left the office quietly.

"Tell Mabel everything is fine," he said as he went out.

It turned out to be routine. I sent a wire to an agency in Honolulu and followed it with an airmail containing the photos and whatever information I had left out of the wire. They found her working as a chambermaid's helper in a luxury hotel, scrubbing bathtubs and bathroom floors and so on. Kerrigan had done just what Mr. Edelweiss expected, cleaned her out while she was asleep and skipped, leaving her stuck with the hotel bill. She pawned a ring which Kerrigan couldn't have taken without violence, and got enough out of it to pay the hotel but not enough to buy her way home. So Edelweiss hopped a plane and went after her.

He was too good for her. I sent him a bill for twenty dollars and the cost of a long telegram. The Honolulu agency grabbed the two hundred. With a portrait of Madison in my office safe I could afford to be underpriced.

So passed a day in the life of a P.I. Not exactly a typical day but not totally untypical either. What makes a man stay with it nobody knows. You don't get rich, you don't often have much fun. Sometimes you get beaten up or shot at or tossed into the jailhouse. Once in a long while you get dead. Every other month you decide to give it up and find some sensible occupation while you can still walk without shaking your head. Then the door buzzer rings and you open the inner door to the waiting room and there stands a new face with a new problem, a new load of grief, and a small piece of money.

"Come in, Mr. Thingummy. What can I do for you?"

There must be a reason.

Three days later in the shank of the afternoon Eileen Wade called me up, and asked me to come around to the house for a drink the next evening. They were having a few friends in for cocktails. Roger would like to see me and thank me adequately. And would I please send in a bill?

"You don't owe me anything, Mrs. Wade. What little I did I got paid for."

"I must have looked very silly acting Victorian about it," she said. "A kiss doesn't seem to mean much nowadays. You will come, won't you?"

"I guess so. Against my better judgment."

"Roger is quite well again. He's working."

"Good."

"You sound very solemn today. I guess you take life pretty seriously."

"Now and then. Why?"

She laughed very gently and said goodbye and hung up. I sat there for a while taking life seriously. Then I tried to think of something funny so that I could have a great big laugh. Neither way worked, so I got Terry Lennox's letter of farewell out of the safe and reread it. It reminded me that I had never gone to Victor's for that gimlet he asked me to drink for him. It was just about the right time of day for the bar to be quiet, the way he would have liked it himself, if he had been around to go with me. I thought of him with a vague sadness and with a puckering bitterness too. When I got to Victor's I almost kept going. Almost, but not quite. I had too much of his money. He had made a fool of me but he had paid well for the privilege.

22

IT WAS SO QUIET IN VICTOR'S that you almost heard the temperature drop as you came in at the door. On a bar stool a woman in a black tailormade, which couldn't at that time of year have been anything but some synthetic fabric like orlon, was sitting alone with a pale greenish-colored drink in front of her and smoking a cigarette in a long jade holder. She had that fine-drawn intense look that is sometimes neurotic, sometimes sex-hungry, and sometimes just the result of drastic dieting.

I sat down two stools away and the barkeep nodded to me, but didn't smile.

"A gimlet," I said. "No bitters."

He put the little napkin in front of me and kept looking at me. "You know something," he said in a pleased voice. "I heard you and your friend talking one night and I got me in a bottle of that Rose's Lime Juice. Then you didn't come back any more and I only opened it tonight."

"My friend left town," I said. "A double if it's all right with you. And thanks for taking the trouble."

He went away. The woman in black gave me a quick glance, then looked down into her glass. "So few people drink them around here," she said so quietly that I didn't realize at first that she was speaking to me. Then she looked my way again. She had very large dark eyes. She had the reddest fingernails I had ever seen. But she didn't look like a pickup and there was no trace of come-on in her voice. "Gimlets I mean."

"A fellow taught me to like them," I said.

"He must be English."

"Why?"

"The lime juice. It's as English as boiled fish with that awful anchovy sauce that looks as if the cook had bled into it. That's how they got called limeys. The English — not the fish."

"I thought it was more a tropical drink, hot weather stuff. Malaya or some place like that."

"You may be right." She turned away again.

The bartender set the drink in front of me. With the lime juice it has a sort of pale greenish yellowish misty look. I tasted it. It was both sweet and sharp at the same time. The woman in black watched me. Then she lifted her own glass towards me. We both drank. Then I knew hers was the same drink.

The next move was routine, so I didn't make it. I just sat there. "He wasn't English," I said after a moment. "I guess maybe he had been there during the war. We used to come in here once in a while, early like now. Before the mob started boiling."

"It's a pleasant hour," she said. "In a bar almost the only pleasant hour." She emptied her glass. "Perhaps I knew your friend," she said. "What was his name?"

I didn't answer her right away. I lit a cigarette and watched her tap the stub of hers out of the jade holder and fit another in its place. I reached across with a lighter. "Lennox," I said.

She thanked me for the light and gave me a brief searching glance. Then she nodded. "Yes, I knew him very well. Perhaps a little too well."

The barkeep drifted over and glanced at my glass. "A couple more of the same," I said. "In a booth."

I got down off the stool and stood waiting. She might or might not blow me down. I didn't particularly care. Once in a while in this much too sex-conscious country a man and a woman can meet and talk without dragging bedrooms into it. This could be it, or she could just think I was on the make. If so, the hell with her.

She hesitated, but not for long. She gathered up a pair of black gloves and a black suede bag with a gold frame and clasp and walked across into a corner booth and sat down without a word. I sat down across the small table.

"My name is Marlowe."

"Mine is Linda Loring," she said calmly. "A bit of a sentimentalist, aren't you, Mr. Marlowe?"

"Because I came in here to drink a gimlet? How about yourself?"

"I might have a taste for them."

"So might I. But it would be a little too much coincidence."

She smiled at me vaguely. She had emerald earrings and an emerald lapel pin. They looked like real stones because of the way they were cut — flat with beveled edges. And even in the dim light of a bar they had an inner glow.

"So you're the man," she said.

The bar waiter brought the drinks over and set them down. When he went away I said: "I'm a fellow who knew Terry Lennox, liked him, and had an occasional drink with him. It was kind of a side deal, an accidental friendship. I never went to his home or knew his wife. I saw her once in a parking lot."

"There was a little more to it than that, wasn't there?"

She reached for her glass. She had an emerald ring set in a nest of diamonds. Beside it a thin platinum band said she was married. I put her in the second half of the thirties, early in the second half.

"Maybe," I said. "The guy bothered me. He still does. How about you?"

She leaned on an elbow and looked up at me without any particular expression. "I said I knew him rather too well. Too well to think it mattered much what happened to him. He had a rich wife who gave him all the luxuries. All she asked in return was to be let alone."

"Seems reasonable," I said.

"Don't be sarcastic, Mr. Marlowe. Some women are like that. They can't help it. It wasn't as if he didn't know in the beginning. If he had to get proud, the door was open. He didn't have to kill her."

"I agree with you."

She straightened up and looked hard at me. Her lip curled. "So he ran away and, if what I hear is true, you helped him. I suppose you feel proud about that."

"Not me," I said. "I just did it for the money."

"That is not amusing, Mr. Marlowe. Frankly I don't know why I sit here drinking with you."

"That's easily changed, Mrs. Loring." I reached for my glass and dropped the contents down the hatch. "I thought perhaps you could tell me something about Terry that I didn't know. I'm not interested in speculating why Terry Lennox beat his wife's face to a bloody sponge."

"That's a pretty brutal way to put it," she said angrily.

"You don't like the words? Neither do I. And I wouldn't be here drinking a gimlet if I believed he did anything of the sort."

She stared. After a moment she said slowly: "He killed himself and left a full confession. What more do you want?"

"He had a gun," I said. "In Mexico that might be enough excuse for some jittery cop to pour lead into him. Plenty of American police have done their killings the same way — some of them through doors that didn't open fast enough to suit them. As for the confession, I haven't seen it."

"No doubt the Mexican police faked it," she said tartly.

"They wouldn't know how, not in a little place like Otatoclán. No, the confession is probably real enough, but it doesn't prove he killed his wife. Not to me anyway. All it proves to me is that he didn't see any way out. In a spot like that a certain sort of man — you can call him weak or soft or sentimental if it amuses you — might decide to save some other people from a lot of very painful publicity."

"That's fantastic," she said. "A man doesn't kill himself or deliberately get himself killed to save a little scandal. Sylvia was already dead. As for her sister and her father — they could take care of themselves very efficiently. People with enough money, Mr. Marlowe, can always protect themselves."

"Okay, I'm wrong about the motive. Maybe I'm wrong all down the line. A minute ago you were mad at me. You want me to leave now — so you can drink your gimlet?"

Suddenly she smiled. "I'm sorry. I'm beginning to think you are sincere. What I thought then was that you were trying to justify yourself, far more than Terry. I don't think you are, somehow."

"I'm not. I did something foolish and I got the works for it. Up to a point anyway. I don't deny that his confession saved me a lot worse. If they had brought him back and tried him, I guess they would have hung one on me too. The least it would have cost me would have been far more money than I could afford."

"Not to mention your license," she said dryly.

"Maybe. There was a time when any cop with a hangover could get me busted. It's a little different now. You get a hearing before a commission of the state licensing authority. Those people are not too crazy about the city police."

She tasted her drink and said slowly: "All things considered, don't you think it was best the way it was? No trial, no sensational headlines, no mud-slinging just to sell newspapers without the slightest regard for truth or fairplay or for the feelings of innocent people."

"Didn't I just say so? And you said it was fantastic."

She leaned back and put her head against the upper curve of the padding on the back of the booth. "Fantastic that Terry Lennox should have killed himself just to achieve that. Not fantastic that it was better for all parties that there should be no trial."

"I need another drink," I said, and waved at the waiter. "I feel an icy breath on the back of my neck. Could you by any chance be related to the Potter family, Mrs. Loring?"

"Sylvia Lennox was my sister," she said simply. "I thought you would know."

The waiter drifted over and I gave him an urgent message. Mrs. Loring shook her head and said she didn't want anything more.

When the waiter took off I said:

"With the hush old man Potter — excuse me, Mr. Harlan Potter — put on this affair, I would be lucky to know for sure that Terry's wife even had a sister."

"Surely you exaggerate. My father is hardly that powerful, Mr. Marlowe — and certainly not that ruthless. I'll admit he does have very old-fashioned ideas about his personal privacy. He never gives interviews even to his own newspapers. He is never photographed, he never makes speeches, he travels mostly by car or in his own plane with his own crew. But he is quite human for all that. He liked Terry. He said Terry was a gentleman twenty-four hours a day instead of for the fifteen minutes between the time the guests arrive and the time they feel their first cocktail."

"He slipped a little at the end. Terry did."

The waiter trotted up with my third gimlet. I tried it for flavor and then sat there with a finger on the edge of the round base of the glass.

"Terry's death was quite a blow to him, Mr. Marlowe. And you're getting sarcastic again. Please don't. Father knew it would all look far too neat to some people. He would much rather Terry had just disappeared. If Terry had asked him for help, I think he would have given it."

"Oh no, Mrs. Loring. His own daughter had been murdered."

She made an irritable motion and eyed me coldly.

"This is going to sound pretty blunt, I'm afraid. Father had written my sister off long ago. When they met he barely spoke to her. If he expressed himself, which he hasn't and won't, I feel sure he would be just as doubtful about Terry as you are. But once Terry was dead, what did it matter? They could have been killed in a plane crash or a fire or a highway accident. If she had to die, it was the best possible time for her to die. In another ten years she would have been a sex-ridden hag like some of these frightful women you see at Hollywood parties, or used to a few years back. The dregs of the international set."

All of a sudden I got mad, for no good reason. I stood up and looked over the booth. The next one was still empty. In the one beyond a guy was reading a paper all by himself, quietly. I sat down with a bump, pushed my glass out of the way, and leaned across the table. I had sense enough to keep my voice down.

"For hell's sake, Mrs. Loring, what are you trying to sell me? That Harlan Potter is such a sweet lovely character he wouldn't dream of using his influence on a political D.A. to drop the blanket on a murder investigation so that the murder was never really investigated at all? That he had doubts about Terry's guilt but didn't let anyone lift a finger to find out who was really the killer? That he didn't use the political power of his newspapers and his bank account and the nine hundred guys who would trip over their chins trying to guess what he wanted done before he knew himself? That he didn't arrange it so that a tame lawyer and nobody else, nobody from the D.A.'s office or the city cops, went down to Mexico to make sure Terry actually had put a slug in his head instead of being knocked off by some Indian with a hot gun just for kicks? Your old man is worth a hundred million bucks, Mrs. Loring. I wouldn't know just how he got it, but I know damn well he didn't get it without building himself a pretty far-reaching organization. He's no softie. He's a hard tough man. You've got to be in these days to make that kind of money. And you do business with some funny people. You may not meet them or shake hands with them, but they are there on the fringe doing business with you."

"You're a fool," she said angrily. "I've had enough of you."

"Oh sure. I don't make the kind of music you like to hear. Let me tell you something. Terry talked to your old man the night Sylvia died. What about? What did your old man say to him? 'Just run on down to Mexico and shoot yourself, old boy. Let's keep this in the family. I know my daughter is a tramp and that any one of a dozen drunken bastards might have blown his top and pushed her pretty face down her throat for her. But that's incidental, old boy. The guy will be sorry when he sobers up. You've had it soft and now is the time you pay back. What we want is to keep the fair Potter name as sweet as mountain lilac. She married you because she needed a front. She needs it worse than ever now she's dead. And you're it. If you can get lost and stay lost, fine. But if you get found, you check out. See you in the morgue.'"

"Do you really think," the woman in black asked with dry ice in her voice, "that my father talks like that?"

I leaned back and laughed unpleasantly. "We could polish up the dialogue a little if that helps."

She gathered her stuff together and slid along the seat. "I'd like to give you a word of warning," she said slowly and very carefully, "a very simple word of warning. If you think my father is that kind of man and if you go around broadcasting the kind of thoughts you have just expressed to me, your career in this city in your business or in any business is apt to be extremely short and terminated very suddenly."

"Perfect, Mrs. Loring. Perfect. I get it from the law, I get it from the hoodlum element, I get it from the carriage trade. The words change, but the meaning is the same. Lay off. I came in here to drink a gimlet because a man asked me to. Now look at me. I'm practically in the boneyard."

She stood up and nodded briefly. "Three gimlets. Doubles. Perhaps you're drunk."

I dropped too much money on the table and stood up beside her. "You had one and a half, Mrs. Loring. Why even that much? Did a man ask you too, or was it all your own idea? Your own tongue got a little loose."

"Who knows, Mr. Marlowe? Who knows? Who really knows anything? There's a man over there at the bar watching us. Would it be anyone you know?"

I looked around, surprised that she had noticed. A lean dark character sat on the end stool nearest the door.

"His name is Chick Agostino," I said. "He's a gun toter for a gambling boy named Menendez. Let's knock him down and jump on him."

"You certainly are drunk," she said quickly and started to walk. I went after her. The man on the stool swung around and looked to his front. When I came abreast I stepped up behind him and reached in under both his arms quickly. Maybe I *was* a little drunk.

He swung around angrily and slid off the stool. "Watch it, kiddo," he snarled. Out of the corner of my eye I saw that she had stopped just inside the door to glance back.

"No guns, Mr. Agostino? How reckless of you. It's almost dark. What if you should run into a tough midget?"

"Scram!" he said savagely.

"Aw, you stole that line from the *New Yorker*."

His mouth worked but he didn't move. I left him and followed Mrs. Loring out through the door into the space under the awning. A gray-haired colored chauffeur stood there talking to the kid from the parking lot. He touched his cap and went off and came back with a flossy Cadillac limousine. He opened the door and Mrs. Loring got in. He shut the door as though he was putting down the lid of a jewel box. He went around the car to the driver's seat.

She ran the window down and looked out at me, half smiling.

"Goodnight, Mr. Marlowe. It's been nice — or has it?"

"We had quite a fight."

"You mean you had — and mostly with yourself."

"It usually is. Goodnight, Mrs. Loring. You don't live around here, do you?"

"Not exactly. I live in Idle Valley. At the far end of the lake. My husband is a doctor."

"Would you happen to know any people named Wade?"

She frowned. "Yes, I know the Wades. Why?"

"Why do I ask? They're the only people in Idle Valley that I know."

"I see. Well, goodnight again, Mr. Marlowe."

She leaned back in the seat and the Cadillac purred politely and slid away into the traffic along the Strip.

Turning I almost bumped into Chick Agostino.

"Who's the doll?" he sneered. "And next time you crack wise, be missing."

"Nobody that would want to know you," I said.

"Okay, bright boy. I got the license number. Mendy likes to know little things like that."

The door of a car banged open and a man about seven feet high and four feet wide jumped out of it, took one look at Agostino, then one long stride, and grabbed him by the throat with one hand.

"How many times I gotta tell you cheap hoods not to hang around where I eat?" he roared.

He shook Agostino and hurled him across the sidewalk against the wall. Chick crumpled up coughing.

"Next time," the enormous man yelled, "I sure as hell put the blast on you, and believe me, boy, you'll be holding a gun when they pick you up."

Chick shook his head and said nothing. The big man gave me a raking glance and grinned. "Nice night," he said, and strolled into Victor's.

I watched Chick straighten himself out and regain some of his composure. "Who's your buddy?" I asked him.

"Big Willie Magoon," he said thickly. "A vice squad bimbo. He thinks he's tough."

"You mean he isn't sure?" I asked him politely.

He looked at me emptily and walked away. I got my car out of the lot and drove home. In Hollywood anything can happen, anything at all.

23

A LOW-SWUNG JAGUAR swept around the hill in front of me and slowed down so as not to bathe me in the granite dust from the half mile of neglected paving at the entrance to Idle Valley. It seemed they wanted it left that way to discourage the Sunday drivers spoiled by drifting along on superhighways. I caught a glimpse of a bright scarf and a pair of sun goggles. A hand waved at me casually, neighbor to neighbor. Then the dust slid across the road and added itself to the white film already well spread over the scrub and the sunbaked grass. Then I was around the outcrop and the paving started up in proper shape and everything was smooth and cared for. Live oaks clustered towards the road, as if they were curious to see who went by, and sparrows with rosy heads hopped about pecking at things only a sparrow would think worth pecking at.

Then there were a few cottonwoods but no eucalyptus. Then a thick growth of Carolina poplars screening a white house. Then a girl walking a horse along the shoulder of the road. She had levis on and a loud shirt and she was chewing on a twig. The horse looked hot but not lathered and the girl was crooning to him gently.

THE LONG GOODBYE 561

Beyond a fieldstone wall a gardener was guiding a power lawn-mower over a huge undulating lawn that ended far back in the portico of a Williamsburg Colonial mansion, the large de luxe size. Somewhere someone was playing left-handed exercises on a grand piano.

Then all this wheeled away and the glisten of the lake showed hot and bright and I began to watch numbers on gateposts. I had seen the Wades' house only once and in the dark. It wasn't as big as it had looked by night. The driveway was full of cars, so I parked on the side of the road and walked in. A Mexican butler in a white coat opened the door for me. He was a slender neat good-looking Mexican and his coat fitted him elegantly and he looked like a Mexican who was getting fifty a week and not killing himself with hard work.

He said: "Buenas tardes, señor," and grinned as if he had put one over. "Su nombre de Usted, por favor?"

"Marlowe," I said, "and who are you trying to upstage, Candy? We talked on the phone, remember?"

He grinned and I went in. It was the same old cocktail party, everybody talking too loud, nobody listening, everybody hanging on for dear life to a mug of the juice, eyes very bright, cheeks flushed or pale and sweaty according to the amount of alcohol consumed and the capacity of the individual to handle it. Then Eileen Wade materialized beside me in a pale blue something which did her no harm. She had a glass in her hand but it didn't look as if it was more than a prop.

"I'm so glad you could come," she said gravely. "Roger wants to see you in his study. He hates cocktail parties. He's working."

"With this racket going on?"

"It never seems to bother him. Candy will get you a drink — or if you'd rather go to the bar —"

"I'll do that," I said. "Sorry about the other night."

She smiled. "I think you apologized already. It was nothing."

"The hell it was nothing."

She kept the smile long enough to nod and turn and walk away. I spotted the bar over in the corner by some very large french windows. It was one of those things you push around. I was halfway across the room, trying not to bump anybody, when a voice said:

"Oh, Mr. Marlowe."

I turned and saw Mrs. Loring on a couch beside a prissy-looking man in rimless cheaters with a smear on his chin that might have been a goatee. She had a drink in her hand and looked bored. He sat still with his arms folded and scowled.

I went over there. She smiled at me and gave me her hand. "This is my husband, Dr. Loring. Mr. Philip Marlowe, Edward."

The guy with the goatee gave me a brief look and a still briefer nod. He didn't move otherwise. He seemed to be saving his energy for better things.

"Edward is very tired," Linda Loring said. "Edward is always very tired."

"Doctors often are," I said. "Can I get you a drink, Mrs. Loring? Or you, Doctor?"

"She's had enough," the man said without looking at either of us. "I don't drink. The more I see of people who do, the more glad I am that I don't."

"Come back, little Sheba," Mrs. Loring said dreamily.

He swung around and did a take. I got away from there and made it to the bar. In the company of her husband Linda Loring seemed like a different person. There was an edge to her voice and a sneer in her expression which she hadn't used on me even when she was angry.

Candy was behind the bar. He asked me what I would drink.

"Nothing right now, thanks. Mr. Wade wants to see me."

"Es muy occupado, señor. Very busy."

I didn't think I was going to like Candy. When I just looked at him he added: "But I go see. De pronto, señor."

He threaded his way delicately through the mob and was back in no time at all. "Okay, chum, let's go," he said cheerfully.

I followed him across the room the long way of the house. He opened a door, I went through, he shut it behind me, and a lot of the noise was dimmed. It was a corner room, big and cool and quiet, with french windows and roses outside and an airconditioner set in a window to one side. I could see the lake, and I could see Wade lying flat out on a long blond leather couch. A big bleached wood desk had a typewriter on it and there was a pile of yellow paper beside the typewriter.

"Good of you to come, Marlowe," he said lazily. "Park yourself. Did you have a drink or two?"

"Not yet." I sat down and looked at him. He still looked a bit pale and pinched. "How's the work going?"

"Fine, except that I get tired too quick. Pity a four-day drunk is so painful to get over. I often do my best work after one. In my racket it's so easy to tighten up and get all stiff and wooden. Then the stuff is no good. When it's good it comes easy. Anything you have read or heard to the contrary is a lot of mishmash."

"Depends who the writer is, maybe," I said. "It didn't come easy to Flaubert, and his stuff is good."

"Okay," Wade said, sitting up. "So you have read Flaubert, so that makes you an intellectual, a critic, a savant of the literary world." He rubbed his forehead. "I'm on the wagon and I hate it. I hate everybody with a drink in his hand. I've got to go out there and smile at those creeps. Every damn one of them knows I'm an alcoholic. So they wonder what I'm running away from. Some Freudian bastard has made that a commonplace. Every ten-year-old kid knows it by now. If I had a ten-year-old kid, which God forbid, the brat would be asking me, 'What are you running away from when you get drunk, Daddy?'"

"The way I got it, all this was rather recent," I said.

"It's got worse, but I was always a hard man with a bottle. When you're young and in hard condition you can absorb a lot of punishment. When you are pushing forty you don't snap back the same way."

I leaned back and lit a cigarette. "What did you want to see me about?"

"What do *you* think I'm running away from, Marlowe?"

"No idea. I don't have enough information. Besides, everybody is running away from something."

"Not everybody gets drunk. What are *you* running away from? Your youth or a guilty conscience or the knowledge that you're a small time operator in a small time business?"

"I get it," I said. "You need somebody to insult. Fire away, chum. When it begins to hurt I'll let you know."

He grinned and rumpled his thick curly hair. He speared his chest with a forefinger. "You're looking right at a small time operator in a small time business, Marlowe. All writers are punks and I am one of the punkest. I've written twelve best sellers, and if I ever finish that stack of magoozlum on the desk there I may possibly have written thirteen. And not a damn one of them worth the powder to blow it to hell. I have a lovely home in a highly restricted residential neighborhood that belongs to a highly restricted multimillionaire. I have a lovely wife who loves me and a lovely publisher who loves me and I love me the best of all. I'm an egotistical son of a bitch, a literary prostitute or pimp — choose your own word — and an all-round heel. So what can you do for me?"

"Well, what?"

"Why don't you get sore?"

"Nothing to get sore about. I'm just listening to you hate yourself. It's boring but it doesn't hurt my feelings."

He laughed roughly. "I like you," he said. "Let's have a drink."

"Not in here, chum. Not you and me alone. I don't care to watch you take the first one. Nobody can stop you and I don't guess anyone would try. But I don't have to help."

He stood up. "We don't have to drink in here. Let's go outside and glance at a choice selection of the sort of people you get to know when you make enough lousy money to live where they live."

"Look," I said. "Shove it. Knock it off. They're no different from anybody else."

"Yeah," he said tightly, "but they ought to be. If they're not, what use are they? They're the class of the county and they're no better than a bunch of truckdrivers full of cheap whiskey. Not as good."

"Knock it off," I said again. "You want to get boiled, get boiled. But don't take it out on a crowd that can get boiled without having to lie up with Dr. Verringer or get loose in the head and throw their wives down the stairs."

"Yeah," he said, and he was suddenly calm and thoughtful. "You pass the test, chum. How about coming to live here for a while? You could do me a lot of good just being here."

"I don't see how."

"But I do. Just by being here. Would a thousand a month interest you? I'm dangerous when I'm drunk. I don't want to be dangerous and I don't want to be drunk."

"I couldn't stop you."

"Try it for three months. I'd finish the damn book and then go far off for a while. Lie up some place in the Swiss mountains and get clean."

"The book, huh? Do you have to have the money?"

"No. I just have to finish something I started. If I don't I'm through. I'm asking you as a friend. You did more than that for Lennox."

I stood up and walked over close to him and gave him a hard stare. "I got Lennox killed, mister. I got him killed."

"Phooey. Don't go soft on me, Marlowe." He put the edge of his hand against his throat. "I'm up to here in the soft babies."

"Soft?" I asked. "Or just kind?"

He stepped back and stumbled against the edge of the couch, but didn't lose his balance.

"The hell with you," he said smoothly. "No deal. I don't blame you, of course. There's something I want to know, that I have to know. You don't know what it is and I'm not sure I know myself. All I'm positive of is that there *is* something, and I have to know it."

"About who? Your wife?"

He moved his lips one over the other. "I think it's about me," he said. "Let's go get that drink."

He walked to the door and threw it open and we went out.

If he had been trying to make me uncomfortable, he had done a first class job.

24

When he opened the door the buzz from the living room exploded into our faces. It seemed louder than before, if possible. About two drinks louder. Wade said hello here and there and people seemed glad to see him. But by that time they would have been glad to see Pittsburgh Phil with his custom-built icepick. Life was just one great big vaudeville show.

On the way to the bar we came face to face with Dr. Loring and his wife. The doctor stood up and stepped forward to face Wade. He had a look on his face that was almost sick with hatred.

"Nice to see you, Doctor," Wade said amiably. "Hi, Linda. Where have you been keeping yourself lately? No, I guess that was a stupid question. I — "

"Mr. Wade," Loring said in a voice that had a tremor to it, "I have something to say to you. Something very simple, and I hope very conclusive. Stay away from my wife."

Wade looked at him curiously. "Doctor, you're tired. And you don't have a drink. Let me get you one."

"I don't drink, Mr. Wade. As you very well know. I am here for one purpose and I have expressed that purpose."

"Well, I guess I get your point," Wade said, still amiable. "And since you are a guest in my house, I have nothing to say except that I think you are a little off the beam."

There had been a drop in the talk near by. The boys and girls were all ears. Big production. Dr. Loring took a pair of gloves out of his pocket, straightened them, took hold of one by the finger end, and swung it hard against Wade's face.

Wade didn't bat an eye. "Pistols and coffee at dawn?" he asked quietly.

I looked at Linda Loring. She was flushed with anger. She stood up slowly and faced the doctor.

"Dear God, what a ham you are, darling. Stop acting like a damn fool, will you, darling? Or would you rather stick around until somebody slaps *your* face?"

Loring swung around to her and raised the gloves. Wade stepped in front of him. "Take it easy, Doc. Around here we only hit our wives in private."

"If you are speaking for yourself, I am well aware of it," Loring sneered. "And I don't need lessons in manners from you."

"I only take promising pupils," Wade said. "Sorry you have to leave so soon." He raised his voice. "Candy! Que el Doctor Loring salga de aqui en el acto!" He swung back to Loring. "In case you don't know Spanish, Doctor, that means the door is over there." He pointed.

Loring stared at him without moving. "I have warned you, Mr. Wade," he said icily. "And a number of people have heard me. I shall not warn you again."

"Don't," Wade said curtly. "But if you do, make it on neutral territory. Gives me a little more freedom of action. Sorry, Linda. But you married him." He rubbed his cheek gently where the heavy end of the glove had hit him. Linda Loring was smiling bitterly. She shrugged.

"We are leaving," Loring said. "Come, Linda."

She sat down again and reached for her glass. She gave her husband a glance of quiet contempt. "You are," she said. "You have a number of calls to make, remember."

"You are leaving with me," he said furiously.

She turned her back on him. He reached suddenly and took hold of her arm. Wade took him by the shoulder and spun him around.

"Take it easy, Doc. You can't win them all."

"Take your hand off me!"

"Sure, just relax," Wade said. "I have a good idea, Doctor. Why don't you see a good doctor?"

Somebody laughed loudly. Loring tensed like an animal all set to spring. Wade sensed it and neatly turned his back and moved away. Which left Dr. Loring holding the bag. If he went after Wade, he would look sillier than he looked now. There was nothing for him to do but leave, and he did it. He marched quickly across the room staring straight in front of him to where Candy was holding the door open. He went out. Candy shut the door, wooden-faced, and went back to the bar. I went over there and asked for some Scotch. I didn't see where Wade went. He just disappeared. I didn't see Eileen either. I turned my back on the room and let them sizzle while I drank my Scotch.

A small girl with mud-colored hair and a band around her forehead popped up beside me and put a glass on the bar and bleated. Candy nodded and made her another drink.

The small girl turned to me. "Are you interested in Communism?" she asked me. She was glassy-eyed and she was running a small red tongue along her lips as if looking for a crumb of chocolate. "I think everyone ought to be," she went on. "But when you ask any of the men here they just want to paw you."

I nodded and looked over my glass at her snub nose and sun-coarsened skin.

"Not that I mind too much if it's done nicely," she told me, reaching for the fresh drink. She showed me her molars while she inhaled half of it.

"Don't rely on me," I said.

"What's your name?"

"Marlowe."

"With an 'e' or not?"

"With."

"Ah, Marlowe," she intoned. "Such a sad beautiful name." She put her glass down damn nearly empty and closed her eyes and threw her head back and her arms out, almost hitting me in the eye. Her voice throbbed with emotion, saying:

> *"Was this the face that launch'd a thousand ships*
> *And burnt the topless towers of Ilium?*
> *Sweet Helen, make me immortal with a kiss."*

She opened her eyes, grabbed her glass, and winked at me. "You were pretty good in there, chum. Been writing any poetry lately?"

"Not very much."

"You can kiss me if you like," she said coyly.

A guy in a shantung jacket and an open neck shirt came up behind her and grinned at me over the top of her head. He had short red hair and a face like a collapsed lung. He was as ugly a guy as I ever saw. He patted the top of the little girl's head.

"Come on kitten. Time to go home."

She rounded on him furiously. "You mean you got to water those goddamned tuberous begonias again?" she yelled.

"Aw listen, kitten——"

"Take your hands off me, you goddamned rapist," she screamed, and threw the rest of her drink in his face. The rest wasn't more than a teaspoonful and two lumps of ice.

"For Chrissake, baby, I'm your husband," he yelled back, grabbing for a handkerchief and mopping his face. "Get it? Your husband."

She sobbed violently and threw herself into his arms. I stepped around them and got out of there. Every cocktail party is the same, even the dialogue.

The house was leaking guests out into the evening air now. Voices were fading, cars were starting, goodbyes were bouncing around like rubber balls. I went to the french windows and out onto a flagged terrace. The ground sloped towards the lake which was as motionless as a sleeping cat. There was a short wooden pier down there with a rowboat tied to it by a white painter. Towards the far shore, which wasn't very far, a black waterhen was doing lazy curves, like a skater. They didn't seem to cause as much as a shallow ripple.

I stretched out on a padded aluminum chaise and lit a pipe and smoked peacefully and wondered what the hell I was doing there. Roger Wade seemed to have enough control to handle himself if he really wanted to. He had done all right with Loring. I wouldn't have been too surprised if he had hung one on Loring's sharp little chin. He would have been out of line by the rules, but Loring was much farther out of line.

If the rules mean anything at all any more, they mean that you don't pick a roomful of people as the spot to threaten a man and hit him across the face with a glove when your wife is standing right beside you and you are practically accusing her of a little double time. For a man still shaky from a hard bout with the hard stuff Wade had done all right. He had done more than all right. Of course I hadn't seen him drunk. I didn't know what he would be like drunk. I didn't even know that he was an alcoholic. There's a big difference. A man who drinks too much on occasion is still the same man as he was sober. An alcoholic, a real alcoholic, is not the same man at all. You can't predict anything about him for sure except that he will be someone you never met before.

Light steps sounded behind me and Eileen Wade came across the terrace and sat down beside me on the edge of a chaise.

"Well, what did you think?" she asked quietly.

"About the gentleman with the loose gloves?"

"Oh no." She frowned. Then she laughed. "I hate people who make stagy scenes like that. Not that he isn't a fine doctor. He has played that scene with half the men in the valley. Linda Loring is no tramp. She doesn't look like one, talk like one, or behave like one. I don't know what makes Dr. Loring behave as if she was."

"Maybe he's a reformed drunk," I said. "A lot of them grow pretty puritanical."

"It's possible," she said, and looked towards the lake. "This is a very peaceful place. One would think a writer would be happy here — if a writer is ever happy anywhere." She turned to look at me. "So you won't be persuaded to do what Roger asked."

"There's no point in it, Mrs. Wade. Nothing I could do. I've said all this before. I couldn't be sure of being around at the right time. I'd have to be around *all* the time. That's impossible, even if I had nothing else to do. If he went wild, for example, it would happen in a flash. And I haven't seen any indications that he does get wild. He seems pretty solid to me."

She looked down at her hands. "If he could finish his book, I think things would be much better."

"I can't help him do that."

She looked up and put her hands on the edge of the chaise beside her. She leaned forward a little. "You can if he thinks you can. That's the whole point. Is it that you would find it distasteful to be a guest in our house and be paid for it?"

"He needs a psychiatrist, Mrs. Wade. If you know one that isn't a quack."

She looked startled. "A psychiatrist? Why?"

I knocked the ashes out of my pipe and sat holding it, waiting for the bowl to get cooler before I put it away.

"You want an amateur opinion, here it is. He thinks he has a secret buried in his mind and he can't get at it. It may be a guilty secret about himself, it may be about someone else. He thinks that's what makes him drink, because he can't get at this thing. He probably thinks that whatever happened, happened while he was drunk and he ought to find it wherever people go when they're drunk — really bad drunk, the way he gets. That's a job for a psychiatrist. So far, so good. If that is wrong, then he gets drunk because he wants to or can't help it, and the idea about the secret is just his excuse. He can't write his book, or anyway can't finish it. Because he gets drunk. That is, the assumption seems to be that he can't finish his book because he knocks himself out by drinking. It could be the other way around."

"Oh no," she said. "No. Roger has a great deal of talent. I feel quite sure that his best work is still to come."

"I told you it was an amateur opinion. You said the other morning that he might have fallen out of love with his wife. That's something else that could go the other way around."

She looked towards the house, then turned so that she had her back to it. I looked the same way. Wade was standing inside the doors, looking out at us. As I watched he moved behind the bar and reached for a bottle.

"There's no use interfering," she said quickly. "I never do. Never. I suppose you're right, Mr. Marlowe. There just isn't anything to do but let him work it out of his system."

The pipe was cool now and I put it away. "Since we're groping around in the back of the drawer, how about that other way around?"

"I love my husband," she said simply. "Not as a young girl loves, perhaps. But I love him. A woman is only a young girl once. The man I loved then is dead. He died in the war. His name, strangely enough, had the same initials as yours. It doesn't matter now — except that sometimes I can't quite believe that he is dead. His body was never found. But that happened to many men."

She gave me a long searching look. "Sometimes — not often, of course — when I go into a quiet cocktail lounge or the lobby of a good hotel at a dead hour, or along the deck of a liner early in the morning or very late at night, I think I may see him waiting for me in some shadowy corner." She paused and dropped her eyes. "It's very silly. I'm ashamed of it. We were very much in love — the wild, mysterious, improbable kind of love that never comes but once."

She stopped talking and sat there half in a trance looking out over the lake. I looked back at the house again. Wade was standing just inside the open french windows with a glass in his hand. I looked back at Eileen. For her I wasn't there any more. I got up and went into the house. Wade stood there with the drink and the drink looked pretty heavy. And his eyes looked wrong.

"How you making out with my wife, Marlowe?" It was said with a twist of the mouth.

"No passes, if you mean it that way."

"That's exactly the way I mean it. You got to kiss her the other night. Probably fancy yourself as a fast worker, but you're wasting your time, bud. Even if you had the right kind of polish."

I tried to move around him but he blocked me with a solid shoulder. "Don't hurry away, old man. We like you around. We get so few private dicks in our house."

"I'm the one too many," I said.

He hoisted the glass and drank from it. When he lowered it he leered at me.

"You ought to give yourself a little more time to build resistance," I told him. "Empty words, huh?"

"Okay, coach. Some little character builder, aren't you? You ought to have more sense than to try educating a drunk. Drunks don't educate, my friend. They disintegrate. And part of the process is a lot of fun." He drank from the glass again, leaving it nearly empty. "And part of it is damned awful. But if I may quote the scintillating words of the good Dr. Loring, a bastardly bastard with a little black bag, stay away from my wife, Marlowe. Sure you go for her. They all do. You'd like to sleep with her. They all would. You'd like to share her dreams and sniff the rose of her memories. Maybe I would too. But there is nothing to share, chum — nothing, nothing, nothing. You're all alone in the dark."

He finished his drink and turned the glass upside down.

"Empty like that, Marlowe. Nothing there at all. I'm the guy that knows."

He put the glass on the edge of the bar and walked stiffly to the foot of the stairs. He made about a dozen steps up, holding on to the rail, and stopped and leaned against it. He looked down at me with a sour grin.

"Forgive the corny sarcasm, Marlowe. You're a nice guy. I wouldn't want anything to happen to you."

"Anything like what?"

"Perhaps she didn't get around yet to that haunting magic of her first love, the guy that went missing in Norway. You wouldn't want to be missing, would you, chum? You're my own special private eye. You find me when I'm lost in the savage splendor of Sepulveda Canyon." He moved the palm of his hand in a circular motion on the polished wood banister. "It would hurt me to the quick if you got lost yourself. Like that character who hitched up with the limeys. He got so lost a man sometimes wonders if he ever existed. You figure she could have maybe just invented him to have a toy to play with?"

"How would I know?"

He looked down at me. There were deep lines between his eyes now and his mouth was twisted with bitterness.

"How would anybody know? Maybe she don't know herself. Baby's tired. Baby been playing too long with broken toys. Baby wants to go bye-bye."

He went on up the stairs.

I stood there until Candy came in and started tidying up around the bar, putting glasses on a tray, examining bottles to see what was left, paying no attention to me. Or so I thought. Then he said:

"Señor. One good drink left. Pity to waste him." He held up a bottle.

"You drink it."

"Gracias, señor, no me gusta. Un vaso de cerveza, no más. A glass of beer is my limit."

"Wise man."

"One lush in the house is enough," he said, staring at me. "I speak good English, not?"

"Sure, fine."

"But I think Spanish. Sometimes I think with a knife. The boss is my guy. He don't need any help, hombre. I take care of him, see."

"A great job you're doing, punk."

"Hijo de la flauta," he said between his white teeth. He picked up a loaded tray and swung it up on the edge of his shoulder and the flat of his hand, bus boy style.

I walked to the door and let myself out, wondering how an expression meaning 'son of a flute' had come to be an insult in Spanish. I didn't wonder very long. I had too many other things to wonder about. Something more than alcohol was the matter with the Wade family. Alcohol was no more than a disguised reaction.

Later that night, between nine-thirty and ten, I called the Wades' number. After eight rings I hung up, but I had only just taken my hand off the instrument when it started to ring me. It was Eileen Wade.

"Someone just rang here," she said. "I had a sort of hunch it might be you. I was just getting ready to take a shower."

"It was me, but it wasn't important, Mrs. Wade. He seemed a little woolly-headed' when I left — Roger did. I guess maybe I feel a little responsibility for him by now."

"He's quite all right," she said. "Fast asleep in bed. I think Dr. Loring upset him more than he showed. No doubt he talked a lot of nonsense to you."

"He said he was tired and wanted to go to bed. Pretty sensible, I thought."

"If that is all he said, yes. Well, goodnight and thank you for calling, Mr. Marlowe."

"I didn't say it was all he said. I said he said it."

There was a pause, then: "Everyone gets fantastic ideas once in a while. Don't take Roger too seriously, Mr. Marlowe. After all, his imagination is rather highly developed. Naturally it would be. He shouldn't have had anything to drink so soon after the last time. Please try to forget all about it. I suppose he was rude to you among other things."

"He wasn't rude to me. He made quite a lot of sense. Your husband is a guy who can take a long hard look at himself and see what is there. It's not a very common gift. Most people go through life using up half their energy trying to protect a dignity they never had. Goodnight, Mrs. Wade."

She hung up and I set out the chess board. I filled a pipe, paraded the chessmen and inspected them for French shaves and loose buttons, and played a championship tournament game between Gortchakoff and Meninkin, seventy-two moves to a draw, a prize specimen of the irresistible force meeting the immovable object, a battle without armor, a war without blood, and as elaborate a waste of human intelligence as you could find anywhere outside an advertising agency.

25

NOTHING HAPPENED FOR A WEEK except that I went about my business which just then didn't happen to be very much business. One morning George Peters of The Carne Organization called me up and told me he had happened to be down Sepulveda Canyon way and had looked in on Dr. Verringer's place just out of curiosity. But Dr. Verringer was no longer there. Half a dozen teams of surveyors were mapping the tract for a subdivision. Those he spoke to had never even heard of Dr. Verringer.

"The poor sucker got closed out on a trust deed," Peters said. "I checked. They gave him a grand for a quitclaim just to save time and expense, and now somebody is going to make a million bucks clear, out of cutting the place up for residential property. That's the difference between crime and business. For business you gotta have capital. Sometimes I think it's the only difference."

"A properly cynical remark," I said, "but big time crime takes capital too."

"And where does it come from, chum? Not from guys that hold up liquor stores. So long. See you soon."

It was ten minutes to eleven on a Thursday night when Wade called me up. His voice was thick, almost gurgling, but I recognized it somehow. And I could hear short hard rapid breathing over the telephone.

"I'm in bad shape, Marlowe. Very bad. I'm slipping my anchor. Could you make it out here in a hurry?"

"Sure — but let me talk to Mrs. Wade a minute."

He didn't answer. There was a crashing sound, then a dead silence, then in a short while a kind of banging around. I yelled something into the phone without getting any answer. Time passed. Finally the light click of the receiver being replaced and the buzz of an open line.

In five minutes I was on the way. I made it in slightly over half an hour and I still don't know how. I went over the pass on wings and hit Ventura Boulevard with the light against me and made a left turn anyhow and dodged between trucks and generally made a damn fool of myself. I went through Encino at close to sixty with a spotlight on the outer edge of the parked cars so that it would freeze anyone with a notion to step out suddenly. I had the kind of luck you only get when you don't care. No cops, no sirens, no red flashers. Just visions of what might be happening in the Wade residence and not very pleasant visions. She was alone in the house with a drunken maniac, she was lying at the bottom of the stairs with her neck broken, she was behind a locked door and somebody was howling outside and trying to break it in, she was running down a moonlit road barefoot and a big buck Negro with a meat cleaver was chasing her.

It wasn't like that at all. When I swung the Olds into their drive-way lights were on all over the house and she was standing in the open doorway with a cigarette in her mouth. I got out and walked over the flagstones to her. She had slacks on and a shirt with an open collar. She looked at me calmly. If there was any excitement around there I had brought it with me.

The first thing I said was as loony as the rest of my behavior. "I thought you didn't smoke."

"What? No, I don't usually." She took the cigarette out and looked at it and dropped it and stepped on it. "Once in a long while. He called Dr. Verringer."

It was a remote placid voice, a voice heard at night over water. Completely relaxed.

"He couldn't," I said. "Dr. Verringer doesn't live there any more. He called me."

"Oh really? I just heard him telephoning and asking someone to come in a hurry. I thought it must be Dr. Verringer."

"Where is he now?"

"He fell down," she said. "He must have tipped the chair too far back. He's done it before. He cut his head on something. There's a little blood, not much."

"Well, that's fine," I said. "We wouldn't want a whole lot of blood. Where is he now, I asked you."

She looked at me solemnly. Then she pointed. "Out there some-where. By the edge of the road or in the bushes along the fence."

I leaned forward and peered at her. "Chrissake, didn't you look?"

I decided by this time that she was in shock. Then I looked back across the lawn. I didn't see anything but there was heavy shadow near the fence.

"No, I didn't look," she said quite calmly. "You find him. I've had all of it I can take. I've had more than I can take. You find him."

She turned and walked back into the house, leaving the door open. She didn't walk very far. About a yard inside the door she just crumpled to the floor and lay there. I scooped her up and spread her out on one of the two big davenports that faced each other across a long blond cocktail table. I felt her pulse. It didn't seem very weak or unsteady. Her eyes were closed and the lids were blue. I left her there and went back out.

He was there all right, just as she had said. He was lying on his side in the shadow of the hibiscus. He had a fast thumping pulse and his breathing was unnatural. Something on the back of his head was sticky. I spoke to him and shook him a little. I slapped his face a couple of times. He mumbled but didn't come to. I dragged him up into a sitting position and dragged one of his arms over my shoulder and heaved him up with my back turned to him and grabbed for a leg. I lost. He was as heavy as a block of cement. We both sat down on the grass and I took a short breather and tried again. Finally I got him hoisted into a fireman's lift position and plowed across the lawn in the direction of the open front door. It seemed about the same distance as a round trip to Siam. The two steps of the porch were ten feet high. I staggered over to the couch and went down on my knees and rolled him off. When I straightened up again my spine felt as if it had cracked in at least three places.

Eileen Wade wasn't there any more. I had the room to myself. I was too bushed at the moment to care where anybody was. I sat down and looked at him and waited for some breath. Then I looked at his head. It was smeared with blood. His hair was sticky with it. It didn't look very bad but you never know with a head wound.

Then Eileen Wade was standing beside me, quietly looking down at him with that same remote expression.

"I'm sorry I fainted," she said. "I don't know why."

"I guess we'd better call a doctor."

"I telephoned Dr. Loring. He is my doctor, you know. He didn't want to come."

"Try somebody else then."

"Oh he's coming," she said. "He didn't want to. But he's coming as soon as he can manage."

"Where's Candy?"

"This is his day off. Thursday. The cook and Candy have Thursdays off. It's the usual thing around here. Can you get him up to bed?"

"Not without help. Better get a rug or blanket. It's a warm night, but cases like this get pneumonia very easily."

She said she would get a rug. I thought it was damn nice of her. But I wasn't thinking very intelligently. I was too bushed from carrying him.

We spread a steamer rug over him and in fifteen minutes Dr. Loring came, complete with starched collar and rimless cheaters and the expression of a man who has been asked to clean up after the dog got sick.

He examined Wade's head. "A superficial cut and bruise," he said. "No chance of concussion. I should say his breath would indicate his condition rather obviously."

He reached for his hat. He picked up his bag.

"Keep him warm," he said. "You might bathe his head gently and get rid of the blood. He'll sleep it off."

"I can't get him upstairs alone, Doctor," I said.

"Then leave him where he is." He looked at me without interest. "Goodnight, Mrs. Wade. As you know I don't treat alcoholics. Even if I did, your husband would not be one of my patients. I'm sure you understand that."

"Nobody's asking you to treat him," I said. "I'm asking for some help to get him into his bedroom so that I can undress him."

"And just who are you?" Dr. Loring asked me freezingly.

"My name's Marlowe. I was here a week ago. Your wife introduced me."

"Interesting," he said. "In what connection do you know my wife?"

"What the hell does that matter? All I want is — "

"I'm not interested in what you want," he cut in on me. He turned to Eileen, nodded briefly, and started out. I got between him and the door and put my back to it.

"Just a minute, Doc. Must be a long time since you glanced at that little piece of prose called the Hippocratic Oath. This man called me on the phone and I live some way off. He sounded bad and I broke every traffic law in the state getting over here. I found him lying out on the ground and I carried him in here and believe me he isn't any bunch of feathers. The houseboy is away and there's nobody here to help me upstairs with Wade. How does it look to you?"

"Get out of my way," he said between his teeth. "Or I shall call the sheriff's substation and have them send over a deputy. As a professional man — "

"As a professional man you're a handful of flea dirt," I said, and moved out of his way.

He turned red — slowly but distinctly. He choked on his own bile. Then he opened the door and went out. He shut it carefully. As he pulled it shut he looked in at me. It was as nasty a look as I ever got and on as nasty a face as I ever saw.

When I turned away from the door Eileen was smiling.

"What's funny?" I snarled.

"You. You don't care what you say to people, do you? Don't you know who Dr. Loring is?"

"Yeah — and I know what he is."

She glanced at her wrist watch. "Candy ought to be home by now," she said. "I'll go see. He has a room behind the garage."

She went out through an archway and I sat down and looked at Wade. The great big writer man went on snoring. His face was sweaty but I left the rug over him. In a minute or two Eileen came back and she had Candy with her.

26

THE MEX HAD a black and white checked sport shirt, heavily pleated black slacks without a belt, two-tone black and white buckskin shoes, spotlessly clean. His thick black hair was brushed straight back and shining with some kind of hair oil or cream.

"Señor," he said, and sketched a brief sarcastic bow.

"Help Mr. Marlowe carry my husband upstairs, Candy. He fell and hurt himself a little. I'm sorry to trouble you."

"De nada, señora," Candy said smiling.

"I think I'll say goodnight," she said to me. "I'm tired out. Candy will get you anything you want."

She went slowly up the stairs. Candy and I watched her.

"Some doll," he said confidentially. "You stay the night?"

"Hardly."

"Es lástima. She is very lonely, that one."

"Get that gleam out of your eye, kid. Let's put this to bed."

He looked sadly at Wade snoring on the couch. "Pobrecito," he murmured as if he meant it. "Borracho como una cuba."

"He may be drunk as a sow but he sure ain't little," I said. "You take the feet."

We carried him and even for two he was as heavy as a lead coffin. At the top of the stairs we went along an open balcony past a closed door. Candy pointed to it with his chin.

"La señora," he whispered. "You knock very light maybe she let you in."

I didn't say anything because I needed him. We went on with the carcass and turned in at another door and dumped him on the bed. Then I took hold of Candy's arm high up near the shoulder where dug-in fingers can hurt. I made mine hurt him. He winced a little and then his face set hard.

"What's your name, cholo?"

"Take your hand off me," he snapped. "And don't call me a cholo. I'm no wetback. My name is Juan García de Soto y Sotomayor. I am Chileno."

"Okay, Don Juan. Just don't get out of line around here. Keep your nose and mouth clean when you talk about the people you work for."

He jerked loose and stepped back, his black eyes hot with anger. His hand slipped inside his shirt and came out with a long thin knife. He balanced it by the point on the heel of his hand, hardly even glancing at it. Then he dropped the hand and caught the handle of the knife while it hung in the air. It was done very fast and without any apparent effort. His hand went up to shoulder height, then snapped forward and the knife sailed through the air and hung quivering in the wood of the window frame.

"Cuidado, señor!" he said with a sharp sneer. "And keep your paws to yourself. Nobody fools with me."

He walked lithely across the room and plucked the knife out of the wood, tossed it in the air, spun on his toes and caught it behind him. With a snap it disappeared under his shirt.

"Neat," I said, "but just a little on the gaudy side."

He strolled up to me smiling derisively.

"And it might get you a broken elbow," I said. "Like this."

I took hold of his right wrist, jerked him off balance, swung to one side and a little behind him, and brought my bent forearm up under the back of his elbow joint. I bore down on it, using my forearm as a fulcrum.

"One hard jerk," I said, "and your elbow joint cracks. A crack is enough. You'd be out of commission as a knife thrower for several months. Make the jerk a little harder and you'd be through permanently. Take Mr. Wade's shoes off."

I let go of him and he grinned at me. "Good trick," he said. "I will remember."

He turned to Wade and reached for one of his shoes, then stopped. There was a smear of blood on the pillow.

"Who cut the boss?"

"Not me, chum. He fell and cut his head on something. It's only a shallow cut. The doctor has been here."

Candy let his breath out slowly. "You see him fall?"

"Before I got here. You like this guy, don't you?"

He didn't answer me. He took the shoes off. We got Wade undressed little by little and Candy dug out a pair of green and silver pajamas. We got Wade into those and got him inside the bed and well covered up. He was still sweaty and still snoring. Candy looked down at him sadly, shaking his sleek head from side to side, slowly.

"Somebody's got to take care of him," he said. "I go change my clothes."

"Get some sleep. I'll take care of him. I can call you if I need you."

He faced me. "You better take care of him good," he said in a quiet voice. "Very good."

He went out of the room. I went into the bathroom and got a wet washcloth and a heavy towel. I turned Wade over a little and spread the towel on the pillow and washed the blood off his head gently so as not to start the bleeding again. Then I could see a sharp shallow cut about two inches long. It was nothing. Dr. Loring had been right that much. It wouldn't have hurt to stitch it but it probably was not really necessary. I found a pair of scissors and cut the hair away enough so that I could put on a strip of adhesive. Then I turned him on his back and washed his face. I guess that was a mistake.

He opened his eyes. They were vague and unfocused at first, then they cleared and he saw me standing beside the bed. His hand moved and went up to his head and felt the adhesive. His lips mumbled something, then his voice cleared up also.

"Who hit me? You?" His hand felt for the adhesive.

"Nobody hit you. You took a fall."

"Took a fall? When? Where?"

"Wherever you telephoned from. You called me. I heard you fall. Over the wire."

"I called you?" He grinned slowly. "Always available, aren't you, fella? What time is it?"

"After one A.M."

"Where's Eileen?"

"Gone to bed. She had it rough."

He thought that over silently. His eyes were full of pain. "Did I —" He stopped and winced.

"You didn't touch her as far as I know. If that's what you mean.

You just wandered outdoors and passed out near the fence. Quit talking. Go to sleep."

"Sleep," he said quietly and slowly, like a child reciting its lesson. "What would that be?"

"Maybe a pill would help. Got any?"

"In the drawer. Night table."

I opened it and found a plastic bottle with red capsules in it. Seconal, 1½ grains. Prescription by Dr. Loring. That nice Dr. Loring. Mrs. Roger Wade's prescription.

I shook two of them loose and put the bottle back and poured a glass of water from a thermos jug on the night table. He said one capsule would be enough. He took it and drank some water and lay back and stared at the ceiling again. Time passed. I sat in a chair and watched him. He didn't seem to get sleepy. Then he said slowly:

"I remember something. Do me a favor, Marlowe. I wrote some crazy stuff I don't want Eileen to see. It's on top of the typewriter under the cover. Tear it up for me."

"Sure. That all you remember?"

"Eileen is all right? Positive about that?"

"Yes. She's just tired. Let it ride, Wade. Stop thinking. I shouldn't have asked you."

"Stop thinking, the man says." His voice was a little drowsy now. He was talking as if to himself. "Stop thinking, stop dreaming, stop loving, stop hating. Goodnight, sweet prince. I'll take that other pill."

I gave it to him with some more water. He lay back again, this time with his head turned so that he could see me. "Look, Marlowe, I wrote some stuff I don't want Eileen — "

"You told me already. I'll attend to it when you go to sleep."

"Oh. Thanks. Nice to have you around. Very nice."

Another longish pause. His eyelids were getting heavy.

"Ever kill a man, Marlowe?"

"Yes."

"Nasty feeling, isn't it?"

"Some people like it."

His eyes went shut all the way. Then they opened again, but they looked vague. "How could they?"

I didn't answer. The eyelids came down again, very gradually, like a slow curtain in the theater. He began to snore. I waited a little longer. Then I dimmed the light in the room and went out.

27

I stopped outside Eileen's door and listened. I didn't hear any sound of movement inside, so I didn't knock. If she wanted to know how he was, it was up to her. Downstairs the living room looked bright and empty. I put out some of the lights. From over near the front door I looked up at the balcony. The middle part of the living room rose to the full height of the house walls and was crossed by open beams that also supported the balcony. The balcony was wide and edged on two sides by a solid railing which looked to be about three and a half feet high. The top and the uprights were cut square to match the cross beams. The dining room was through a square arch closed off by double louvered doors. Above it I guessed there were servants' quarters. This part of the second floor was walled off so there would be another stairway reaching it from the kitchen part of the house. Wade's room was in the corner over his study. I could see the light from his open door reflected against the high ceiling and I could see the top foot of his doorway.

I cut all the lights except in one standing lamp and crossed to the study. The door was shut but two lamps were lit, a standing lamp at the end of the leather couch and a cowled desk lamp. The typewriter was on a heavy stand under this and beside it on the desk there was a disorderly mess of yellow paper. I sat in a padded chair and studied the layout. What I wanted to know was how he had cut his head. I sat in his desk chair with the phone at my left hand.

The spring was set very weak. If I tilted back and went over, my head might have caught the corner of the desk. I moistened my handkerchief and rubbed the wood. No blood, nothing there. There was a lot of stuff on the desk, including a row of books between bronze elephants, and an old-fashioned square glass inkwell. I tried that without result. Not much point to it anyway, because if someone else had slugged him, the weapon didn't have to be in the room. And there wasn't anyone else to do it. I stood up and switched on the cornice lights. They reached into the shadowy corners and of course the answer was simple enough after all. A square metal wastebasket was lying on its side over against the wall, with paper spilled. It couldn't have walked there, so it had been thrown or kicked. I tried its sharp corners with my moistened handkerchief. I got the red-brown smear of blood this time. No mystery at all. Wade had fallen over and struck his head on the sharp corner of the wastebasket — a glancing blow most likely — picked himself up and booted the damn thing across the room. Easy.

Then he would have another quick drink. The drinking liquor was on the cocktail table in front of the couch. An empty bottle, another three quarters full, a thermos jug of water and a silver bowl containing water which had been ice cubes. There was only one glass and it was the large economy size.

Having taken his drink he felt a little better. He noticed the phone off the hook in a bleary sort of way and very likely didn't remember any more what he had been doing with it. So he just walked across and put it back in its cradle. The time had been just about right. There is something compulsive about a telephone. The gadget-ridden man of our age loves it, loathes it, and is afraid of it. But he always treats it with respect, even when he is drunk. The telephone is a fetish.

Any normal man would have said hello into the mouthpiece before hanging up, just to be sure. But not necessarily a man who was bleary with drink and had just taken a fall. It didn't matter anyhow. His wife might have done it, she might have heard the fall and the bang as the wastebasket bounced against the wall and come into the study. About that time the last drink would kick him in the face and he would stagger out of the house and across the front lawn and pass out where I had found him. Somebody was coming for him. By this time he didn't know who it was. Maybe the good Dr. Verringer.

So far, so good. So what would his wife do? She couldn't handle him or reason with him and she might well be afraid to try. So she would call somebody to come and help. The servants were out, so it would have to be by the telephone. Well, she *had* called somebody. She had called that nice Dr. Loring. I'd just assumed she called him after I got there. She hadn't said so.

From here on it didn't quite add up. You'd expect her to look for him and find him and make sure he wasn't hurt. It wouldn't hurt him to lie out on the ground on a warm summer night for a while. She couldn't move him. It had taken all I had to do that. But you wouldn't quite expect to find her standing in the open doorway smoking a cigarette, not knowing except very vaguely where he was. Or would you? I didn't know what she had been through with him, how dangerous he was in that condition, how much afraid she might be to go near him. "I've had all of it I can take," she had said to me when I arrived. "You find him." Then she had gone inside and pulled a faint.

It still bothered me, but I had to leave it at that. I had to assume that when she had been up against the situation often enough to know there was nothing she could do about it except to let it ride, then that would be what she would do. Just that. Let it ride. Let him lie out there on the ground until somebody came around with the physical equipment to handle him.

It still bothered me. It bothered me also that she had checked out and gone into her own room while Candy and I got him upstairs to bed. She said she loved the guy. He was her husband, they had been married for five years, he was a very nice guy indeed when sober — those were her own words. Drunk, he was something else, something to stay away from because he was dangerous. All right, forget it. But somehow it still bothered me. If she was really scared, she wouldn't have been standing there in the open door smoking a cigarette. If she was just bitter and withdrawn and disgusted, she wouldn't have fainted.

There was something else. Another woman, perhaps. Then she had only just found out. Linda Loring? Maybe. Dr. Loring thought so and said so in a very public manner.

I stopped thinking about it and took the cover off the typewriter. The stuff was there, several loose sheets of typed yellow paper that I was supposed to destroy so Eileen wouldn't see them. I took them over to the couch and decided I deserved a drink to go with the reading matter. There was a half bath off the study. I rinsed the tall glass out and poured a libation and sat down with it to read. And what I read was really wild. Like this:

28

The moon's four days off the full and there's a square patch of moonlight on the wall and it's looking at me like a big blind milky eye, a wall eye. Joke. Goddam silly simile. Writers. Everything has to be like something else. My head is as fluffy as whipped cream but not as sweet. More similes. I could vomit just thinking about the lousy racket. I could vomit anyway. I probably will. Don't push me. Give me time. The worms in my solar plexus crawl and crawl and crawl. I would be better off in bed but there would be a dark animal underneath the bed and the dark animal would crawl around rustling and hump himself and bump the underside of the bed, then I would let out a yell that wouldn't make any sound except to me. A dream yell, a yell in a nightmare. There is nothing to be afraid of and I am not afraid because there is nothing to be afraid of, but just the same I was lying like that once in bed and the dark animal was doing it to me, bumping himself against the underside of the bed, and I had an orgasm. That disgusted me more than any other of the nasty things I have done.

I'm dirty. I need a shave. My hands are shaking. I'm sweating. I smell foul to myself. The shirt under my arms is wet and on the chest and back. The sleeves are wet in the folds of the elbows. The glass on the table is empty. It would take both hands to pour the stuff now. I could get one out of the bottle maybe to brace me. The taste of the stuff is sickening. And it wouldn't get me anywhere. In the end I won't be able to sleep even and the whole world will moan in the horror of tortured nerves. Good stuff, huh, Wade? More.

It's all right for the first two or three days and then it is negative. You suffer and you take a drink and for a little while it is better, but the price keeps getting higher and higher and what you get for it is less and less and then there is always the point where you get nothing but nausea. Then you call Verringer. All right, Verringer, here I come. There isn't any Verringer any more. He's gone to Cuba or he is dead. The queen has killed him. Poor old Verringer, what a fate, to die in bed with a queen — that kind of queen. Come on, Wade, let's get up and go places. Places where we haven't ever been and aren't ever going back to when we have been. Does this sentence make sense? No. Okay, I'm not asking any money for it. A short pause here for a long commercial.

Well, I did it. I got up. What a man. I went over to the couch and here I am kneeling beside the couch with my hands down on it and my face in my hands, crying. Then I prayed and despised myself for praying. Grade Three drunk despising himself. What the hell are you praying to, you fool? If a well man prays, that's faith. A sick man prays and he is just scared. Nuts to prayer. This is the world you made and you make it all by yourself and what little outside help you got — well you made that too. Stop praying, you jerk. Get up on your feet and take that drink. It's too late for anything else now.

Well, I took it. Both hands. Poured it in the glass too. Hardly spilled a drop. Now if I can hold it without vomiting. Better add some water. Now lift it slow. Easy, not too much at a time. It gets warm. It gets hot. If I could stop sweating. The glass is empty. It's down on the table again.

There's a haze over the moonlight but I set that glass down in spite of it, carefully, carefully, like a spray of roses in a tall vase. The roses nod their heads with dew. Maybe I'm a rose. Brother, have I got dew. Now to get upstairs. Maybe a short one straight for the journey. No? Okay, whatever you say. Take it upstairs when I get there. If I get there, something to look forward to. If I make it upstairs I am entitled to compensation. A token of regard from me to me. I have such a beautiful love for myself — and the sweet part of it — no rivals. Double space. Been up and came down. Didn't like it upstairs. The altitude makes my heart flutter. But I keep hitting these typewriter keys. What a magician is the subconscious. If only it would work regular hours. There was moonlight upstairs too. Probably the same moon. No variety about the moon. It comes and goes like the milkman and the moon's milk is always the same. The milk's moon is always — hold it, chum. You've got your feet crossed. This is no time to get involved in the case history of the moon. You got enough case history to take care of the whole damn valley.

She was sleeping on her side without sound. Her knees drawn up. Too still I thought. You always make some sound when you sleep. Maybe not asleep, maybe just trying to sleep. If I went closer I would know. Might fall down too. One of her eyes opened — or did it? She looked at me or did she? No. Would have sat up and said, Are you sick, darling? Yes, I am sick, darling. But don't give it a thought, darling, because this sick is my sick and not your sick, and let you sleep still and lovely and never remember and no slime from me to you and nothing come near you that is grim and gray and ugly.

You're a louse, Wade. Three adjectives, you lousy writer. Can't you even stream-of-consciousness you louse without getting it in three adjectives for Chrissake? I came downstairs again holding on to the rail. My guts lurched with the steps and I held them together with a promise. I made the main floor and I made the study and I made the couch and I waited for my heart to slow down. The bottle is handy. One thing you can say about Wade's arrangements the bottle is always handy. Nobody hides it, nobody locks it up. Nobody says, Don't you think you've had enough, darling? You'll make yourself sick, darling. Nobody says that. Just sleep on side softly like roses.

I gave Candy too much money. Mistake. Should have started him with a bag of peanuts and worked up to a banana. Then a little real change, slow and easy, always keep him eager. You give him a big slug of the stuff to begin with and pretty soon he has a stake. He can live in Mexico for a month, live high wide and nasty, on what it costs here for a day. So when he gets that stake, what does he do? Well, does a man ever have enough money, if he thinks he can get more? Maybe it's all right. Maybe I ought to kill the shiny-eyed bastard. A good man died for me once, why not a cockroach in a white jacket?

Forget Candy. There's always a way to blunt a needle. The other I shall never forget. It's carved on my liver in green fire. Better telephone. Losing control. Feel them jumping, jumping, jumping. Better call someone quick before the pink things crawl on my face. Better call, call, call. Call Sioux City Sue. Hello, Operator, give me Long Distance. Hello, Long Distance, get me Sioux City Sue. What's her number? No have number, just name, Operator. You'll find her walking along Tenth Street, on the shady side, under the tall corn trees with their spreading ears. . . . All right, Operator, all right. Just cancel the whole program and let me tell you something, I mean, ask you something. Who's going to pay for all those snazzy parties Gifford is throwing in London, if you cancel my long distance call? Yeah, you think your job is solid. You think. Here, I better talk to Gifford direct. Get him on the line. His valet just brought in his tea. If he can't talk we'll send over somebody that can.

Now what did I write that for? What was I trying not to think about? Telephone. Better telephone now. Getting very bad, very, very . . .

That was all. I folded the sheets up small and pushed them down into my inside breast pocket behind the note case. I went over to the french windows and opened them wide and stepped out onto the terrace. The moonlight was a little spoiled. But it was summer in Idle Valley and summer is never quite spoiled. I stood there looking at the motionless colorless lake and thought and wondered. Then I heard a shot.

29

ON THE BALCONY two lighted doors were open now — Eileen's and his. Her room was empty. There was a sound of struggling from his and I came through the door in a jump to find her bending over the bed wrestling with him. The black gleam of a gun shot up into the air, two hands, a large male hand and a woman's small hand were both holding it, neither by the butt. Roger was sitting up in bed and leaning forward pushing. She was in a pale blue house coat, one of those quilted things, her hair was all over her face and now she had both hands on the gun and with a quick jerk she got it away from him. I was surprised that she had the strength, even dopey as he was. He fell back glaring and panting and she stepped away and bumped into me.

She stood there leaning against me, holding the gun with both hands pressed hard against her body. She was racked with panting sobs. I reached around her body and put my hand on the gun.

She spun around as if it took that to make her realize I was there. Her eyes widened and her body sagged against me. She let go of the gun. It was a heavy clumsy weapon, a Webley double-action hammerless. The barrel was warm. I held her with one arm, dropped the gun in my pocket, and looked past her head at him. Nobody said anything.

Then he opened his eyes and that weary smile played on his lips. "Nobody hurt," he muttered. "Just a wild shot into the ceiling."

I felt her go stiff. Then she pulled away. Her eyes were focused and clear. I let her go.

"Roger," she said in a voice not much more than a sick whisper, "did it have to be that?"

He stared owlishly, licked his lip and said nothing. She went and leaned against the dressing table. Her hand moved mechanically and threw the hair back from her face. She shuddered once from head to foot, shaking her head from side to side. "Roger," she whispered again. "Poor Roger. Poor miserable Roger."

He was staring straight up at the ceiling now. "I had a nightmare," he said slowly. "Somebody with a knife was leaning over the bed. I don't know who. Looked a little like Candy. Couldn't of been Candy."

"Of course not, darling," she said softly. She left the dressing table and sat down on the side of the bed. She put her hand out and began to stroke his forehead. "Candy has gone to bed long ago. And why would Candy have a knife?"

"He's a Mex. They all have knives," Roger said in the same remote impersonal voice. "They like knives. And he doesn't like me."

"Nobody likes you," I said brutally.

She turned her head swiftly. "Please — please don't talk like that. He didn't know. He had a dream —"

"Where was the gun?" I growled, watching her, not paying any attention to him.

"Night table. In the drawer." He turned his head and met my stare. There hadn't been any gun in the drawer, and he knew I knew it. The pills had been in there and some odds and ends, but no gun.

"Or under the pillow," he added. "I'm vague about it. I shot once —" he lifted a heavy hand and pointed — "up there."

I looked up. There seemed to be a hole in the ceiling plaster all right. I went where I could look up at it. Yes. The kind of hole a bullet might make. From that gun it would go on through, into the attic. I went back close to the bed and stood looking down at him, giving him the hard eye.

"Nuts. You meant to kill yourself. You didn't have any nightmare. You were swimming in a sea of self-pity. You didn't have any gun in the drawer or under your pillow either. You got up and got the gun and got back into bed and there you were all ready to wipe out the whole messy business. But I don't think you had the nerve. You fired a shot not meant to hit anything. And your wife came running — that's what you wanted. Just pity and sympathy, pal. Nothing else. Even the struggle was mostly fake. She couldn't take a gun away from you if you didn't want her to."

"I'm sick," he said. "But you could be right. Does it matter?"

"It matters like this. They'd put you in the psycho ward, and believe me, the people who run that place are about as sympathetic as Georgia chain-gang guards."

Eileen stood up suddenly. "That's enough," she said sharply. "He *is* sick, and you know it."

"He wants to be sick. I'm just reminding him of what it would cost him."

"This is not the time to tell him."

"Go on back to your room."

Her blue eyes flashed. "How dare you —"

"Go on back to your room. Unless you want me to call the police. These things are supposed to be reported."

He almost grinned. "Yeah, call the police," he said, "like you did on Terry Lennox."

I didn't pay any attention to that. I was still watching her. She looked exhausted now, and frail, and very beautiful. The moment of flashing anger was gone. I put a hand out and touched her arm. "It's all right," I said. "He won't do it again. Go back to bed."

She gave him a long look and went out of the room. When the open door was empty of her I sat down on the side of the bed where she had been sitting.

"More pills?"

"No thanks. It doesn't matter whether I sleep. I feel a lot better."

"Did I hit right about that shot? It was just a crazy bit of acting?"

"More or less." He turned his head away. "I guess I was light-headed."

"Nobody can stop you from killing yourself, if you really want to. I realize that. So do you."

"Yes." He was still looking away. "Did you do what I asked you — that stuff in the typewriter?"

"Uh huh. I'm surprised you remember. It's pretty crazy writing. Funny thing, it's clearly typed."

"I can always do that — drunk or sober — up to a point anyway."

"Don't worry about Candy," I said. "You're wrong about his not liking you. And I was wrong to say nobody did. I was trying to jar Eileen, make her mad."

"Why?"

"She pulled one faint already tonight."

He shook his head slightly. "Eileen never faints."

"Then it was a phony."

He didn't like that either.

"What did you mean — a good man died for you?" I asked.

He frowned, thinking about it. "Just rubbish. I told you I had a dream — "

"I'm talking about that guff you typed out."

He looked at me now, turning his head on the pillow as if it had enormous weight. "Another dream."

"I'll try again. What's Candy got on you?"

"Shove it, Jack," he said, and closed his eyes.

I got up and closed the door. "You can't run forever, Wade. Candy could be a blackmailer, sure. Easy. He could even be nice about it — like you and lift your dough at the same time. What is it — a woman?"

"You believe that fool, Loring," he said with his eyes closed.

"Not exactly. What about the sister — the one that's dead?"

It was a wild pitch in a sense but it happened to split the plate. His eyes snapped wide open. A bubble of saliva showed on his lips.

"Is that — why you're here?" he asked slowly, and in a whispering voice.

"You know better. I was invited. You invited me."

His head rolled back and forth on the pillow. In spite of the seconal he was eaten up by his nerves. His face was covered with sweat.

"I'm not the first loving husband who has been an adulterer. Leave me alone, damn you. Leave me alone."

I went into the bathroom and got a face towel and wiped his face off. I grinned at him sneeringly. I was the heel to end all heels. Wait until the man is down, then kick him and kick him again. He's weak. He can't resist or kick back.

"One of these days we'll get together on it," I said.

"I'm not crazy," he said.

"You just hope you're not crazy."

"I've been living in hell."

"Oh sure. That's obvious. The interesting point is why. Here — take this." I had another seconal out of the night table and another glass of water. He got up on one elbow and grabbed for the glass and missed it by a good four inches. I put it in his hand. He managed to drink and swallow his pill. Then he lay back flat and deflated, his face drained of emotion. His nose had that pinched look. He could almost have been a dead man. He wasn't throwing anybody down any stairs tonight. Most likely not any night.

When his eyelids got heavy I went out of the room. The weight of the Webley was against my hip, dragging at my pocket. I started back downstairs again. Eileen's door was open. Her room was dark but there was enough light from the moon to frame her standing just inside the door. She called out something that sounded like a name, but it wasn't mine. I stepped close to her.

"Keep your voice down," I said. "He's gone back to sleep."

"I always knew you would come back," she said softly. "Even after ten years."

I peered at her. One of us was goofy.

"Shut the door," she said in the same caressing voice. "All these years I have kept myself for you."

I turned and shut the door. It seemed like a good idea at the moment. When I faced her she was already falling towards me. So I caught her. I damn well had to. She pressed herself hard against me and her hair brushed my face. Her mouth came up to be kissed. She was trembling. Her lips opened and her teeth opened and her tongue darted. Then her hands dropped and jerked at something and the robe she was wearing came open and underneath it she was as naked as September Morn but a darn sight less coy.

"Put me on the bed," she breathed.

I did that. Putting my arms around her I touched bare skin, soft skin, soft yielding flesh. I lifted her and carried her the few steps to the bed and lowered her. She kept her arms around my neck. She was making some kind of a whistling noise in her throat. Then she thrashed about and moaned. This was murder. I was as erotic as a stallion. I was losing control. You don't get that sort of invitation from that sort of woman very often anywhere.

Candy saved me. There was a thin squeak and I swung around to see the doorknob moving. I jerked loose and jumped for the door. I got it open and barged out through it and the Mex was tearing along the hall and down the stairs. Halfway down he stopped and turned and leered at me. Then he was gone.

I went back to the door and shut it — from the outside this time. Some kind of weird noises were coming from the woman on the bed, but that's all they were now. Weird noises. The spell was broken.

I went down the stairs fast and crossed into the study and grabbed the bottle of Scotch and tilted it. When I couldn't swallow any more I leaned against the wall and panted and let the stuff burn in me until the fumes reached my brain.

It was a long time since dinner. It was a long time since anything that was normal. The whiskey hit me hard and fast and I kept guzzling it until the room started to get hazy and the furniture was all in the wrong places and the lamplight was like wildfire or summer lightning. Then I was flat out on the leather couch, trying to balance the bottle on my chest. It seemed to be empty. It rolled away and thumped on the floor.

That was the last incident of which I took any precise notice.

30

A SHAFT OF SUNLIGHT tickled one of my ankles. I opened my eyes and saw the crown of a tree moving gently against a hazed blue sky. I rolled over and leather touched my cheek. An axe split my head. I sat up. There was a rug over me. I threw that off and got my feet on the floor. I scowled at a clock. The clock said a minute short of six-thirty.

I got up on my feet and it took character. It took will power. It took a lot out of me, and there wasn't as much to spare as there once had been. The hard heavy years had worked me over.

I plowed across to the half bath and stripped off my tie and shirt and sloshed cold water in my face with both hands and sloshed it on my head. When I was dripping wet I toweled myself off savagely. I put my shirt and tie back on and reached for my jacket and the gun in the pocket banged against the wall. I took it out and swung the cylinder away from the frame and tipped the cartridges into my hand, five full, one just a blackened shell. Then I thought, what's the use, there are always more of them. So I put them back where they had been before and carried the gun into the study and put it away in one of the drawers of the desk.

When I looked up Candy was standing in the doorway, spick and span in his white coat, his hair brushed back and shining black, his eyes bitter.

"You want some coffee?"

"Thanks."

"I put the lamps out. The boss is okay. Asleep. I shut his door. Why you get drunk?"

"I had to."

He sneered at me. "Didn't make her, huh? Got tossed out on your can, shamus."

"Have it your own way."

"You ain't tough this morning, shamus. You ain't tough at all."

"Get the goddam coffee," I yelled at him.

"Hijo de la puta!"

In one jump I had him by the arm. He didn't move. He just looked at me contemptuously. I laughed and let go of his arm.

"You're right, Candy. I'm not tough at all."

He turned and went out. In no time at all he was back with a silver tray and a small silver pot of coffee on it and sugar and cream and a neat triangular napkin. He set it down on the cocktail table and removed the empty bottle and the rest of the drinking materials. He picked another bottle off the floor.

"Fresh. Just made," he said, and went out.

I drank two cups black. Then I tried a cigarette. It was all right. I still belonged to the human race. Then Candy was back in the room again.

"You want breakfast?" he asked morosely.

"No, thanks."

"Okay, scram out of here. We don't want you around."

"Who's we?"

He lifted the lid of a box and helped himself to a cigarette. He lit it and blew smoke at me insolently.

"I take care of the boss," he said.

"You making it pay?"

He frowned, then nodded. "Oh yes. Good money."

"How much on the side — for not spilling what you know?"

He went back to Spanish. "No entendido."

"You understand all right. How much you shake him for? I bet it's not more than a couple of yards."

"What's that? Couple of yards?"

"Two hundred bucks."

He grinned. "You give me couple of yards, shamus. So I don't tell the boss you come out of her room last night."

"That would buy a whole busload of wetbacks like you."

He shrugged that off. "The boss gets pretty rough when he blows his top. Better pay up, shamus."

"Pachuco stuff," I said contemptuously. "All you're touching is the small money. Lots of men play around when they're lit. Anyhow she knows all about it. You don't have anything to sell."

There was a gleam in his eye. "Just don't come round any more, tough boy."

"I'm leaving."

I stood up and walked around the table. He moved enough to keep facing towards me. I watched his hand but he evidently wasn't wearing a knife this morning. When I was close enough I slapped a hand across his face.

"I don't get called a son of a whore by the help, greaseball. I've got business here and I come around whenever I feel like it. Watch your lip from now on. You might get pistol-whipped. That pretty face of yours would never look the same again."

He didn't react at all, not even to the slap. That and being called a greaseball must have been deadly insults to him. But this time he just stood there wooden-faced, motionless. Then without a word he picked up the coffee tray and carried it out.

"Thanks for the coffee," I said to his back.

He kept going. When he was gone I felt the bristles on my chin, shook myself, and decided to be on my way. I had had a skinful of the Wade family.

As I crossed the living room Eileen was coming down the stairs in white slacks and open-toed sandals and a pale blue shirt. She looked at me with complete surprise. "I didn't know you were here, Mr.

Marlowe," she said, as thought she hadn't seen me for a week and at that time I had just dropped in for tea.

"I put his gun in the desk," I said.

"Gun?" Then it seemed to dawn on her. "Oh, last night was a little hectic, wasn't it? But I thought you had gone home."

I walked over closer to her. She had a thin gold chain around her neck and some kind of fancy pendant in gold and blue on white enamel. The blue enameled part looked like a pair of wings, but not spread out. Against these there was a broad white enamel and gold dagger that pierced a scroll. I couldn't read the words. It was some kind of military insigne.

"I got drunk," I said. "Deliberately and not elegantly. I was a little lonely."

"You didn't have to be," she said, and her eyes were as clear as water. There wasn't a trace of guile in them.

"A matter of opinion," I said. "I'm leaving now and I'm not sure I'll be back. You heard what I said about the gun?"

"You put it in his desk. It might be a good idea to put it somewhere else. But he didn't really mean to shoot himself, did he?"

"I can't answer that. But next time he might."

She shook her head. "I don't think so. I really don't. You were a wonderful help last night, Mr. Marlowe. I don't know how to thank you."

"You made a pretty good try."

She got pink. Then she laughed. "I had a very curious dream in the night," she said slowly, looking off over my shoulder. "Someone I used to know was here in the house. Someone who has been dead for ten years." Her fingers went up and touched the gold and enamel pendant. "That's why I am wearing this today. He gave it to me."

"I had a curious dream myself," I said. "But I'm not telling mine. Let me know how Roger gets on and if there is anything I can do."

She lowered her eyes and looked into mine. "You said you were not coming back."

"I said I wasn't sure. I may have to come back. I hope I won't. There is something very wrong in this house. And only part of it came out of a bottle."

She stared at me, frowning. "What does that mean?"

"I think you know what I'm talking about."

She thought it over carefully. Her fingers were still touching the pendant gently. She let out a slow patient sigh. "There's always another woman," she said quietly. "At some time or other. It's not necessarily fatal. We're talking at cross purposes, aren't we? We are not even talking about the same thing, perhaps."

"Could be," I said. She was still standing on the steps, the third step from the bottom. She still had her fingers on the pendant. She still looked like a golden dream. "Especially if you have in mind that the other woman is Linda Loring."

She dropped her hand from the pendant and came down one more step of the stairs.

"Dr. Loring seems to agree with me," she said indifferently. "He must have some source of information."

"You said he had played that scene with half the males in the valley."

"Did I? Well — it was the conventional sort of thing to say at the time." She came down another step.

"I haven't shaved," I said.

That startled her. Then she laughed. "Oh, I wasn't expecting you to make love to me."

"Just what did you expect of me, Mrs. Wade — in the beginning, when you first persuaded me to go hunting? Why me — what have I got to offer?"

"You kept faith," she said quietly. "When it couldn't have been very easy."

"I'm touched. But I don't think that was the reason."

She came down the last step and then she was looking up at me. "Then what was the reason?"

"Or if it was — it was a damn poor reason. Just about the worst reason in the world."

She frowned a tiny frown. "Why?"

"Because what I did — this keeping faith — is something even a fool doesn't do twice."

"You know," she said lightly, "this is getting to be a very enigmatic conversation."

"You're a very enigmatic person, Mrs. Wade. So long and good luck and if you really care anything about Roger, you'd better find him the right kind of doctor — and quick."

She laughed again. "Oh, that was a mild attack last night. You ought to see him in a bad one. He'll be up and working by this afternoon."

"Like hell he will."

"But believe me he will. I know him so well."

I gave her the last shot right in the teeth and it sounded pretty nasty.

"You don't really want to save him, do you? You just want to look as if you are trying to save him."

"That," she said deliberately, "was a very beastly thing to say to me."

She stepped past me and walked through the dining room doors and then the big room was empty and I crossed to the front door and let myself out. It was a perfect summer morning in that bright secluded valley. It was too far from the city to get any smog and cut off by the low mountains from the dampness of the ocean. It was going to be hot later, but in a nice refined exclusive sort of way, nothing brutal like the heat of the desert, not sticky and rank like the heat of the city. Idle Valley was a perfect place to live. Perfect. Nice people with nice homes, nice cars, nice horses, nice dogs, possibly even nice children.

But all a man named Marlowe wanted from it was out. And fast.

31

I WENT HOME AND SHOWERED and shaved and changed clothes and began to feel clean again. I cooked some breakfast, ate it, washed up, swept the kitchen and the service porch, filled a pipe and called the phone answering service. I shot a blank. Why go to the office?

There would be nothing there but another dead moth and another layer of dust. In the safe would be my portrait of Madison. I could go down and play with that, and with the five crisp hundred dollar bills that still smelled of coffee. I could do that, but I didn't want to. Something inside me had gone sour. None of it really belonged to me. What was it supposed to buy? How much loyalty can a dead man use? Phooey: I was looking at life through the mists of a hangover.

It was the kind of morning that seems to go on forever. I was flat and tired and dull and the passing minutes seemed to fall into a void, with a soft whirring sound, like spent rockets. Birds chirped in the shrubbery outside and the cars went up and down Laurel Canyon Boulevard endlessly. Usually I wouldn't even hear them. But I was brooding and irritable and mean and oversensitive. I decided to kill the hangover.

Ordinarily I was not a morning drinker. The Southern California climate is too soft for it. You don't metabolize fast enough. But I mixed a tall cold one this time and sat in an easy chair with my shirt open and pecked at a magazine, reading a crazy story about a guy that had two lives and two psychiatrists, one was human and one was some kind of insect in a hive. The guy kept going from one to the other and the whole thing was as crazy as a crumpet, but funny in an off-beat sort of way. I was handling the drink carefully, a sip at a time, watching myself.

It was about noon when the telephone rang and the voice said: "This is Linda Loring. I called your office and your phone service told me to try your home. I'd like to see you."

"Why?"

"I'd rather explain that in person. You go to your office from time to time, I suppose."

"Yeah. From time to time. Is there any money in it?"

"I hadn't thought of it that way. But I have no objection, if you want to be paid. I could be at your office in about an hour."

"Goody."

"What's the matter with you?" she asked sharply.

"Hangover. But I'm not paralyzed. I'll be there. Unless you'd rather come here."

"Your office would suit me better."

"I've got a nice quiet place here. Dead-end street, no near neighbors."

"The implication does not attract me — if I understand you."

"Nobody understands me, Mrs. Loring. I'm enigmatic. Okay, I'll struggle down to the coop."

"Thank you so much." She hung up.

I was slow getting down there because I stopped on the way for a sandwich. I aired out the office and switched on the buzzer and poked my head through the communicating door and she was there already, sitting in the same chair where Mendy Menendez had sat and looking through what could have been the same magazine. She had a tan gabardine suit on today and she looked pretty elegant. She put the magazine aside, gave me a serious look and said:

"Your Boston fern needs watering. I think it needs repotting too. Too many air roots."

I held the door open for her. The hell with the Boston fern. When she was inside and I had let the door swing shut I held the customer's chair for her and she gave the office the usual once-over. I got around to my side of the desk.

"You're establishment isn't exactly palatial," she said. "Don't you even have a secretary?"

"It's a sordid life, but I'm used to it."

"And I shouldn't think very lucrative," she said.

"Oh I don't know. Depends. Want to see a portrait of Madison?"

"A what?"

"A five-thousand-dollar bill. Retainer. I've got it in the safe." I got up and started over there. I spun the knob and opened it and unlocked a drawer inside, opened an envelope, and dropped it in front of her. She stared at it in something like amazement.

"Don't let the office fool you," I said. "I worked for an old boy one time that would cash in at about twenty millions. Even your old man would say hello to him. His office was no better than mine, except he was a bit deaf and had that soundproofing stuff on the ceiling. On the floor brown linoleum, no carpet."

She picked the portrait of Madison up and pulled it between her fingers and turned it over. She put it down again.

"You got this from Terry, didn't you?"

"Gosh, you know everything, don't you Mrs. Loring?"

She pushed the bill away from her, frowning. "He had one. He carried it on him ever since he and Sylvia were married the second time. He called it his mad money. It was not found on his body."

"There could be other reasons for that."

"I know. But how many people carry a five-thousand-dollar bill around with them? How many who could afford to give you that much money would give it to you in this form?"

It wasn't worth answering. I just nodded. She went on brusquely. "And what were you supposed to do for it, Mr. Marlowe? Or would you tell me? On that last ride down to Tijuana he had plenty of time to talk. You made it very clear the other evening that you didn't believe his confession. Did he give you a list of his wife's lovers so that you might find a murderer among them?"

I didn't answer that either, but for different reasons.

"And would the name of Roger Wade appear on that list by any chance?" she asked harshly. "If Terry didn't kill his wife, the murderer would have to be some violent and irresponsible man, a lunatic or a savage drunk. Only that sort of man could, to use your own repulsive phrase, beat her face into a bloody sponge. Is that why you are making yourself so very useful to the Wades — a regular mother's helper who comes on call to nurse him when he is drunk, to find him when he is lost, to bring him home when he is helpless?"

"Let me set you right on a couple of points, Mrs. Loring. Terry may or may not have given me that beautiful piece of engraving. But he gave me no list and mentioned no names. There was nothing he asked me to do except what you seem to feel sure I did do, drive him to Tijuana. My getting involved with the Wades was the work of a New York publisher who is desperate to have Roger Wade finish his book, which involves keeping him fairly sober, which in turn involves finding out if there is any special trouble that makes him get drunk. If there is and it can be found out, then the next step would be an effort to remove it. I say effort, because the chances are you couldn't do it. But you could try."

"I could tell you in one simple sentence why he gets drunk," she said contemptuously. "That anemic blond show piece he's married to."

"Oh I don't know," I said. "I wouldn't call her anemic."

"Really? How interesting." Her eyes glittered.

I picked up my portrait of Madison. "Don't chew too long on that one, Mrs. Loring. I am not sleeping with the lady. Sorry to disappoint you."

I went over to the safe and put my money away in the locked compartment. I shut the safe and spun the dial.

"On second thought," she said to my back, "I doubt very much that anyone is sleeping with her."

I went back and sat on the corner of the desk. "You're getting bitchy, Mrs. Loring. Why? Are you carrying a torch for our alcoholic friend?"

"I hate remarks like that," she said bitingly. "I hate them. I suppose that idiotic scene my husband made makes you think you have the right to insult me. No, I am not carrying a torch for Roger Wade. I never did — even when he was a sober man who behaved himself. Still less now that he is what he is."

I flopped into my chair, reached for a matchbox, and stared at her. She looked at her watch.

"You people with a lot of money are really something," I said. "You think anything you choose to say, however nasty, is perfectly all right. You can make sneering remarks about Wade and his wife to a man you hardly know, but if I hand you back a little change, that's an insult. Okay, let's play it low down. Any drunk will eventually turn up with a loose woman. Wade is a drunk, but you're not a loose woman. That's just a casual suggestion your high-bred husband drops to brighten up a cocktail party. He doesn't mean it, he's just saying it for laughs. So we rule you out, and look for a loose woman elsewhere. How far do we have to look, Mrs. Loring — to find one that would involve you enough to bring you down here trading sneers with me? It has to be somebody rather special, doesn't it — otherwise why should you care?"

She sat perfectly silent, just looking. A long half minute went by. The corners of her mouth were white and her hands were rigid on her gabardine bag that matched her suit.

"You haven't exactly wasted your time, have you?" she said at last. "How convenient that this publisher should have thought of employing you! So Terry named no names to you! Not a name. But it really didn't matter, did it, Mr. Marlowe? Your instinct was unerring. May I ask what you propose to do next?"

"Nothing."

"Why, what a waste of talent! How can you reconcile it with your obligation to your portrait of Madison? Surely there must be something you can do."

"Just between the two of us," I said, "you're getting pretty corny. So Wade knew your sister. Thanks for telling me, however indirectly. I already guessed it. So what? He's just one of what was most likely a fairly rich collection. Let's leave it there. And let's get around to why you wanted to see me. That kind of got lost in the shuffle, didn't it?"

She stood up. She glanced at her watch once more. "I have a car downstairs. Could I prevail upon you to drive home with me and drink a cup of tea?"

"Go on," I said. "Let's have it."

"Do I sound so suspicious? I have a guest who would like to make your acquaintance."

"The old man?"

"I don't call him that," she said evenly.

I stood up and leaned across the desk. "Honey, you're awful cute sometimes. You really are. Is it all right if I carry a gun?"

"Surely you're not afraid of an old man." She wrinkled her lip at me.

"Why not? I'll bet you are — plenty."

She sighed. "Yes, I'm afraid I am. I always have been. He can be rather terrifying."

"Maybe I'd better take two guns," I said, then wished I hadn't.

32

IT WAS THE DAMNDEST-LOOKING HOUSE I ever saw. It was a square gray box three stories high, with a mansard roof, steeply sloped and broken by twenty or thirty double dormer windows with a lot of wedding cake decoration around them and between them. The entrance had double stone pillars on each side but the cream of the joint was an outside spiral staircase with a stone railing, topped by a tower room from which there must have been a view the whole length of the lake.

The motor yard was paved with stone. What the place really seemed to need was a half mile of poplar-lined driveway and a deer park and a wild garden and a terrace on three levels and a few hundred roses outside the library window and a long green vista from every window ending in forest and silence and quiet emptiness. What it had was a wall of fieldstone around a comfortable ten or fifteen acres, which is a fair hunk of real estate in our crowded little country. The driveway was lined with a cypress hedge trimmed round. There were all sorts of ornamental trees in clumps here and there and they didn't look like California trees. Imported stuff. Whoever built that place was trying to drag the Atlantic seaboard over the Rockies. He was trying hard, but he hadn't made it.

Amos, the middle-aged colored chauffeur, stopped the Caddy gently in front of the pillared entrance, hopped out, and came around to hold the open door for Mrs. Loring. I got out first and helped him hold it. I helped her get out. She had hardly spoken to me since we got into the car in front of my building. She looked tired and nervous. Maybe this idiotic hunk of architecture depressed her. It would have depressed a laughing jackass and made it coo like a mourning dove.

"Who built this place?" I asked her. "And who was he mad at?"

She finally smiled. "Hadn't you seen it before?"

"Never been this far into the valley."

She walked me over to the other side of the driveway and pointed up. "The man who built it jumped out of that tower room and landed about where you are standing. He was a French count named La Tourelle and unlike most French counts he had a lot of money. His wife was Ramona Desborough, who was not exactly threadbare herself. In the silent-picture days she made thirty thousand a week. La Tourelle built this place for their home. It's supposed to be a miniature of the Château de Blois. You know that, of course."

"Like the back of my hand," I said. "I remember now. It was one of those Sunday paper stories once. She left him and he killed himself. There was some kind of queer will too, wasn't there?"

She nodded. "He left his ex-wife a few millions for carfare and tied the rest up in a trust. The estate was to be kept on just as it was. Nothing was to be changed, the dining table was to be laid in style every night, and nobody was to be allowed inside the grounds except the servants and the lawyers. The will was broken, of course. Eventually the estate was carved up to some extent and when I married Dr. Loring my father gave it to me for a wedding present. It must have cost him a fortune merely to make it fit to live in again. I loathe it. I always have."

"You don't have to stay here, do you?"

She shrugged in a tired sort of way. "Part of the time, at least. One of his daughters has to show him some sign of stability. Dr. Loring likes it here."

"He would. Any guy who could make the kind of scene he made at Wade's house ought to wear spats with his pajamas."

She arched her eyebrows. "Why, thank you for taking such an interest, Mr. Marlowe. But I think enough has been said on that subject. Shall we go in? My father doesn't like to be kept waiting."

We crossed the driveway again and went up the stone steps and half of the big double doors swung open noiselessly and an expensive and very snooty looking character stood aside for us to enter. The hallway was bigger than all the floor space in the house I was living in. It had a tesselated floor and there seemed to be stained-glass windows at the back and if there had been any light coming through them I might have been able to see what else was there. From the hallway we went through some more double carved doors into a dim room that couldn't have been less than seventy feet long. A man was sitting there waiting, silent. He stared at us coldly.

"Am I late, Father?" Mrs. Loring asked hurriedly. "This is Mr.

Philip Marlowe. Mr. Harlan Potter."

The man just looked at me and moved his chin down about half an inch.

"Ring for tea," he said. "Sit down, Mr. Marlowe."

I sat down and looked at him. He looked at me like an entomologist looking at a beetle. Nobody said anything. There was complete silence until the tea came. It was put down on a huge silver tray on a Chinese table. Linda sat at a table and poured.

"Two cups," Harlan Potter said. "You can have your tea in another room, Linda."

"Yes, Father. How do you like your tea, Mr. Marlowe?"

"Any way at all," I said. My voice seemed to echo off into the distance and get small and lonely.

She gave the old man a cup and then gave me a cup. Then she stood up silently and went out of the room. I watched her go. I took a sip of tea and got a cigarette out.

"Don't smoke, please. I am subject to asthma."

I put the cigarette back in the pack. I stared at him. I don't know how it feels to be worth a hundred million or so, but he didn't look as if he was having any fun. He was an enormous man, all of six feet five and built to scale. He wore a gray tweed suit with no padding. His shoulders didn't need any. He wore a white shirt and a dark tie and no display handkerchief. A spectacle case showed in the outside breast pocket. It was black, like his shoes. His hair was black too, no gray at all. It was brushed sideways across his skull in a MacArthur sweep. And I had a hunch there was nothing under it but bare skull. His eyebrows were thick and black. His voice seemed to come from a long way off. He drank his tea as if he hated it.

"It will save time, Mr. Marlowe, if I put my position before you. I believe you are interfering in my affairs. If I am correct, I propose to stop it."

"I don't know enough about your affairs to interfere in them, Mr. Potter."

"I disagree."

He drank some more tea and put the cup aside. He leaned back in the big chair he was sitting in and took me to pieces with his hard gray eyes.

"I know who you are, naturally. And how you make your living — if you make one — and how you became involved with Terry Lennox. It has been reported to me that you helped Terry get out of the country, that you have doubts about his guilt, and that you have since made contact with a man who was known to my dead daughter. For what purpose has not been explained to me. Explain it."

"If the man has a name," I said, "name it."

He smiled very slightly but not as if he was falling for me. "Wade. Roger Wade. Some sort of writer, I believe. A writer, they tell me, of rather prurient books which I should not be interested to read. I further understand that this man is a dangerous alcoholic. That may have given you a strange notion."

"Maybe you had better let me have my own notions, Mr. Potter. They are not important, naturally, but they're all I have. First, I do not believe Terry killed his wife, because of the way it was done and because I don't think he was that kind of man. Second, I didn't make contact with Wade. I was asked to live in his house and do what I could to keep him sober while he finished a job of writing. Third, if he is a dangerous alcoholic, I haven't seen any sign of it. Fourth, my first contact was at the request of his New York publisher and I didn't at that time have any idea that Roger Wade even knew your daughter. Fifth, I refused this offer of employment and then Mrs. Wade asked me to find her husband who was away somewhere taking a cure. I found him and took him home."

"Very methodical," he said dryly.

"I'm not finished being methodical, Mr. Potter. Sixth — you or someone on your instructions sent a lawyer named Sewell Endicott to get me out of jail. He didn't say who sent him, but there wasn't anyone else in the picture. Seventh, when I got out of jail a hoodlum named Mendy Menendez pushed me around and warned me to keep my nose clean and gave me a song and dance about how Terry had saved his life and the life of a gambler at Las Vegas named Randy Starr. The story could be true for all I know. Menendez pretended to be sore that Terry hadn't asked him for help getting to Mexico and had asked a punk like me instead. He, Menendez, could have done it two ways from the jack by lifting one finger, and done it much better."

"Surely," Harlan Potter said with a bleak smile, "you are not under the impression that I number Mr. Menendez and Mr. Starr among my acquaintances."

"I wouldn't know, Mr. Potter. A man doesn't make your kind of money in any way I can understand. The next person to warn me off the courthouse lawn was your daughter, Mrs. Loring. We met by accident at a bar and we spoke because we were both drinking gimlets, Terry's favorite drink, but an uncommon one around here. I didn't know who she was until she told me. I told her a little of how I felt about Terry and she gave me the idea that I would have a short unhappy career if I got you mad. Are you mad, Mr. Potter?"

"When I am," he said coldly, "you will not have to ask me. You will be in no uncertainty about it."

"What I thought. I've been kind of expecting the goon squad to drop around, but they haven't shown so far. I haven't been bothered by the cops either. I could have been. I could have been given a rough time. I think all you wanted, Mr. Potter, was quiet. Just what have I done to disturb you?"

He grinned. It was a sour kind of grin, but it was a grin. He put his long yellow fingers together and crossed a leg over his knee and leaned back comfortably.

"A pretty good pitch, Mr. Marlowe, and I have let you make it. Now listen to me. You are exactly right in thinking all I want is quiet. It's quite possible that your connection with the Wades may be incidental, accidental, and coincidental. Let it remain so. I am a family man in an age when it means almost nothing. One of my daughters married a Bostonian prig and the other made a number of foolish marriages, the last being with a complaisant pauper who allowed her to live a worthless and immoral life until he suddenly and for no good reason lost his self-control and murdered her. You think that impossible to accept because of the brutality with which it was done. You are wrong. He shot her with a Mauser automatic, the very gun he took with him to Mexico. And after he shot her he did what he did in order to cover the bullet wound. I admit the brutality of this, but remember the man had been in a war, had been badly wounded, had suffered a great deal and seen others suffer. He may not have intended to kill her. There may have been some sort of scuffle, since the gun belonged to my daughter. It was a small but powerful gun, 7.65 m/m caliber, a model called P.P.K. The bullet went completely through her head and lodged in the wall behind a chintz curtain. It was not found immediately and the fact was not published at all. Now let us consider the situation." He broke off and stared at me. "Are you very badly in need of a cigarette?"

"Sorry, Mr. Potter. I took it out without thinking. Force of habit." I put the cigarette back for the second time.

"Terry had just killed his wife. He had ample motive from the rather limited police point of view. But he also had an excellent defense — that it was her gun in her possession and that he tried to take it away from her and failed and she shot herself with it. A good trial lawyer could have done a lot with that. He would probably have been acquitted. If he had called me up then, I would have helped him. But by making the murder a brutal affair to cover the traces of the bullet, he made it impossible. He had to run away and even that he did clumsily."

"He certainly did, Mr. Potter. But he called you up in Pasadena first, didn't he? He told me he did."

The big man nodded. "I told him to disappear and I would still see what I could do. I didn't want to know where he was. That was imperative. I could not hide a criminal."

"Sounds good, Mr. Potter."

"Do I detect a note of sarcasm? No matter. When I learned the details there was nothing to be done. I could not permit the sort of trial that kind of killing would result in. To be frank, I was very glad when I learned that he had shot himself in Mexico and left a confession."

"I can understand that, Mr. Potter."

He beetled his eyebrows at me. "Be careful, young man. I don't like irony. Can you understand now that I cannot tolerate any further investigation of any sort by any person? And why I have used all my influence to make what investigation there was as brief as possible and as little publicized as possible?"

"Sure — if you're convinced he killed her."

"Of course he killed her. With what intent is another matter. It is no longer important. I am not a public character and I do not intend to be. I have always gone to a great deal of trouble to avoid any kind of publicity. I have influence but I don't abuse it. The District Attorney of Los Angeles County is an ambitious man who has too much good sense to wreck his career for the notoriety of the moment. I see a glint in your eye, Marlowe. Get rid of it. We live in what is called a democracy, rule by the majority of the people. A fine ideal if it could be made to work. The people elect, but the party machines nominate, and the party machines to be effective must spend a great deal of money. Somebody has to give it to them, and that somebody, whether it be an individual, a financial group, a trade union or what have you, expects some consideration in return. What I and people of my kind expect is to be allowed to live our lives in decent privacy. I own newspapers, but I don't like them. I regard them as a constant menace to whatever privacy we have left. Their constant yelping about a free press means, with a few honorable exceptions, freedom to peddle scandal, crime, sex, sensationalism, hate, innuendo, and the political and financial uses of propaganda. A newspaper is a business out to make money through advertising revenue. That is predicated on its circulation and you know what the circulation depends on."

I got up and walked around my chair. He eyed me with cold attention. I sat down again. I needed a little luck. Hell, I needed it in carload lots.

"Okay, Mr. Potter, what goes from here?"

He wasn't listening. He was frowning at his own thoughts. "There's a peculiar thing about money," he went on. "In large quantities it tends to have a life of its own, even a conscience of its own. The power of money becomes very difficult to control. Man has always been a venal animal. The growth of populations, the huge costs of wars, the incessant pressure of confiscatory taxation — all these things make him more and more venal. The average man is tired and scared, and a tired, scared man can't afford ideals. He has to buy food for his family. In our time we have seen a shocking decline in both public and private morals. You can't expect quality from people whose lives are a subjection to a lack of quality. You can't have quality with mass production. You don't want it because it lasts too long. So you substitute styling, which is a commercial swindle intended to produce artificial obsolescence. Mass production couldn't sell its goods next year unless it made what it sold this year look unfashionable a year from now. We have the whitest kitchens and the most shining bathrooms in the world. But in the lovely white kitchen the average American housewife can't produce a meal fit to eat, and the lovely shining bathroom is mostly a receptacle for deodorants, laxatives, sleeping pills, and the products of that confidence racket called the cosmetic industry. We make the finest packages in the world, Mr. Marlowe. The stuff inside is mostly junk."

He took out a large white handkerchief and touched his temples with it. I was sitting there with my mouth open, wondering what made the guy tick. He hated everything.

"It's a little too warm for me in these parts," he said. "I'm used to a cooler climate. I'm beginning to sound like an editorial that has forgotten the point it wanted to make."

"I got your point all right, Mr. Potter. You don't like the way the world is going so you use what power you have to close off a private corner to live in as near as possible to the way you remember people lived fifty years ago before the age of mass production. You've got a hundred million dollars and all it has bought you is a pain in the neck."

He pulled the handkerchief taut by two opposite corners, then crumpled it into a ball and stuffed it in a pocket.

"And then?" he asked shortly.

"That's all there is, there isn't any more. You don't care who murdered your daughter, Mr. Potter. You wrote her off as a bad job long ago. Even if Terry Lennox didn't kill her, and the real murderer is still walking around free, you don't care. You wouldn't want him caught, because that would revive the scandal and there would have to be a trial and his defense would blow your privacy as high as the Empire State Building. Unless, of course, he was obliging enough to commit suicide, before there was any trial. Preferably in Tahiti or Guatemala or the middle of the Sahara Desert. Anywhere where the County would hate the expense of sending a man to verify what had happened."

He smiled suddenly, a big rugged smile with a reasonable amount of friendliness in it.

"What do you want from me, Marlowe?"

"If you mean how much money, nothing. I didn't ask myself

here. I was brought. I told the truth about how I met Roger Wade. But he did know your daughter and he does have a record of violence, although I haven't seen any of it. Last night the guy tried to shoot himself. He's a haunted man. He has a massive guilt complex. If I happened to be looking for a good suspect, he might do. I realize he's only one of many, but he happens to be the only one I've met."

He stood up and standing up he was really big. Tough too. He came over and stood in front of me.

"A telephone call, Mr. Marlowe, would deprive you of your license. Don't fence with me. I won't put up with it."

"Two telephone calls and I'd wake up kissing the gutter — with the back of my head missing."

He laughed harshly. "I don't operate that way. I suppose in your quaint line of business it is natural for you to think so. I've given you too much of my time. I'll ring for the butler to show you out."

"Not necessary," I said, and stood up myself. "I came here and got told. Thanks for the time."

He held his hand out. "Thank you for coming. I think you're a pretty honest sort of fellow. Don't be a hero, young man. There's no percentage in it."

I shook hands with him. He had a grip like a pipe wrench. He smiled at me benignantly now. He was Mr. Big, the winner, everything under control.

"One of these days I might be able to throw some business your way," he said. "And don't go away thinking that I buy politicians or law enforcement officers. I don't have to. Goodbye, Mr. Marlowe. And thank you again for coming."

He stood there and watched me out of the room. I had my hand on the front door when Linda Loring popped out of a shadow somewhere.

"Well?" she asked me quietly. "How did you get on with Father?"

"Fine. He explained civilization to me. I mean how it looks to him. He's going to let it go on for a little while longer. But it better be careful and not interfere with his private life. If it does, he's apt to make a phone call to God and cancel the order."

"You're hopeless," she said.

"Me? I'm hopeless? Lady, take a look at your old man. Compared with him I'm a blue-eyed baby with a brand new rattle."

I went on out and Amos had the Caddy there waiting. He drove me back to Hollywood. I offered him a buck but he wouldn't take it. I offered to buy him the poems of T. S. Eliot. He said he already had them.

33

A WEEK WENT BY and I heard nothing from the Wades. The weather was hot and sticky and the acid sting of the smog had crept as far west as Beverly Hills. From the top of Mulholland Drive you could see it leveled out all over the city like a ground mist. When you were in it you could taste it and smell it and it made your eyes smart. Everybody was griping about it. In Pasadena, where the stuffy millionaires holed up after Beverly Hills was spoiled for them by the movie crowd, the city fathers screamed with rage. Everything was the fault of the smog. If the canary wouldn't sing, if the milk-man was late, if the Pekinese had fleas, if an old coot in a starched collar had a heart attack on the way to church, that was the smog. Where I lived it was usually clear in the early morning and nearly always at night. Once in a while a whole day would be clear, no-body quite knew why.

It was on a day like that — it happened to be a Thursday — that Roger Wade called me up. "How are you? This is Wade." He sounded fine.

"Fine, and you?"

"Sober, I'm afraid. Scratching a hard buck. We ought to have a talk. And I think I owe you some dough."

"Nope."

"Well, how about lunch today? Could you make it here some-where around one?"

"I guess so. How's Candy?"

"Candy?" He sounded puzzled. He must have blacked out plenty that night. "Oh, he helped you put me to bed that night."

"Yeah. He's a helpful little guy — in spots. And Mrs. Wade?"

"She's fine too. She's in town shopping today."

We hung up and I sat and rocked in my swivel chair. I ought to have asked him how the book was going. Maybe you always ought to ask a writer how the book is going. And then again maybe he gets damned tired of that question.

I had another call in a little while, a strange voice.

"This is Roy Ashterfelt. George Peters told me to call you up, Marlowe."

"Oh yes, thanks. You're the fellow that knew Terry Lennox in New York. Called himself Marston then."

"That's right. He was sure on the sauce. But it's the same guy all right. You couldn't very well mistake him. Out here I saw him in Chasen's one night with his wife. I was with a client. The client knew them. Can't tell you the client's name, I'm afraid."

"I understand. It's not very important now, I guess. What was his first name?"

"Wait a minute while I bite my thumb. Oh yeah, Paul. Paul Marston. And there was one thing more, if it interests you. He was wearing a British Army service badge. Their version of the ruptured duck."

"I see. What happened to him?"

"I don't know. I came west. Next time I saw him he was here too — married to Harlan Potter's somewhat wild daughter. But you know all that."

"They're both dead now. But thanks for telling me."

"Not at all. Glad to help. Does it mean anything to you?"

"Not a thing," I said, and I was a liar. "I never asked him about himself. He told me once he had been brought up in an orphanage. Isn't it just possible you made a mistake?"

"With that white hair and that scarred face, brother? Not a chance. I won't say I never forget a face, but not that one."

"Did he see you?"

"If he did, he didn't let on. Hardly expect him to in the circumstances. Anyhow he might not have remembered me. Like I said, he was always pretty well lit back in New York."

I thanked him some more and he said it was a pleasure and we hung up.

I thought about it for a while. The noise of the traffic outside the building on the boulevard made an unmusical obbligato to my thinking. It was too loud. In summer in hot weather everything is too loud. I got up and shut the lower part of the window and called Detective-Sergeant Green at Homicide. He was obliging enough to be in.

"Look," I said, after the preliminaries, "I heard something about Terry Lennox that puzzles me. A fellow I know used to know him in New York under another name. You check his war record?"

"You guys never learn," Green said harshly. "You just never learn to stay on your own side of the street. That matter is closed, locked up, weighted with lead and dropped in the ocean. Get it?"

"I spent part of an afternoon with Harlan Potter last week at his daughter's house in Idle Valley. Want to check?"

"Doing what?" he asked sourly. "Supposing I believe you."

"Talking things over. I was invited. He likes me. Incidentally, he told me the girl was shot with a Mauser P.P.K. 7.65 m/m. That news to you?"

"Go on."

"Her own gun, chum. Makes a little difference, maybe. But don't get me wrong. I'm not looking into any dark corners. This is a personal matter. Where did he get that wound?"

Green was silent. I heard a door close in the background. Then he said quietly, "Probably in a knife fight south of the border."

"Aw hell, Green, you had his prints. You sent them to Washington like always. You got a report back — like always. All I asked was something about his service record."

"Who said he had one?"

"Well, Mendy Menendez for one. Seems Lennox saved his life one time and that's how he got the wound. He was captured by the Germans and they gave him the face he had."

"Menendez, huh? You believe that son of a bitch? You got a hole in your own head. Lennox didn't have any war record. Didn't have any record of any kind under any name. You satisfied?"

"If you say so," I said. "But I don't see why Menendez would bother to come up here and tell me a yarn and warn me to keep my nose clean on account of Lennox was a pal of him and Randy Starr in Vegas and they didn't want anybody fooling around. After all Lennox was already dead."

"Who knows what a hoodlum figures?" Green asked bitterly. "Or why? Maybe Lennox was in a racket with them before he married all that money and got respectable. He was a floor manager at Starr's place in Vegas for a while. That's where he met the girl. A smile and a bow and a dinner jacket. Keep the customers happy and keep an eye on the house players. I guess he had class for the job."

"He had charm," I said. "They don't use it in police business. Much obliged, Sergeant. How is Captain Gregorius these days?"

"Retirement leave. Don't you read the papers?"

"Not the crime news, Sergeant. Too sordid."

I started to say goodbye but he chopped me off. "What did Mr. Money want with you?"

"We just had a cup of tea together. A social call. He said he might put some business my way. He also hinted — just hinted, not in so many words — that any cop that looked cross-eyed at me would be facing a grimy future."

"He don't run the police department," Green said.

"He admits it. Doesn't even buy commissioners or D.A.'s, he said. They just kind of curl up in his lap when he's having a doze."

"Go to hell," Green said, and hung up in my ear.

A difficult thing, being a cop. You never know whose stomach it's safe to jump up and down on.

34

THE STRETCH OF BROKEN-PAVED ROAD from the highway to the curve of the hill was dancing in the noon heat and the scrub that dotted the parched land on both sides of it was flour-white with granite dust by this time. The weedy smell was almost nauseating. A thin hot acrid breeze was blowing. I had my coat off and my sleeves rolled up, but the door was too hot to rest an arm on. A tethered horse dozed wearily under a clump of live oaks. A brown Mexican sat on the ground and ate something out of a newspaper. A tumbleweed rolled lazily across the road and came to rest against a piece of granite outcrop, and a lizard that had been there an instant before disappeared without seeming to move at all.

Then I was around the hill on the blacktop and in another country. In five minutes I turned into the driveway of the Wades' house, parked and walked across the flagstones and rang the bell. Wade answered the door himself, in a brown and white checked shirt with short sleeves, pale blue denim slacks, and house slippers. He looked tanned and he looked good. There was an inkstain on his hand and a smear of cigarette ash on one side of his nose.

He led the way into his study and parked himself behind his desk. On it there was a thick pile of yellow typescript. I put my coat on a chair and sat on the couch.

"Thanks for coming, Marlowe. Drink?"

I got that look on my face you get when a drunk asks you to have a drink. I could feel it. He grinned.

"I'll have a coke," he said.

"You pick up fast," I said. "I don't think I want a drink right now. I'll take a coke with you."

He pressed something with his foot and after a while Candy came. He looked surly. He had a blue shirt on and an orange scarf and no white coat. Two-tone black and white shoes, elegant high-waisted gabardine pants.

Wade ordered the cokes. Candy gave me a hard stare and went away.

"Book?" I said, pointing to the stack of paper.

"Yeah. Stinks."

"I don't believe it. How far along?"

"About two thirds of the way — for what it's worth. Which is damn little. You know how a writer can tell when he's washed up?"

"Don't know anything about writers." I filled my pipe.

"When he starts reading his old stuff for inspiration. That's absolute. I've got five hundred pages of typescript here, well over a hundred thousand words. My books run long. The public likes long books. The damn fool public thinks if there's a lot of pages there must be a lot of gold. I don't dare read it over. And I can't remember half of what's in it. I'm just plain scared to look at my own work."

"You look good yourself," I said. "From the other night I wouldn't have believed it. You've got more guts than you think you have."

"What I need right now is more than guts. Something you don't get by wishing for it. A belief in yourself. I'm a spoiled writer who doesn't believe any more. I have a beautiful home, a beautiful wife, and a beautiful sales record. But all I really want is to get drunk and forget."

He leaned his chin in his cupped hands and stared across the desk.

"Eileen said I tried to shoot myself. Was it that bad?"

"You don't remember?"

He shook his head. "Not a damn thing except that I fell down and cut my head. And after a while I was in bed. And you were there. Did Eileen call you?"

"Yeah. Didn't she say?"

"She hasn't been talking to me very much this last week. I guess she's had it. Up to here." He put the edge of one hand against his neck just under his chin. "That show Loring put on here didn't help any."

"Mrs. Wade said it meant nothing."

"Well, she would, wouldn't she? It happened to be the truth, but I don't suppose she believed it when she said it. The guy is just abnormally jealous. You have a drink or two with his wife in the corner and laugh a little and kiss her goodbye and right off he assumes you are sleeping with her. One reason being that he isn't."

"What I like about Idle Valley," I said, "is that everybody is living just a comfortable normal life."

He frowned and then the door opened and Candy came in with two cokes and glasses and poured the cokes. He set one in front of me without looking at me.

"Lunch in half an hour," Wade said, "and where's the white coat?"

"This my day off," Candy said, deadpan. "I ain't the cook, boss."

"Cold cuts or sandwiches and beer will do," Wade said. "The cook's off today, Candy. I've got a friend to lunch."

"You think he is your friend?" Candy sneered. "Better ask your wife."

Wade leaned back in his chair and smiled at him. "Watch your lip, little man. You've got it soft here. I don't often ask a favor of you, do I?"

Candy looked down at the floor. After a moment he looked up and grinned. "Okay, boss. I put the white coat on. I get the lunch, I guess."

He turned softly and went out. Wade watched the door close. Then he shrugged and looked at me.

"We used to call them servants. Now we call them domestic help. I wonder how long it will be before we have to give them breakfast in bed. I'm paying the guy too much money. He's spoiled."

"Wages — or something on the side?"

"Such as what?" he asked sharply.

I got up and handed him some folded yellow sheets. "You'd better read it. Evidently you don't remember asking me to tear it up. It was in your typewriter, under the cover."

He unfolded the yellow pages and leaned back to read them. The glass of coke fizzed unnoticed on the desk in front of him. He read slowly, frowning. When he came to the end he refolded the sheets and ran a finger along the edge.

"Did Eileen see this?" he asked carefully.

"I wouldn't know. She might have."

"Pretty wild, isn't it?"

"I liked it. Especially the part about a good man dying for you."

He opened the paper again and tore it into long strips viciously and dumped the strips into his wastebasket.

"I suppose a drunk will write or say or do anything," he said slowly. "It's meaningless to me. Candy's not blackmailing me. He likes me."

"Maybe you'd better get drunk again. You might remember what you meant. You might remember a lot of things. We've been through this before — that night when the gun went off. I suppose the seconal blanked you out too. You sounded sober enough. But now you pretend not to remember writing that stuff I just gave you. No wonder you can't write your book, Wade. It's a wonder you can stay alive."

He reached sideways and opened a drawer of his desk. His hand fumbled in it and came up with a three-decker check book. He opened it and reached for a pen.

"I owe you a thousand dollars," he said quietly. He wrote in the book. Then on the counterfoil. He tore the check out, came around the desk with it, and dropped it in front of me. "Is that all right?"

I leaned back and looked up at him and didn't touch the check and didn't answer him. His face was tight and drawn. His eyes were deep and empty.

"I suppose you think I killed her and let Lennox take the rap," he said slowly. "She was a tramp all right. But you don't beat a woman's head in just because she's a tramp. Candy knows I went there sometimes. The funny part of it is I don't think he would tell. I could be wrong, but I don't think so."

"Wouldn't matter if he did," I said. "Harlan Potter's friends wouldn't listen to him. Also, she wasn't killed with that bronze thing. She was shot through the head with her own gun."

"She maybe had a gun," he said almost dreamily. "But I didn't know she had been shot. It wasn't published."

"Didn't know or didn't remember?" I asked him. "No, it wasn't published."

"What are you trying to do to me, Marlowe?" His voice was still dreamy, almost gentle. "What do you want me to do? Tell my wife? Tell the police? What good would it do?"

"You said a good man died for you."

"All I meant was that if there had been any real investigation I might have been identified as one — but only one — of the possible suspects. It would have finished me in several ways."

"I didn't come here to accuse you of a murder, Wade. What's eating you is that you're not sure yourself. You have a record of violence to your wife. You black out when you're drunk. It's no argument to say you don't beat a woman's head in just because she's a tramp. That is exactly what somebody did do. And the guy who got credit for the job seemed to me a lot less likely than you."

He walked to the open french windows and stood looking out at the shimmer of heat over the lake. He didn't answer me. He hadn't moved or spoken a couple of minutes later when there was a light knock at the door and Candy came in wheeling a tea wagon, with a crisp white cloth, silver-covered dishes, a pot of coffee, and two bottles of beer.

"Open the beer, boss?" he asked Wade's back.

"Bring me a bottle of whiskey." Wade didn't turn around.

"Sorry, boss. No whiskey."

Wade spun around and yelled at him, but Candy didn't budge. He looked down at the check lying on the cocktail table and his head twisted as he read it. Then he looked up at me and hissed something between his teeth. Then he looked at Wade.

"I go now. This my day off."

He turned and went. Wade laughed.

"So I get it myself," he said sharply, and went.

I lifted one of the covers and saw some neatly trimmed three-cornered sandwiches. I took one and poured some beer and ate the sandwich standing up. Wade came back with a bottle and a glass. He sat down on the couch and poured a stiff jolt and sucked it down. There was the sound of a car going away from the house, probably Candy leaving by the service driveway. I took another sandwich.

"Sit down and make yourself comfortable," Wade said. "We have all afternoon to kill." He had a glow on already. His voice was vibrant and cheerful. "You don't like me, do you, Marlowe?"

"That question has already been asked and answered."

"Know something? You're a pretty ruthless son of a bitch. You'd do anything to find what you want. You'd even make love to my wife while I was helpless drunk in the next room."

"You believe everything that knife thrower tells you?"

He poured some more whiskey into his glass and held it up against the light. "Not everything, no. A pretty color whiskey is, isn't it? To drown in a golden flood — that's not so bad. 'To cease upon the midnight with no pain.' How does that go on? Oh, sorry, you wouldn't know. Too literary. You're some kind of a dick, aren't you? Mind telling me why you're here?"

He drank some more whiskey and grinned at me. Then he spotted the check lying on the table. He reached for it and read it over his glass.

"Seems to be made out to somebody named Marlowe. I wonder why, what for. Seems I signed it. Foolish of me. I'm a gullible chap."

"Stop acting," I said roughly. "Where's your wife?"

He looked up politely. "My wife will be home in due course. No doubt by that time I shall be passed out and she can entertain you at her leisure. The house will be yours."

"Where's the gun?" I asked suddenly.

He looked blank. I told him I had put it in his desk. "Not there now, I'm sure," he said. "You may search if it pleases you. Just don't steal any rubber bands."

I went to the desk and frisked it. No gun. That was something. Probably Eileen had hidden it.

"Look, Wade, I asked you where your wife was. I think she ought to come home. Not for my benefit, friend, for yours. Somebody has to look out for you, and I'll be goddamned if it's going to be me."

He stared vaguely. He was still holding the check. He put his glass down and tore the check across, then again and again, and let the pieces fall to the floor.

"Evidently the amount was too small," he said. "Your services come very high. Even a thousand dollars *and* my wife fail to satisfy you. Too bad, but I can't go any higher. Except on this." He patted the bottle.

"I'm leaving," I said.

"But why? You wanted me to remember. Well — here in the bottle is my memory. Stick around, pal. When I get lit enough I'll tell you about all the women I have murdered."

"All right, Wade. I'll stick around for a while. But not in here. If you need me, just smash a chair against the wall."

I went out and left the door open. I walked across the big living room and out to the patio and pulled one of the chaises into the shadow of the overhang and stretched out on it. Across the lake there was a blue haze against the hills. The ocean breeze had begun to filter through the low mountains to the west. It wiped the air clean and it wiped away just enough of the heat. Idle Valley was having a perfect summer. Somebody had planned it that way. Paradise Incorporated, and also Highly Restricted. Only the nicest people. Absolutely no Central Europeans. Just the cream, the top drawer crowd, the lovely, lovely people. Like the Lorings and the Wades. Pure gold.

35

I LAY THERE FOR HALF AN HOUR trying to make up my mind what to do. Part of me wanted to let him get good and drunk and see if anything came out. I didn't think anything much would happen to him in his own study in his own house. He might fall down again but it would be a long time. The guy had capacity. And somehow a drunk never hurts himself very badly. He might get back his mood of guilt. More likely, this time he would just go to sleep.

The other part of me wanted to get out and stay out, but this was the part I never listened to. Because if I ever had I would have stayed in the town where I was born and worked in the hardware store and married the boss's daughter and had five kids and read them the funny paper on Sunday morning and smacked their heads when they got out of line and squabbled with the wife about how much spending money they were to get and what programs they could have on the radio or TV set. I might even have got rich — small-town rich, an eight-room house, two cars in the garage, chicken every Sunday and the *Reader's Digest* on the living room table, the wife with a cast iron permanent and me with a brain like a sack of Portland cement. You take it, friend. I'll take the big sordid dirty crooked city.

I got up and went back to the study. He was just sitting there staring at nothing, the Scotch bottle more than half empty, a loose frown on his face and a dull glitter in his eyes. He looked at me like a horse looking over a fence.

"What d'you want?"

"Nothing. You all right?"

"Don't bother me. I have a little man on my shoulder telling me stories."

I got another sandwich off the tea wagon and another glass of beer. I munched the sandwich and drank the beer, leaning against his desk.

"Know something?" he asked suddenly, and his voice suddenly seemed much more clear. "I had a male secretary once. Used to dictate to him. Let him go. He bothered me sitting there waiting for me to create. Mistake. Ought to have kept him. Word would have got around I was a homo. The clever boys that write book reviews because they can't write anything else would have caught on and started giving me the buildup. Have to take care of their own, you know. They're all queers, every damn one of them. The queer is the artistic arbiter of our age, chum. The pervert is the top guy now."

"That so? Always been around, hasn't he?"

He wasn't looking at me. He was just talking. But he heard what I said.

"Sure, thousands of years. And especially in all the great ages of art. Athens, Rome, the Renaissance, the Elizabethan Age, the Romantic Movement in France — loaded with them. Queers all over the place. Ever read *The Golden Bough?* No, too long for you. Shorter version though. Ought to read it. Proves our sexual habits are pure conventions — like wearing a black tie with a dinner jacket. Me. I'm a sex writer, but with frills and straight."

He looked up at me and sneered. "You know something? I'm a liar. My heroes are eight feet tall and my heroines have callouses on their bottoms from lying in bed with their knees up. Lace and ruffles, swords and coaches, elegance and leisure, duels and gallant death. All lies. They used perfume instead of soap, their teeth rotted because they never cleaned them, their fingernails smelled of stale gravy. The nobility of France urinated against the walls in the marble corridors of Versailles, and when you finally got several sets of underclothes off the lovely marquise the first thing you noticed was that she needed a bath. I ought to write it that way."

"Why don't you?"

He chuckled. "Sure, and live in a five-room house in Compton — if I was that lucky." He reached down and patted the whiskey bottle. "You're lonely, pal. You need company."

He got up and walked fairly steadily out of the room. I waited, thinking about nothing. A speedboat came racketing down the lake. When it came in sight I could see that it was high out of the water on its step and towing a surfboard with a husky sunburned lad on it. I went over to the french windows and watched it make a sweeping turn. Too fast, the speedboat almost turned over. The surfboard rider danced on one foot trying to hold his balance, then went shooting off into the water. The speedboat drifted to a stop and the man in the water came up to it in a lazy crawl, then went back along the tow rope and rolled himself on to the surfboard.

Wade came back with another bottle of whiskey. The speedboat picked up and went off into the distance. Wade put his fresh bottle down beside the other. He sat down and brooded.

"Christ, you're not going to drink all that, are you?"

He squinted his eyes at me. "Take off, buster. Go on home and mop the kitchen floor or something. You're in my light." His voice was thick again. He had taken a couple in the kitchen, as usual.

"If you want me, holler."

"I couldn't get low enough to want you."

"Yeah, thanks. I'll be around until Mrs. Wade comes home. Ever hear of anybody named Paul Marston?"

His head came up slowly. His eyes focused, but with effort. I could see him fighting for control. He won the fight — for the moment. His face became expressionless.

"Never did," he said carefully, speaking very slowly. "Who's he?"

The next time I looked in on him he was asleep, with his mouth open, his hair damp with sweat, and reeking of Scotch. His lips were pulled back from his teeth in a loose grimace and the furred surface of his tongue looked dry.

One of the whiskey bottles was empty. A glass on the table had about two inches in it and the other bottle was about three quarters full. I put the empty on the tea wagon and rolled it out of the room, then went back to close the french windows and turn the slats of the blinds. The speedboat might come back and wake him. I shut the study door.

I wheeled the tea wagon out to the kitchen, which was blue and white and large and airy and empty. I was still hungry. I ate another sandwich and drank what was left of the beer, then poured a cup of coffee and drank that. The beer was flat but the coffee was still hot. Then I went back to the patio. It was quite a long time before the speedboat came tearing down the lake again. It was almost four o'clock when I heard its distant roar swell into an ear-splitting howl of noise. There ought to be a law. Probably was and the guy in the speedboat didn't give a damn. He enjoyed making a nuisance of himself, like other people I was meeting. I walked down to the edge of the lake.

He made it this time. The driver slowed just enough on the turn and the brown lad on the surfboard leaned far out against the centrifugal pull. The surfboard was almost out of the water, but one edge stayed in and then the speedboat straightened out and the surfboard still had a rider and they went back the way they had come and that was that. The waves stirred up by the boat came charging in towards the shore of the lake at my feet. They slapped hard against the piles of the short landing and jumped the tied boat up and down. They were still slapping it around when I turned back to the house.

As I reached the patio I heard a bell chiming from the direction of the kitchen. When it sounded again I decided that only the front door would have chimes. I crossed to it and opened it.

Eileen Wade was standing there looking away from the house. As she turned she said: "I'm sorry, I forgot my key." Then she saw me. "Oh — I thought it was Roger or Candy."

"Candy isn't here. It's Thursday."

She came in and I shut the door. She put a bag down on the table between the two davenports. She looked cool and also distant. She pulled off a pair of white pigskin gloves.

"Is anything wrong?"

"Well, there's a little drinking being done. Not bad. He's asleep on the couch in his study."

"He called you?"

"Yes, but not for that. He asked me to lunch. I'm afraid he didn't have any himself."

"Oh." She sat down slowly on a davenport. "You know, I completely forgot it was Thursday. The cook's away too. How stupid."

"Candy got the lunch before he left. I guess I'll blow now. I hope my car wasn't in your way."

She smiled. "No. There was plenty of room. Won't you have some tea? I'm going to have some."

"All right." I didn't know why I said that. I didn't want any tea. I just said it.

She slipped off a linen jacket. She hadn't worn a hat. "I'll just look in and see if Roger is all right."

I watched her cross to the study door and open it. She stood there a moment and closed the door and came back.

"He's still asleep. Very soundly. I have to go upstairs for a moment. I'll be right down."

I watched her pick up her jacket and gloves and bag and go up the stairs and into her room. The door closed. I crossed to the study with the idea of removing the bottle of hooch. If he was still asleep, he wouldn't need it.

36

THE SHUTTING OF THE FRENCH WINDOWS had made the room stuffy and the turning of the venetian blinds had made it dim. There was an acrid smell on the air and there was too heavy a silence. It was not more than sixteen feet from the door to the couch and I didn't need more than half of that to know a dead man lay on that couch.

He was on his side with his face to the back of the couch, one arm crooked under him and the forearm of the other lying almost across his eyes. Between his chest and the back of the couch there was a pool of blood and in that pool lay the Webley Hammerless. The side of his face was a smeared mask.

I bent over him, peering at the edge of the wide open eye, the bare and gaudy arm, at the inner curve of which I could see the puffed and blackened hole in his head from which the blood oozed still.

I left him like that. His wrist was warm but there was no doubt he was quite dead. I looked around for some kind of note or scribble. There was nothing but the pile of script on the desk. They don't always leave notes. The typewriter was uncovered on its stand. There was nothing in that. Otherwise everything looked natural enough. Suicides prepare themselves in all sorts of ways, some with liquor, some with elaborate champagne dinners. Some in evening clothes, some in no clothes. People have killed themselves on the tops of walls, in ditches, in bathrooms, in the water, over the water, on the water. They have hanged themselves in barns and gassed themselves in garages. This one looked simple. I hadn't heard the shot but it must have gone off when I was down by the lake watching the surfboard rider make his turn. There was plenty of noise. Why that should have mattered to Roger Wade I didn't know. Perhaps it hadn't. The final impulse had coincided with the run of the speedboat. I didn't like it, but nobody cared what I liked.

The torn pieces of the check were still on the floor but I left them. The torn strips of that stuff he had written that other night were in the wastebasket. These I did not leave. I picked them out and made sure I had them all and stuffed them into my pocket. The basket was almost empty, which made it easy. No use wondering where the gun had been. There were too many places to hide it in. It could have been in a chair or in the couch, under one of the cushions. It could have been on the floor, behind the books, anywhere.

I went out and shut the door. I listened. From the kitchen, sounds. I went out there. Eileen had a blue apron on and the kettle was just beginning to whistle. She turned the flame down and gave me a brief impersonal glance.

"How do you like your tea, Mr. Marlowe?"

"Just out of the pot as it comes."

I leaned against the wall and got a cigarette out just to have something to do with my fingers. I pinched and squeezed it and broke it in half and threw one half on the floor. Her eyes followed it down.

I bent and picked it up. I squeezed the two halves together into a little ball.

She made the tea. "I always take cream and sugar," she said over her shoulder. "Strange, when I drink my coffee black. I learned tea drinking in England. They were using saccharin instead of sugar. When the war came they had no cream, of course."

"You lived in England?"

"I worked there. I stayed all through the Blitz. I met a man — but I told you about that."

"Where did you meet Roger?"

"In New York."

"Married there?"

She swung around, frowning. "No, we were not married in New York. Why?"

"Just talking while the tea draws."

She looked out of the window over the sink. She could see down to the lake from there. She leaned against the edge of the drain-board and her fingers fiddled with a folded tea towel.

"It has to be stopped," she said, "and I don't know how. Perhaps he'll have to be committed to an institution. Somehow I can't quite see myself doing that. I'd have to sign something, wouldn't I?"

She turned around when she asked that.

"He could do it himself," I said. "That is, he could have up to now."

The tea timer rang its bell. She turned back to the sink and poured the tea from one pot into another. Then she put the fresh pot on the tray she had already fixed up with cups. I went over and got the tray and carried it to the table between the two davenports in the living room. She sat down opposite me and poured two cups. I reached for mine and set it down in front of me for it to cool. I watched her fix hers with two lumps of sugar and the cream. She tasted it.

"What did you mean by that last remark?" she asked suddenly. "That he could have up to now — committed himself to some institution, you meant, didn't you?"

"I guess it was a wild pitch. Did you hide the gun I told you about? You know, the morning after he made that play upstairs."

"Hide it?" she repeated frowning. "No. I never do anything like that. I don't believe in it. Why are you asking?"

"And you forgot your house keys today?"

"I told you I did."

"But not the garage key. Usually in this kind of house the outside keys are mastered."

"I don't need a key for the garage," she said sharply. "It opens by a switch. There's a relay switch inside the front door you push up as you go out. Then another switch beside the garage operates that door. Often we leave the garage open. Or Candy goes out and closes it."

"I see."

"You are making some rather strange remarks," she said with acid in her voice. "You did the other morning."

"I've had some rather strange experiences in this house. Guns going off in the night, drunks lying out on the front lawn and doctors coming that won't do anything. Lovely women wrapping their arms around me and talking as if they thought I was someone else, Mexican houseboys throwing knives. It's a pity about that gun. But you don't really love your husband, do you? I guess I said that before too."

She stood up slowly. She was as calm as a custard, but her violet eyes didn't seem quite the same color, nor of quite the same softness. Then her mouth began to tremble.

"Is — is something — wrong in there?" she asked very slowly, and looked towards the study.

I barely had time to nod before she was running. She was at the door in a flash. She threw it open and darted in. If I expected a wild scream I was fooled. I didn't hear anything. I felt lousy. I ought to have kept her out and eased into that corny routine about bad news, prepare yourself, won't you sit down, I'm afraid something rather serious has happened. Blah, blah, blah. And when you have worked your way through it you haven't saved anybody a thing. Often enough you have made it worse.

I got up and followed her into the study. She was kneeling beside the couch with his head pulled against her breast, smearing herself with his blood. She wasn't making a sound of any kind. Her eyes were shut. She was rocking back and forth on her knees as far as she could, holding him tight.

I went back out and found a telephone and a book. I called the sheriff's substation that seemed to be nearest. Didn't matter, they'd relay it by radio in any case. Then I went out to the kitchen and turned the water on and fed the strips of yellow paper from my pocket down the electric garbage grinder. I dumped the tea leaves from the other pot after it. In a matter of seconds the stuff was gone. I shut off the water and switched off the motor. I went back to the living room and opened the front door and stepped outside.

There must have been a deputy cruising close by because he was there in about six minutes. When I took him into the study she was still kneeling by the couch. He went over to her at once.

"I'm sorry, ma'am. I understand how you must feel, but you shouldn't be touching anything."

She turned her head, then scrambled to her feet. "It's my husband. He's been shot."

He took his cap off and put it on the desk. He reached for the telephone.

"His name is Roger Wade," she said in a high brittle voice. "He's the famous novelist."

"I know who he is, ma'am," the deputy said, and dialed.

She looked down at the front of her blouse. "May I go upstairs and change this?"

"Sure." He nodded to her and spoke into the phone, then hung up and turned. "You say he's been shot. That mean somebody else shot him?"

"I think this man murdered him," she said without looking at me, and went quickly out of the room.

The deputy looked at me. He got a notebook out. He wrote something in it. "I better have your name," he said casually, "and address. You the one called in?"

"Yes." I told him my name and address.

"Just take it easy until Lieutenant Ohls gets here."

"Bernie Ohls?"

"Yeah. You know him?"

"Sure. I've known him a long time. He used to work out of the D.A.'s office."

"Not lately," the deputy said. "He's Assistant Chief of Homicide, working out of the L.A. Sheriff's office. You a friend of the family, Mr. Marlowe?"

"Mrs. Wade didn't make it sound that way."

He shrugged and half smiled. "Just take it easy, Mr. Marlowe. Not carrying a gun, are you?"

"Not today."

"I better make sure." He did. He looked towards the couch then. "In spots like this you can't expect the wife to make much sense. We better wait outside."

37

OHLS WAS A MEDIUM-SIZED THICK MAN with short-cropped faded blond hair and faded blue eyes. He had stiff white eyebrows and in the days before he stopped wearing a hat you were always a little surprised when he took it off — there was so much more head than you expected. He was a hard tough cop with a grim outlook on life but a very decent guy underneath. He ought to have made captain years ago. He had passed the examination among the top three half a dozen times. But the Sheriff didn't like him and he didn't like the Sheriff.

He came down the stairs rubbing the side of his jaw. Flashlights had been going off in the study for a long time. Men had gone in and out. I had just sat in the living room with a plain-clothes dick and waited.

Ohls sat down on the edge of a chair and dangled his hands. He was chewing on an unlit cigarette. He looked at me broodingly.

"Remember the old days when they had a gatehouse and a private police force in Idle Valley?"

I nodded. "And gambling also."

"Sure. You can't stop it. This whole valley is still private property. Like Arrowhead used to be, and Emerald Bay. Long time since I was on a case with no reporters jumping around. Somebody must have whispered in Sheriff Petersen's ear. They kept it off the teletype."

"Real considerate of them," I said. "How is Mrs. Wade?"

"Too relaxed. She must of grabbed some pills. There's a dozen kinds up there — even demerol. That's bad stuff. Your friends don't have a lot of luck lately, do they? They get dead."

I didn't have anything to say to that.

"Gunshot suicides always interest me," Ohls said loosely. "So easy to fake. The wife says you killed him. Why would she say that?"

"She doesn't mean it literally."

"Nobody else was here. She says you knew where the gun was, knew he was getting drunk, knew he had fired off the gun the other night when she had to fight with him to get the gun away from him. You were there that night too. Don't seem to help much, do you?"

"I searched his desk this afternoon. No gun. I'd told her where it was and to put it away. She says now she didn't believe in that sort of thing."

"Just when would 'now' be?" Ohls asked gruffly.

"After she came home and before I phoned the substation."

"You searched the desk. Why?" Ohls lifted his hands and put them on his knees. He was looking at me indifferently, as if he didn't care what I said.

"He was getting drunk. I thought it just as well to have the gun somewhere else. But he didn't try to kill himself the other night. It was just show-off."

Ohls nodded. He took the chewed cigarette out of his mouth, dropped it into a tray, and put a fresh one in place of it.

"I quit smoking," he said. "Got me coughing too much. But the goddam things still ride me. Can't feel right without one in my mouth. You supposed to watch the guy when he's alone?"

"Certainly not. He asked me to come out and have lunch. We talked and he was kind of depressed about his writing not going well. He decided to hit the bottle. Think I should have taken it away from him?"

"I'm not thinking yet. I'm just trying to get a picture. How much drinking did you do?"

"Beer."

"It's your tough luck you were here, Marlowe. What was the check for? The one he wrote and signed and tore up?"

"They all wanted me to come and live here and keep him in line. All means himself, his wife, and his publisher, a man named Howard Spencer. He's in New York, I guess. You can check with him. I turned it down. Afterwards she came to me and said her husband was off on a toot and she was worried and would I find him and bring him home. I did that. Next thing I knew I was carrying him in off his front lawn and putting him to bed. I didn't want any part of it, Bernie. It just kind of grew up around me."

"Nothing to do with the Lennox case, huh?"

"Aw, for Pete's sake. There isn't any Lennox case."

"How true," Ohls said dryly. He squeezed his kneecaps. A man came in at the front door and spoke to the other dick, then came across to Ohls.

"There's a Dr. Loring outside, Lieutenant. Says he was called. He's the lady's doctor."

"Let him in."

The dick went back and Dr. Loring came in with his neat black bag. He was cool and elegant in a tropical worsted suit. He went past me without looking at me.

"Upstairs?" he asked Ohls.

"Yeah — in her room." Ohls stood up. "What you give her that demerol for, Doc?"

Dr. Loring frowned at him. "I prescribe for my patient as I think proper," he said coldly. "I am not required to explain why. Who says I gave Mrs. Wade demerol?"

"I do. The bottle's up there with your name on it. She's got a regular drugstore in her bathroom. Maybe you don't know it, Doc, but we have a pretty complete exhibit of the little pills downtown. Bluejays, redbirds, yellow jackets, goofballs, and all the rest of the list. Demerol's about the worst of the lot. That's the stuff Goering lived on, I heard somewhere. Took eighteen a day when they caught him. Took the army doctors three months to cut him down."

"I don't know what those words mean," Dr. Loring said frigidly.

"You don't? Pity. Bluejays are sodium amytal. Redbirds are seconal. Yellow jackets are nembutal. Goofballs are one of the barbiturates laced with benzedrine. Demerol is a synthetic narcotic that is very habit forming. You just hand 'em out, huh? Is the lady suffering from something serious?"

"A drunken husband can be a very serious complaint indeed for a sensitive woman," Dr. Loring said.

"You didn't get around to him, huh? Pity. Mrs. Wade's upstairs, Doc. Thanks for the time."

"You are impertinent, sir. I shall report you."

"Yeah, do that," Ohls said. "But before you report me, do something else. Keep the lady clear in her head. I've got questions to ask."

"I shall do exactly what I think best for her condition. Do you know who I am, by any chance? And just to make matters clear, Mr. Wade was not my patient. I don't treat alcoholics."

"Just their wives, huh?" Ohls snarled at him. "Yeah, I know who you are, Doc. I'm bleeding internally. My name is Ohls. Lieutenant Ohls."

Dr. Loring went on up the stairs. Ohls sat down again and grinned at me.

"You got to be diplomatic with this kind of people," he said.

A man came out of the study and came up to Ohls. A thin serious-looking man with glasses and a brainy forehead.

"Lieutenant."

"Shoot."

"The wound is contact, typically suicidal, with a good deal of distention from gas pressure. The eyes are exophthalmic from the same cause. I don't think there will be any prints on the outside of the gun. It's been bled on too freely."

"Could it be homicide if the guy was asleep or passed out drunk?" Ohls asked him.

"Of course, but there's no indication of it. The gun's a Webley Hammerless. Typically, this gun takes a very stiff pull to cock it, but a very light pull to discharge it. The recoil explains the position of the gun. I see nothing against suicide so far. I expect a high figure on alcoholic concentration. If it's high enough — " the man stopped and shrugged meaningly — "I might be inclined to doubt suicide."

"Thanks. Somebody call the coroner?"

The man nodded and went away. Ohls yawned and looked at his watch. Then he looked at me.

"You want to blow?"

"Sure, if you'll let me. I thought I was a suspect."

"We might oblige you later on. Stick around where you can be found, that's all. You were a dick once, you know how they go. Some you got to work fast before the evidence gets away from you. This one is just the opposite. If it was a homicide, who wanted him dead? His wife? She wasn't here. You? Fine, you had the house to yourself and knew where the gun was. A perfect setup. Everything but a motive, and we might perhaps give some weight to your experience. I figure if you wanted to kill a guy, you could maybe do it a little less obviously."

"Thanks, Bernie. I could at that."

"The help wasn't here. They're out. So it must have been somebody that just happened to drop by. That somebody had to know where Wade's gun was, had to find him drunk enough to be asleep or passed out, and had to pull the trigger when that speedboat was making enough noise to drown the shot, and had to get away before you came back into the house. That I don't buy on any knowledge I have now. The only person who had the means and opportunity was the one guy who wouldn't have used them — for the simple reason he *was* the one guy who had them."

I stood up to go. "Okay, Bernie. I'll be home all evening."

"There's just one thing," Ohls said musingly. "This man Wade was a big time writer. Lots of dough, lots of reputation. I don't go for his sort of crap myself. You might find nicer people than his characters in a whorehouse. That's a matter of taste and none of my business as a cop. With all this money he had a beautiful home in one of the best places to live in in the county. He had a beautiful wife, lots of friends, and no troubles at all. What I want to know is what made all that so tough that he had to pull a trigger? Sure as hell something did. If you know, you better get ready to lay it on the line. See you."

I went to the door. The man on the door looked back at Ohls, got the sign, and let me out. I got into my car and had to edge over on the lawn to get around the various official cars that jammed the driveway. At the gate another deputy looked me over but didn't say anything. I slipped my dark glasses on and drove back towards the main highway. The road was empty and peaceful. The afternoon sun beat down on the manicured lawns and the large roomy expensive houses behind them.

A man not unknown to the world had died in a pool of blood in a house in Idle Valley, but the lazy quiet had not been disturbed. So far as the newspapers were concerned it might have happened in Tibet.

At a turn of the road the walls of two estates came down to the shoulder and a dark green sheriff's car was parked there. A deputy got out and held up his hand. I stopped. He came to the window.

"May I see your driver's license, please?"

I took out my wallet and handed it to him open.

"Just the license, please. I'm not allowed to touch your wallet."

I took it out and gave it to him. "What's the trouble?"

He glanced into my car and handed me back my license.

"No trouble," he said. "Just a routine check. Sorry to have troubled you."

He waved me on and went back to the parked car. Just like a cop. They never tell you why they are doing anything. That way you don't find out they don't know themselves.

I drove home, bought myself a couple of cold drinks, went out to dinner, came back, opened the windows and my shirt and waited for something to happen. I waited a long time. It was nine o'clock when Bernie Ohls called up and told me to come in and not stop on the way to pick any flowers.

38

THEY HAD CANDY IN A HARD CHAIR against the wall of the Sheriff's anteroom. He hated me with his eyes as I went by him into the big square room where Sheriff Petersen held court in the middle of a collection of testimonials from a grateful public to his twenty years of faithful public service. The walls were loaded with photographs of horses and Sheriff Petersen made a personal appearance in every photograph. The corners of his carved desk were horses' heads. His inkwell was a mounted polished horse's hoof and his pens were planted in the mate to it filled with white sand. A gold plate on each of these said something or other about a date. In the middle of a spotless desk blotter lay a bag of Bull Durham and a pack of brown cigarette papers. Petersen rolled his own. He could roll one with one hand on horseback and often did, especially when leading a parade on a big white horse with a Mexican saddle loaded with beautiful Mexican silverwork. On horseback he wore a flat-crowned Mexican sombrero. He rode beautifully and his horse always knew exactly when to be quiet, when to act up so that the Sheriff with his calm inscrutable smile could bring the horse back under control with one hand. The Sheriff had a good act. He had a handsome hawklike profile, getting a little saggy under the chin by now, but he knew how to hold his head so it wouldn't show too much. He put a lot of hard work into having his picture taken. He was in his middle fifties and his father, a Dane, had left him a lot of money. The Sheriff didn't look like a Dane, because his hair was dark and his skin was brown and he had the impassive poise of a cigar store Indian and about the same kind of brains. But nobody had ever called him a crook. There had been crooks in his department and they had fooled him as well as they had fooled the public, but none of the crookedness rubbed off on Sheriff Petersen. He just went right on getting elected without even trying, riding white horses at the head of parades, and questioning suspects in front of cameras. That's what the captions said. As a matter of fact he never questioned anybody. He wouldn't have known how. He just sat at his desk looking sternly at the suspect, showing his profile to the camera. The flash bulbs would go off, the camera men would thank the Sheriff deferentially, and the suspect would be removed not having opened his mouth, and the Sheriff would go home to his ranch in the San Fernando Valley. There he could always be reached. If you couldn't reach him in person, you could talk to one of his horses.

Once in a while, come election time, some misguided politician would try to get Sheriff Petersen's job, and would be apt to call him things like The Guy With The Built-In Profile or The Ham That Smokes Itself, but it didn't get him anywhere. Sheriff Petersen just went right on getting re-elected, a living testimonial to the fact that you can hold an important public office forever in our country with no qualifications for it but a clean nose, a photogenic face, and a close mouth. If on top of that you look good on a horse, you are unbeatable.

As Ohls and I went in, Sheriff Petersen was standing behind his desk and the camera boys were filing out by another door. The Sheriff had his white stetson on. He was rolling a cigarette. He was all set to go home. He looked at me sternly.

"Who's this?" he asked in a rich baritone voice.

"Name's Philip Marlowe, Chief," Ohls said. "Only person in the house when Wade shot himself. You want a picture?"

The Sheriff studied me. "I don't think so," he said, and turned to a big tired-looking man with iron-gray hair. "If you need me, I'll be at the ranch, Captain Hernandez."

"Yes, sir."

Petersen lit his cigarette with a kitchen match. He lit it on his thumbnail. No lighters for Sheriff Petersen. He was strictly a roll-your-own-and-light-'em-with-one-hand type.

He said goodnight and went out. A deadpan character with hard black eyes went with him, his personal bodyguard. The door closed. When he was gone Captain Hernandez moved to the desk and sat in the Sheriff's enormous chair and a stenotype operator in the corner moved his stand out from the wall to get elbow room. Ohls sat at the end of the desk and looked amused.

"All right, Marlowe," Hernandez said briskly. "Let's have it."

"How come I don't get my photo taken?"

"You heard what the Sheriff said."

"Yeah, but why?" I whined.

Ohls laughed. "You know damn well why."

"You mean on account of I'm tall, dark, and handsome and somebody might look at me?"

"Cut it," Hernandez said coldly. "Let's get on with your statement. Start from the beginning."

I gave it to them from the beginning: my interview with Howard Spencer, my meeting with Eileen Wade, her asking me to find Roger, my finding him, her asking me to the house, what Wade asked me to do and how I found him passed out near the hibiscus bushes and the rest of it. The stenotype operator took it down. Nobody interrupted me. All of it was true. The truth and nothing but the truth. But not quite all the truth. What I left out was my business.

"Nice," Hernandez said at the end. "But not quite complete." This was a cool competent dangerous guy, this Hernandez. Somebody in the Sheriff's office had to be. "The night Wade shot off the gun in his bedroom you went into Mrs. Wade's room and were in there for some time with the door shut. What were you doing in there?"

"She called me in and asked me how he was."

"Why shut the door?"

"Wade was half asleep and I didn't want to make any noise. Also the houseboy was hanging around with his ear out. Also she asked me to shut the door. I didn't realize it was going to be important."

"How long were you in there?"

"I don't know. Three minutes maybe."

"I suggest you were in there a couple of hours," Hernandez said coldly. "Do I make myself clear?"

I looked at Ohls. Ohls didn't look at anything. He was chewing on an unlighted cigarette as usual.

"You are misinformed, Captain."

"We'll see. After you left the room you went downstairs to the study and spent the night on the couch. Perhaps I should say the rest of the night."

"It was ten minutes to eleven when he called me at home. It was long past two o'clock when I went into the study for the last time that night. Call it the rest of the night if you like."

"Get the houseboy in here," Hernandez said.

Ohls went out and came back with Candy. They put Candy in a chair. Hernandez asked him a few questions to establish who he was and so on. Then he said: "All right, Candy — we'll call you that for convenience — after you helped Marlowe put Roger Wade to bed, what happened?"

I knew what was coming more or less. Candy told his story in a quiet savage voice with very little accent. It seemed as if he could turn that on and off at will. His story was that he had hung around downstairs in case he was wanted again, part of the time in the kitchen where he got himself some food, part of the time in the living room. While in the living room sitting in a chair near the front door he had seen Eileen Wade standing in the door of her room and he had seen her take her clothes off. He had seen her put a robe on with nothing under it and he had seen me go into her room and I shut the door and stayed in there a long time, a couple of hours he thought. He had gone up the stairs and listened. He had heard the bedsprings making sounds. He had heard whispering. He made his meaning very obvious. When he had finished he gave me a corrosive look and his mouth was twisted tight with hatred.

"Take him out," Hernandez said.

"Just a minute," I said. "I want to question him."

"I ask the questions here," Hernandez said sharply.

"You don't know how, Captain. You weren't there. He's lying and he knows it and I know it."

Hernandez leaned back and picked up one of the Sheriff's pens. He bent the handle of the pen. It was long and pointed and made of stiffened horsehair. When he let go of the point it sprang back.

"Shoot," he said at last.

I faced Candy. "Where were you when you saw Mrs. Wade take her clothes off?"

"I was sitting down in a chair near the front door," he said in a surly tone.

"Between the front door and the two facing davenports?"

"What I said."

"Where was Mrs. Wade?"

"Just inside the door of her room. The door was open."

"What light was there in the living room?"

"One lamp. Tall lamp what they call a bridge lamp."

"What light was on the balcony?"

"No light. Light in her bedroom."

"What kind of light in her bedroom?"

"Not much light. Night table lamp, maybe."

"Not a ceiling light?"

"No."

"After she took her clothes off — standing just inside the door of her room, you said — she put on a robe. What kind of robe?"

"Blue robe. Long thing like a house coat. She tie it with a sash."

"So if you hadn't actually seen her take her clothes off you wouldn't know what she had on under the robe?"

He shrugged. He looked vaguely worried. "Sí. That's right. But I see her take her clothes off."

"You're a liar. There isn't any place in the living room from which you could see her take her clothes off right bang in her doorway, much less inside her room. She would have to come out to the edge of the balcony. If she had done that she would have seen you."

He just glared at me. I turned to Ohls. "You've seen the house. Captain Hernandez hasn't — or has he?"

Ohls shook his head slightly. Hernandez frowned and said nothing.

"There is no spot in that living room, Captain Hernandez, from which he could see even the top of Mrs. Wade's head — even if he was standing up — and he says he was sitting down — provided she was as far back as her own doorway or inside it. I'm four inches taller than he is and I could only see the top foot of an open door when I was standing just inside the front door of the house. She would have to come out to the edge of the balcony for him to see what he says he saw. Why would she do that? Why would she undress in her doorway even? There's no sense to it."

Hernandez just looked at me. Then he looked at Candy. "How about the time element?" he asked softly, speaking to me.

"That's his word against mine. I'm talking about what can be proved."

Hernandez spit Spanish at Candy too fast for me to understand. Candy just stared at him sulkily.

"Take him out," Hernandez said.

Ohls jerked a thumb and opened the door. Candy went out. Hernandez brought out a box of cigarettes, stuck one on his lip, and lit it with a gold lighter.

Ohls came back into the room. Hernandez said calmly: "I just told him that if there was an inquest and he told that story on the stand, he'd find himself doing a one-to-three up in Q for perjury. Didn't seem to impress him much. It's obvious what's eating him. An old-fashioned case of hot pants. If he'd been around and we had any reason to suspect murder, he'd make a pretty good pigeon —

except that he would have used a knife. I got the impression earlier that he felt pretty bad about Wade's death. Any questions you want to ask, Ohls?"

Ohls shook his head. Hernandez looked at me and said: "Come back in the morning and sign your statement. We'll have it typed out by then. We ought to have a P.M. report by ten o'clock, preliminary anyway. Anything you don't like about this setup, Marlowe?"

"Would you mind rephrasing the question? The way you put it suggests there might be something I do like about it."

"Okay," he said wearily. "Take off. I'm going home."

I stood up.

"Of course I never did believe that stuff Candy pulled on us," he said. "Just used it for a corkscrew. No hard feelings, I hope."

"No feelings at all, Captain. No feelings at all."

They watched me go out and didn't say goodnight. I walked down the long corridor to the Hill Street entrance and got into my car and drove home.

No feelings at all was exactly right. I was as hollow and empty as the spaces between the stars. When I got home I mixed a stiff one and stood by the open window in the living room and sipped it and listened to the groundswell of the traffic on Laurel Canyon Boulevard and looked at the glare of the big angry city hanging over the shoulder of the hills through which the boulevard had been cut. Far off the banshee wail of police or fire sirens rose and fell, never for very long completely silent. Twenty-four hours a day somebody is running, somebody else is trying to catch him. Out there in the night of a thousand crimes people were dying, being maimed, cut by flying glass, crushed against steering wheels or under heavy tires. People were being beaten, robbed, strangled, raped, and murdered. People were hungry, sick, bored, desperate with loneliness or remorse or fear, angry, cruel, feverish, shaken by sobs. A city no worse than others, a city rich and vigorous and full of pride, a city lost and beaten and full of emptiness.

It all depends on where you sit and what your own private score is. I didn't have one. I didn't care.

I finished the drink and went to bed.

39

THE INQUEST WAS A FLOP. The coroner sailed into it before the medical evidence was complete, for fear the publicity would die on him. He needn't have worried. The death of a writer — even a loud writer — is not news for long, and that summer there was too much to compete. A king abdicated and another was assassinated. In one week three large passenger planes crashed. The head man of a big wire service was shot to pieces in Chicago in his own automobile. Twenty-four convicts were burned to death in a prison fire. The Coroner of Los Angeles County was out of luck. He was missing the good things in life.

As I left the stand I saw Candy. He had a bright malicious grin on his face — I had no idea why — and as usual he was dressed just a little too well, in a cocoa brown gabardine suit with a white nylon shirt and a midnight blue bow tie. On the witness stand he was quiet and made a good impression. Yes, the boss had been pretty drunk lately a lot of times. Yes, he had helped put him to bed the night the gun went off upstairs. Yes, the boss had demanded whiskey before he, Candy, left on the last day, but he had refused to get it. No, he didn't know anything about Mr. Wade's literary work, but he knew the boss had been discouraged. He kept throwing it away and then getting it out of the wastebasket again. No, he had never heard Mr. Wade quarreling with anyone. And so on. The coroner milked him but it was thin stuff. Somebody had done a good coaching job on Candy.

Eileen Wade wore black and white. She was pale and spoke in a low clear voice which even the amplifier could not spoil. The coroner handled her with two pairs of velvet gloves. He talked to her as if he had trouble keeping the sobs out of his voice. When she left the stand he stood up and bowed and she gave him a faint fugitive smile that nearly made him choke on his saliva.

She almost passed me without a glance on the way out, then at the last moment turned her head a couple of inches and nodded very slightly, as if I was somebody she must have met somewhere a long time ago, but couldn't quite place in her memory.

Outside on the steps when it was all over I ran into Ohls. He was watching the traffic down below, or pretending to.

"Nice job," he said without turning his head. "Congratulations."

"You did all right on Candy."

"Not me, kid. The D.A. decided the sexy stuff was irrelevant."

"What sexy stuff was that?"

He looked at me then. "Ha, ha, ha," he said. "And I don't mean you." Then his expression got remote. "I been looking at them for too many years. It wearies a man. This one came out of the special bottle. Old private stock. Strictly for the carriage trade. So long, sucker. Call me when you start wearing twenty-dollar shirts. I'll drop around and hold your coat for you."

People eddied around us going up and down the steps. We just stood there. Ohls took a cigarette out of his pocket and looked at it and dropped it on the concrete and ground it to nothing with his heel.

"Wasteful," I said.

"Only a cigarette, pal. It's not a life. After a while maybe you marry the girl, huh?"

"Shove it."

He laughed sourly. "I been talking to the right people about the wrong things," he said acidly. "Any objection?"

"No objection, Lieutenant," I said, and went on down the steps. He said something behind me but I kept going.

I went over to a corn-beef joint on Flower. It suited my mood. A rude sign over the entrance said: "Men Only. Dogs and Women Not Admitted." The service inside was equally polished. The waiter who tossed your food at you needed a shave and deducted his tip without being invited. The food was simple but very good and they had a brown Swedish beer which could hit as hard as a martini.

When I got back to the office the phone was ringing. Ohls said: "I'm coming by your place. I've got things to say."

He must have been at or near the Hollywood substation because he was in the office inside twenty minutes. He planted himself in the customer's chair and crossed his legs and growled:

"I was out of line. Sorry. Forget it."

"Why forget it? Let's open up the wound."

"Suits me. Under the hat, though. To some people you're a wrong gee. I never knew you to do anything too crooked."

"What was the crack about twenty-dollar shirts?"

"Aw hell, I was just sore," Ohls said. "I was thinking of old man Potter. Like he told a secretary to tell a lawyer to tell District Attorney Springer to tell Captain Hernandez you were a personal friend of his."

"He wouldn't take the trouble."

"You met him. He gave you time."

"I met him, period. I didn't like him, but perhaps it was only envy. He sent for me to give me some advice. He's big and he's tough and I don't know what else. I don't figure he's a crook."

"There ain't no clean way to make a hundred million bucks," Ohls said. "Maybe the head man thinks his hands are clean but somewhere along the line guys got pushed to the wall, nice little businesses got the ground cut from under them and had to sell out for nickels, decent people lost their jobs, stocks got rigged on the market, proxies got bought up like a pennyweight of old gold, and the five per centers and the big law firms got paid hundred-grand fees for beating some law the people wanted but the rich guys didn't, on account of it cut into their profits. Big money is big power and big power gets used wrong. It's the system. Maybe it's the best we can get, but it still ain't any Ivory Soap deal."

"You sound like a Red," I said, just to needle him.

"I wouldn't know," he said contemptuously. "I ain't been investigated yet. You liked the suicide verdict, didn't you?"

"What else could it be?"

"Nothing else, I guess." He put his hard blunt hands on the desk and looked at the big brown freckles on the backs of them. "I'm getting old. Keratosis, they call those brown spots. You don't get them until you're past fifty. I'm an old cop and an old cop is an old bastard. I don't like a few things about this Wade death."

"Such as?" I leaned back and watched the tight sun wrinkles around his eyes.

"You get so you can smell a wrong setup, even when you know you can't do a damn thing about it. Then you just sit and talk like now. I don't like that he left no note."

"He was drunk. Probably just a sudden crazy impulse."

Ohls lifted his pale eyes and dropped his hands off the desk. "I went through his desk. He wrote letters to himself. He wrote and wrote and wrote. Drunk or sober he hit that typewriter. Some of it is wild, some of it kind of funny, and some of it is sad. The guy had something on his mind. He wrote all around it but he never quite touched it. That guy would have left a two-page letter if he knocked himself off."

"He was drunk," I said again.

"With him that didn't matter," Ohls said wearily. "The next thing I don't like is he did it there in that room and left his wife to find him. Okay, he was drunk. I still don't like it. The next thing I don't like is he pulled the trigger just when the noise of that speedboat could drown out the shot. What difference would it make to him? More coincidence, huh? More coincidence still that the wife forgot her door keys on the help's day off and had to ring the bell to get into the house."

"She could have walked around to the back," I said.

"Yeah, I know. What I'm talking about is a situation. Nobody to answer the door but you, and she said on the stand she didn't know you were there. Wade wouldn't have heard the bell if he had been alive and working in his study. His door is soundproofed. The help was away. That was Thursday. That she forgot. Like she forgot her keys."

"You're forgetting something yourself, Bernie. My car was in the driveway. So she knew I was there — or that somebody was there — before she rang the bell."

He grinned. "I forgot that, didn't I? All right, here's the picture. You were down at the lake, the speedboat was making all that racket — incidentally it was a couple of guys from Lake Arrowhead just visiting, had their boat on a trailer — Wade was asleep in his study or passed out, somebody took the gun out of his desk already, and she knew you had put it there because you told her that other time. Now suppose she didn't forget her keys, that she goes into the house, looks across and sees you down at the water, looks into the study and sees Wade asleep, knows where the gun is, gets it, waits for the right moment, plugs him, drops the gun where it was found, goes back outside the house, waits a little while for the speedboat to go away, and then rings the doorbell and waits for you to open it. Any objections?"

"With what motive?"

"Yeah," he said sourly. "That knocks it. If she wanted to slough the guy, it was easy. She had him over a barrel, habitual drunk, record of violence to her. Plenty alimony, nice fat property settlement. No motive at all. Anyhow the timing was too neat. Five minutes earlier and she couldn't have done it unless you were in on it."

I started to say something but he put his hand up. "Take it easy. I'm not accusing anybody, just speculating. Five minutes later and you get the same answer. She had ten minutes to pull it off."

"Ten minutes," I said irritably, "that couldn't possibly have been foreseen, much less planned."

He leaned back in the chair and sighed. "I know. You've got all the answers, I've got all the answers. And I still don't like it. What the hell were you doing with these people anyway? The guy writes you a check for a grand, then tears it up. Got mad at you, you say. You didn't want it anyway, wouldn't have taken it, you say. Maybe. Did he think you were sleeping with his wife?"

"Lay off, Bernie."

"I didn't ask were you, I asked did he think you were."

"Same answer."

"Okay, try this. What did the Mex have on him?"

"Nothing that I know of."

"The Mex has too much money. Over fifteen hundred in the bank, all kinds of clothes, a brand new Chevvy."

"Maybe he peddles dope," I said.

Ohls pushed himself up out of the chair and scowled down at me. "You're an awful lucky boy, Marlowe. Twice you've slid out from under a heavy one. You could get overconfident. You were pretty helpful to those people and you didn't make a dime. You were pretty helpful to a guy named Lennox too, the way I hear it. And you didn't make a dime out of that one either. What do you do for eating money, pal? You got a lot saved so you don't have to work any more?"

I stood up and walked around the desk and faced him. "I'm a

romantic, Bernie. I hear voices crying in the night and I go see what's the matter. You don't make a dime that way. You got sense, you shut your windows and turn up more sound on the TV set. Or you shove down on the gas and get far away from there. Stay out of other people's troubles. All it can get you is the smear. The last time I saw Terry Lennox we had a cup of coffee together that I made myself in my house, and we smoked a cigarette. So when I heard he was dead I went out to the kitchen and made some coffee and poured a cup for him and lit a cigarette for him and when the coffee was cold and the cigarette was burned down I said goodnight to him. You don't make a dime that way. *You* wouldn't do it. That's why you're a good cop and I'm a private eye. Eileen Wade is worried about her husband, so I go out and find him and bring him home. Another time he's in trouble and calls me up and I go out and carry him in off the lawn and put him to bed, and I don't make a dime out of it. No percentage at all. No nothing, except sometimes I get my face pushed in or get tossed in the can or get threatened by some fast money boy like Mendy Menendez. But no money, not a dime. I've got a five-thousand-dollar bill in my safe but I'll never spend a nickel of it. Because there was something wrong with the way I got it. I played with it a little at first and I still get it out once in a while and look at it. But that's all — not a dime of spending money."

"Must be a phony," Ohls said dryly, "except they don't make them that big. So what's your point with all this yap?"

"No point. I told you I was a romantic."

"I heard you. And you don't make a dime at it. I heard that too."

"But I can always tell a cop to go to hell. Go to hell, Bernie."

"You wouldn't tell me to go to hell if I had you in the back room under the light, chum."

"Maybe we'll find out about that some day."

He walked to the door and yanked it open. "You know something, kid? You think you're cute but you're just stupid. You're a shadow on the wall. I've got twenty years on the cops without a mark against me. I know when I'm being kidded and I know when a guy is holding out on me. The wise guy never fools anybody but himself. Take it from me, chum. I know."

He pulled his head back out of the doorway and let the door close. His heels hammered down the corridor. I could still hear them when the phone on my desk started to sound. The voice said in that clear professional tone:

"New York is calling Mr. Philip Marlowe."

"I'm Philip Marlowe."

"Thank you. One moment, please, Mr. Marlowe. Here is your party."

The next voice I knew. "Howard Spencer, Mr. Marlowe. We've heard about Roger Wade. It was a pretty hard blow. We haven't the full details, but your name seems to be involved."

"I was there when it happened. He just got drunk and shot himself. Mrs. Wade came home a little later. The servants were away — Thursday's the day off."

"You were alone with him?"

"I wasn't with him. I was outside the house, just hanging around waiting for his wife to come home."

"I see. Well, I suppose there will be an inquest."

"It's all over, Mr. Spencer. Suicide. And remarkably little publicity."

"Really? That's curious." He didn't exactly sound disappointed — more like puzzled and surprised. "He was so well known. I should have thought — well, never mind what I thought. I guess I'd better fly out there, but I can't make it before the end of next week. I'll send a wire to Mrs. Wade. There may be something I could do for her — and also about the book. I mean there may be enough of it so that we could get someone to finish it. I assume you did take the job after all."

"No. Although he asked me to himself. I told him right out I couldn't stop him from drinking."

"Apparently you didn't even try."

"Look, Mr. Spencer, you don't know the first damn thing about this situation. Why not wait until you do before jumping to conclusions? Not that I don't blame myself a little. I guess that's inevitable when something like this happens, and you're the guy on the spot."

"Of course," he said. "I'm sorry I made that remark. Most uncalled for. Will Eileen Wade be at her home now — or wouldn't you know?"

"I wouldn't know, Mr. Spencer. Why don't you just call her up?"

"I hardly think she would want to speak to anyone yet," he said slowly.

"Why not? She talked to the Coroner and never batted an eye."

He cleared his throat. "You don't sound exactly sympathetic."

"Roger Wade is dead, Spencer. He was a bit of a bastard and maybe a bit of a genius too. That's over my head. He was an egotistical drunk and he hated his own guts. He made me a lot of trouble and in the end a lot of grief. Why the hell should I be sympathetic?"

"I was talking about Mrs. Wade," he said shortly.

"So was I."

"I'll call you when I get in," he said abruptly. "Goodbye."

He hung up. I hung up. I stared at the telephone for a couple of minutes without moving. Then I got the phone book up on the desk and looked for a number.

40

I CALLED SEWELL ENDICOTT'S OFFICE. Somebody said he was in court and would not be available until late in the afternoon. Would I care to leave my name? No.

I dialed the number of Mendy Menendez's joint on the Strip. It was called El Tapado this year, not a bad name either. In American Spanish that means buried treasure among other things. It had been called other names in the past, quite a few other names. One year it was just a blue neon number on a blank high wall facing south on the Strip, with its back against the hill and a driveway curving around one side out of sight of the street. Very exclusive.

Nobody knew much about it except vice cops and mobsters and people who could afford thirty bucks for a good dinner and any amount up to fifty grand in the big quiet room upstairs.

I got a woman who didn't know from nothing. Then I got a captain with a Mex accent.

"You wish to speak with Mr. Menendez? Who is calling?"

"No names, amigo. Private matter."

"Un momento, por favor."

There was a longish wait. I got a hard boy this time. He sounded as if he was talking through the slit in an armored car. It was probably just the slit in his face.

"Talk it up. Who wants him?"

"The name's Marlowe."

"Who's Marlowe?"

"This Chick Agostino?"

"No, this ain't Chick. Come on, let's have the password."

"Go fry your face."

There was a chuckle. "Hold the line."

Finally another voice said: "Hello, cheapie. What's the time by you?"

"You alone?"

"You can talk, cheapie. I been looking over some acts for the floor show."

"You could cut your throat for one."

"What would I do for an encore?"

I laughed. He laughed. "Been keeping your nose clean?" he asked.

"Haven't you heard? I got to be friends with another guy who suicided. They're going to call me the 'Kiss-of-Death Kid' from now on."

"That's funny, huh?"

"No, it isn't funny. Also the other afternoon I had tea with Harlan Potter."

"Nice going. I never drink the stuff myself."

"He said for you to be nice to me."

"I never met the guy and I don't figure to."

"He casts a long shadow. All I want is a little information, Mendy. Like about Paul Marston."

"Never heard of him."

"You said that too quick. Paul Marston was the name Terry Lennox used one time in New York before he came west."

"So?"

"His prints were checked through the F.B.I. files. No record. That means he never served in the Armed Forces."

"So?"

"Do I have to draw you a picture? Either that foxhole yarn of yours was all spaghetti or it happened somewhere else."

"I didn't say where it happened, cheapie. Take a kind word and forget the whole thing. You got told, you better stay told."

"Oh sure. I do something you don't like and I'm swimming to Catalina with a streetcar on my back. Don't try to scare me, Mendy. I've been up against the pros. You ever been in England?"

"Be smart, cheapie. Things can happen to a guy in this town. Things can happen to big strong boys like Big Willie Magoon. Take a look at the evening paper."

"I'll get one if you say so. It might even have my picture in it. What about Magoon?"

"Like I said — things can happen. I wouldn't know how except what I read. Seems Magoon tried to shake down four boys in a car with Nevada plates. Was parked right by his house. Nevada plates with big numbers like they don't have. Must have been some kind of a rib. Only Magoon ain't feeling funny, what with both arms in casts, and his jaw wired in three places, and one leg in high traction. Magoon ain't tough any more. It could happen to you."

"He bothered you, huh? I saw him bounce your boy Chick off the wall in front of Victor's. Should I ring up a friend in the Sheriff's office and tell him?"

"You do that, cheapie," he said very slowly. "You do that."

"And I'll mention that at the time I was just through having a drink with Harlan Potter's daughter. Corroborative evidence, in a sense, don't you think? You figure to smash her up too?"

"Listen to me careful, cheapie — "

"Were you ever in England, Mendy? You and Randy Starr and Paul Marston or Terry Lennox or whatever his name was? In the British Army perhaps? Had a little racket in Soho and got hot and figured the Army was a cooling-off spot?"

"Hold the line."

I held it. Nothing happened except that I waited and my arm got tired. I switched the receiver to the other side. Finally he came back.

"Now listen careful, Marlowe. You stir up that Lennox case and you're dead. Terry was a pal and I got feelings too. So you got feelings. I'll go along with you just this far. It was a Commando outfit. It was British. It happened in Norway, one of those islands off the coast. They got a million of them. November 1942. Now will you lie down and rest that tired brain of yours?"

"Thank you, Mendy. I will do that. Your secret is safe with me. I'm not telling it to anybody but the people I know."

"Buy yourself a paper, cheapie. Read and remember. Big tough Willie Magoon. Beat up in front of his own house. Boy, was he surprised when he come out of the ether!"

He hung up. I went downstairs and bought a paper and it was just as Menendez had said. There was a picture of Big Willie Magoon in his hospital bed. You could see half his face and one eye. The rest of him was bandages. Seriously but not critically injured. The boys had been very careful about that. They wanted him to live. After all he was a cop. In our town the mobs don't kill a cop. They leave that to the juveniles. And a live cop who has been put through the meat grinder is a much better advertisement. He gets well eventually and goes back to work. But from that time on something is missing — the last inch of steel that makes all the difference. He's a walking lesson that it is a mistake to push the racket boys too hard — especially if you are on the vice squad and eating at the best places and driving a Cadillac.

I sat there and brooded about it for a while and then I dialed the number of The Carne Organization and asked for George Peters. He was out. I left my name and said it was urgent. He was expected in about five-thirty.

I went over to the Hollywood Public Library and asked questions in the reference room, but couldn't find what I wanted. So I had to go back for my Olds and drive downtown to the Main Library. I found it there, in a smallish red-bound book published in England.

I copied what I wanted from it and drove home. I called The Carne Organization again. Peters was still out, so I asked the girl to re-route the call to me at home.

I put the chessboard on the coffee table and set out a problem called The Sphynx. It is printed on the end papers of a book on chess by Blackburn, the English chess wizard, probably the most dynamic chess player who ever lived, although he wouldn't get to first base in the cold war type of chess they play nowadays. The Sphynx is an eleven-mover and it justifies its name. Chess problems seldom run to more than four or five moves. Beyond that the diffi-culty of solving them rises in almost geometrical progression. An eleven-mover is sheer unadulterated torture.

Once in a long while when I feel mean I enough I set it out and look for a new way to solve it. It's a nice quiet way to go crazy. You don't even scream, but you come awfully close.

George Peters called me at five-forty. We exchanged pleasantries and condolences.

"You've got yourself in another jam, I see," he said cheerfully. "Why don't you try some quiet business like embalming?"

"Takes too long to learn. Listen, I want to become a client of your agency, if it doesn't cost too much."

"Depends what you want done, old boy. And you'd have to talk to Carne."

"No."

"Well, tell me."

"London is full of guys like me, but I wouldn't know one from the other. They call them private enquiry agents. Your outfit would have connections. I'd just have to pick a name at random and probably get hornswoggled. I want some information that should be easy enough to get, and I want it quick. Must have it before the end of next week."

"Spill."

"I want to know something about the war service of Terry Lennox or Paul Marston, whatever name he used. He was in the Commandos over there. He was captured wounded in November 1942 in a raid on some Norwegian island. I want to know what outfit he was posted from and what happened to him. The War Office will have all that. It's not secret information, or I wouldn't think so. Let's say a question of inheritance is involved."

"You don't need a P.I. for that. You could get it direct. Write them a letter."

"Shove it, George. I might get an answer in three months. I want one in five days."

"You have a thought there, pal. Anything else?"

"One thing more. They keep all their vital records over there in a place they call Somerset House. I want to know if he figures there in any connection — birth, marriage, naturalization, anything at all."

"Why?"

"What do you mean, why? Who's paying the bill?"

"Suppose the names don't show?"

"Then I'm stuck. If they do, I want certified copies of anything your man turns up. How much you soaking me?"

"I'll have to ask Carne. He may thumb it out altogether. We don't want the kind of publicity you get. If he lets me handle it, and you agree not to mention the connection, I'd say three hundred bucks. Those guys over there don't get much by dollar standards. He might hit us for ten guineas, less than thirty bucks. On top of that any expenses he might have. Say fifty bucks altogether and Carne wouldn't open a file for less than two-fifty."

"Professional rates."

"Ha, ha. He never heard of them."

"Call me, George. Want to eat dinner?"

"Romanoff's?"

"All right," I growled, "if they'll give me a reservation — which I doubt."

"We can have Carne's table. I happen to know he's dining privately. He's a regular at Romanoff's. It pays off in the upper brackets of the business. Carne is a pretty big boy in this town."

"Yeah, sure. I know somebody — and know him personally —, who could lose Carne under his little fingernail."

"Good work, kid. I always knew you would come through in the clutch. See you about seven o'clock in the bar at Romanoff's. Tell the head thief you're waiting for Colonel Carne. He'll clear a space around you so you don't get elbowed by any riffraff like screenwriters or television actors."

"See you at seven," I said.

We hung up and I went back to the chess board. But The Sphinx didn't seem to interest me any more. In a little while Peters called me back and said it was all right with Carne provided the name of their agency was not connected with my problems. Peters said he would get a night letter off to London at once.

41

HOWARD SPENCER CALLED ME on the following Friday morning. He was at the Ritz-Beverly and suggested I drop over for a drink in the bar.

"Better make it in your room," I said.

"Very well, if you prefer it. Room 828. I've just talked to Eileen Wade. She seems quite resigned. She has read the script Roger left and says she thinks it can be finished off very easily. It will be a good deal shorter than his other books, but that is balanced by the publicity value. I guess you think we publishers are a pretty callous bunch. Eileen will be home all afternoon. Naturally she wants to see me and I want to see her."

"I'll be over in half an hour, Mr. Spencer."

He had a nice roomy suite on the west side of the hotel. The living room had tall windows opening on a narrow iron-railed balcony. The furniture was upholstered in some candy-striped material and that with the heavily flowered design of the carpet gave it an old-fashioned air, except that everything you could put a drink down on had a plate glass top and there were nineteen ash trays spotted around. A hotel room is a pretty sharp indication of the manners of the guests. The Ritz-Beverly wasn't expecting them to have any.

Spencer shook hands. "Sit down," he said. "What will you drink?"

"Anything or nothing. I don't have to have a drink."

"I fancy a glass of Amontillado. California is poor drinking country in the summer. In New York you can handle four times as much for one half the hangover."

"I'll take a rye whiskey sour."

He went to the phone and ordered. Then he sat down on one of the candy-striped chairs and took off his rimless glasses to polish them on a handkerchief. He put them back on, adjusted them carefully, and looked at me.

"I take it you have something on your mind. That's why you wanted to see me up here rather than in the bar."

"I'll drive you out to Idle Valley. I'd like to see Mrs. Wade too."

He looked a little uncomfortable. "I'm not sure that she wants to see you," he said.

"I know she doesn't. I can get in on your ticket."

"That would not be very diplomatic of me, would it?"

"She tell you she didn't want to see me?"

"Not exactly, not in so many words." He cleared his throat. "I get the impression that she blames you for Roger's death."

"Yeah. She said that right out — to the deputy who came the afternoon he died. She probably said it to the Sheriff's homicide lieutenant that investigated the death. She didn't say it to the Coroner, however."

He leaned back and scratched the inside of his hand with a finger, slowly. It was just a sort of doodling gesture.

"What good would it do for you to see her, Marlowe? It was a pretty dreadful experience for her. I imagine her whole life had been pretty dreadful for some time. Why make her live it over? Do you expect to convince her that you didn't miss out a little?"

"She told the deputy I killed him."

"She couldn't have meant that literally. Otherwise — "

The door buzzer rang. He got up to go to the door and open it. The room service waiter came in with the drinks and put them down with as much flourish as if he was serving a seven course dinner. Spencer signed the check and gave him four bits. The guy went away. Spencer picked up his glass of sherry and walked away as if he didn't want to hand me my drink. I let it stay where it was.

"Otherwise what?" I asked him.

"Otherwise she *would* have said something to the Coroner, wouldn't she?" He frowned at me. "I think we are talking non-sense. Just what did you want to see me about?"

"You wanted to see me."

"Only," he said coldly, "because when I talked to you from New York you said I was jumping to conclusions. That implied to me that you had something to explain. Well, what is it?"

"I'd like to explain it in front of Mrs. Wade."

"I don't care for the idea. I think you had better make your own arrangements. I have a great regard for Eileen Wade. As a business-man I'd like to salvage Roger's work if it can be done. If Eileen feels about you as you suggest, I can't be the means of getting you into her house. Be reasonable."

"That's all right," I said. "Forget it. I can get to see her without any trouble. I just thought I'd like to have somebody along with me as a witness."

"Witness to what?" he almost snapped at me.

"You'll hear it in front of her or you won't hear it at all."

"Then I won't hear it at all."

I stood up. "You're probably doing the right thing, Spencer. You want that book of Wade's — if it can be used. And you want to be a nice guy. Both laudable ambitions. I don't share either of them. The best of luck to you and goodbye."

He stood up suddenly and started towards me. "Now just a minute, Marlowe. I don't know what's on your mind but you seem to take it hard. Is there some mystery about Roger Wade's death?"

"No mystery at all. He was shot through the head with a Webley Hammerless revolver. Didn't you see a report of the inquest?"

"Certainly." He was standing close to me now and he looked bothered. "That was in the eastern papers and a couple of days later a much fuller account in the Los Angeles papers. He was alone in the house, although you were not far away. The servants were away, Candy and the cook, and Eileen had been uptown shop-ping and arrived home just after it happened. At the moment it happened a very noisy motorboat on the lake drowned the sound of the shot, so that even you didn't hear it."

"That's correct," I said. "Then the motorboat went away, and I walked back from the lake edge and into the house, heard the doorbell ringing, and opened it to find Eileen Wade had forgotten her keys. Roger was already dead. She looked into the study from the doorway, thought he was asleep on the couch, went up to her room, then out to the kitchen to make some tea. A little later than she did I also looked into the study, noticed there was no sound of breathing, and found out why. In due course I called the law."

"I see no mystery," Spencer said quietly, all the sharpness gone from his voice. "It was Roger's own gun, and only the week before he had shot it off in his own room. You found Eileen struggling to get it away from him. His state of mind, his behavior, his depressions over his work — all that was brought out."

"She told you the stuff is good. Why should he be depressed over it?"

"That's just her opinion, you know. It may be very bad. Or he may have thought it worse than it was. Go on. I'm not a fool. I can see there is more."

"The homicide dick who investigated the case is an old friend of mine. He's a bulldog and a bloodhound and an old wise cop. He doesn't like a few things. Why did Roger leave no note — when he was a writing fool? Why did he shoot himself in such a way as to leave the shock of discovery to his wife? Why did he bother to pick the moment when I couldn't hear the gun go off? Why did she forget her house keys so that she had to be let in to the house? Why did she leave him alone on the day the help got off? Remember, she said she didn't know I would be there. If she did, those two cancel out."

"My God," Spencer bleated, "are you telling me the damn fool cop suspects Eileen?"

"He would if he could think of a motive."

"That's ridiculous. Why not suspect you? You had all afternoon. There could have been only a few minutes when she could have done it — and she had forgotten her house keys."

"What motive could I have?"

He reached back and grabbed my whiskey sour and swallowed it whole. He put the glass down carefully and got a handkerchief out and wiped his lips and his fingers where the chilled glass had moistened them. He put the handkerchief away. He stared at me.

"Is the investigation still going on?"

"Couldn't say. One thing is sure. They know by now whether he had drunk enough hooch to pass him out. If he had, there may still be trouble."

"And you want to talk to her," he said slowly, "in the presence of a witness."

"That's right."

"That means only one of two things to me, Marlowe. Either you are badly scared or you think she ought to be."

I nodded.

"Which one?" he asked grimly.

"I'm not scared."

He looked at his watch. "I hope to God you're crazy."

We looked at each other in silence.

42

NORTH THROUGH COLDWATER CANYON it began to get hot. When we topped the rise and started to wind down towards the San Fernando Valley it was breathless and blazing. I looked sideways at Spencer. He had a vest on, but the heat didn't seem to bother him. He had something else to bother him a lot more. He looked straight ahead through the windshield and said nothing. The valley had a thick layer of smog nuzzling down on it. From above it looked like a ground mist and then we were in it and it jerked Spencer out of his silence.

"My God, I thought Southern California had a climate," he said. "What are they doing — burning old truck tires?"

"It'll be all right in Idle Valley," I told him soothingly. "They get an ocean breeze in there."

"I'm glad they get something besides drunk," he said. "From what I've seen of the local crowd in the rich suburbs I think Roger made a tragic mistake in coming out here to live. A writer needs stimulation — and not the kind they bottle. There's nothing around here but one great big suntanned hangover. I'm referring to the upper crust people of course."

I turned off and slowed down for the dusty stretch to the entrance of Idle Valley, then hit the paving again and in a little while the ocean breeze made itself felt, drifting down through the gap in the hills at the far end of the lake. High sprinklers revolved over the big smooth lawns and the water made a swishing sound as it licked at the grass. By this time most of the well-heeled people were away somewhere else. You could tell by the shuttered look of the houses and the way the gardener's truck was parked smack in the middle of the driveway. Then we reached the Wades' place and I swung through the gateposts and stopped behind Eileen's Jaguar. Spencer got out and marched solidly across the flagstones to the portico of the house. He rang the bell and the door opened almost at once. Candy was there in the white jacket and the dark good-looking face and the sharp black eyes. Everything was in order.

Spencer went in. Candy gave me a brief look and neatly shut the door in my face. I waited and nothing happened. I leaned on the bell and heard the chimes. The door swung wide and Candy came out snarling.

"Beat it! Turn blue. You want a knife in the belly?"

"I came to see Mrs. Wade."

"She don't want any part of you."

"Out of my way, peasant. I got business here."

"Candy!" It was her voice, and it was sharp.

He gave me a final scowl and backed into the house. I went in and shut the door. She was standing at the end of one of the facing davenports, and Spencer was standing beside her. She looked like a million. She had white slacks on, very high-waisted, and a white sport shirt with half sleeves, and a lilac-colored handkerchief budding from the pocket over her left breast.

"Candy is getting rather dictatorial lately," she said to Spencer. "It's so good to see you, Howard. And so nice of you to come all this way. I didn't realize you were bringing someone with you."

"Marlowe drove me out," Spencer said. "Also he wanted to see you."

"I can't imagine why," she said coolly. Finally she looked at me, but not as if not seeing me for a week had left an emptiness in her life. "Well?"

"It's going to take a little time," I said.

She sat down slowly. I sat down on the other davenport. Spencer was frowning. He took his glasses off and polished them. That gave him a chance to frown more naturally. Then he sat on the other end of the davenport from me.

"I was sure you would come in time for lunch," she told him, smiling.

"Not today, thanks."

"No? Well, of course if you are too busy. Then you just want to see that script."

"If I may."

"Of course. Candy! Oh, he's gone. It's on the desk in Roger's study. I'll get it."

Spencer stood up. "May I get it?"

Without waiting for an answer he started across the room. Ten feet behind her he stopped and gave me a strained look. Then he went on. I just sat there and waited until her head came around and her eyes gave me a cool impersonal stare.

"What was it you wanted to see me about?" she asked curtly.

"This and that. I see you are wearing that pendant again."

"I often wear it. It was given to me by a very dear friend a long time ago."

"Yeah. You told me. It's a British military badge of some sort, isn't it?"

She held it out at the end of the thin chain. "It's a jeweler's reproduction of one. Smaller than the original and in gold and enamel."

Spencer came back across the room and sat down again and put a thick pile of yellow paper on the corner of the cocktail table in front of him. He glanced at it idly, then his eyes were watching Eileen.

"Could I look at it a little closer?" I asked her.

She pulled the chain around until she could unfasten the clasp. She handed the pendant to me, or rather she dropped it in my hand. Then she folded her hands in her lap and just looked curious. "Why are you so interested? It's the badge of a regiment called the Artists Rifles, a Territorial regiment. The man who gave it to me was lost soon afterwards. At Andalsnes in Norway, in the spring of that terrible year — 1940." She smiled and made a brief gesture with one hand. "He was in love with me."

"Eileen was in London all through the Blitz," Spencer said in an empty voice. "She couldn't get away."

We both ignored Spencer. "And you were in love with him," I said.

She looked down and then raised her head and our glances locked. "It was a long time ago," she said. "And there was a war. Strange things happen."

"There was a little more to it than that, Mrs. Wade. I guess you forget how much you opened up about him. 'The wild mysterious improbable kind of love that never comes but once.' I'm quoting you. In a way you're still in love with him. It's darn nice of me to have the same initials. I suppose that had something to do with your picking me out."

"His name was nothing like yours," she said coldly. "And he is dead, dead, dead."

I held the gold and enamel pendant out to Spencer. He took it reluctantly. "I've seen it before," he muttered.

"Check me on the design," I said. "It consists of a broad dagger in white enamel with a gold edge. The dagger points downwards and the flat of the blade crosses in front of a pair of upward-curling pale blue enamel wings. Then it crosses in back of a scroll. On the scroll are the words: WHO DARES WINS."

"That seems to be correct," he said. "What makes it important?"

"She says it's a badge of the Artists Rifles, a Territorial outfit. She says it was given to her by a man who was in that outfit and was lost in the Norwegian campaign with the British Army in the spring of 1940 at Andalsnes."

I had their attention. Spencer watched me steadily. I wasn't talking to the birds and he knew it. Eileen knew it too. Her tawny eyebrows were crimped in a puzzled frown which could have been genuine. It was also unfriendly.

"This is a sleeve badge," I said. "It came into existence because the Artists Rifles were made over or attached or seconded or whatever the correct term is into a Special Air Service Outfit. They had originally been a Territorial Regiment of infantry. This badge didn't even exist until 1947. Therefore nobody gave it to Mrs. Wade in 1940. Also, no Artists Rifles were landed at Andalsnes in Norway in 1940. Sherwood Foresters and Leicestershires, yes. Both Territorial. Artists Rifles, no. Am I being nasty?"

Spencer put the pendant down on the coffee table and pushed it slowly across until it was in front of Eileen. He said nothing.

"Do you think I wouldn't know?" Eileen asked me contemptuously.

"Do you think the British War Office wouldn't know?" I asked her right back.

"Obviously there must be some mistake," Spencer said mildly.

I swung around and gave him a hard stare. "That's one way of putting it."

"Another way of putting it is that I am a liar," Eileen said icily. "I never knew anyone named Paul Marston, never loved him or he me. He never gave me a reproduction of his regimental badge, he was never missing in action, he never existed. I bought this badge myself in a shop in New York where they specialize in imported British luxuries, things like leather goods, hand-made brogues, regimental and school ties and cricket blazers, knickknacks with coats of arms on them and so on. Would an explanation like that satisfy you, Mr. Marlowe?"

"The last part would. Not the first. No doubt somebody told you it was an Artists Rifles badge and forgot to mention what kind, or didn't know. But you did know Paul Marston and he did serve in that outfit, and he was missing in action in Norway. But it didn't happen in 1940, Mrs. Wade. It happened in 1942 and he was in the Commandos then, and it wasn't at Andalsnes, but on a little island off the coast where the Commando boys pulled a fast raid."

"I see no need to be so hostile about it," Spencer said in an executive sort of voice. He was fooling with the yellow sheets in front of him now. I didn't know whether he was trying to stooge for me or was just sore. He picked up a slab of yellow script and weighed it on his hand.

"You going to buy that stuff by the pound?" I asked him.

He looked startled, then he smiled a small difficult smile.

"Eileen had a pretty rough time in London," he said. "Things get confused in one's memory."

I took a folded paper out of my pocket. "Sure," I said. "Like who you got married to. This is a certified copy of a marriage certificate. The original came from Caxton Hall Registry Office. The date of the marriage is August 1942. The parties named are Paul Edward Marston and Eileen Victoria Sampsell. In a sense Mrs. Wade is right. There was no such person as Paul Edward Marston. It was a fake name because in the army you have to get permission to get married. The man faked an identity. In the army he had another name. I have his whole army history. It's a wonder to me that people never seem to realize that all you have to do is ask."

Spencer was very quiet now. He leaned back and stared. But not at me. He stared at Eileen. She looked back at him with one of those faint half deprecatory, half seductive smiles women are so good at.

"But he was dead, Howard. Long before I met Roger. What could it possibly matter? Roger knew all about it. I never stopped using my unmarried name. In the circumstances I had to. It was on my passport. Then after he was killed in action ——" She stopped and drew a slow breath and let her hand fall slowly and softly to her knee. "All finished, all done for, all lost."

"You're sure Roger knew?" he asked her slowly.

"He knew something," I said. "The name Paul Marston had a meaning for him. I asked him once and he got a funny look in his eyes. But he didn't tell me why."

She ignored that and spoke to Spencer.

"Why, of course Roger knew all about it." Now she was smiling at Spencer patiently as if he was being a little slow on the take. The tricks they have.

"Then why lie about the dates?" Spencer asked dryly. "Why say the man was lost in 1940 when he was lost in 1942? Why wear a badge that he couldn't have given you and make a point of saying that he did give it to you?"

"Perhaps I was lost in a dream," she said softly. "Or a nightmare, more accurately. A lot of my friends were killed in the bombing. When you said goodnight in those days you tried not to make it sound like goodbye. But that's what it often was. And when you said goodbye to a soldier — it was worse. It's always the kind and gentle ones that get killed."

He didn't say anything. I didn't say anything. She looked down at the pendant lying on the table in front of her. She picked it up and fitted it to the chain around her neck again and leaned back composedly.

"I know I haven't any right to cross-examine you, Eileen," Spencer said slowly. "Let's forget it. Marlowe made a big thing out of the badge and the marriage certificate and so on. Just for a moment I guess he had me wondering."

"Mr. Marlowe," she told him quietly, "makes a big thing out of trifles. But when it comes to a really big thing — like saving a man's life — he is out by the lake watching a silly speedboat."

"And you never saw Paul Marston again," I said.

"How could I when he was dead?"

"You didn't know he was dead. There was no report of his death from the Red Cross. He might have been taken prisoner."

She shuddered suddenly. "In October 1942," she said slowly, "Hitler issued an order that all Commando prisoners were to be turned over to the Gestapo. I think we all know what that meant. Torture and a nameless death in some Gestapo dungeon." She shuddered again. Then she blazed at me: "You're a horrible man. You want me to live that over again, to punish me for a trivial lie. Suppose someone you loved had been caught by those people and you knew what had happened, what must have happened to him or her? Is it so strange that I tried to build another kind of memory — even a false one?"

"I need a drink," Spencer said. "I need a drink badly. May I have one?"

She clapped her hands and Candy drifted up from nowhere as he always did. He bowed to Spencer.

"What you like to drink, Señor Spencer?"

"Straight Scotch, and plenty of it," Spencer said.

Candy went over in the corner and pulled the bar out from the wall. He got a bottle up on it and poured a stiff jolt into a glass. He came back and set it down in front of Spencer. He started to leave again.

"Perhaps, Candy," Eileen said quietly, "Mr. Marlowe would like a drink too."

He stopped and looked at her, his face dark and stubborn.

"No, thanks," I said. "No drink for me."

Candy made a snorting sound and walked off. There was another silence. Spencer put down half of his drink. He lit a cigarette. He spoke to me without looking at me.

"I'm sure Mrs. Wade or Candy could drive me back to Beverly Hills. Or I can get a cab. I take it you've said your piece."

I refolded the certified copy of the marriage license. I put it back in my pocket.

"Sure that's the way you want it?" I asked him.

"That's the way everybody wants it."

"Good." I stood up. "I guess I was a fool to try to play it this way. Being a big time publisher and having the brains to go with it — if it takes any — you might have assumed I didn't come out here just to play the heavy. I didn't revive ancient history or spend my own money to get the facts just to twist them around somebody's neck. I didn't investigate Paul Marston because the Gestapo murdered him, because Mrs. Wade was wearing the wrong badge, because she got mixed up on her dates, because she married him in one of those quickie wartime marriages. When I started investigating him I didn't know any of those things. All I knew was his name. Now how do you suppose I knew that?"

"No doubt somebody told you," Spencer said curtly.

"Correct, Mr. Spencer. Somebody who knew him in New York after the war and later on saw him out here in Chasen's with his wife."

"Marston is a pretty common name," Spencer said, and sipped his whiskey. He turned his head sideways and his right eyelid drooped a fraction of an inch. So I sat down again. "Even Paul Marstons could hardly be unique. There are nineteen Howard Spencers in the Greater New York area telephone directories, for instance. And four of them are just plain Howard Spencer with no middle initial."

"Yeah. How may Paul Marstons would you say had had one side of their faces smashed by a delayed-action mortar shell and showed the scars and marks of the plastic surgery that repaired the damage?"

Spencer's mouth fell open. He made some kind of heavy breathing sound. He got out a handkerchief and tapped his temples with it.

"How many Paul Marstons would you say had saved the lives of a couple of tough gamblers named Mendy Menendez and Randy Starr on that same occasion? They're still around, they've got good memories. They can talk when it suits them. Why ham it up any more, Spencer? Paul Marston and Terry Lennox were the same man. It can be proved beyond any shadow of a doubt."

I didn't expect anyone to jump six feet into the air and scream and nobody did. But there is a kind of silence that is almost as loud as a shout. I had it. I had it all around me, thick and hard. In the kitchen I could hear water run. Outside on the road I could hear the dull thump of a folded newspaper hit the driveway, then the light inaccurate whistling of a boy wheeling away on his bicycle.

I felt a tiny sting on the back of my neck. I jerked away from it and swung around. Candy was standing there with his knife in his hand. His dark face was wooden but there was something in his eyes I hadn't seen before.

"You are tired, amigo," he said softly. "I fix you a drink, no?"

"Bourbon on the rocks, thanks," I said.

"De pronto, señor."

He snapped the knife shut, dropped it into the side pocket of his white jacket and went softly away.

Then at last I looked at Eileen. She sat leaning forward, her hands clasped tightly. The downward tilt of her face hid her expression if she had any. And when she spoke her voice had the lucid emptiness of that mechanical voice on the telephone that tells you the time and if you keep on listening, which people don't because they have no reason to, it will keep on telling you the passing seconds forever, without the slightest change of inflection.

"I saw him once, Howard. Just once. I didn't speak to him at all. Nor he to me. He was terribly changed. His hair was white and his face — it wasn't quite the same face. But of course I knew him, and of course he knew me. We looked at each other. That was all. Then he was gone out of the room and the next day he was gone from her house. It was at the Lorings' I saw him — and her. One afternoon late. You were there, Howard. And Roger was there. I suppose you saw him too."

"We were introduced," Spencer said. "I knew who he was married to."

"Linda Loring told me he just disappeared. He gave no reason. There was no quarrel. Then after a while that woman divorced him. And still later I heard she found him again. He was down and out. And they were married again. Heaven knows why. I suppose he had no money and it didn't matter to him any more. He knew that I was married to Roger. We were lost to each other."

"Why?" Spencer asked.

Candy put my drink in front of me without a word. He looked at Spencer and Spencer shook his head. Candy drifted away. Nobody paid any attention to him. He was like the prop man in a Chinese play, the fellow that moves things around on the stage and the actors and audience alike behave as if he wasn't there.

"Why?" she repeated. "Oh, you wouldn't understand. What we had was lost. It could never be recovered. The Gestapo didn't get him after all. There must have been *some* decent Nazis who didn't obey Hitler's order about the Commandos. So he survived, he came back. I used to pretend to myself that I would find him again, but as he had been, eager and young and unspoiled. But to find him married to that redheaded whore — that was disgusting. I already knew about her and Roger. I have no doubt Paul did too. So did Linda Loring, who is a bit of a tramp herself, but not completely so. They all are in that set. You ask me why I didn't leave Roger and go back to Paul. After he had been in her arms and Roger had been in those same willing arms? No thank you. I need a little more inspiration than that. Roger I could forgive. He drank, he didn't know what he was doing. He worried about his work and he hated himself because he was just a mercenary hack. He was a weak man, unreconciled, frustrated, but understandable. He was just a husband. Paul was either much more or he was nothing. In the end he was nothing."

I took a swig of my drink. Spencer had finished his. He was scratching at the material of the davenport. He had forgotten the pile of paper in front of him, the unfinished novel of the very much finished popular author.

"I wouldn't say he was nothing," I said.

She lifted her eyes and looked at me vaguely and dropped them again.

"Less than nothing," she said, with a new note of sarcasm in her voice. "He knew what she was, he married her. Then because she was what he knew she was, he killed her. And then ran away and killed himself."

"He didn't kill her," I said, "and you know it."

She came upright with a smooth motion and stared at me blankly. Spencer let out a noise of some kind.

"Roger killed her," I said, "and you also know that."

"Did he tell you?" she asked quietly.

"He didn't have to. He did give me a couple of hints. He would have told me or someone in time. It was tearing him to pieces not to."

She shook her head slightly. "No, Mr. Marlowe. That was not why he was tearing himself to pieces. Roger didn't know he had killed her. He had blacked out completely. He knew something was wrong and he tried to bring it to the surface, but he couldn't. The shock had destroyed his memory of it. Perhaps it would have come back and perhaps in the last moments of his life it did come back. But not until then. Not until then."

Spencer said in a sort of growl: "That sort of thing just doesn't happen, Eileen."

"Oh yes, it does," I said. "I know of two well established instances. One was a blackout drunk who killed a woman he picked up in a bar. He strangled her with a scarf she was wearing fastened with a fancy clasp. She went home with him and what went on then is not known except that she got dead and when the law caught up with him he was wearing the fancy clasp on his own tie and he didn't have the faintest idea where he got it."

"Never?" Spencer asked. "Or just at the time?"

"He never admitted it. And he's not around any more to be asked. They gassed him. The other case was a head wound. He was living with a rich pervert, the kind that collects first editions and does fancy cooking and has a very expensive secret library behind a panel in the wall. The two of them had a fight. They fought all over the house, from room to room, the place was a shambles and the rich guy eventually got the low score. The killer, when they caught him, had dozens of bruises on him and a broken finger. All he knew for sure was that he had a headache and he couldn't find his way back to Pasadena. He kept circling around and stopping to ask directions at the same service station. The guy at the service station decided he was nuts and called the cops. Next time around they were waiting for him."

"I don't believe that about Roger," Spencer said. "He was no more psycho than I am."

"He blacked out when he was drunk," I said.

"I was there. I *saw* him do it," Eileen said calmly.

I grinned at Spencer. It was some kind of grin, not the cheery kind probably, but I could feel my face doing its best.

"She's going to tell us about it," I told him. "Just listen. She's going to tell us. She can't help herself now."

"Yes, that is true," she said gravely. "There are things no one likes to tell about an enemy, much less about one's own husband. And if I have to tell them publicly on a witness stand, you are not going to enjoy it, Howard. Your fine, talented, ever so popular and lucrative author is going to look pretty cheap. Sexy as all get out, wasn't he? On paper, that is. And how the poor fool tried to live up to it! All that woman was to him was a trophy. I spied on them. I should be ashamed of that. One has to say these things. I am ashamed of nothing. I saw the whole nasty scene. The guest house she used for her amours happens to be a nice secluded affair with its own garage and entrance on a side street, a dead end, shaded by big trees. The time came, as it must to people like Roger, when he was no longer a satisfactory lover. Just a little too drunk. He tried to leave but she came out after him screaming and stark naked, waving some kind of small statuette. She used language of a depth of filth and depravity I couldn't attempt to describe. Then she tried to hit him with the statuette. You are both men and you must know that nothing shocks a man quite so much as to hear a supposedly refined woman use the language of the gutter and the public urinal. He was drunk, he had had sudden spells of violence, and he had one then. He tore the statuette out of her hand. You can guess the rest."

"There must have been a lot of blood," I said.

"Blood?" She laughed bitterly. "You should have seen him when he got home. When I ran for my car to get away he was just standing there looking down at her. Then he bent and picked her up in his arms and carried her into the guest house. I knew then that the shock had partially sobered him. He got home in about an hour. He was very quiet. It shook him when he saw me waiting. But he wasn't drunk then. He was dazed. There was blood on his face, on his hair, all over the front of his coat. I got him into the lavatory off the study and got him stripped and cleaned off enough to get him upstairs into the shower. I put him to bed. I got an old suitcase and went downstairs and gathered up the bloody clothes and put them in the suitcase. I cleaned the basin and the floor and then I took a wet towel out and made sure his car was clean. I put it away and got mine out. I drove to the Chatsworth Reservoir and you can guess what I did with the suitcase full of bloody clothes and towels."

She stopped. Spencer was scratching at the palm of his left hand. She gave him a quick glance and went on.

"While I was away he got up and drank a lot of whiskey. And the next morning he didn't remember a single thing. That is, he didn't say a word about it or behave as if he had anything on his mind but a hangover. And I said nothing."

"He must have missed the clothes," I said.

She nodded. "I think he did eventually — but he didn't say so. Everything seemed to happen at once about that time. The papers were full of it, then Paul was missing, and then he was dead in Mexico. How was I to know that would happen? Roger was my husband. He had done an awful thing, but she was an awful woman. And he hadn't known what he was doing. Then almost as suddenly as it began the papers dropped it. Linda's father must have had something to do with that. Roger read the papers, of course, and he made just the sort of comments one would expect from an innocent bystander who had just happened to know the people involved."

"Weren't you afraid?" Spencer asked her quietly.

"I was sick with fear, Howard. If he remembered, he would probably kill me. He was a good actor — most writers are — and perhaps he already knew and was just waiting for a chance. But I couldn't be sure. He might — just might — have forgotten the whole thing permanently. And Paul was dead."

"If he never mentioned the clothes that you had dumped in the reservoir, that proved he suspected something," I said. "And remember, in that stuff he left in the typewriter the other time — the time he shot the gun off upstairs and I found you trying to get it away from him — he said a good man had died for him."

"He said that?" Her eyes widened just the right amount.

"He wrote it — on the typewriter. I destroyed it, he asked me to. I supposed you had already seen it."

"I never read anything he wrote in his study."

"You read the note he left the time Verringer took him away. You even dug something out of the wastebasket."

"That was different," she said coolly. "I was looking for a clue to where he might have gone."

"Okay," I said, and leaned back. "Is there any more?"

She shook her head slowly, with a deep sadness. "I suppose not. At the very last, the afternoon he killed himself, he may have remembered. We'll never know. Do we want to know?"

Spencer cleared his throat. "What was Marlowe supposed to do in all this? It was your idea to get him here. You talked me into that, you know."

"I was terribly afraid. I was afraid of Roger and I was afraid *for* him. Mr. Marlowe was Paul's friend, almost the last person to see him who knew him. Paul might have told him something. I had to be sure. If he was dangerous, I wanted him on my side. If he found out the truth, there might still be some way to save Roger."

Suddenly and for no reason that I could see, Spencer got tough. He leaned forward and pushed his jaw out.

"Let me get this straight, Eileen. Here was a private detective who was already in bad with the police. They'd had him in jail. He was supposed to have helped Paul — I call him that because you do — jump the country to Mexico. That's a felony, if Paul was a murderer. So if he found out the truth and could clear himself, he would just sit on his hands and do nothing. Was that your idea?"

"I was afraid, Howard. Can't you understand that? I was living in the house with a murderer who might be a maniac. I was alone with him a large part of the time."

"I understand that," Spencer said, still tough. "But Marlowe didn't take it on, and you were still alone. Then Roger fired the gun off and for a week after that you were alone. Then Roger killed himself and very conveniently it was Marlowe who was alone that time."

"That is true," she said. "What of it? Could I help it?"

"All right," Spencer said. "Is it just possible you thought Marlowe might find the truth and with the background of the gun going off once already, just kind of hand it to Roger and say something like, 'Look, old man, you're a murderer and I know it and your wife knows it. She's a fine woman. She has suffered enough. Not to mention Sylvia Lennox's husband. Why not do the decent thing and pull the trigger and everybody will assume it was just a case of too much wild drinking? So I'll stroll down by the lake and smoke a cigarette, old man. Good luck and goodbye. Oh, here's the gun. It's loaded and it's all yours.' "

"You're getting horrible, Howard. I didn't think anything of the sort."

"You told the deputy Marlowe had killed Roger. What was that supposed to mean?"

She looked at me briefly, almost shyly. "I was very wrong to say that. I didn't know what I was saying."

"Maybe you thought Marlowe had shot him," Spencer suggested calmly.

Her eyes narrowed. "Oh no, Howard. Why? Why would he do that? That's an abominable suggestion."

"Why?" Spencer wanted to know. "What's abominable about it? The police had the same idea. And Candy gave them a motive. He said Marlowe was in your room for two hours the night Roger shot a hole in his ceiling — after Roger had been put to sleep with pills."

She flushed to the roots of her hair. She stared at him dumbly.

"And you didn't have any clothes on," Spencer said brutally. "That's what Candy told them."

"But at the inquest —" she began to say in a shattered kind of voice. Spencer cut her off.

"The police didn't believe Candy. So he didn't tell it at the inquest."

"Oh." It was a sigh of relief.

"Also," Spencer went on coldly, "the police suspected you. They still do. All they need is a motive. Looks to me like they might be able to put one together now."

She was up on her feet. "I think you had both better leave my house," she said angrily. "The sooner the better."

"Well, did you or didn't you?" Spencer asked calmly, not moving except to reach for his glass and find it empty.

"Did I or didn't I what?"

"Shoot Roger?"

She was standing there staring at him. The flush had gone. Her face was white and tight and angry.

"I'm just giving you the sort of thing you'd get in court."

"I was out. I had forgotten my keys. I had to ring to get into the house. He was dead when I got home. All that is known. What has got into you, for God's sake?"

He took a handkerchief out and wiped his lips. "Eileen, I've stayed in this house twenty times. I've never known that front door to be locked during the daytime. I don't say you shot him. I just asked you. And don't tell me it was impossible. The way things worked out it was easy."

"I shot my own husband?" she asked slowly and wonderingly.

"Assuming," Spencer said in the same indifferent voice, "that he was your husband. You had another when you married him."

"Thank you, Howard. Thank you very much. Roger's last book, his swan song, is there in front of you. Take it and go. And I think you had better call the police and tell them what you think. It will be a charming ending to our friendship. Most charming. Goodbye, Howard. I am very tired and I have a headache. I'm going to my room and lie down. As for Mr. Marlowe — and I suppose he put you up to all this — I can only say to him that if he didn't kill Roger in a literal sense, he certainly drove him to his death."

She turned to walk away. I said sharply: "Mrs. Wade, just a moment. Let's finish the job. No sense in being bitter. We are all trying to do the right thing. That suitcase you threw into the Chatsworth Reservoir — was it heavy?"

She turned and stared at me. "It was an old one, I said. Yes, it was very heavy."

"How did you get it over the high wire fence around the reservoir?"

"What? The fence?" She made a helpless gesture. "I suppose in emergencies one has an abnormal strength to do what has to be done. Somehow or other I did it. That's all."

"There isn't any fence," I said.

"Isn't any fence?" She repeated it dully, as if it didn't mean anything.

"And there was no blood on Roger's clothes. And Sylvia Lennox wasn't killed outside the guest house, but inside it on the bed. And there was practically no blood, because she was already dead — shot dead with a gun — and when the statuette was used to beat her face to a pulp, it was beating a dead woman. And the dead, Mrs. Wade, bleed very little."

She curled her lip at me contemptuously. "I suppose you were there," she said scornfully.

Then she went away from us.

We watched her go. She went up the stairs slowly, moving with calm elegance. She disappeared into her room and the door closed softly but firmly behind her. Silence.

"What was that about the wire fence?" Spencer asked me vaguely. He was moving his head back and forth. He was flushed and sweating. He was taking it gamely but it wasn't easy for him to take.

"Just a gag," I said. "I've never been close enough to the Chatsworth Reservoir to know what it looks like. Maybe it has a fence around it, maybe not."

"I see," he said unhappily. "But the point is she didn't know either."

"Of course not. She killed both of them."

43

THEN SOMETHING MOVED softly and Candy was standing at the end of the couch looking at me. He had his switch knife in his hand. He pressed the button and the blade shot out. He pressed the button and the blade went back into the handle. There was a sleek glitter in his eye.

"Million de pardones, señor," he said. "I was wrong about you. She killed the boss. I think I —" He stopped and the blade shot out again.

"No." I stood up and held my hand out. "Give me the knife, Candy. You're just a nice Mexican houseboy. They'd hang it onto you and love it. Just the kind of smoke screen that would make them grin with delight. You don't know what I'm talking about. But I do. They fouled it up so bad that they couldn't straighten it out now if they wanted to. And they don't want to. They'd blast a confession out of you so quick you wouldn't even have time to tell them your full name. And you'd be sitting on your fanny up in San Quentin with a life sentence three weeks from Tuesday."

"I tell you before I am not a Mexican. I am Chileno from Viña del Mar near Valparaíso."

"The knife, Candy. I know all that. You're free. You've got money saved. You've probably got eight brothers and sisters back home. Be smart and go back where you came from. This job here is dead."

"Lots of jobs," he said quietly. Then he reached out and dropped the knife into my hand. "For you I do this."

I dropped the knife into my pocket. He glanced up towards the balcony. "La señora — what do we do now?"

"Nothing. We do nothing at all. The señora is very tired. She has been living under a great strain. She doesn't want to be disturbed."

"We've got to call the police," Spencer said grittily.

"Why?"

"Oh my God, Marlowe — we have to."

"Tomorrow. Pick up your pile of unfinished novel and let's go."

"We've got to call the police. There is such a thing as law."

"We don't have to do anything of the sort. We haven't enough evidence to swat a fly with. Let the law enforcement people do their own dirty work. Let the lawyers work it out. They write the laws for other lawyers to dissect in front of other lawyers called judges so that other judges can say the first judges were wrong and the Supreme Court can say the second lot were wrong. Sure there's such a thing as law. We're up to our necks in it. About all it does is make business for lawyers. How long do you think the big-shot mobsters would last if the lawyers didn't show them how to operate?"

Spencer said angrily: "That has nothing to do with it. A man was killed in this house. He happened to be an author and a very successful and important one, but that has nothing to do with it either. He was a man and you and I know who killed him. There's such a thing as justice."

"Tomorrow."

"You're just as bad as she is if you let her get away with it. I'm beginning to wonder about you a little, Marlowe. You could have saved his life if you had been on your toes. In a sense you did let her get away with it. And for all I know this whole performance this afternoon has been just that — a performance."

"That's right. A disguised love scene. You could see Eileen is crazy about me. When things quiet down we may get married. She ought to be pretty well fixed. I haven't made a buck out of the Wade family yet. I'm getting impatient."

He took his glasses off and polished them. He wiped perspiration from the hollows under his eyes, replaced the glasses and looked at the floor.

"I'm sorry," he said. "I've taken a pretty stiff punch this afternoon. It was bad enough to know Roger had killed himself. But this other version makes me feel degraded — just knowing about it." He looked up at me. "Can I trust you?"

"To do what?"

"The right thing — whatever it is." He reached down and picked up the pile of yellow script and tucked it under his arm. "No, forget it. I guess you know what you are doing. I'm a pretty good publisher but this is out of my line. I guess what I really am is just a goddam stuffed shirt."

He walked past me and Candy stepped out of his way, then went quickly to the front door and held it open. Spencer went out past him with a brief nod. I followed. I stopped beside Candy and looked into his dark shining eyes.

"No tricks, amigo," I said.

"The señora is very tired," he said quietly. "She has gone to her room. She will not be disturbed. I know nothing, señor. No me acuerdo de nada . . . A sus órdenes, señor."

I took the knife out of my pocket and held it out to him. He smiled.

"Nobody trusts me, but I trust you, Candy."

"Lo mismo, señor. Muchas gracias."

Spencer was already in the car. I got in and started it and backed down the driveway and drove him back to Beverly Hills. I let him out at the side entrance of the hotel.

"I've been thinking all the way back," he said as he got out. "She must be a little insane. I guess they'd never convict her."

"They won't even try," I said. "But she doesn't know that."

He struggled with the batch of yellow paper under his arm, got it straightened out, and nodded to me. I watched him heave open the door and go on in. I eased up on the brake and the Olds slid out from the white curb, and that was the last I saw of Howard Spencer.

I got home late and tired and depressed. It was one of those nights when the air is heavy and the night noises seem muffled and far away. There was a high misty indifferent moon. I walked the floor, played a few records, and hardly heard them. I seemed to hear a steady ticking somewhere, but there wasn't anything in the house to tick. The ticking was in my head. I was a one-man death watch.

I thought of the first time I had seen Eileen Wade and the second and the third and the fourth. But after that something in her got out of drawing. She no longer seemed quite real. A murderer is always unreal once you know he is a murderer. There are people who kill out of hate or fear or greed. There are the cunning killers who plan and expect to get away with it. There are the angry killers who do not think at all. And there are the killers who are in love with death, to whom murder is a remote kind of suicide. In a sense they are all insane, but not in the way Spencer meant it.

It was almost daylight when I finally went to bed.

The jangle of the telephone dragged me up out of a black well of sleep. I rolled over on the bed, fumbled for slippers, and realized that I hadn't been asleep for more than a couple of hours. I felt like a half-digested meal eaten in a greasy-spoon joint. My eyes were stuck together and my mouth was full of sand. I heaved up on the feet and lumbered into the living room and pulled the phone off the cradle and said into it: "Hold the line."

I put the phone down and went into the bathroom and hit myself in the face with some cold water. Outside the window something went snip, snip, snip. I looked out vaguely and saw a brown expressionless face. It was the once-a-week Jap gardener I called Hardhearted Harry. He was trimming the tecoma — the way a Japanese gardener trims your tecoma. You ask him four times and he says, "next week" and then he comes by at six o'clock in the morning and trims it outside your bedroom window.

I rubbed my face dry and went back to the telephone.

"Yeah?"

"This is Candy, señor."

"Good morning, Candy."

"La señora es muerta."

Dead. What a cold black noiseless word it is in any language. The lady is dead.

"Nothing you did, I hope."

"I think the medicine. It is called demerol. I think forty, fifty in the bottle. Empty now. No dinner last night. This morning I climb up on the ladder and look in the window. Dressed just like yesterday afternoon. I break the screen open. La señora es muerta. Frio como agua de nieve."

Cold as icewater. "You call anybody?"

"Sí. El Doctor Loring. He call the cops. Not here yet."

"Dr. Loring, huh? Just the man to come too late."

"I don't show him the letter," Candy said.

"Letter to who?"

"Señor Spencer."

"Give it to the police, Candy. Don't let Dr. Loring have it. Just the police. And one more thing, Candy. Don't hide anything, don't tell them any lies. We were there. Tell the truth. This time the truth and all the truth."

There was a little pause. Then he said: "Sí. I catch. Hasta la vista, amigo." He hung up.

I dialed the Ritz-Beverly and asked for Howard Spencer.

"One moment, please. I'll give you the desk."

A man's voice said: "Desk speaking. May I help you?"

"I asked for Howard Spencer. I know it's early, but it's urgent."

"Mr. Spencer checked out last evening. He took the eight o'clock plane to New York."

"Oh, sorry. I didn't know."

I went out to the kitchen to make coffee — yards of coffee. Rich, strong, bitter, boiling hot, ruthless, depraved. The lifeblood of tired men.

It was a couple of hours later that Bernie Ohls called me.

"Okay, wise guy," he said. "Get down here and suffer."

44

IT WAS LIKE THE OTHER TIME except that it was day and we were in Captain Hernandez's office and the Sheriff was up in Santa Barbara opening Fiesta Week. Captain Hernandez was there and Bernie Ohls and a man from the coroner's office and Dr. Loring, who looked as if he had been caught performing an abortion, and a man named Lawford, a deputy from the D.A.'s office, a tall gaunt expressionless man whose brother was vaguely rumored to be a boss of the numbers racket in the Central Avenue district.

Hernandez had some handwritten sheets of note paper in front of him, flesh-pink paper, deckle-edged, and written on with green ink.

"This is informal," Hernandez said, when everybody was as comfortable as you can get in hard chairs. "No stenotype or recording equipment. Say what you like. Dr. Weiss represents the coroner who will decide whether an inquest is necessary. Dr. Weiss?"

He was fat, cheerful, and looked competent. "I think no inquest," he said. "There is every surface indication of narcotic poisoning. When the ambulance arrived the woman was still breathing very faintly and she was in a deep coma and all the reflexes were negative. At that stage you don't save one in a hundred. Her skin was cold and respiration would not be noticed without close examination. The houseboy thought she was dead. She died approximately an hour after that. I understand the lady was subject to occasional violent attacks of bronchial asthma. The demerol was prescribed by Dr. Loring as an emergency measure."

"Any information or deduction about the amount of demerol taken, Dr. Weiss?"

"A fatal dose," he said, smiling faintly. "There is no quick way of determining that without knowing the medical history, the acquired or natural tolerance. According to her confession she took twenty-three hundred milligrams, four or five times the minimal lethal dose for a non-addict." He looked questioningly at Dr. Loring.

"Mrs. Wade was not an addict," Dr. Loring said coldly. "The prescribed dose would be one or two fifty-milligram tablets. Three or four during a twenty-four-hour period would be the most I'd permit."

"But you gave her fifty at a whack," Captain Hernandez said. "A pretty dangerous drug to have around in that quantity, don't you think? How bad was this bronchial asthma, Doctor?"

Dr. Loring smiled contemptuously. "It was intermittent, like all asthma. It never amounted to what we term *status asthmaticus*, an attack so severe that the patient seems in danger of suffocating."

"Any comment, Dr. Weiss?"

"Well," Dr. Weiss said slowly, "assuming the note didn't exist and assuming we had no other evidence of how much of the stuff she took, it could be an accidental overdose. The safety margin isn't very wide. We'll know for sure tomorrow. You don't want to suppress the note, Hernandez, for Pete's sake?"

Hernandez scowled down at his desk. "I was just wondering. I didn't know narcotics were standard treatment for asthma. Guy learns something every day."

Loring flushed. "An emergency measure, I said, Captain. A doctor can't be everywhere at once. The onset of an asthmatic flare-up can be very sudden."

Hernandez gave him a brief glance and turned to Lawford. "What happens to your office, if I give this letter to the press?"

The D.A.'s deputy glanced at me emptily. "What's this guy doing here, Hernandez?"

"I invited him."

"How do I know he won't repeat everything said in here to some reporter?"

"Yeah, he's a great talker. You found that out. The time you had him pinched."

Lawford grinned, then cleared his throat. "I've read that purported confession," he said carefully. "And I don't believe a word of it. You've got a background of emotional exhaustion, bereavement, some use of drugs, the strain of wartime life in England under bombing, this clandestine marriage, the man coming back here, and so on. Undoubtedly she developed a feeling of guilt and tried to purge herself of it by a sort of transference."

He stopped and looked around, but all he saw was faces with no expression. "I can't speak for the D.A. but my own feeling is that your confession would be no grounds to seek an indictment even if the woman had lived."

"And having already believed one confession you wouldn't care to believe another that contradicted the first one," Hernandez said caustically.

"Take it easy, Hernandez. Any law enforcement agency has to consider public relations. If the papers printed that confession we'd be in trouble. That's for sure. We've got enough eager beaver reformer groups around just waiting for that kind of chance to stick a knife into us. We've got a grand jury that's already jittery about the working-over your vice squad lieutenant got last week — it's about ten days."

Hernandez said: "Okay, it's your baby. Sign the receipt for me."

He shuffled the pink deckle-edged pages together and Lawford leaned down to sign a form. He picked up the pink pages, folded them, put them in his breast pocket and walked out.

Dr. Weiss stood up. He was tough, good-natured, unimpressed. "We had the last inquest on the Wade family too quick," he said. "I guess we won't bother to have this one at all."

He nodded to Ohls and Hernandez, shook hands formally with Loring, and went out. Loring stood up to go, then hesitated.

"I take it that I may inform a certain interested party that there will be no further investigation of this matter?" he said stiffly.

"Sorry to have kept you away from your patients so long, Doctor."

"You haven't answered my question," Loring said sharply. "I'd better warn you — "

"Get lost, Jack," Hernandez said.

Dr. Loring almost staggered with shock. Then he turned and fumbled his way rapidly out of the room. The door closed and it was a half minute before anybody said anything. Hernandez shook himself and lit a cigarette. Then he looked at me.

"Well?" he said.

"Well what?"

"What are you waiting for?"

"This is the end, then? Finished? Kaput."

"Tell him, Bernie."

"Yeah, sure it's the end," Ohls said. "I was all set to pull her in for questioning. Wade didn't shoot himself. Too much alcohol in his brain. But like I told you, where was the motive? Her confession could be wrong in details, but it proves she spied on him. She knew the layout of the guest house in Encino. The Lennox frail had taken both her men from her. What happened in the guest house is just what you want to imagine. One question you forgot to ask Spencer. Did Wade own a Mauser P.P.K.? Yeah, he owned a small Mauser automatic. We talked to Spencer already today on the phone. Wade was a blackout drunk. The poor unfortunate bastard either thought he had killed Sylvia Lennox or he actually had killed her or else he had some reason to know his wife had. Either way he was going to lay it on the line eventually. Sure, he'd been hitting the hooch long before, but he was a he guy married to a beautiful nothing. The Mex knows all about it. The little bastard knows damn near everything. That was a dream girl. Some of her was here and now, but a lot of her was there and then. If she ever got hot pants, it wasn't for her husband. Get what I'm talking about?"

I didn't answer him.

"Damn near made her yourself, didn't you?"

I gave him the same no answer.

Ohls and Hernandez both grinned sourly. "Us guys aren't exactly brainless," Ohls said. "We knew there was something in that story about her taking her clothes off. You outtalked him and he let you. He was hurt and confused and he liked Wade and he wanted to be sure. When he got sure he'd have used his knife. This was a personal matter with him. He never snitched on Wade. Wade's wife did, and she deliberately fouled up the issue just to confuse Wade. It all adds. In the end I guess she was scared of him. And Wade never threw her down any stairs. That was an accident. She tripped and the guy tried to catch her. Candy saw that too."

"None of it explains why she wanted me around."

"I could think of reasons. One of them is old stuff. Every cop has run into it a hundred times. You were the loose end, the guy that helped Lennox escape, his friend, and probably to some extent his confidant. What did he know and what did he tell you? He took the gun that had killed her and he knew it had been fired. She could have thought he did it for her. That made her think he knew she had used it. When he killed himself she was sure. But what about you? You were still the loose end. She wanted to milk you, and she had the charm to use, and a situation ready-made for an excuse to get next to you. And if she needed a fall guy, you were it. You might say she was collecting fall guys."

"You're imputing too much knowledge to her," I said.

Ohls broke a cigarette in half and started chewing on one half. The other half he stuck behind his ear.

"Another reason is she wanted a man, a big, strong guy that could crush her in his arms and make her dream again."

"She hated me," I said. "I don't buy that one."

"Of course," Hernandez put in dryly. "You turned her down. But she would have got over that. And then you blew the whole thing up in her face with Spencer listening in."

"You two characters been seeing any psychiatrists lately?"

"Jesus," Ohls said, "hadn't you heard? We got them in our hair all the time these days. We've got two of them on the staff. This ain't police business any more. It's getting to be a branch of the medical racket. They're in and out of jail, the courts, the interrogation rooms. They write reports fifteen pages long on why some punk of a juvenile held up a liquor store or raped a schoolgirl or peddled tea to the senior class. Ten years from now guys like Hernandez and me will be doing Rohrschach tests and word associations instead of chin-ups and target practice. When we go out on a case we'll carry little black bags with portable lie detectors and bottles of truth serum. Too bad we didn't grab the four hard monkeys that poured it on Big Willie Magoon. We might have been able to unmaladjust them and make them love their mothers."

"Okay for me to blow?"

"What are you not convinced about?" Hernandez asked, snapping a rubber band.

"I'm convinced. The case is dead. She's dead, they're all dead. A nice smooth routine all around. Nothing to do but go home and forget it ever happened. So I'll do that."

Ohls reached the half cigarette from behind his ear, looked at it as if wondering how it got there, and tossed it over his shoulder.

"What are you crying about?" Hernandez said. "If she hadn't been fresh out of guns she might have made it a perfect score."

"Also," Ohls said grimly, "the telephone was working yesterday."

"Oh sure," I said. "You'd have come running and what you would have found would have been a mixed up story that admitted nothing but a few silly lies. This morning you have what I suppose is a full confession. You haven't let me read it, but you wouldn't have called in the D.A. if it was just a love note. If any real solid work had been done on the Lennox case at the time, somebody would have dug up his war record and where he got wounded and all the rest of it. Somewhere along the line a connection with the Wades would have turned up. Roger Wade knew who Paul Marston was. So did another P.I. I happened to get in touch with."

"It's possible," Hernandez admitted, "but that isn't how police investigations work. You don't fool around with an open-shut case, even if there's no heat on to get it finalized and forgotten. I've investigated hundreds of homicides. Some are all of a piece, neat, tidy, and according to the book. Most of them make sense here, don't make sense there. But when you get motive, means, opportunity, flight, a written confession, and a suicide immediately afterwards, you leave it lay. No police department in the world has the men or the time to question the obvious. The only thing against Lennox being a killer was that somebody thought he was a nice guy who wouldn't have done it and that there were others who could equally well have done it. But the others didn't take it on the lam, didn't confess, didn't blow their brains out. He did. And as for being a nice guy I figure sixty to seventy per cent of all the killers that end up in the gas chamber or the hot seat or on the end of a rope are people the neighbors thought were just as harmless as a Fuller Brush salesman. Just as harmless and quiet and well bred as Mrs. Roger Wade. You want to read what she wrote in that letter? Okay, read it. I've got to go down the hall."

He stood up and pulled a drawer open and put a folder on the top of the desk. "There are five photostats in here, Marlowe. Don't let me catch you looking at them."

He started for the door and then turned his head and said to Ohls: "You want to talk to Peshorek with me?"

Ohls nodded and followed him out. When I was alone in the office I lifted the cover of the file folder and looked at the white-on-black photostats. Then touching only the edges I counted them. There were six, each of several pages clipped together. I took one and rolled it up and slipped it into my pocket. Then I read over the next one in the pile. When I had finished I sat down and waited. In about ten minutes Hernandez came back alone. He sat down behind his desk again, tallied the photostats in the file folder, and put the file back in his desk.

He raised his eyes and looked at me without any expression. "Satisfied?"

"Lawford know you have those?"

"Not from me. Not from Bernie. Bernie made them himself. Why?"

"What would happen if one got loose?"

He smiled unpleasantly. "It won't. But if it did, it wouldn't be anybody in the Sheriff's office. The D.A. has photostat equipment too."

"You don't like District Attorney Springer too well, do you, Captain?"

He looked surprised. "Me? I like everybody, even you. Get the hell out of here. I've got work to do."

I stood up to go. He said suddenly: "You carry a gun these days?"

"Part of the time."

"Big Willie Magoon carried two. I wonder why he didn't use them."

"I guess he figured he had everybody scared."

"That could be it," Hernandez said casually. He picked up a

rubber band and stretched it between his thumbs. He stretched it farther and farther. Finally with a snap it broke. He rubbed his thumb where the loose end had snapped back against it. "Anybody can be stretched too far," he said. "No matter how tough he looks. See you around."

I went out of the door and got out of the building fast. Once a patsy, always a patsy.

45

BACK IN MY DOG HOUSE on the sixth floor of the Cahuenga Building I went through my regular double play with the morning mail. Mail slot to desk to wastebasket, Tinker to Evers to Chance. I blew a clear space on the top of the desk and unrolled the photostat on it. I had rolled it so as not to make creases.

I read it over again. It was detailed enough and reasonable enough to satisfy any open mind. Eileen Wade had killed Terry's wife in a fit of jealous fury and later when the opportunity was set up she had killed Roger because she was sure he knew. The gun fired into the ceiling of his room that night had been part of the setup. The unanswered and forever unanswerable question was why Roger Wade had stood still and let her put it over. He must have known how it would end. So he had written himself off and didn't care. Words were his business, he had words for almost everything, but none for this.

"I have forty-six demerol tablets left from my last prescription," she wrote. "I now intend to take them all and lie down on the bed. The door is locked. In a very short time I shall be beyond saving. This, Howard, is to be understood. What I write is in the presence of death. Every word is true. I have no regrets — except possibly that I could not have found them together and killed them together. I have no regrets for Paul whom you have heard called Terry Lennox. He was the empty shell of the man I loved and married.

He meant nothing to me. When I saw him that afternoon for the only time after he came back from the war — at first I didn't know him. Then I did and he knew me at once. He should have died young in the snow of Norway, my lover that I gave to death. He came back a friend of gamblers, the husband of a rich whore, a spoiled and ruined man, and probably some kind of crook in his past life. Time makes everything mean and shabby and wrinkled. The tragedy of life, Howard, is not that the beautiful things die young, but that they grow old and mean. It will not happen to me. Goodbye, Howard."

I put the photostat in the desk and locked it up. It was time for lunch but I wasn't in the mood. I got the office bottle out of the deep drawer and poured a slug and then got the phone book off the hook at the desk and looked up the number of the *Journal*. I dialed it and asked the girl for Lonnie Morgan.

"Mr. Morgan doesn't come in until around four o'clock. You might try the press room at the City Hall."

I called that. And I got him. He remembered me well enough. "You've been a pretty busy guy, I heard."

"I've got something for you, if you want it. I don't think you want it."

"Yeah? Such as?"

"A photostat of a confession to two murders."

"Where are you?"

I told him. He wanted more information. I wouldn't give him any over the phone. He said he wasn't on a crime beat. I said he was still a newspaperman and on the only independent paper in the city. He still wanted to argue.

"Where did you get this whatever it is? How do I know it's worth my time?"

"The D.A.'s office has the original. They won't release it. It breaks open a couple of things they hid behind the icebox."

"I'll call you. I have to check with the brass."

We hung up. I went down to the drugstore and ate a chicken salad sandwich and drank some coffee. The coffee was overtrained and the sandwich was as full of rich flavor as a piece torn off an old shirt. Americans will eat anything if it is toasted and held together with a couple of toothpicks and has lettuce sticking out of the sides, preferably a little wilted.

At three-thirty or so Lonnie Morgan came in to see me. He was the same long thin wiry piece of tired and expressionless humanity as he had been the night he drove me home from the jailhouse. He shook hands listlessly and rooted in a crumpled pack of cigarettes. "Mr. Sherman — that's the M.E. — said I could look you up and see what you have."

"It's off the record unless you agree to my terms." I unlocked the desk and handed him the photostat. He read the four pages rapidly and then again more slowly. He looked very excited — about as excited as a mortician at a cheap funeral.

"Gimme the phone."

I pushed it across the desk. He dialed, waited, and said: "This is Morgan. Let me talk to Mr. Sherman." He waited and got some other female and then got his party and asked him to ring back on another line.

He hung up and sat holding the telephone in his lap with the forefinger pressing the button down. It rang again and he lifted the receiver to his ear.

"Here it is, Mr. Sherman."

He read slowly and distinctly. At the end there was a pause. Then, "One moment, sir." He lowered the phone and glanced across the desk. "He wants to know how you got hold of this."

I reached across the desk and took the photostat away from him. "Tell him it's none of his goddam business how I got hold of it. Where is something else. The stamp on the back of the pages show that."

"Mr. Sherman, it's apparently an official document of the Los Angeles Sheriff's office. I guess we could check its authenticity easy enough. Also there's a price."

He listened some more and then said: "Yes, sir. Right here. " He pushed the phone across the desk. "Wants to talk to you."

It was a brusque authoritative voice. "Mr. Marlowe, what are your terms? And remember the *Journal* is the only paper in Los Angeles which would even consider touching this matter."

"You didn't do much on the Lennox case, Mr. Sherman."

"I realize that. But at that time it was purely a question of scandal for scandal's sake. There was no question of who was guilty. What we have now, if your document is genuine, is something quite different. What are your terms?"

"You print the confession in full in the form of a photographic reproduction. Or you don't print it at all."

"It will be verified. You understand that?"

"I don't see how, Mr. Sherman. If you ask the D.A. he will either deny it or give it to every paper in town. He'd have to. If you ask the Sheriff's office they will put it up to the D.A."

"Don't worry about that, Mr. Marlowe. We have ways. How about your terms?"

"I just told you."

"Oh. You don't expect to be paid?"

"Not with money."

"Well, you know your own business, I suppose. May I have Morgan again?"

I gave the phone back to Lonnie Morgan.

He spoke briefly and hung up. "He agrees," he said. "I take that photostat and he checks it. He'll do what you say. Reduced to half size it will take about half of page 1A."

I gave him back the photostat. He held it and pulled at the tip of his long nose. "Mind my saying I think you're a damn fool?"

"I agree with you."

"You can still change your mind."

"Nope. Remember that night you drove me home from the City Bastille? You said I had a friend to say goodbye to. I've never really said goodbye to him. If you publish this photostat, that will be it. It's been a long time — a long, long time."

"Okay, chum." He grinned crookedly. "But I still think you're a damn fool. Do I have to tell you why?"

"Tell me anyway."

"I know more about you than you think. That's the frustrating part of newspaper work. You always know so many things you can't use. You get cynical. If this confession is printed in the *Journal*, a lot of people will be sore. The D.A., the coroner, the Sheriff's crowd, an influential and powerful private citizen named Potter, and a couple of toughies called Menendez and Starr. You'll probably end up in the hospital or in jail again."

"I don't think so."

"Think what you like, pal. I'm telling you what *I* think. The D.A. will be sore because he dropped a blanket on the Lennox case. Even if the suicide and confession of Lennox made him look justified, a lot of people will want to know how Lennox, an innocent man, came to make a confession, how he got dead, did he really commit suicide or was he helped, why was there no investigation into the circumstances, and how come the whole thing died so fast. Also, if he has the original of this photostat he will think he has been double-crossed by the Sheriff's people."

"You don't have to print the identifying stamp on the back."

"We won't. We're pals with the Sheriff. We think he's a straight guy. We don't blame him because he can't stop guys like Menendez. Nobody can stop gambling as long as its legal in all forms in some places and legal in some forms in all places. You stole this from the Sheriff's office. I don't know how you got away with it. Want to tell me?"

"No."

"Okay. The coroner will be sore because he buggered up the Wade suicide. The D.A. helped him with that too. Harlan Potter will be sore because something is reopened that he used a lot of power to close up. Menendez and Starr will be sore for reasons I'm not sure of, but I know you got warned off. And when those boys get sore at somebody he gets hurt. You're apt to get the treatment Big Willie Magoon got."

"Magoon was probably getting too heavy for his job."

"Why?" Morgan drawled. "Because those boys have to make it stick. If they take the trouble to tell you to lay off, you lay off. If you don't and they let you get away with it they look weak. The hard boys that run the business, the big wheels, the board of directors, don't have any use for weak people. They're dangerous. And then there's Chris Mady."

"He just about runs Nevada, I heard."

"You heard right, chum. Mady is a nice guy but he knows what's right for Nevada. The rich hoodlums that operate in Reno and Vegas are very careful not to annoy Mr. Mady. If they did, their taxes would go up fast and their police co-operation would go down the same way. Then the top guys back East would decide some changes were necessary. An operator who can't get along with Chris

Mady ain't operating correctly. Get him the hell out of there and put somebody else in. Getting him out of there means only one thing to them. Out in a wooden box."

"They never heard of me," I said.

Morgan frowned and whipped an arm up and down in a meaningless gesture. "They don't have to. Mady's estate on the Nevada side of Tahoe is right next to Harlan Potter's estate. Could be they say hello once in a while. Could be some character that is on Mady's payroll hears from another guy on Potter's payroll that a punk named Marlowe is buzzing too loud about things that are not any of his business. Could be that this passing remark gets passed on down to where the phone rings in some apartment in L.A. and a guy with large muscles gets a hint to go out and exercise himself and two or three of his friends. If somebody wants you knocked off or smashed, the muscle men don't have to have it explained why. It's mere routine to them. No hard feelings at all. Just sit still while we break your arm. You want this back?"

He held out the photostat.

"You know what I want," I said.

Morgan stood up slowly and put the photostat in his inside pocket. "I could be wrong," he said. "You may know more about it than I do. I wouldn't know how a man like Harlan Potter looks at things."

"With a scowl," I said. "I've met him. But he wouldn't operate with a goon squad. He couldn't reconcile it with his opinion of how he wants to live."

"For my money," Morgan said sharply, "stopping a murder investigation with a phone call and stopping it by knocking off the witnesses is just a question of method. And both methods stink in the nostrils of civilization. See you around — I hope."

He drifted out of the office like something blown by the wind.

46

I DROVE OUT TO VICTOR'S with the idea of drinking a gimlet and sitting around until the evening edition of the morning papers was on the street. But the bar was crowded and it wasn't any fun. When the barkeep I knew got around to me he called me by name.

"You like a dash of bitters in it, don't you?"

"Not usually. Just for tonight two dashes of bitters."

"I haven't seen your friend lately. The one with the green ice."

"Neither have I."

He went away and came back with the drink. I pecked at it to make it last, because I didn't feel like getting a glow on. Either I would get really stiff or stay sober. After a while I had another of the same. It was just past six when the kid with the papers came into the bar. One of the barkeeps yelled at him to beat it, but he managed one quick round of the customers before a waiter got hold of him and threw him out. I was one of the customers. I opened up the *Journal* and glanced at page 1A. They had made it. It was all there. They had reversed the photostat by making it black on white and by reducing it in size they had fitted it into the top half of the page. There was a short brusque editorial on another page. There was a half column by Lonnie Morgan with a by-line, on still another page.

I finished my drink and left and went to another place to eat dinner and then drove home.

Lonnie Morgan's piece was a straightforward factual recapitulation of the facts and happenings involved in the Lennox case and the "suicide" of Roger Wade — the facts as they had been published. It added nothing, deduced nothing, imputed nothing. It was clear concise businesslike reporting. The editorial was something else. It asked questions — the kind a newspaper asks of public officials when they are caught with jam on their faces.

About nine-thirty the telephone rang and Bernie Ohls said he would drop by on his way home.

"Seen the *Journal?*" he asked coyly, and hung up without waiting for an answer.

When he got there he grunted about the steps and said he would drink a cup of coffee if I had one. I said I would make some. While I made it he wandered around the house and made himself very much at home.

"You live pretty lonely for a guy that could get himself disliked," he said. "What's over the hill in back?"

"Another street. Why?"

"Just asking. Your shrubbery needs pruning."

I carried some coffee into the living room and he parked himself and sipped it. He lit one of my cigarettes and puffed at it for a minute or two, then put it out. "Getting so I don't care for the stuff," he said. "Maybe it's the TV commercials. They make you hate everything they try to sell. God, they must think the public is a halfwit. Every time some jerk in a white coat with a stethoscope hanging around his neck holds up some toothpaste or a pack of cigarettes or a bottle of beer or a mouthwash or a jar of shampoo or a little box of something that makes a fat wrestler smell like mountain lilac I always make a note never to buy any. Hell, I wouldn't buy the product even if I liked it. You read the *Journal*, huh?"

"A friend of mine tipped me off. A reporter."

"You got friends?" he asked wonderingly. "Didn't tell you how they got hold of the material, did he?"

"No. And in this state he doesn't have to tell you."

"Springer is hopping mad. Lawford, the deputy D.A. that got the letter this morning, claims he took it straight to his boss, but it makes a guy wonder. What the *Journal* printed looks like a straight reproduction from the original."

I sipped coffee and said nothing.

"Serves him right," Ohls went on. "Springer ought to have handled it himself. Personally I don't figure it was Lawford that leaked. He's a politician too." He stared at me woodenly.

"What are you here for, Bernie? You don't like me. We used to be friends — as much as anybody can be friends with a tough cop. But it soured a little."

He leaned forward and smiled — a little wolfishly. "No cop likes it when a private citizen does police work behind his back. If you had connected up Wade and the Lennox frail for me the time Wade got dead I'd have made out. If you had connected up Mrs. Wade and this Terry Lennox I'd have had her in the palm of my hand — alive. If you had come clean from the start Wade might be still alive. Not to mention Lennox. You figure you're a pretty smart monkey, don't you?"

"What would you like me to say?"

"Nothing. It's too late. I told you a wise guy never fools anybody but himself. I told you straight and clear. So it didn't take. Right now it might be smart for you to leave town. Nobody likes you and a couple of guys that don't like people do something about it. I had the word from a stoolie."

"I'm not that important, Bernie. Let's stop snarling at each other. Until Wade was dead you didn't even enter the case. After that it didn't seem to matter to you and to the coroner or to the D.A. or to anybody. Maybe I did some things wrong. But the truth came out. You could have had her yesterday afternoon — with what?"

"With what you had to tell us about her."

"Me? With the police work I did behind your back?"

He stood up abruptly. His face was red. "Okay, wise guy. She'd have been alive. We could have booked her on suspicion. You *wanted* her dead, you punk, and you know it."

"I wanted her to take a good long quiet look at herself. What she did about it was her business. I wanted to clear an innocent man. I didn't give a good goddam how I did it and I don't now. I'll be around when you feel like doing something about me."

"The hard boys will take care of you, buster. I won't have to bother. You think you're not important enough to bother them. As a P.I. named Marlowe, check. You're not. As a guy who was told where to get off and blew a raspberry in their faces publicly in a newspaper, that's different. That hurts their pride."

"That's pitiful," I said. "Just thinking about it makes me bleed internally, to use your own expression."

He went across to the door and opened it. He stood looking down the redwood steps and at the trees on the hill across the way and up the slope at the end of the street.

"Nice and quiet here," he said. "Just quiet enough."

He went on down the steps and got into his car and left. Cops never say goodbye. They're always hoping to see you again in the line-up.

47

FOR A SHORT TIME THE NEXT DAY things looked like getting lively. District Attorney Springer called an early press conference and delivered a statement. He was the big florid black-browed prematurely gray-haired type that always does so well in politics.

"I have read the document which purports to be a confession by the unfortunate and unhappy woman who recently took her life, a document which may or may not be genuine, but which, if genuine, is obviously the product of a disordered mind. I am willing to assume that the *Journal* published this document in good faith, in spite of its many absurdities and inconsistencies, and these I shall not bore you with enumerating. If Eileen Wade wrote these words, and my office in conjunction with the staff of my respected coadjutor, Sheriff Petersen, will soon determine whether or no she did, then I say to you that she did not write them with a clear head, nor with a steady hand. It is only a matter of weeks since the unfortunate lady found her husband wallowing in his own blood, spilled by his own hand. Imagine the shock, the despair, the utter loneliness which must have followed so sharp a disaster! And now she has joined him in the bitterness of death. Is anything to be gained by disturbing the ashes of the dead? Anything, my friends, beyond the sale of a few copies of a newspaper which is badly in need of circulation? Nothing, my friends, nothing. Let us leave it at that. Like Ophelia in that great dramatic masterpiece called *Hamlet,* by the immortal William Shakespeare, Eileen Wade wore her rue with a difference. My political enemies would like to make much of that difference, but my friends and fellow voters will not be deceived. They know that this office has long stood for wise and mature law enforcement, for justice tempered with mercy, for solid, stable, and conservative government. The *Journal* stands for I know not what, and for what it stands I do not much or greatly care. Let the enlightened public judge for itself."

The *Journal* printed this guff in its early edition (it was a round-the-clock newspaper) and Henry Sherman, the Managing Editor, came right back at Springer with a signed comment.

Mr. District-Attorney Springer was in good form this morning. He is a fine figure of a man and he speaks with a rich baritone voice that is a pleasure to listen to. He did not bore us with any facts. Any time Mr. Springer cares to have the authenticity of the document in question proved to him, the *Journal* will be most happy to oblige. We do not expect Mr. Springer to take any action to reopen cases which have been officially closed with his sanction or under his direction, just as we do not expect Mr. Springer to stand on his head on the tower of the City Hall. As Mr. Springer so aptly phrases it, is anything to be gained by disturbing the ashes of the dead? Or, as the *Journal* would prefer to phrase it less elegantly, is anything to be gained by finding out who committed a murder when the murderee is already dead? Nothing, of course, but justice and truth.

On behalf of the late William Shakespeare, the *Journal* wishes to thank Mr. Springer for his favorable mention of *Hamlet,* and for his substantially, although not exactly, correct allusion to Ophelia. 'You must wear your rue with a difference' was not said of Ophelia but by her, and just what she meant has never been very clear to our less erudite minds. But let that pass. It sounds well and helps to confuse the issue. Perhaps we may be permitted to quote, also from that officially approved dramatic production known as *Hamlet,* a good thing that happened to be said by a bad man: "And where the offence is let the great axe fall."

Lonnie Morgan called me up about noon and asked me how I liked it. I told him I didn't think it would do Springer any harm. "Only with the eggheads," Lonnie Morgan said, "and they already had his number. I meant what about you?"

"Nothing about me. I'm just sitting here waiting for a soft buck to rub itself against my cheek."

"That wasn't exactly what I meant."

"I'm still healthy. Quit trying to scare me. I got what I wanted. If Lennox was still alive he could walk right up to Springer and spit in his eye."

"You did it for him. And by this time Springer knows that. They got a hundred ways to frame a guy they don't like. I don't figure what made it worth your time. Lennox wasn't that much man."

"What's that got to do with it?"

He was silent for a moment. Then he said: "Sorry, Marlowe. Shut my big mouth. Good luck."

We hung up after the usual goodbyes.

About two in the afternoon Linda Loring called me. "No names, please," she said. "I've just flown in from that big lake up north. Somebody up there is boiling over something that was in the *Journal* last night. My almost ex-husband got it right between the eyes. The poor man was weeping when I left. He flew up to report."

"What do you mean, almost ex-husband?"

"Don't be stupid. For once Father approves. Paris is an excellent place to get a quiet divorce. So I shall soon be leaving to go there. And if you have any sense left you could do worse than spend a little of that fancy engraving you showed me going a long way off yourself."

"What's it got to do with me?"

"That's the second stupid question you've asked. You're not fooling anyone but yourself, Marlowe. Do you know how they shoot tigers?"

"How would I?"

"They tie a goat to a stake and then hide out in a blind. It's apt to be rough on the goat. I like you. I'm sure I don't know why, but I do. I hate the idea of your being the goat. You tried so hard to do the right thing — as you saw it."

"Nice of you," I said. "If I stick my neck out and it gets chopped, it's still my neck."

"Don't be a hero, you fool," she said sharply. "Just because someone we knew chose to be a fall guy, you don't have to imitate him."

"I'll buy you a drink if you're going to be around long enough."

"Buy me one in Paris. Paris is lovely in the fall."

"I'd like to do that too. I hear it was even better in the spring. Never having been there I wouldn't know."

"The way you're going you never will."

"Goodbye, Linda. I hope you find what you want."

"Goodbye," she said coldly. "I always find what I want. But when I find it, I don't want it any more."

She hung up. The rest of the day was a blank. I ate dinner and left the Olds at an all night garage to have the brake linings checked. I took a cab home. The street was as empty as usual. In the wooden mailbox was a free soap coupon. I went up the steps slowly. It was a soft night with a little haze in the air. The trees on the hill hardly moved. No breeze. I unlocked the door and pushed it part way open and then stopped. The door was about ten inches open from the frame. It was dark inside, there was no sound. But I had the feeling that the room beyond was not empty. Perhaps a spring squeaked faintly or I caught the gleam of a white jacket across the room. Perhaps on a warm still night like this one the room beyond the door was not warm enough, not still enough. Perhaps there was a drifting smell of man on the air. And perhaps I was just on edge.

I stepped sideways off the porch on to the ground and leaned down against the shrubbery. Nothing happened. No light went on inside, there was no movement anywhere that I heard. I had a gun in a belt holster on the left side, butt forward, a short-barreled Police .38. I jerked it out and it got me nowhere. The silence continued. I decided I was a damn fool. I straightened up and lifted a foot to go back to the front door, and then a car turned the corner and came fast up the hill and stopped almost without sound at the foot of my steps. It was a big black sedan with the lines of a Cadillac. It could have been Linda Loring's car, except for two things. Nobody opened a door and the windows on my side were all shut tight. I waited and listened, crouched against the bush, and there was nothing to listen to and nothing to wait for. Just a dark car motionless at the foot of my redwood steps, with the windows closed. If its motor was still running I couldn't hear it. Then a big red spotlight clicked on and the beam struck twenty feet beyond the corner of the house. And then very slowly the big car backed until the spotlight could swing across the front of the house, across the hood and up.

Policemen don't drive Cadillacs. Cadillacs with red spotlights belong to the big boys, mayors and police commissioners, perhaps District Attorneys. Perhaps hoodlums.

THE LONG GOODBYE 705

The spotlight traversed. I went down flat, but it found me just the same. It held on me. Nothing else. Still the car door didn't open, still the house was silent and without light.

Then a siren growled in low pitch just for a second or two and stopped. And then at last the house was full of lights and a man in a white dinner jacket came out to the head of the steps and looked sideways along the wall and the shrubbery.

"Come on in, cheapie," Menendez said with a chuckle. "You've got company."

I could have shot him with no trouble at all. Then he stepped back and it was too late — even if I could have done it. Then a window went down at the back of the car and I could hear the thud as it opened. Then a machine pistol went off and fired a short burst into the slope of the bank thirty feet away from me.

"Come on in, cheapie," Menendez said again from the doorway. "There just ain't anywhere else to go."

So I straightened up and went and the spotlight followed me accurately. I put the gun back in the holster on my belt. I stepped up onto the small redwood landing and went in through the door and stopped just inside. A man was sitting across the room with his legs crossed and a gun resting sideways on his thigh. He looked rangy and tough and his skin had that dried-out look of people who live in sun-bleached climates. He was wearing a dark brown gabardine-type windbreaker and the zipper was open almost to his waist. He was looking at me and neither his eyes nor the gun moved. He was as calm as an adobe wall in the moonlight.

<h1 style="text-align:center">48</h1>

I LOOKED AT HIM TOO LONG. There was a brief half-seen move at my side and a numbing pain in the point of my shoulder. My whole arm went dead to the fingertips. I turned and looked at a big mean-looking Mexican. He wasn't grinning, he was just watching me.

The .45 in his brown hand dropped to his side. He had a mustache and his head bulged with oily black hair brushed up and back and over and down. There was a dirty sombrero on the back of his head and the leather chin strap hung loose in two strands down the front of a stitched shirt that smelled of sweat. There is nothing tougher than a tough Mexican, just as there is nothing gentler than a gentle Mexican, nothing more honest than an honest Mexican, and above all nothing sadder than a sad Mexican. This guy was one of the hard boys. They don't come any harder anywhere.

I rubbed my arm. It tingled a little but the ache was still there and the numbness. If I had tried to pull a gun I should probably have dropped it.

Menendez held his hand out towards the slugger. Without seeming to look he tossed the gun and Menendez caught it. He stood in front of me now and his face glistened. "Where would you like it, cheapie?" His black eyes danced.

I just looked at him. There is no answer to a question like that.

"I asked you a question, cheapie."

I wet my lips and asked one back. "What happened to Agostino? I thought he was your gun handler."

"Chick went soft," he said gently.

"He was always soft — like his boss."

The man in the chair flicked his eyes. He almost but not quite smiled. The tough boy who had paralyzed my arm neither moved nor spoke. I knew he was breathing. I could smell that.

"Somebody bump into your arm, cheapie?"

"I tripped over an enchilada."

Negligently, not quite looking at me even, he slashed me across the face with the gun barrel.

"Don't get gay with me, cheapie. You're out of time for all that. You got told and you got told nice. When I take the trouble to call around personally and tell a character to lay off — he lays off. Or else he lays down and don't get up."

I could feel a trickle of blood down my cheek. I could feel the full numbing ache of the blow in my cheekbone. It spread until my whole head ached. It hadn't been a hard blow, but the thing he used was hard. I could still talk and nobody tried to stop me.

"How come you do your own slugging, Mendy? I thought that

was coolie labor for the sort of boys that beat up Big Willie Magoon."

"It's the personal touch," he said softly, "on account of I had personal reasons for telling you. The Magoon job was strictly business. He got to thinking he could push me around — me that bought his clothes and his cars and stocked his safe deposit box and paid off the trust deed on his house. These vice squad babies are all the same. I even paid school bills for his kid. You'd think the bastard would have some gratitude. So what does he do? He walks into my private office and slaps me around in front of the help."

"On account of why?" I asked him, in the vague hope of getting him mad at somebody else.

"On account of some lacquered chippie said we used loaded dice. Seems like the bim was one of his sleepy-time gals. I had her put out of the club — with every dime she brought in with her."

"Seems understandable," I said. "Magoon ought to know no professional gambler plays crooked games. He doesn't have to. But what have I done to you?"

He hit me again, thoughtfully. "You made me look bad. In my racket you don't tell a guy twice. Not even a hard number. He goes out and does it, or you ain't got control. You ain't got control, you ain't in business."

"I've got a hunch that there's a little more to it than that," I said. "Excuse me if I reach for a handkerchief."

The gun watched me while I got one out and touched the blood on my face.

"A two-bit peeper," Menendez said slowly, "figures he can make a monkey out of Mendy Menendez. He can get me laughed at. He can get me the big razzoo — me, Menendez. I ought to use a knife on you, cheapie. I ought to cut you into slices of raw meat."

"Lennox was your pal," I said, and watched his eyes. "He got dead. He got buried like a dog without even a name over the dirt where they put his body. And I had a little something to do with proving him innocent. So that makes you look bad, huh? He saved your life and he lost his, and that didn't mean a thing to you. All that means anything to you is playing the big shot. You didn't give a hoot in hell for anybody but yourself. You're not big, you're just loud."

His face froze and he swung his arm back to slug me a third time and this time with the power behind it. His arm was still going back when I took a half step forward and kicked him in the pit of the stomach.

I didn't think, I didn't plan, I didn't figure my chances or whether I had any. I just got enough of his yap and I ached and bled and maybe I was just a little punch drunk by this time.

He jackknifed, gasping, and the gun fell out of his hand. He groped for it wildly making strained sounds deep in his throat. I put a knee into his face. He screeched.

The man in the chair laughed. That staggered me. Then he stood up and the gun in his hand came up with him.

"Don't kill him," he said mildly. "We want to use him for live bait."

Then there was movement in the shadows of the hall and Ohls came through the door, blank-eyed, expressionless and utterly calm. He looked down at Menendez. Menendez was kneeling with his head on the floor.

"Soft," Ohls said. "Soft as mush."

"He's not soft," I said. "He's hurt. Any man can be hurt. Was Big Willie Magoon soft?"

Ohls looked at me. The other man looked at me. The tough Mex at the door hadn't made a sound.

"Take that goddam cigarette out of your face," I snarled at Ohls. "Either smoke it or leave it alone. I'm sick of watching you. I'm sick of you, period. I'm sick of cops."

He looked surprised. Then he grinned.

"That was a plant, kiddo," he said cheerfully. "You hurt bad? Did the nasty mans hit your facey-wacey? Well for my money you had it coming and it was damn useful that you had." He looked down at Mendy. Mendy had his knees under him. He was climbing out of a well, a few inches at a time. He breathed gaspingly.

"What a talkative lad he is," Ohls said, "when he doesn't have three shysters with him to button his lip."

He jerked Menendez to his feet. Mendy's nose was bleeding. He fumbled the handkerchief out of his white dinner jacket and held it to his nose. He said no word.

"You got crossed up, sweetheart," Ohls told him carefully. "I ain't grieving a whole lot over Magoon. He had it coming. But he was a cop and punks like you lay off cops — always and forever."

Menendez lowered the handkerchief and looked at Ohls. He looked at me. He looked at the man who had been sitting in the chair. He turned slowly and looked at the tough Mex by the door. They all looked at him. There was nothing in their faces. Then a knife shot into view from nowhere and Mendy lunged for Ohls. Ohls side-stepped and took him by the throat with one hand and chopped the knife out of his hand with ease, almost indifferently. Ohls spread his feet and straightened his back and bent his legs slightly and lifted Menendez clear off the floor with one hand holding his neck. He walked him across the floor and pinned him against the wall. He let him down, but didn't let go of his throat.

"Touch me with one finger and I'll kill you," Ohls said. "One finger." Then he dropped his hands.

Mendy smiled at him scornfully, looked at his handkerchief, and refolded it to hide the blood. He held it to his nose again. He looked down at the gun he had used to hit me. The man from the chair said loosely: "Not loaded, even if you could grab it."

"A cross," Mendy said to Ohls. "I heard you the first time."

"You ordered three muscles," Ohls said. "What you got was three deputies from Nevada. Somebody in Vegas don't like the way you forget to clear with them. The somebody wants to talk to you. You can go along with the deputies or you can go downtown with me and get hung on the back of the door by a pair of handcuffs. There's a couple of boys down there would like to see you close up."

"God help Nevada," Mendy said quietly, looking around again at the tough Mex by the door. Then he crossed himself quickly and walked out of the front door. The tough Mex followed him. Then the other one, the dried out desert type, picked up the gun and the knife and went out too. He shut the door. Ohls waited motionless. There was a sound of doors banging shut, then a car went off into the night.

"You sure those mugs were deputies?" I asked Ohls.

He turned as if surprised to see me there. "They had stars," he said shortly.

"Nice work, Bernie. Very nice. Think he'll get to Vegas alive, you coldhearted son of a bitch?"

I went to the bathroom and ran cold water and held a soaked towel against my throbbing cheek. I looked at myself in the glass. The cheek was puffed out of shape and bluish and there were jagged wounds on it from the force of the gun barrel hitting against the cheekbone. There was a discoloration under my left eye too. I wasn't going to be beautiful for a few days.

Then Ohls' reflection showed behind me in the mirror. He was rolling his damn unlighted cigarette along his lips, like a cat teasing a half-dead mouse, trying to get it to run away just once more.

"Next time don't try to outguess the cops," he said gruffly. "You think we let you steal that photostat just for laughs? We had a hunch Mendy would come gunning for you. We put it up to Starr cold. We told him we couldn't stop gambling in the county, but we could make it tough enough to cut way into the take. No mobster beats up a cop, not even a bad cop, and gets away with it in our territory. Starr convinced us he had nothing to do with it, that the outfit was sore about it and Menendez was going to get told. So when Mendy called for a squad of out-of-town hard boys to come and give you the treatment, Starr sent him three guys he knew, in one of his own cars, at his own expense. Starr is a police comissioner in Vegas."

I turned around and looked at Ohls. "The coyotes out in the desert will get fed tonight. Congratulations. Cop business is wonderful uplifting idealistic work, Bernie. The only thing wrong with cop business is the cops that are in it."

"Too bad for you, hero," he said with a sudden cold savagery. "I could hardly help laughing when you walked into your own parlor to take your beating. I got a rise out of that, kiddo. It was a dirty job and it had to be done dirty. To make these characters talk you got to give them a sense of power. You ain't hurt bad, but we had to let them hurt you some."

"So sorry," I said. "So very sorry you had to suffer like that."

He shoved his taut face at me. "I hate gamblers," he said in a rough voice. "I hate them the way I hate dope pushers. They pander to a disease that is every bit as corrupting as dope. You think those palaces in Reno and Vegas are just for harmless fun? Nuts, they're there for the little guy, the something-for-nothing sucker, the lad that stops off with his pay envelope in his pocket and loses the week-end grocery money. The rich gambler loses forty grand and laughs it off and comes back for more. But the rich gambler don't make the big racket, pal. The big steal is in dimes and quarters and half dollars and once in a while a buck or even a five-spot. The big racket money comes in like water from the pipe in your bathroom, a steady stream that never stops flowing. Any time anybody wants to knock off a professional gambler, that's for me. I like it. And any time a state government takes money from gambling and calls it taxes, that government is helping to keep the mobs in business. The barber or the beauty parlor girl puts two bucks on the nose. That's for the Syndicate, that's what really makes the profits. The people want an honest police force, do they? What for? To protect the guys with courtesy cards? We got legal horse tracks in this state, we got them all year round. They operate honest and the state gets its cut, and for every dollar laid at the track there's fifty laid with the bookies. There's eight or nine races on a card and in half of them, the little ones nobody notices, the fix can be in any time somebody says so. There's only one way a jock can win a race, but there's twenty ways he can lose one, with a steward at every eighth pole watching, and not able to do a damn thing about it if the jock knows his stuff. That's legal gambling, pal, clean honest business, state approved. So it's right, is it? Not by my book, it ain't. Because it's gambling and it breeds gamblers and when you add it all up there's one kind of gambling — the wrong kind."

"Feel better?" I asked him, putting some white iodine on my wounds.

"I'm an old tired beat-up cop. All I feel is sore."

I turned around and stared at him. "You're a damn good cop, Bernie, but just the same you're all wet. In one way cops are all the same. They all blame the wrong things. If a guy loses his pay check at a crap table, stop gambling. If he gets drunk, stop liquor. If he kills somebody in a car crash, stop making automobiles. If he gets pinched with a girl in a hotel room, stop sexual intercourse. If he falls downstairs, stop building houses."

"Aw shut up!"

"Sure, shut me up. I'm just a private citizen. Get off it, Bernie.

We don't have mobs and crime syndicates and goon squads because we have crooked politicians and their stooges in the City Hall and the legislatures. Crime isn't a disease, it's a symptom. Cops are like a doctor that gives you aspirin for a brain tumor, except that the cop would rather cure it with a blackjack. We're a big rough rich wild people and crime is the price we pay for it, and organized crime is the price we pay for organization. We'll have it with us a long time. Organized crime is just the dirty side of the sharp dollar."

"What's the clean side?"

"I never saw it. Maybe Harlan Potter could tell you. Let's have a drink."

"You looked pretty good walking in that door," Ohls said.

"You looked better when Mendy pulled the knife on you."

"Shake," he said, and put his hand out.

We had the drink and he left by the back door, which he had jimmied to get in, having dropped by the night before for scouting purposes. Back doors are a soft touch if they open out and are old enough for the wood to have dried and shrunk. You knock the pins out of the hinges and the rest is easy. Ohls showed me a dent in the frame when he left to go back over the hill to where he had left his car on the next street. He could have opened the front door almost as easily but that would have broken the lock. It would have showed up too much.

I watched him climb through the trees with the beam of a torch in front of him and disappear over the rise. I locked the door and mixed another mild drink and went back to the living room and sat down. I looked at my watch. It was still early. It only seemed a long time since I had come home.

I went to the phone and dialed the operator and gave her the Lorings' phone number. The butler asked who was calling, then went to see if Mrs. Loring was in. She was.

"I was the goat all right," I said, "but they caught the tiger alive. I'm bruised up a little."

"You must tell me about it sometime." She sounded about as far away as if she had got to Paris already.

"I could tell you over a drink — if you had time."

"Tonight? Oh, I'm packing my things to move out. I'm afraid that would be impossible."

"Yes, I can see that. Well, I just thought you might like to know. It was kind of you to warn me. It had nothing at all to do with your old man."

"Are you sure?"

"Positive."

"Oh. Just a minute." She was gone for a time, then she came back and sounded warmer. "Perhaps I could fit a drink in. Where?"

"Anywhere you say. I haven't a car tonight, but I can get a cab."

"Nonsense, I'll pick you up, but it will be an hour or longer. What is the address there?"

I told her and she hung up and I put the porch light on and then stood in the open door inhaling the night. It had got much cooler.

I went back in and tried to phone Lonnie Morgan but couldn't reach him. Then just for the hell of it I put a call in to the Terrapin Club at Las Vegas, Mr. Randy Starr. He probably wouldn't take it. But he did. He had a quiet, competent, man-of-affairs voice.

"Nice to hear from you, Marlowe. Any friend of Terry's is a friend of mine. What can I do for you?"

"Mendy is on his way."

"On his way where?"

"To Vegas, with the three goons you sent after him in a big black Caddy with a red spotlight and siren. Yours, I presume?"

He laughed. "In Vegas, as some newspaper guy said, we use Cadillacs for trailers. What's this all about?"

"Mendy staked out here in my house with a couple of hard boys. His idea was to beat me up — putting it low — for a piece in the paper he seemed to think was my fault."

"Was it your fault?"

"I don't own any newspapers, Mr. Starr."

"I don't own any hard boys in Cadillacs, Mr. Marlowe."

"They were deputies maybe."

"I couldn't say. Anything else?"

"He pistol-whipped me. I kicked him in the stomach and used my knee on his nose. He seemed dissatisfied. All the same I hope he gets to Vegas alive."

"I'm sure he will, if he started this way. I'm afraid I'll have to cut this conversation short now."

"Just a second, Starr. Were you in on that caper at Otatoclán —

or did Mendy work it alone?"

"Come again?"

"Don't kid, Starr. Mendy wasn't sore at me for why he said — not to the point of staking out in my house and giving me the treatment he gave Big Willie Magoon. Not enough motive. He warned me to keep my nose clean and not to dig into the Lennox case. But I did, because it just happened to work out that way. So he did what I've just told you. So there was a better reason."

"I see," he said slowly and still mildly and quietly. "You think there was something not quite kosher about how Terry got dead? That he didn't shoot himself, for instance, but someone else did?"

"I think the details would help. He wrote a confession which was false. He wrote a letter to me which got mailed. A waiter or hop in the hotel was going to sneak it out and mail it for him. He was holed up in the hotel and couldn't get out. There was a big bill in the letter and the letter was finished just as a knock came at his door. I'd like to know who came into the room."

"Why?"

"If it had been a bellhop or a waiter, Terry would have added a line to the letter and said so. If it was a cop, the letter wouldn't have been mailed. So who was it — and why did Terry write that confession?"

"No idea, Marlowe. No idea at all."

"Sorry I bothered you, Mr. Starr."

"No bother, glad to hear from you. I'll ask Mendy if he has any ideas."

"Yeah — if you ever see him again — alive. If you don't — find out anyway. Or somebody else will."

"You?" His voice hardened now, but it was still quiet.

"No, Mr. Starr. Not me. Somebody that could blow you out of Vegas without taking a long breath. Believe me, Mr. Starr. Just believe me. This is strictly on the level."

"I'll see Mendy alive. Don't worry about that, Marlowe."

"I figured you knew all about that. Goodnight, Mr. Starr."

49

WHEN THE CAR STOPPED out front and the door opened I went out and stood at the top of the steps to call down. But the middle-aged colored driver was holding the door for her to get out. Then he followed her up the steps carrying a small overnight case. So I just waited.

She reached the top and turned to the driver: "Mr. Marlowe will drive me to my hotel, Amos. Thank you for everything. I'll call you in the morning."

"Yes, Mrs. Loring. May I ask Mr. Marlowe a question?"

"Certainly, Amos."

He put the overnight case down inside the door and she went in past me and left us.

" 'I grow old . . . I grow old . . . I shall wear the bottoms of my trousers rolled.' What does that mean, Mr. Marlowe?"

"Not a bloody thing. It just sounds good."

He smiled. "That is from the 'Love Song of J. Alfred Prufrock.' Here's another one. 'In the room the women come and go/Talking of Michael Angelo.' Does that suggest anything to you, sir?"

"Yeah — it suggests to me that the guy didn't know very much about women."

"My sentiments exactly, sir. Nonetheless I admire T. S. Eliot very much."

"Did you say 'nonetheless'?"

"Why, yes I did, Mr. Marlowe. Is that incorrect?"

"No, but don't say it in front of a millionaire. He might think you were giving him the hotfoot."

He smiled sadly. "I shouldn't dream of it. Have you had an accident, sir?"

"Nope. It was planned that way. Goodnight, Amos."

"Goodnight, sir."

He went back down the steps and I went back into the house. Linda Loring was standing in the middle of the living room looking around her.

"Amos is a graduate of Howard University," she said. "You don't live in a very safe place — for such an unsafe man, do you?"

"There aren't any safe places."

"Your poor face. Who did that to you?"

"Mendy Menendez."

"What did you do to him?"

"Nothing much. Kicked him a time or two. He walked into a trap. He's on his way to Nevada in the company of three or four tough Nevada deputies. Forget him."

She sat down on the davenport.

"What would you like to drink?" I asked. I got a cigarette box and held it out to her. She said she didn't want to smoke. She said anything would do to drink.

"I thought of champagne," I said. "I haven't any ice bucket, but it's cold. I've been saving it for years. Two bottles. Cordon Rouge. I guess it's good. I'm no judge."

"Saving it for what?" she asked.

"For you."

She smiled, but she was still staring at my face. "You're all cut." She reached her fingers up and touched my cheek lightly. "Saving it for me? That's not very likely. It's only a couple of months since we met."

"Then I was saving it until we met. I'll go get it." I picked up her overnight bag and started across the room with it.

"Just where are you going with that?" she asked sharply.

"It's an overnight bag, isn't it?"

"Put it down and come back here."

I did that. Her eyes were bright and at the same time they were sleepy.

"This is something new," she said slowly. "Something quite new."

"In what way?"

"You've never laid a finger on me. No passes, no suggestive remarks, no pawing, no nothing. I thought you were tough, sarcastic, mean, and cold."

"I guess I am — at times."

"Now I'm here and I suppose without preamble, after we have had a reasonable quantity of champagne you plan to grab me and throw me on the bed. Is that it?"

"Frankly," I said, "some such idea did stir at the back of my mind."

"I'm flattered, but suppose I don't want it that way? I like you. I like you very much. But it doesn't follow that I want to go to bed with you. Aren't you rather jumping at conclusions — just because I happen to bring an overnight bag with me?"

"Could be I made an error," I said. I went and got her overnight bag and put it back by the front door. "I'll get the champagne."

"I didn't mean to hurt your feelings. Perhaps you would rather save the champagne for some more auspicious occasion."

"It's only two bottles," I said. "A really auspicious occasion would call for a dozen."

"Oh, I see," she said, suddenly angry. "I'm just to be a fill-in until someone more beautiful and attractive comes along. Thank you so very much. Now you've hurt my feelings, but I suppose it's something to know that I'm safe here. If you think a bottle of champagne will make a loose woman out of me, I can assure you that you are very much mistaken."

"I admitted the mistake already."

"The fact that I told you I was going to divorce my husband and that I had Amos drop me by here with an overnight bag doesn't make me as easy as all that," she said, still angry.

"Damn the overnight bag!" I growled. "The hell with the overnight bag! Mention it again and I'll throw the damn thing down the front steps. I asked you to have a drink. I'm going out to the kitchen to get the drink. That's all. I hadn't the least idea of getting you drunk. You don't want to go to bed with me. I understand perfectly. No reason why you should. But we can still have a glass or two of champagne, can't we? This doesn't have to be a wrangle about who is going to get seduced and when and where and on how much champagne."

"You don't have to lose your temper," she said, flushing.

"That's just another gambit," I snarled. "I know fifty of them and I hate them all. They're all phony and they all have a sort of leer at the edges."

She got up and came over close to me and ran the tips of her fingers gently over the cuts and swollen places on my face. "I'm sorry. I'm a tired and disappointed woman. Please be kind to me.

I'm no bargain to anyone."

"You're not tired and you're no more disappointed than most people are. By all the rules you ought to be the same sort of shallow spoiled promiscuous brat your sister was. By some miracle you're not. You've got all the honesty and a large part of the guts in your family. You don't need anyone to be kind to you."

I turned and walked out of the room down the hall to the kitchen and got one of the bottles of champagne out of the icebox and popped the cork and filled a couple of shallow goblets quickly and drank one down. The sting of it brought tears to my eyes, but I emptied the glass. I filled it again. Then I put the whole works on a tray and carted it into the living room.

She wasn't there. The overnight bag wasn't there. I put the tray down and opened the front door. I hadn't heard any sound of its opening and she had no car. I hadn't heard any sound at all.

Then she spoke from behind me. "Idiot, did you think I was going to run away?"

I shut the door and turned. She had loosened her hair and she had tufted slippers on her bare feet and a silk robe the color of a sunset in a Japanese print. She came towards me slowly with a sort of unexpectedly shy smile. I held a glass out to her. She took it, took a couple of sips of the champagne, and handed it back.

"It's very nice," she said. Then very quietly and without a trace of acting or affectation she came into my arms and pressed her mouth against mine and opened her lips and her teeth. The tip of her tongue touched mine. After a long time she pulled her head back but kept her arms around my neck. She was starry-eyed.

"I meant to all the time," she said. "I just had to be difficult. I don't know why. Just nerves perhaps. I'm not really a loose woman at all. Is that a pity?"

"If I had thought you were I'd have made a pass at you the first time I met you in the bar at Victor's."

She shook her head slowly and smiled. "I don't think so. That's why I am here."

"Perhaps not that night," I said. "That night belonged to something else."

"Perhaps you don't ever make passes at women in bars."

"Not often. The light's too dim."

"But a lot of women go to bars just to have passes made at them."

"A lot of women get up in the morning with the same idea."

"But liquor is an aphrodisiac — up to a point."

"Doctors recommend it."

"Who said anything about doctors? I want my champagne."

I kissed her some more. It was light, pleasant work.

"I want to kiss your poor cheek," she said, and did. "It's burning hot," she said.

"The rest of me is freezing."

"It is not. I want my champagne."

"Why?"

"It'll get flat if we don't drink it. Besides I like the taste of it."

"All right."

"Do you love me very much? Or will you if I go to bed with you?"

"Possibly."

"You don't have to go to bed with me, you know. I don't absolutely insist on it."

"Thank you."

"I want my champagne."

"How much money have you got?"

"Altogether? How would I know? About eight million dollars."

"I've decided to go to bed with you."

"Mercenary," she said.

"I paid for the champagne."

"The hell with the champagne," she said.

50

AN HOUR LATER she stretched out a bare arm and tickled my ear and said: "Would you consider marrying me?"

"It wouldn't last six months."

"Well, for God's sake," she said, "suppose it didn't. Wouldn't it be worth it? What do you expect from life — full coverage against all possible risks?"

"I'm forty-two years old. I'm spoiled by independence. You're spoiled a little — not too much — by money."

"I'm thirty-six. It's no disgrace to have money and no disgrace to marry it. Most of those who have it don't deserve it and don't know how to behave with it. But it won't be long. We'll have another war and at the end of that nobody will have any money — except the crooks and the chiselers. We'll all be taxed to nothing, the rest of us."

I stroked her hair and wound some of it around my finger. "You may be right."

"We could fly to Paris and have a wonderful time." She raised herself on an elbow and looked down at me. I could see the shine of her eyes but I couldn't read her expression. "Do you have something against marriage?"

"For two people in a hundred it's wonderful. The rest just work at it. After twenty years all the guy has left is a work bench in the garage. American girls are terrific. American wives take in too damn much territory. Besides — "

"I want some champagne."

"Besides," I said, "it would be just an incident to you. The first divorce is the only tough one. After that it's merely a problem in economics. No problem to you. Ten years from now you might pass me on the street and wonder where the hell you had seen me before. If you noticed me at all."

"You self-sufficient, self-satisfied, self-confident, untouchable bastard. I want some champagne."

"This way you will remember me."

"Conceited too. A mass of conceit. Slightly bruised at the moment. You think I'll remember you? No matter how many men I marry or sleep with, you think I'll remember you? Why should I?"

"Sorry. I overstated my case. I'll get you some champagne."

"Aren't we sweet and reasonable?" she said sarcastically. "I'm a rich woman, darling, and I shall be infinitely richer. I could buy you the world if it were worth buying. What have you now? An empty house to come home to, with not even a dog or cat, a small stuffy office to sit in and wait. Even if I divorced you I'd never let you go back to that."

"How would you stop me? I'm no Terry Lennox."

"Please. Don't let's talk about him. Nor about that golden icicle, the Wade woman. Nor about her poor drunken sunken husband. Do you want to be the only man who turned me down? What kind of pride is that? I've paid you the greatest compliment I know how to pay. I've asked you to marry me."

"You paid me a greater compliment."

She began to cry. "You fool, you utter fool!" Her cheeks were wet. I could feel the tears on them. "Suppose it lasted six months or a year or two years. What would you have lost except the dust on your office desk and the dirt on your venetian blinds and the loneliness of a pretty empty kind of life?"

"You still want some champagne?"

"All right."

I pulled her close and she cried against my shoulder. She wasn't in love with me and we both knew it. She wasn't crying over me. It was just time for her to shed a few tears.

Then she pulled away and I got out of bed and she went into the bathroom to fix her face. I got the champagne. When she came back she was smiling.

"I'm sorry I blubbered," she said. "In six months from now I won't even remember your name. Bring it into the living room. I want to see lights."

I did what she said. She sat on the davenport as before. I put the champagne in front of her. She looked at the glass but didn't touch it.

"I'll introduce myself," I said. "We'll have a drink together."

"Like tonight?"

"It won't ever be like tonight again."

She raised her glass of champagne, drank a little of it slowly, turned her body on the davenport and threw the rest in my face. Then she began to cry again. I got a handkerchief out and wiped my face off and wiped hers for her.

"I don't know why I did that," she said. "But for God's sake don't say I'm a woman and a woman never knows why she does anything."

I poured some more champagne into her glass and laughed at her. She drank it slowly and then turned the other way and fell across my knees.

"I'm tired," she said. "You'll have to carry me this time."

After a while she went to sleep.

In the morning she was still asleep when I got up and made coffee. I showered and shaved and dressed. She woke up then. We had breakfast together. I called a cab and carried her overnight case down the steps.

We said goodbye. I watched the cab out of sight. I went back up the steps and into the bedroom and pulled the bed to pieces and remade it. There was a long dark hair on one of the pillows. There was a lump of lead at the pit of my stomach.

The French have a phrase for it. The bastards have a phrase for everything and they are always right.

To say goodbye is to die a little.

51

SEWELL ENDICOTT SAID he was working late and I could drop around in the evening about seven-thirty.

He had a corner office with a blue carpet, a red mahogany desk with carved corners, very old and obviously very valuable, the usual glass-front bookshelves of mustard-yellow legal books, the usual cartoons by Spy of famous English judges, and a large portrait of Justice Oliver Wendell Holmes on the south wall, alone. Endicott's chair was quilted in black leather. Near him was an open rolltop desk jammed with papers. It was an office no decorator had had a chance to pansy up.

He was in his shirtsleeves and he looked tired, but he had that kind of face. He was smoking one of his tasteless cigarettes. Ashes from it had fallen on his loosened tie. His limp black hair was all over the place.

He stared at me silently after I sat down. Then he said: "You're a stubborn son of a bitch, if ever I met one. Don't tell me you're still digging into that mess."

"Something worries me a little. Would it be all right now if I assumed you were representing Mr. Harlan Potter when you came to see me in the birdcage?"

He nodded. I touched the side of my face gently with my finger-tips. It was all healed up and the swelling was gone, but one of the blows must have damaged a nerve. Part of the cheek was still numb. I couldn't let it alone. It would get all right in time.

"And that when you went to Otatoclán you were temporarily deputized as a member of the D.A.'s staff?"

"Yes, but don't rub it in, Marlowe. It was a valuable connection. Perhaps I gave it too much weight."

"Still is, I hope."

He shook his head. "No. That's finished. Mr. Potter does his legal business through San Francisco, New York, and Washington firms."

"I guess he hates my guts — if he thinks about it."

Endicott smiled. "Curiously enough, he put all the blame on his son-in-law, Dr. Loring. A man like Harlan Potter has to blame somebody. He couldn't possibly be wrong himself. He felt that if Loring hadn't been feeding the woman dangerous drugs, none of it would have happened."

"He's wrong. You saw Terry Lennox's body in Otatoclán, didn't you?"

"I did indeed. In the back of a cabinet maker's shop. They have no proper mortuary there. He was making the coffin too. The body was ice-cold. I saw the wound in the temple. There's no question of identity, if you had any ideas along those lines."

"No, Mr. Endicott, I didn't, because in his case it could hardly be possible. He was disguised a little though, wasn't he?"

"Face and hands darkened, hair dyed black. But the scars were still obvious. And the fingerprints, of course, were easily checked from things he had handled at home."

"What kind of police force do they have down there?"

"Primitive. The jefe could just about read and write. But he knew about fingerprints. It was hot weather, you know. Quite hot." He frowned and took his cigarette out of his mouth and dropped it negligently into an enormous black basalt sort of receptacle. "They had to get ice from the hotel," he added. "Plenty of ice." He looked at me again. "No embalming there. Things have to move fast."

"You speak Spanish, Mr. Endicott?"

"Only a few words. The hotel manager interpreted." He smiled. "A well-dressed smoothie, that fellow. Looked tough, but he was very polite and helpful. It was all over in no time."

"I had a letter from Terry. I guess Mr. Potter would know about it. I told his daughter, Mrs. Loring. I showed it to her. There was a portrait of Madison in it."

"A what?"

"Five-thousand-dollar bill."

He raised his eyebrows. "Really. Well, he could certainly afford it. His wife gave him a cool quarter of a million the second time they were married. I've an idea he meant to go to Mexico to live anyhow — quite apart from what happened. I don't know what happened to the money. I wasn't in on that."

"Here's the letter, Mr. Endicott, if you care to read it."

I took it out and gave it to him. He read it carefully, the way lawyers read everything. He put it down on the desk and leaned back and stared at nothing.

"A little literary, isn't it?" he said quietly. "I wonder why he did it."

"Killed himself, confessed, or wrote me the letter?"

"Confessed and killed himself, of course," Endicott said sharply. "The letter is understandable. At least you got a reasonable recompense for what you did for him — and since."

"The mailbox bothers me," I said. "Where he says there was a mailbox on the street under his window and the hotel waiter was going to hold his letter up before he mailed it, so Terry could see that it was mailed."

Something in Endicott's eyes went to sleep. "Why?" he asked indifferently. He picked another of his filtered cigarettes out of a square box. I held my lighter across the desk for him.

"They wouldn't have one in a place like Otatoclán," I said.

"Go on."

"I didn't get it at first. Then I looked the place up. It's a mere village. Population say ten or twelve hundred. One street partly paved. The jefe has a Model A Ford as an official car. The post office is in the corner of a store, the chanceria, the butcher shop. One hotel, a couple of cantinas, no good roads, a small airfield. There's hunting around there in the mountains — lots of it. Hence the airfield. Only decent way to get there."

"Go on. I know about the hunting."

"So there's a mailbox on the street. Like there's a race course and a dog track and a golf course and a jai alai frontón and park with a colored fountain and a bandstand."

"Then he made a mistake," Endicott said coldly. "Perhaps it was something that looked like a mailbox to him — say a trash receptacle."

I stood up. I reached for the letter and refolded it and put it back in my pocket.

"A trash receptacle," I said. "Sure, that's it. Painted with the Mexican colors, green, white, red, and a sign on it stenciled in large clear print: KEEP OUR CITY CLEAN. In Spanish, of course. And lying around it seven mangy dogs."

"Don't get cute, Marlowe."

"Sorry if I let my brains show. Another small point I have already raised with Randy Starr. How come the letter got mailed at all? According to the letter the method was prearranged. So somebody told him about the mailbox. So somebody lied. So somebody mailed the letter with five grand in it just the same. Intriguing, don't you agree?"

He puffed smoke and watched it float away.

"What's your conclusion — and why ring Starr in on it?"

"Starr and a heel named Menendez, now removed from our midst, were pals of Terry's in the British Army. They are wrong gees in a way — I should say in almost every way — but they still have room for personal pride and so on. There was a cover-up here engineered for obvious reasons. There was another sort of cover-up in Otatoclán, for entirely different reasons."

"What's your conclusion?" he asked me again and much more sharply.

"What's yours?"

He didn't answer me. So I thanked him for his time and left.

He was frowning as I opened the door, but I thought it was an honest frown of puzzlement. Or maybe he was trying to remember how it looked outside the hotel and whether there was a mailbox there.

It was another wheel to start turning — no more. It turned for a solid month before anything came up.

Then on a certain Friday morning I found a stranger waiting for me in my office. He was a well-dressed Mexican or Suramericano of some sort. He sat by the open window smoking a brown cigarette that smelled strong. He was tall and very slender and very elegant, with a neat dark mustache and dark hair, rather longer than we wear it, and a fawn-colored suit of some loosely woven material. He wore those green sunglasses. He stood up politely.

"Señor Marlowe?"

"What can I do for you?"

He handed me a folded paper. "Un aviso de parte del Señor Starr en Las Vegas, señor. Habla Usted Español?"

"Yeah, but not fast. English would be better."

"English then," he said. "It is all the same to me."

I took the paper and read it. "This introduces Cisco Maioranos, a friend of mine. I think he can fix you up. S."

"Let's go inside, Señor Maioranos," I said.

I held the door open for him. He smelled of perfume as he went by. His eyebrows were awfully damned dainty too. But he probably wasn't as dainty as he looked because there were knife scars on both sides of his face.

52

HE SAT DOWN in the customer's chair and crossed his knees. "You wish certain information about Señor Lennox, I am told."

"The last scene only."

"I was there at the time, señor. I had a position in the hotel." He shrugged. "Unimportant and of course temporary. I was the day clerk." He spoke perfect English but with a Spanish rhythm. Spanish — American Spanish that is — has a definite rise and fall which to an American ear seems to have nothing to do with the meaning. It's like the swell of the ocean.

"You don't look the type," I said.

"One has difficulties."

"Who mailed the letter to me?"

He held out a box of cigarettes. "Try one of these."

I shook my head. "Too strong for me. Colombian cigarettes I like. Cuban cigarettes are murder."

He smiled faintly, lit another pill himself, and blew smoke. The guy was so goddam elegant he was beginning to annoy me.

"I know about the letter, señor. The mozo was afraid to go up to the room of this Señor Lennox after the guarda was posted. The cop or dick, as you say. So I myself took the letter to the correo. After the shooting, you understand."

"You ought to have looked inside. It had a large piece of money in it."

"The letter was sealed," he said coldly. "El honor no se mueve de lado como los congrejos. That is, honor does not move side-wise like a crab, señor."

"My apologies. Please continue."

"Señor Lennox had a hundred-peso note in his left hand when I went into the room and shut the door in the face of the guarda. In his right hand was a pistol. On the table before him was the letter. Also another paper which I did not read. I refused the note."

"Too much money," I said, but he didn't react to the sarcasm.

"He insisted. So I took the note finally and gave it to the mozo later. I took the letter out under the napkin on the tray from the previous service of coffee. The dick looked hard at me. But he said nothing. I was halfway down the stairs when I heard the shot. Very quickly I hid the letter and ran back upstairs. The dick was trying to kick the door open. I used my key. Señor Lennox was dead."

He moved his fingertips gently along the edge of the desk and sighed. "The rest no doubt you know."

"Was the hotel full?"

"Not full, no. There were half a dozen guests."

"Americans?"

"Two Americanos del Norte. Hunters."

"Real Gringos or just transplanted Mexicans?"

He drew a fingertip slowly along the fawn-colored cloth above his knee. "I think one of them could well have been of Spanish origin. He spoke border Spanish. Very inelegant."

"They go near Lennox's room at all?"

He lifted his head sharply but the green cheaters didn't do a thing for me. "Why should they, señor?"

I nodded. "Well, it was damn nice of you to come in here and tell me about it, Señor Maioranos. Tell Randy I'm ever so grateful, will you?"

"No hay de que, señor. It is nothing."

"And later on, if he has time, he could send me somebody who knows what he is talking about."

"Señor?" His voice was soft, but icy. "You doubt my word?"

"You guys are always talking about honor. Honor is the cloak of thieves — sometimes. Don't get mad. Sit quiet and let me tell it another way."

He leaned back superciliously.

"I'm only guessing, mind. I could be wrong. But I could be right too. These two Americanos were there for a purpose. They came in on a plane. They pretended to be hunters. One of them was named Menendez, a gambler. He registered under some other name or not. I wouldn't know. Lennox knew they were there. He knew why. He wrote me that letter because he had a guilty conscience. He had played me for a sucker and he was too nice a guy for that to rest easy on him. He put the bill — five thousand dollars it was — in the letter because he had a lot of money and he knew I hadn't. He also put in a little off-beat hint which might or might not register. He was the kind of guy who always wants to do the right thing but somehow winds up doing something else. You say you took the letter to the correo. Why didn't you mail it in the box in front of the hotel?"

"The box, señor?"

"The mailbox. The cajón cartero, you call it, I think."

He smiled. Otatoclán is not Mexico City, señor. It is a very primitive place. A street mailbox in Otatoclán? No one there would understand what it was for. No one would collect letters from it."

I said: "Oh. Well, skip it. You did not take any coffee on any tray up to Señor Lennox's room, Señor Maioranos. You did not go into the room past the dick. But the two Americanos did go in. The dick was fixed, of course. So were several other people. One of the Americanos slugged Lennox from behind. Then he took the Mauser pistol and opened up one of the cartridges and took out the bullet and put the cartridge back in the breech. Then he put this gun to Lennox's temple and pulled the trigger. It made a nasty-looking wound, but it did not kill him. Then he was carried out on a stretcher covered up and well hidden. Then when the American lawyer arrived, Lennox was doped and packed in ice and kept in a dark corner of the carpintería where the man was making a coffin. The American lawyer saw Lennox there, he was ice-cold, in a deep stupor, and there was a bloody blackened wound in his temple. He looked plenty dead. The next day the coffin was buried with stones in it. The American lawyer went home with the finger-prints and some kind of document which was a piece of cheese. How do you like that, Señor Maioranos?"

He shrugged. "It would be possible, señor. It would require money and influence. It would be possible, perhaps, if this Señor Menendez was closely related to important people in Otatoclán, the alcalde, the hotel proprietor and so on."

"Well, that's possible too. It's a good idea. It would explain why they picked a remote little place like Otatoclán."

He smiled quickly. "Then Señor Lennox may still be alive, no?"

"Sure. The suicide had to be some kind of fake to back up the confession. It had to be good enough to fool a lawyer who had been a district attorney, but it would make a very sick monkey out of the current D.A. if it backfired. This Menendez is not as tough as he thinks he is, but he was tough enough to pistol-whip me for not keeping my nose clean. So he had to have reasons. If the fake got exposed, Menendez would be right in the middle of an inter-national stink. The Mexicans don't like crooked police work any more than we do."

"All that is possible, señor, as I very well know. But you accused me of lying. You said I did not go into the room where Señor

Lennox was and get his letter."

"You were already in there, chum — writing the letter."

He reached up and took the dark glasses off. Nobody can change the color of a man's eyes.

"I suppose it's a bit too early for a gimlet," he said.

53

THEY HAD DONE A WONDERFUL JOB on him in Mexico City, but why not? Their doctors, technicians, hospitals, painters, architects are as good as ours. Sometimes a little better. A Mexican cop invented the paraffin test for powder nitrates. They couldn't make Terry's face perfect, but they had done plenty. They had even changed his nose, taken out some bone and made it look flatter, less Nordic. They couldn't eliminate every trace of a scar, so they had put a couple on the other side of his face too. Knife scars are not uncommon in Latin countries.

"They even did a nerve graft up here," he said, and touched what had been the bad side of his face.

"How close did I come?"

"Close enough. A few details wrong, but they are not important. It was a quick deal and some of it was improvised and I didn't know myself just what was going to happen. I was told to do certain things and to leave a clear trail. Mendy didn't like my writing to you, but I held out for that. He undersold you a little. He never noticed the bit about the mailbox."

"You knew who killed Sylvia?"

He didn't answer me directly. "It's pretty tough to turn a woman in for murder — even if she never meant much to you."

"It's a tough world. Was Harlan Potter in on all this?"

He smiled again. "Would he be likely to let anyone know that? My guess is not. My guess is he thinks I am dead. Who would tell him otherwise — unless you did?"

"What I'd tell him you could fold into a blade of grass. How's Mendy these days — or is he?"

"He's doing all right. In Acapulco. He slipped by because of Randy. But the boys don't go for rough work on cops. Mendy's not as bad as you think. He has a heart."

"So has a snake."

"Well, what about that gimlet?"

I got up without answering him and went to the safe. I spun the knob and got out the envelope with the portrait of Madison on it and the five C notes that smelled of coffee. I dumped the lot out on the desk and then picked up the five C notes.

"These I keep. I spent almost all of it on expenses and research. The portrait of Madison I enjoyed playing with. It's all yours now."

I spread it on the edge of the desk in front of him. He looked at it but didn't touch it.

"It's yours to keep," he said. "I've got plenty. You could have let things lie."

"I know. After she killed her husband and got away with it she might have gone on to better things. He was of no real importance, of course. Just a human being with blood and a brain and emotions. He knew what happened too and he tried pretty hard to live with it. He wrote books. You may have heard of him."

"Look, I couldn't very well help what I did," he said slowly. "I didn't want anyone to get hurt. I wouldn't have had a dog's chance up here. A man can't figure every angle that quick. I was scared and I ran. What should I have done?"

"I don't know."

"She had a mad streak. She might have killed him anyway."

"Yeah, she might."

"Well, thaw out a little. Let's go have a drink somewhere where it's cool and quiet."

"No time right now, Señor Maioranos."

"We were pretty good friends once," he said unhappily.

"Were we? I forget. That was two other fellows, seems to me. You permanently in Mexico?"

"Oh yes. I'm not here legally even. I never was. I told you I was born in Salt Lake City. I was born in Montreal. I'll be a Mexican national pretty soon now. All it takes is a good lawyer. I've always liked Mexico. It wouldn't be much risk going to Victor's for that gimlet."

"Pick up your money, Señor Maioranos. It has too much blood on it."

"You're a poor man."

"How would you know?"

He picked the bill up and stretched it between his thin fingers and slipped it casually into an inside pocket. He bit his lip with the very white teeth you can have when you have a brown skin.

"I couldn't tell you any more than I did that morning you drove me to Tijuana. I gave you a chance to call the law and turn me in."

"I'm not sore at you. You're just that kind of guy. For a long time I couldn't figure you at all. You had nice ways and nice qualities, but there was something wrong. You had standards and you lived up to them, but they were personal. They had no relation to any kind of ethics or scruples. You were a nice guy because you had a nice nature. But you were just as happy with mugs or hoodlums as with honest men. Provided the hoodlums spoke fairly good English and had fairly acceptable table manners. You're a moral defeatist. I think maybe the war did it and again I think maybe you were born that way."

"I don't get it," he said. "I really don't. I'm trying to pay you back and you won't let me. I couldn't have told you any more than I did. You wouldn't have stood for it."

"That's as nice a thing as was ever said to me."

"I'm glad you like something about me. I got in a bad jam. I happened to know the sort of people who know how to deal with bad jams. They owed me for an incident that happened long ago in the war. Probably the only time in my life I ever did the right thing quick like a mouse. And when I needed them, they delivered. And for free. You're not the only guy in the world that has no price tag, Marlowe."

He leaned across the desk and snapped at one of my cigarettes. There was an uneven flush on his face under the deep tan. The scars showed up against it. I watched him spring a fancy gas cartridge lighter loose from a pocket and light the cigarette. I got a whiff of perfume from him.

"You bought a lot of me, Terry. For a smile and a nod and a wave of the hand and a few quiet drinks in a quiet bar here and there. It was nice while it lasted. So long, amigo. I won't say goodbye. I said it to you when it meant something. I said it when it was sad and lonely and final."

"I came back too late," he said. "These plastic jobs take time."

"You wouldn't have come at all if I hadn't smoked you out."

There was suddenly a glint of tears in his eyes. He put his dark glasses back on quickly.

"I wasn't sure about it," he said. "I hadn't made up my mind. They didn't want me to tell you anything. I just hadn't made up my mind."

"Don't worry about it, Terry. There's always somebody around to do it for you."

"I was in the Commandos, bud. They don't take you if you're just a piece of fluff. I got badly hurt and it wasn't any fun with those Nazi doctors. It did something to me."

"I know all that, Terry. You're a very sweet guy in a lot of ways. I'm not judging you. I never did. It's just that you're not here any more. You're long gone. You've got nice clothes and perfume and you're as elegant as a fifty-dollar whore."

"That's just an act," he said almost desperately.

"You get a kick out of it, don't you?"

His mouth dropped in a sour smile. He shrugged an expressive energetic Latin shrug.

"Of course. An act is all there is. There isn't anything else. In here — " he tapped his chest with the lighter — "there isn't anything. I've had it, Marlowe. I had it long ago. Well — I guess that winds things up."

He stood up. I stood up. He put out a lean hand. I shook it.

"So long, Señor Maioranos. Nice to have known you — however briefly."

"Goodbye."

He turned and walked across the floor and out. I watched the door close. I listened to his steps going away down the imitation marble corridor. After a while they got faint, then they got silent. I kept on listening anyway. What for? Did I want him to stop suddenly and turn and come back and talk me out of the way I felt? Well, he didn't. That was the last I saw of him.

I never saw any of them again — except the cops. No way has yet been invented to say goodbye to them.